ESTRANGED

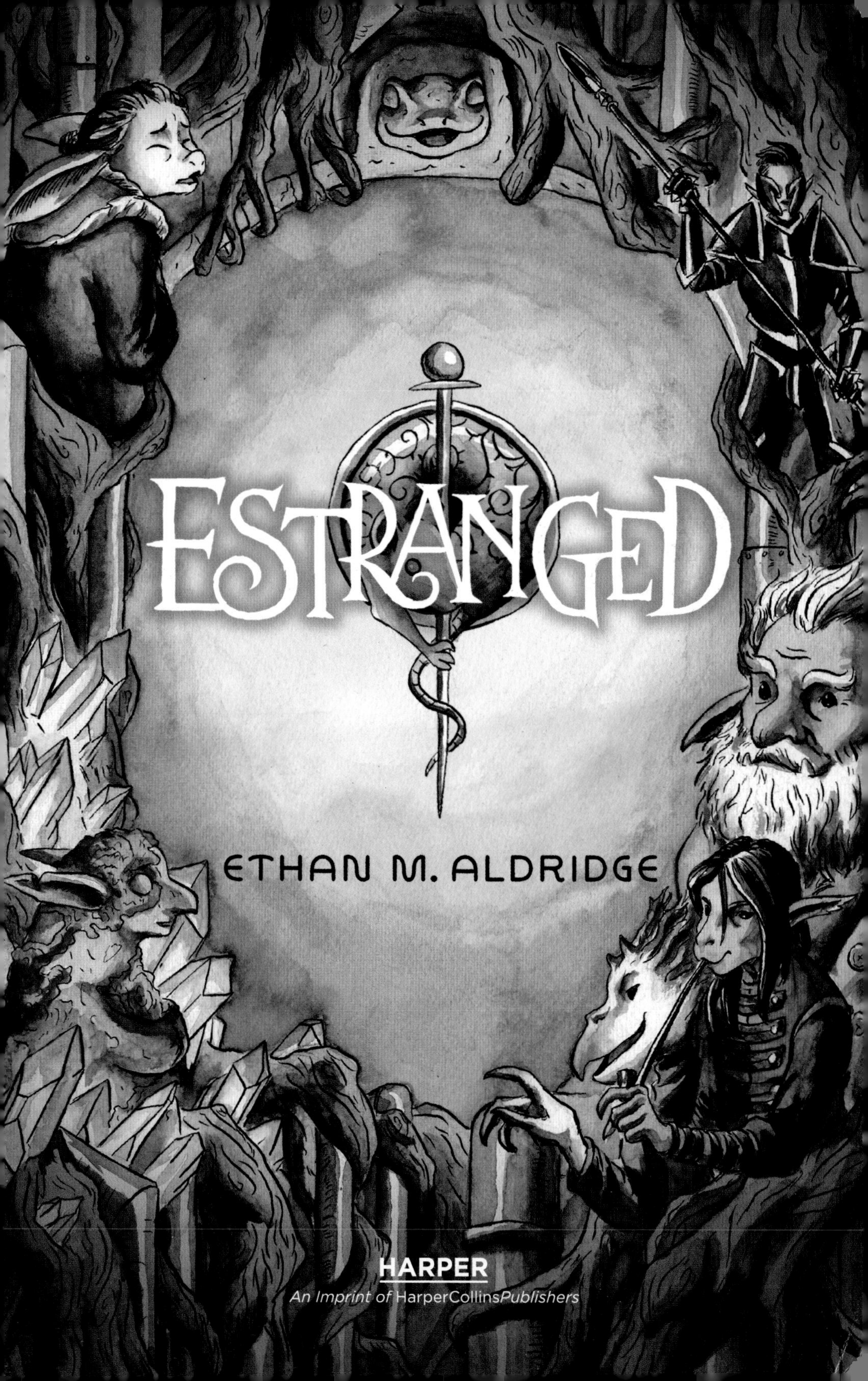
ESTRANGED
ETHAN M. ALDRIDGE
HARPER
An Imprint of HarperCollinsPublishers

Estranged

 For information address HarperCollins Children's Books, a division of HarperCollins Publishers, 195 Broadway, New York, NY 10007.
www.harpercollinschildrens.com

Library of Congress Control Number: 2017949551
ISBN 978-0-06-265386-4 (paperback) – ISBN 978-0-06-265387-1 (hardcover)

The artist used watercolors, ink, and Photoshop to create the illustrations for this book.
Typography by Jim Tierney
18 19 20 21 22 SCP 10 9 8 7 6 5 4 3 2 1
❖
First Edition

To my mother and father

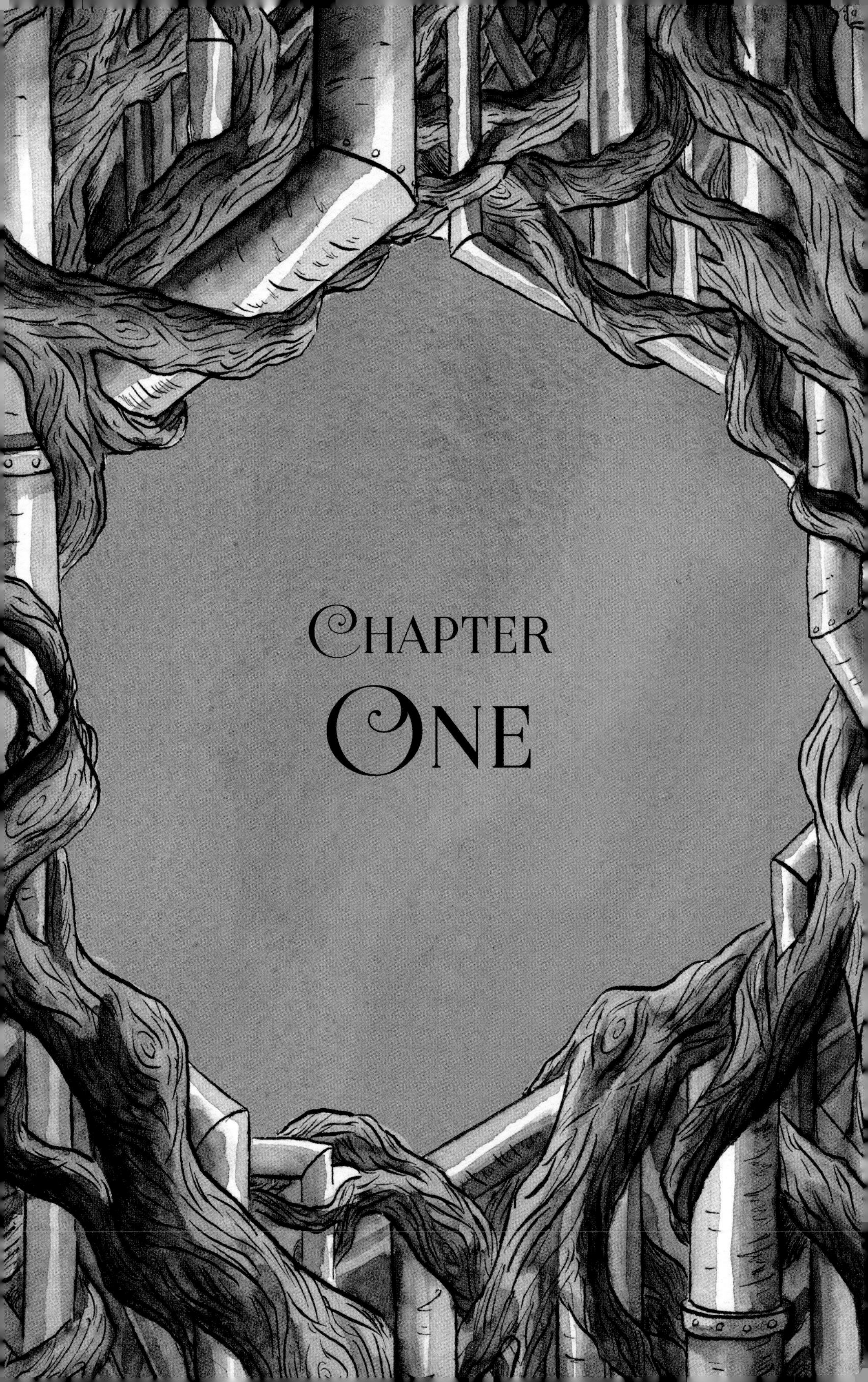

Chapter One

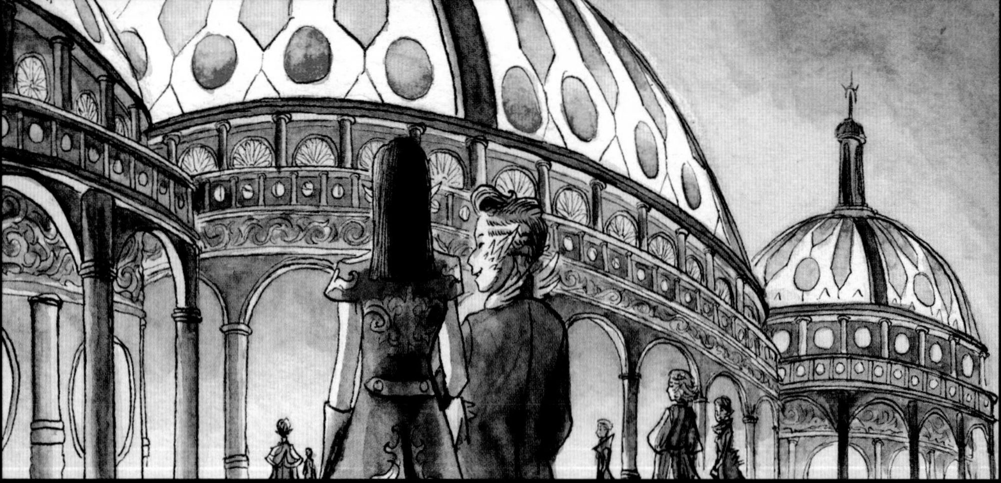

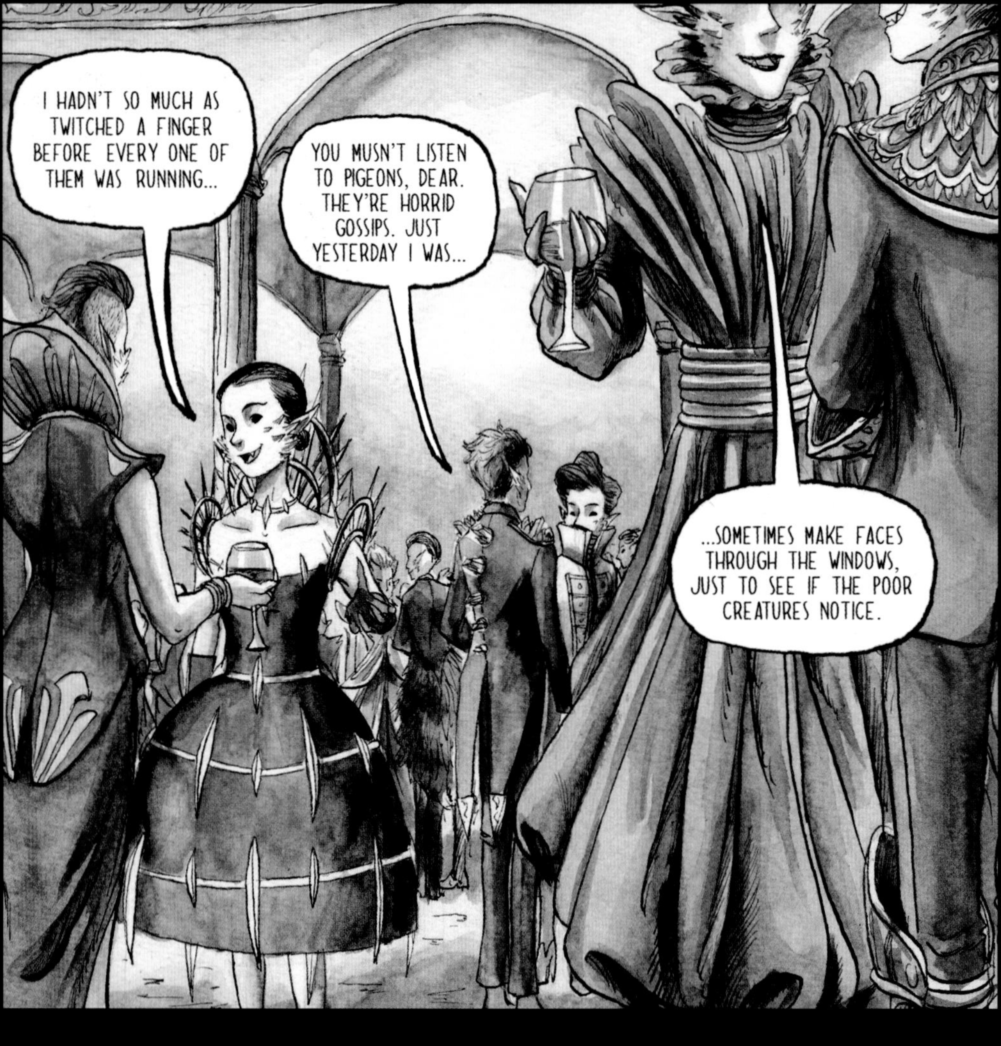
I HADN'T SO MUCH AS TWITCHED A FINGER BEFORE EVERY ONE OF THEM WAS RUNNING...
YOU MUSN'T LISTEN TO PIGEONS, DEAR. THEY'RE HORRID GOSSIPS. JUST YESTERDAY I WAS...
...SOMETIMES MAKE FACES THROUGH THE WINDOWS, JUST TO SEE IF THE POOR CREATURES NOTICE.

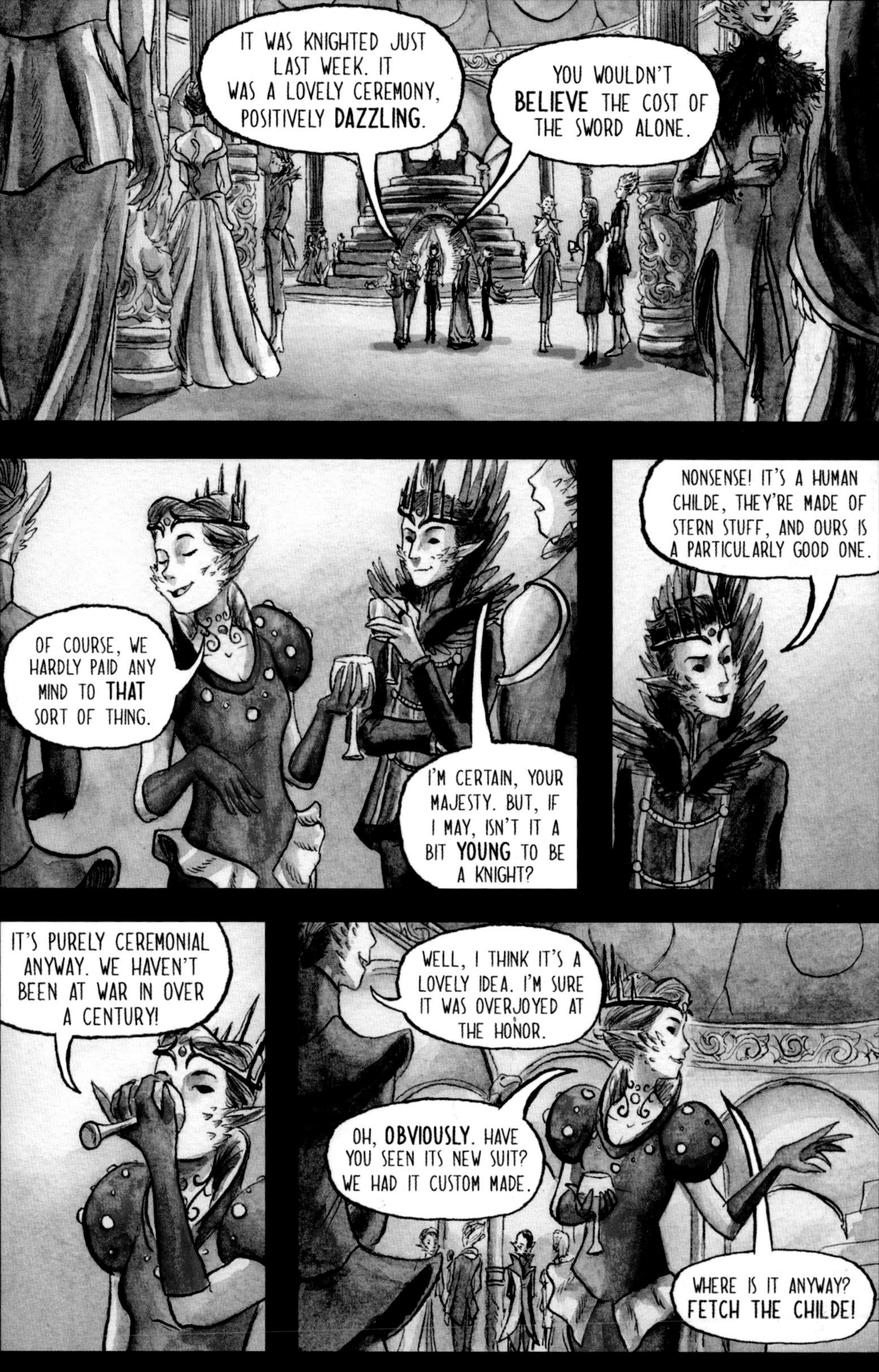
IT WAS KNIGHTED JUST LAST WEEK. IT WAS A LOVELY CEREMONY, POSITIVELY **DAZZLING**.
YOU WOULDN'T **BELIEVE** THE COST OF THE SWORD ALONE.
OF COURSE, WE HARDLY PAID ANY MIND TO **THAT** SORT OF THING.
I'M CERTAIN, YOUR MAJESTY. BUT, IF I MAY, ISN'T IT A BIT **YOUNG** TO BE A KNIGHT?
NONSENSE! IT'S A HUMAN CHILDE, THEY'RE MADE OF STERN STUFF, AND OURS IS A PARTICULARLY GOOD ONE.
IT'S PURELY CEREMONIAL ANYWAY. WE HAVEN'T BEEN AT WAR IN OVER A CENTURY!
WELL, I THINK IT'S A LOVELY IDEA. I'M SURE IT WAS OVERJOYED AT THE HONOR.
OH, **OBVIOUSLY**. HAVE YOU SEEN ITS NEW SUIT? WE HAD IT CUSTOM MADE.
WHERE IS IT ANYWAY? **FETCH THE CHILDE!**

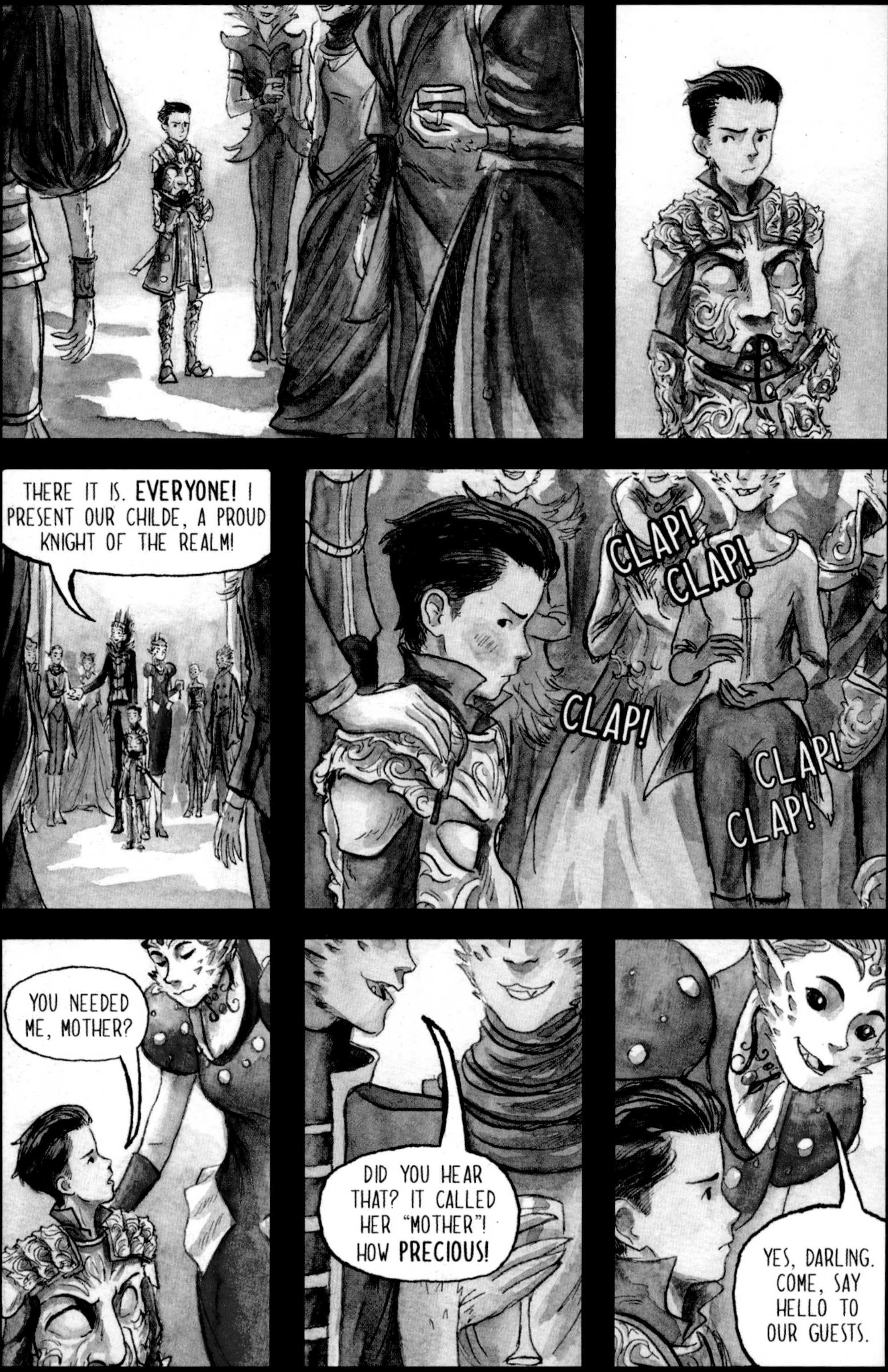
THERE IT IS. EVERYONE! I PRESENT OUR CHILDE, A PROUD KNIGHT OF THE REALM!
CLAP! CLAP!
CLAP!
CLAP! CLAP!
YOU NEEDED ME, MOTHER?
DID YOU HEAR THAT? IT CALLED HER "MOTHER"! HOW PRECIOUS!
YES, DARLING. COME, SAY HELLO TO OUR GUESTS.

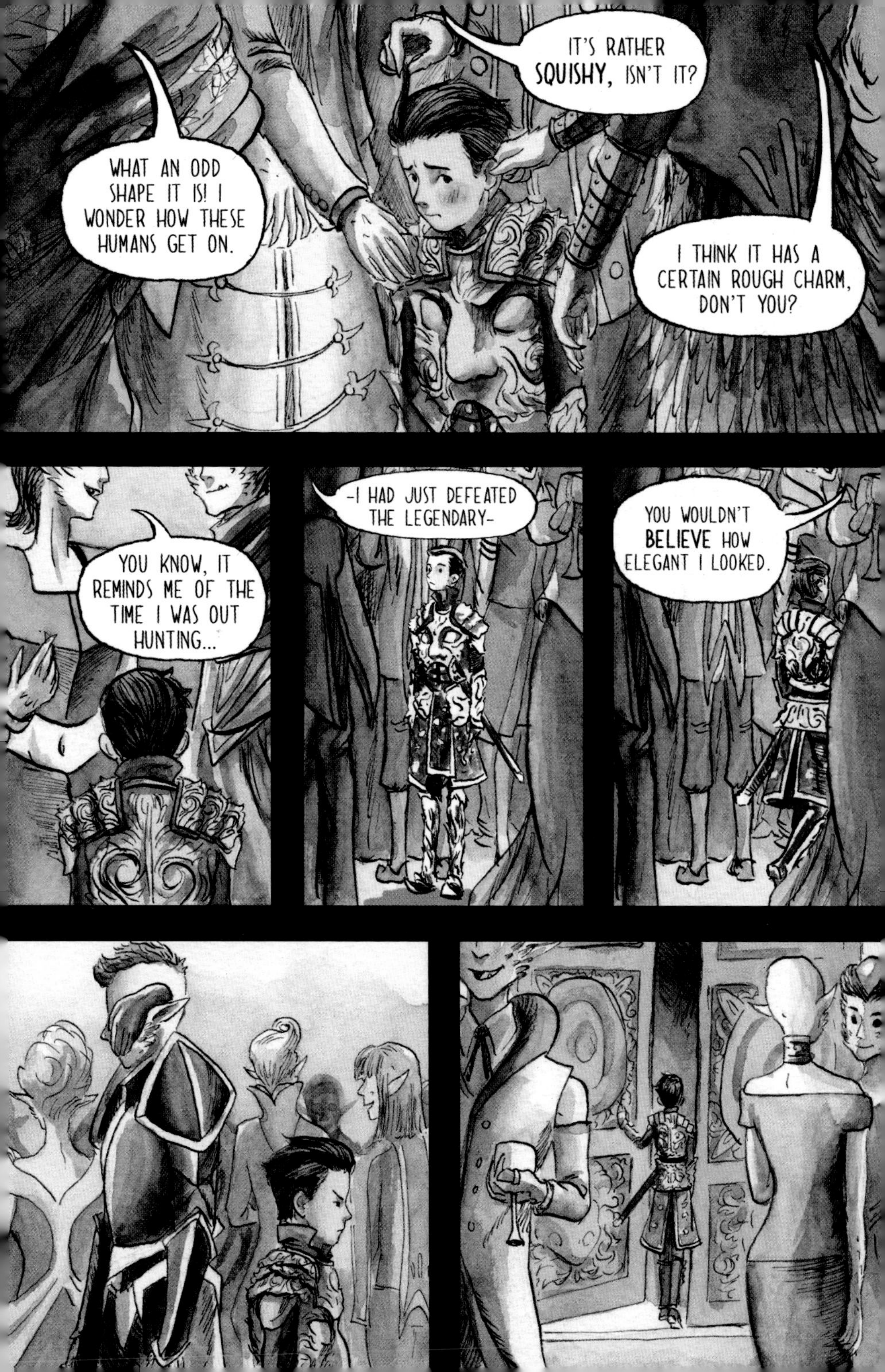
WHAT AN ODD SHAPE IT IS! I WONDER HOW THESE HUMANS GET ON.
IT'S RATHER SQUISHY, ISN'T IT?
I THINK IT HAS A CERTAIN ROUGH CHARM, DON'T YOU?
YOU KNOW, IT REMINDS ME OF THE TIME I WAS OUT HUNTING...
-I HAD JUST DEFEATED THE LEGENDARY-
YOU WOULDN'T BELIEVE HOW ELEGANT I LOOKED.

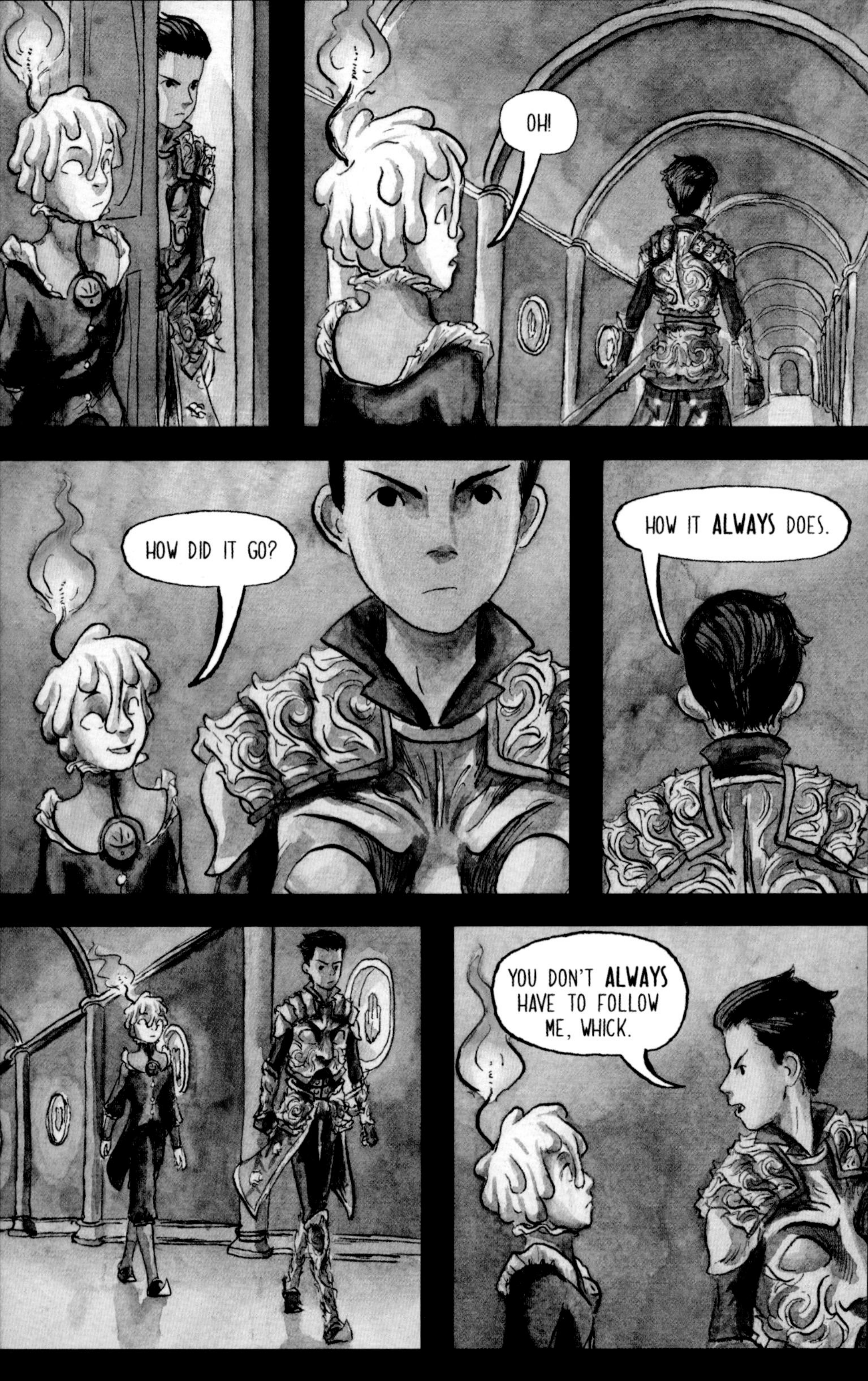
OH!
HOW DID IT GO?
HOW IT ALWAYS DOES.
YOU DON'T ALWAYS HAVE TO FOLLOW ME, WHICK.

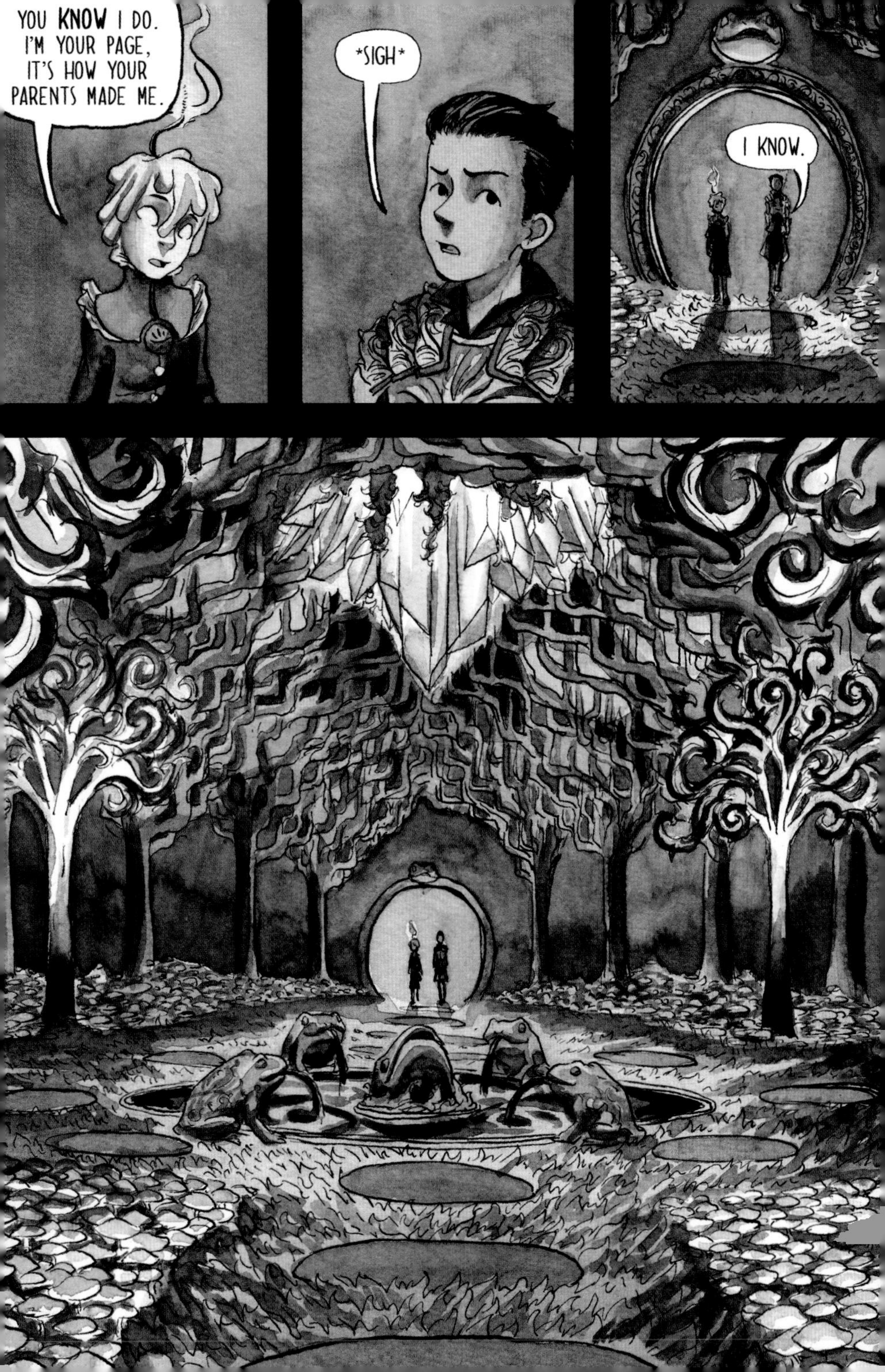
YOU KNOW I DO. I'M YOUR PAGE, IT'S HOW YOUR PARENTS MADE ME.
SIGH
I KNOW.

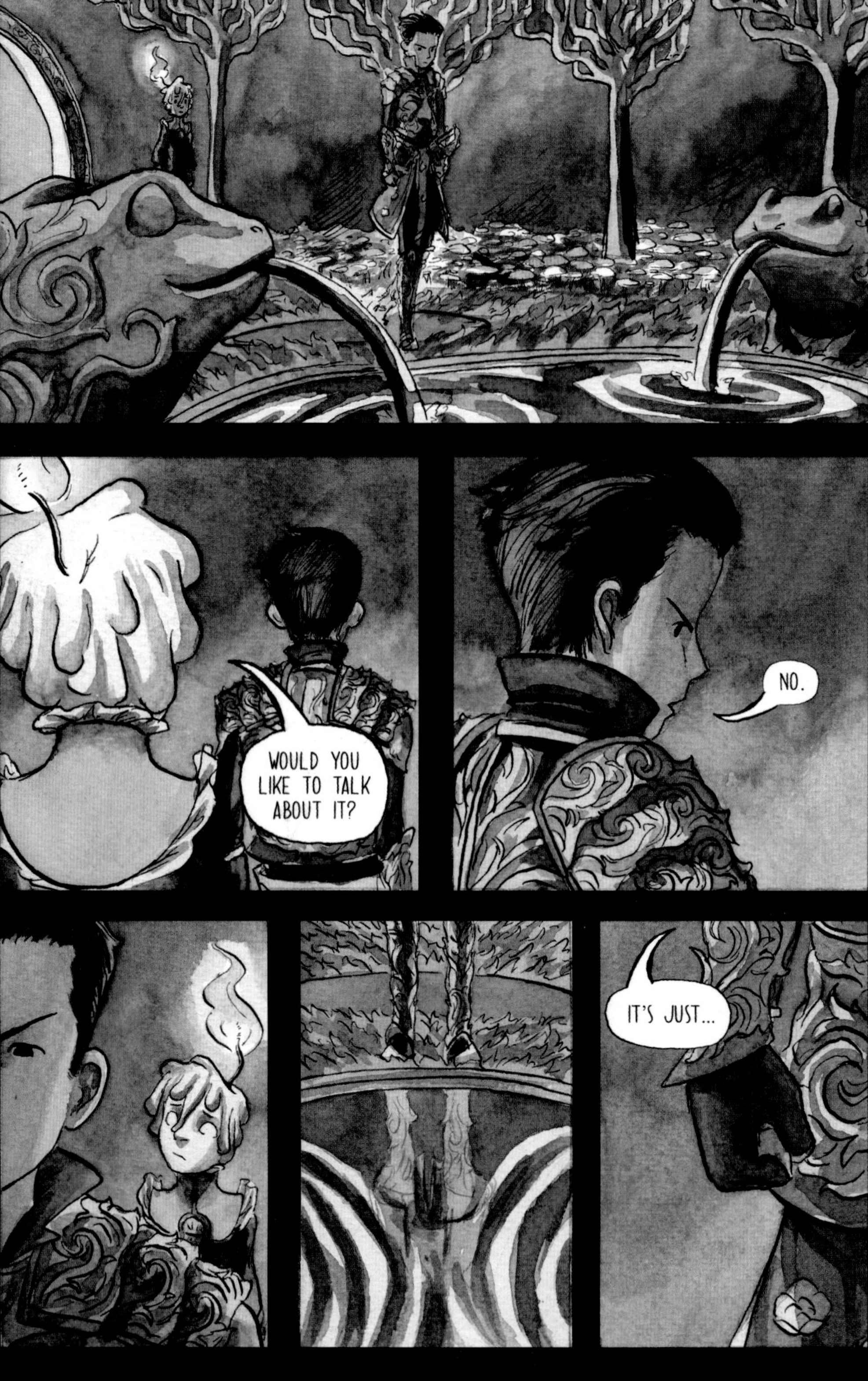
WOULD YOU LIKE TO TALK ABOUT IT?
NO.
IT'S JUST...

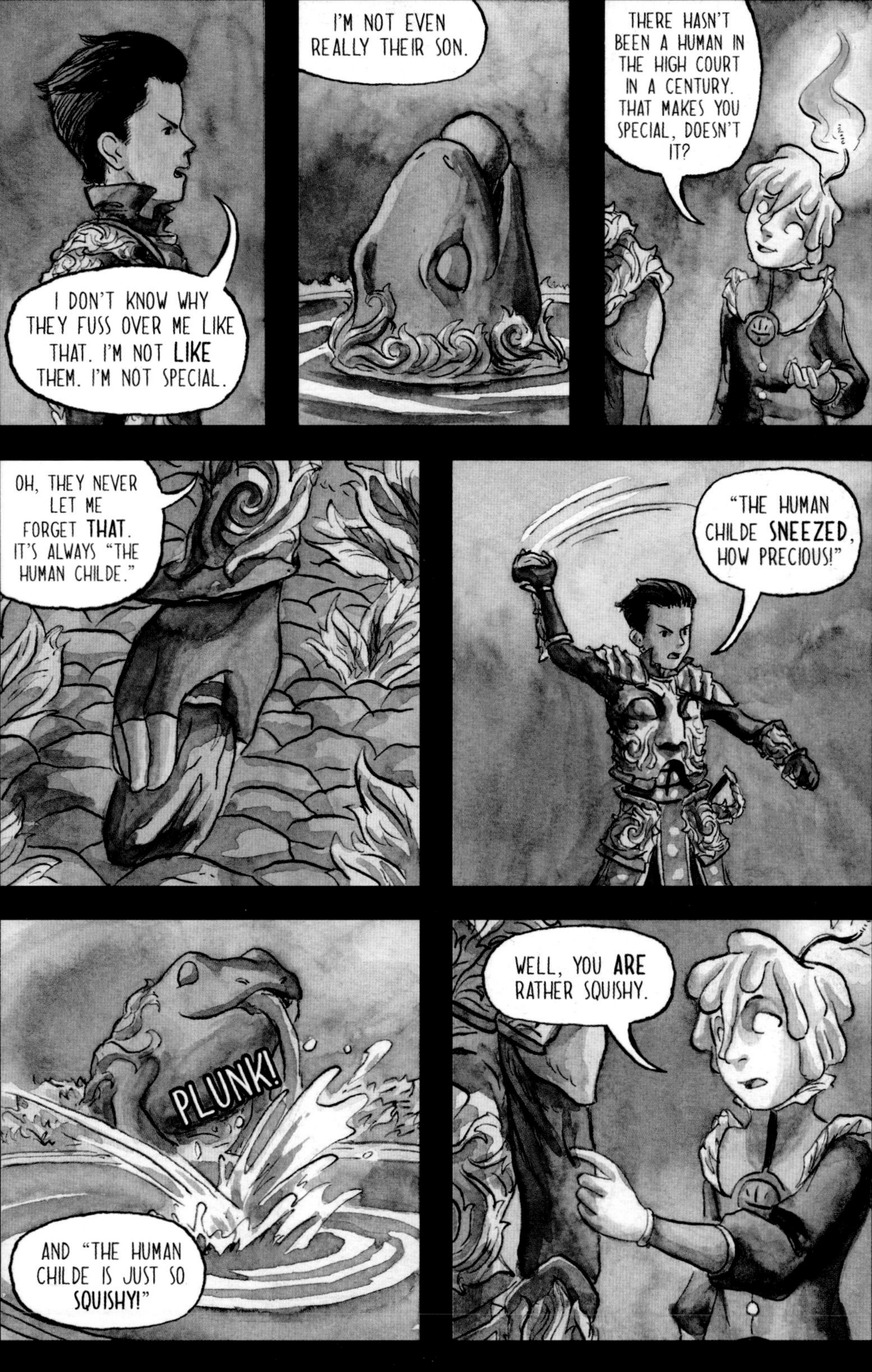
I DON'T KNOW WHY THEY FUSS OVER ME LIKE THAT. I'M NOT **LIKE** THEM. I'M NOT SPECIAL.
I'M NOT EVEN REALLY THEIR SON.
THERE HASN'T BEEN A HUMAN IN THE HIGH COURT IN A CENTURY. THAT MAKES YOU SPECIAL, DOESN'T IT?
OH, THEY NEVER LET ME FORGET **THAT**. IT'S ALWAYS "THE HUMAN CHILDE."
"THE HUMAN CHILDE **SNEEZED**, HOW PRECIOUS!"
PLUNK!
AND "THE HUMAN CHILDE IS JUST SO **SQUISHY**!"
WELL, YOU **ARE** RATHER SQUISHY.

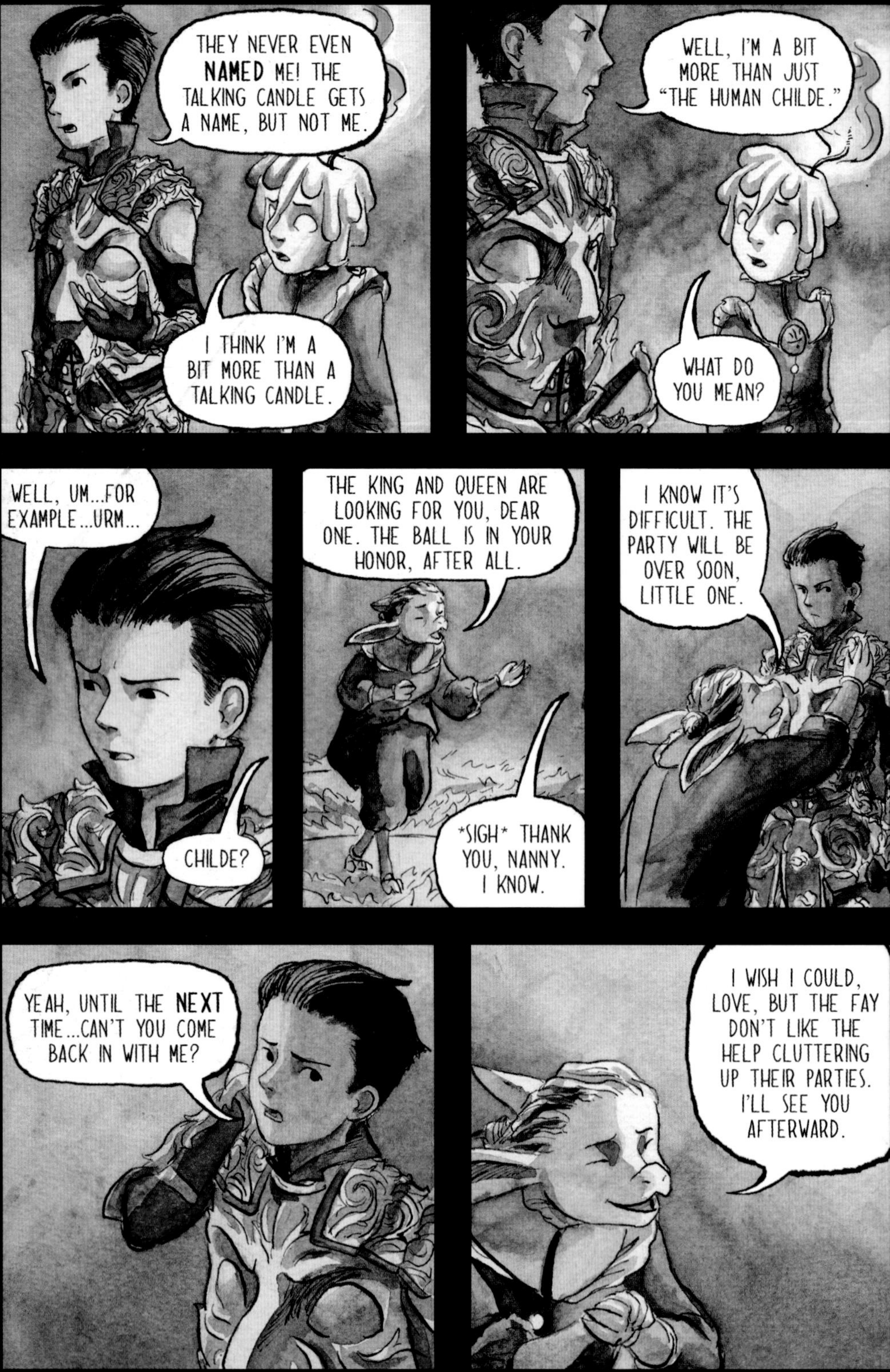

THEY NEVER EVEN **NAMED** ME! THE TALKING CANDLE GETS A NAME, BUT NOT ME.
I THINK I'M A BIT MORE THAN A TALKING CANDLE.
WELL, I'M A BIT MORE THAN JUST "THE HUMAN CHILDE."
WHAT DO YOU MEAN?
WELL, UM...FOR EXAMPLE...URM...
CHILDE?
THE KING AND QUEEN ARE LOOKING FOR YOU, DEAR ONE. THE BALL IS IN YOUR HONOR, AFTER ALL.
SIGH THANK YOU, NANNY. I KNOW.
I KNOW IT'S DIFFICULT. THE PARTY WILL BE OVER SOON, LITTLE ONE.
YEAH, UNTIL THE **NEXT** TIME...CAN'T YOU COME BACK IN WITH ME?
I WISH I COULD, LOVE, BUT THE FAY DON'T LIKE THE HELP CLUTTERING UP THEIR PARTIES. I'LL SEE YOU AFTERWARD.

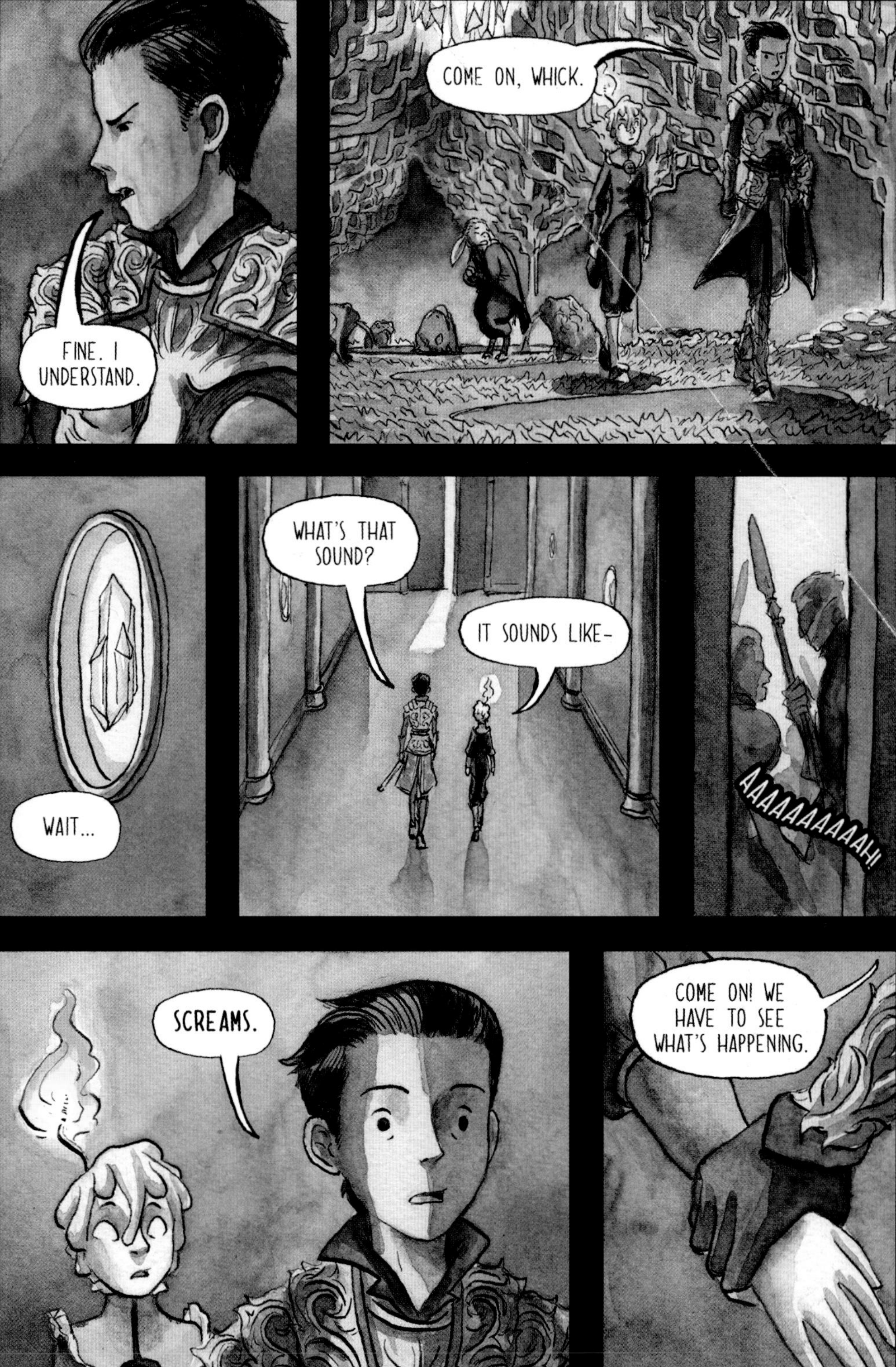
FINE. I UNDERSTAND.
COME ON, WHICK.
WAIT...
WHAT'S THAT SOUND?
IT SOUNDS LIKE-
AAAAAAAAAH!
SCREAMS.
COME ON! WE HAVE TO SEE WHAT'S HAPPENING.

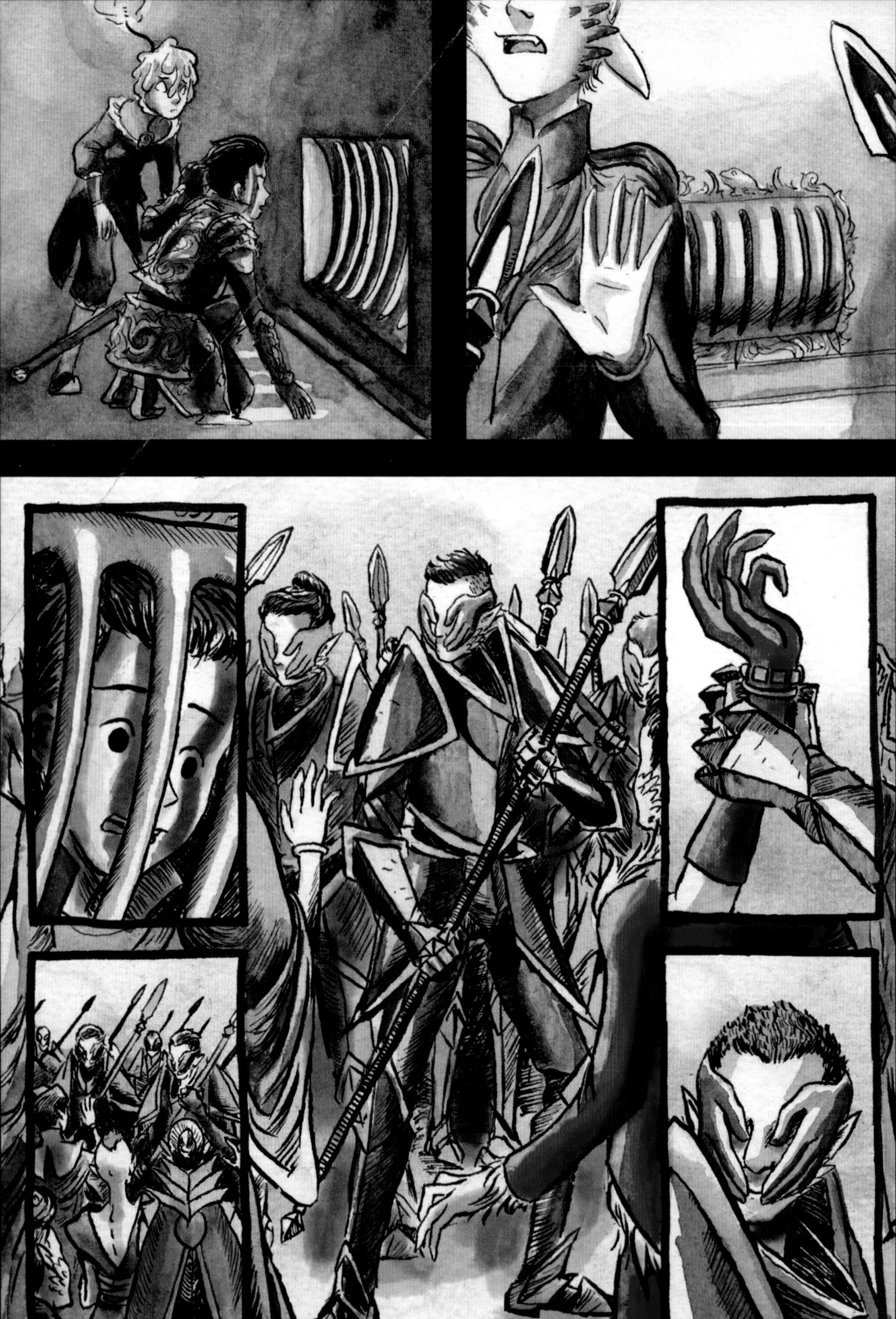

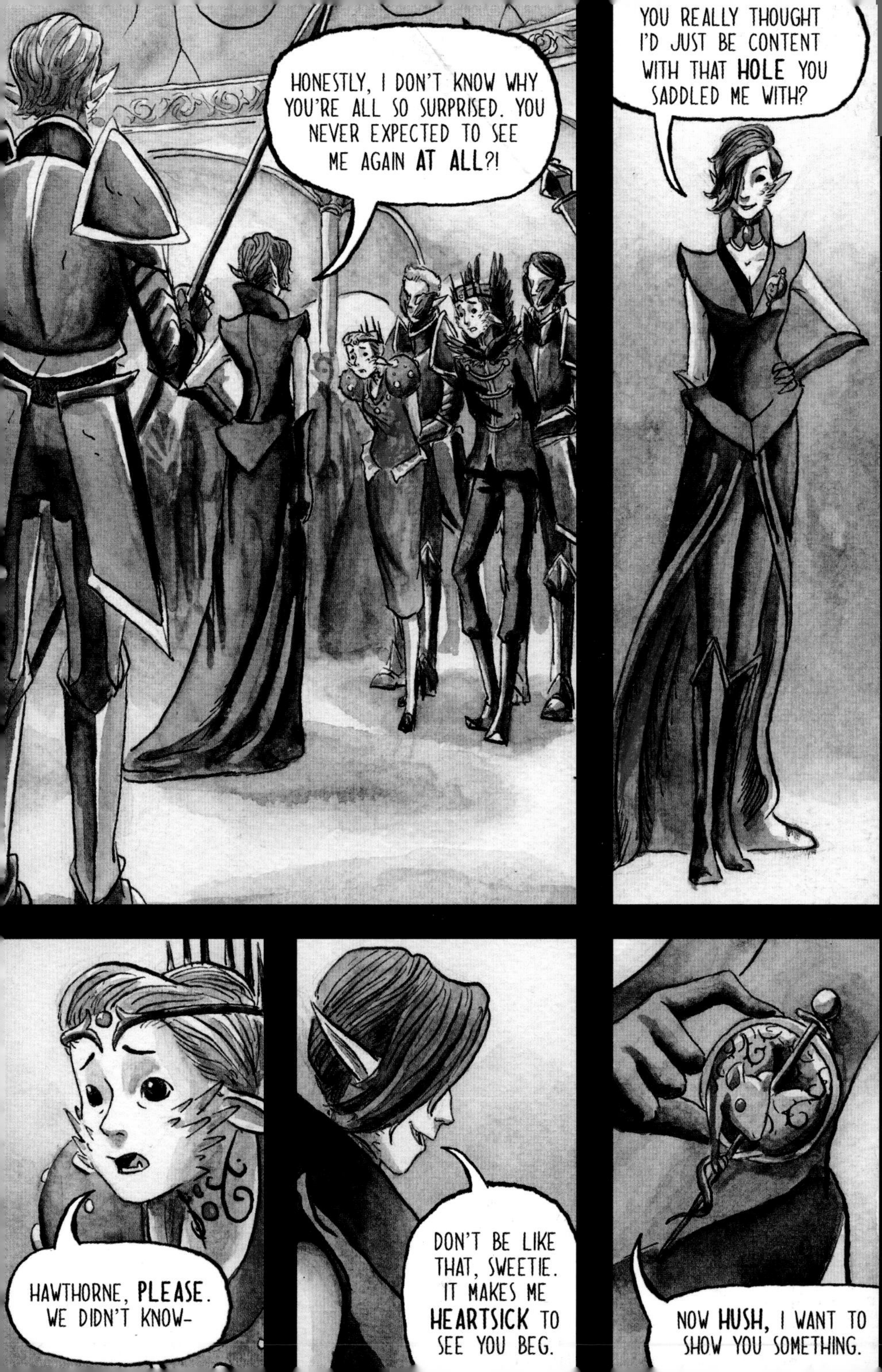
HONESTLY, I DON'T KNOW WHY YOU'RE ALL SO SURPRISED. YOU NEVER EXPECTED TO SEE ME AGAIN **AT ALL**?!
YOU REALLY THOUGHT I'D JUST BE CONTENT WITH THAT **HOLE** YOU SADDLED ME WITH?
HAWTHORNE, **PLEASE**. WE DIDN'T KNOW-
DON'T BE LIKE THAT, SWEETIE. IT MAKES ME **HEARTSICK** TO SEE YOU BEG.
NOW **HUSH**, I WANT TO SHOW YOU SOMETHING.

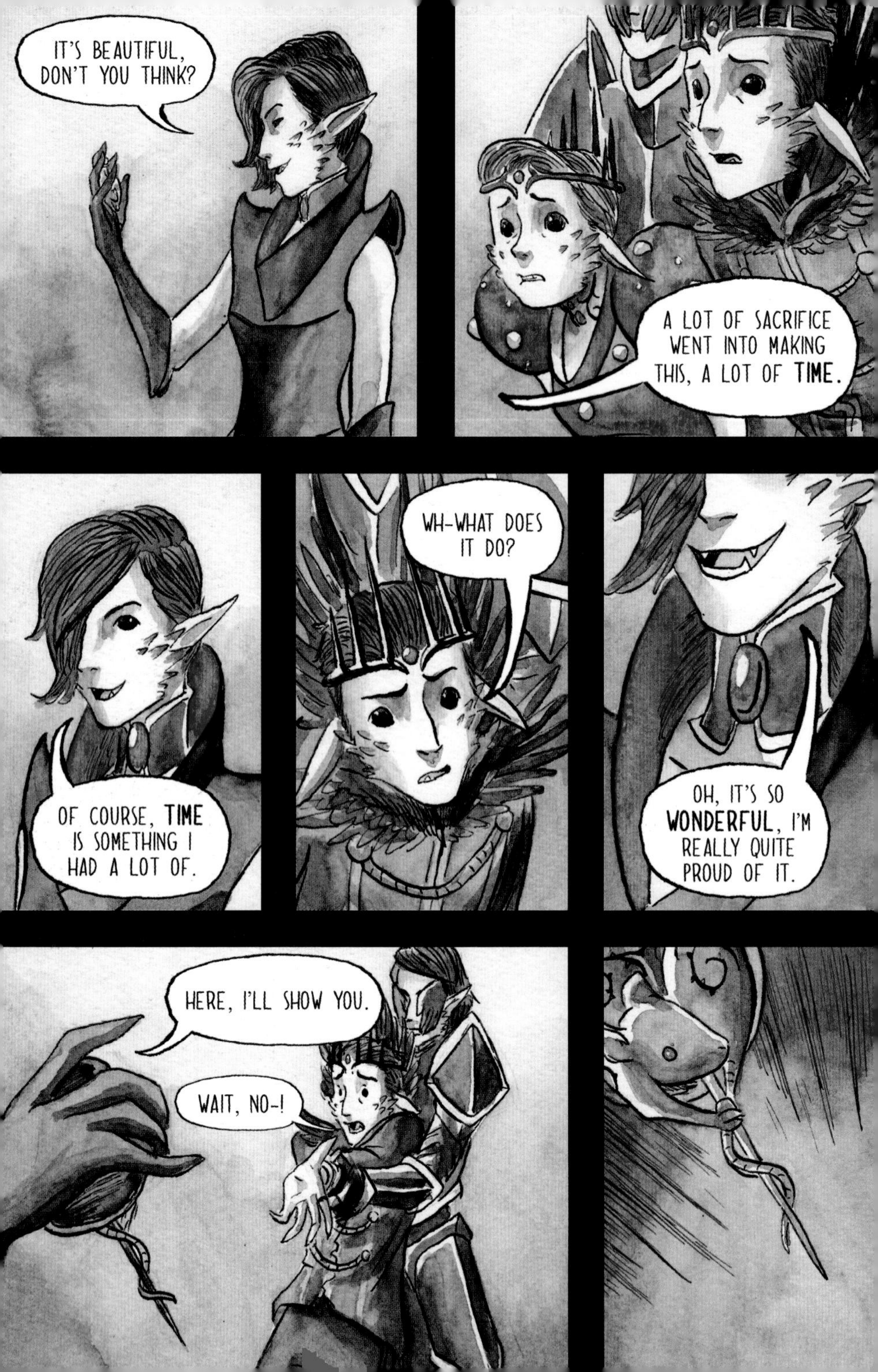
IT'S BEAUTIFUL, DON'T YOU THINK?
A LOT OF SACRIFICE WENT INTO MAKING THIS, A LOT OF **TIME**.
OF COURSE, **TIME** IS SOMETHING I HAD A LOT OF.
WH-WHAT DOES IT DO?
OH, IT'S SO **WONDERFUL**, I'M REALLY QUITE PROUD OF IT.
HERE, I'LL SHOW YOU.
WAIT, NO-!

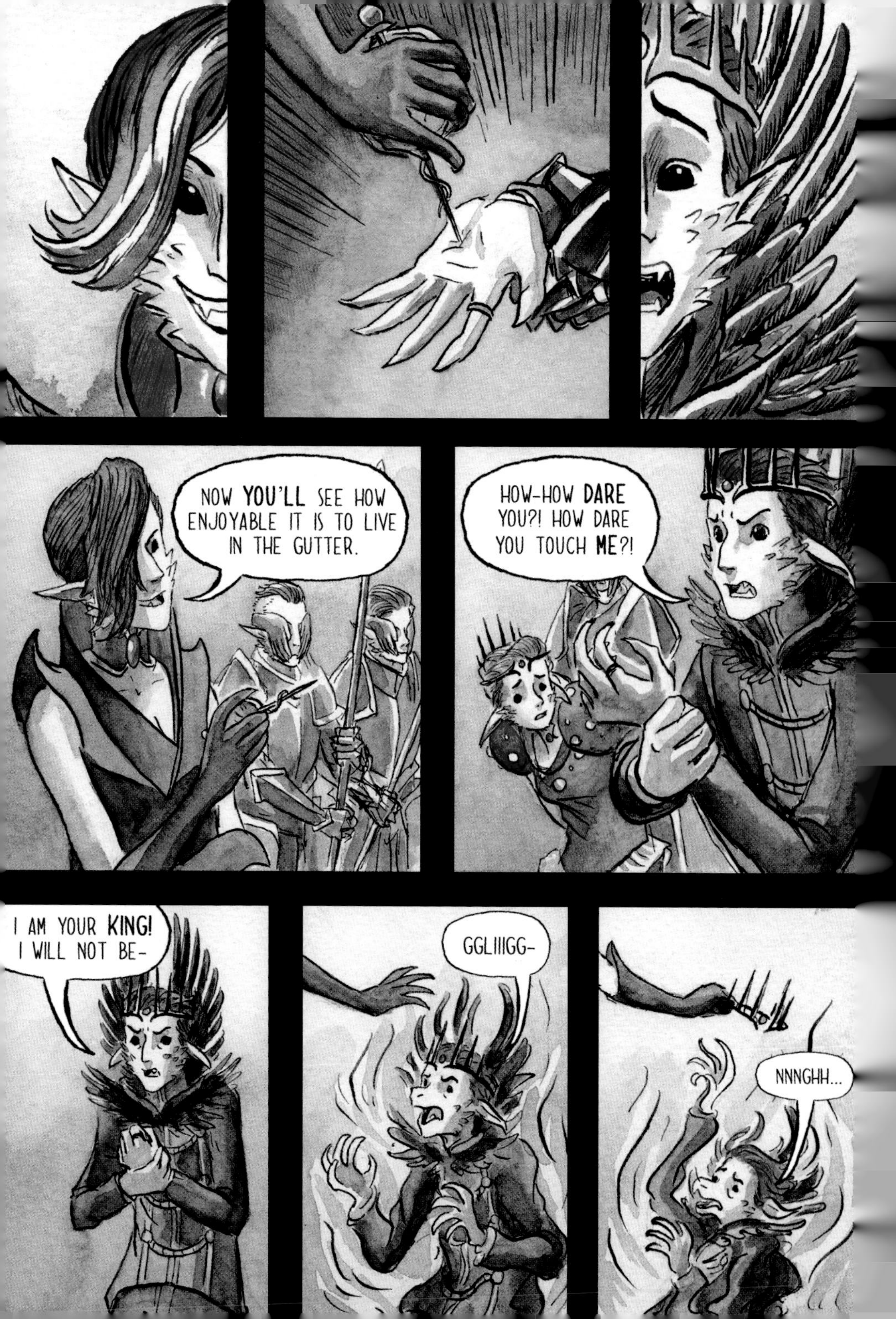
NOW YOU'LL SEE HOW ENJOYABLE IT IS TO LIVE IN THE GUTTER.
HOW-HOW DARE YOU?! HOW DARE YOU TOUCH ME?!
I AM YOUR KING! I WILL NOT BE-
GGLIIIGG-
NNNGHH...

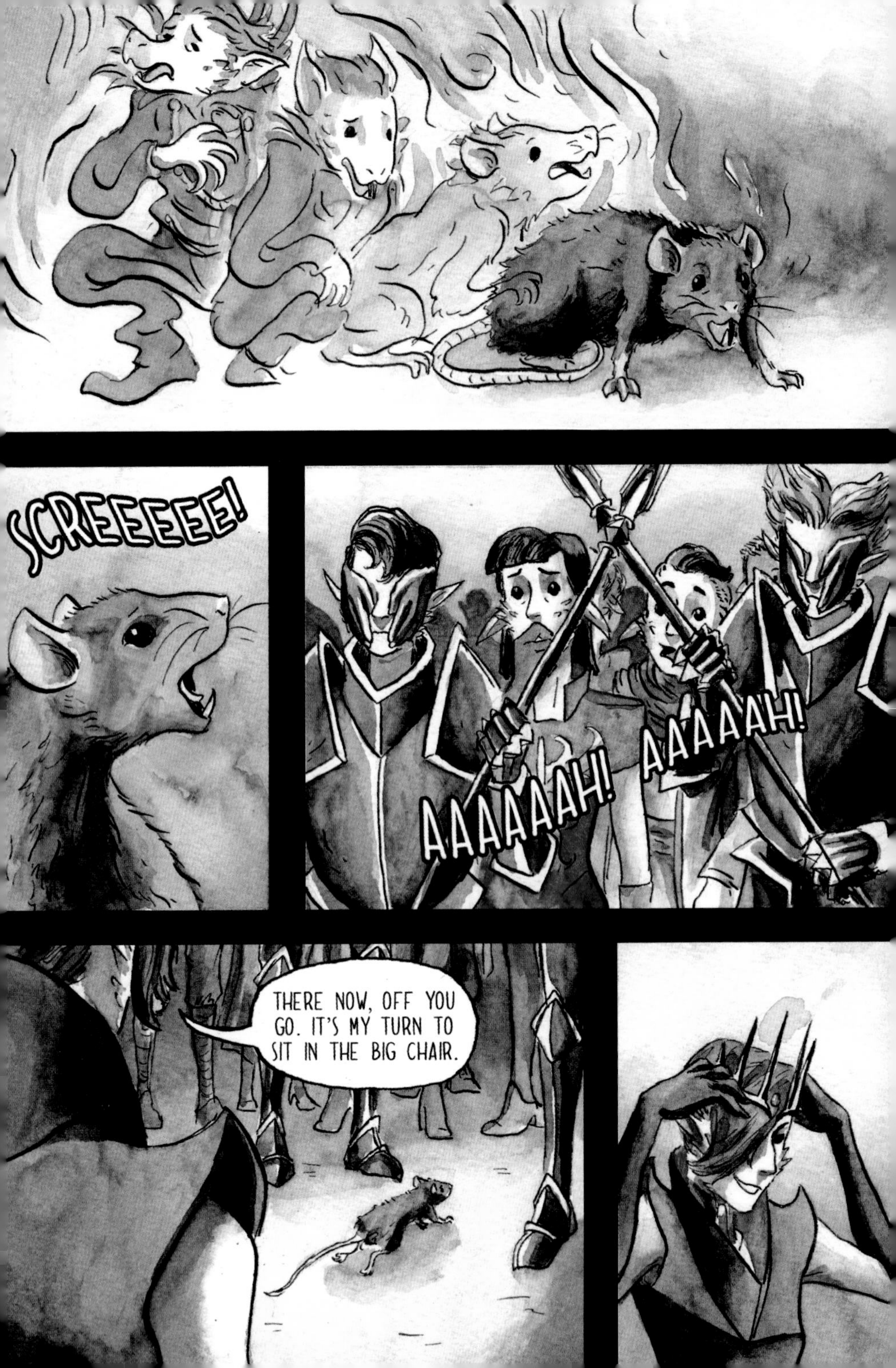
SCREEEEEE!
AAAAAAH!
AAAAAH!
THERE NOW, OFF YOU GO. IT'S MY TURN TO SIT IN THE BIG CHAIR.

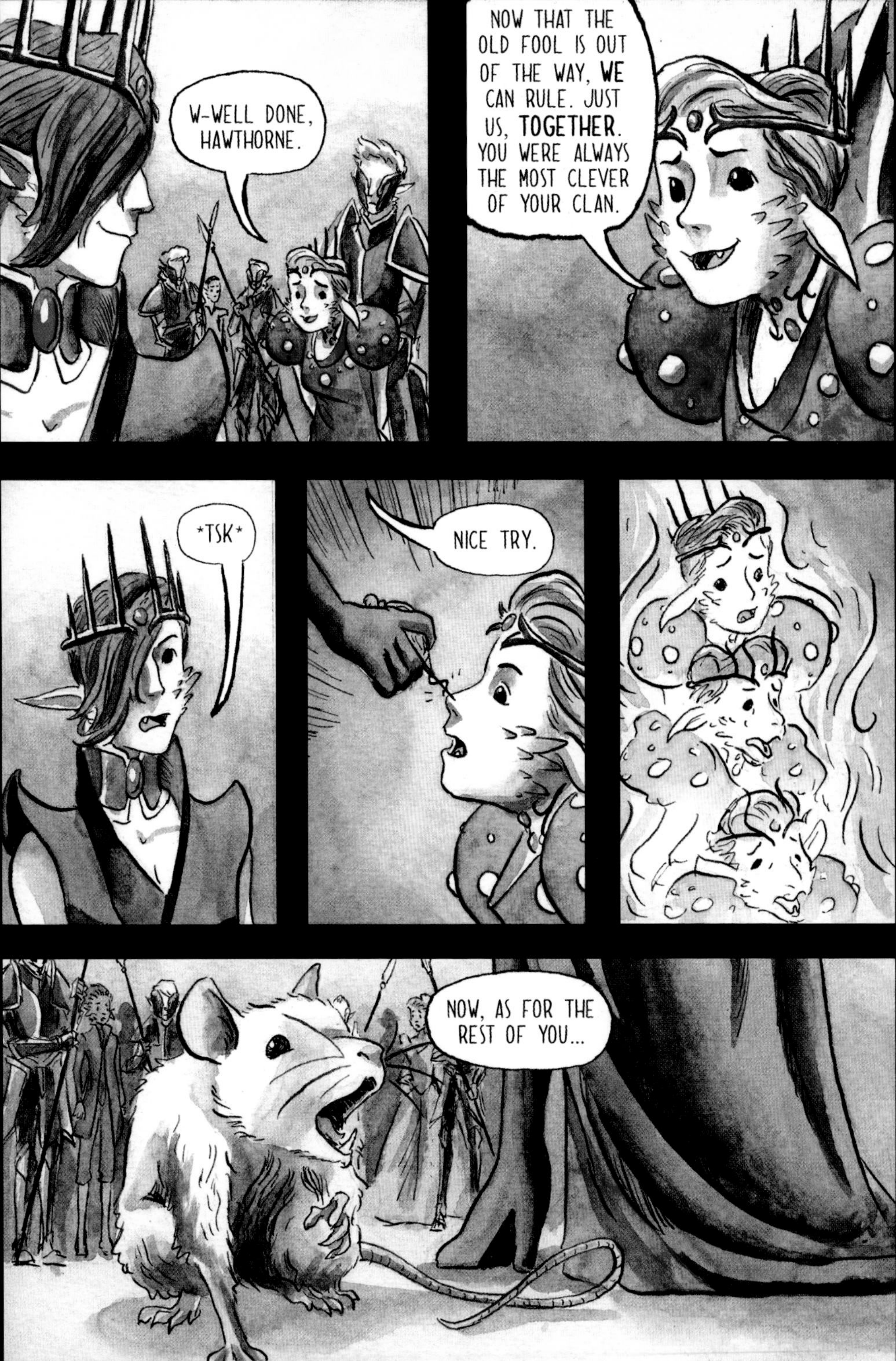
W-WELL DONE, HAWTHORNE.
NOW THAT THE OLD FOOL IS OUT OF THE WAY, **WE** CAN RULE. JUST US, **TOGETHER**. YOU WERE ALWAYS THE MOST CLEVER OF YOUR CLAN.
TSK
NICE TRY.
NOW, AS FOR THE REST OF YOU...

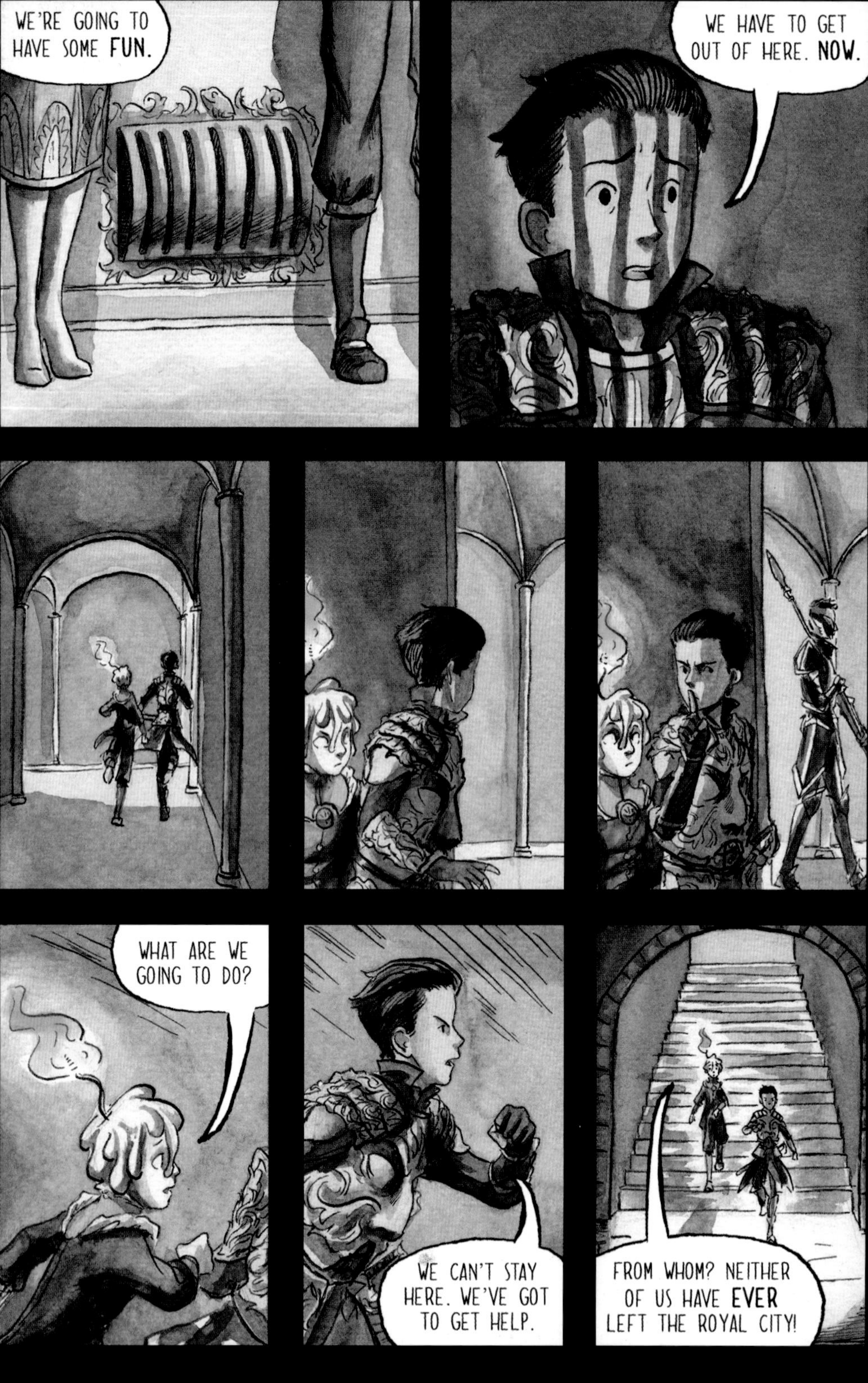
WE'RE GOING TO HAVE SOME **FUN**.
WE HAVE TO GET OUT OF HERE. **NOW**.
WHAT ARE WE GOING TO DO?
WE CAN'T STAY HERE. WE'VE GOT TO GET HELP.
FROM WHOM? NEITHER OF US HAVE **EVER** LEFT THE ROYAL CITY!

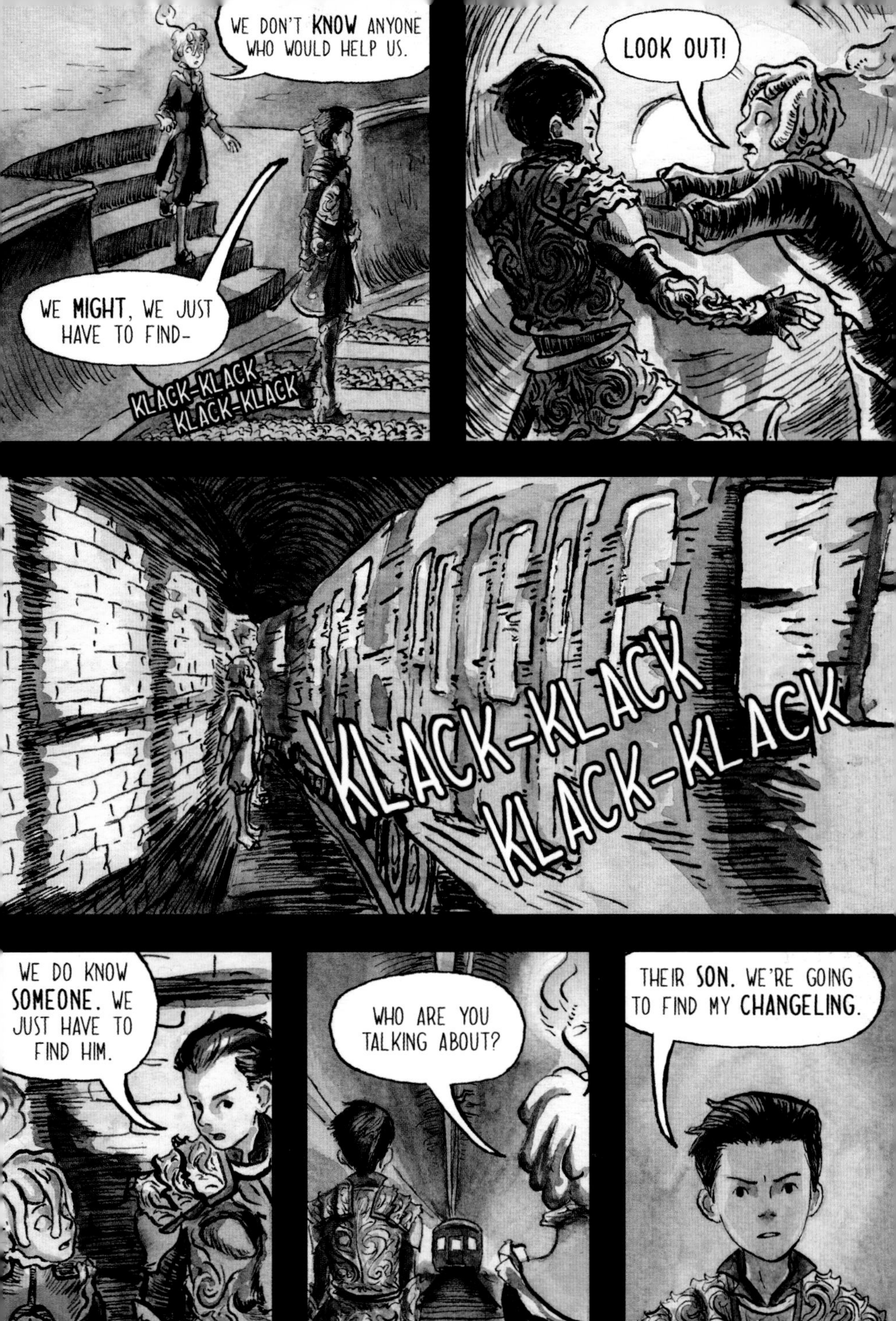
WE DON'T KNOW ANYONE WHO WOULD HELP US.
WE MIGHT, WE JUST HAVE TO FIND-
KLACK-KLACK KLACK-KLACK
LOOK OUT!
KLACK-KLACK KLACK-KLACK
WE DO KNOW SOMEONE. WE JUST HAVE TO FIND HIM.
WHO ARE YOU TALKING ABOUT?
THEIR SON. WE'RE GOING TO FIND MY CHANGELING.

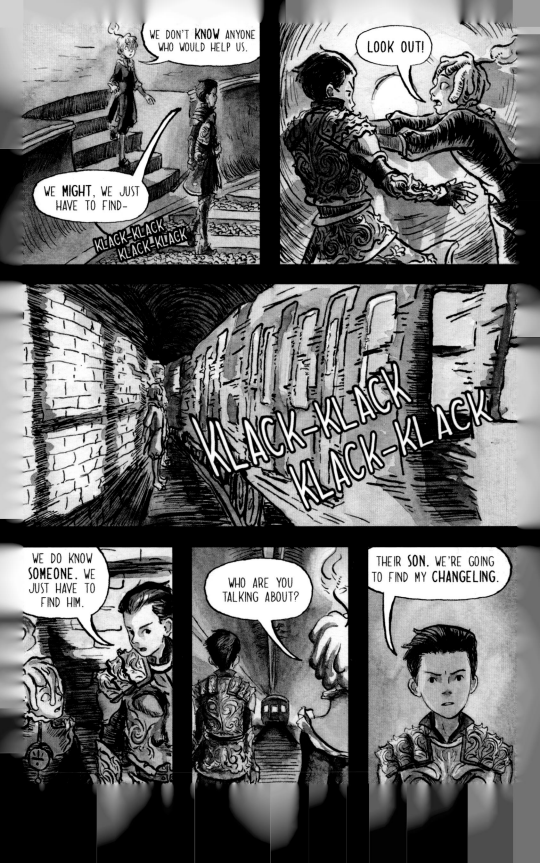

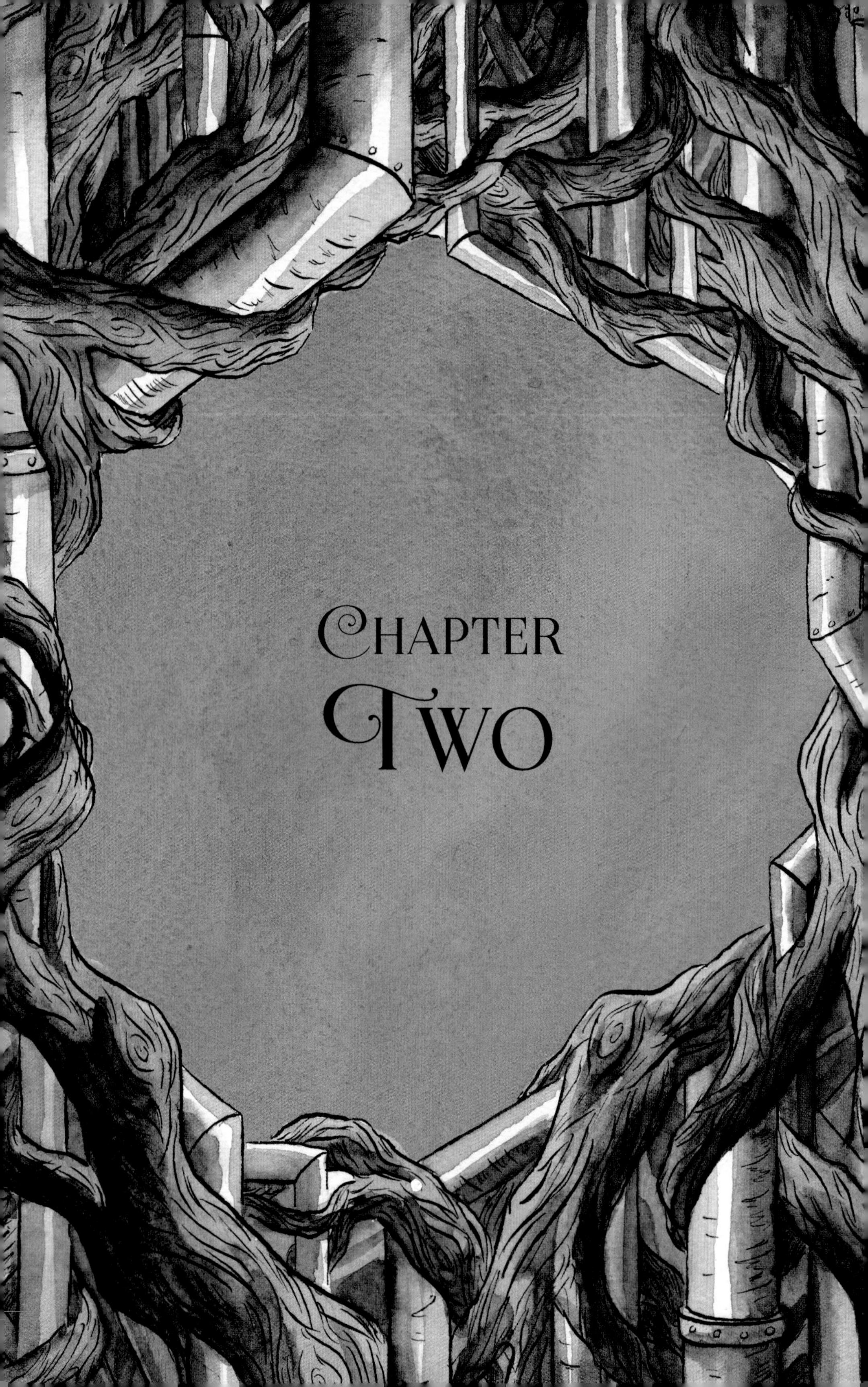

Chapter Two

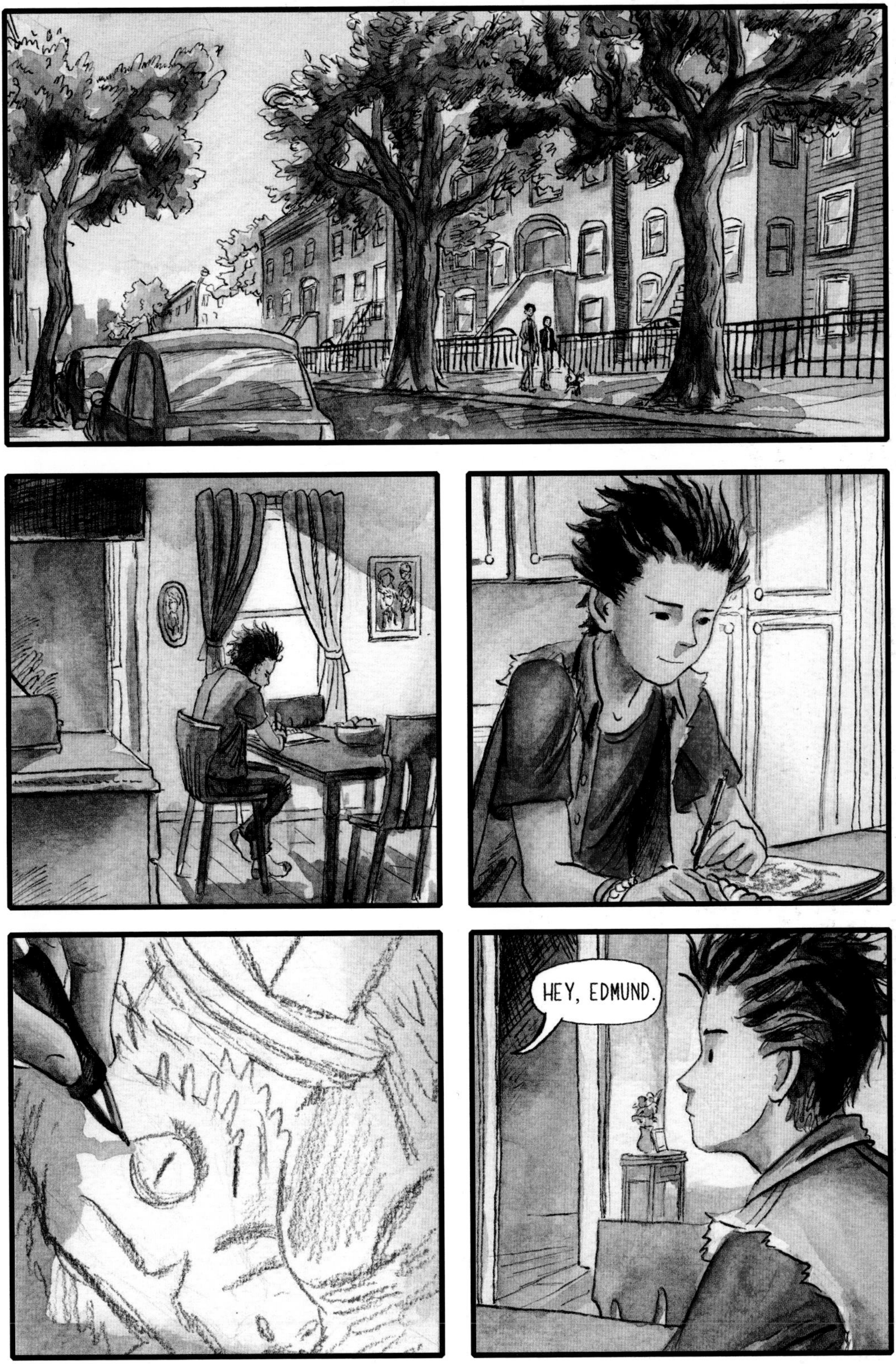
HEY, EDMUND.

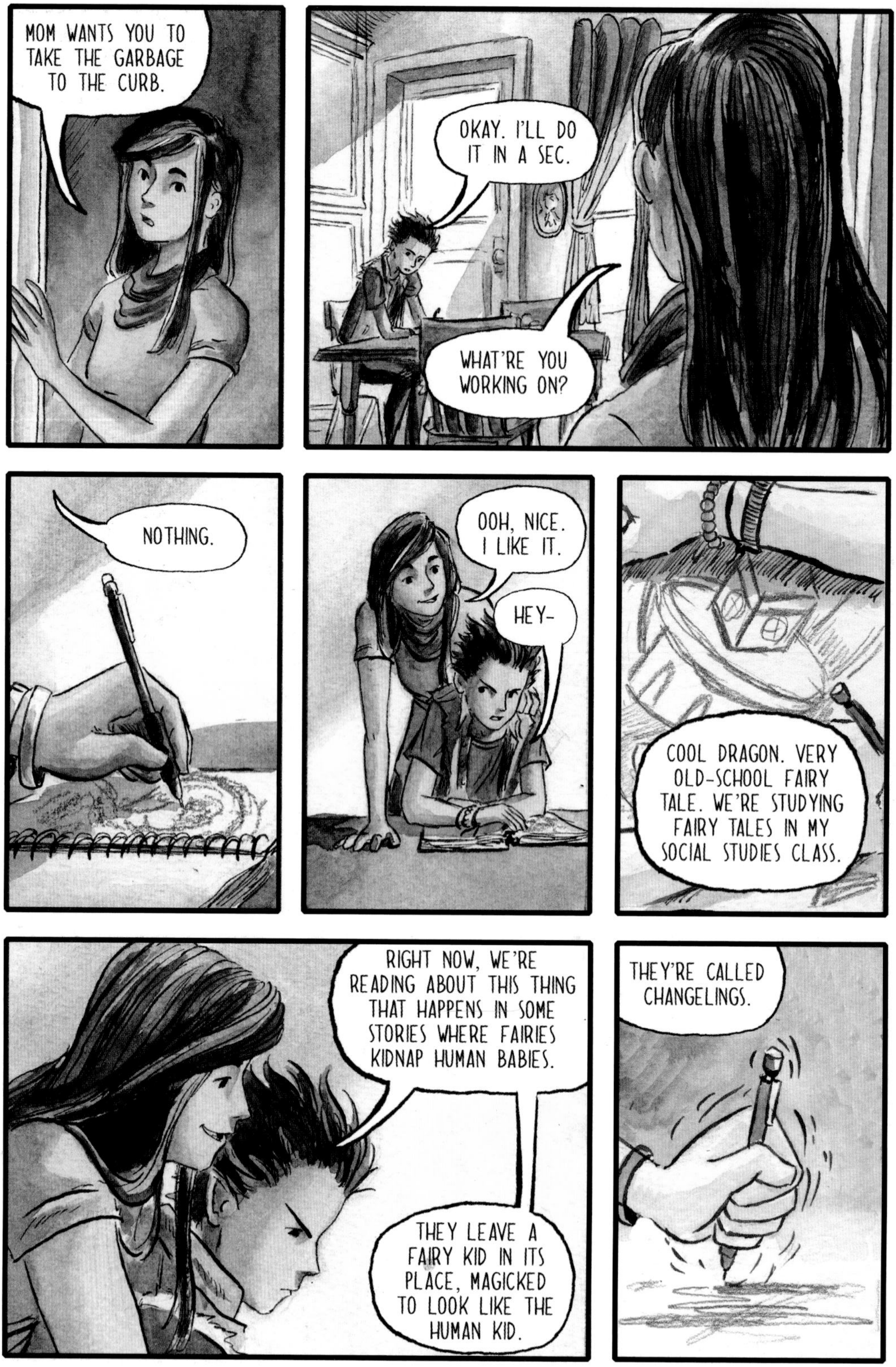
MOM WANTS YOU TO TAKE THE GARBAGE TO THE CURB.
OKAY. I'LL DO IT IN A SEC.
WHAT'RE YOU WORKING ON?
NOTHING.
OOH, NICE. I LIKE IT.
HEY-
COOL DRAGON. VERY OLD-SCHOOL FAIRY TALE. WE'RE STUDYING FAIRY TALES IN MY SOCIAL STUDIES CLASS.
RIGHT NOW, WE'RE READING ABOUT THIS THING THAT HAPPENS IN SOME STORIES WHERE FAIRIES KIDNAP HUMAN BABIES.
THEY LEAVE A FAIRY KID IN ITS PLACE, MAGICKED TO LOOK LIKE THE HUMAN KID.
THEY'RE CALLED CHANGELINGS.

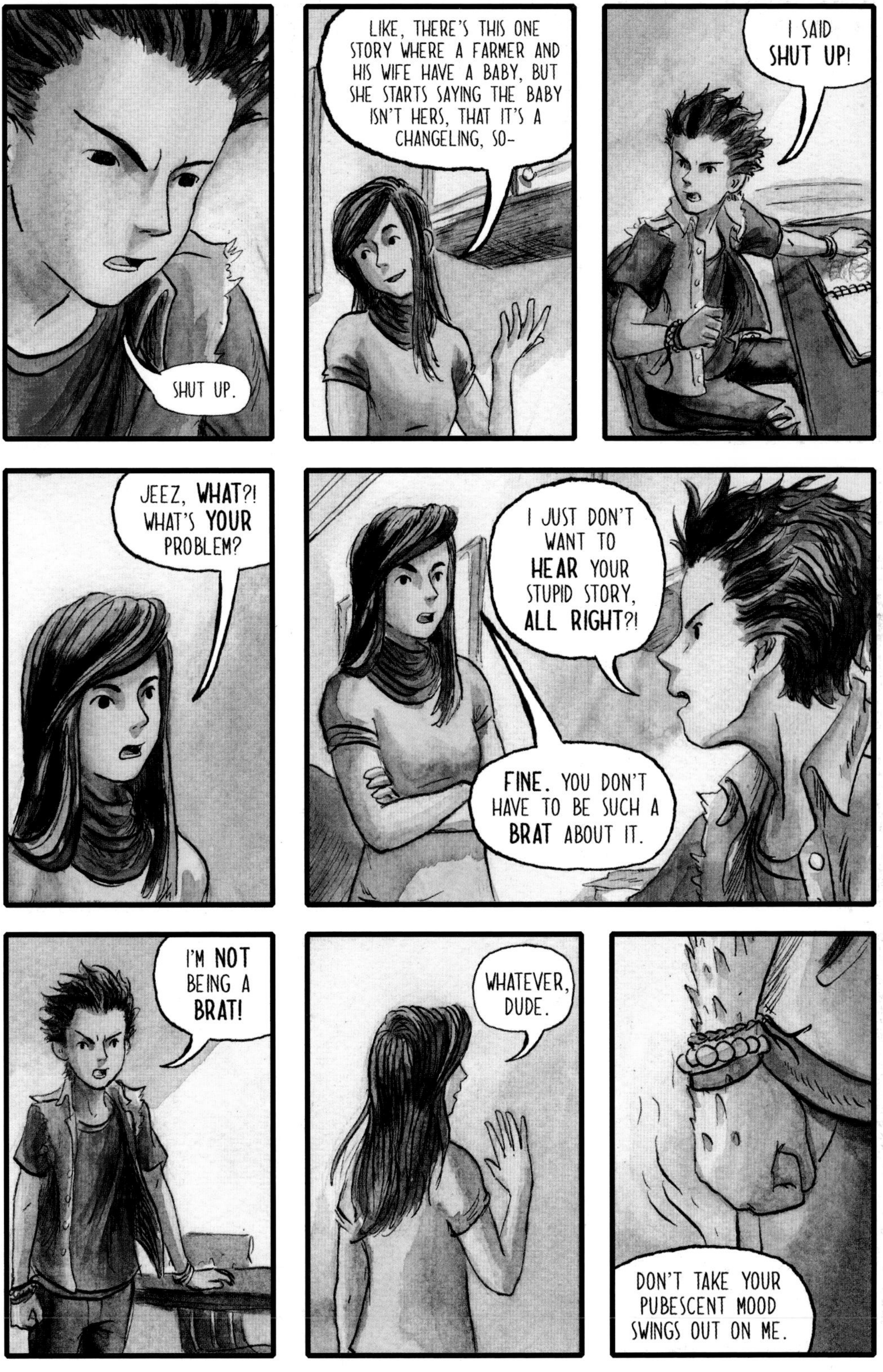
SHUT UP.
LIKE, THERE'S THIS ONE STORY WHERE A FARMER AND HIS WIFE HAVE A BABY, BUT SHE STARTS SAYING THE BABY ISN'T HERS, THAT IT'S A CHANGELING, SO-
I SAID **SHUT UP**!
JEEZ, **WHAT**?! WHAT'S **YOUR** PROBLEM?
I JUST DON'T WANT TO **HEAR** YOUR STUPID STORY, **ALL RIGHT**?!
FINE. YOU DON'T HAVE TO BE SUCH A **BRAT** ABOUT IT.
I'M **NOT** BEING A **BRAT**!
WHATEVER, DUDE.
DON'T TAKE YOUR PUBESCENT MOOD SWINGS OUT ON ME.

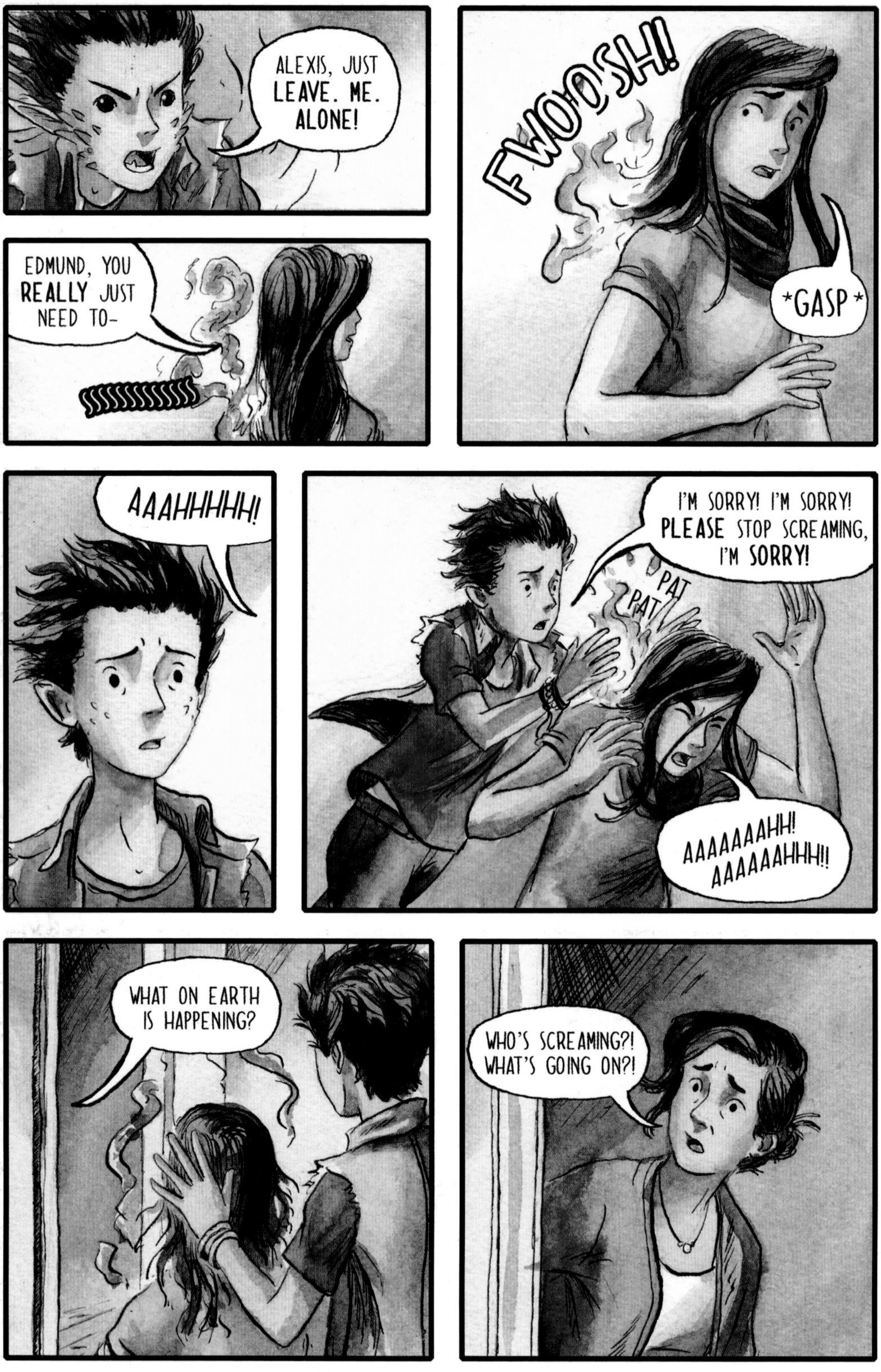
ALEXIS, JUST LEAVE. ME. ALONE!
EDMUND, YOU REALLY JUST NEED TO-
SSSSSSSSSSS
FWOOSH!
GASP
AAAHHHHH!
I'M SORRY! I'M SORRY! PLEASE STOP SCREAMING, I'M SORRY!
PAT PAT
AAAAAAAHH! AAAAAAHHH!!
WHAT ON EARTH IS HAPPENING?
WHO'S SCREAMING?! WHAT'S GOING ON?!

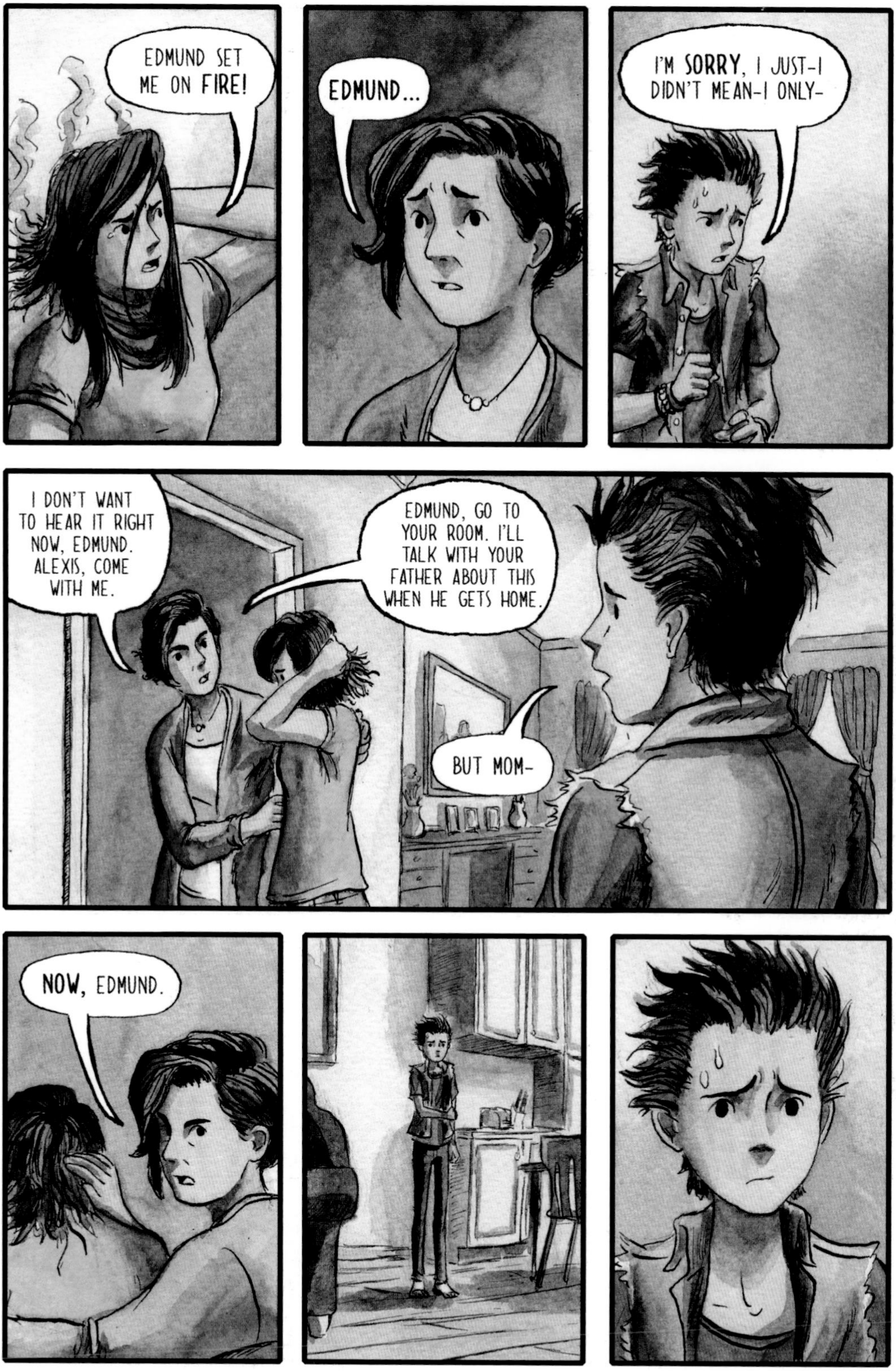
EDMUND SET ME ON FIRE!
EDMUND...
I'M SORRY, I JUST-I DIDN'T MEAN-I ONLY-
I DON'T WANT TO HEAR IT RIGHT NOW, EDMUND. ALEXIS, COME WITH ME.
EDMUND, GO TO YOUR ROOM. I'LL TALK WITH YOUR FATHER ABOUT THIS WHEN HE GETS HOME.
BUT MOM-
NOW, EDMUND.

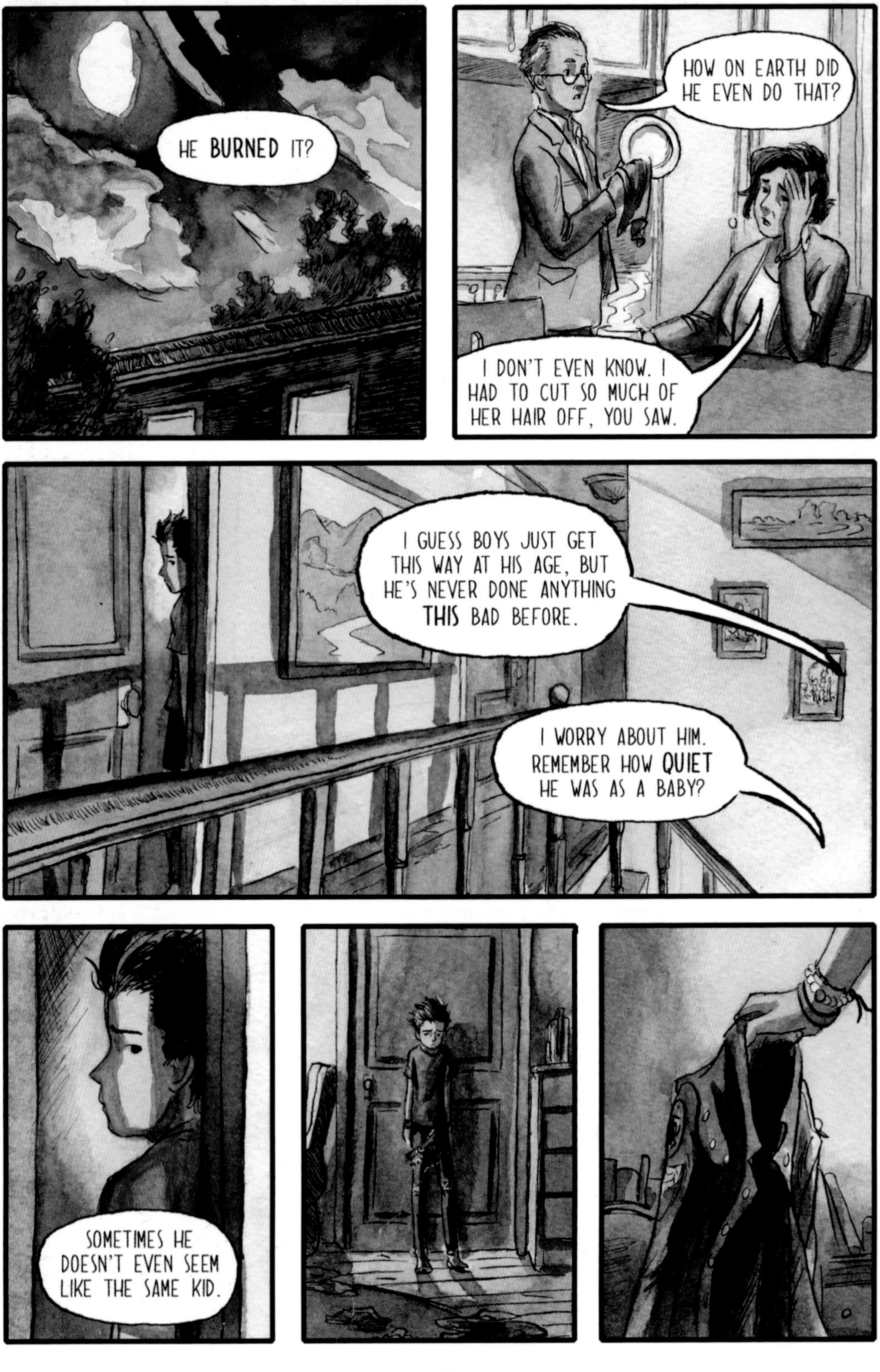
HE BURNED IT?
HOW ON EARTH DID HE EVEN DO THAT?
I DON'T EVEN KNOW. I HAD TO CUT SO MUCH OF HER HAIR OFF, YOU SAW.
I GUESS BOYS JUST GET THIS WAY AT HIS AGE, BUT HE'S NEVER DONE ANYTHING THIS BAD BEFORE.
I WORRY ABOUT HIM. REMEMBER HOW QUIET HE WAS AS A BABY?
SOMETIMES HE DOESN'T EVEN SEEM LIKE THE SAME KID.

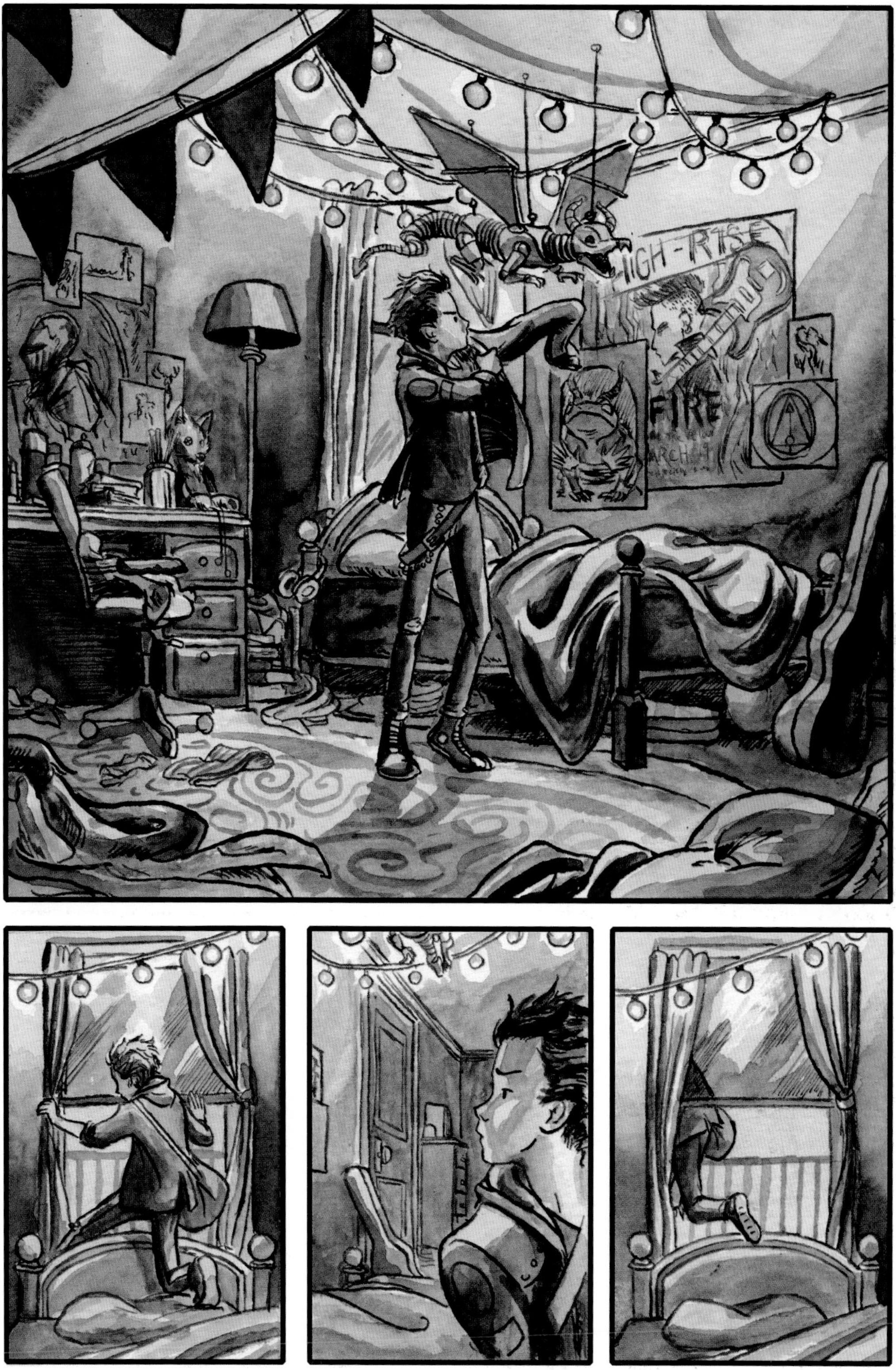
HIGH-RISE
FIRE

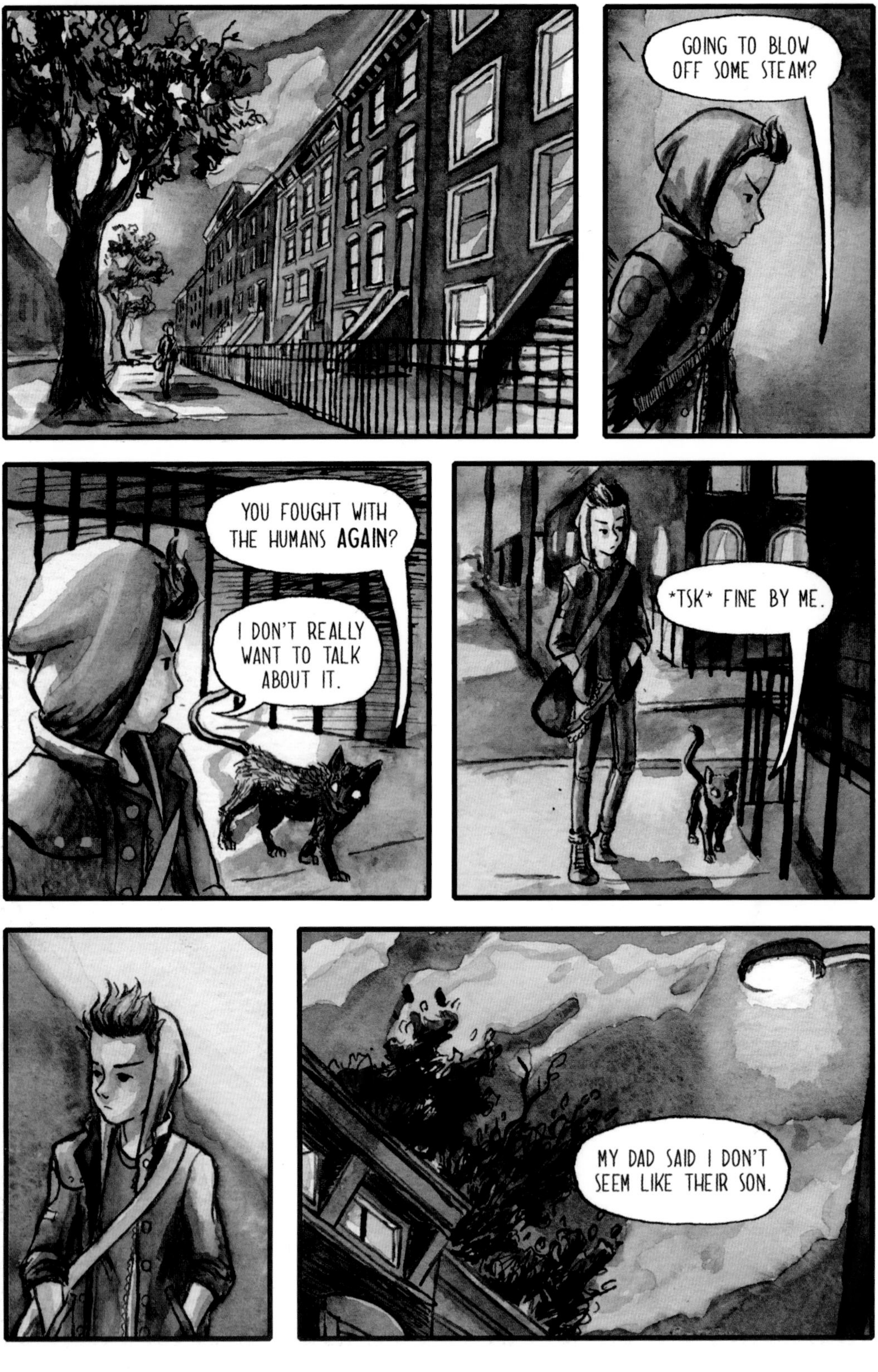
GOING TO BLOW OFF SOME STEAM?
YOU FOUGHT WITH THE HUMANS **AGAIN**?
I DON'T REALLY WANT TO TALK ABOUT IT.
TSK FINE BY ME.
MY DAD SAID I DON'T SEEM LIKE THEIR SON.

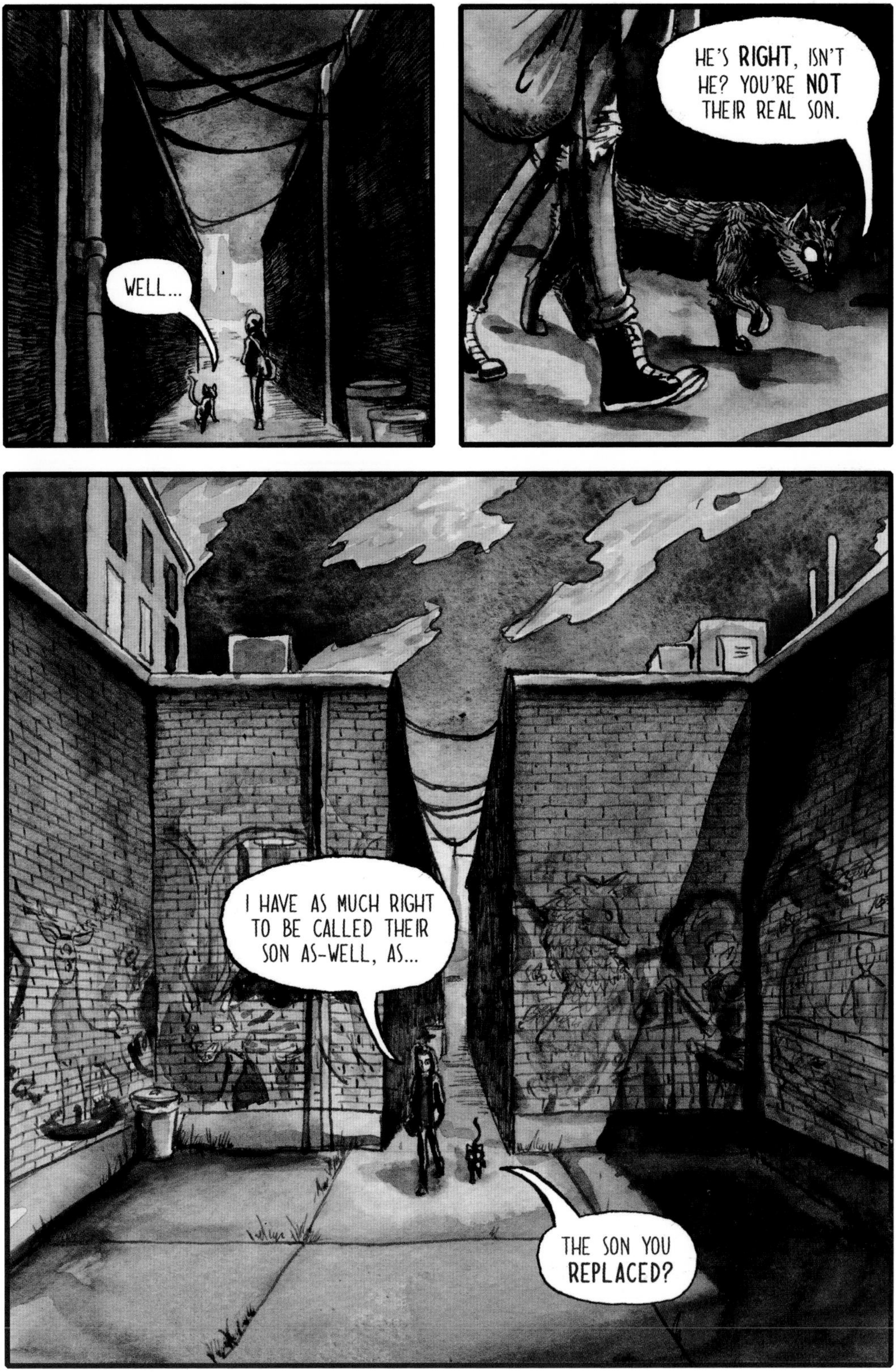
WELL...
HE'S **RIGHT**, ISN'T HE? YOU'RE **NOT** THEIR REAL SON.
I HAVE AS MUCH RIGHT TO BE CALLED THEIR SON AS-WELL, AS...
THE SON YOU **REPLACED?**

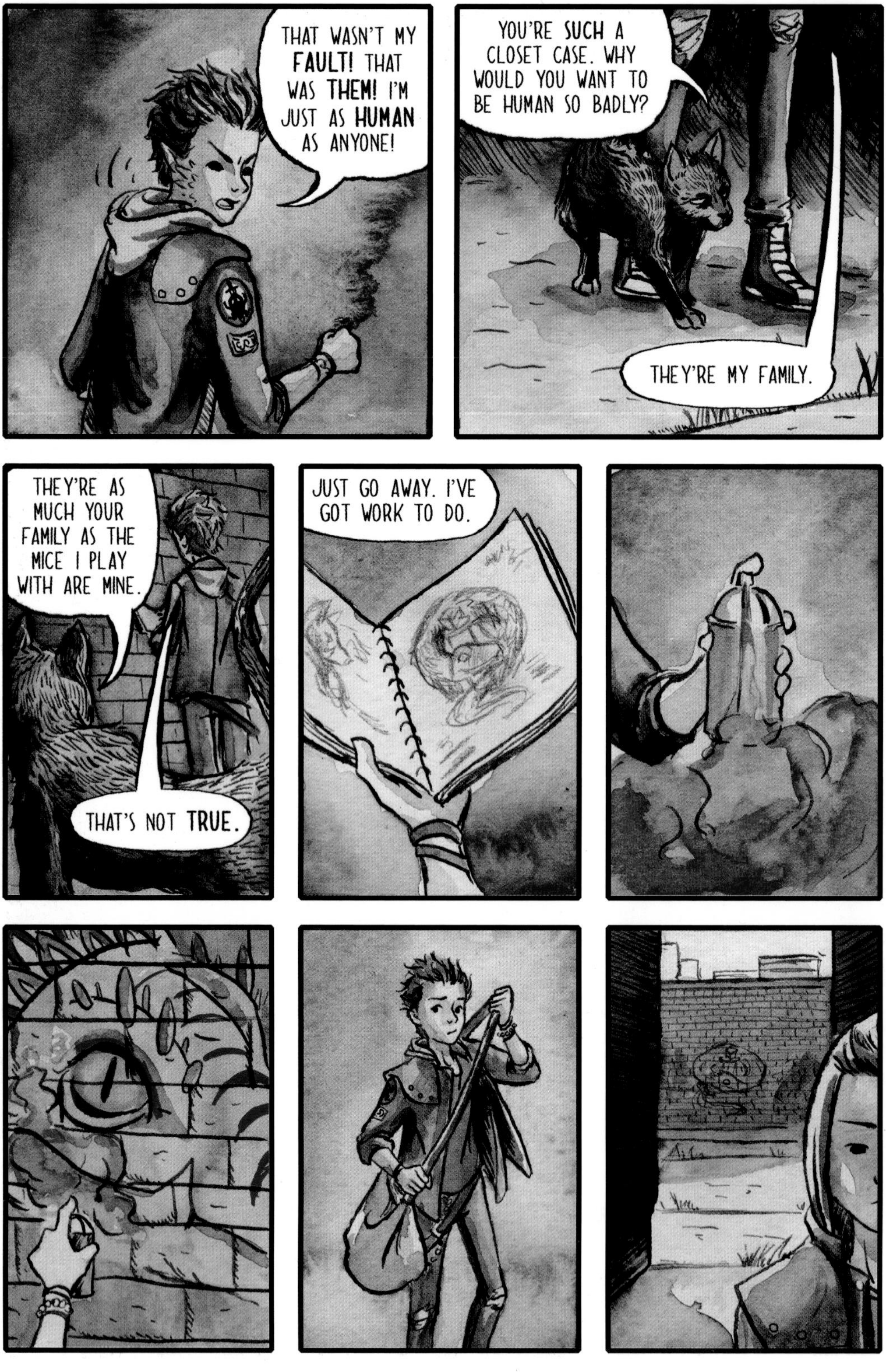
THAT WASN'T MY FAULT! THAT WAS THEM! I'M JUST AS HUMAN AS ANYONE!
YOU'RE SUCH A CLOSET CASE. WHY WOULD YOU WANT TO BE HUMAN SO BADLY?
THEY'RE MY FAMILY.
THEY'RE AS MUCH YOUR FAMILY AS THE MICE I PLAY WITH ARE MINE.
THAT'S NOT TRUE.
JUST GO AWAY. I'VE GOT WORK TO DO.

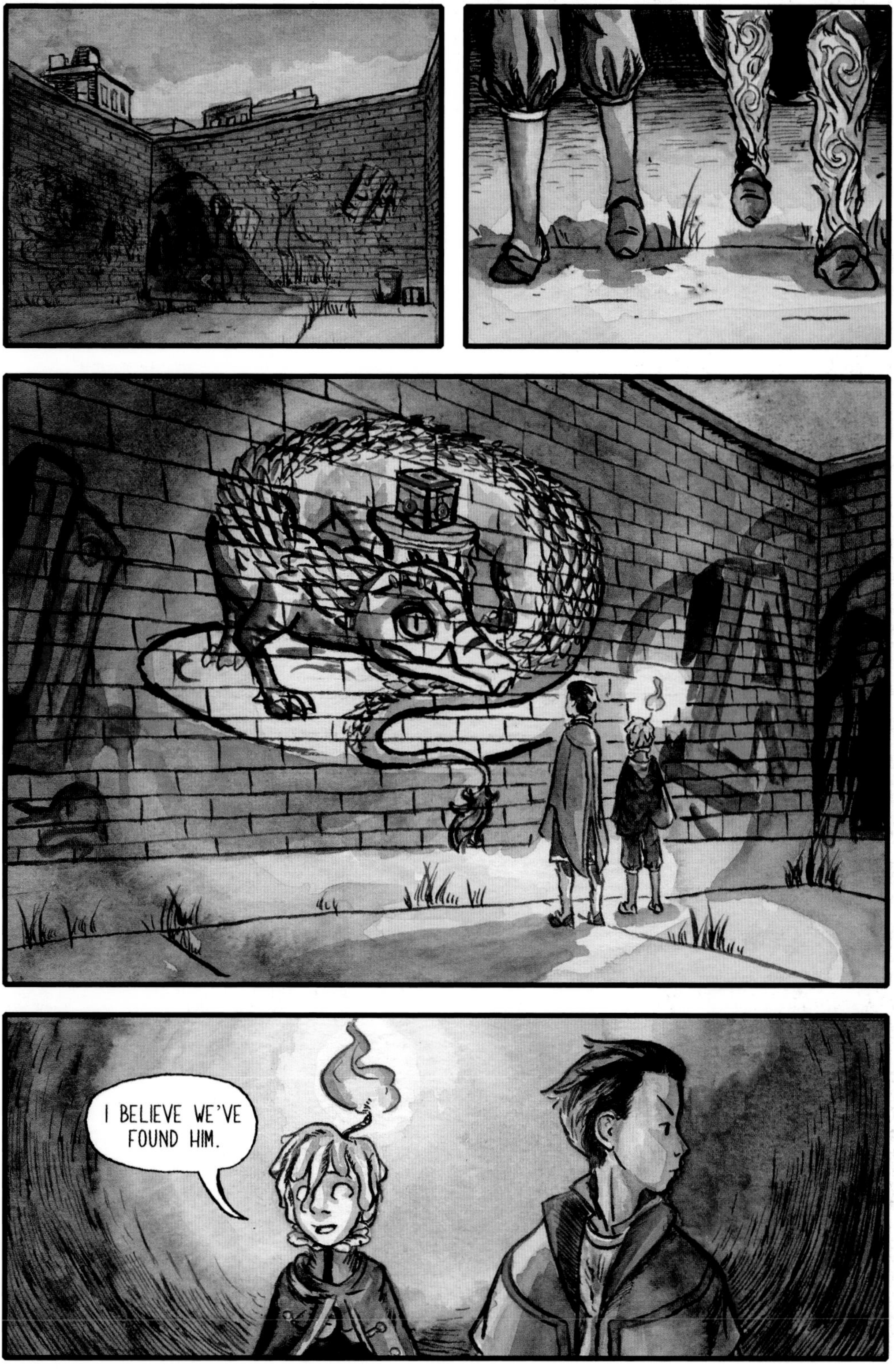
I BELIEVE WE'VE FOUND HIM.

Chapter Three

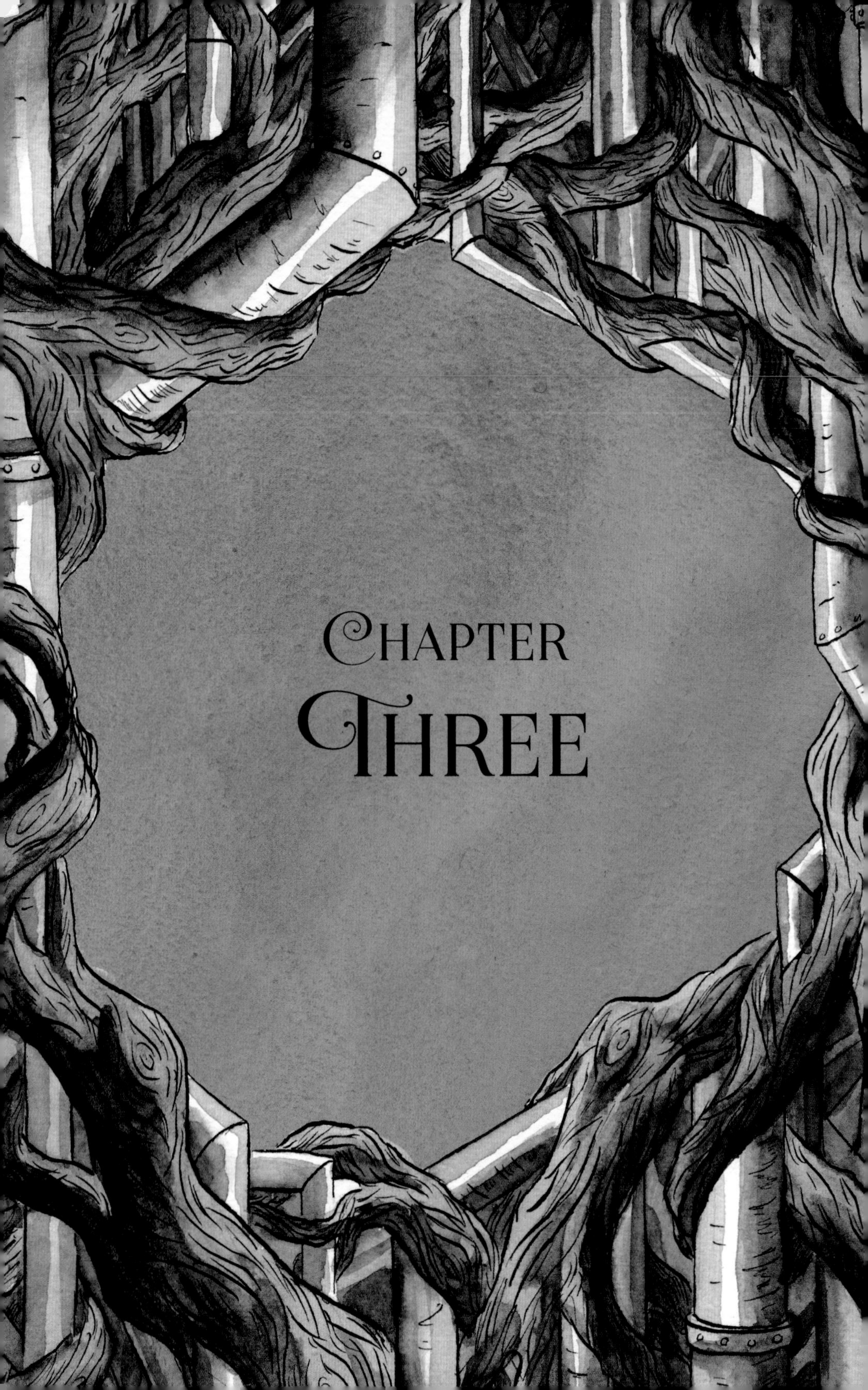

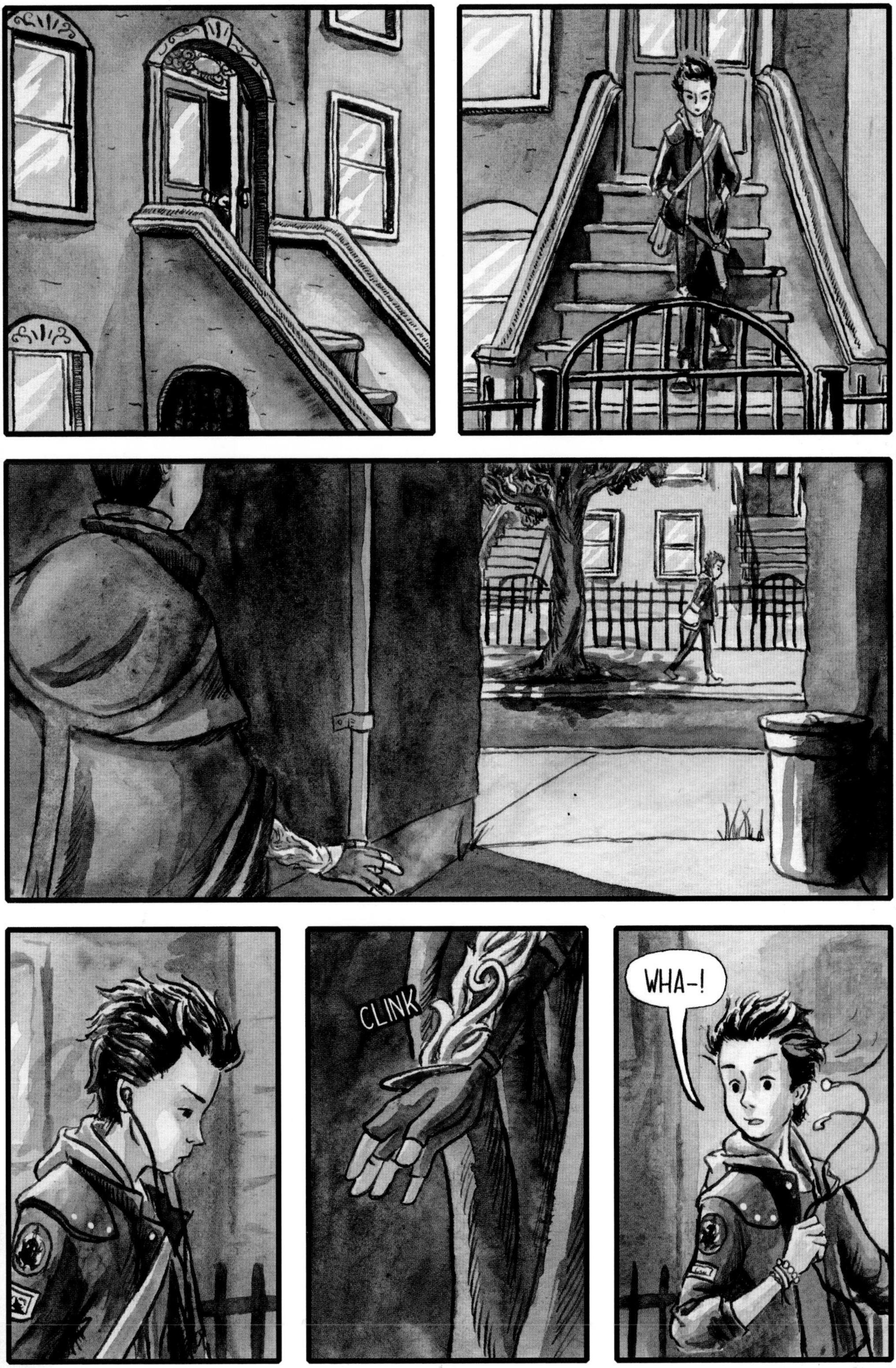
CLINK
WHA-!

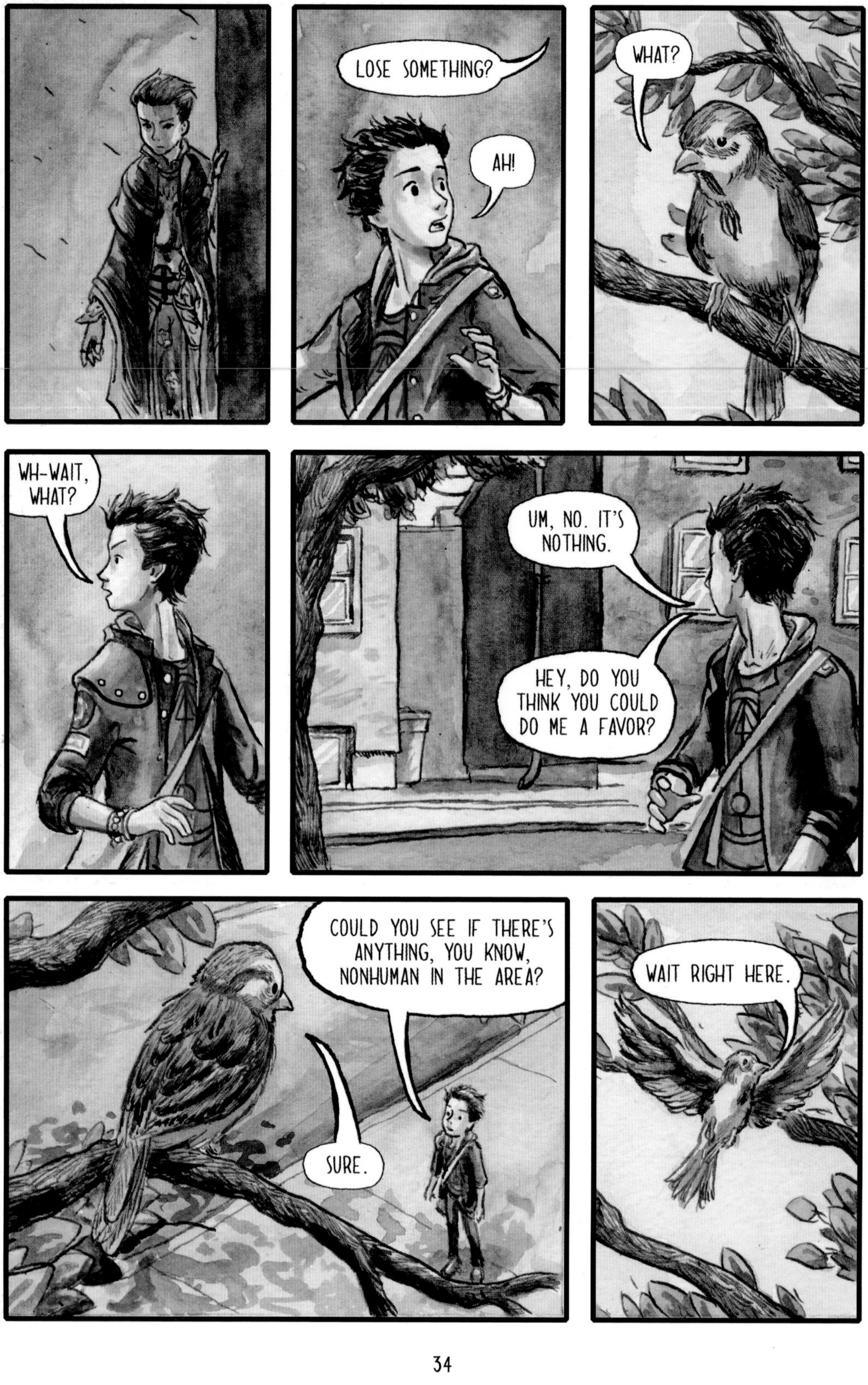
LOSE SOMETHING?
AH!
WHAT?
WH-WAIT, WHAT?
UM, NO. IT'S NOTHING.
HEY, DO YOU THINK YOU COULD DO ME A FAVOR?
COULD YOU SEE IF THERE'S ANYTHING, YOU KNOW, NONHUMAN IN THE AREA?
SURE.
WAIT RIGHT HERE.

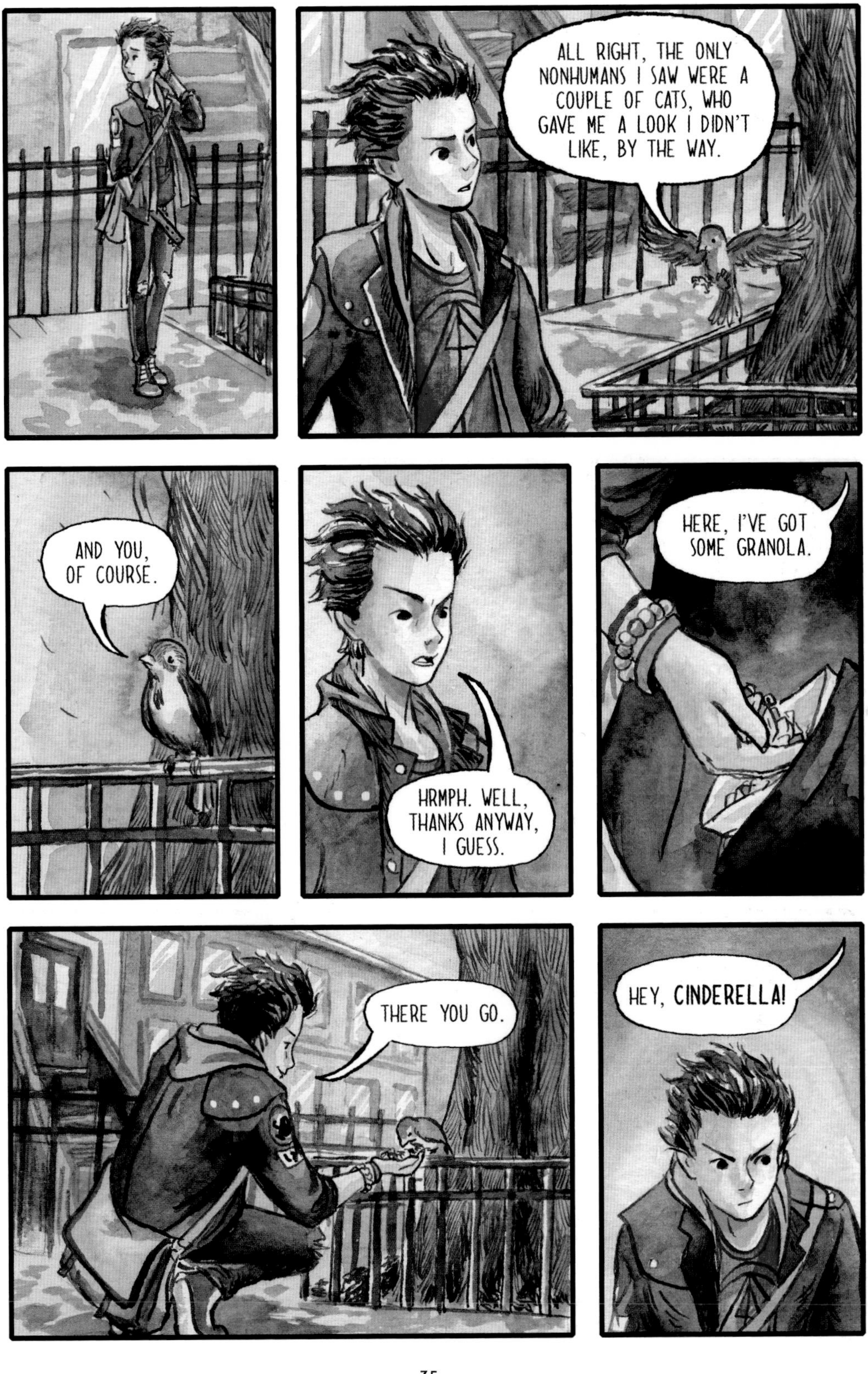
ALL RIGHT, THE ONLY NONHUMANS I SAW WERE A COUPLE OF CATS, WHO GAVE ME A LOOK I DIDN'T LIKE, BY THE WAY.
AND YOU, OF COURSE.
HRMPH. WELL, THANKS ANYWAY, I GUESS.
HERE, I'VE GOT SOME GRANOLA.
THERE YOU GO.
HEY, CINDERELLA!

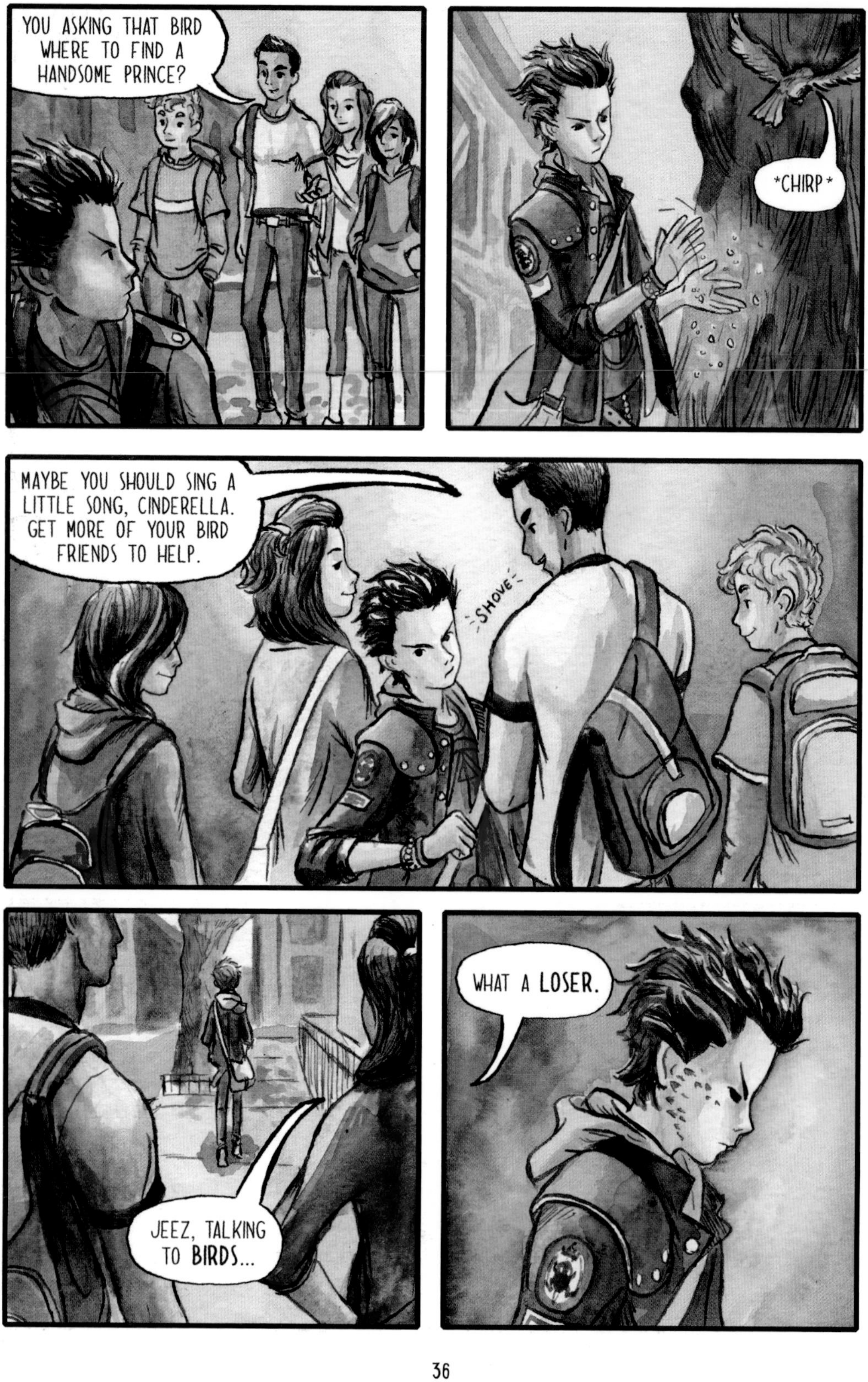
YOU ASKING THAT BIRD WHERE TO FIND A HANDSOME PRINCE?
CHIRP
MAYBE YOU SHOULD SING A LITTLE SONG, CINDERELLA. GET MORE OF YOUR BIRD FRIENDS TO HELP.
SHOVE
JEEZ, TALKING TO BIRDS...
WHAT A LOSER.

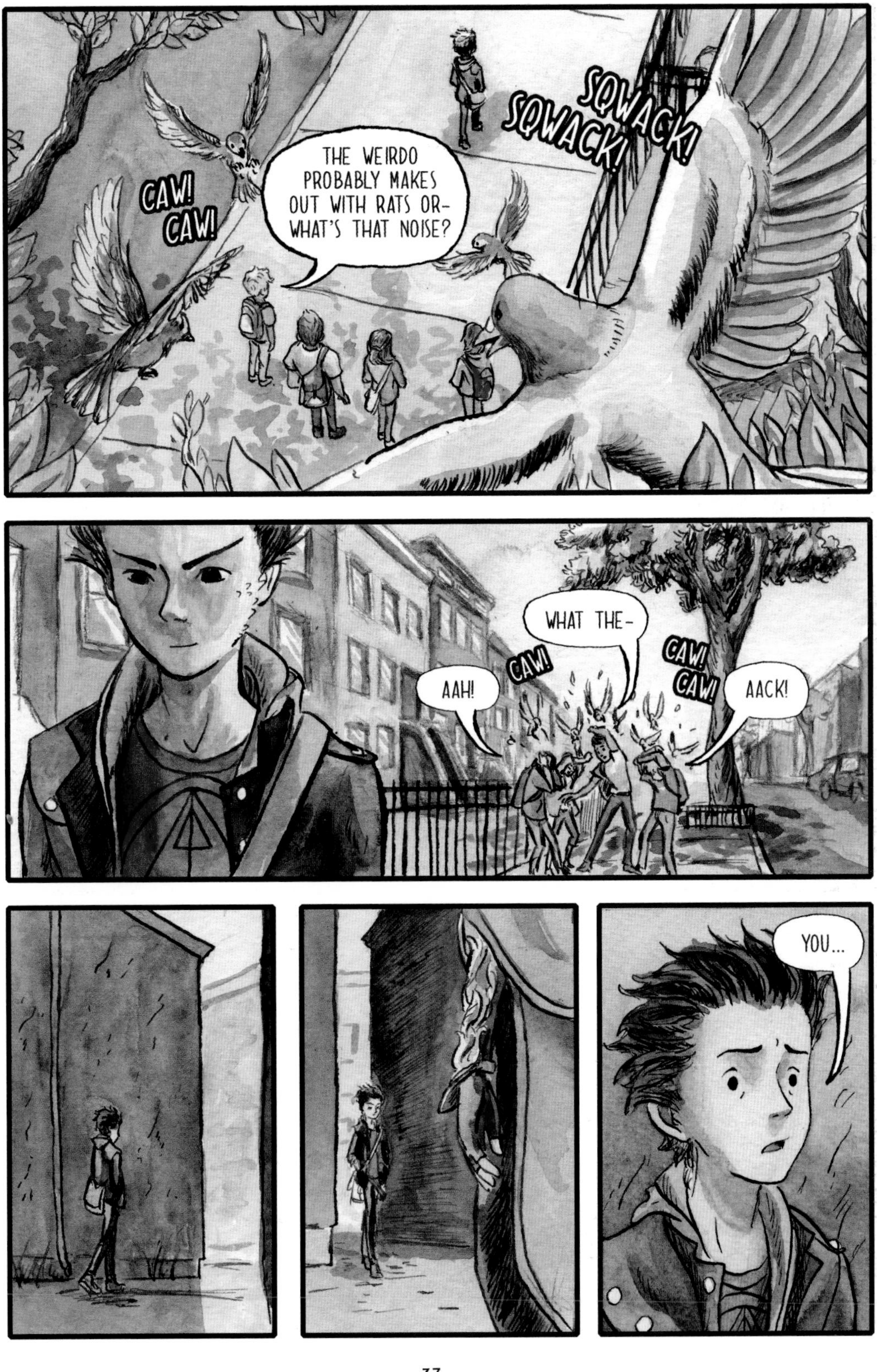
SQWACK!
SQWACK!
CAW!
CAW!
THE WEIRDO PROBABLY MAKES OUT WITH RATS OR- WHAT'S THAT NOISE?
WHAT THE-
CAW!
AAH!
CAW!
CAW!
AACK!
YOU...

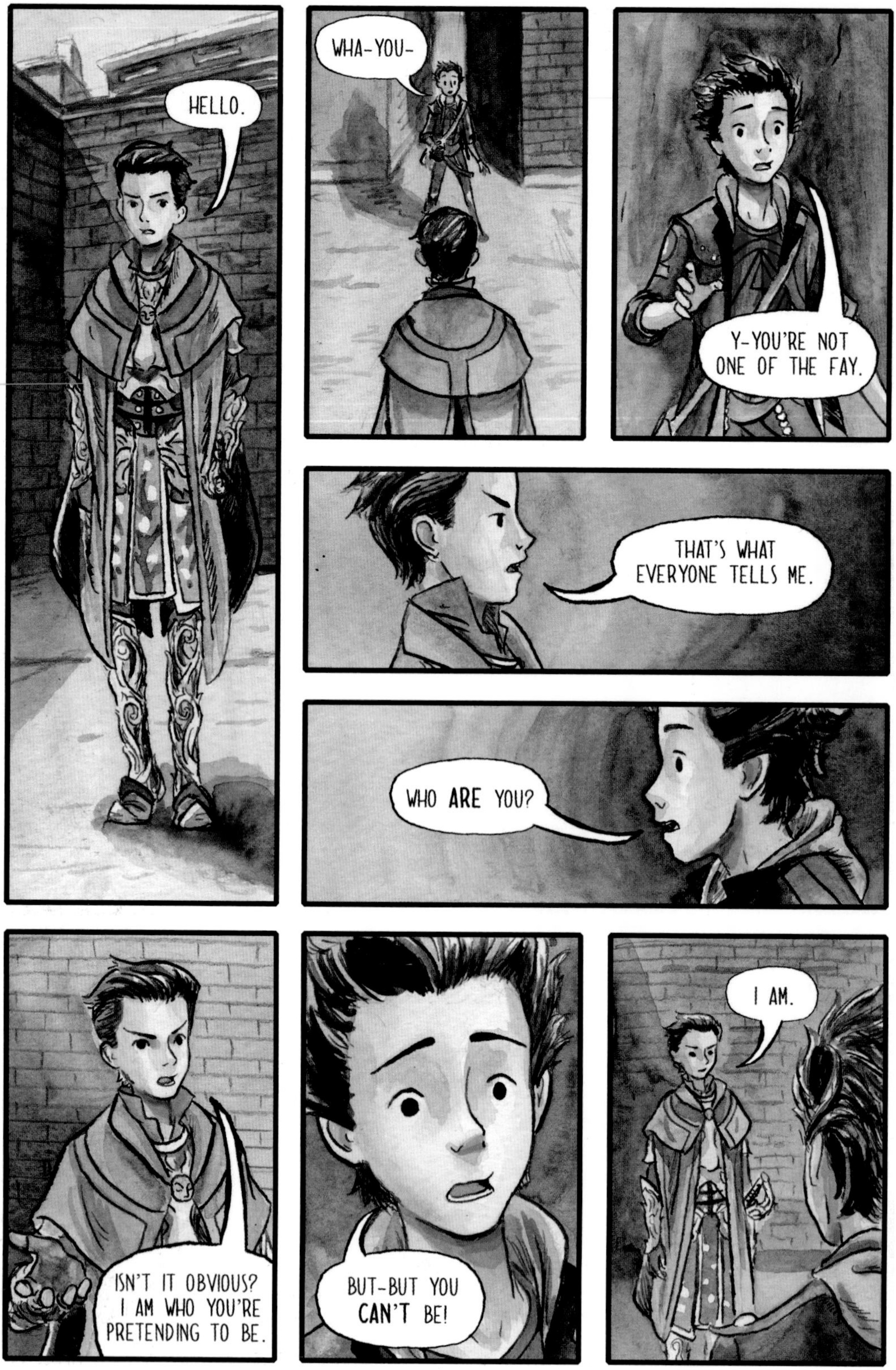
HELLO.
WHA-YOU-
Y-YOU'RE NOT ONE OF THE FAY.
THAT'S WHAT EVERYONE TELLS ME.
WHO **ARE** YOU?
ISN'T IT OBVIOUS? I AM WHO YOU'RE PRETENDING TO BE.
BUT-BUT YOU **CAN'T** BE!
I AM.

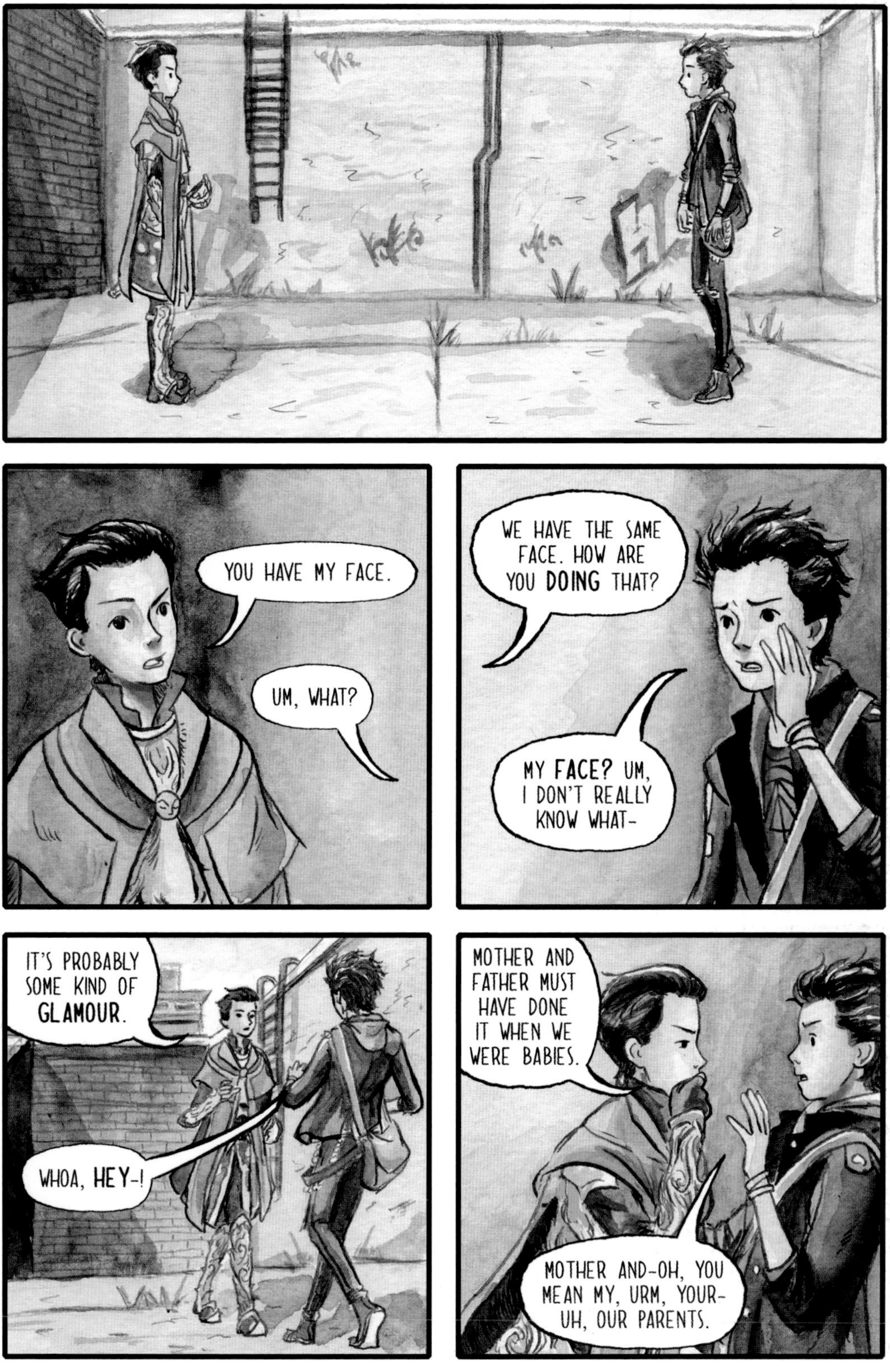
YOU HAVE MY FACE.
UM, WHAT?
WE HAVE THE SAME FACE. HOW ARE YOU DOING THAT?
MY FACE? UM, I DON'T REALLY KNOW WHAT-
IT'S PROBABLY SOME KIND OF GLAMOUR.
WHOA, HEY-!
MOTHER AND FATHER MUST HAVE DONE IT WHEN WE WERE BABIES.
MOTHER AND-OH, YOU MEAN MY, URM, YOUR- UH, OUR PARENTS.

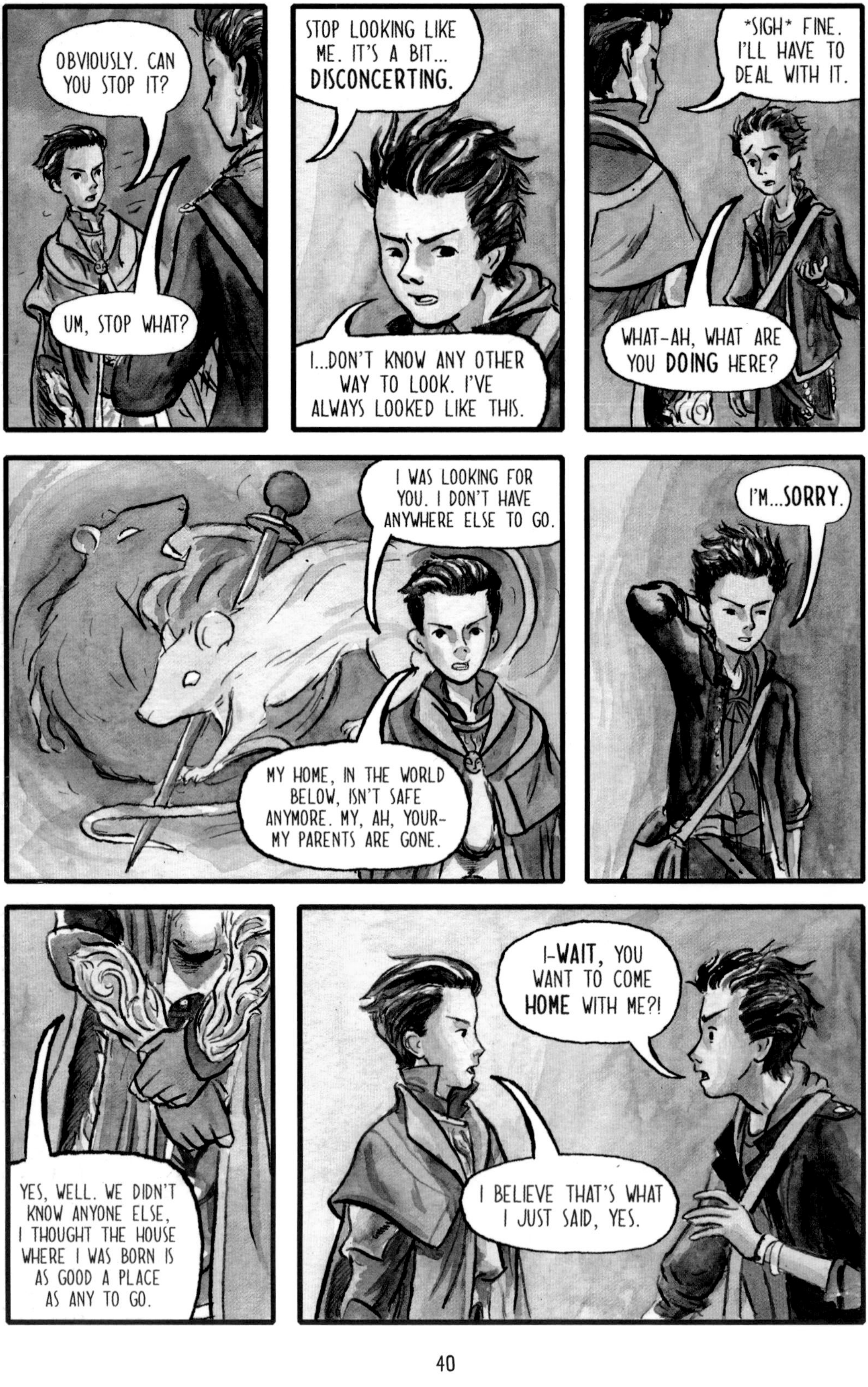
OBVIOUSLY. CAN YOU STOP IT?
UM, STOP WHAT?
STOP LOOKING LIKE ME. IT'S A BIT... DISCONCERTING.
I...DON'T KNOW ANY OTHER WAY TO LOOK. I'VE ALWAYS LOOKED LIKE THIS.
SIGH FINE. I'LL HAVE TO DEAL WITH IT.
WHAT-AH, WHAT ARE YOU DOING HERE?
I WAS LOOKING FOR YOU. I DON'T HAVE ANYWHERE ELSE TO GO.
MY HOME, IN THE WORLD BELOW, ISN'T SAFE ANYMORE. MY, AH, YOUR- MY PARENTS ARE GONE.
I'M...SORRY.
YES, WELL. WE DIDN'T KNOW ANYONE ELSE, I THOUGHT THE HOUSE WHERE I WAS BORN IS AS GOOD A PLACE AS ANY TO GO.
I-WAIT, YOU WANT TO COME HOME WITH ME?!
I BELIEVE THAT'S WHAT I JUST SAID, YES.

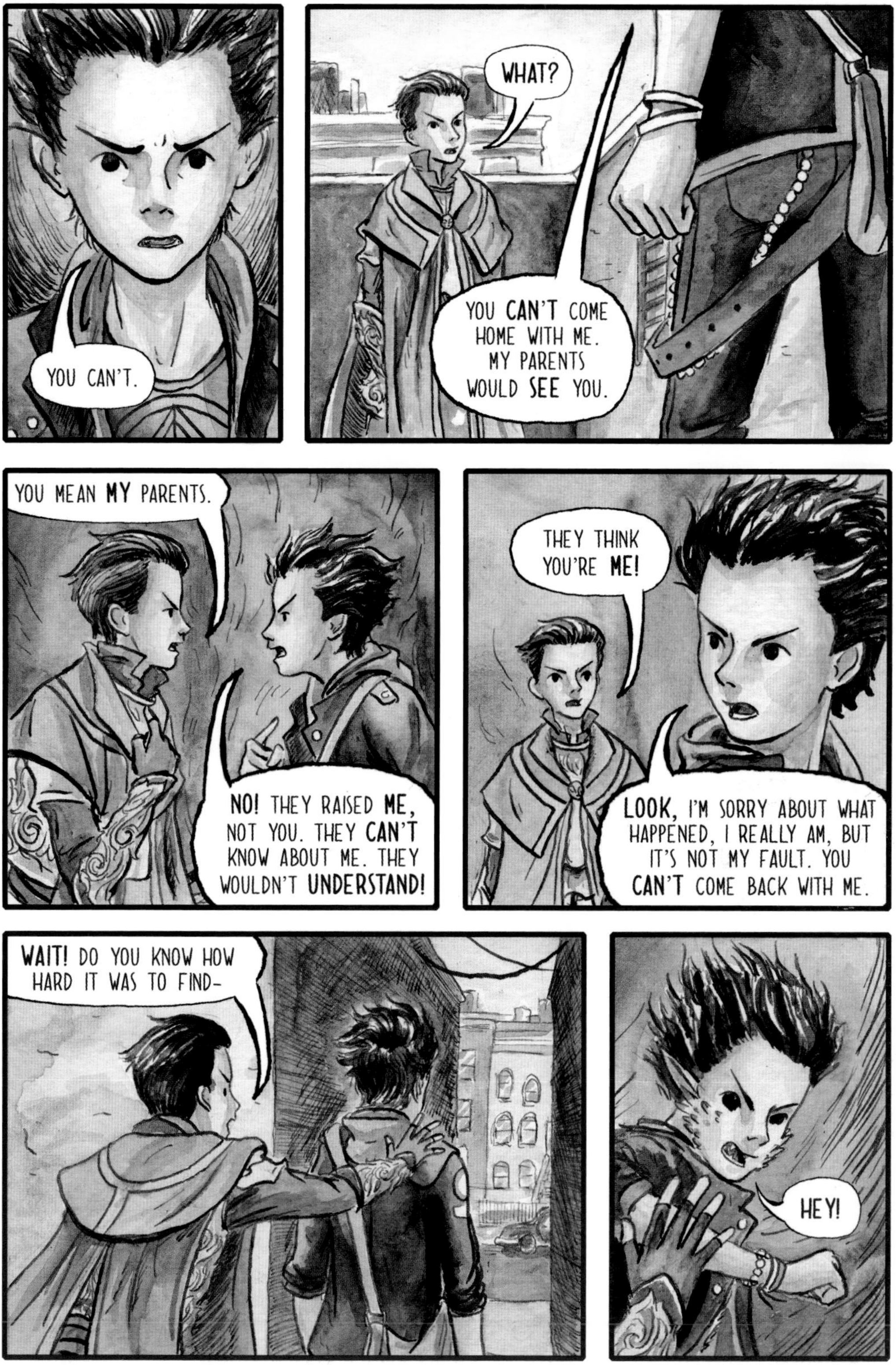
YOU CAN'T.
WHAT?
YOU CAN'T COME HOME WITH ME. MY PARENTS WOULD SEE YOU.
YOU MEAN MY PARENTS.
NO! THEY RAISED ME, NOT YOU. THEY CAN'T KNOW ABOUT ME. THEY WOULDN'T UNDERSTAND!
THEY THINK YOU'RE ME!
LOOK, I'M SORRY ABOUT WHAT HAPPENED, I REALLY AM, BUT IT'S NOT MY FAULT. YOU CAN'T COME BACK WITH ME.
WAIT! DO YOU KNOW HOW HARD IT WAS TO FIND-
HEY!

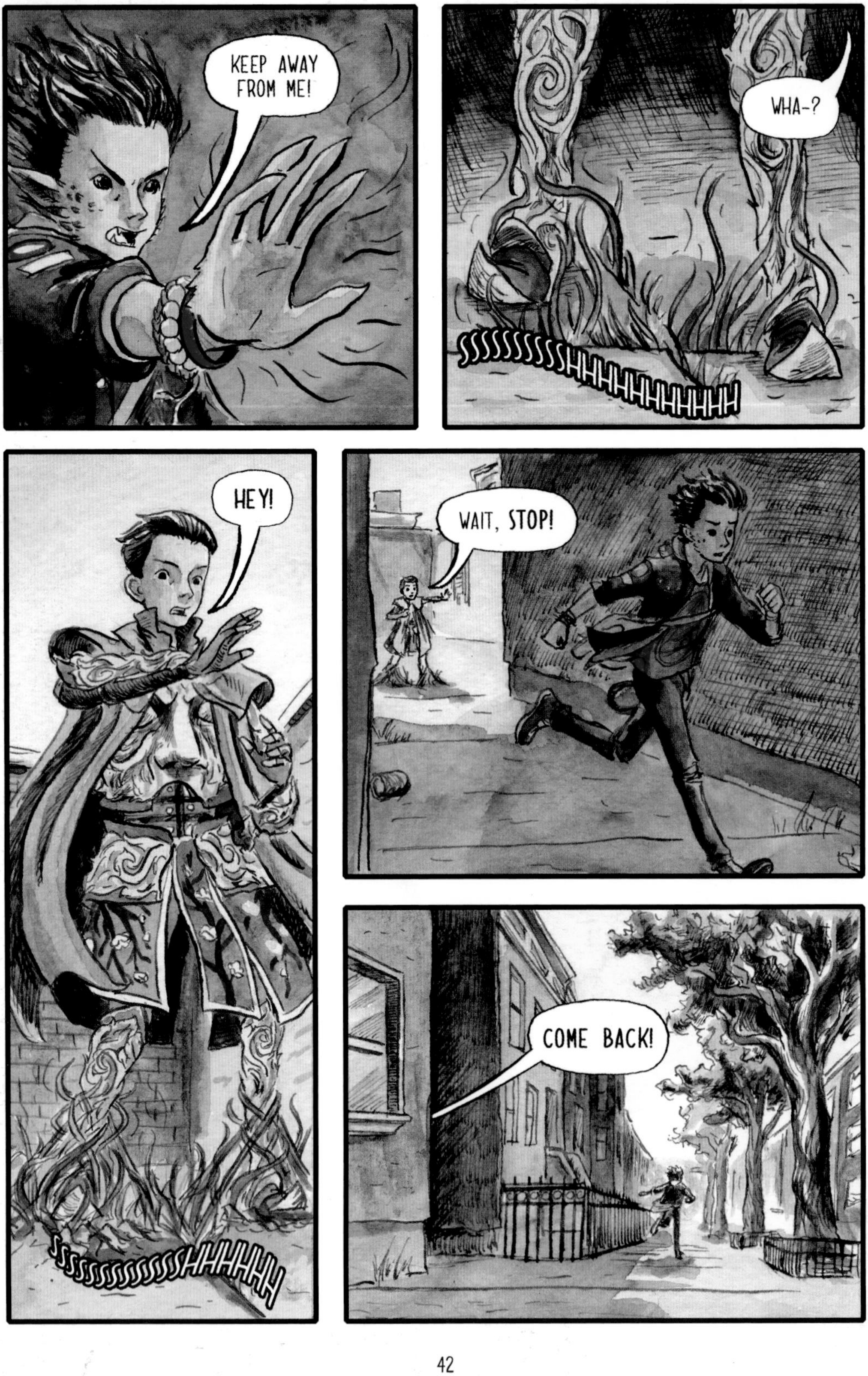
KEEP AWAY FROM ME!
WHA-?
SSSSSSSSSSHHHHHHHHHHHH
HEY!
SSSSSSSSSSSHHHHHH
WAIT, STOP!
COME BACK!

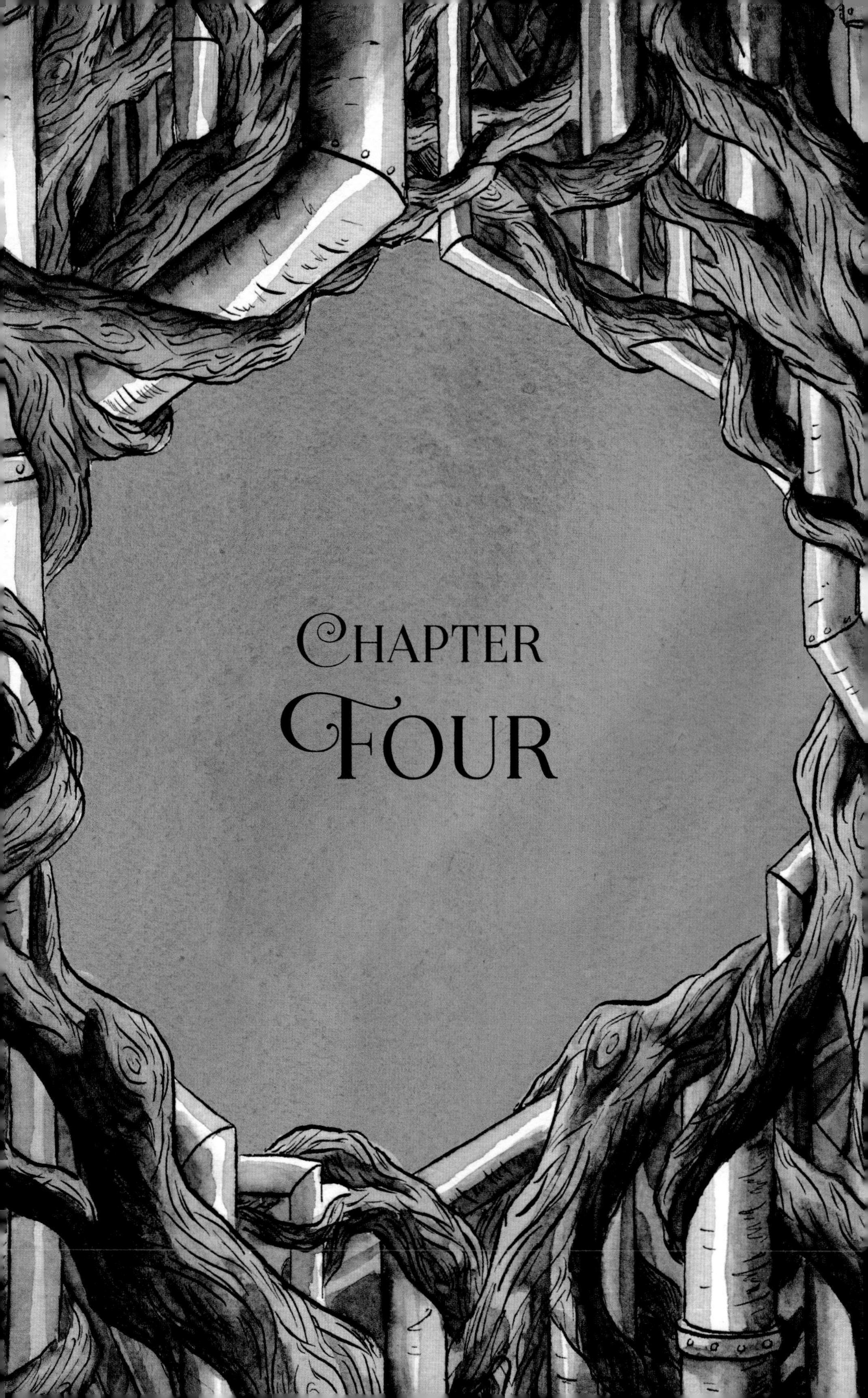

Chapter Four

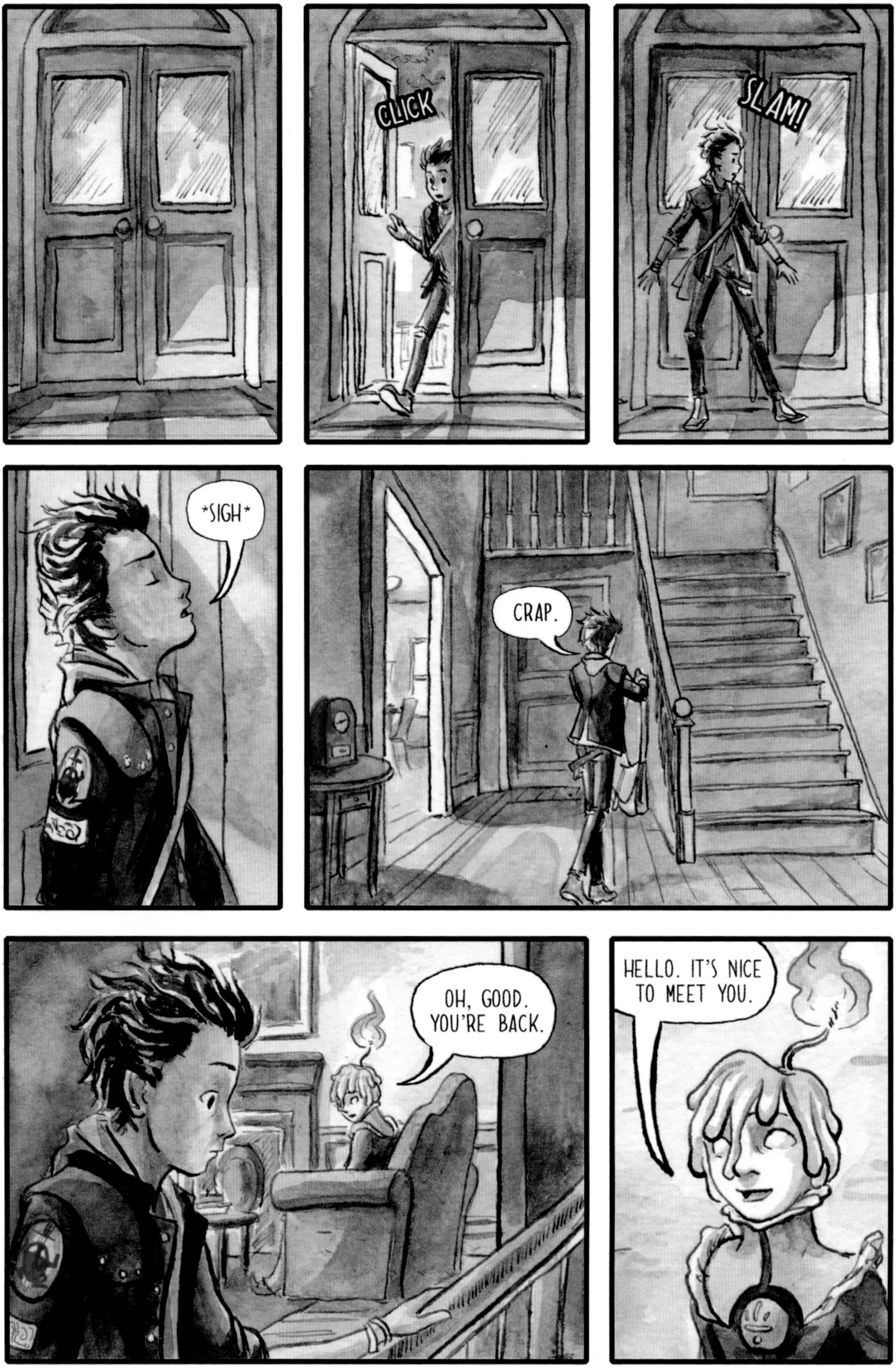
CLICK
SLAM!
SIGH
CRAP.
OH, GOOD. YOU'RE BACK.
HELLO. IT'S NICE TO MEET YOU.

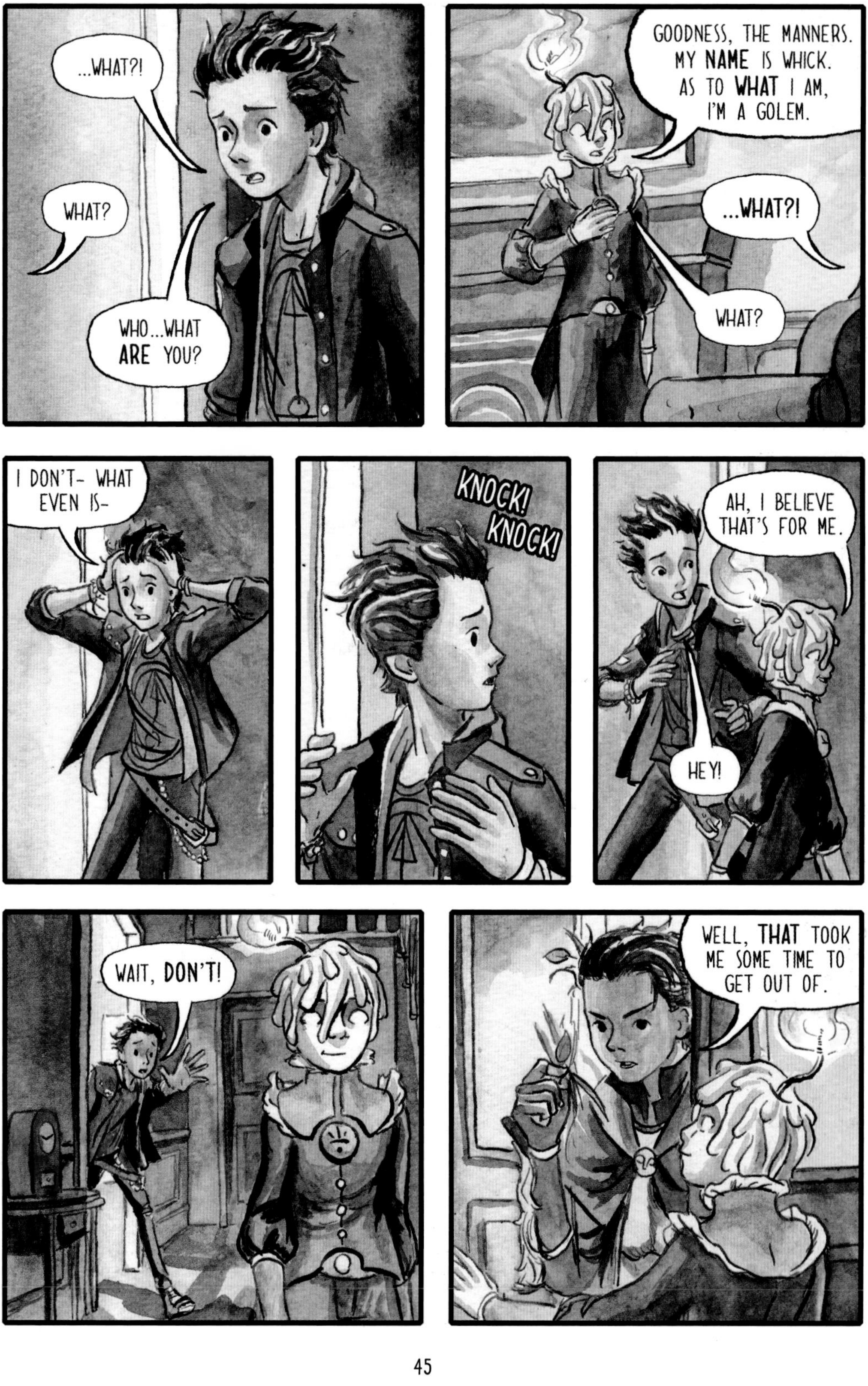
...WHAT?!
WHAT?
WHO...WHAT **ARE** YOU?
GOODNESS, THE MANNERS. MY **NAME** IS WHICK. AS TO **WHAT** I AM, I'M A GOLEM.
...WHAT?!
WHAT?
I DON'T- WHAT EVEN IS-
KNOCK! KNOCK!
AH, I BELIEVE THAT'S FOR ME.
HEY!
WAIT, **DON'T**!
WELL, **THAT** TOOK ME SOME TIME TO GET OUT OF.

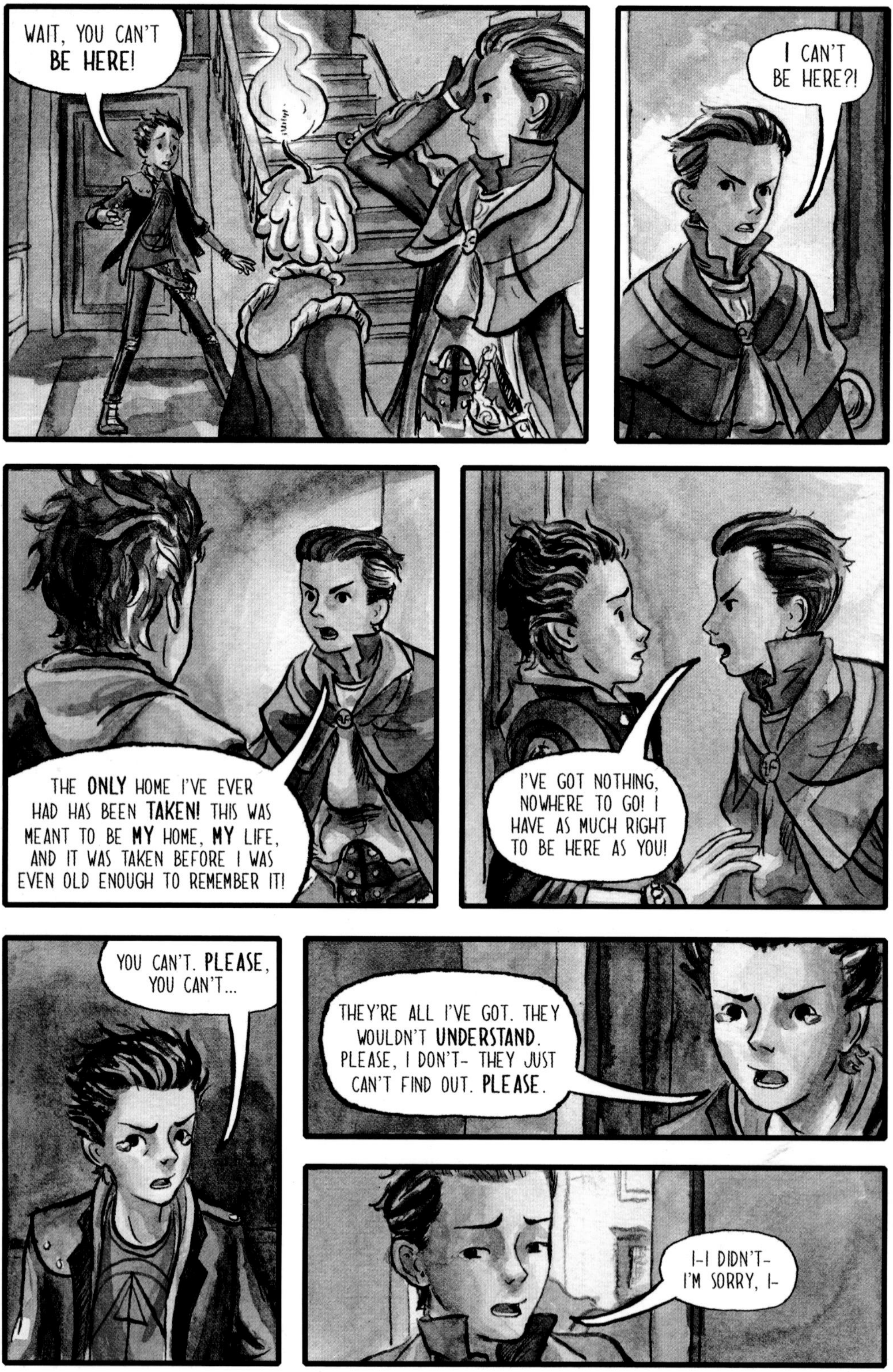
WAIT, YOU CAN'T BE HERE!
I CAN'T BE HERE?!
THE ONLY HOME I'VE EVER HAD HAS BEEN TAKEN! THIS WAS MEANT TO BE MY HOME, MY LIFE, AND IT WAS TAKEN BEFORE I WAS EVEN OLD ENOUGH TO REMEMBER IT!
I'VE GOT NOTHING, NOWHERE TO GO! I HAVE AS MUCH RIGHT TO BE HERE AS YOU!
YOU CAN'T. PLEASE, YOU CAN'T...
THEY'RE ALL I'VE GOT. THEY WOULDN'T UNDERSTAND. PLEASE, I DON'T- THEY JUST CAN'T FIND OUT. PLEASE.
I-I DIDN'T- I'M SORRY, I-

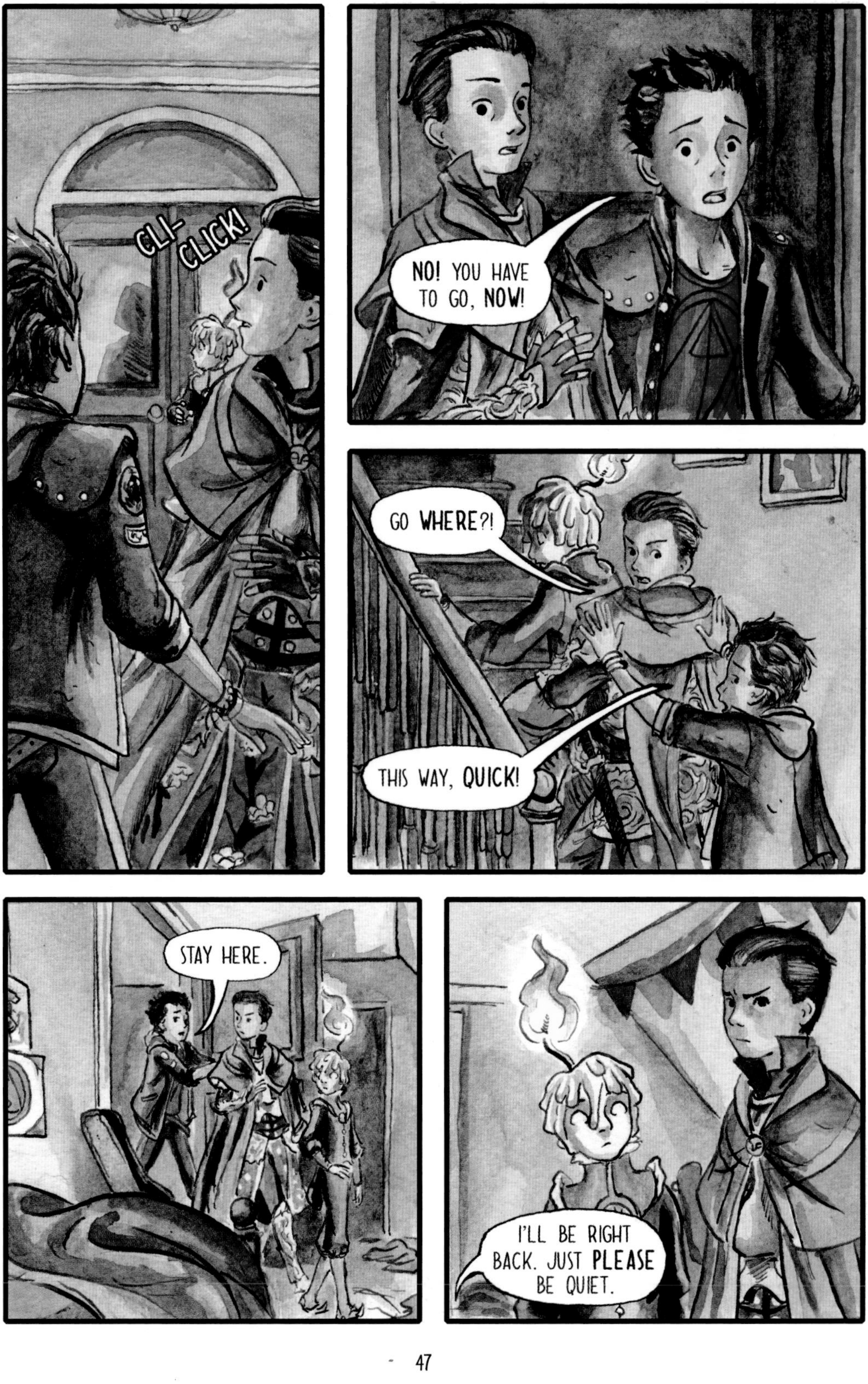
CLI-CLICK!
NO! YOU HAVE TO GO, NOW!
GO WHERE?!
THIS WAY, QUICK!
STAY HERE.
I'LL BE RIGHT BACK. JUST PLEASE BE QUIET.

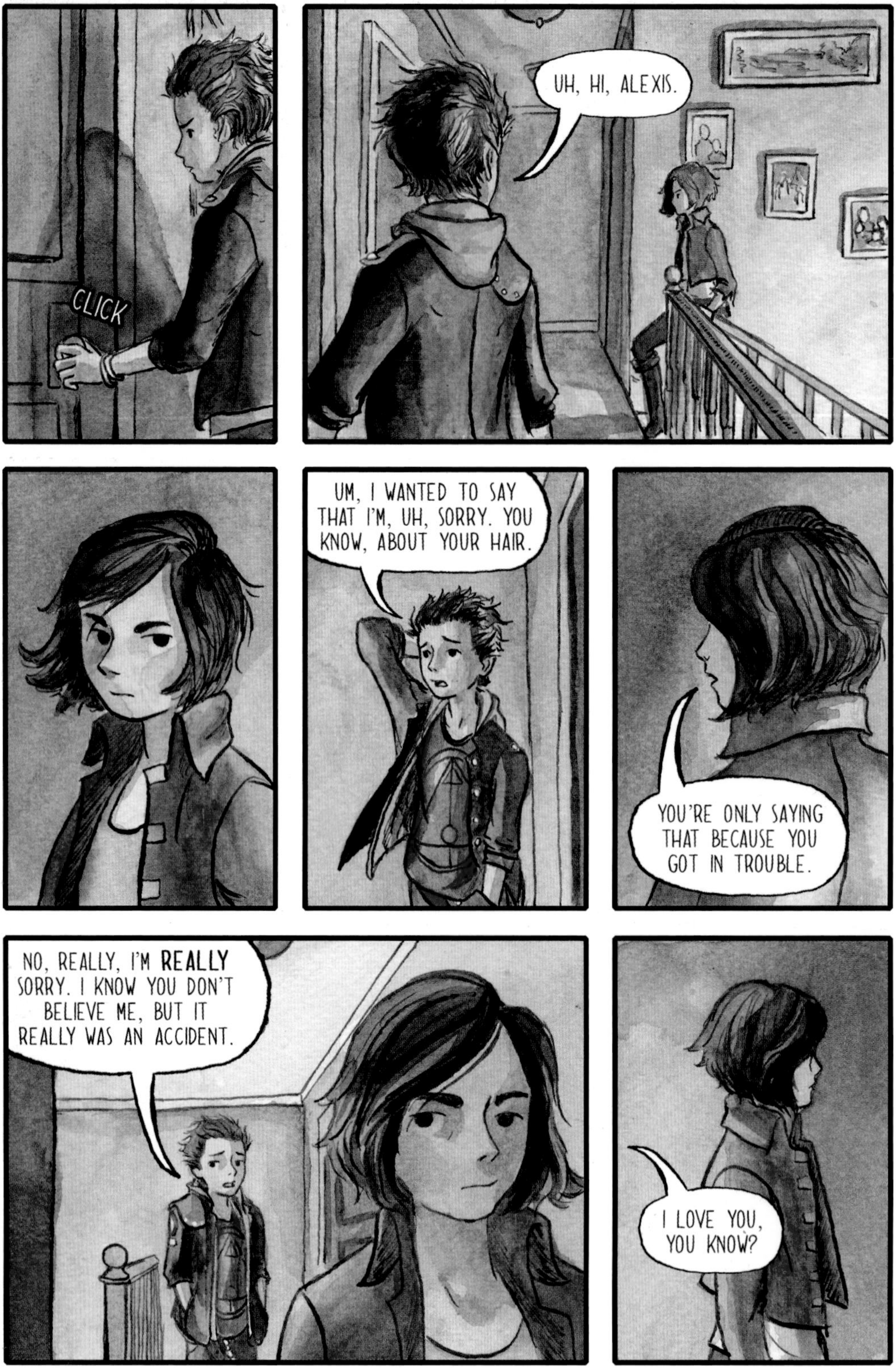
CLICK
UH, HI, ALEXIS.
UM, I WANTED TO SAY THAT I'M, UH, SORRY. YOU KNOW, ABOUT YOUR HAIR.
YOU'RE ONLY SAYING THAT BECAUSE YOU GOT IN TROUBLE.
NO, REALLY, I'M **REALLY** SORRY. I KNOW YOU DON'T BELIEVE ME, BUT IT REALLY WAS AN ACCIDENT.
I LOVE YOU, YOU KNOW?

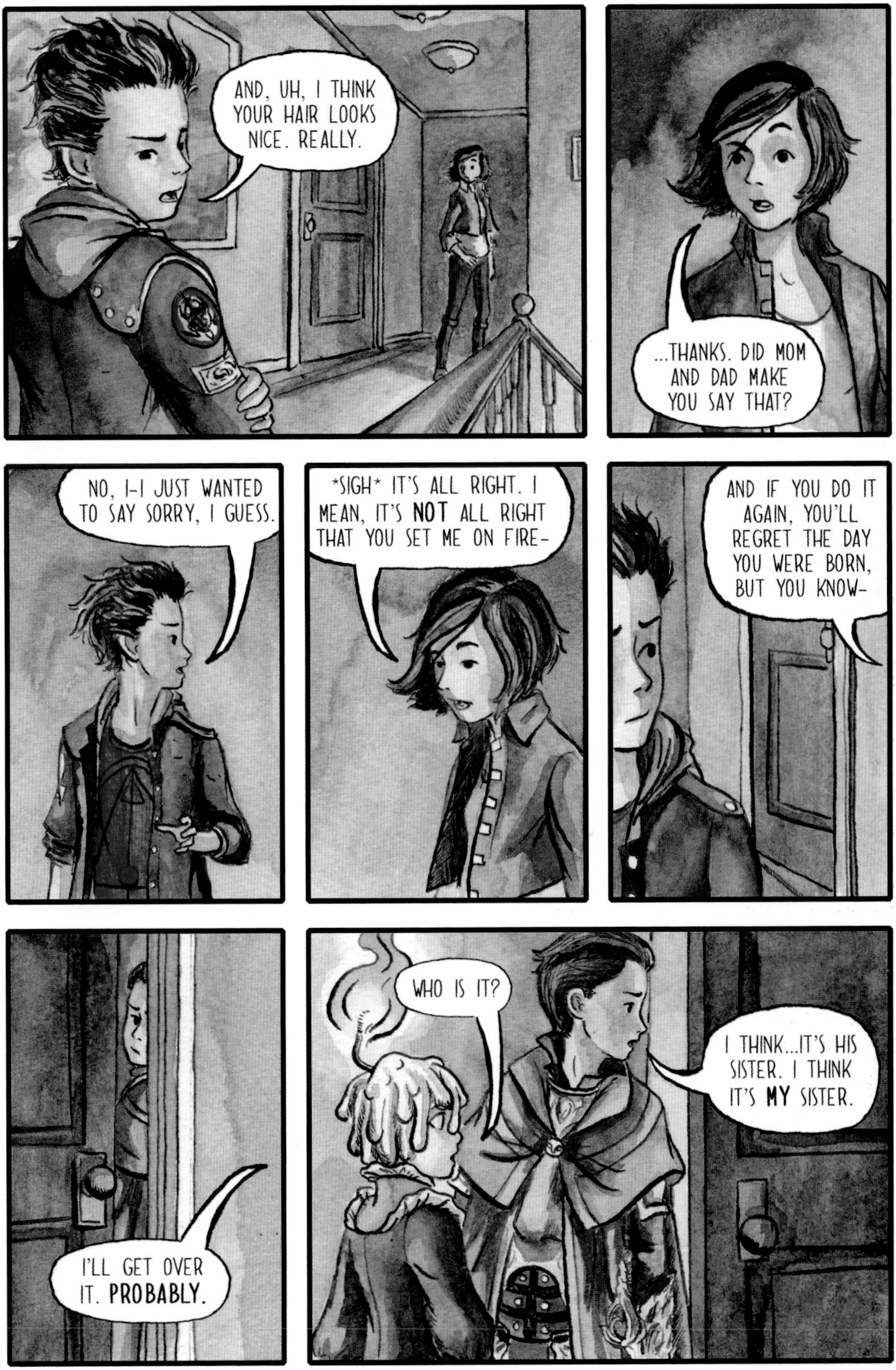
AND, UH, I THINK YOUR HAIR LOOKS NICE. REALLY.
...THANKS. DID MOM AND DAD MAKE YOU SAY THAT?
NO, I-I JUST WANTED TO SAY SORRY, I GUESS.
SIGH IT'S ALL RIGHT. I MEAN, IT'S NOT ALL RIGHT THAT YOU SET ME ON FIRE-
AND IF YOU DO IT AGAIN, YOU'LL REGRET THE DAY YOU WERE BORN, BUT YOU KNOW-
I'LL GET OVER IT. PROBABLY.
WHO IS IT?
I THINK...IT'S HIS SISTER. I THINK IT'S MY SISTER.

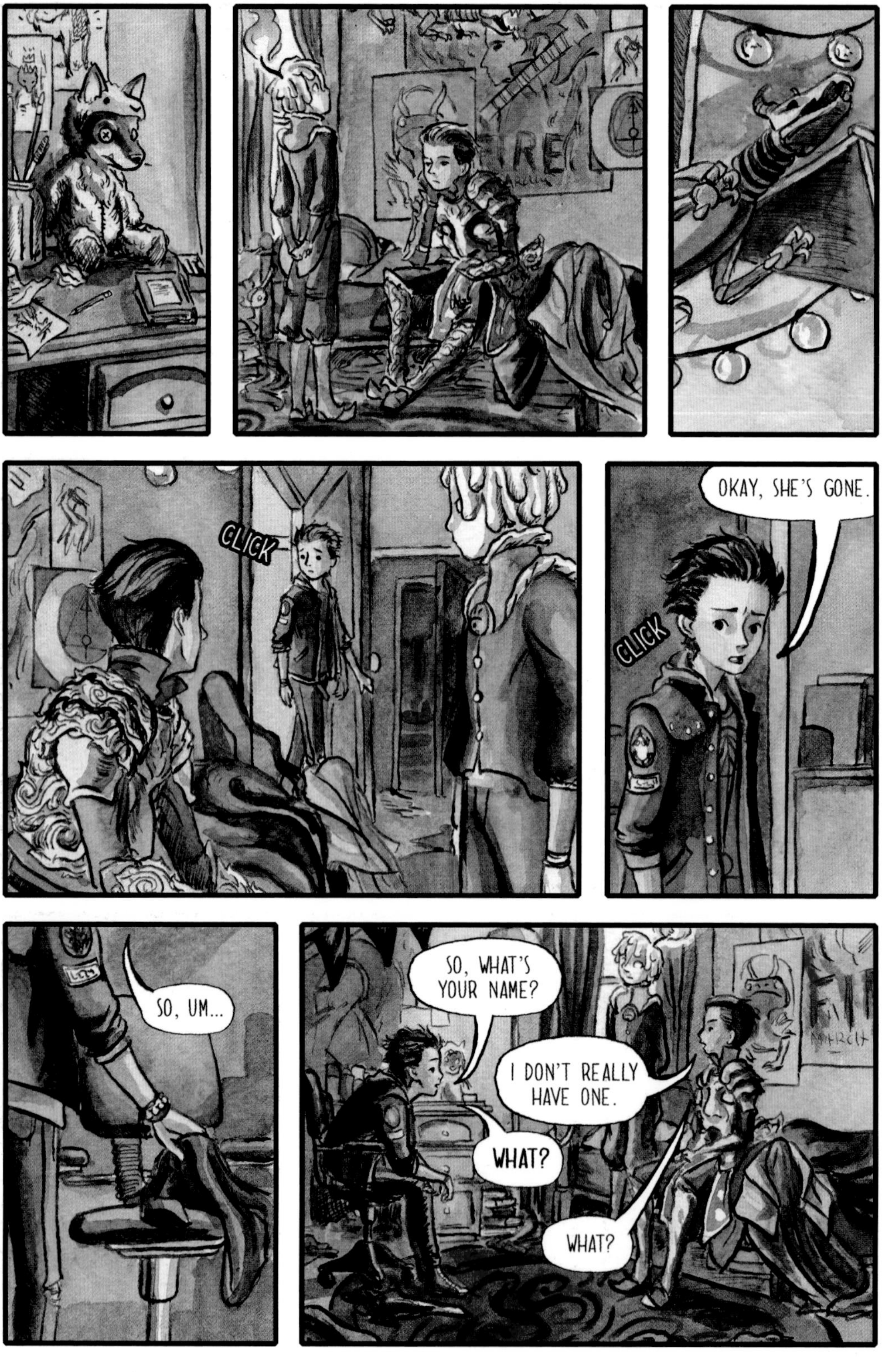
CLICK
OKAY, SHE'S GONE.
CLICK
SO, UM...
SO, WHAT'S YOUR NAME?
I DON'T REALLY HAVE ONE.
WHAT?
WHAT?

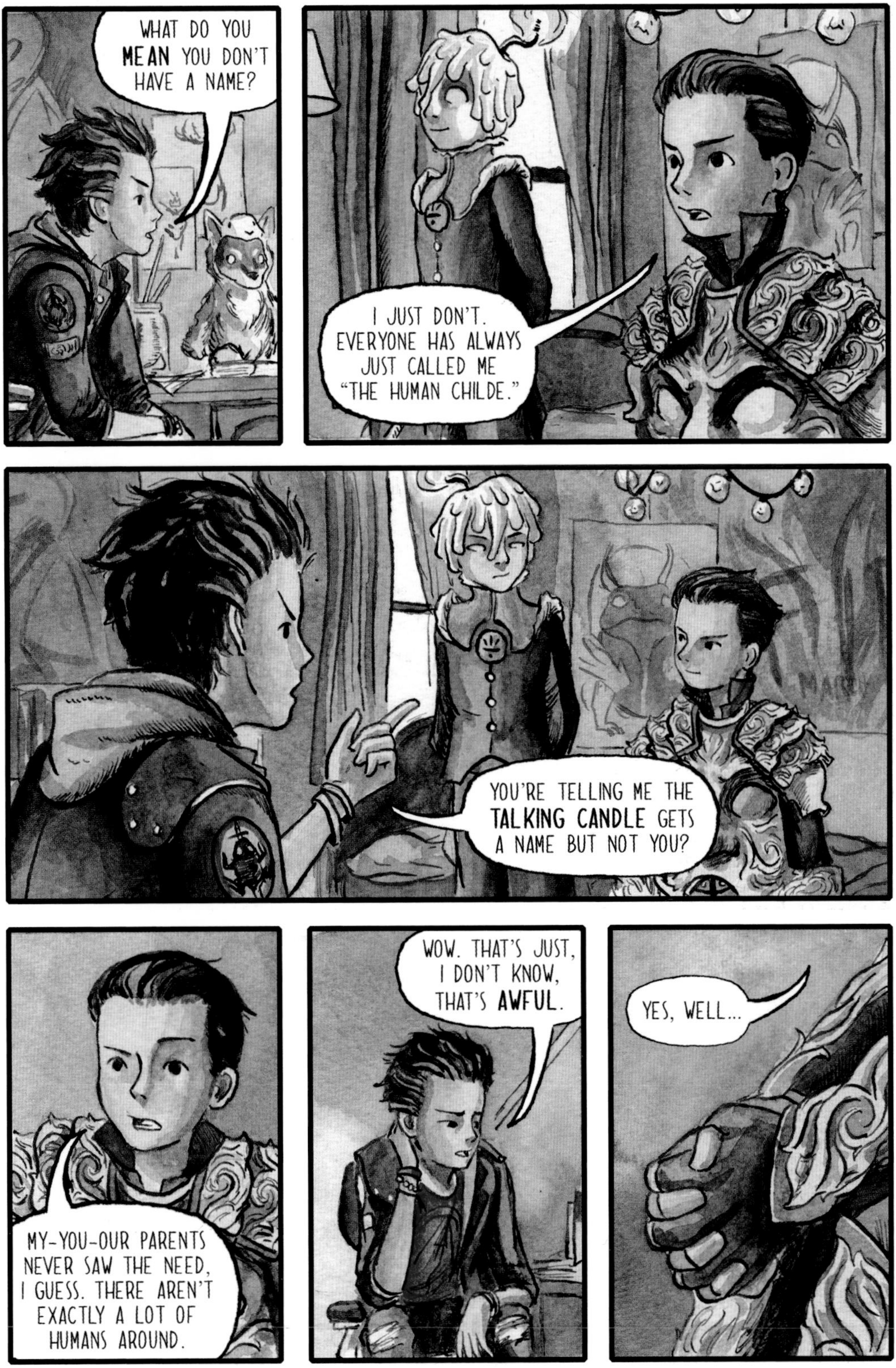
WHAT DO YOU MEAN YOU DON'T HAVE A NAME?
I JUST DON'T. EVERYONE HAS ALWAYS JUST CALLED ME "THE HUMAN CHILDE."
YOU'RE TELLING ME THE TALKING CANDLE GETS A NAME BUT NOT YOU?
MY-YOU-OUR PARENTS NEVER SAW THE NEED, I GUESS. THERE AREN'T EXACTLY A LOT OF HUMANS AROUND.
WOW. THAT'S JUST, I DON'T KNOW, THAT'S AWFUL.
YES, WELL...

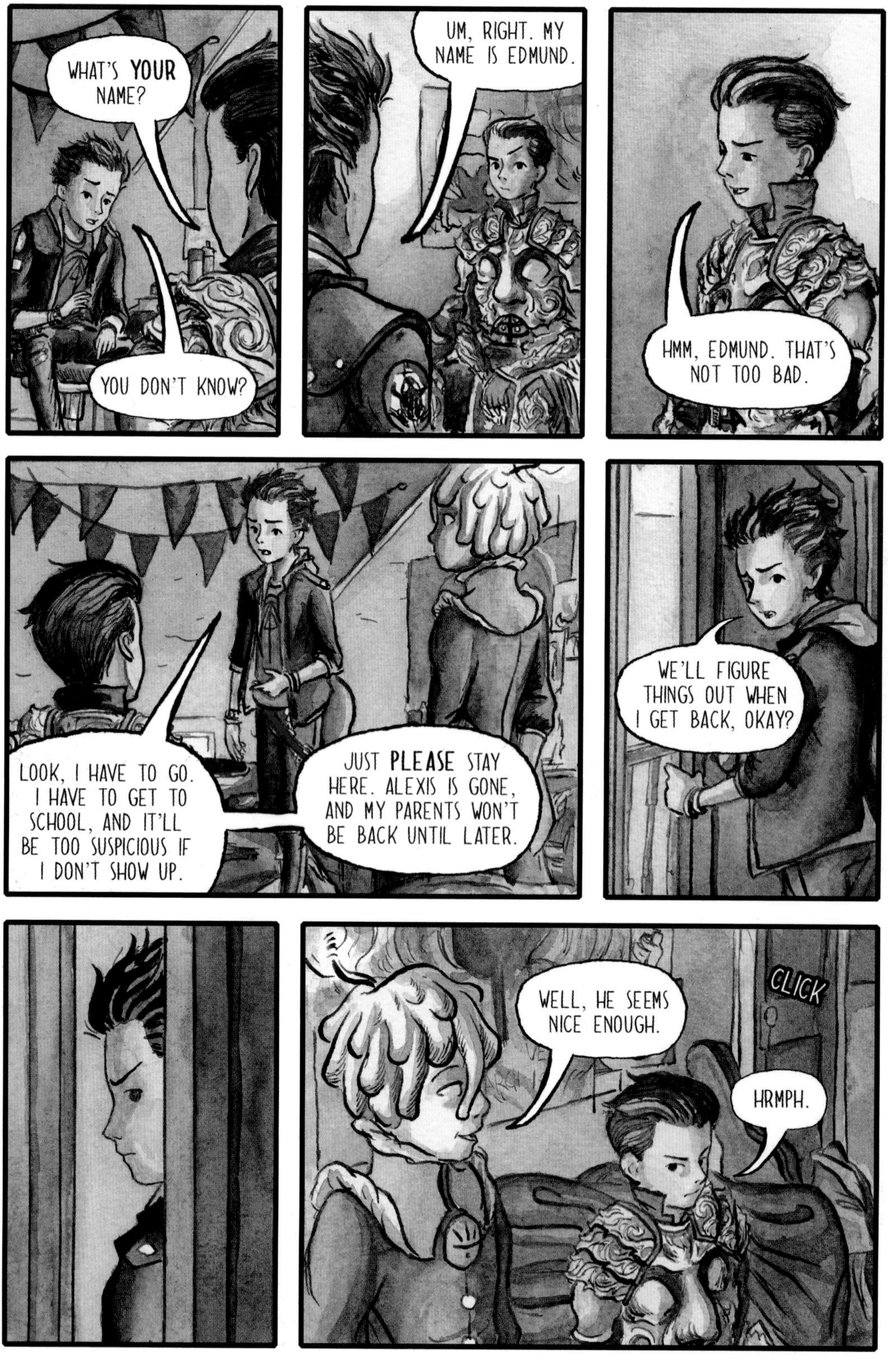
WHAT'S YOUR NAME?
YOU DON'T KNOW?
UM, RIGHT. MY NAME IS EDMUND.
HMM, EDMUND. THAT'S NOT TOO BAD.
LOOK, I HAVE TO GO. I HAVE TO GET TO SCHOOL, AND IT'LL BE TOO SUSPICIOUS IF I DON'T SHOW UP.
JUST PLEASE STAY HERE. ALEXIS IS GONE, AND MY PARENTS WON'T BE BACK UNTIL LATER.
WE'LL FIGURE THINGS OUT WHEN I GET BACK, OKAY?
CLICK
WELL, HE SEEMS NICE ENOUGH.
HRMPH.

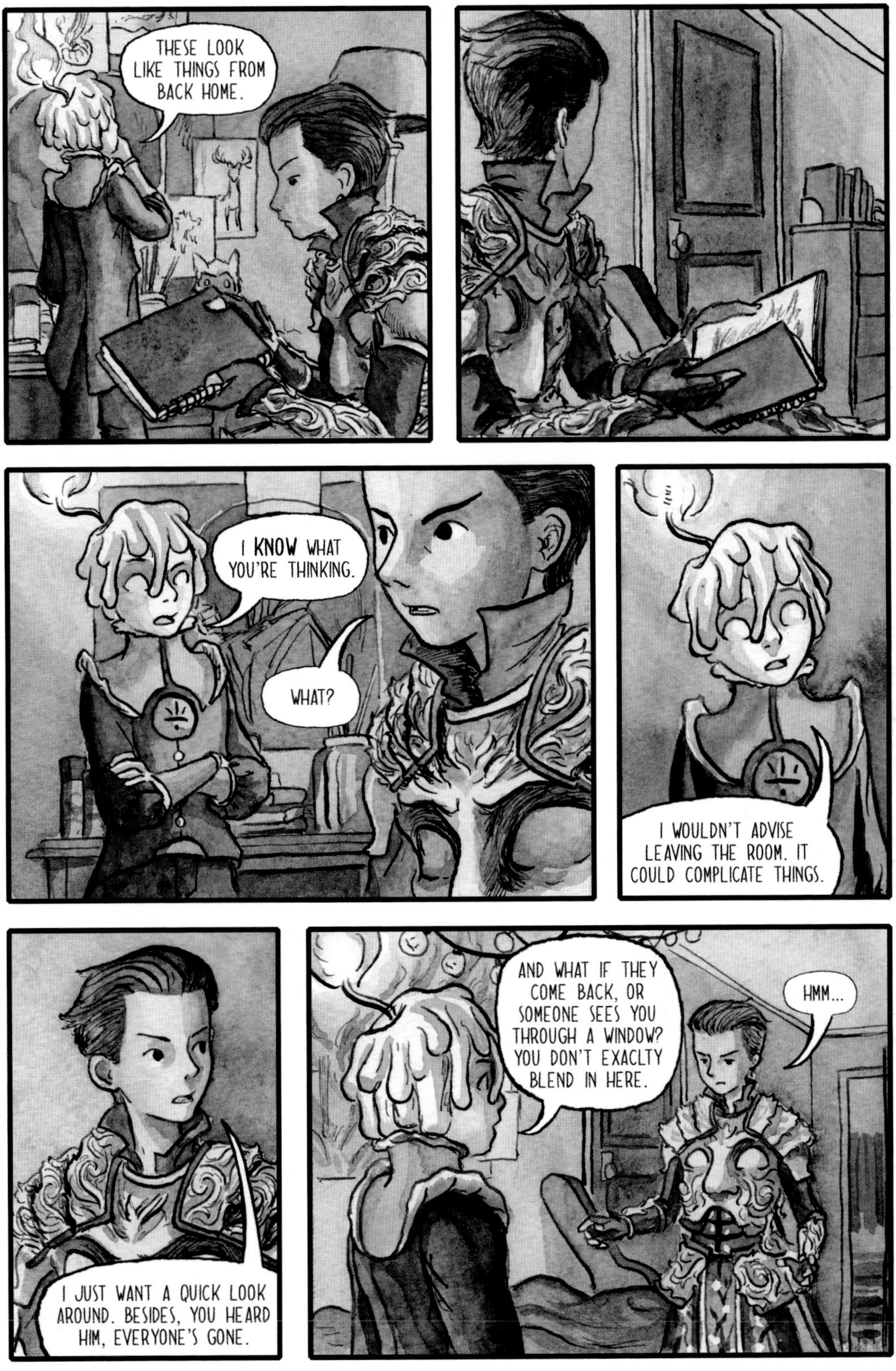
THESE LOOK LIKE THINGS FROM BACK HOME.
I KNOW WHAT YOU'RE THINKING.
WHAT?
I WOULDN'T ADVISE LEAVING THE ROOM. IT COULD COMPLICATE THINGS.
I JUST WANT A QUICK LOOK AROUND. BESIDES, YOU HEARD HIM, EVERYONE'S GONE.
AND WHAT IF THEY COME BACK, OR SOMEONE SEES YOU THROUGH A WINDOW? YOU DON'T EXACLTY BLEND IN HERE.
HMM...

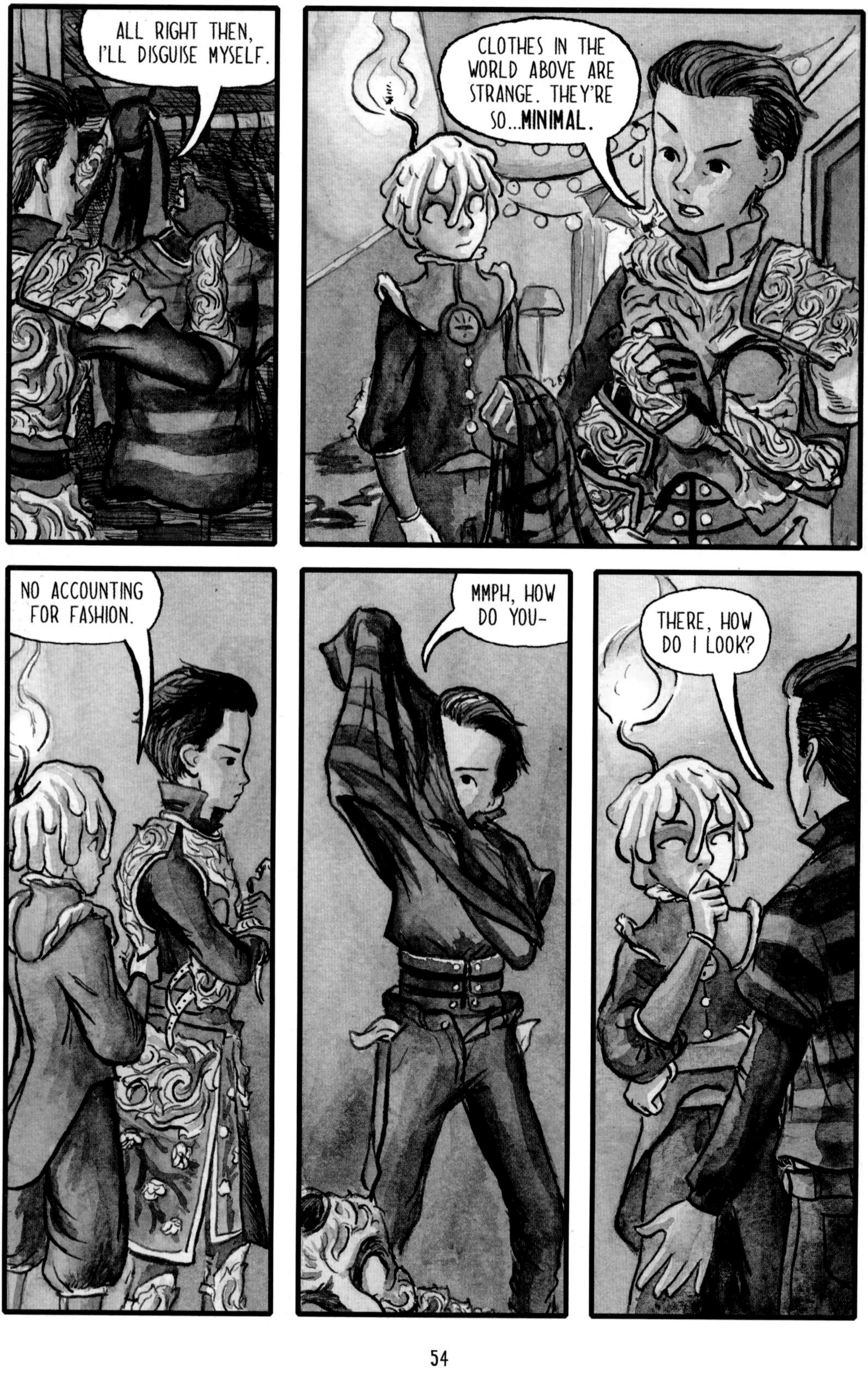

ALL RIGHT THEN, I'LL DISGUISE MYSELF.
CLOTHES IN THE WORLD ABOVE ARE STRANGE. THEY'RE SO...**MINIMAL.**
NO ACCOUNTING FOR FASHION.
MMPH, HOW DO YOU-
THERE, HOW DO I LOOK?

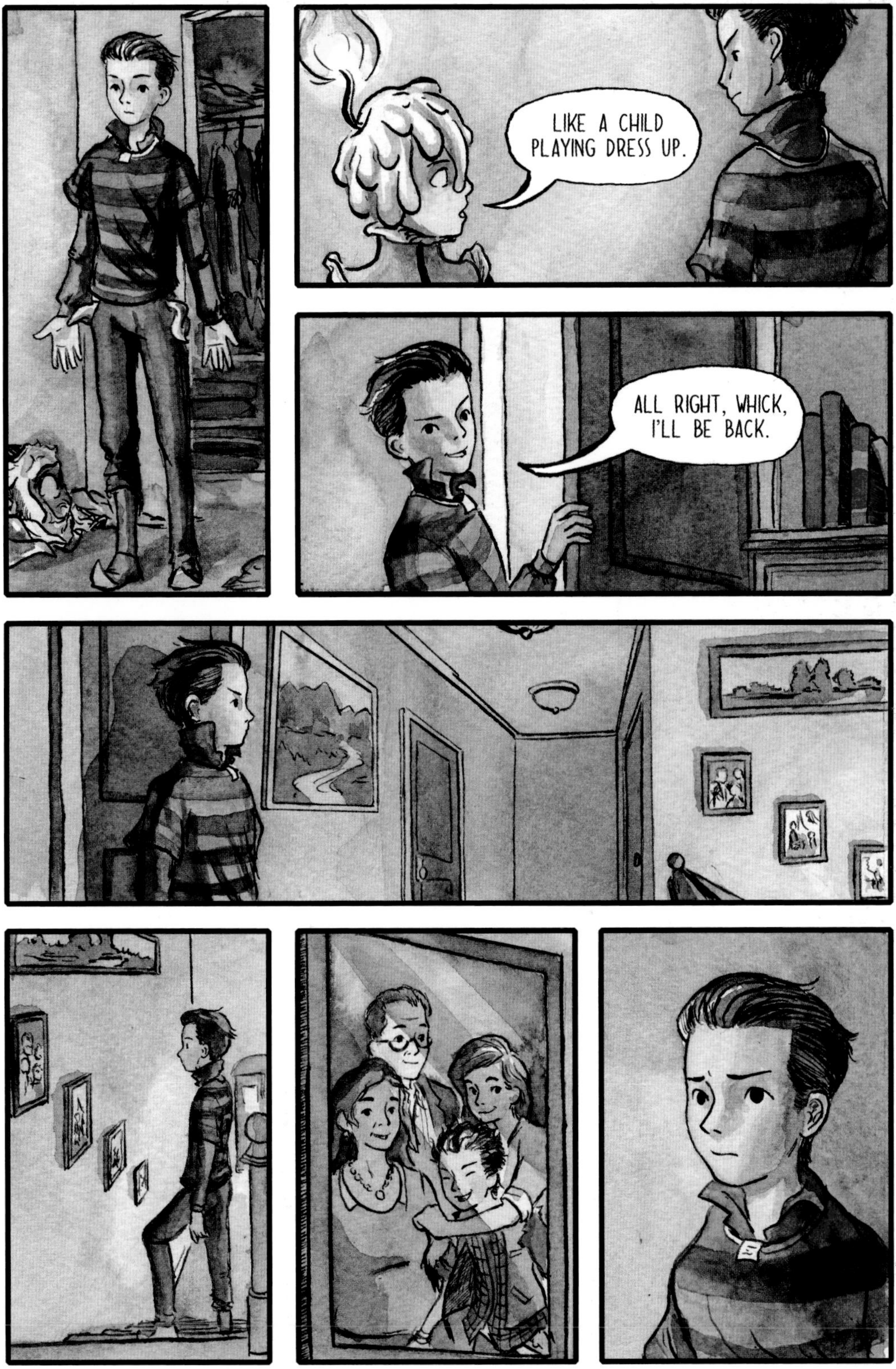
LIKE A CHILD PLAYING DRESS UP.
ALL RIGHT, WHICK, I'LL BE BACK.

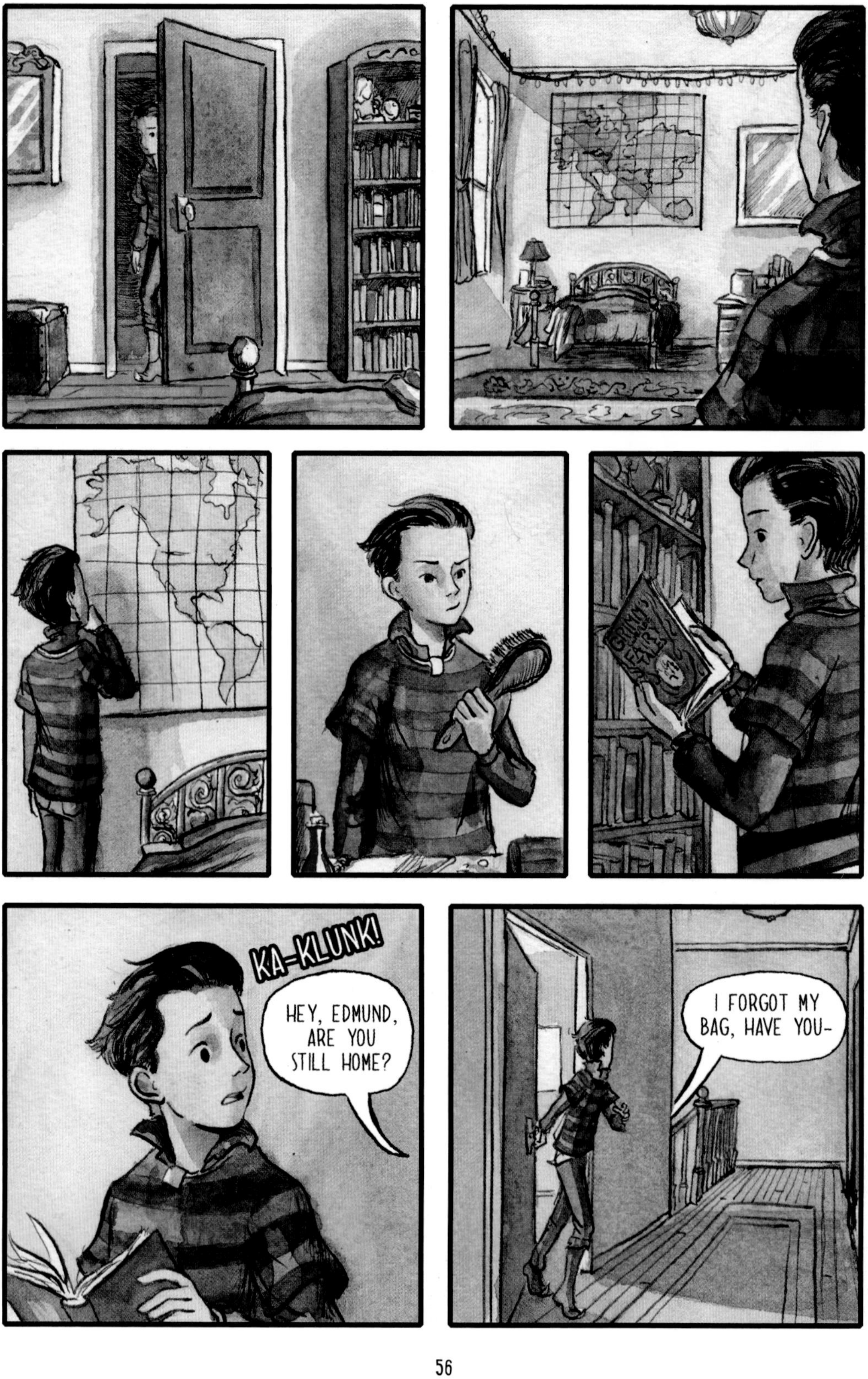
GRIMM'S FAIRY
KA-KLUNK!
HEY, EDMUND, ARE YOU STILL HOME?
I FORGOT MY BAG, HAVE YOU-

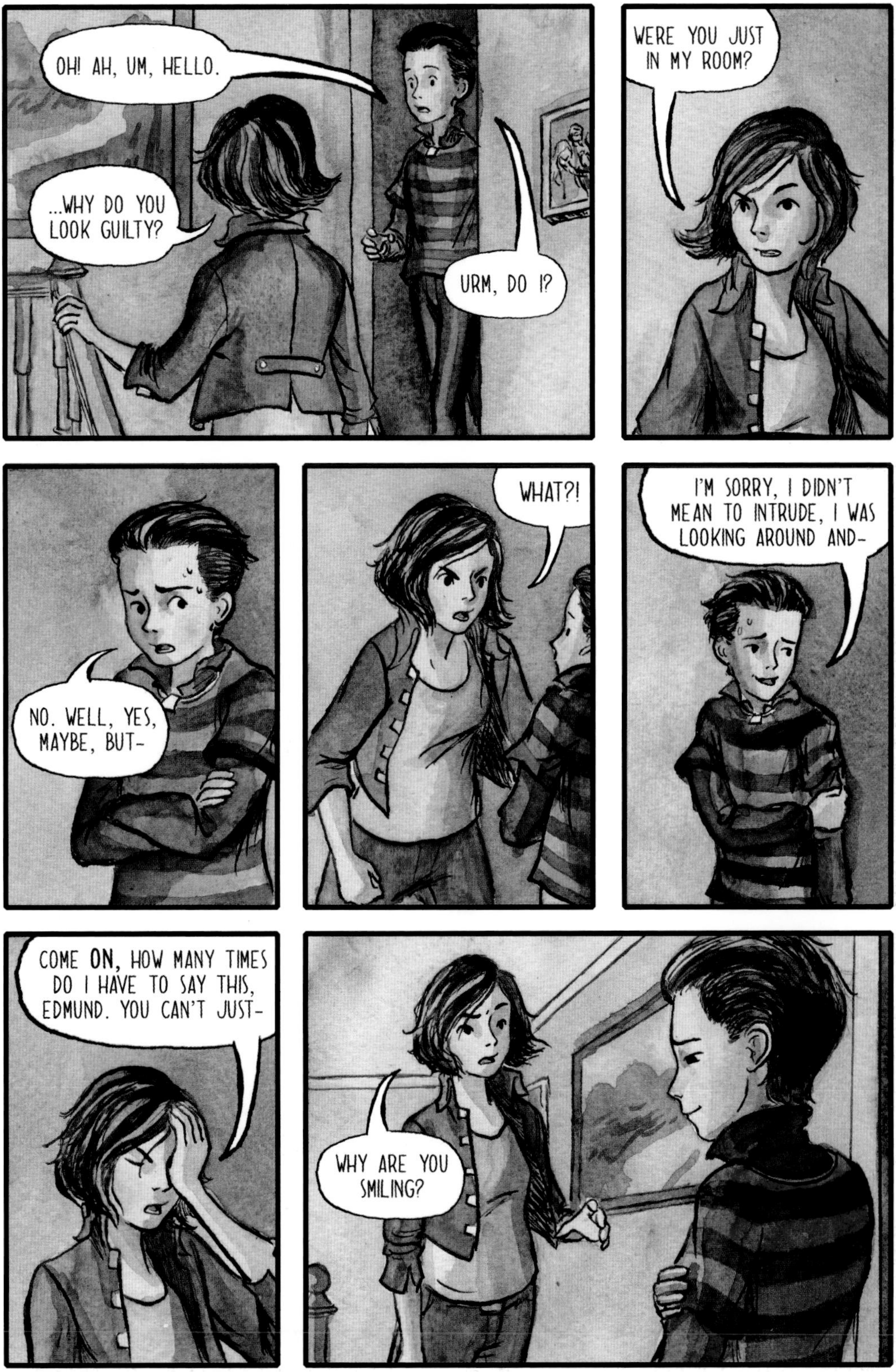

OH! AH, UM, HELLO.
...WHY DO YOU LOOK GUILTY?
URM, DO I?
WERE YOU JUST IN MY ROOM?
NO. WELL, YES, MAYBE, BUT-
WHAT?!
I'M SORRY, I DIDN'T MEAN TO INTRUDE, I WAS LOOKING AROUND AND-
COME **ON,** HOW MANY TIMES DO I HAVE TO SAY THIS, EDMUND. YOU CAN'T JUST-
WHY ARE YOU SMILING?

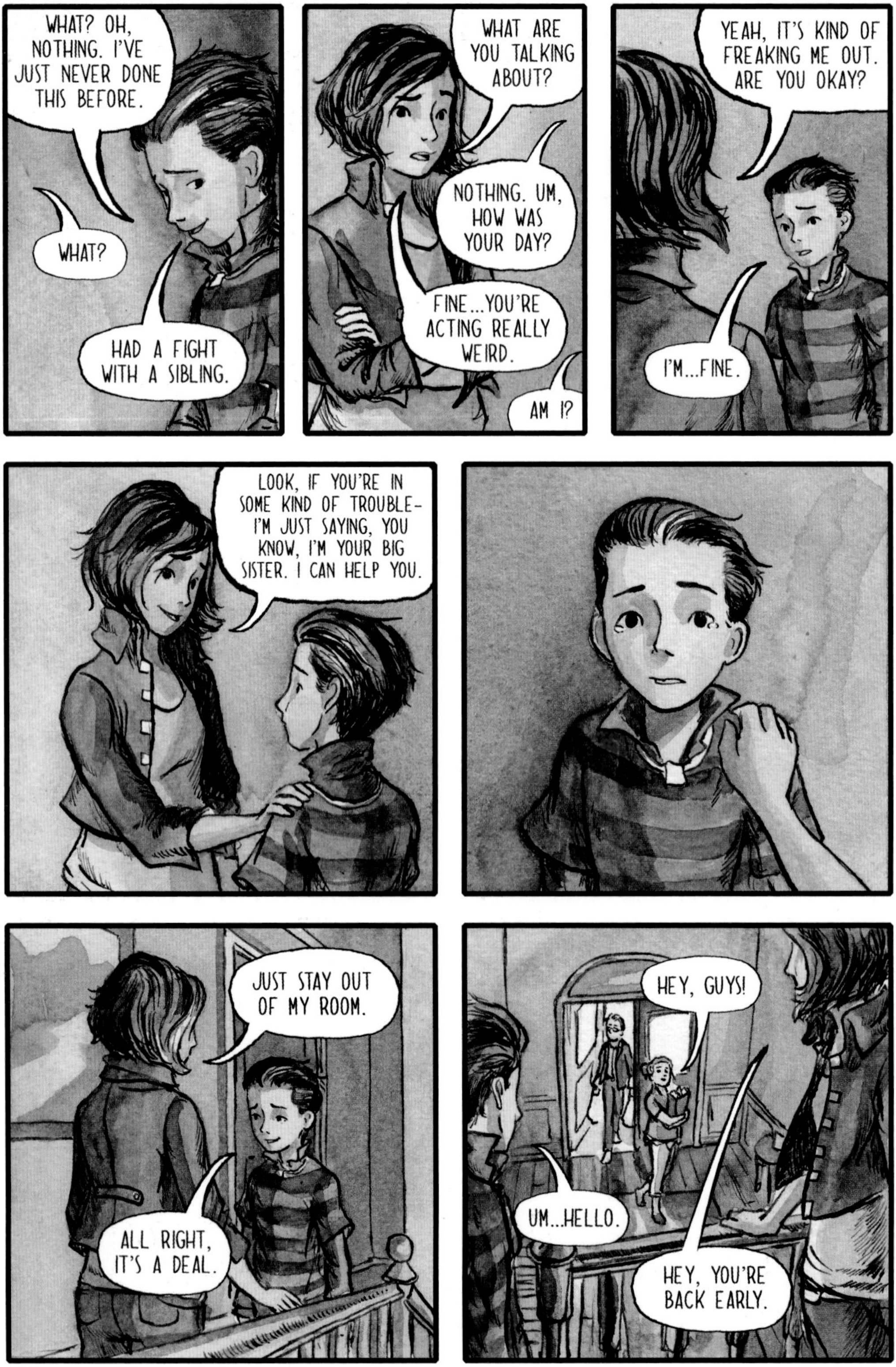
WHAT? OH, NOTHING. I'VE JUST NEVER DONE THIS BEFORE.
WHAT?
HAD A FIGHT WITH A SIBLING.
WHAT ARE YOU TALKING ABOUT?
NOTHING. UM, HOW WAS YOUR DAY?
FINE...YOU'RE ACTING REALLY WEIRD.
AM I?
YEAH, IT'S KIND OF FREAKING ME OUT. ARE YOU OKAY?
I'M...FINE.
LOOK, IF YOU'RE IN SOME KIND OF TROUBLE-I'M JUST SAYING, YOU KNOW, I'M YOUR BIG SISTER. I CAN HELP YOU.
JUST STAY OUT OF MY ROOM.
ALL RIGHT, IT'S A DEAL.
HEY, GUYS!
UM...HELLO.
HEY, YOU'RE BACK EARLY.

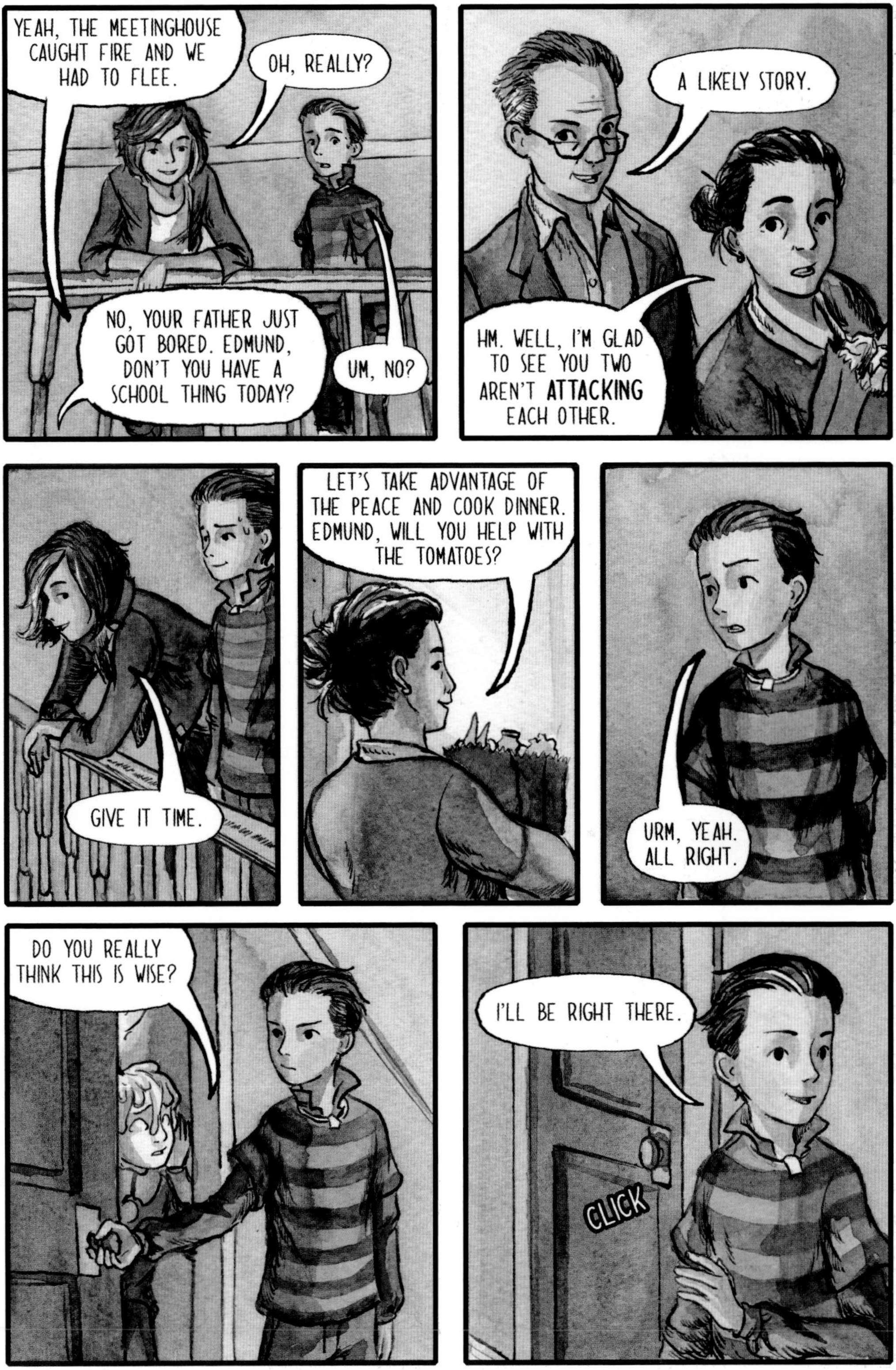
YEAH, THE MEETINGHOUSE CAUGHT FIRE AND WE HAD TO FLEE.
OH, REALLY?
NO, YOUR FATHER JUST GOT BORED. EDMUND, DON'T YOU HAVE A SCHOOL THING TODAY?
UM, NO?
A LIKELY STORY.
HM. WELL, I'M GLAD TO SEE YOU TWO AREN'T **ATTACKING** EACH OTHER.
GIVE IT TIME.
LET'S TAKE ADVANTAGE OF THE PEACE AND COOK DINNER. EDMUND, WILL YOU HELP WITH THE TOMATOES?
URM, YEAH. ALL RIGHT.
DO YOU REALLY THINK THIS IS WISE?
I'LL BE RIGHT THERE.
CLICK

Chapter Five

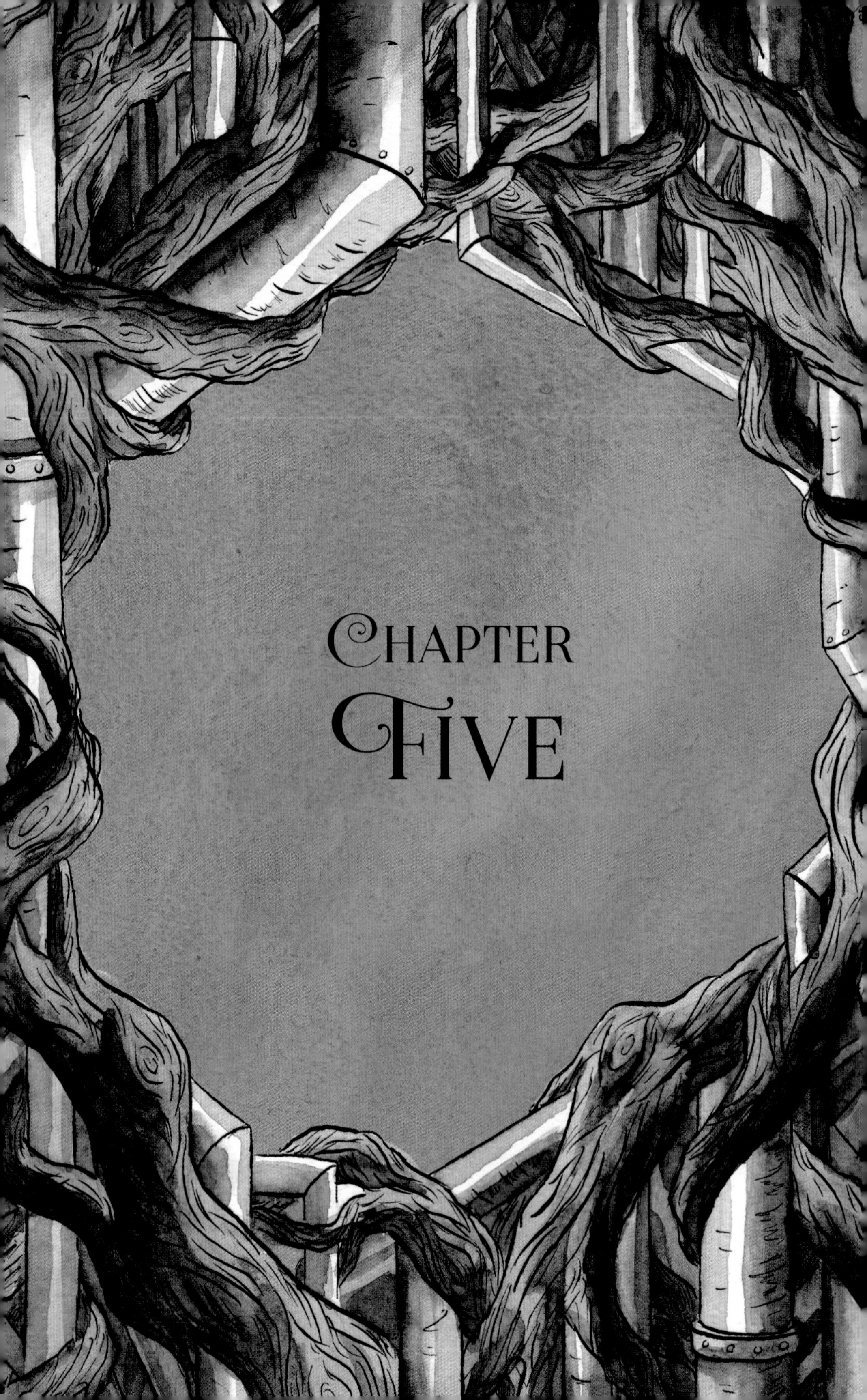

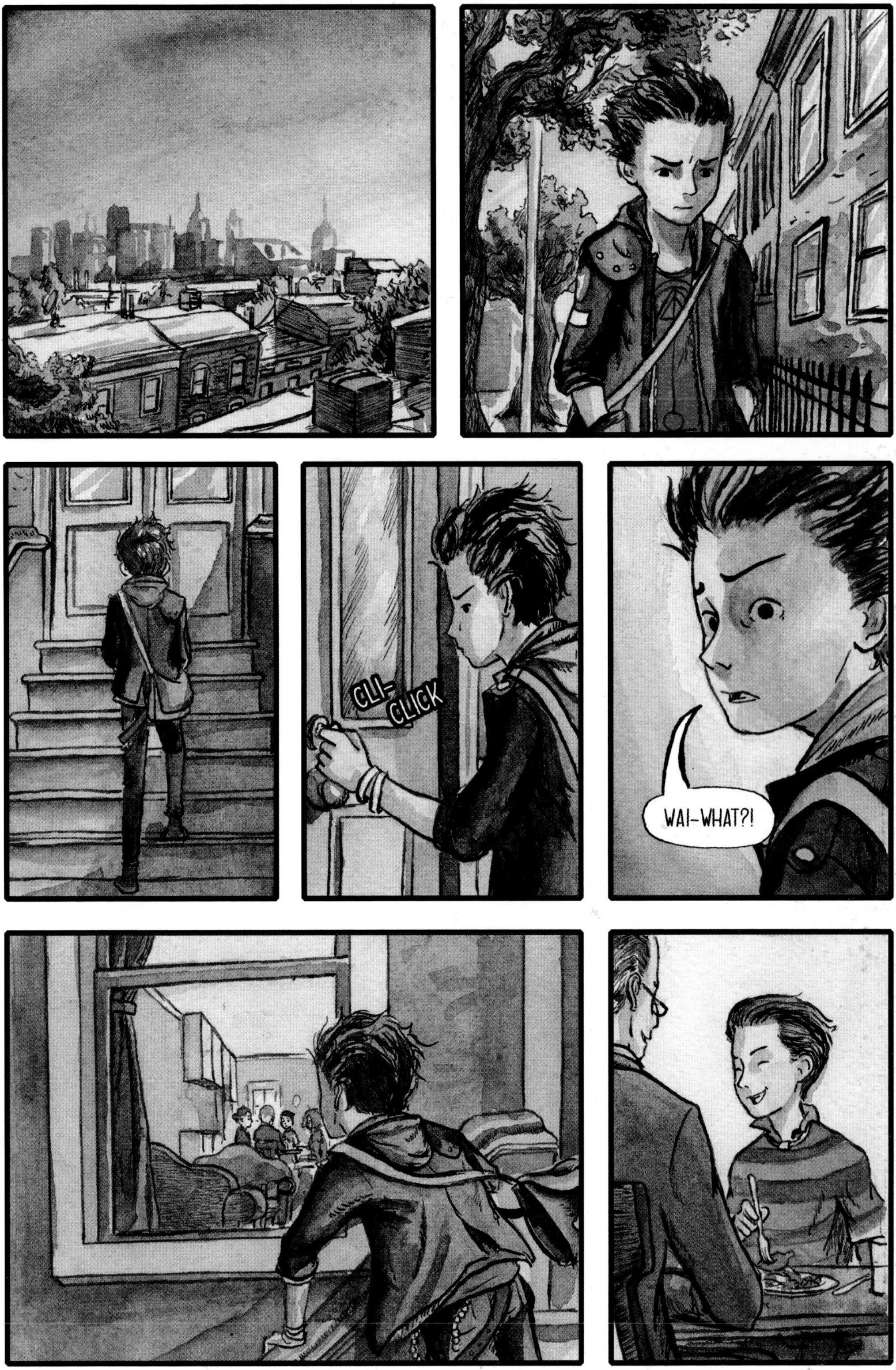
CLI-
CLICK
WAI-WHAT?!

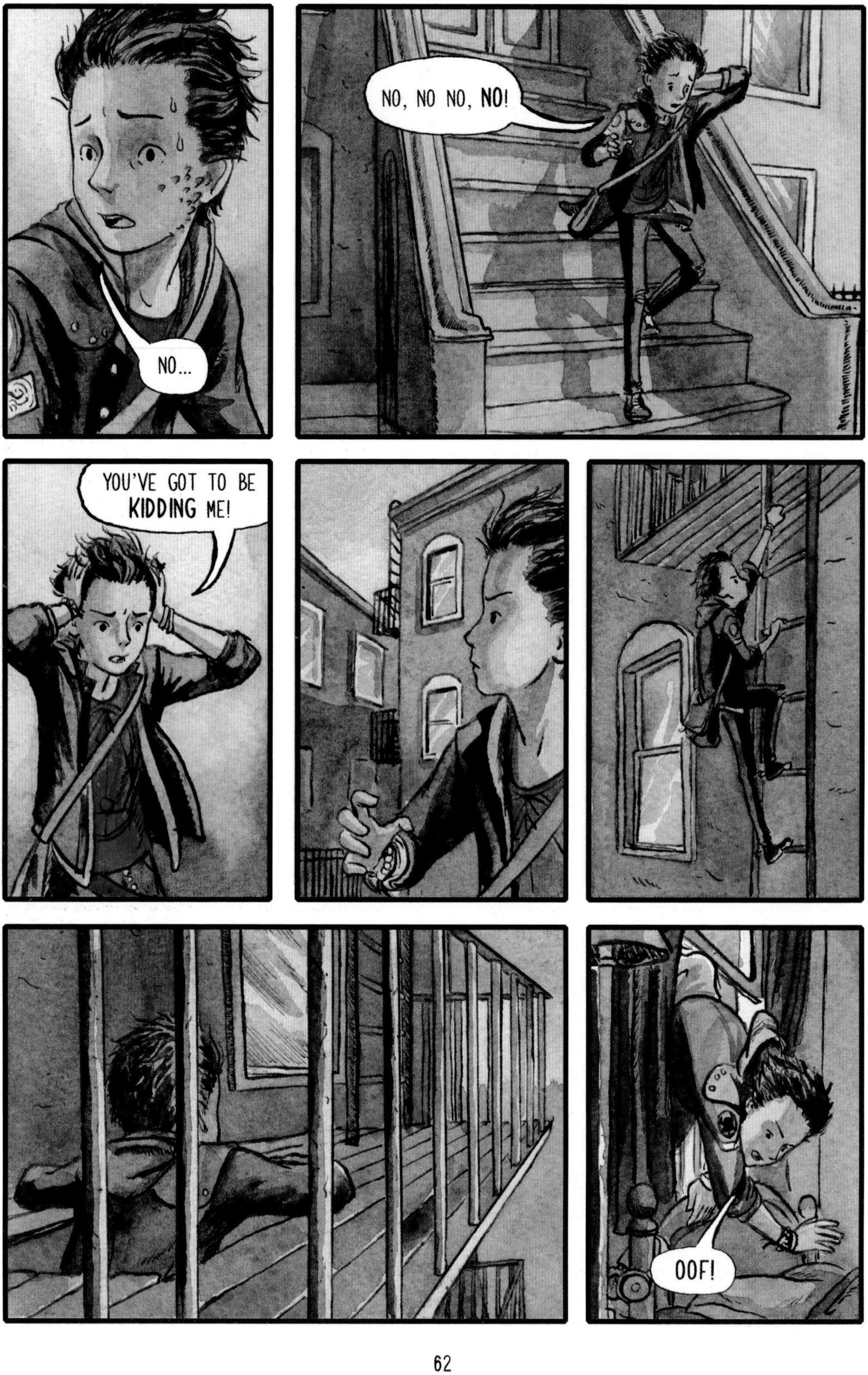
NO...
NO, NO NO, NO!
YOU'VE GOT TO BE KIDDING ME!
OOF!

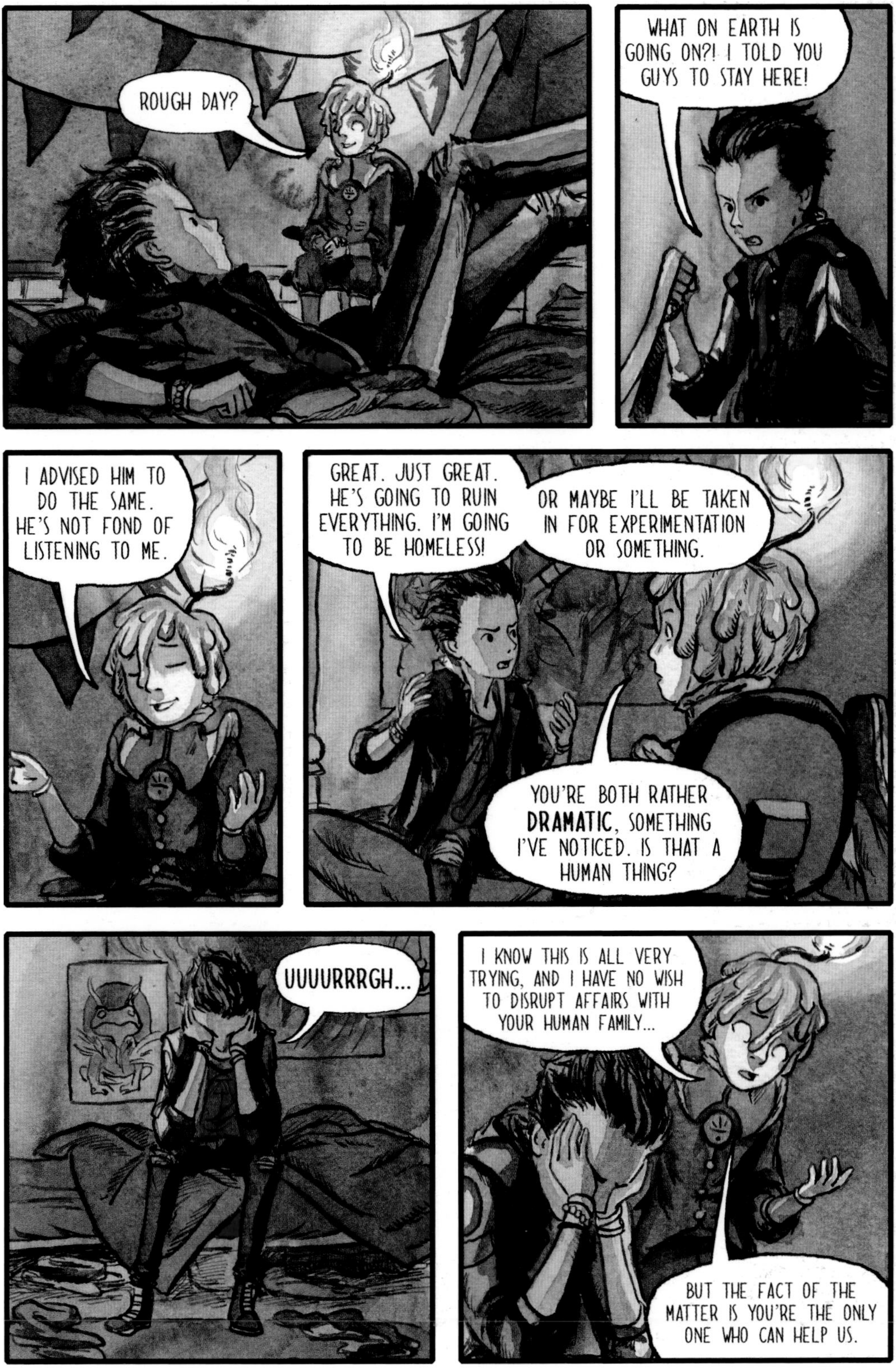
ROUGH DAY?
WHAT ON EARTH IS GOING ON?! I TOLD YOU GUYS TO STAY HERE!
I ADVISED HIM TO DO THE SAME. HE'S NOT FOND OF LISTENING TO ME.
GREAT. JUST GREAT. HE'S GOING TO RUIN EVERYTHING. I'M GOING TO BE HOMELESS!
OR MAYBE I'LL BE TAKEN IN FOR EXPERIMENTATION OR SOMETHING.
YOU'RE BOTH RATHER **DRAMATIC**, SOMETHING I'VE NOTICED. IS THAT A HUMAN THING?
UUUURRRGH...
I KNOW THIS IS ALL VERY TRYING, AND I HAVE NO WISH TO DISRUPT AFFAIRS WITH YOUR HUMAN FAMILY...
BUT THE FACT OF THE MATTER IS YOU'RE THE ONLY ONE WHO CAN HELP US.

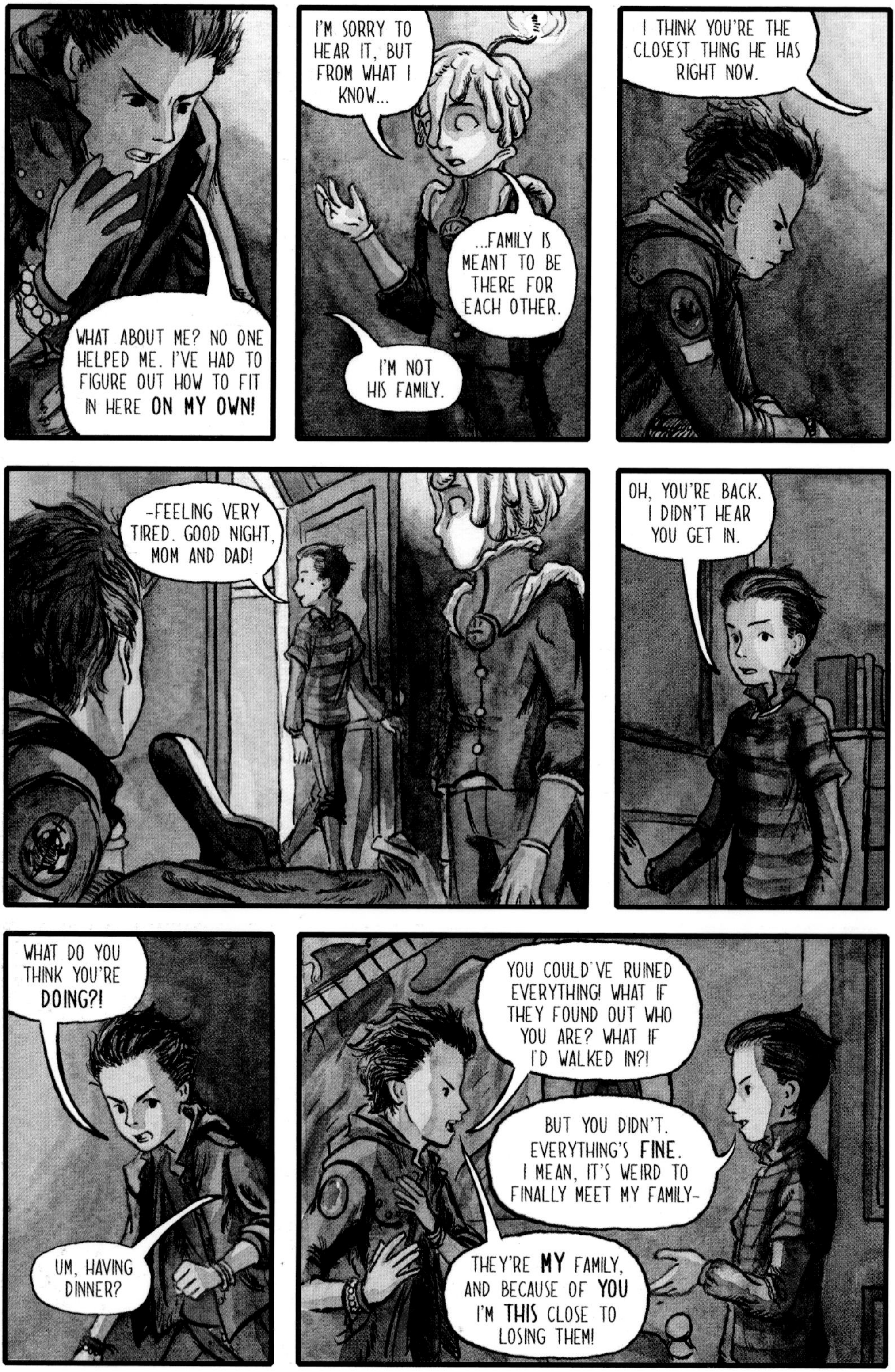
WHAT ABOUT ME? NO ONE HELPED ME. I'VE HAD TO FIGURE OUT HOW TO FIT IN HERE **ON MY OWN!**
I'M SORRY TO HEAR IT, BUT FROM WHAT I KNOW...
...FAMILY IS MEANT TO BE THERE FOR EACH OTHER.
I'M NOT HIS FAMILY.
I THINK YOU'RE THE CLOSEST THING HE HAS RIGHT NOW.
-FEELING VERY TIRED. GOOD NIGHT, MOM AND DAD!
OH, YOU'RE BACK. I DIDN'T HEAR YOU GET IN.
WHAT DO YOU THINK YOU'RE **DOING?!**
UM, HAVING DINNER?
YOU COULD'VE RUINED EVERYTHING! WHAT IF THEY FOUND OUT WHO YOU ARE? WHAT IF I'D WALKED IN?!
BUT YOU DIDN'T. EVERYTHING'S **FINE.** I MEAN, IT'S WEIRD TO FINALLY MEET MY FAMILY-
THEY'RE **MY** FAMILY, AND BECAUSE OF **YOU** I'M **THIS** CLOSE TO LOSING THEM!

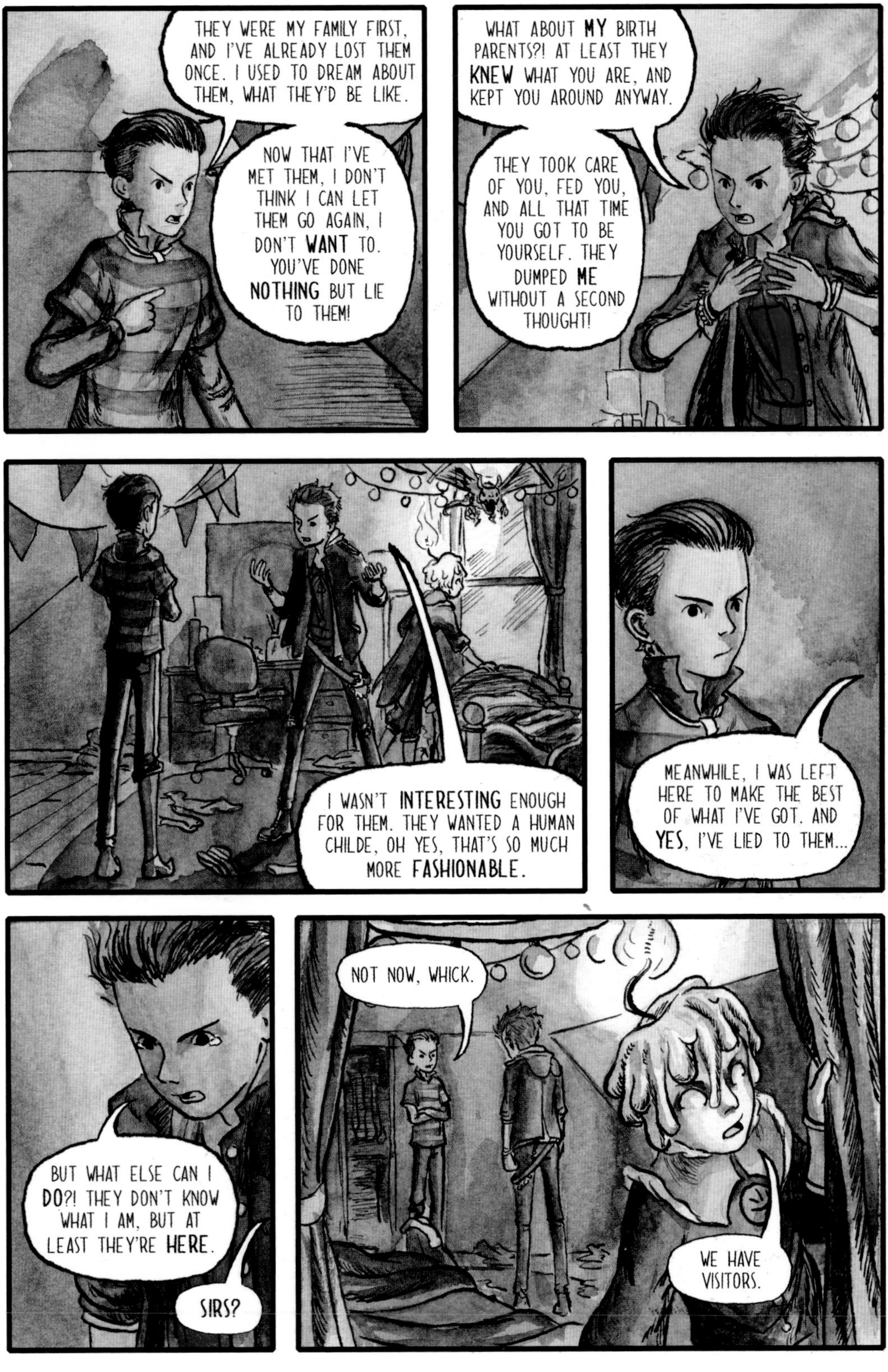
THEY WERE MY FAMILY FIRST, AND I'VE ALREADY LOST THEM ONCE. I USED TO DREAM ABOUT THEM, WHAT THEY'D BE LIKE.
NOW THAT I'VE MET THEM, I DON'T THINK I CAN LET THEM GO AGAIN, I DON'T **WANT** TO. YOU'VE DONE **NOTHING** BUT LIE TO THEM!
WHAT ABOUT **MY** BIRTH PARENTS?! AT LEAST THEY **KNEW** WHAT YOU ARE, AND KEPT YOU AROUND ANYWAY.
THEY TOOK CARE OF YOU, FED YOU, AND ALL THAT TIME YOU GOT TO BE YOURSELF. THEY DUMPED **ME** WITHOUT A SECOND THOUGHT!
I WASN'T **INTERESTING** ENOUGH FOR THEM. THEY WANTED A HUMAN CHILDE, OH YES, THAT'S SO MUCH MORE **FASHIONABLE**.
MEANWHILE, I WAS LEFT HERE TO MAKE THE BEST OF WHAT I'VE GOT. AND **YES**, I'VE LIED TO THEM...
BUT WHAT ELSE CAN I **DO**?! THEY DON'T KNOW WHAT I AM, BUT AT LEAST THEY'RE **HERE**.
SIRS?
NOT NOW, WHICK.
WE HAVE VISITORS.

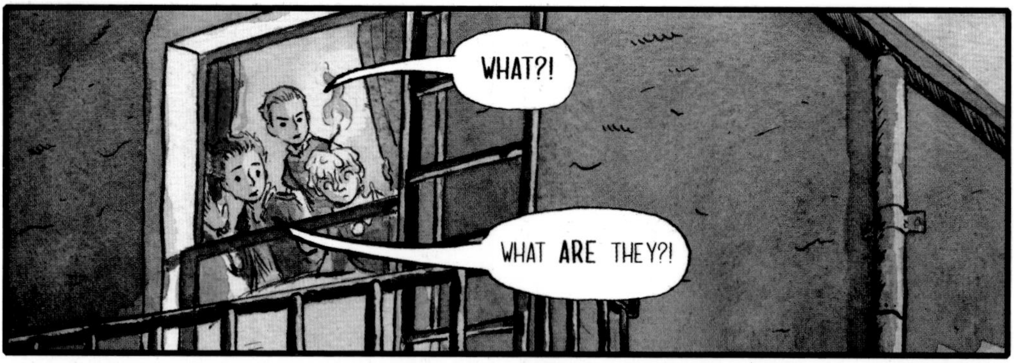
WHAT?!
WHAT ARE THEY?!

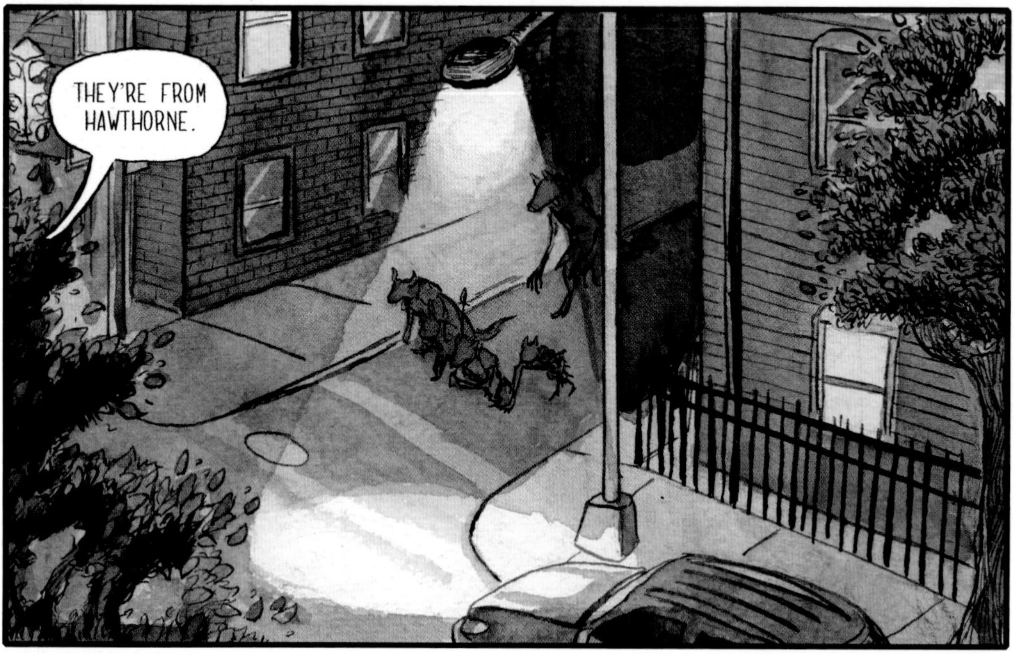
THEY'RE FROM HAWTHORNE.

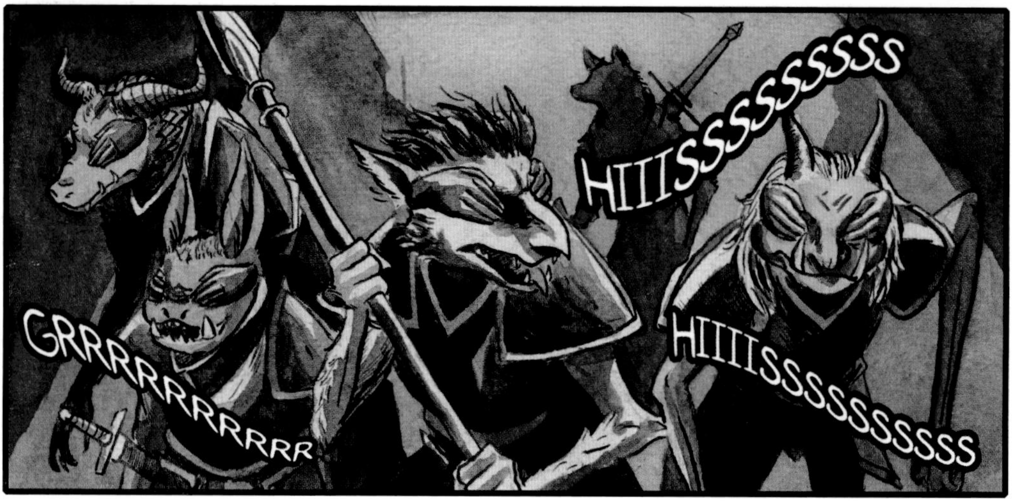
HIIISSSSSSSSS
GRRRRRRRRRRR
HIIIISSSSSSSSSSS

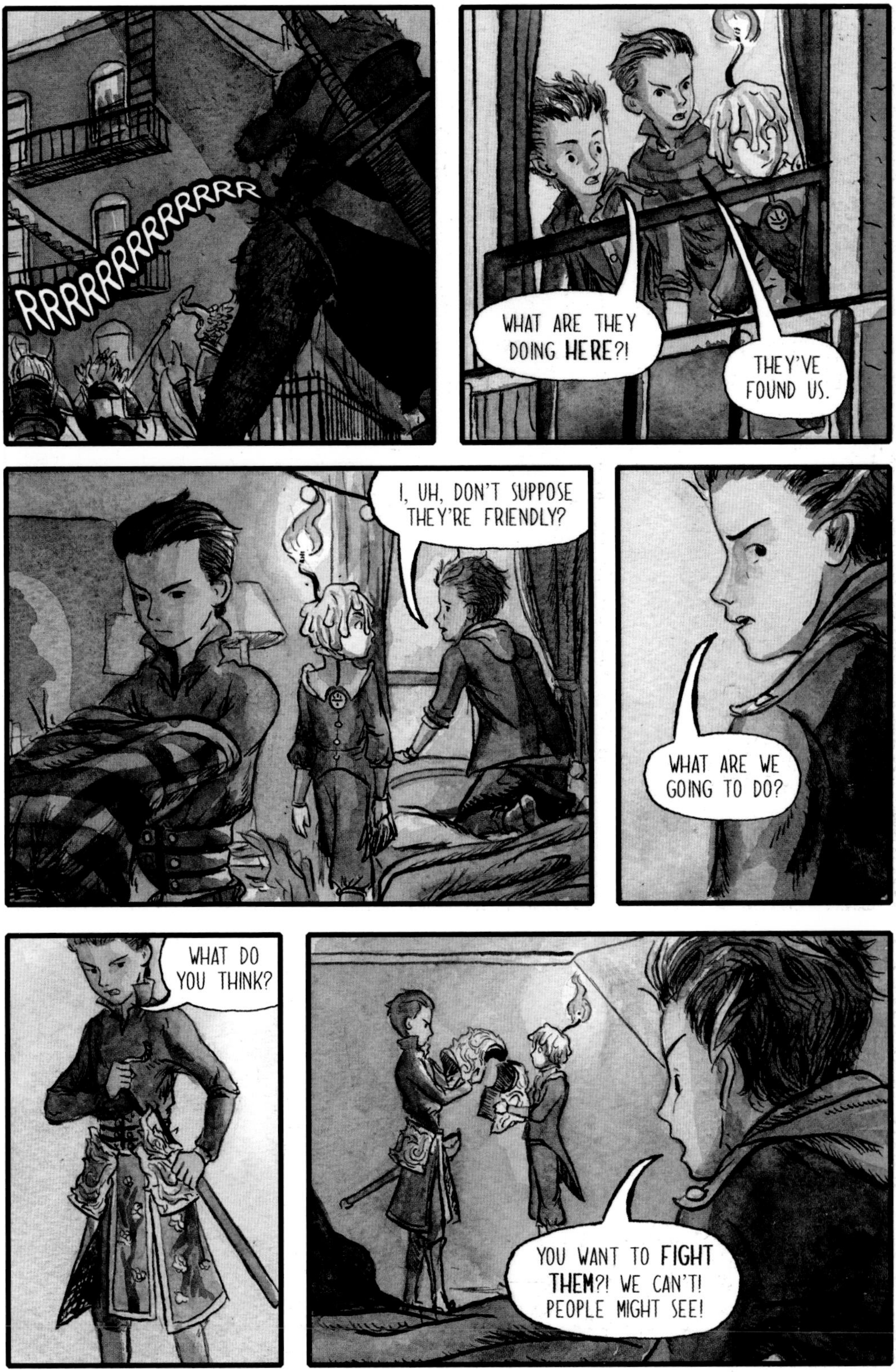
RRRRRRRRRRRRRRRR
WHAT ARE THEY DOING HERE?!
THEY'VE FOUND US.
I, UH, DON'T SUPPOSE THEY'RE FRIENDLY?
WHAT ARE WE GOING TO DO?
WHAT DO YOU THINK?
YOU WANT TO FIGHT THEM?! WE CAN'T! PEOPLE MIGHT SEE!

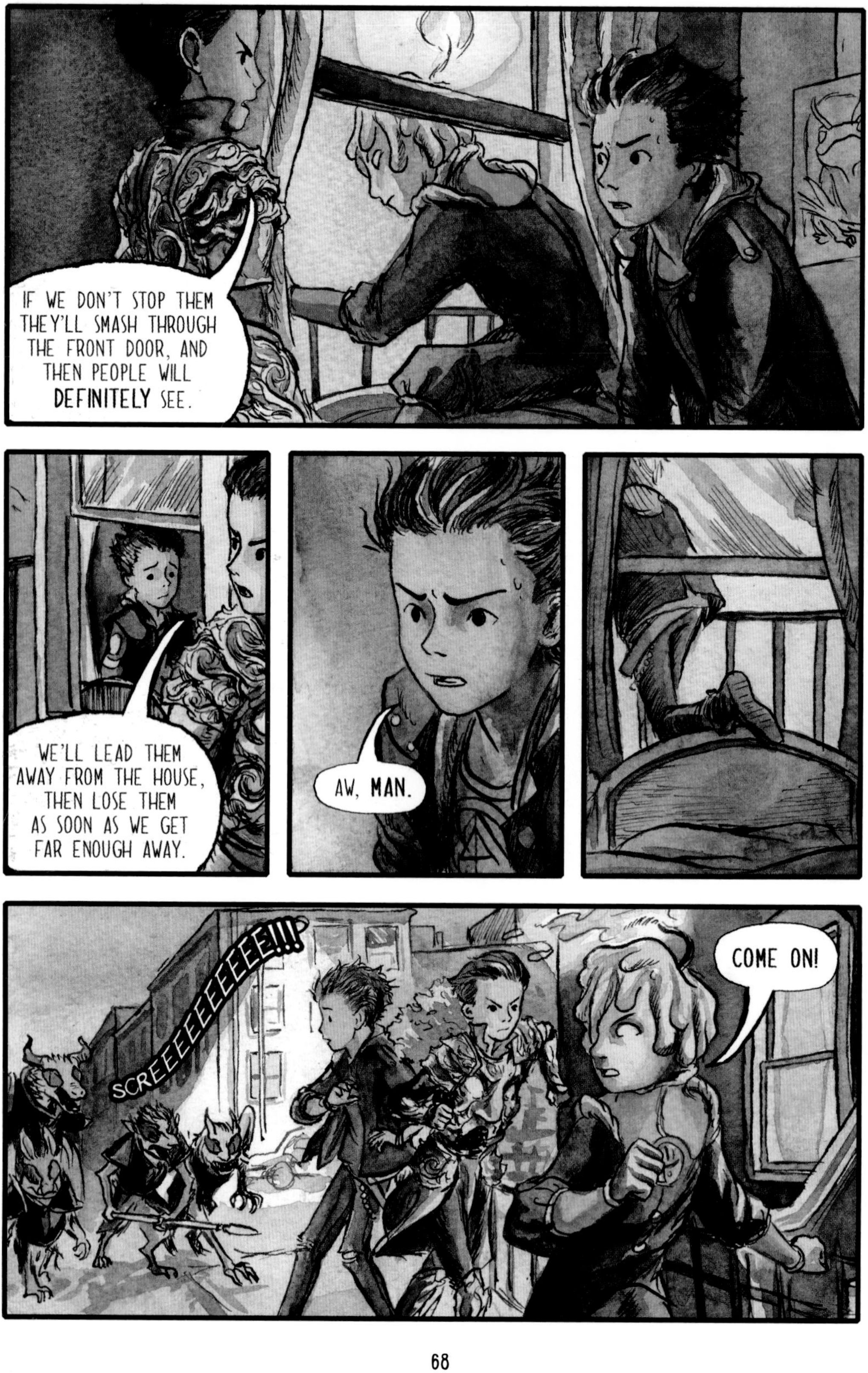
IF WE DON'T STOP THEM THEY'LL SMASH THROUGH THE FRONT DOOR, AND THEN PEOPLE WILL **DEFINITELY** SEE.
WE'LL LEAD THEM AWAY FROM THE HOUSE, THEN LOSE THEM AS SOON AS WE GET FAR ENOUGH AWAY.
AW, **MAN.**
SCREEEEEEEEEEE!!!
COME ON!

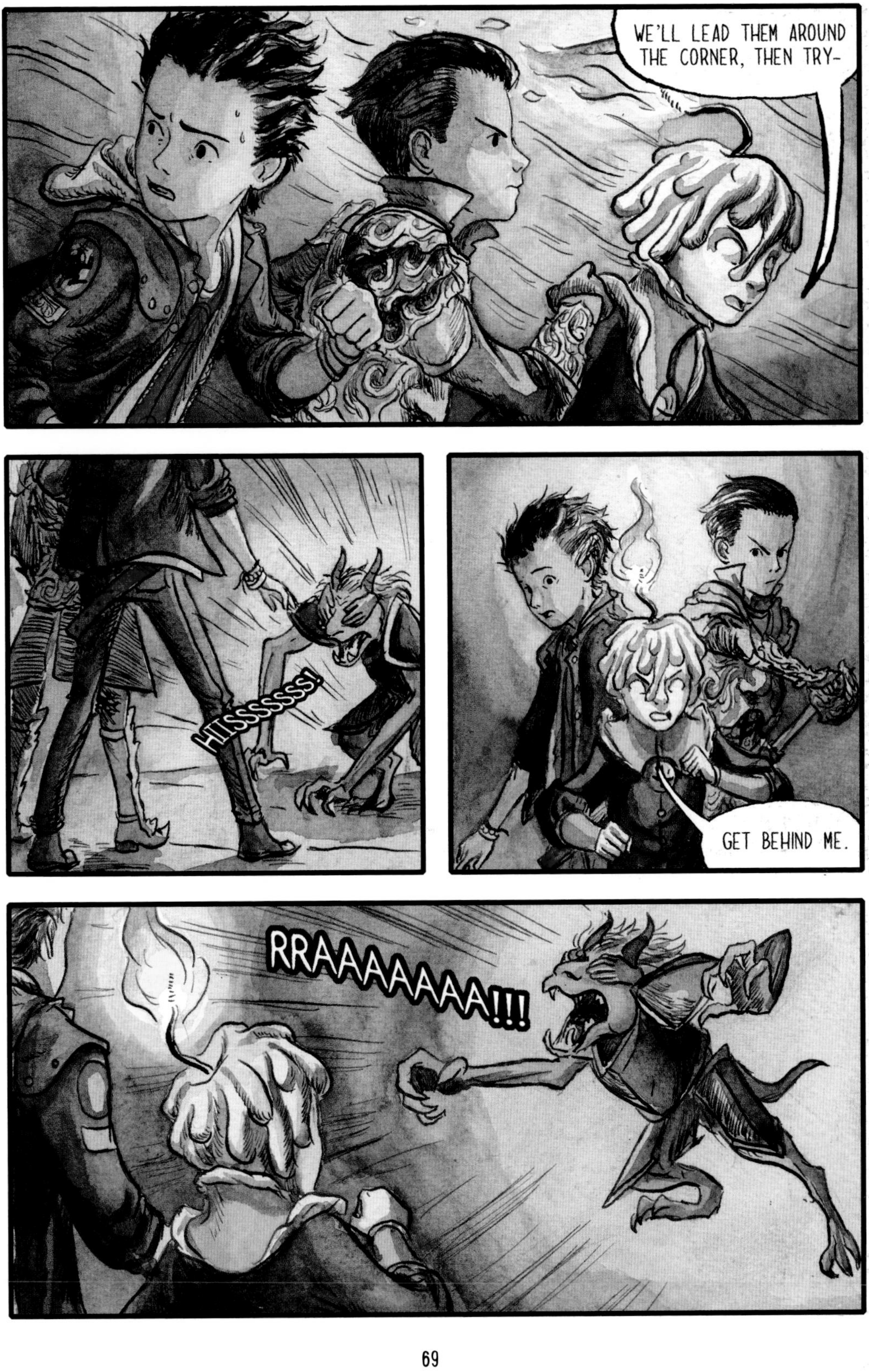
WE'LL LEAD THEM AROUND THE CORNER, THEN TRY-
HISSSSSSS!
GET BEHIND ME.
RRAAAAAAAA!!!

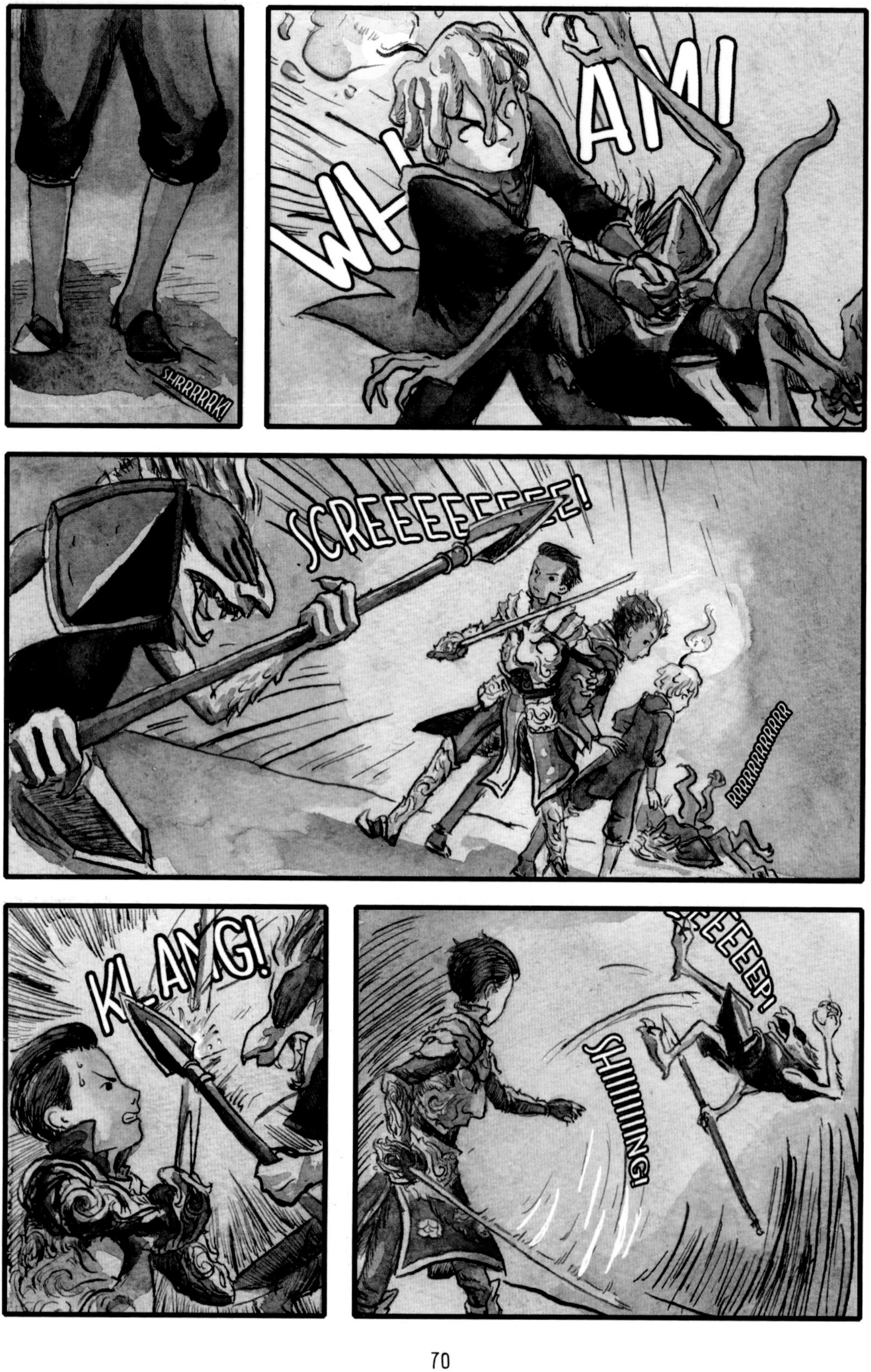
SHRRRRRK!
WH
AM!
SCREEEEEEEEE!
RRRRRRRRRRRR
KLANG!
SHIIIIIING!
EEEEEP!

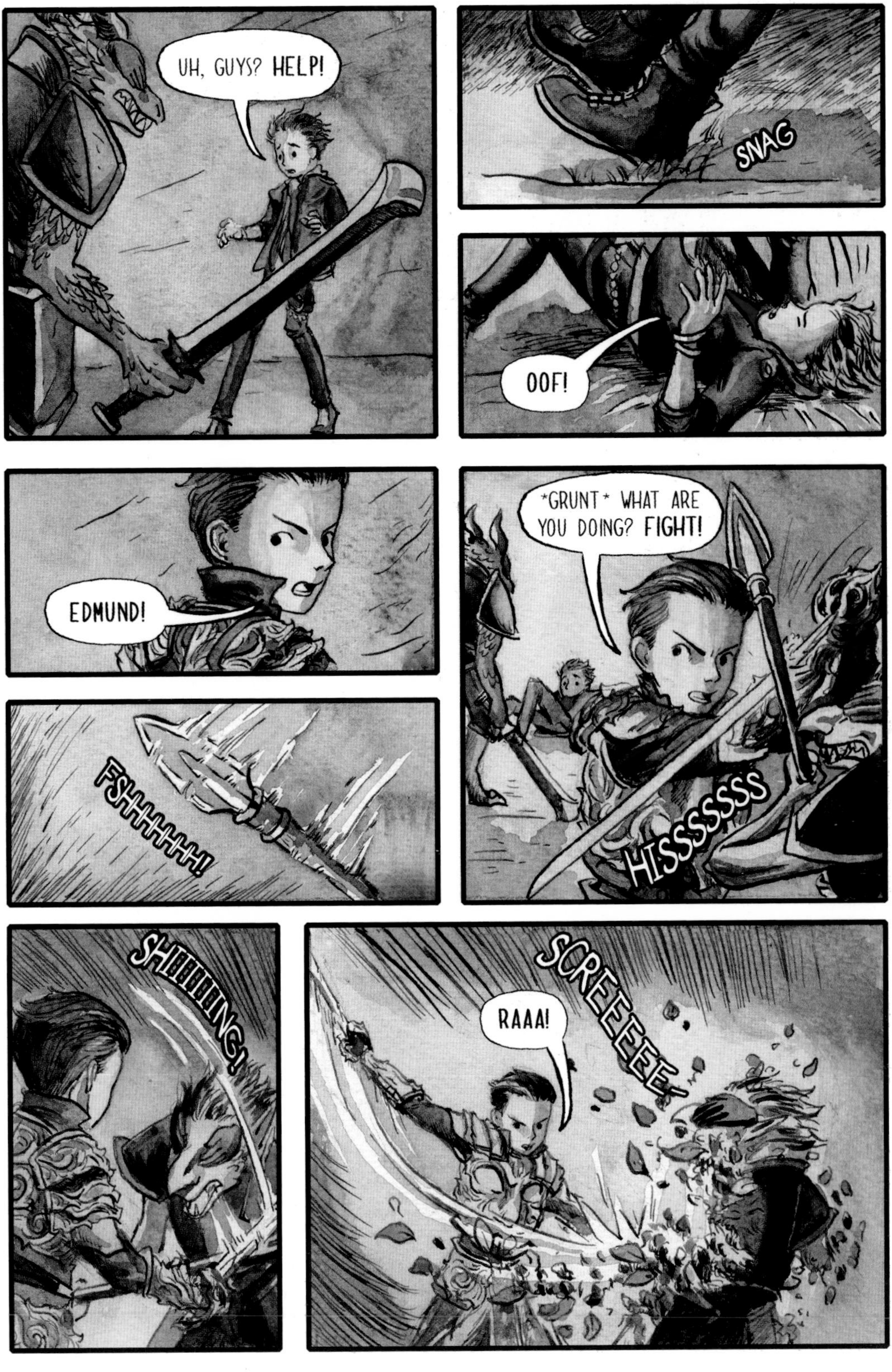
UH, GUYS? HELP!
SNAG
OOF!
EDMUND!
GRUNT WHAT ARE YOU DOING? FIGHT!
FSHHHHHH!
HISSSSSSS
SHIIIIIING!
SCREEEEEE
RAAA!

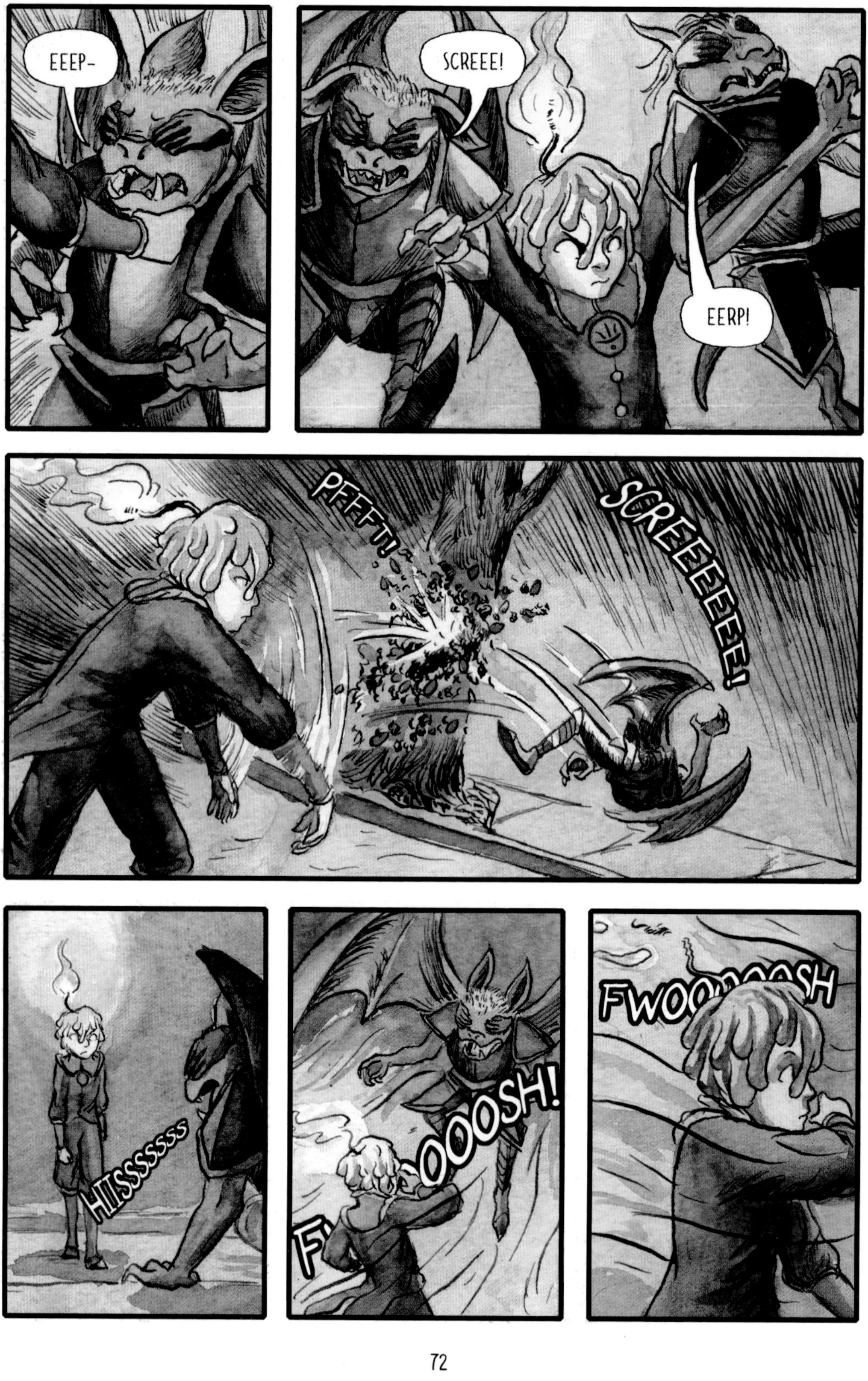
EEEP-
SCREEE!
EERP!
PFFFT!
SCREEEEEEEE!
HISSSSSSS
F
OOOSH!
FWOOOOOSH

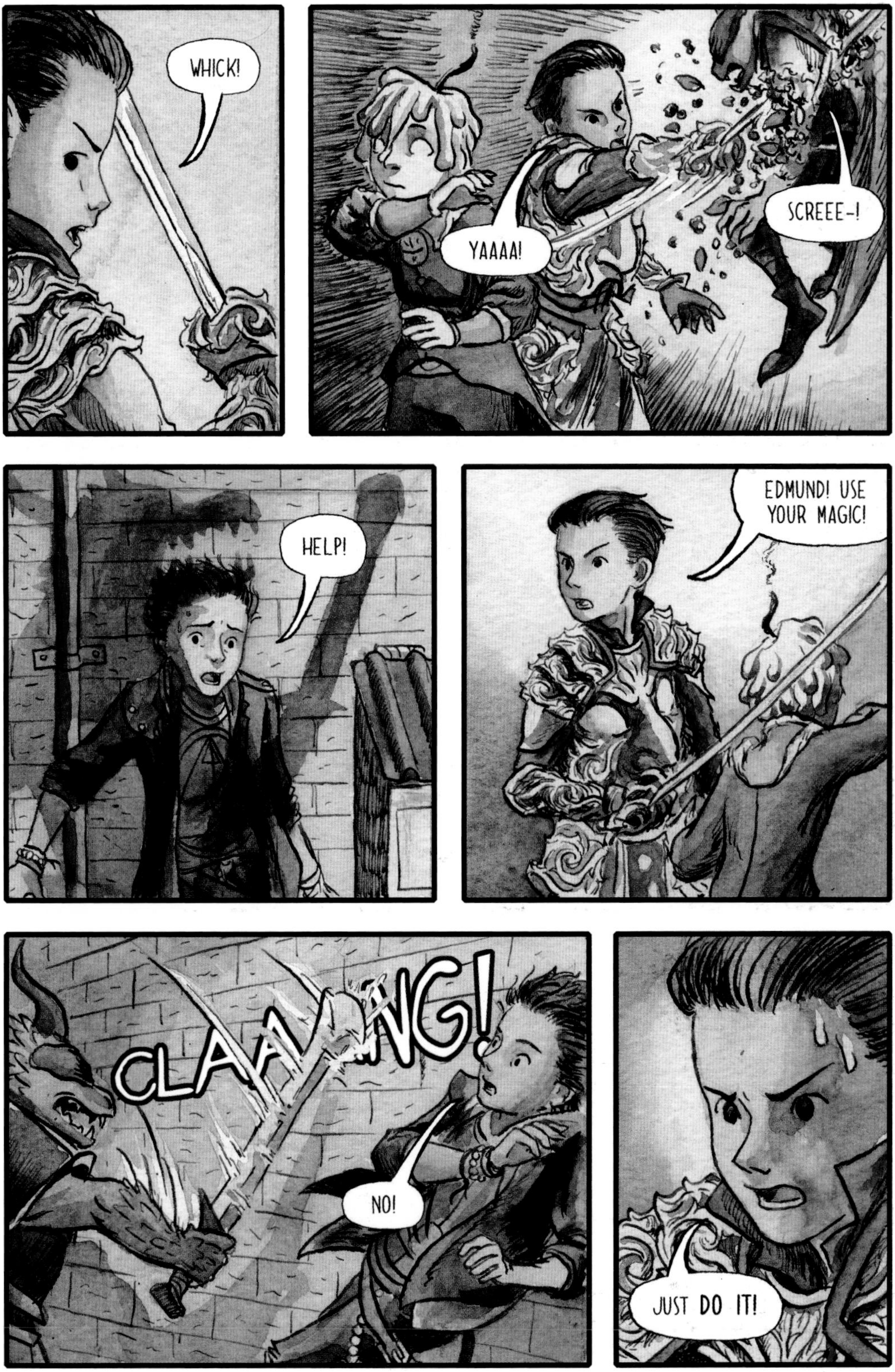
WHICK!
YAAAA!
SCREEE-!
HELP!
EDMUND! USE YOUR MAGIC!
CLAAANG!
NO!
JUST DO IT!

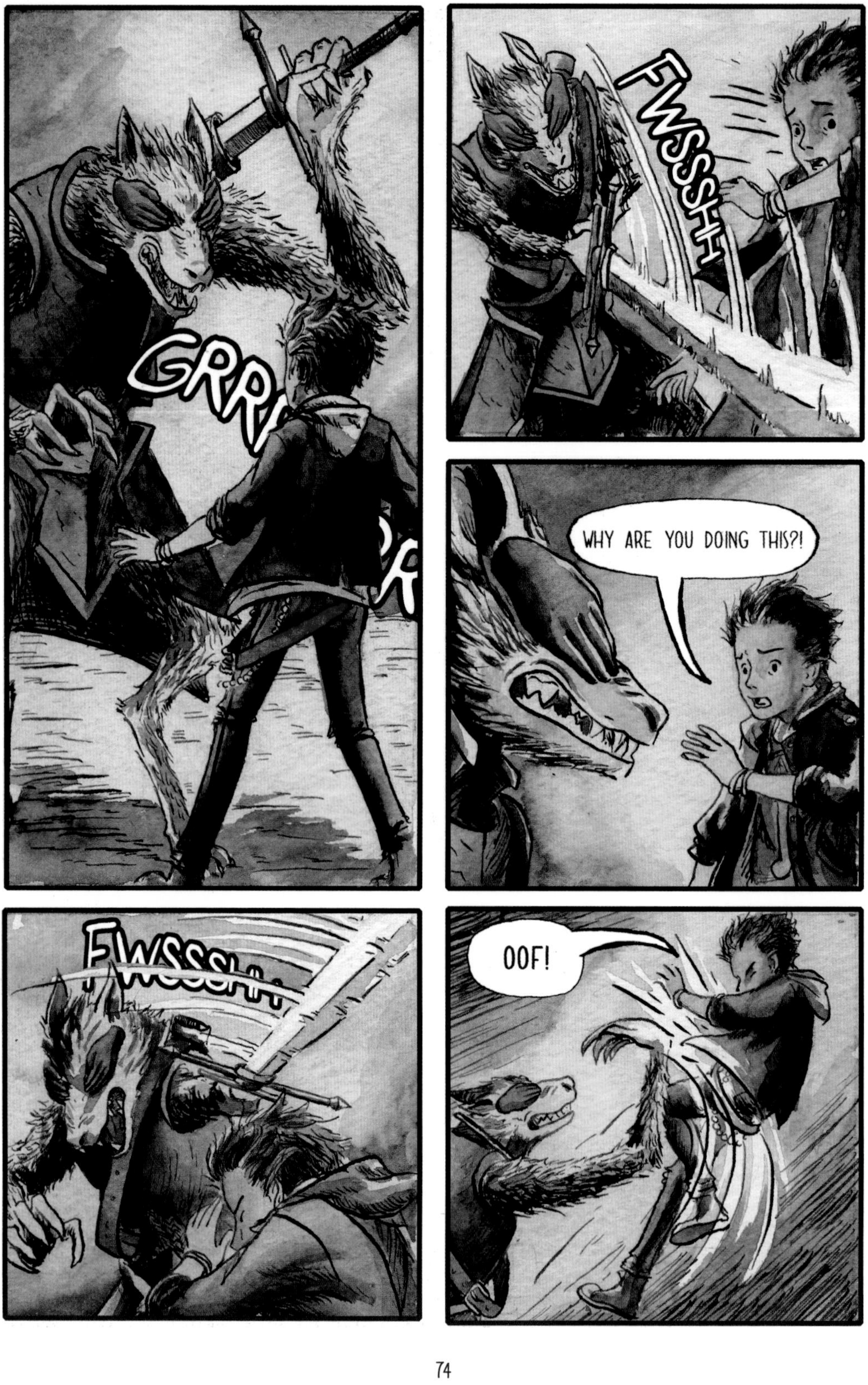
GRRRR
FWSSSHH
WHY ARE YOU DOING THIS?!
FWSSSHH
OOF!

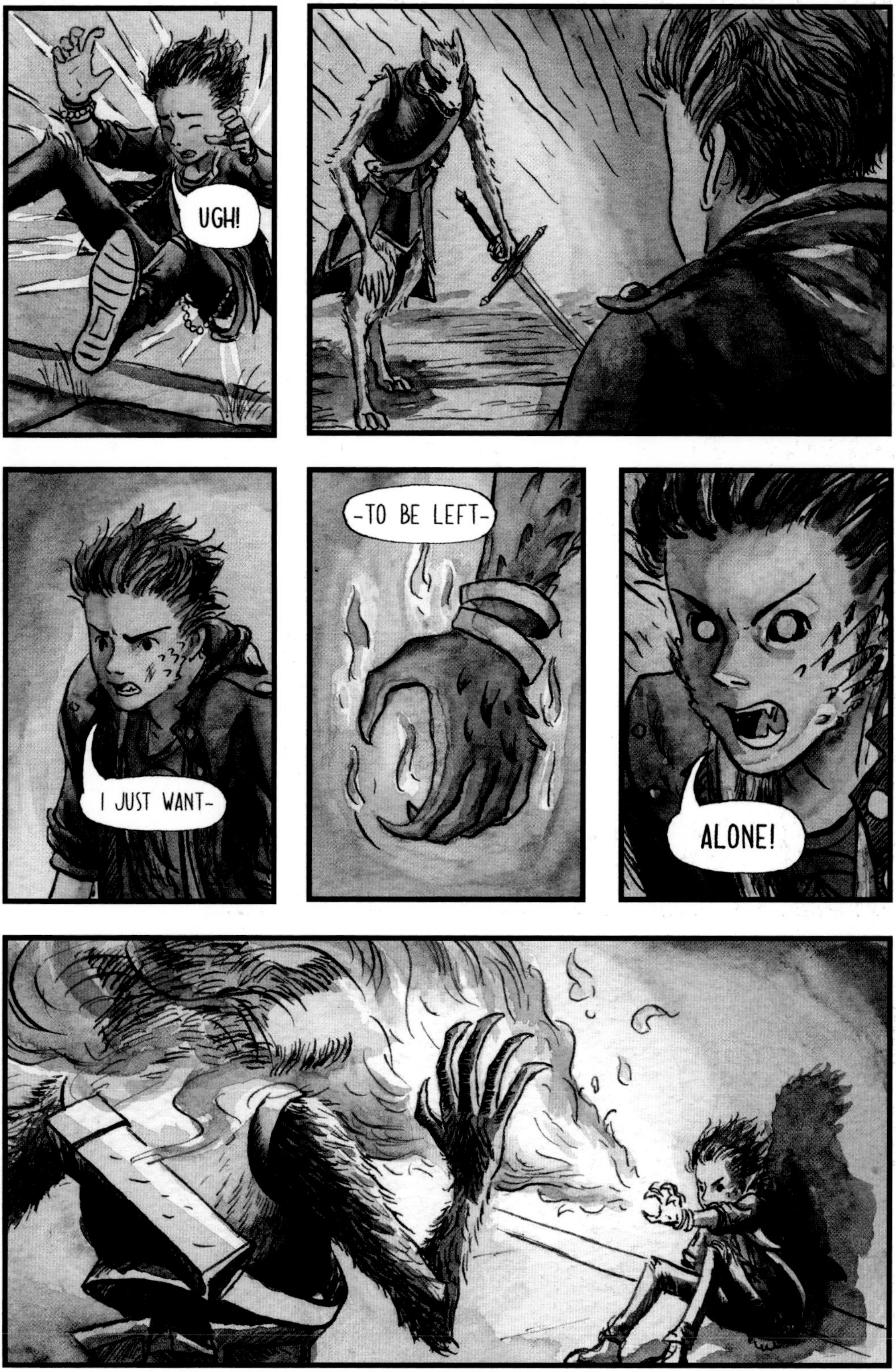
UGH!
I JUST WANT-
-TO BE LEFT-
ALONE!

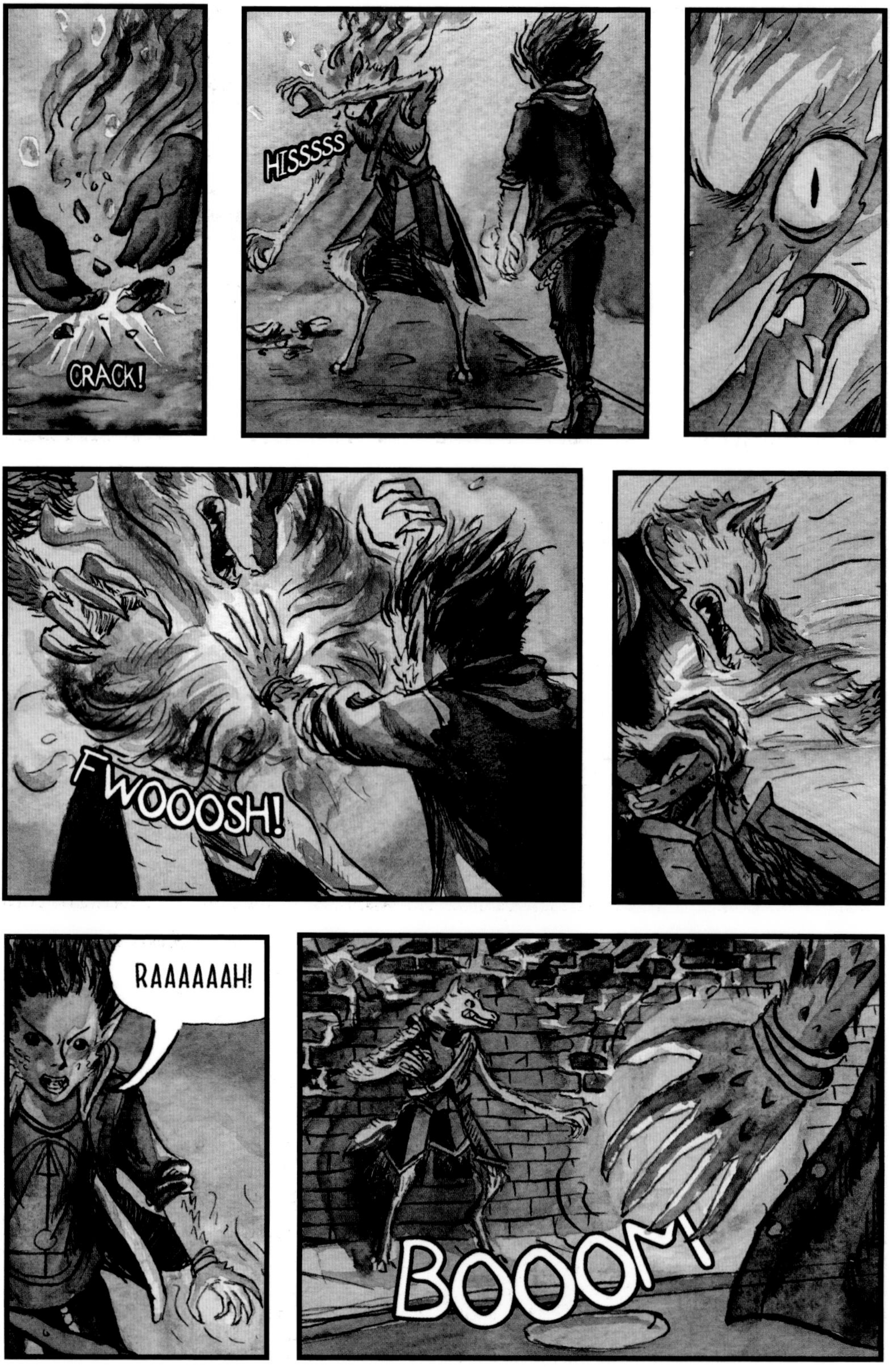
CRACK!
HISSSSS
FWOOOSH!
RAAAAAAH!
BOOOM!

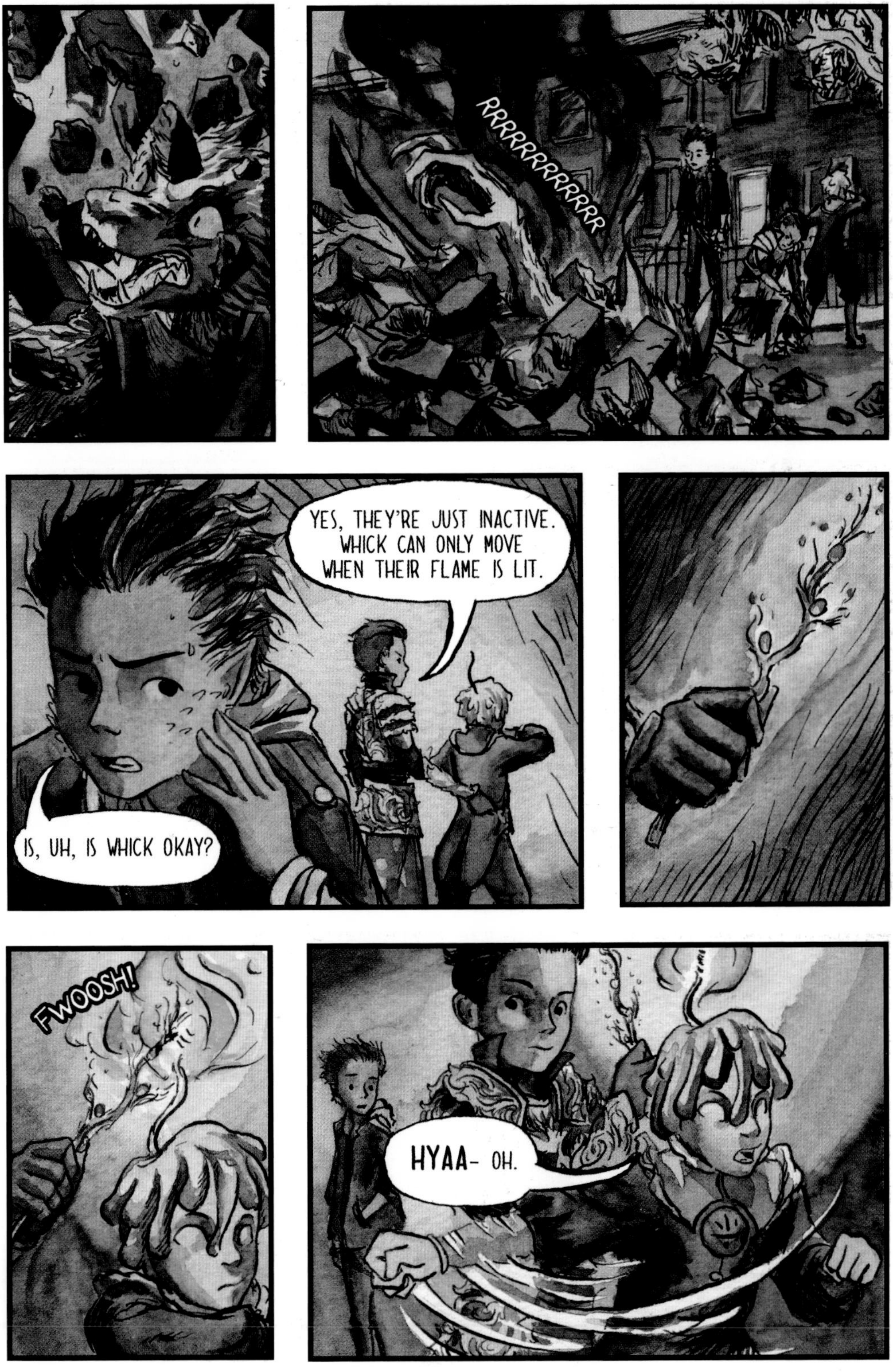
RRRRRRRRRRRR
YES, THEY'RE JUST INACTIVE. WHICK CAN ONLY MOVE WHEN THEIR FLAME IS LIT.
IS, UH, IS WHICK OKAY?
FWOOSH!
HYAA- OH.

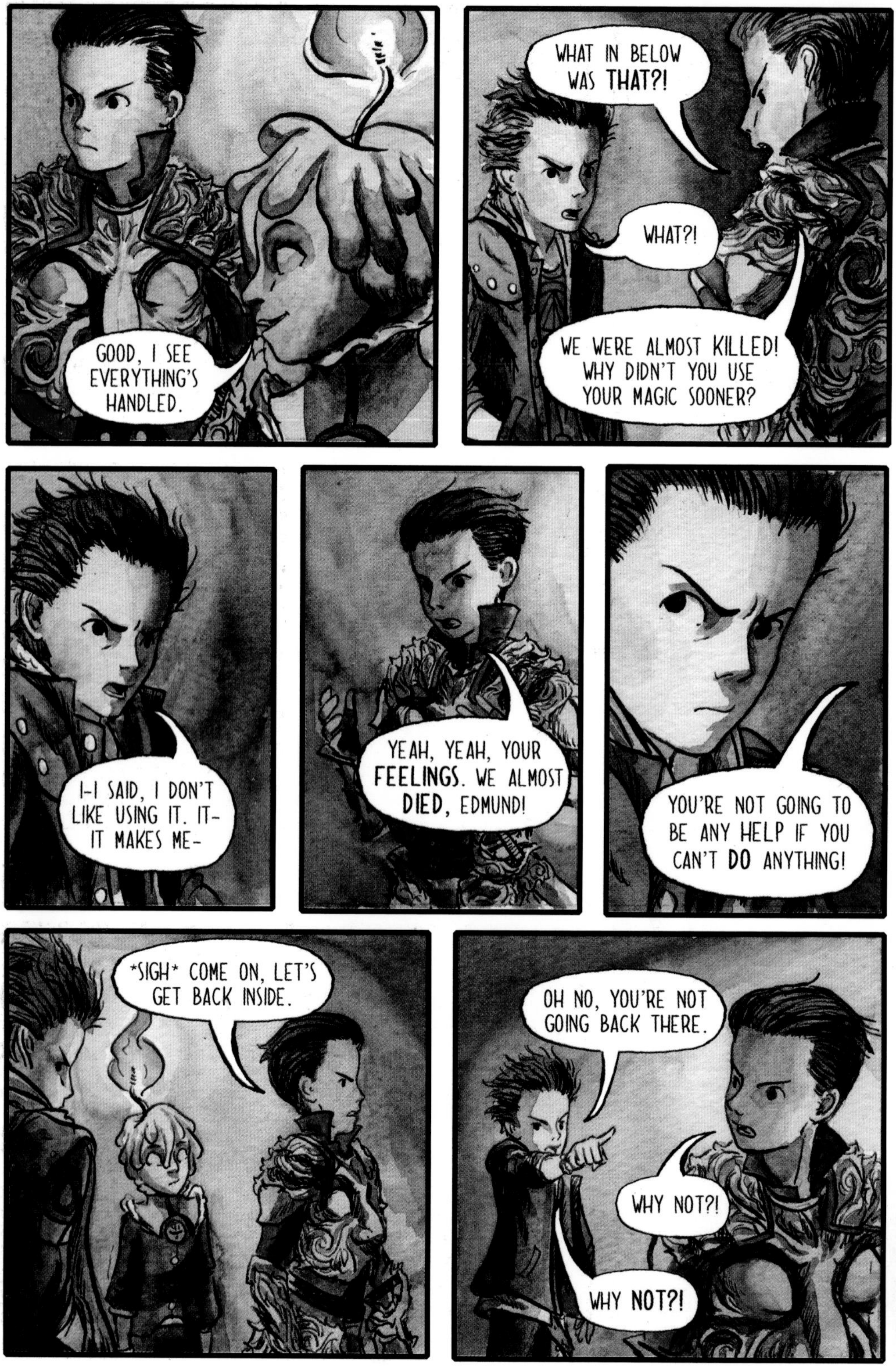
GOOD, I SEE EVERYTHING'S HANDLED.
WHAT IN BELOW WAS THAT?!
WHAT?!
WE WERE ALMOST KILLED! WHY DIDN'T YOU USE YOUR MAGIC SOONER?
I-I SAID, I DON'T LIKE USING IT. IT- IT MAKES ME-
YEAH, YEAH, YOUR FEELINGS. WE ALMOST DIED, EDMUND!
YOU'RE NOT GOING TO BE ANY HELP IF YOU CAN'T DO ANYTHING!
SIGH COME ON, LET'S GET BACK INSIDE.
OH NO, YOU'RE NOT GOING BACK THERE.
WHY NOT?!
WHY NOT?!

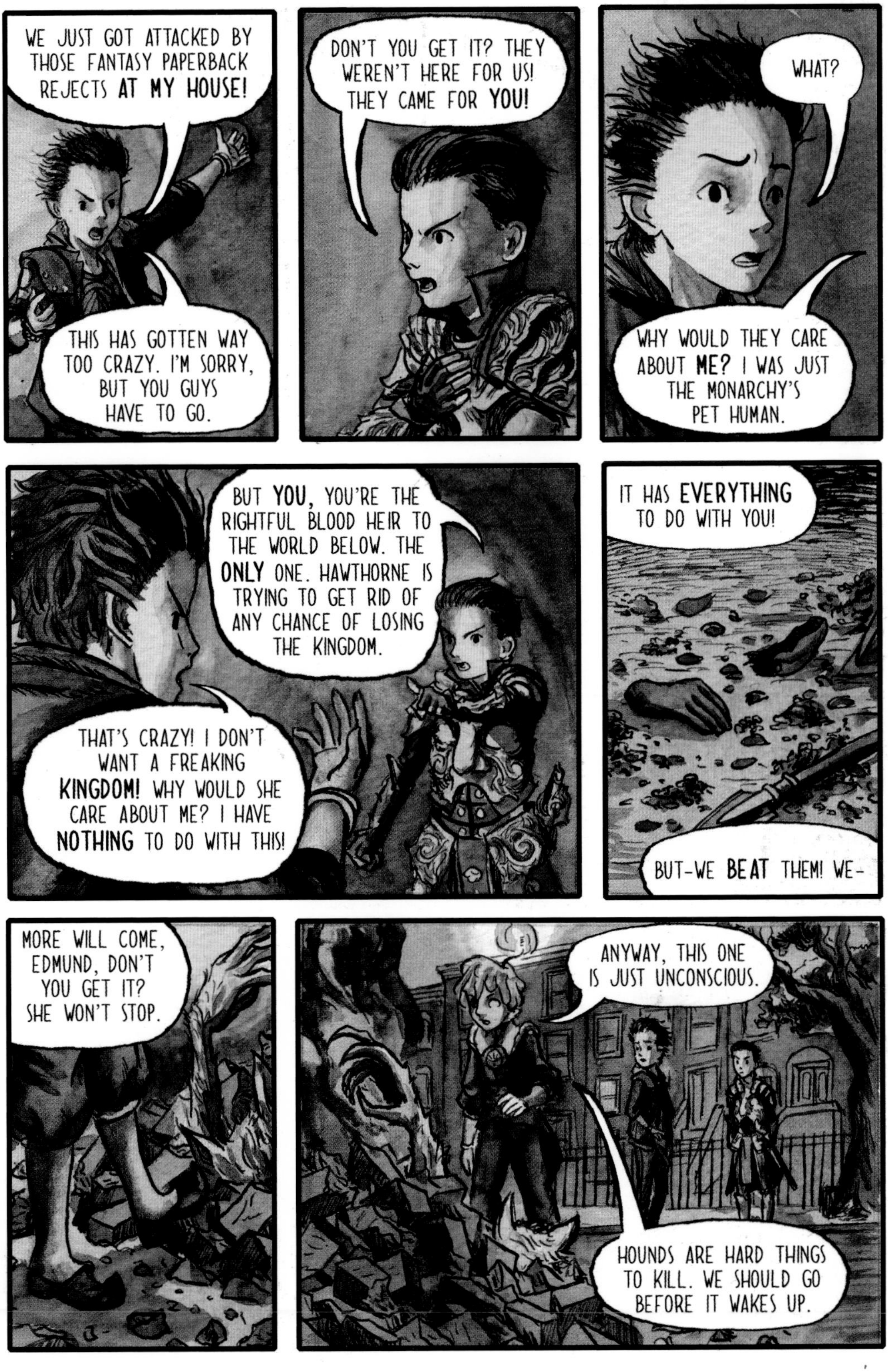
WE JUST GOT ATTACKED BY THOSE FANTASY PAPERBACK REJECTS AT MY HOUSE!
THIS HAS GOTTEN WAY TOO CRAZY. I'M SORRY, BUT YOU GUYS HAVE TO GO.
DON'T YOU GET IT? THEY WEREN'T HERE FOR US! THEY CAME FOR YOU!
WHAT?
WHY WOULD THEY CARE ABOUT ME? I WAS JUST THE MONARCHY'S PET HUMAN.
BUT YOU, YOU'RE THE RIGHTFUL BLOOD HEIR TO THE WORLD BELOW. THE ONLY ONE. HAWTHORNE IS TRYING TO GET RID OF ANY CHANCE OF LOSING THE KINGDOM.
THAT'S CRAZY! I DON'T WANT A FREAKING KINGDOM! WHY WOULD SHE CARE ABOUT ME? I HAVE NOTHING TO DO WITH THIS!
IT HAS EVERYTHING TO DO WITH YOU!
BUT-WE BEAT THEM! WE-
MORE WILL COME, EDMUND, DON'T YOU GET IT? SHE WON'T STOP.
ANYWAY, THIS ONE IS JUST UNCONSCIOUS.
HOUNDS ARE HARD THINGS TO KILL. WE SHOULD GO BEFORE IT WAKES UP.

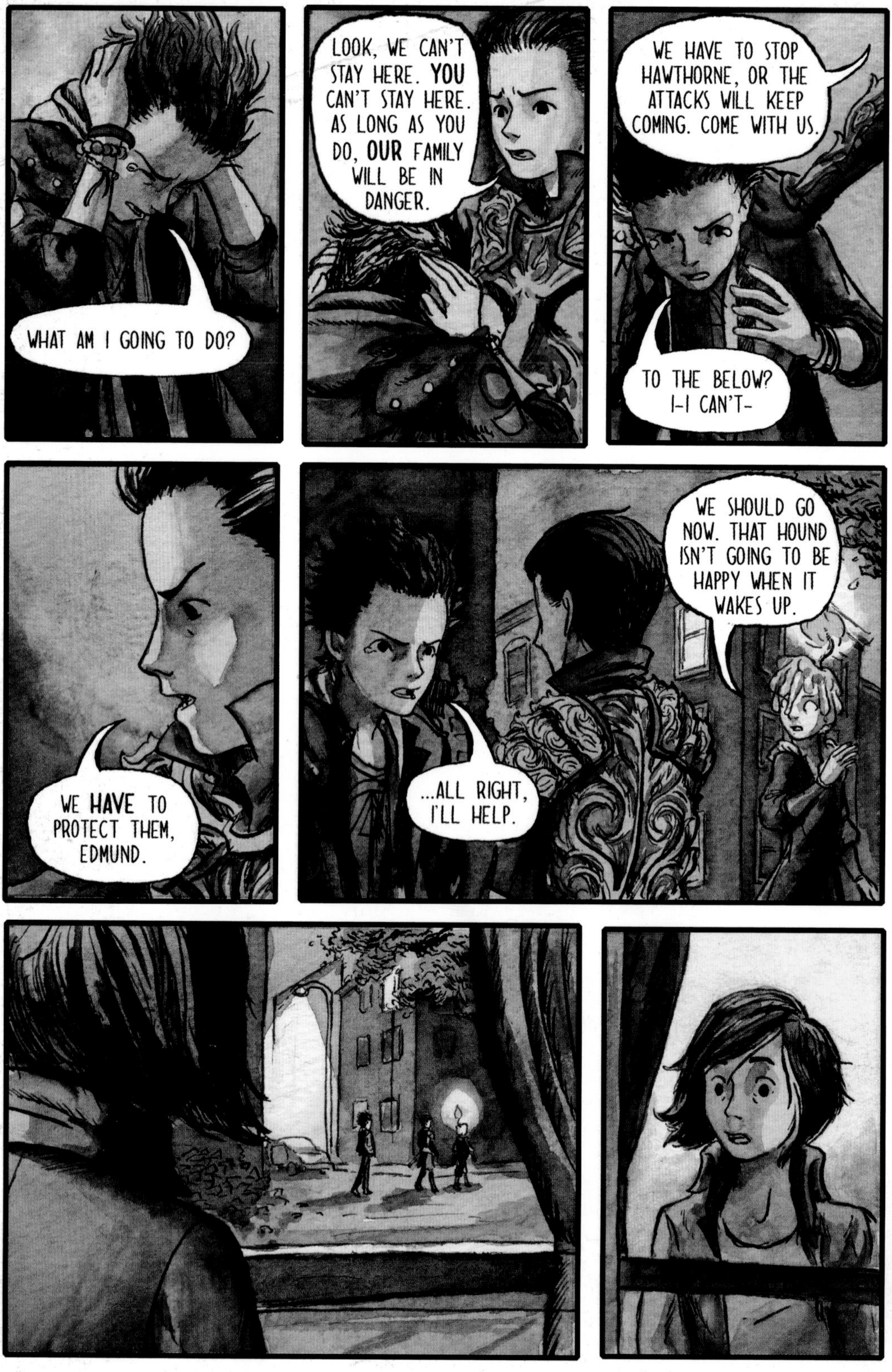
WHAT AM I GOING TO DO?
LOOK, WE CAN'T STAY HERE. YOU CAN'T STAY HERE. AS LONG AS YOU DO, OUR FAMILY WILL BE IN DANGER.
WE HAVE TO STOP HAWTHORNE, OR THE ATTACKS WILL KEEP COMING. COME WITH US.
TO THE BELOW? I-I CAN'T-
WE HAVE TO PROTECT THEM, EDMUND.
WE SHOULD GO NOW. THAT HOUND ISN'T GOING TO BE HAPPY WHEN IT WAKES UP.
...ALL RIGHT, I'LL HELP.

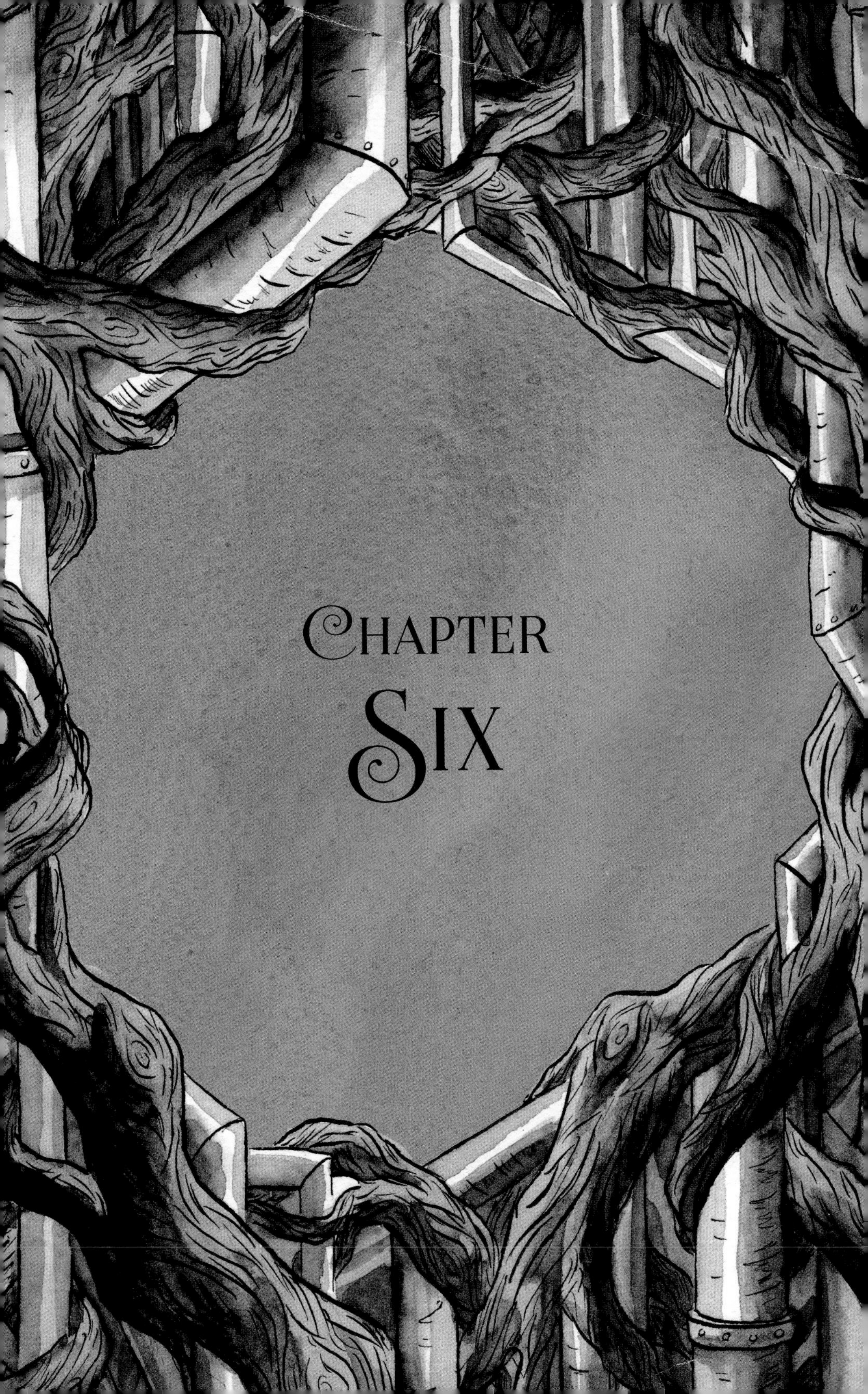

Chapter Six

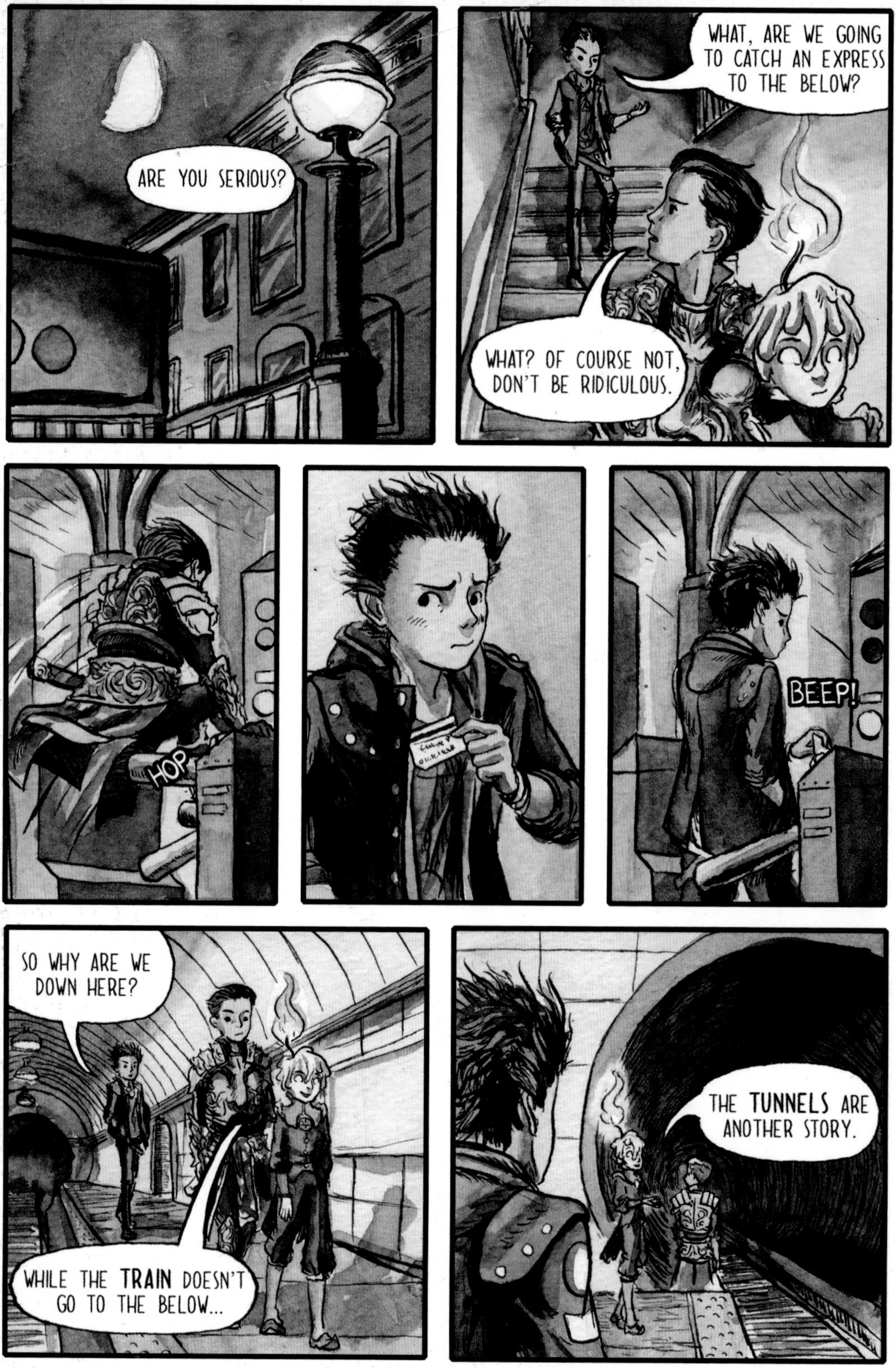
ARE YOU SERIOUS?
WHAT, ARE WE GOING TO CATCH AN EXPRESS TO THE BELOW?
WHAT? OF COURSE NOT, DON'T BE RIDICULOUS.
HOP
BEEP!
SO WHY ARE WE DOWN HERE?
WHILE THE **TRAIN** DOESN'T GO TO THE BELOW...
THE **TUNNELS** ARE ANOTHER STORY.

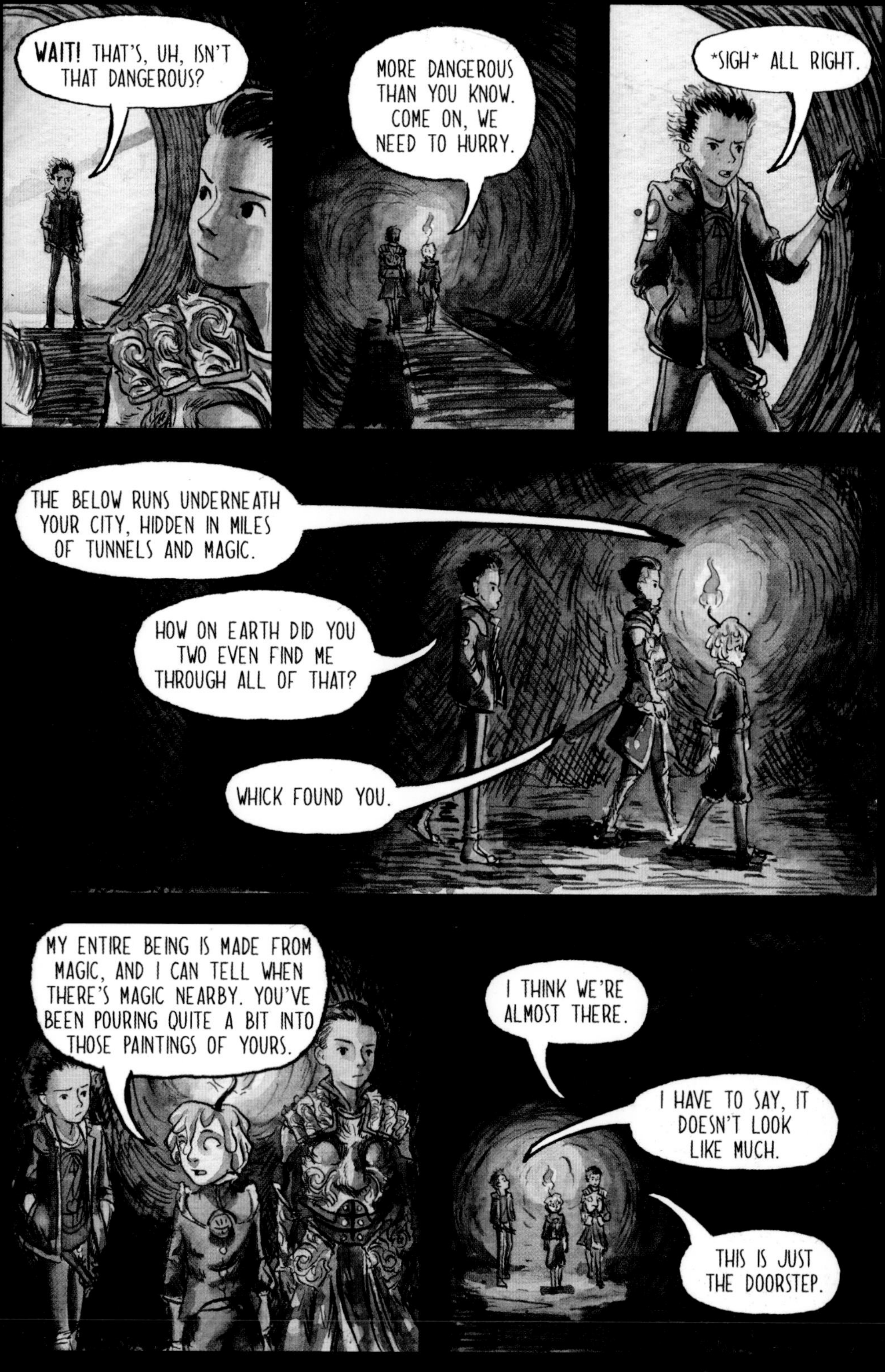
WAIT! THAT'S, UH, ISN'T THAT DANGEROUS?
MORE DANGEROUS THAN YOU KNOW. COME ON, WE NEED TO HURRY.
SIGH ALL RIGHT.
THE BELOW RUNS UNDERNEATH YOUR CITY, HIDDEN IN MILES OF TUNNELS AND MAGIC.
HOW ON EARTH DID YOU TWO EVEN FIND ME THROUGH ALL OF THAT?
WHICK FOUND YOU.
MY ENTIRE BEING IS MADE FROM MAGIC, AND I CAN TELL WHEN THERE'S MAGIC NEARBY. YOU'VE BEEN POURING QUITE A BIT INTO THOSE PAINTINGS OF YOURS.
I THINK WE'RE ALMOST THERE.
I HAVE TO SAY, IT DOESN'T LOOK LIKE MUCH.
THIS IS JUST THE DOORSTEP.

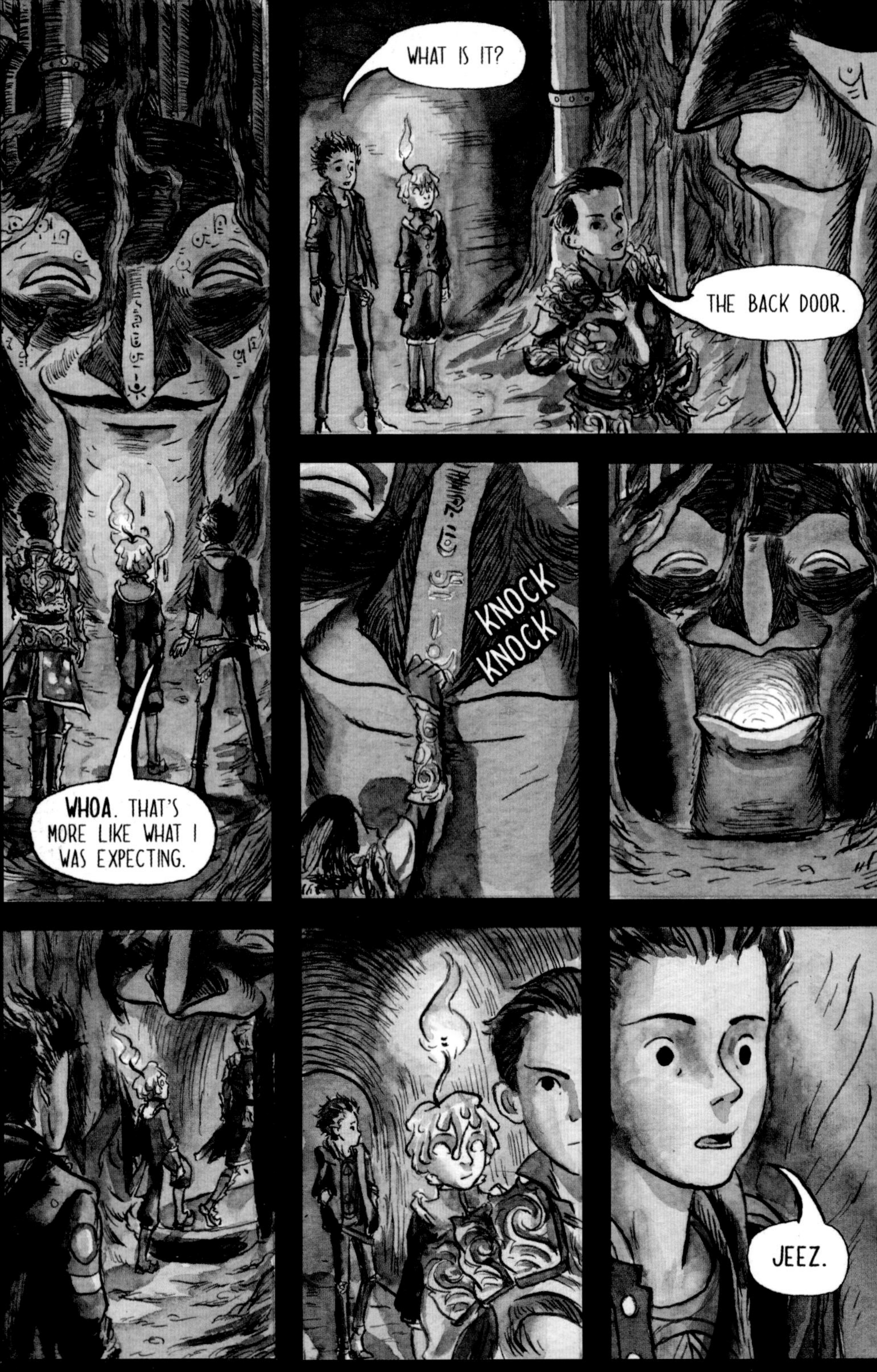
WHAT IS IT?
THE BACK DOOR.
WHOA. THAT'S MORE LIKE WHAT I WAS EXPECTING.
KNOCK KNOCK
JEEZ.

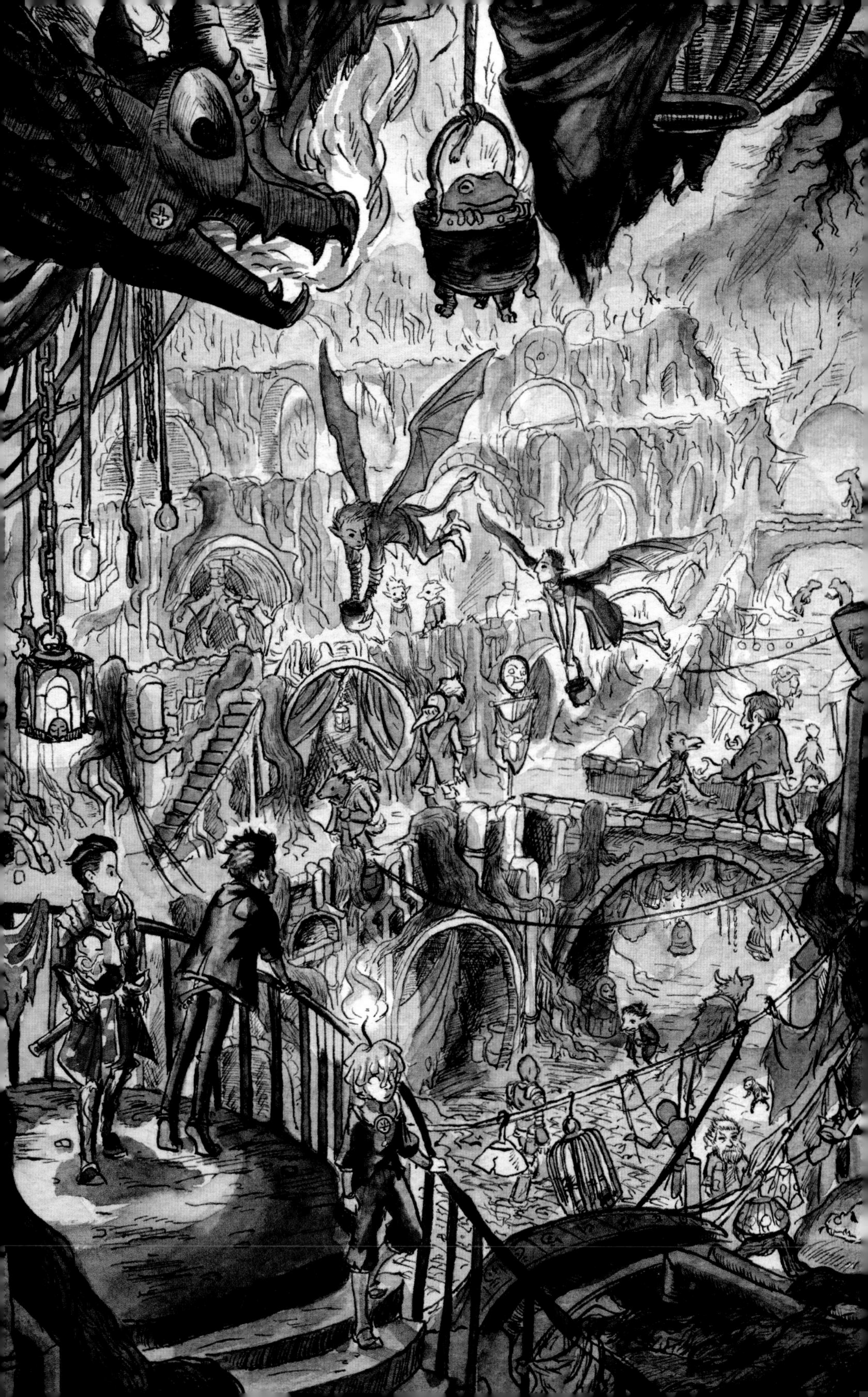

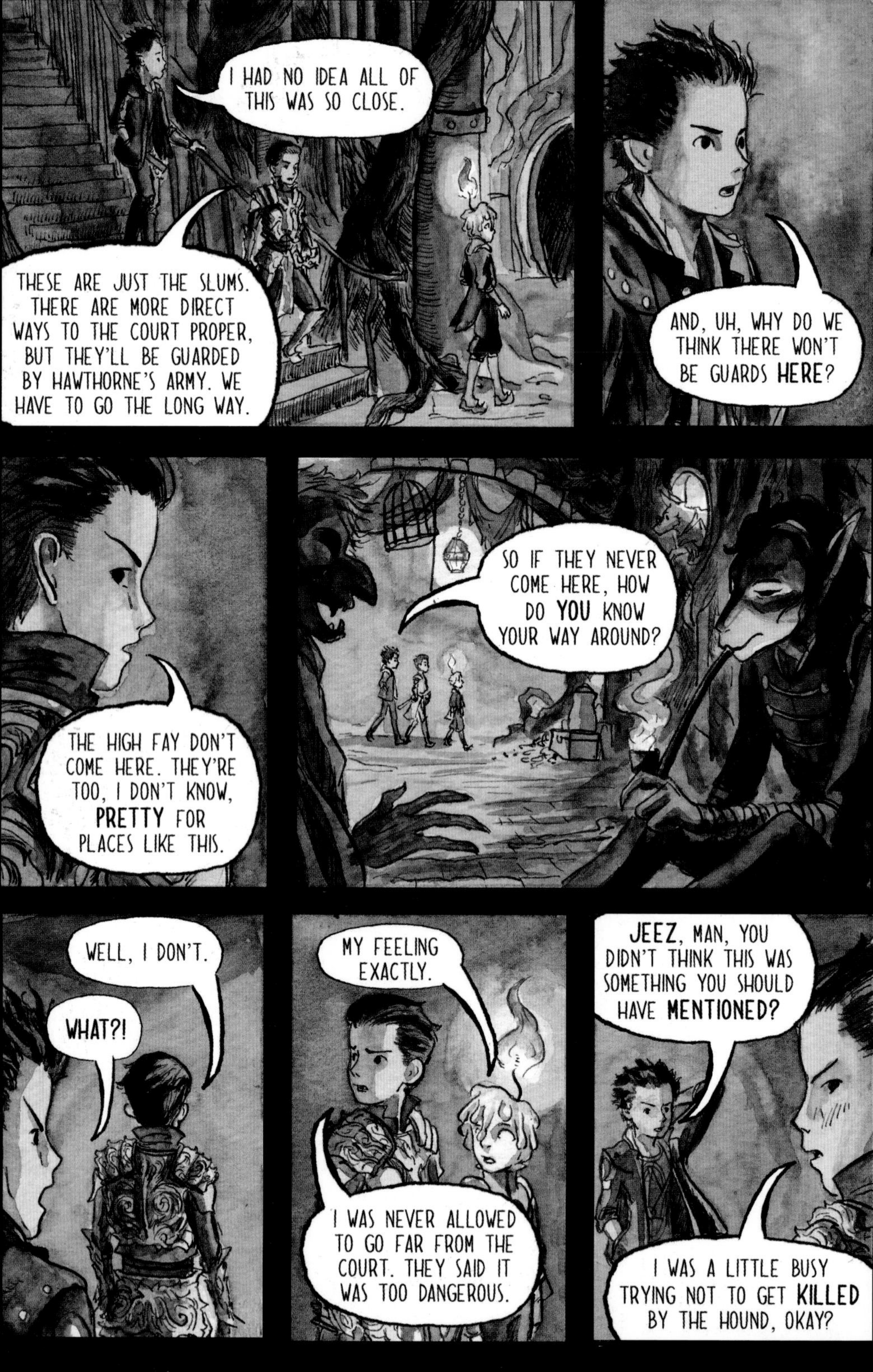
I HAD NO IDEA ALL OF THIS WAS SO CLOSE.
THESE ARE JUST THE SLUMS. THERE ARE MORE DIRECT WAYS TO THE COURT PROPER, BUT THEY'LL BE GUARDED BY HAWTHORNE'S ARMY. WE HAVE TO GO THE LONG WAY.
AND, UH, WHY DO WE THINK THERE WON'T BE GUARDS **HERE**?
THE HIGH FAY DON'T COME HERE. THEY'RE TOO, I DON'T KNOW, **PRETTY** FOR PLACES LIKE THIS.
SO IF THEY NEVER COME HERE, HOW DO **YOU** KNOW YOUR WAY AROUND?
WELL, I DON'T.
WHAT?!
MY FEELING EXACTLY.
I WAS NEVER ALLOWED TO GO FAR FROM THE COURT. THEY SAID IT WAS TOO DANGEROUS.
JEEZ, MAN, YOU DIDN'T THINK THIS WAS SOMETHING YOU SHOULD HAVE **MENTIONED?**
I WAS A LITTLE BUSY TRYING NOT TO GET **KILLED** BY THE HOUND, OKAY?

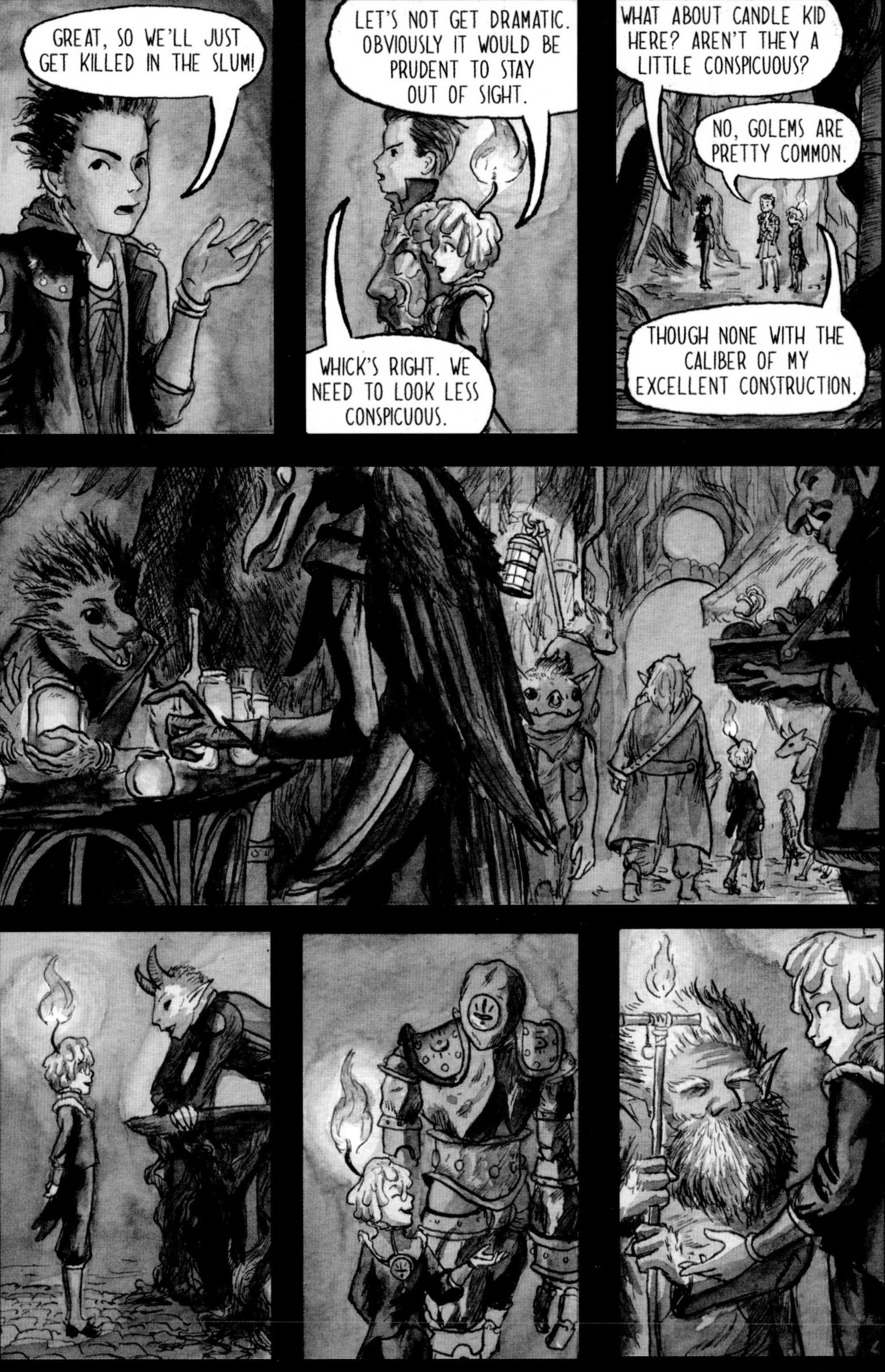
GREAT, SO WE'LL JUST GET KILLED IN THE SLUM!
LET'S NOT GET DRAMATIC. OBVIOUSLY IT WOULD BE PRUDENT TO STAY OUT OF SIGHT.
WHICK'S RIGHT. WE NEED TO LOOK LESS CONSPICUOUS.
WHAT ABOUT CANDLE KID HERE? AREN'T THEY A LITTLE CONSPICUOUS?
NO, GOLEMS ARE PRETTY COMMON.
THOUGH NONE WITH THE CALIBER OF MY EXCELLENT CONSTRUCTION.

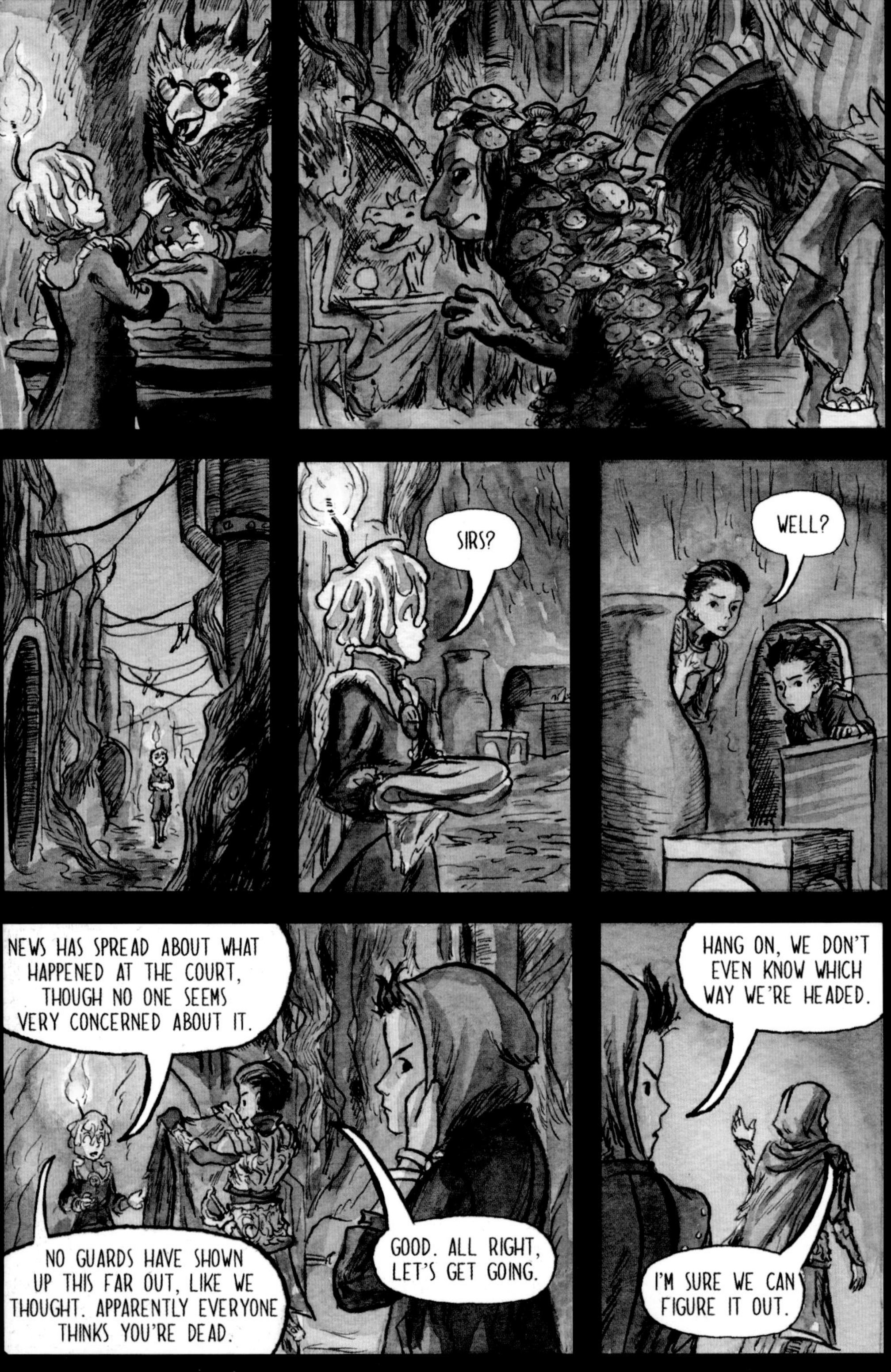
SIRS?
WELL?
NEWS HAS SPREAD ABOUT WHAT HAPPENED AT THE COURT, THOUGH NO ONE SEEMS VERY CONCERNED ABOUT IT.
NO GUARDS HAVE SHOWN UP THIS FAR OUT, LIKE WE THOUGHT. APPARENTLY EVERYONE THINKS YOU'RE DEAD.
GOOD. ALL RIGHT, LET'S GET GOING.
HANG ON, WE DON'T EVEN KNOW WHICH WAY WE'RE HEADED.
I'M SURE WE CAN FIGURE IT OUT.

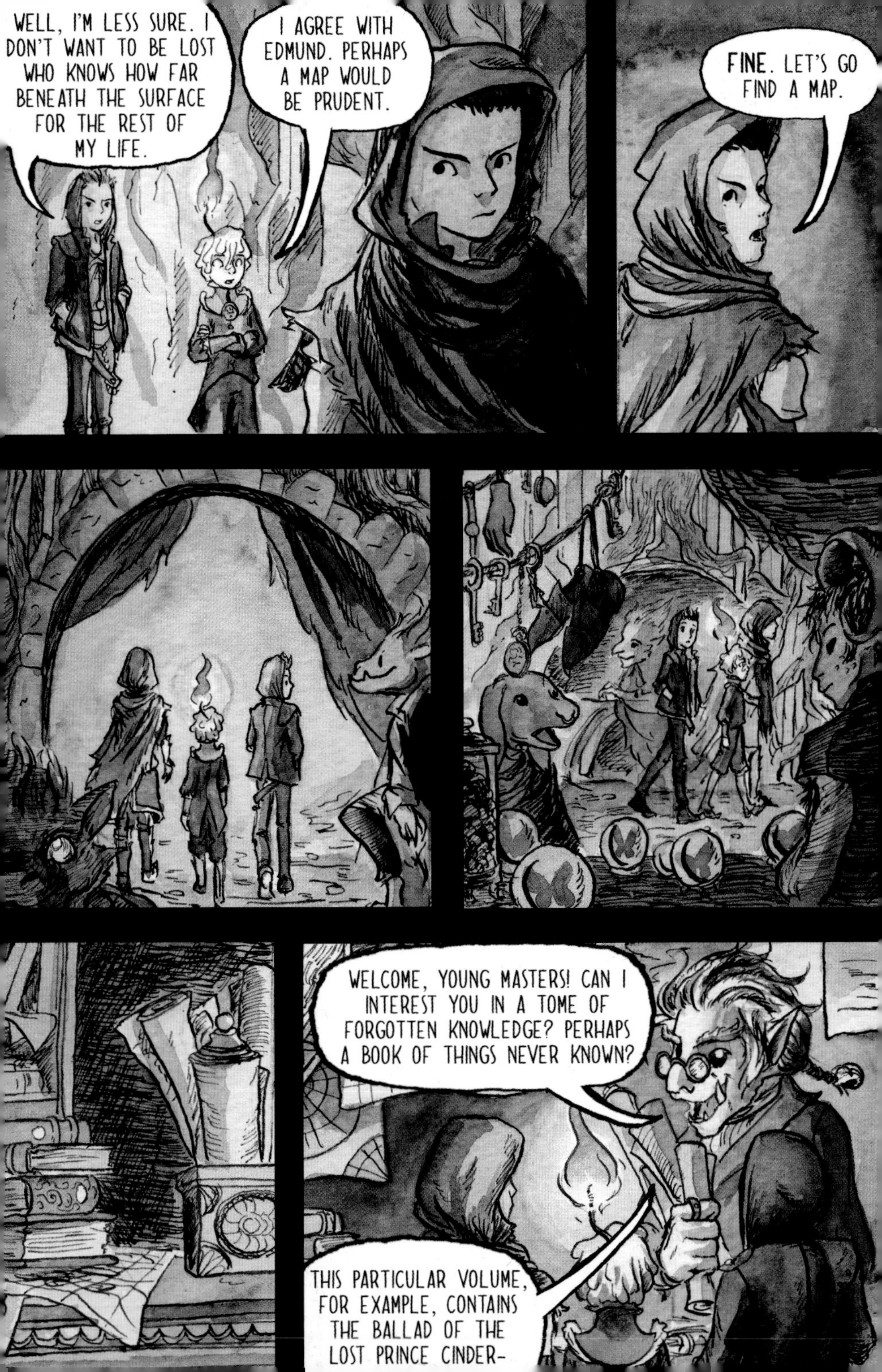
WELL, I'M LESS SURE. I DON'T WANT TO BE LOST WHO KNOWS HOW FAR BENEATH THE SURFACE FOR THE REST OF MY LIFE.
I AGREE WITH EDMUND. PERHAPS A MAP WOULD BE PRUDENT.
FINE. LET'S GO FIND A MAP.
WELCOME, YOUNG MASTERS! CAN I INTEREST YOU IN A TOME OF FORGOTTEN KNOWLEDGE? PERHAPS A BOOK OF THINGS NEVER KNOWN?
THIS PARTICULAR VOLUME, FOR EXAMPLE, CONTAINS THE BALLAD OF THE LOST PRINCE CINDER-

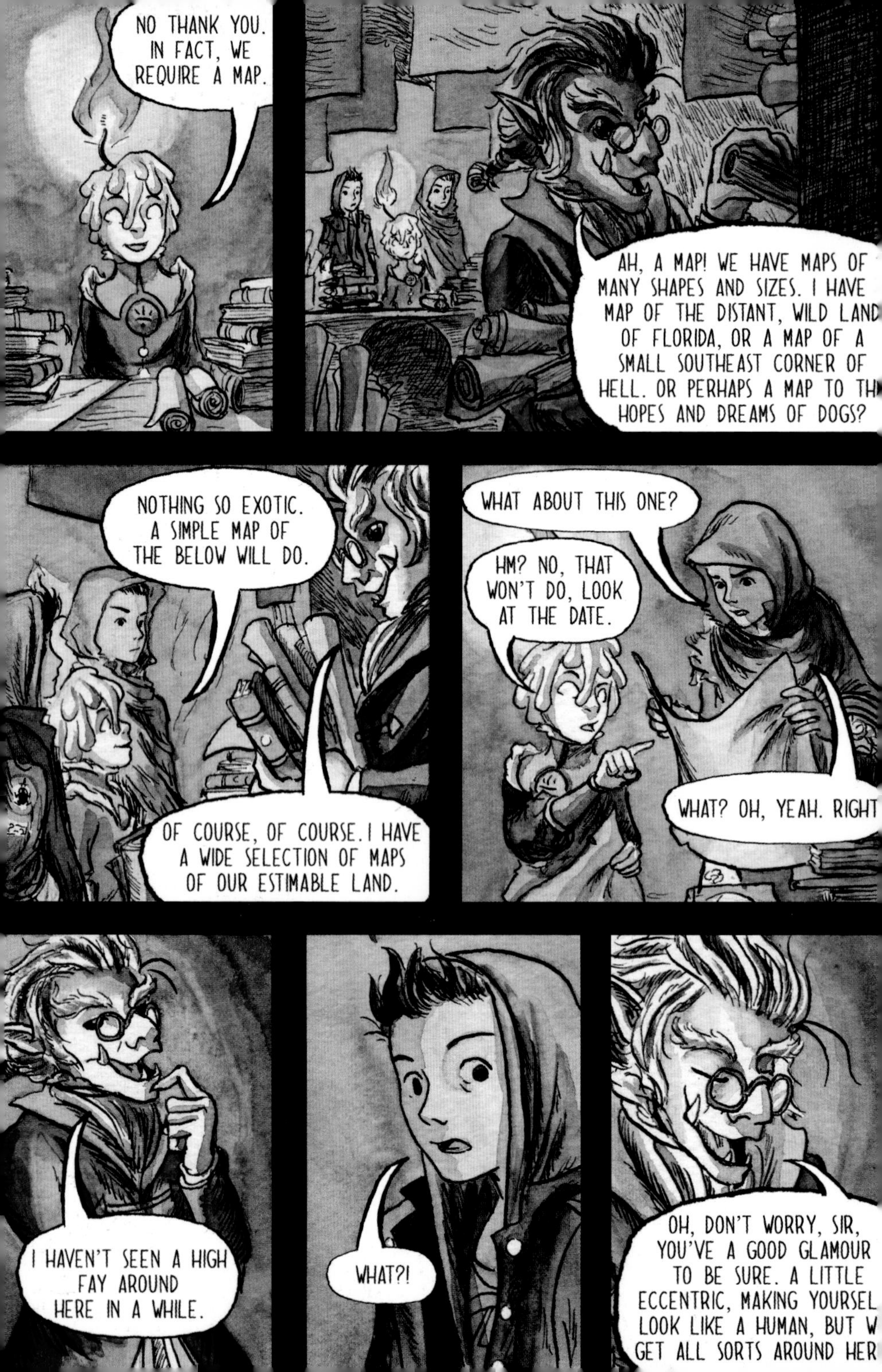
NO THANK YOU. IN FACT, WE REQUIRE A MAP.
AH, A MAP! WE HAVE MAPS OF MANY SHAPES AND SIZES. I HAVE MAP OF THE DISTANT, WILD LAND OF FLORIDA, OR A MAP OF A SMALL SOUTHEAST CORNER OF HELL. OR PERHAPS A MAP TO TH HOPES AND DREAMS OF DOGS?
NOTHING SO EXOTIC. A SIMPLE MAP OF THE BELOW WILL DO.
OF COURSE, OF COURSE. I HAVE A WIDE SELECTION OF MAPS OF OUR ESTIMABLE LAND.
WHAT ABOUT THIS ONE?
HM? NO, THAT WON'T DO, LOOK AT THE DATE.
WHAT? OH, YEAH. RIGHT
I HAVEN'T SEEN A HIGH FAY AROUND HERE IN A WHILE.
WHAT?!
OH, DON'T WORRY, SIR, YOU'VE A GOOD GLAMOUR TO BE SURE. A LITTLE ECCENTRIC, MAKING YOURSEL LOOK LIKE A HUMAN, BUT W GET ALL SORTS AROUND HER

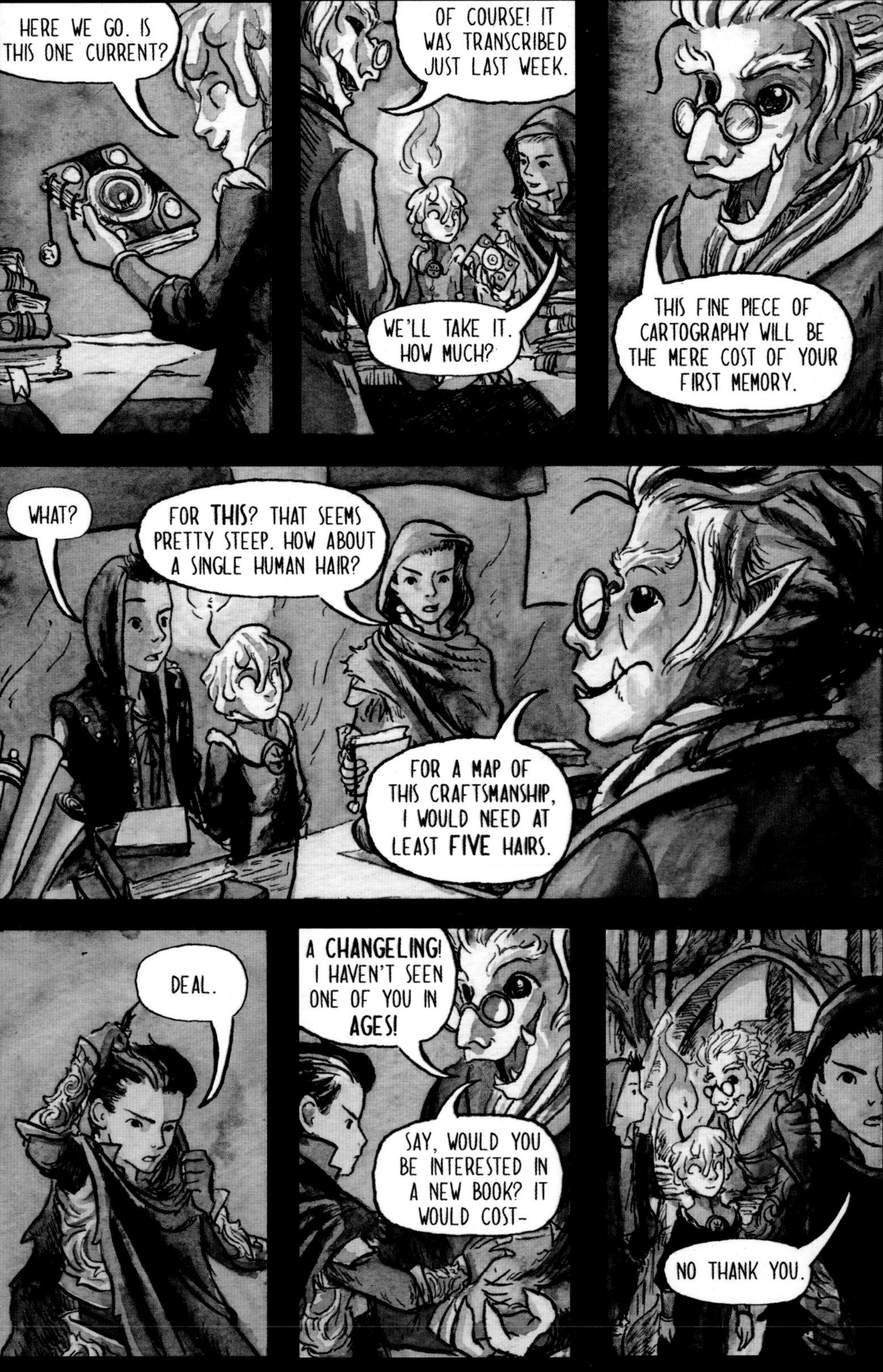
HERE WE GO. IS THIS ONE CURRENT?
OF COURSE! IT WAS TRANSCRIBED JUST LAST WEEK.
WE'LL TAKE IT. HOW MUCH?
THIS FINE PIECE OF CARTOGRAPHY WILL BE THE MERE COST OF YOUR FIRST MEMORY.
WHAT?
FOR **THIS**? THAT SEEMS PRETTY STEEP. HOW ABOUT A SINGLE HUMAN HAIR?
FOR A MAP OF THIS CRAFTSMANSHIP, I WOULD NEED AT LEAST **FIVE** HAIRS.
DEAL.
A **CHANGELING**! I HAVEN'T SEEN ONE OF YOU IN **AGES**!
SAY, WOULD YOU BE INTERESTED IN A NEW BOOK? IT WOULD COST-
NO THANK YOU.

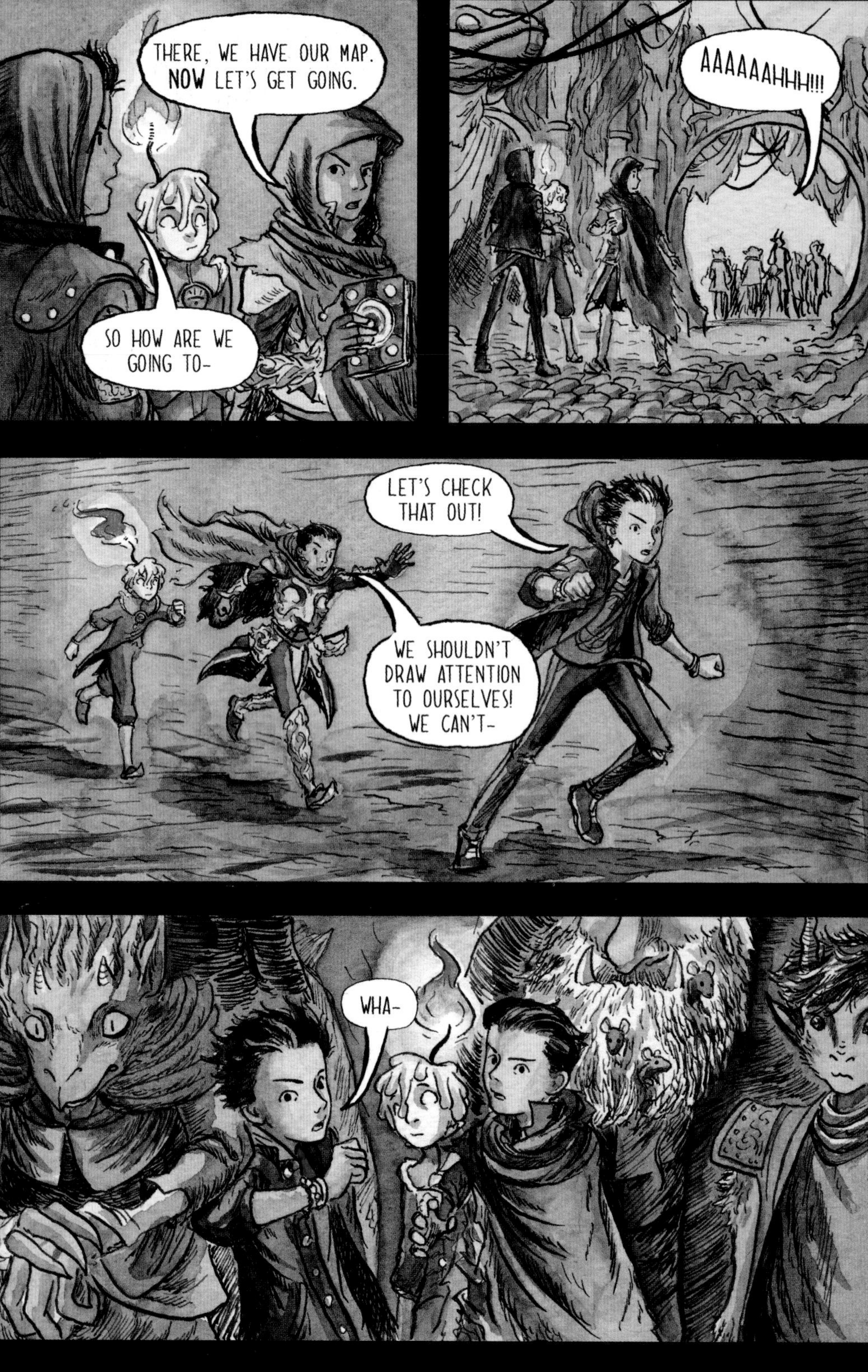
THERE, WE HAVE OUR MAP. **NOW** LET'S GET GOING.
SO HOW ARE WE GOING TO-
AAAAAAHHH!!!
LET'S CHECK THAT OUT!
WE SHOULDN'T DRAW ATTENTION TO OURSELVES! WE CAN'T-
WHA-

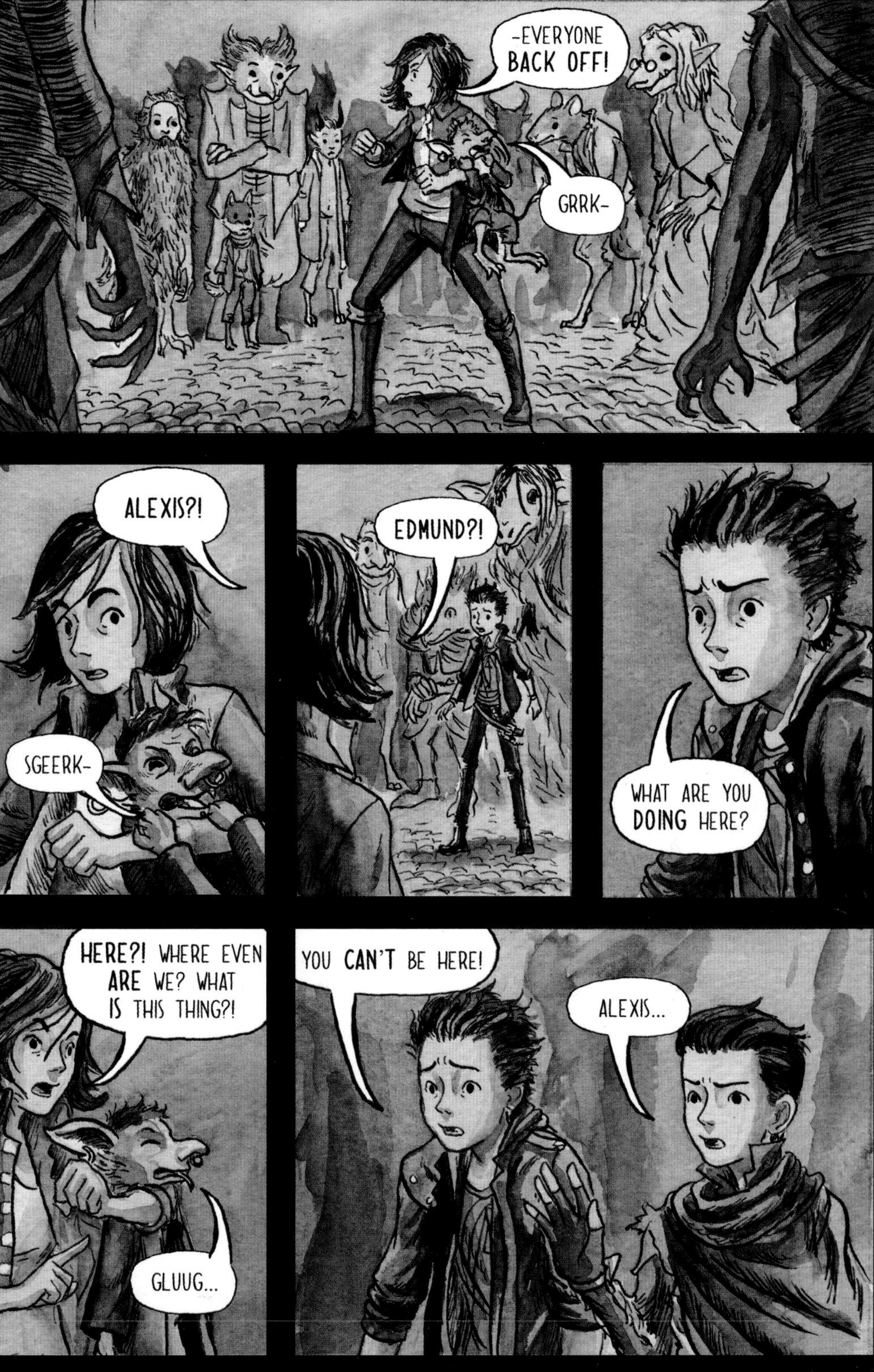
-EVERYONE BACK OFF!
GRRK-
ALEXIS?!
SGEERK-
EDMUND?!
WHAT ARE YOU DOING HERE?
HERE?! WHERE EVEN ARE WE? WHAT IS THIS THING?!
GLUUG...
YOU CAN'T BE HERE!
ALEXIS...

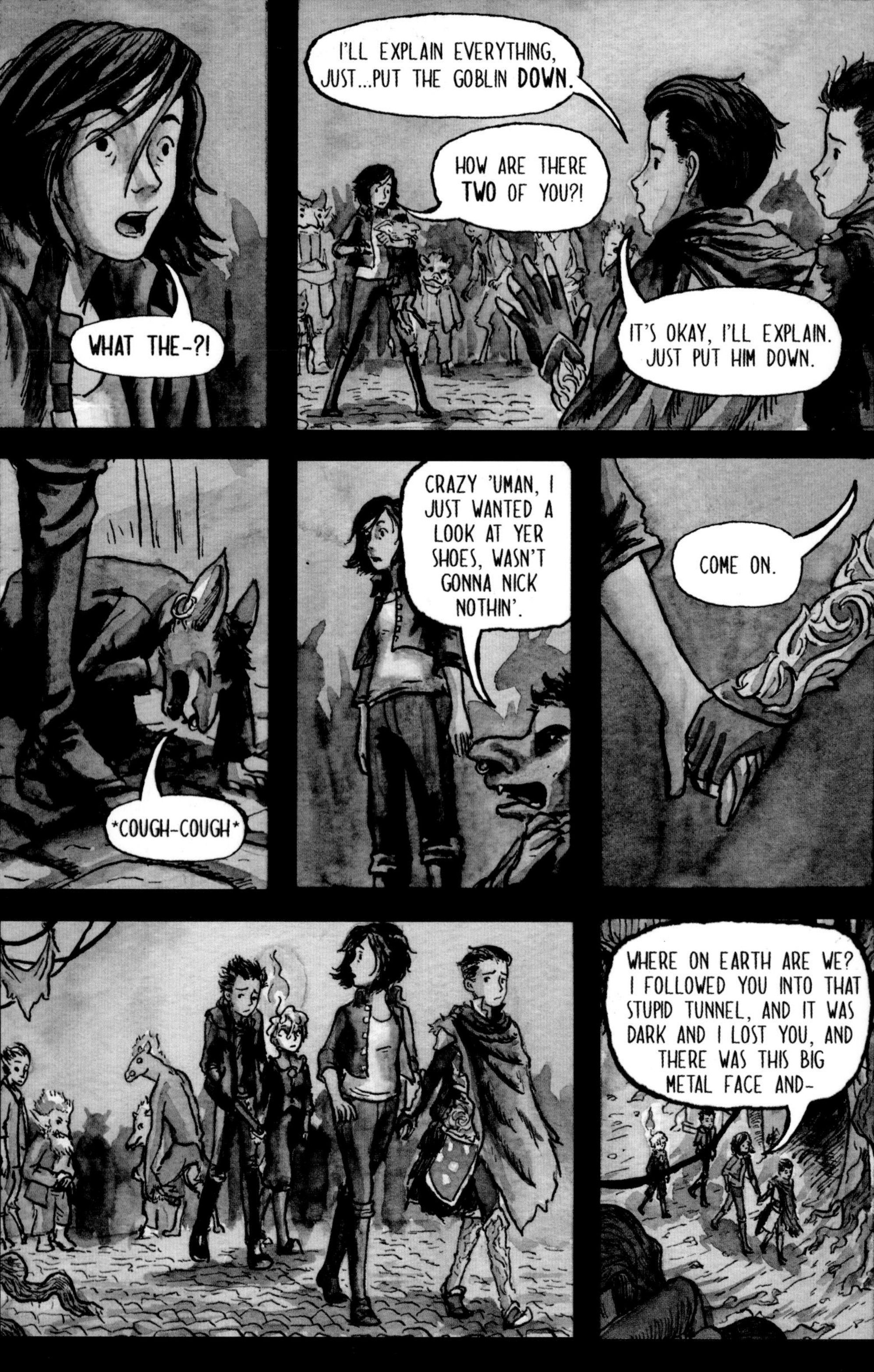
WHAT THE-?!
I'LL EXPLAIN EVERYTHING, JUST...PUT THE GOBLIN DOWN.
HOW ARE THERE TWO OF YOU?!
IT'S OKAY, I'LL EXPLAIN. JUST PUT HIM DOWN.
COUGH-COUGH
CRAZY 'UMAN, I JUST WANTED A LOOK AT YER SHOES, WASN'T GONNA NICK NOTHIN'.
COME ON.
WHERE ON EARTH ARE WE? I FOLLOWED YOU INTO THAT STUPID TUNNEL, AND IT WAS DARK AND I LOST YOU, AND THERE WAS THIS BIG METAL FACE AND-

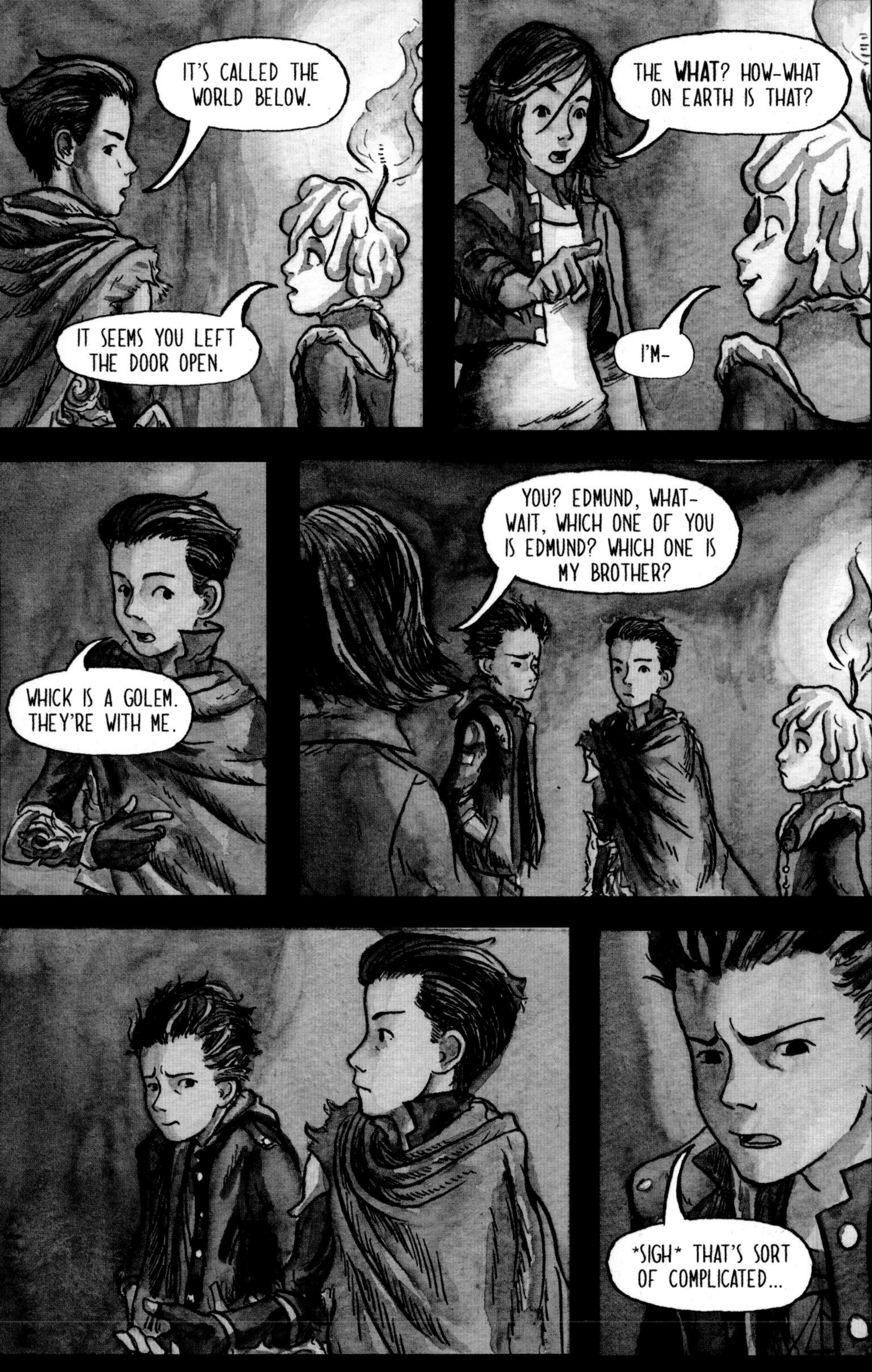
IT'S CALLED THE WORLD BELOW.
IT SEEMS YOU LEFT THE DOOR OPEN.
THE WHAT? HOW-WHAT ON EARTH IS THAT?
I'M-
WHICK IS A GOLEM. THEY'RE WITH ME.
YOU? EDMUND, WHAT- WAIT, WHICH ONE OF YOU IS EDMUND? WHICH ONE IS MY BROTHER?
SIGH THAT'S SORT OF COMPLICATED...

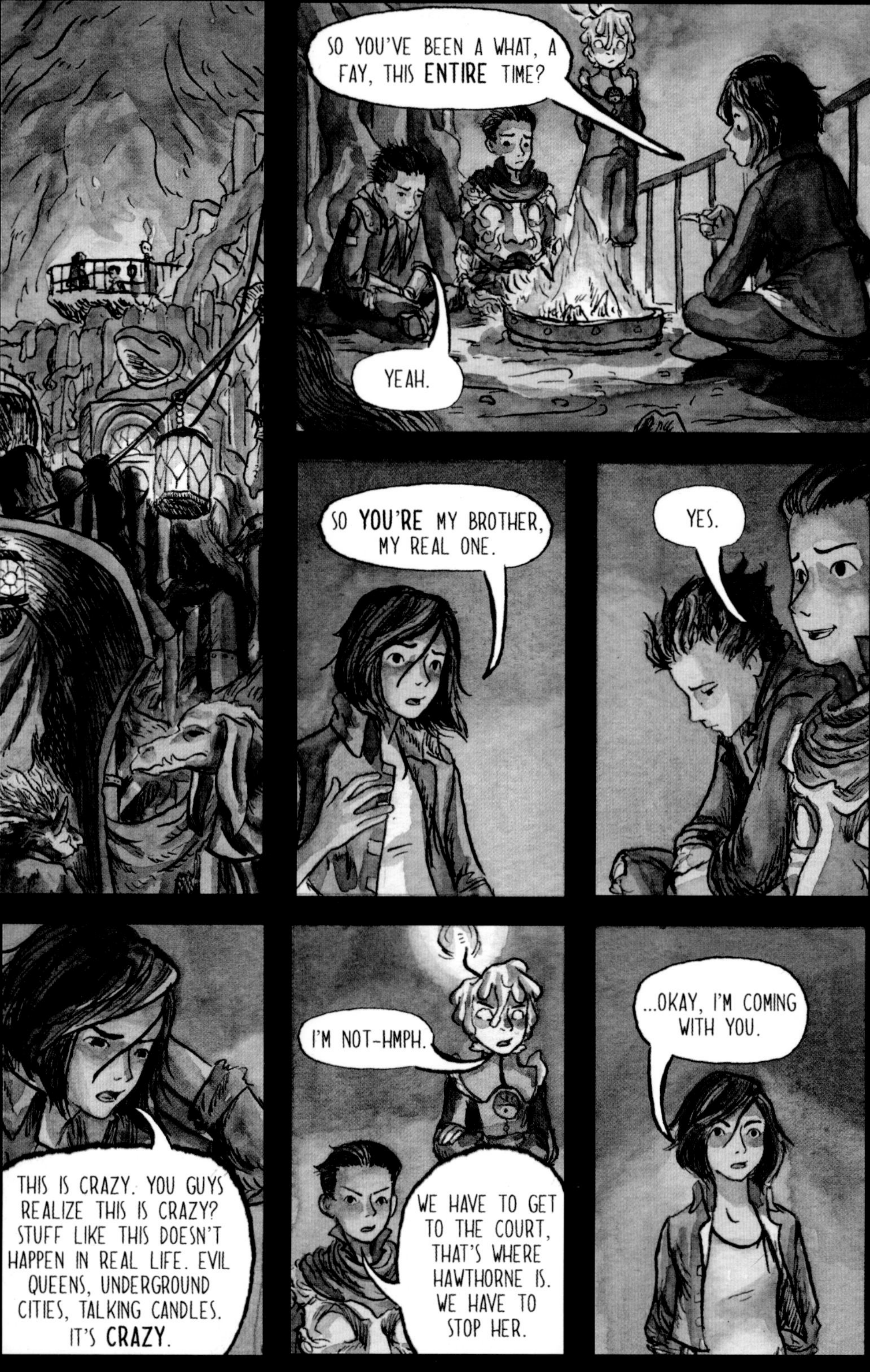
SO YOU'VE BEEN A WHAT, A FAY, THIS ENTIRE TIME?
YEAH.
SO YOU'RE MY BROTHER, MY REAL ONE.
YES.
THIS IS CRAZY. YOU GUYS REALIZE THIS IS CRAZY? STUFF LIKE THIS DOESN'T HAPPEN IN REAL LIFE. EVIL QUEENS, UNDERGROUND CITIES, TALKING CANDLES. IT'S CRAZY.
I'M NOT–HMPH.
WE HAVE TO GET TO THE COURT, THAT'S WHERE HAWTHORNE IS. WE HAVE TO STOP HER.
...OKAY, I'M COMING WITH YOU.

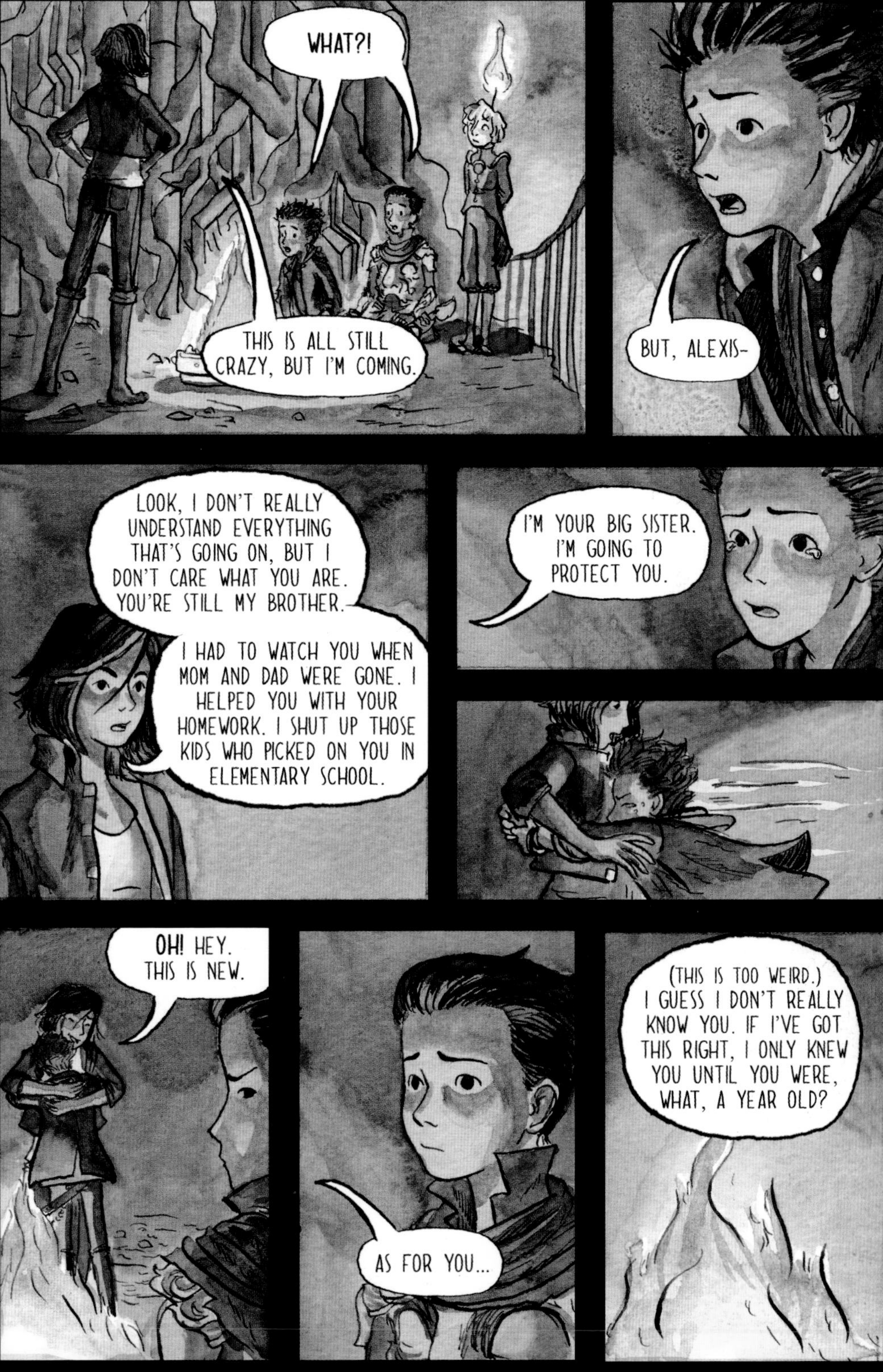

WHAT?!
THIS IS ALL STILL CRAZY, BUT I'M COMING.
BUT, ALEXIS-
LOOK, I DON'T REALLY UNDERSTAND EVERYTHING THAT'S GOING ON, BUT I DON'T CARE WHAT YOU ARE. YOU'RE STILL MY BROTHER.
I HAD TO WATCH YOU WHEN MOM AND DAD WERE GONE. I HELPED YOU WITH YOUR HOMEWORK. I SHUT UP THOSE KIDS WHO PICKED ON YOU IN ELEMENTARY SCHOOL.
I'M YOUR BIG SISTER. I'M GOING TO PROTECT YOU.
OH! HEY. THIS IS NEW.
AS FOR YOU...
(THIS IS TOO WEIRD.) I GUESS I DON'T REALLY KNOW YOU. IF I'VE GOT THIS RIGHT, I ONLY KNEW YOU UNTIL YOU WERE, WHAT, A YEAR OLD?

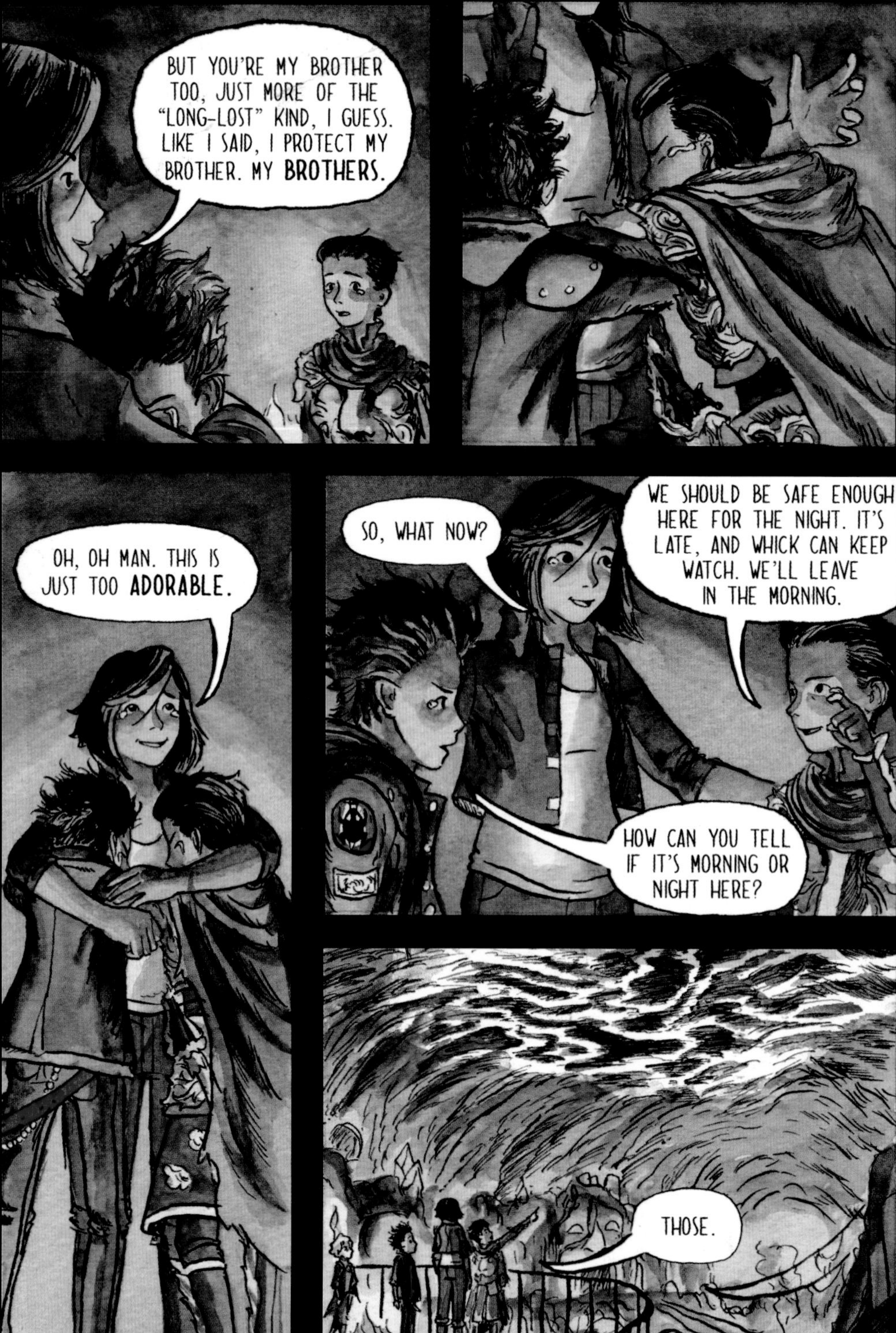
BUT YOU'RE MY BROTHER TOO, JUST MORE OF THE "LONG-LOST" KIND, I GUESS. LIKE I SAID, I PROTECT MY BROTHER. MY **BROTHERS**.
OH, OH MAN. THIS IS JUST TOO **ADORABLE**.
SO, WHAT NOW?
WE SHOULD BE SAFE ENOUGH HERE FOR THE NIGHT. IT'S LATE, AND WHICK CAN KEEP WATCH. WE'LL LEAVE IN THE MORNING.
HOW CAN YOU TELL IF IT'S MORNING OR NIGHT HERE?
THOSE.

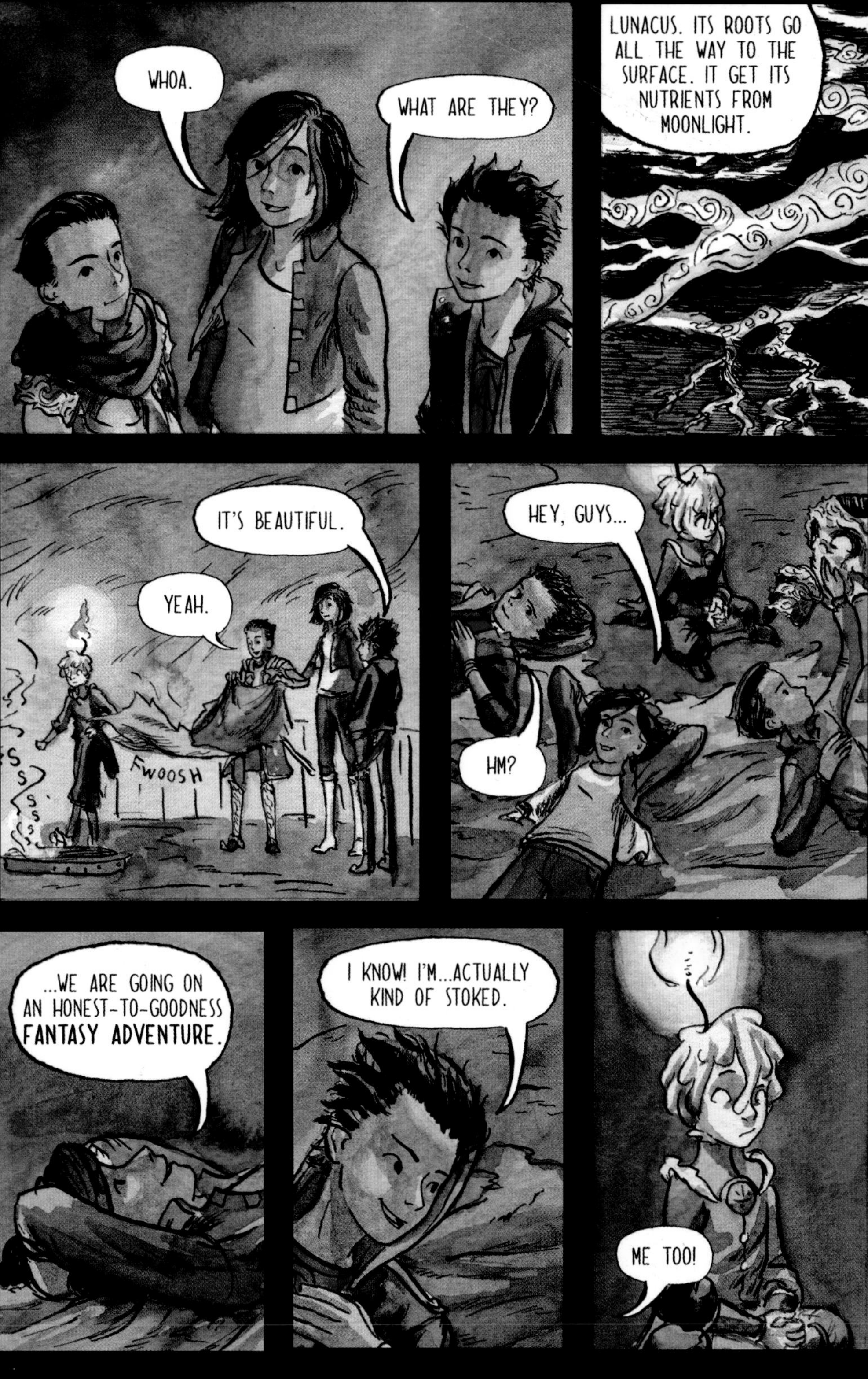
WHOA.
WHAT ARE THEY?
LUNACUS. ITS ROOTS GO ALL THE WAY TO THE SURFACE. IT GET ITS NUTRIENTS FROM MOONLIGHT.
IT'S BEAUTIFUL.
YEAH.
FWOOSH
SSSSS
HEY, GUYS...
HM?
...WE ARE GOING ON AN HONEST-TO-GOODNESS **FANTASY ADVENTURE**.
I KNOW! I'M...ACTUALLY KIND OF STOKED.
ME TOO!

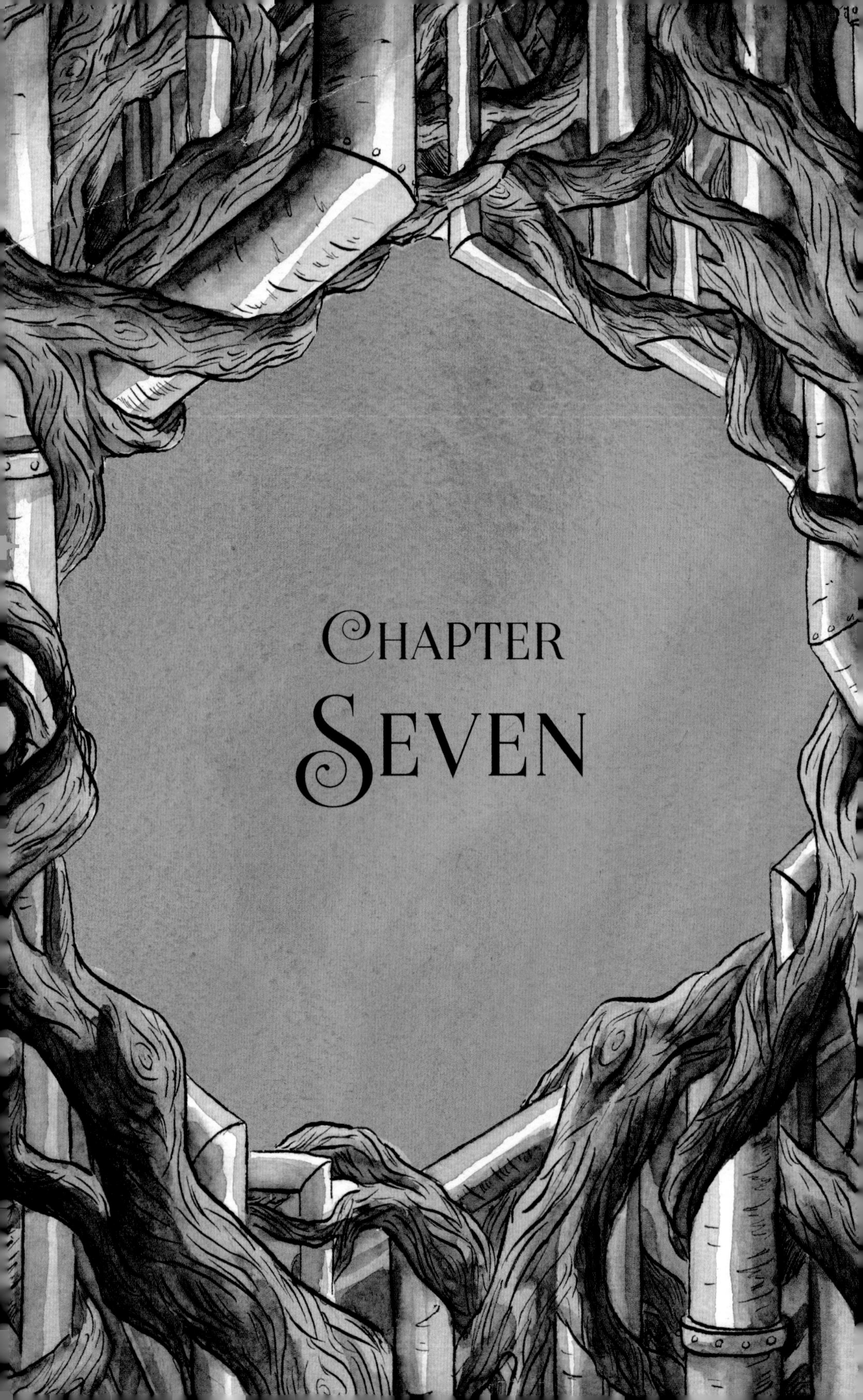

Chapter Seven

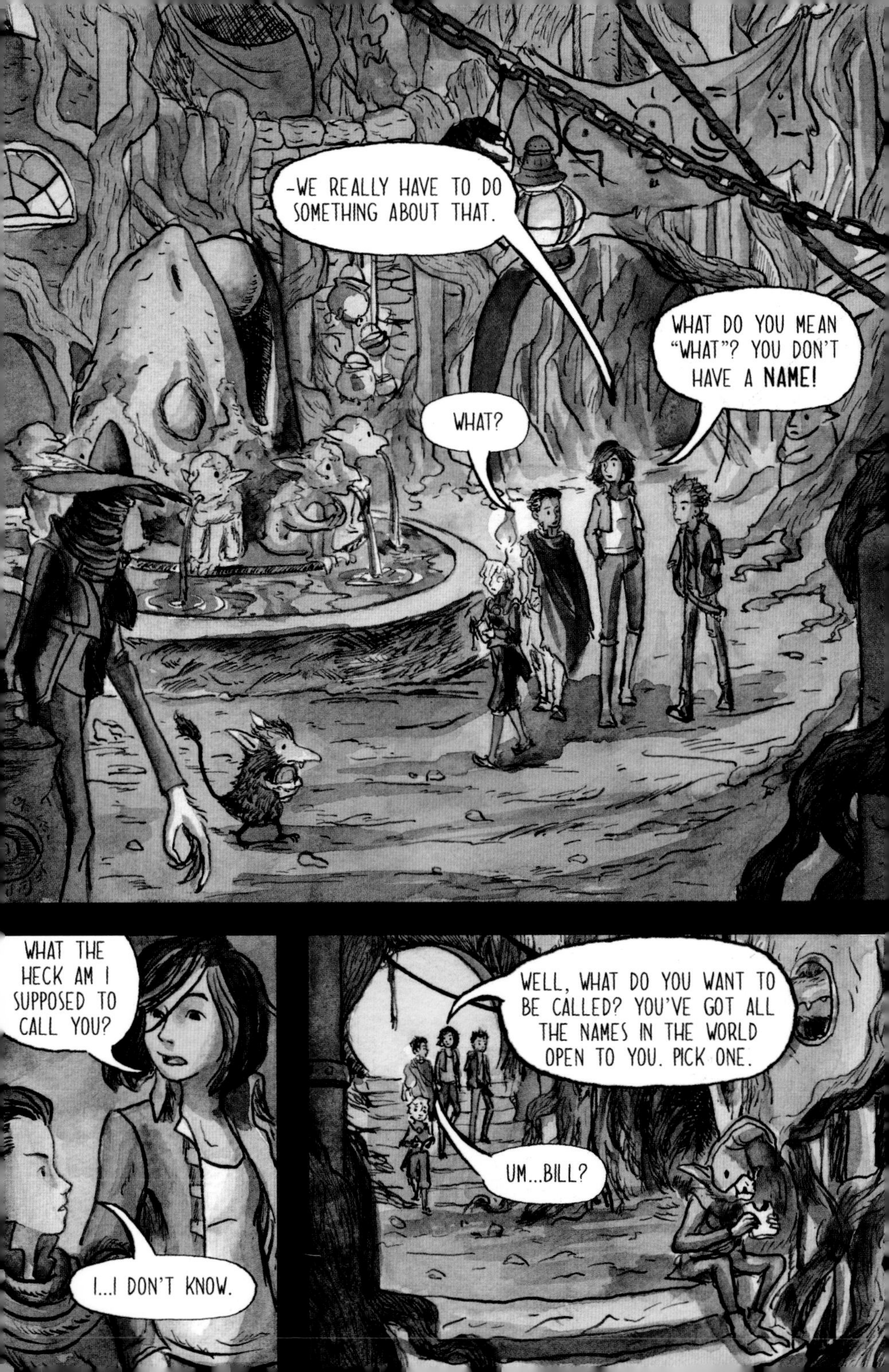
-WE REALLY HAVE TO DO SOMETHING ABOUT THAT.
WHAT?
WHAT DO YOU MEAN "WHAT"? YOU DON'T HAVE A **NAME!**
WHAT THE HECK AM I SUPPOSED TO CALL YOU?
I...I DON'T KNOW.
WELL, WHAT DO YOU WANT TO BE CALLED? YOU'VE GOT ALL THE NAMES IN THE WORLD OPEN TO YOU. PICK ONE.
UM...BILL?

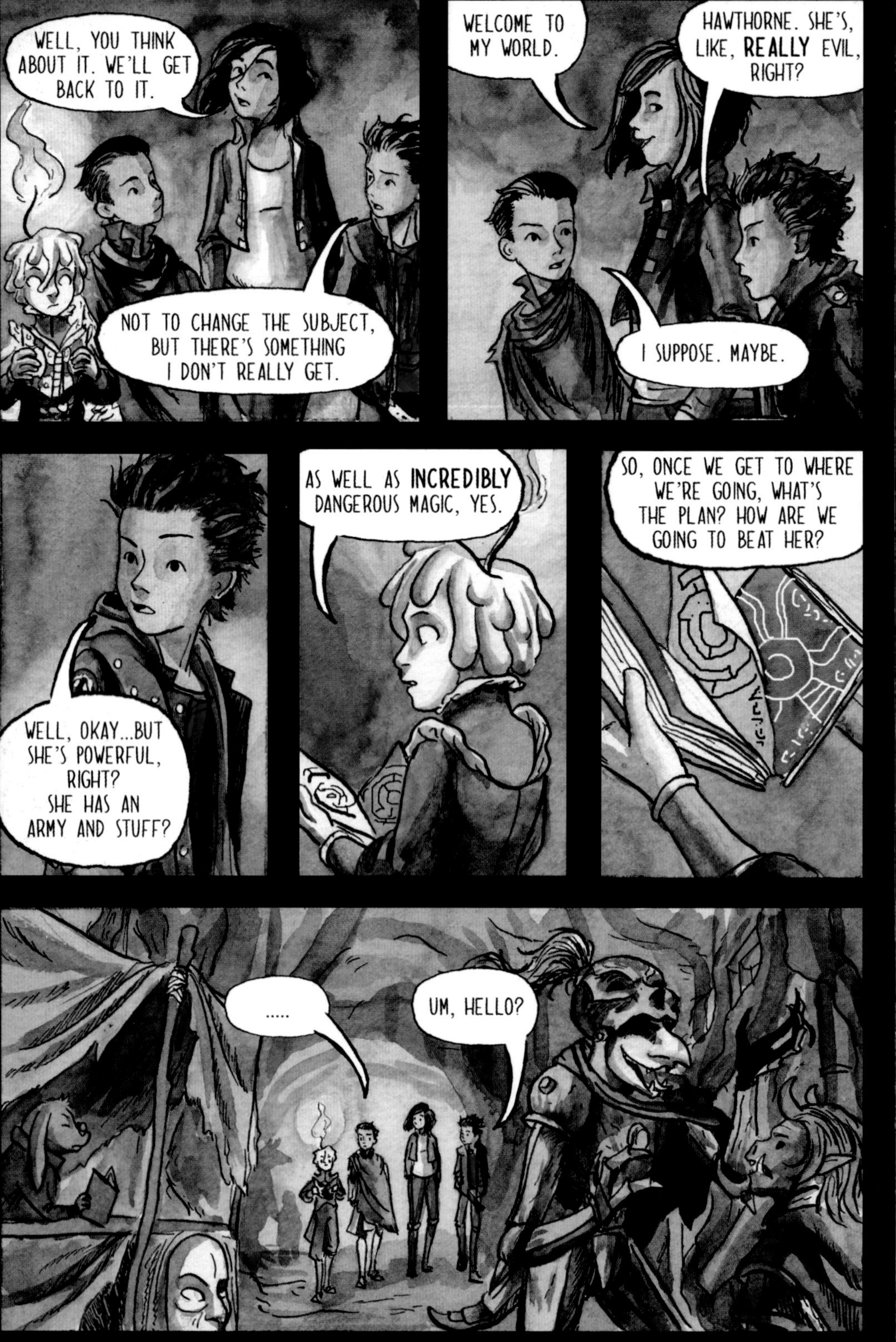
WELL, YOU THINK ABOUT IT. WE'LL GET BACK TO IT.
NOT TO CHANGE THE SUBJECT, BUT THERE'S SOMETHING I DON'T REALLY GET.
WELCOME TO MY WORLD.
HAWTHORNE. SHE'S, LIKE, **REALLY** EVIL, RIGHT?
I SUPPOSE. MAYBE.
WELL, OKAY...BUT SHE'S POWERFUL, RIGHT? SHE HAS AN ARMY AND STUFF?
AS WELL AS **INCREDIBLY** DANGEROUS MAGIC, YES.
SO, ONCE WE GET TO WHERE WE'RE GOING, WHAT'S THE PLAN? HOW ARE WE GOING TO BEAT HER?
.....
UM, HELLO?

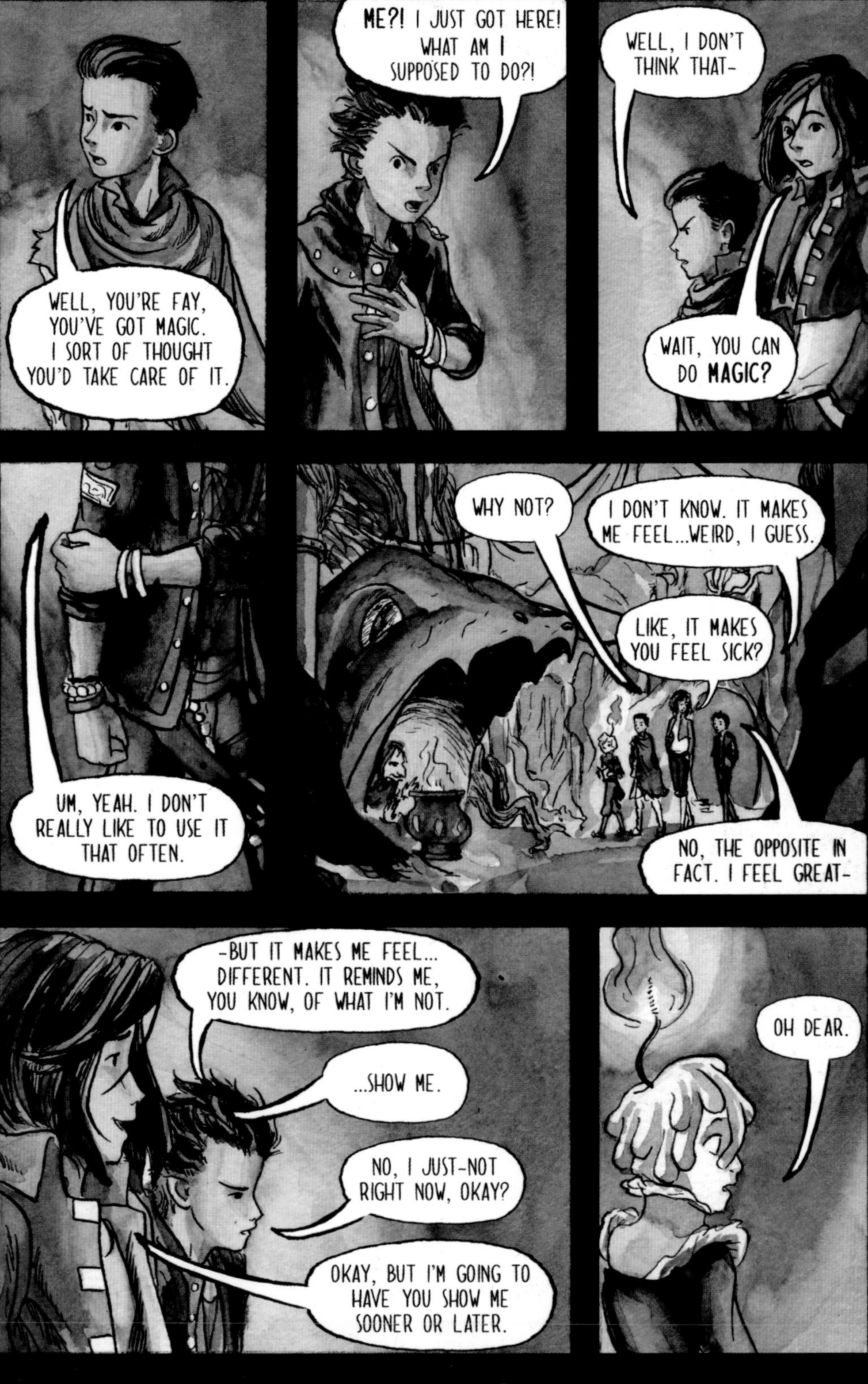
WELL, YOU'RE FAY, YOU'VE GOT MAGIC. I SORT OF THOUGHT YOU'D TAKE CARE OF IT.
ME?! I JUST GOT HERE! WHAT AM I SUPPOSED TO DO?!
WELL, I DON'T THINK THAT-
WAIT, YOU CAN DO MAGIC?
UM, YEAH. I DON'T REALLY LIKE TO USE IT THAT OFTEN.
WHY NOT?
I DON'T KNOW. IT MAKES ME FEEL...WEIRD, I GUESS.
LIKE, IT MAKES YOU FEEL SICK?
NO, THE OPPOSITE IN FACT. I FEEL GREAT-
-BUT IT MAKES ME FEEL... DIFFERENT. IT REMINDS ME, YOU KNOW, OF WHAT I'M NOT.
...SHOW ME.
NO, I JUST-NOT RIGHT NOW, OKAY?
OKAY, BUT I'M GOING TO HAVE YOU SHOW ME SOONER OR LATER.
OH DEAR.

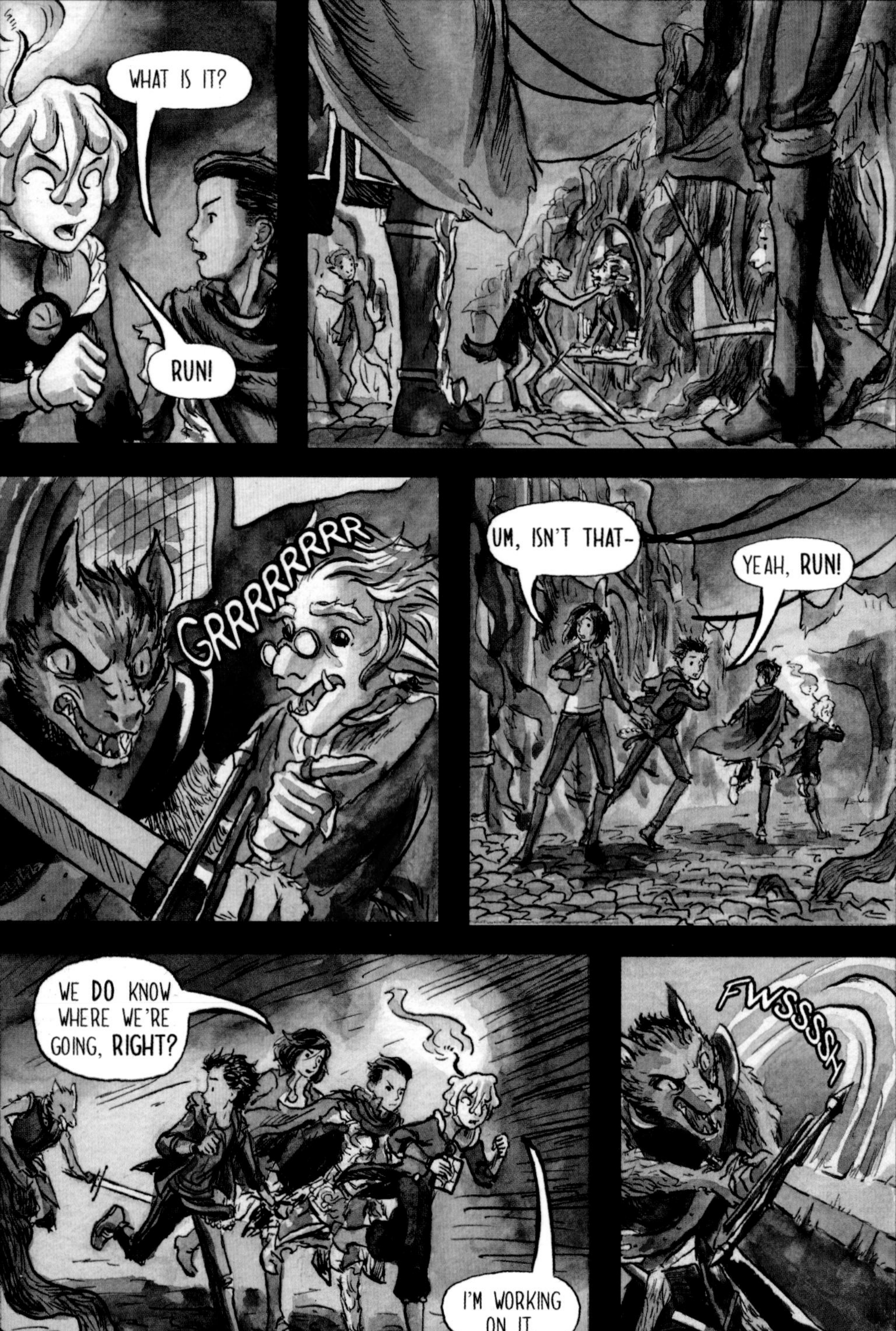
WHAT IS IT?
RUN!
GRRRRRRRR
UM, ISN'T THAT-
YEAH, RUN!
WE DO KNOW WHERE WE'RE GOING, RIGHT?
I'M WORKING ON IT.
FWSSSSH

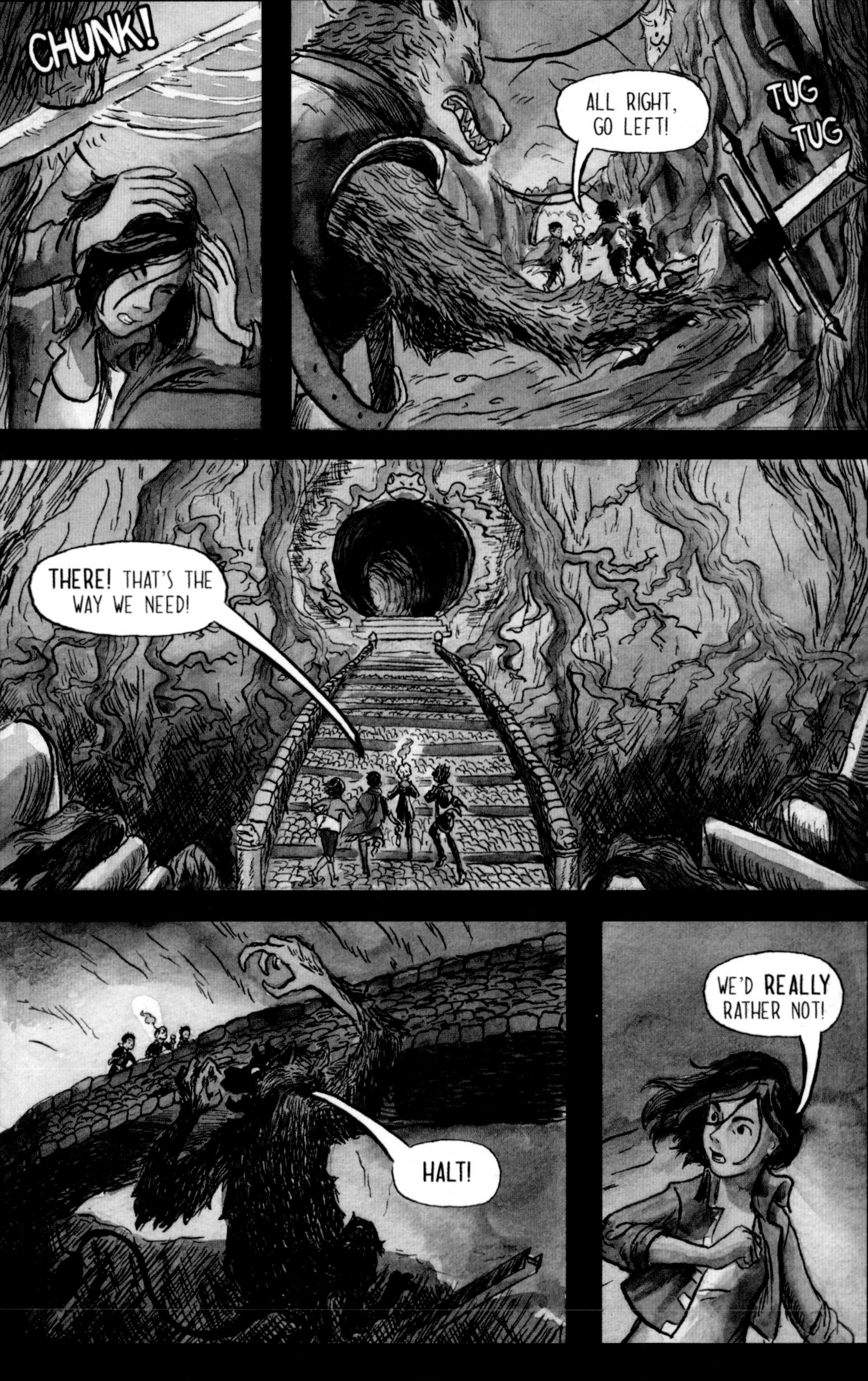
CHUNK!
ALL RIGHT, GO LEFT!
TUG TUG
THERE! THAT'S THE WAY WE NEED!
HALT!
WE'D REALLY RATHER NOT!

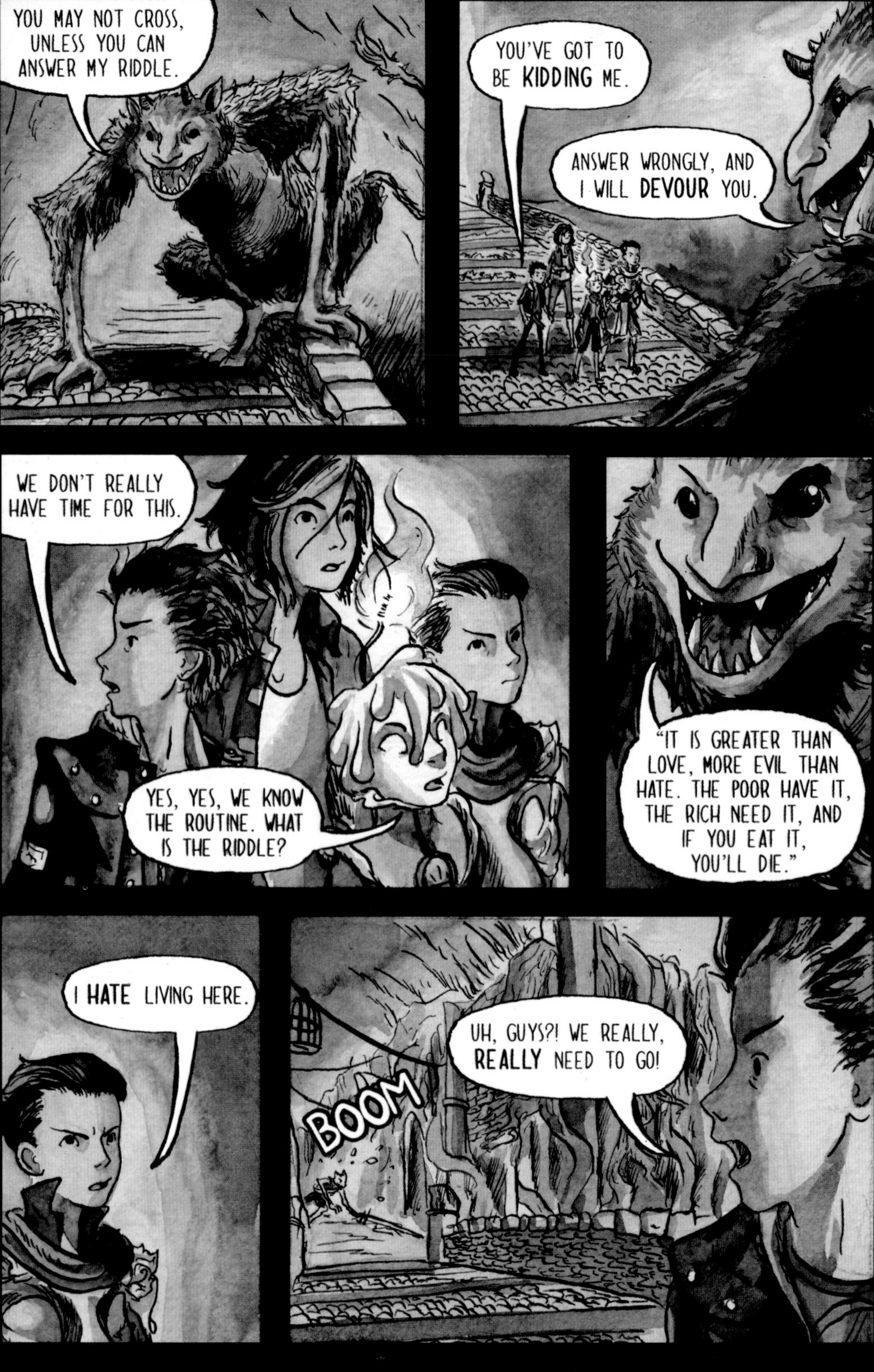
YOU MAY NOT CROSS, UNLESS YOU CAN ANSWER MY RIDDLE.
YOU'VE GOT TO BE KIDDING ME.
ANSWER WRONGLY, AND I WILL DEVOUR YOU.
WE DON'T REALLY HAVE TIME FOR THIS.
YES, YES, WE KNOW THE ROUTINE. WHAT IS THE RIDDLE?
"IT IS GREATER THAN LOVE, MORE EVIL THAN HATE. THE POOR HAVE IT, THE RICH NEED IT, AND IF YOU EAT IT, YOU'LL DIE."
I HATE LIVING HERE.
BOOM
UH, GUYS?! WE REALLY, REALLY NEED TO GO!

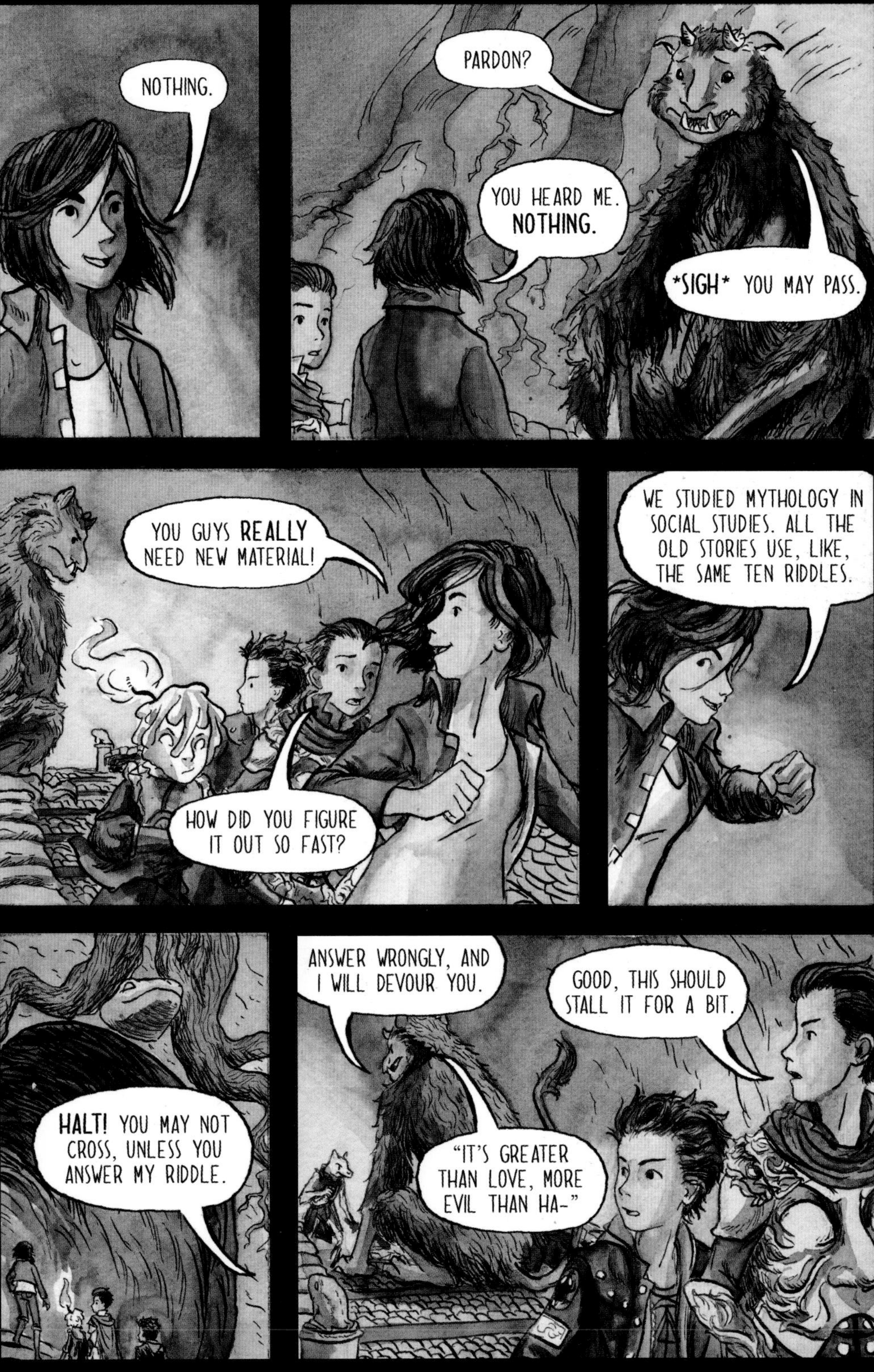
NOTHING.
PARDON?
YOU HEARD ME. NOTHING.
SIGH YOU MAY PASS.
YOU GUYS REALLY NEED NEW MATERIAL!
HOW DID YOU FIGURE IT OUT SO FAST?
WE STUDIED MYTHOLOGY IN SOCIAL STUDIES. ALL THE OLD STORIES USE, LIKE, THE SAME TEN RIDDLES.
HALT! YOU MAY NOT CROSS, UNLESS YOU ANSWER MY RIDDLE.
ANSWER WRONGLY, AND I WILL DEVOUR YOU.
GOOD, THIS SHOULD STALL IT FOR A BIT.
"IT'S GREATER THAN LOVE, MORE EVIL THAN HA-"

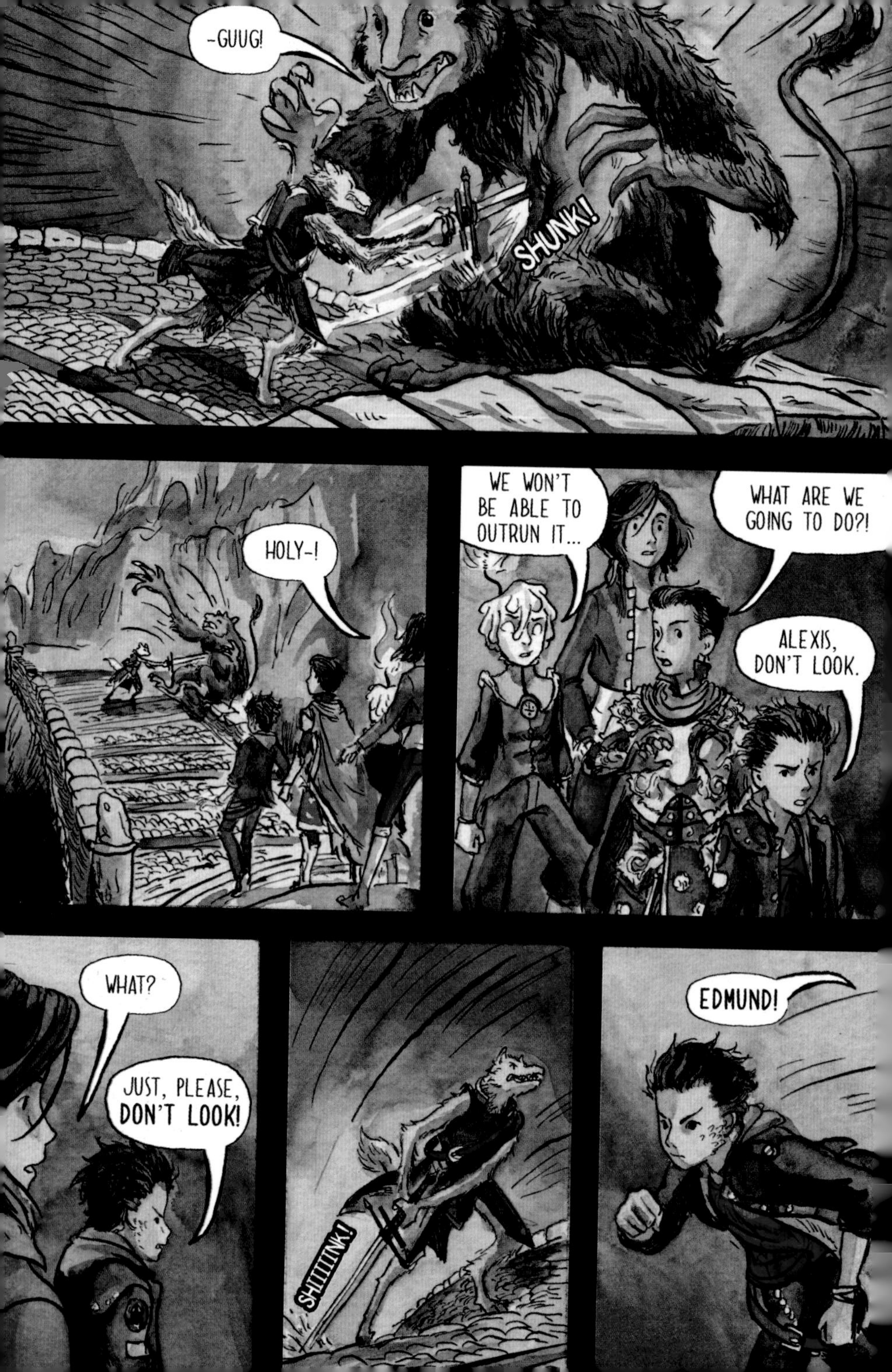
-GUUG!
SHUNK!
HOLY-!
WE WON'T BE ABLE TO OUTRUN IT...
WHAT ARE WE GOING TO DO?!
ALEXIS, DON'T LOOK.
WHAT?
JUST, PLEASE, DON'T LOOK!
SHIIIIINK!
EDMUND!

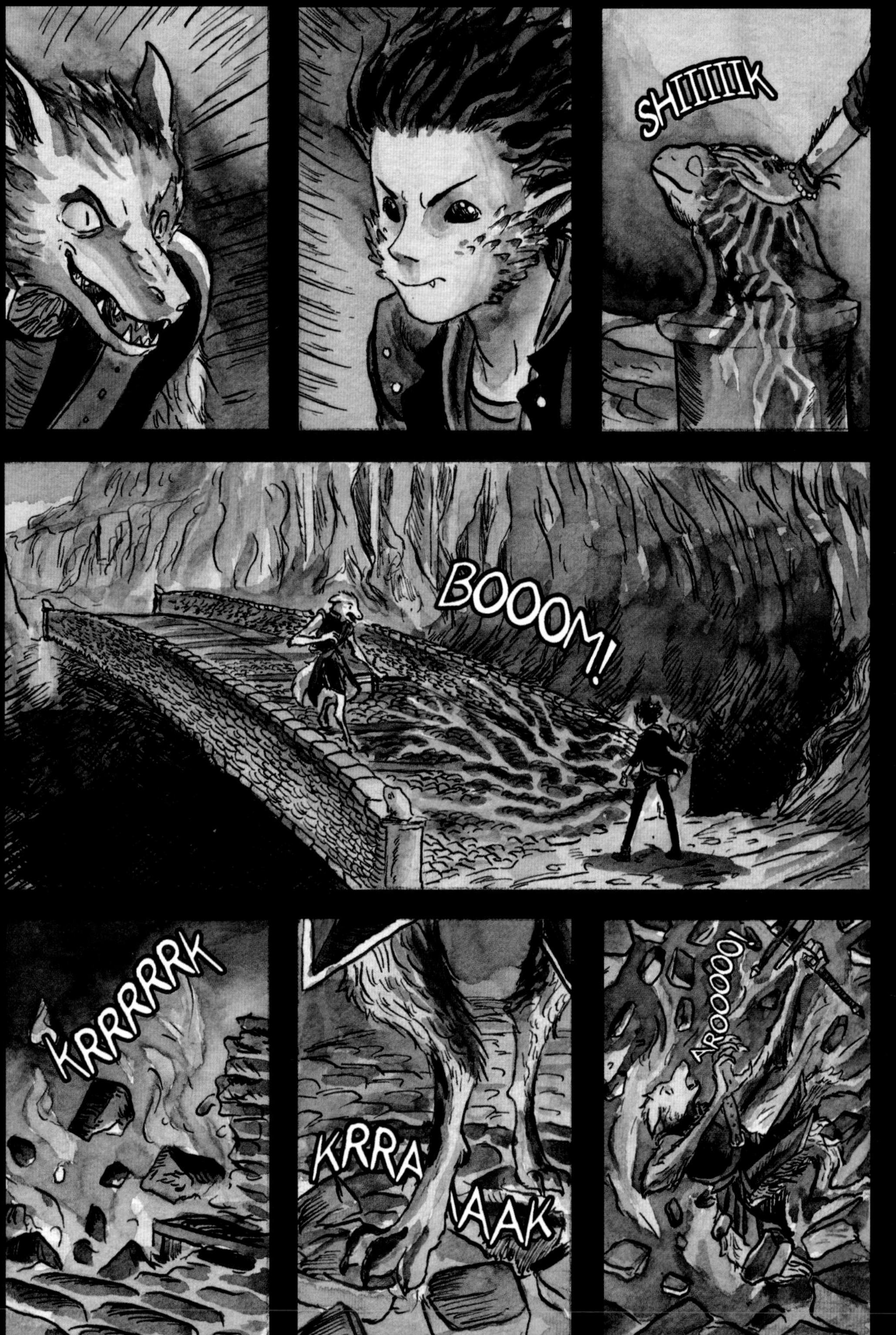
SHIIIIIK
BOOOM!
KRRRRRK
KRRAAAAK
AROOOOOO!

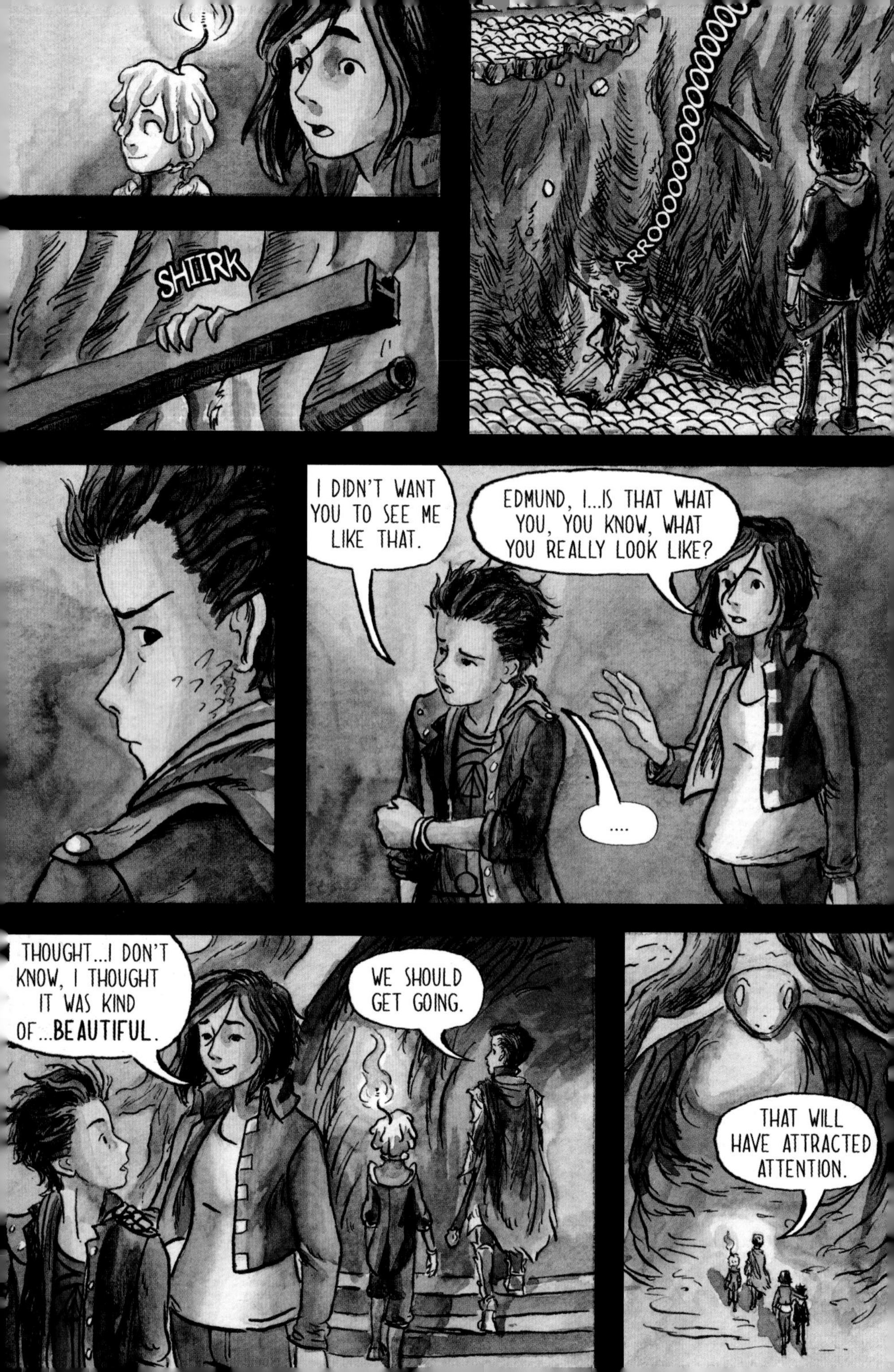
SHIIRK
ARROOOOOOOOOOOOOOO
I DIDN'T WANT YOU TO SEE ME LIKE THAT.
EDMUND, I...IS THAT WHAT YOU, YOU KNOW, WHAT YOU REALLY LOOK LIKE?
....
THOUGHT...I DON'T KNOW, I THOUGHT IT WAS KIND OF...**BEAUTIFUL**.
WE SHOULD GET GOING.
THAT WILL HAVE ATTRACTED ATTENTION.

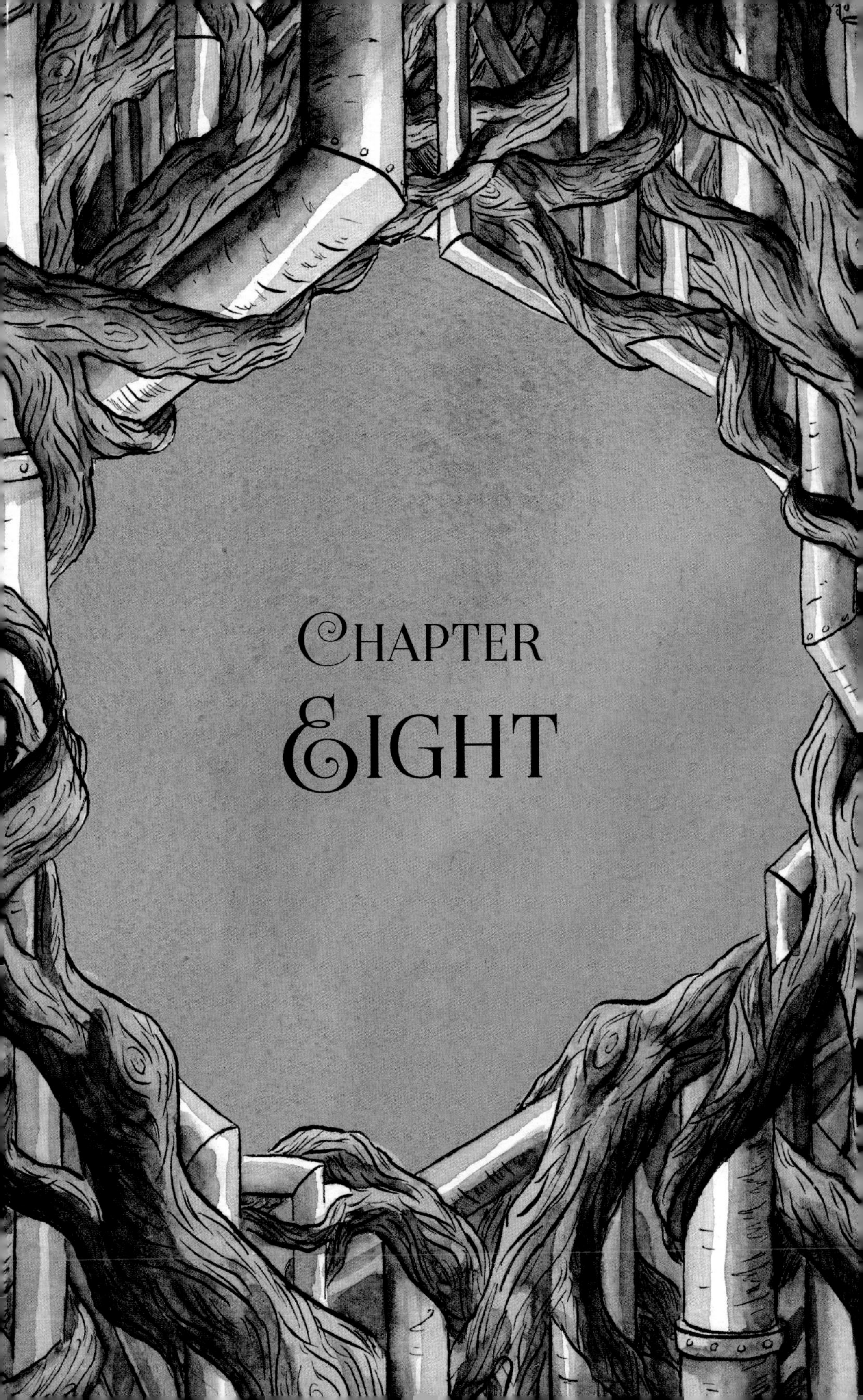

Chapter Eight

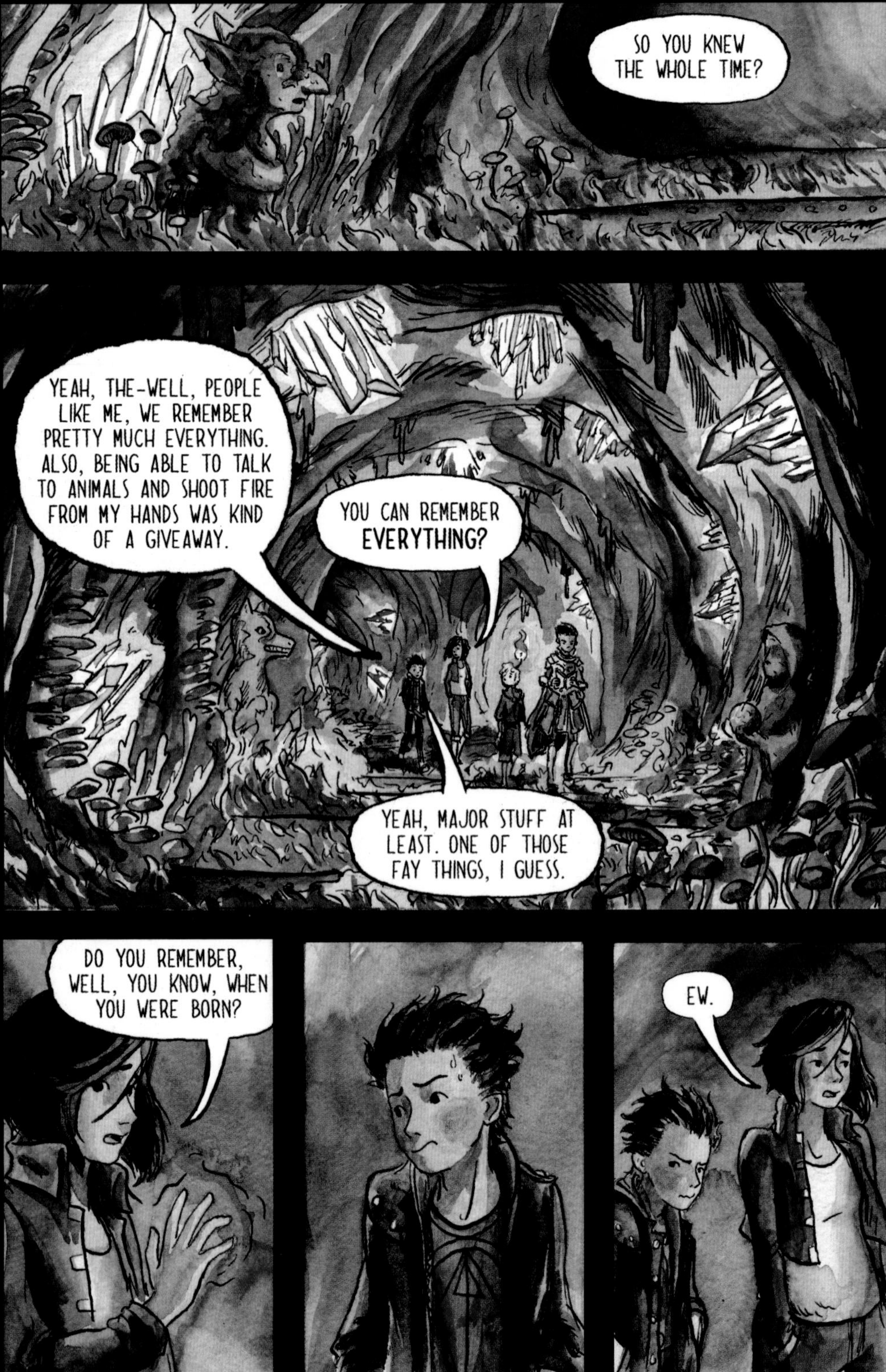
SO YOU KNEW THE WHOLE TIME?
YEAH, THE-WELL, PEOPLE LIKE ME, WE REMEMBER PRETTY MUCH EVERYTHING. ALSO, BEING ABLE TO TALK TO ANIMALS AND SHOOT FIRE FROM MY HANDS WAS KIND OF A GIVEAWAY.
YOU CAN REMEMBER **EVERYTHING?**
YEAH, MAJOR STUFF AT LEAST. ONE OF THOSE FAY THINGS, I GUESS.
DO YOU REMEMBER, WELL, YOU KNOW, WHEN YOU WERE BORN?
EW.

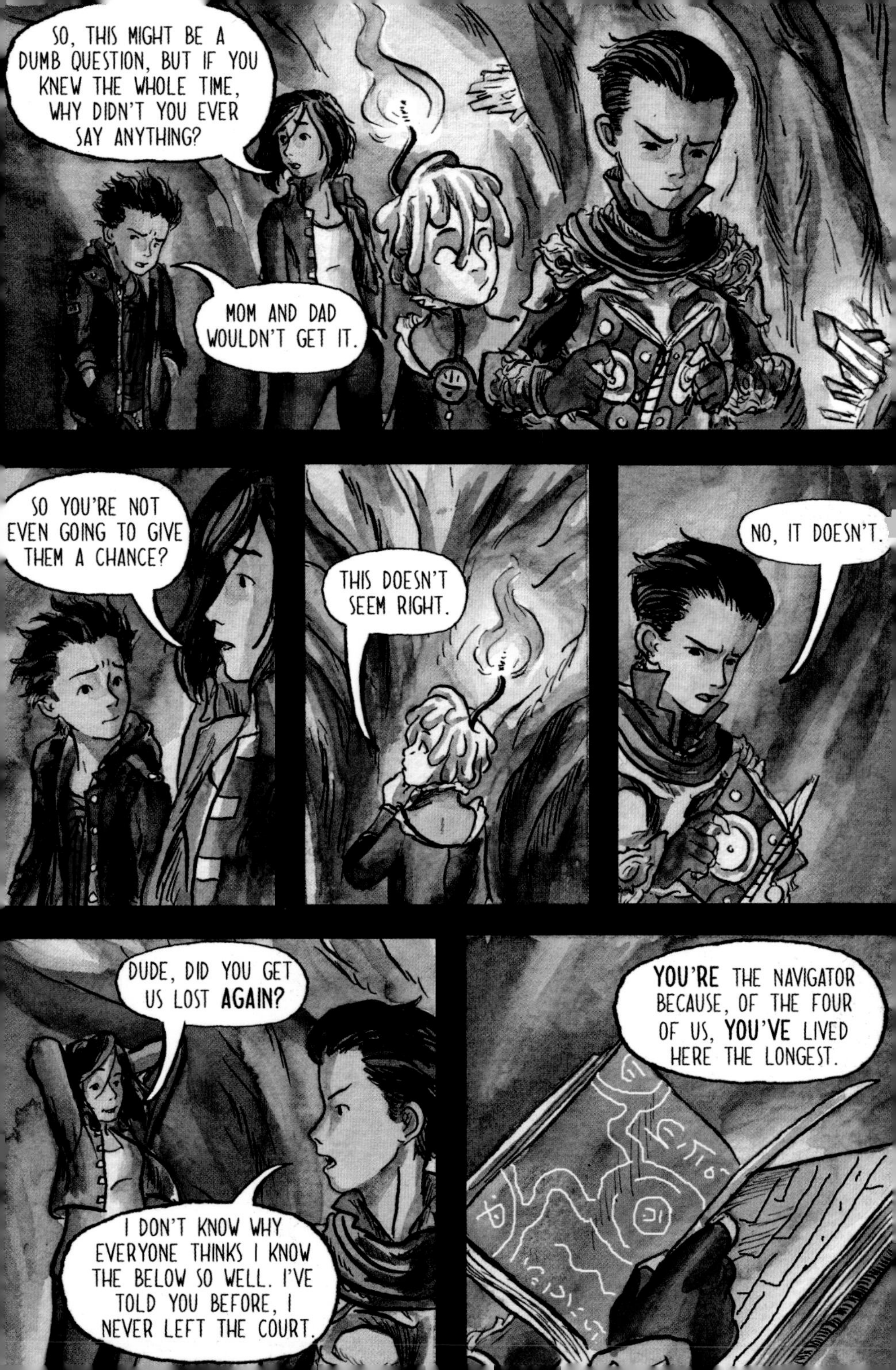
SO, THIS MIGHT BE A DUMB QUESTION, BUT IF YOU KNEW THE WHOLE TIME, WHY DIDN'T YOU EVER SAY ANYTHING?
MOM AND DAD WOULDN'T GET IT.
SO YOU'RE NOT EVEN GOING TO GIVE THEM A CHANCE?
THIS DOESN'T SEEM RIGHT.
NO, IT DOESN'T.
DUDE, DID YOU GET US LOST **AGAIN?**
I DON'T KNOW WHY EVERYONE THINKS I KNOW THE BELOW SO WELL. I'VE TOLD YOU BEFORE, I NEVER LEFT THE COURT.
YOU'RE THE NAVIGATOR BECAUSE, OF THE FOUR OF US, **YOU'VE** LIVED HERE THE LONGEST.

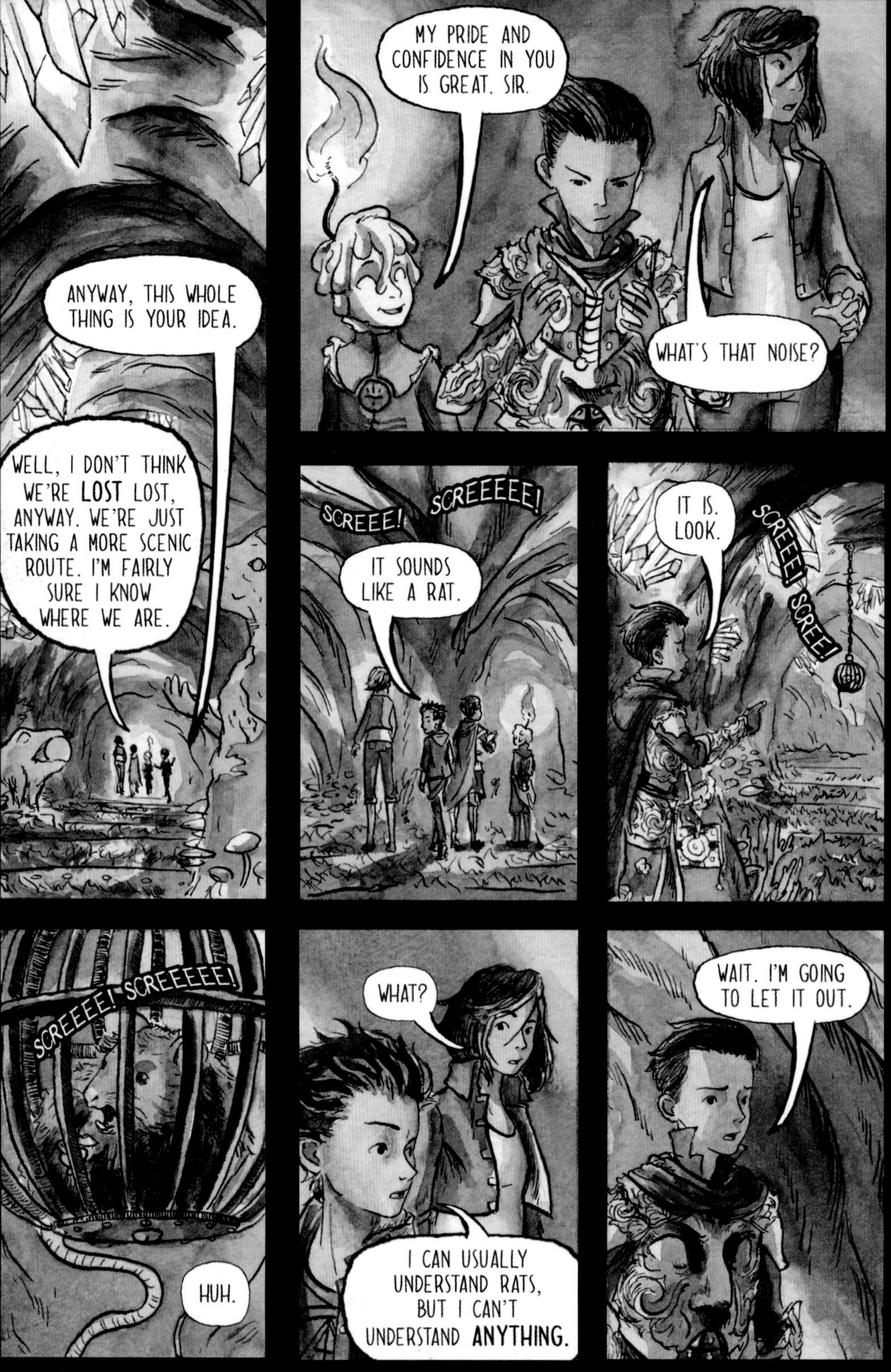
ANYWAY, THIS WHOLE THING IS YOUR IDEA.
WELL, I DON'T THINK WE'RE **LOST** LOST, ANYWAY. WE'RE JUST TAKING A MORE SCENIC ROUTE. I'M FAIRLY SURE I KNOW WHERE WE ARE.
MY PRIDE AND CONFIDENCE IN YOU IS GREAT, SIR.
WHAT'S THAT NOISE?
SCREEE!
SCREEEEE!
IT SOUNDS LIKE A RAT.
IT IS. LOOK.
SCREEE!
SCREE!
SCREEEE!
SCREEEEEE!
HUH.
WHAT?
I CAN USUALLY UNDERSTAND RATS, BUT I CAN'T UNDERSTAND **ANYTHING**.
WAIT. I'M GOING TO LET IT OUT.

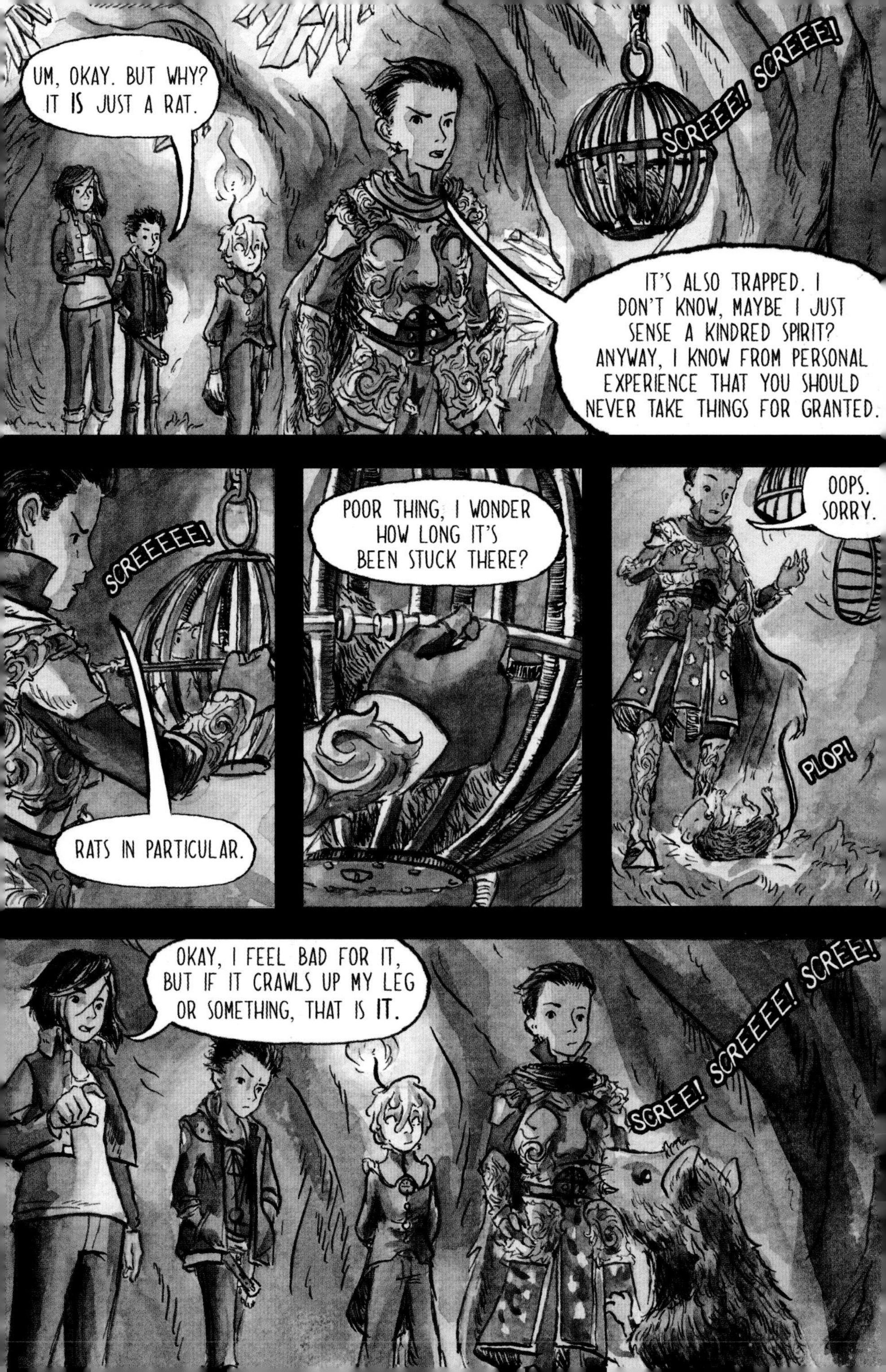
UM, OKAY. BUT WHY? IT IS JUST A RAT.
SCREEE! SCREEE!
IT'S ALSO TRAPPED. I DON'T KNOW, MAYBE I JUST SENSE A KINDRED SPIRIT? ANYWAY, I KNOW FROM PERSONAL EXPERIENCE THAT YOU SHOULD NEVER TAKE THINGS FOR GRANTED.
SCREEEEE!
RATS IN PARTICULAR.
POOR THING, I WONDER HOW LONG IT'S BEEN STUCK THERE?
OOPS. SORRY.
PLOP!
OKAY, I FEEL BAD FOR IT, BUT IF IT CRAWLS UP MY LEG OR SOMETHING, THAT IS IT.
SCREE! SCREEEE! SCREE!

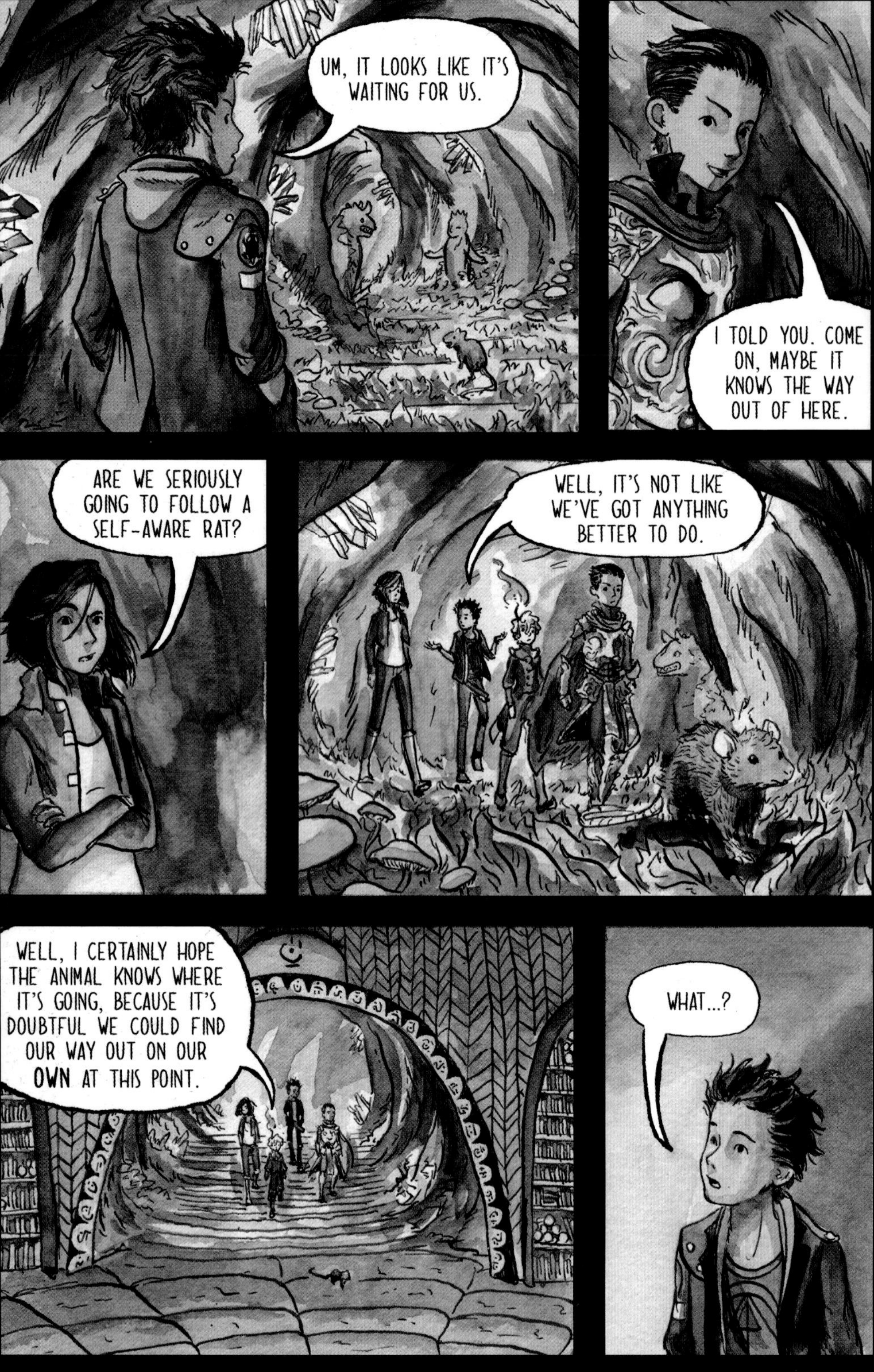
UM, IT LOOKS LIKE IT'S WAITING FOR US.
I TOLD YOU. COME ON, MAYBE IT KNOWS THE WAY OUT OF HERE.
ARE WE SERIOUSLY GOING TO FOLLOW A SELF-AWARE RAT?
WELL, IT'S NOT LIKE WE'VE GOT ANYTHING BETTER TO DO.
WELL, I CERTAINLY HOPE THE ANIMAL KNOWS WHERE IT'S GOING, BECAUSE IT'S DOUBTFUL WE COULD FIND OUR WAY OUT ON OUR **OWN** AT THIS POINT.
WHAT...?

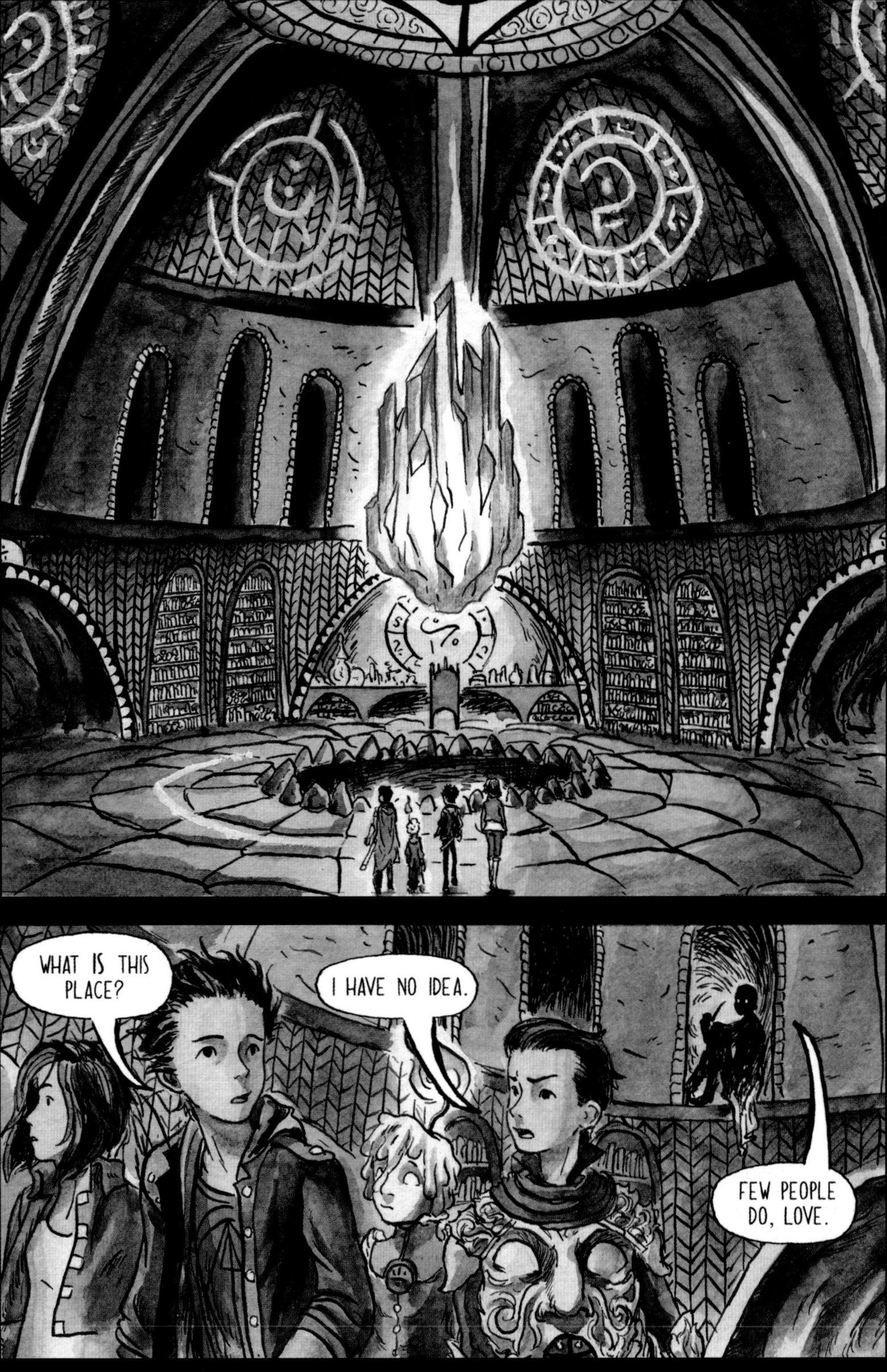
WHAT IS THIS PLACE?
I HAVE NO IDEA.
FEW PEOPLE DO, LOVE.

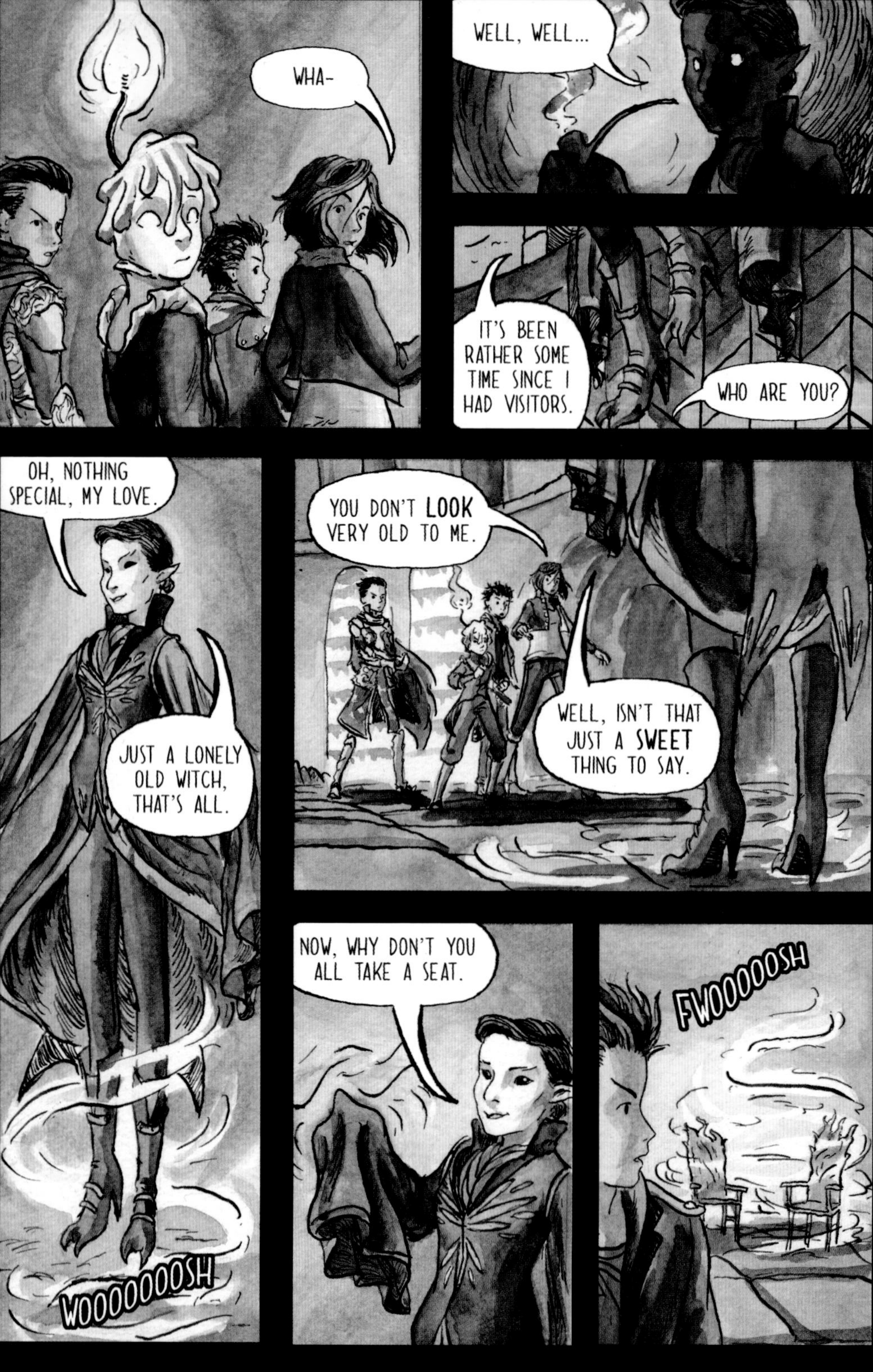
WHA-
WELL, WELL...
IT'S BEEN RATHER SOME TIME SINCE I HAD VISITORS.
WHO ARE YOU?
OH, NOTHING SPECIAL, MY LOVE.
JUST A LONELY OLD WITCH, THAT'S ALL.
YOU DON'T **LOOK** VERY OLD TO ME.
WELL, ISN'T THAT JUST A **SWEET** THING TO SAY.
WOOOOOOOOSH
NOW, WHY DON'T YOU ALL TAKE A SEAT.
FWOOOOOSH

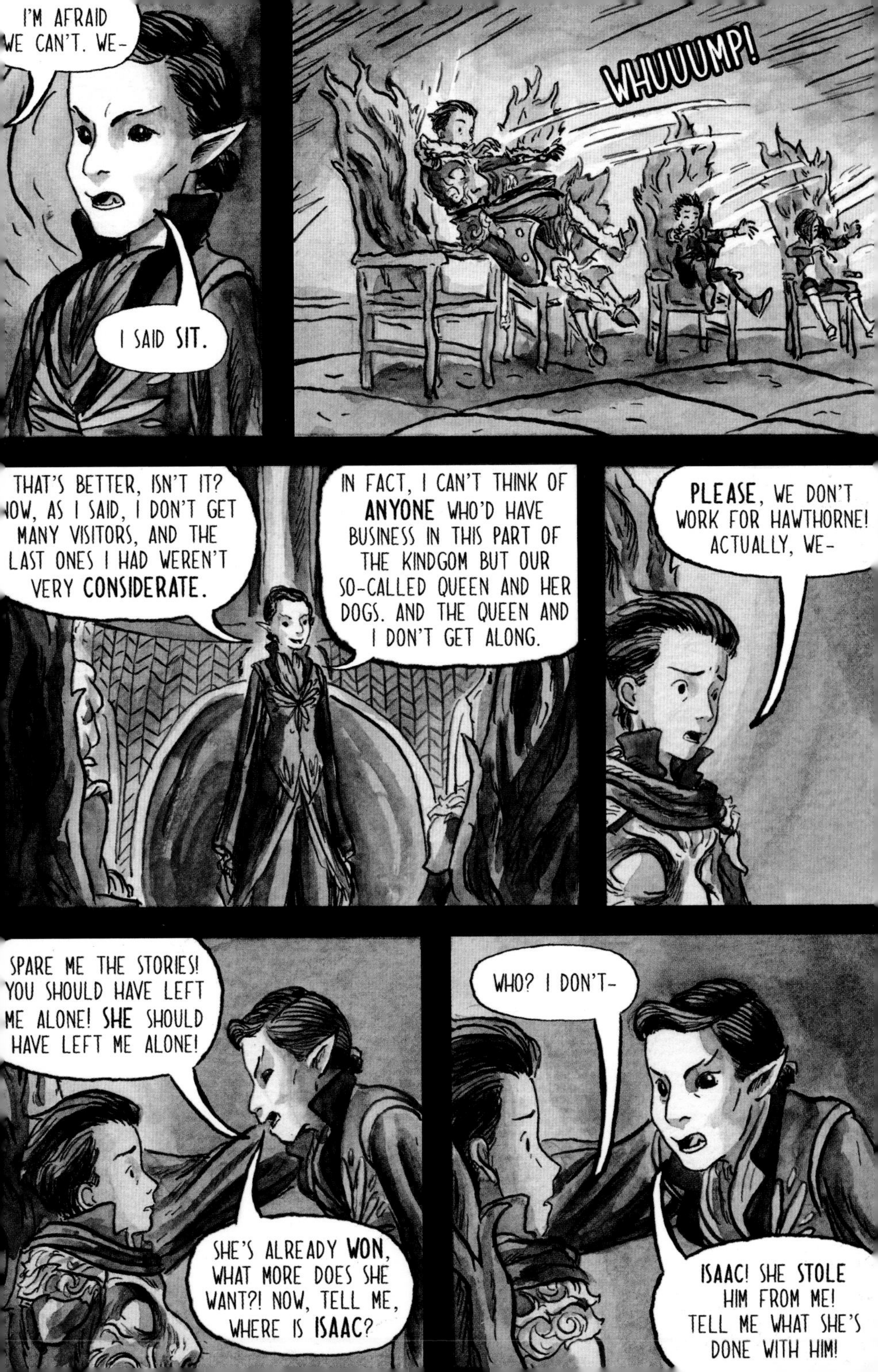
I'M AFRAID WE CAN'T. WE-
I SAID SIT.
WHUUUMP!
THAT'S BETTER, ISN'T IT? NOW, AS I SAID, I DON'T GET MANY VISITORS, AND THE LAST ONES I HAD WEREN'T VERY CONSIDERATE.
IN FACT, I CAN'T THINK OF ANYONE WHO'D HAVE BUSINESS IN THIS PART OF THE KINDGOM BUT OUR SO-CALLED QUEEN AND HER DOGS. AND THE QUEEN AND I DON'T GET ALONG.
PLEASE, WE DON'T WORK FOR HAWTHORNE! ACTUALLY, WE-
SPARE ME THE STORIES! YOU SHOULD HAVE LEFT ME ALONE! SHE SHOULD HAVE LEFT ME ALONE!
SHE'S ALREADY WON, WHAT MORE DOES SHE WANT?! NOW, TELL ME, WHERE IS ISAAC?
WHO? I DON'T-
ISAAC! SHE STOLE HIM FROM ME! TELL ME WHAT SHE'S DONE WITH HIM!

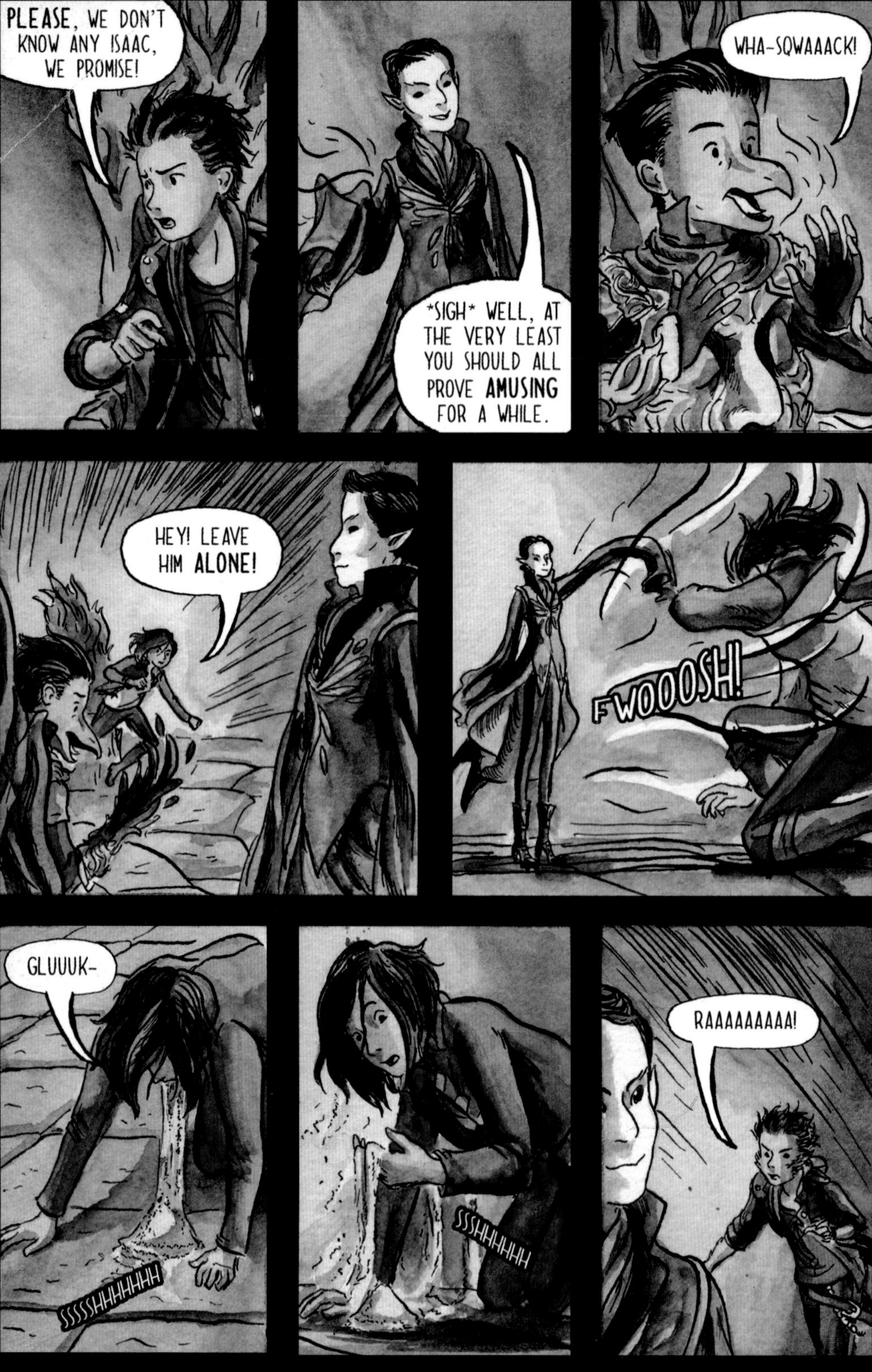
PLEASE, WE DON'T KNOW ANY ISAAC, WE PROMISE!
SIGH WELL, AT THE VERY LEAST YOU SHOULD ALL PROVE AMUSING FOR A WHILE.
WHA-SQWAAACK!
HEY! LEAVE HIM ALONE!
FWOOOSH!
GLUUUK-
SSSSSHHHHHHH
SSSHHHHHH
RAAAAAAAAA!

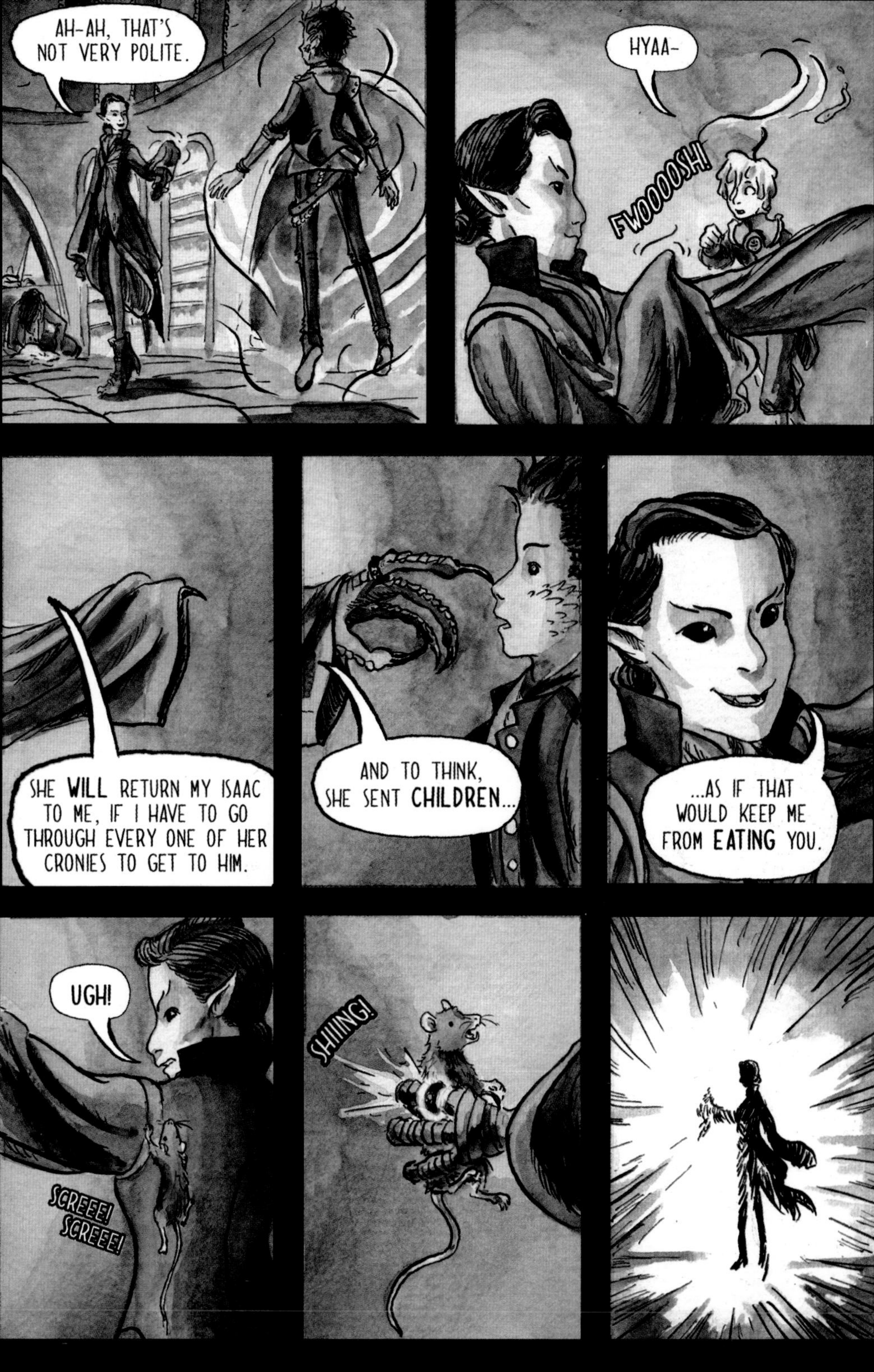
AH-AH, THAT'S NOT VERY POLITE.
HYAA-
FWOOOOSH!
SHE WILL RETURN MY ISAAC TO ME, IF I HAVE TO GO THROUGH EVERY ONE OF HER CRONIES TO GET TO HIM.
AND TO THINK, SHE SENT CHILDREN...
...AS IF THAT WOULD KEEP ME FROM EATING YOU.
UGH!
SCREEE! SCREEE!
SHIIING!

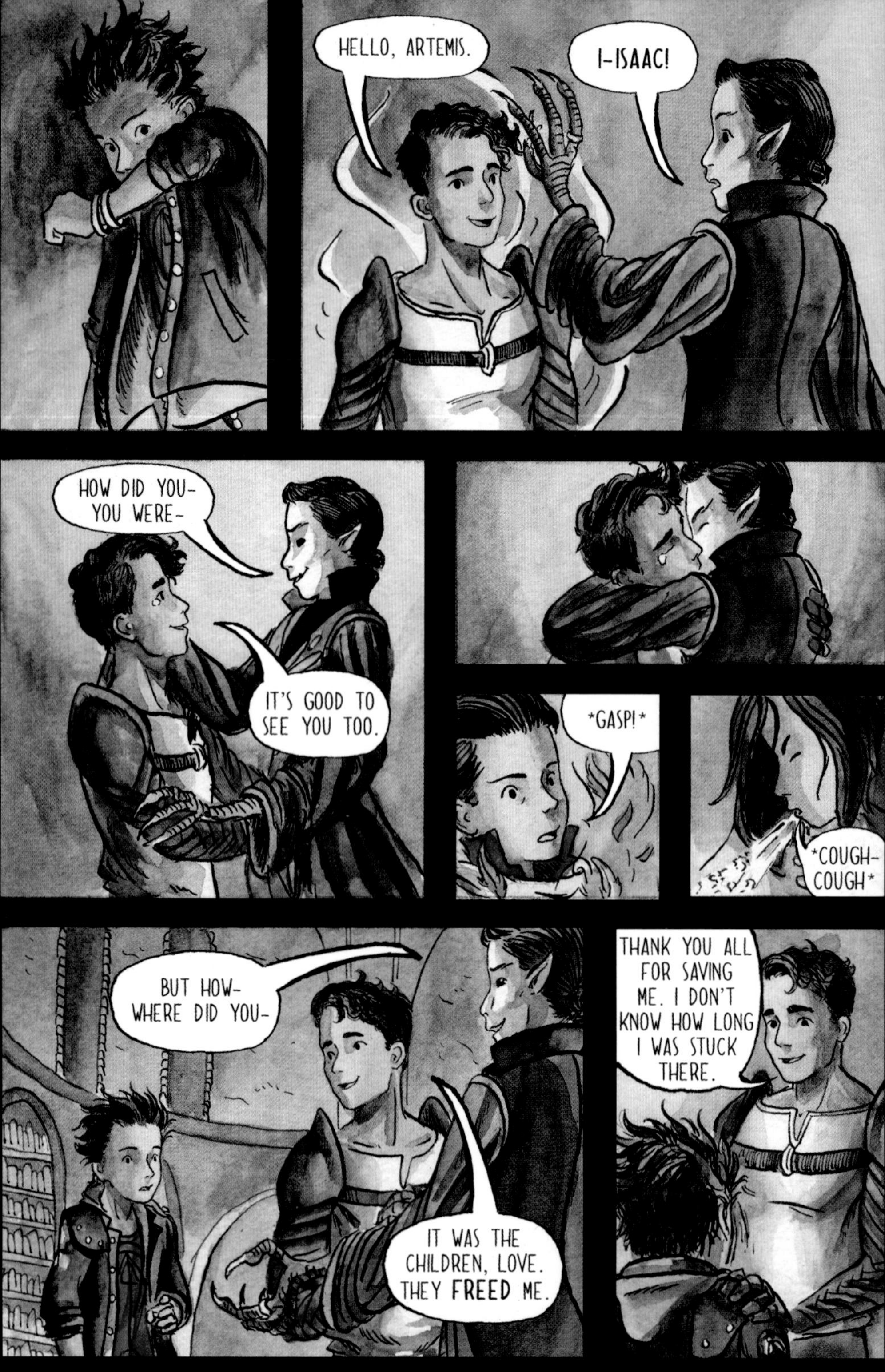

HELLO, ARTEMIS.
I-ISAAC!
HOW DID YOU- YOU WERE-
IT'S GOOD TO SEE YOU TOO.
GASP!
COUGH-COUGH
BUT HOW- WHERE DID YOU-
IT WAS THE CHILDREN, LOVE. THEY **FREED** ME.
THANK YOU ALL FOR SAVING ME. I DON'T KNOW HOW LONG I WAS STUCK THERE.

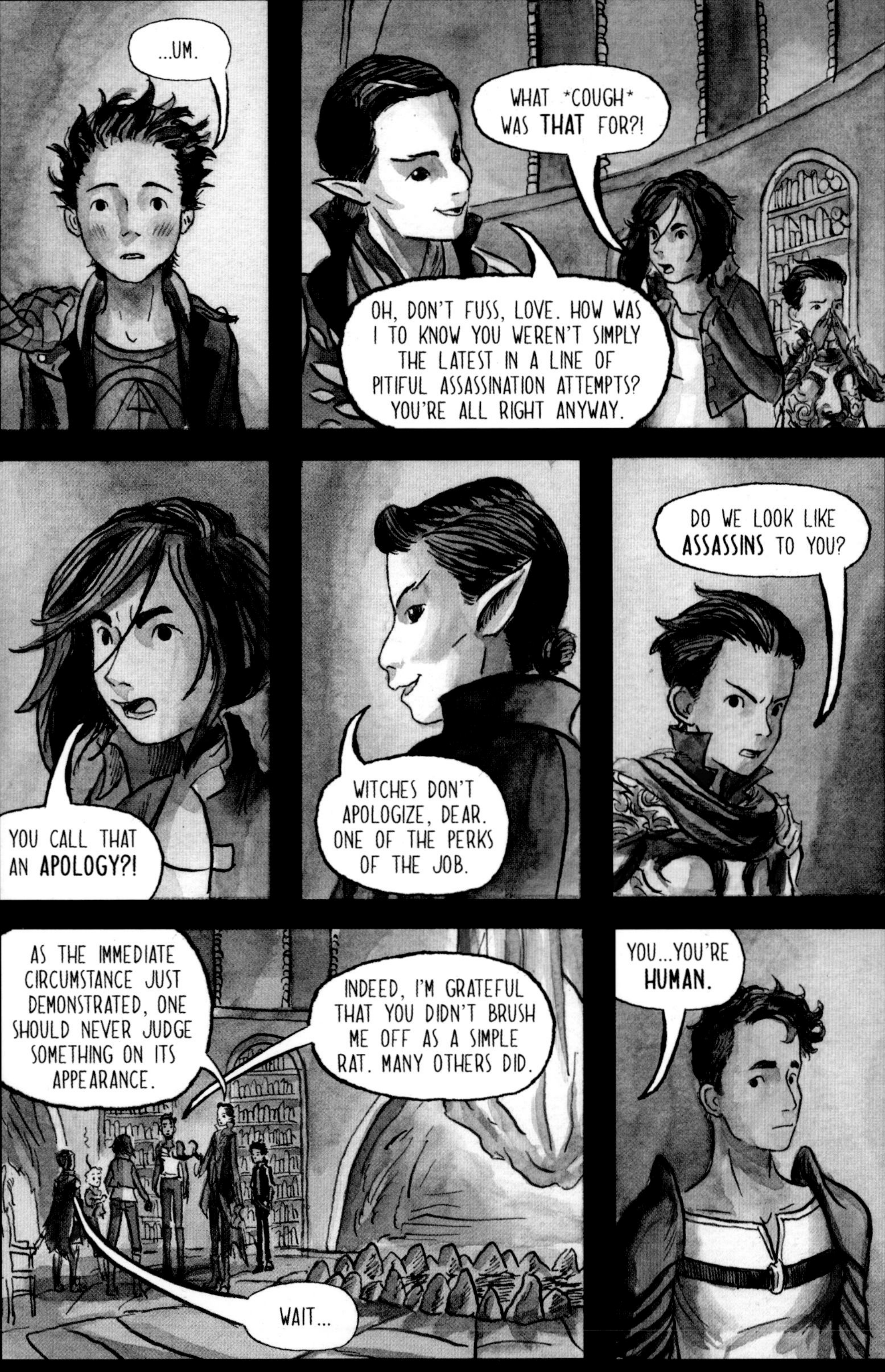
...UM.
WHAT *COUGH* WAS THAT FOR?!
OH, DON'T FUSS, LOVE. HOW WAS I TO KNOW YOU WEREN'T SIMPLY THE LATEST IN A LINE OF PITIFUL ASSASSINATION ATTEMPTS? YOU'RE ALL RIGHT ANYWAY.
YOU CALL THAT AN APOLOGY?!
WITCHES DON'T APOLOGIZE, DEAR. ONE OF THE PERKS OF THE JOB.
DO WE LOOK LIKE ASSASSINS TO YOU?
AS THE IMMEDIATE CIRCUMSTANCE JUST DEMONSTRATED, ONE SHOULD NEVER JUDGE SOMETHING ON ITS APPEARANCE.
INDEED, I'M GRATEFUL THAT YOU DIDN'T BRUSH ME OFF AS A SIMPLE RAT. MANY OTHERS DID.
WAIT...
YOU...YOU'RE HUMAN.

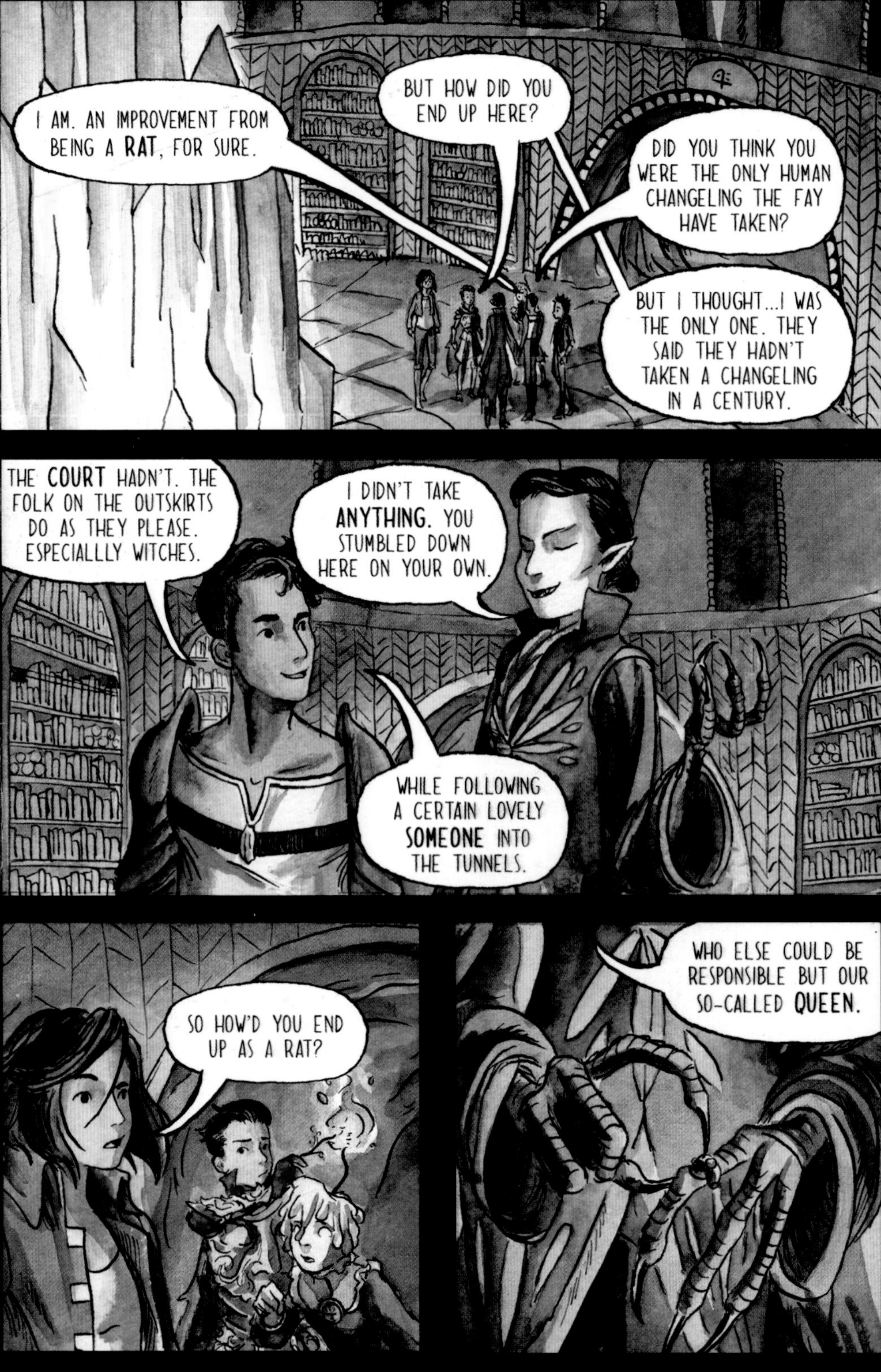
I AM. AN IMPROVEMENT FROM BEING A RAT, FOR SURE.
BUT HOW DID YOU END UP HERE?
DID YOU THINK YOU WERE THE ONLY HUMAN CHANGELING THE FAY HAVE TAKEN?
BUT I THOUGHT...I WAS THE ONLY ONE. THEY SAID THEY HADN'T TAKEN A CHANGELING IN A CENTURY.
THE COURT HADN'T. THE FOLK ON THE OUTSKIRTS DO AS THEY PLEASE. ESPECIALLLY WITCHES.
I DIDN'T TAKE ANYTHING. YOU STUMBLED DOWN HERE ON YOUR OWN.
WHILE FOLLOWING A CERTAIN LOVELY SOMEONE INTO THE TUNNELS.
SO HOW'D YOU END UP AS A RAT?
WHO ELSE COULD BE RESPONSIBLE BUT OUR SO-CALLED QUEEN.

Chapter Nine

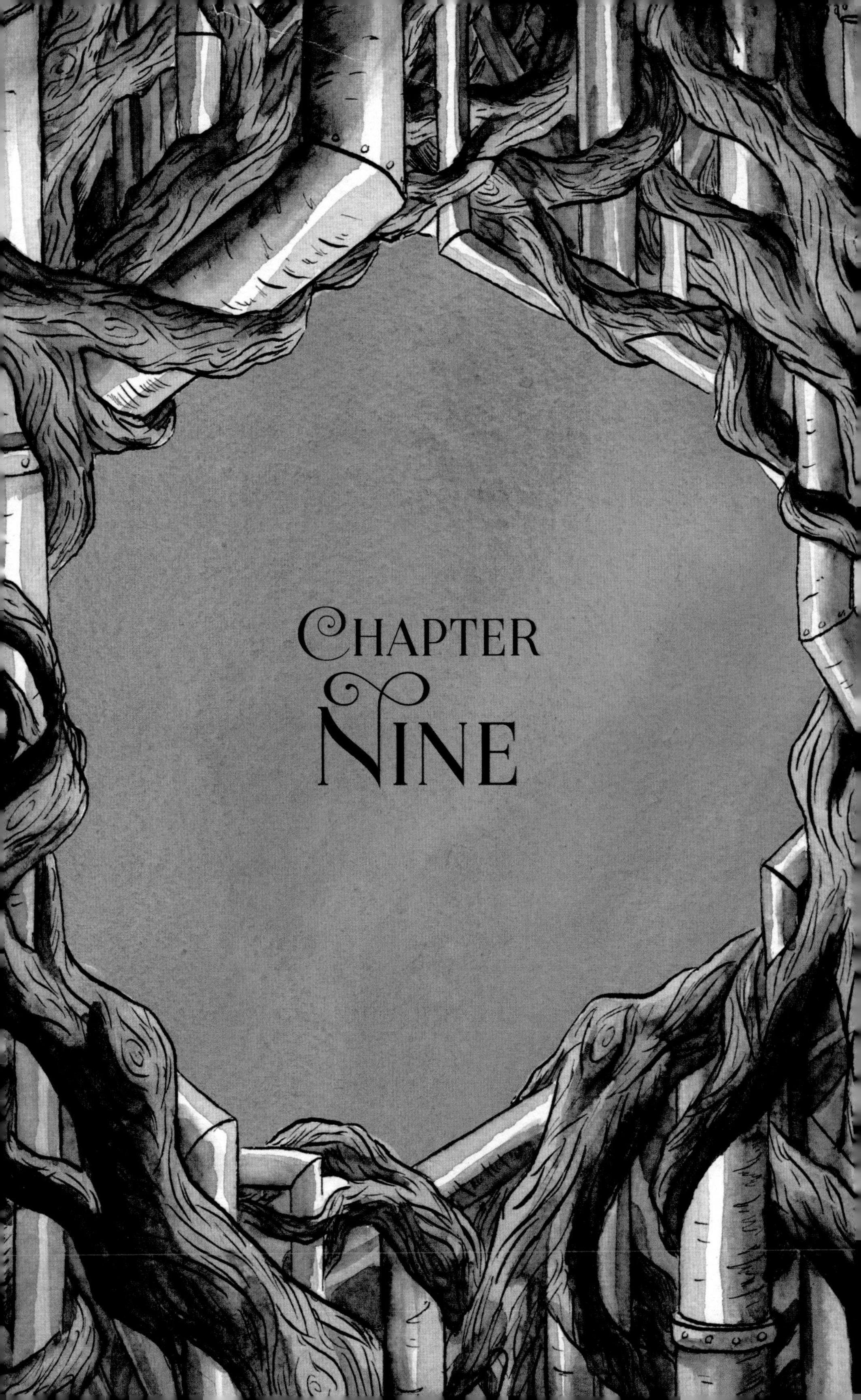

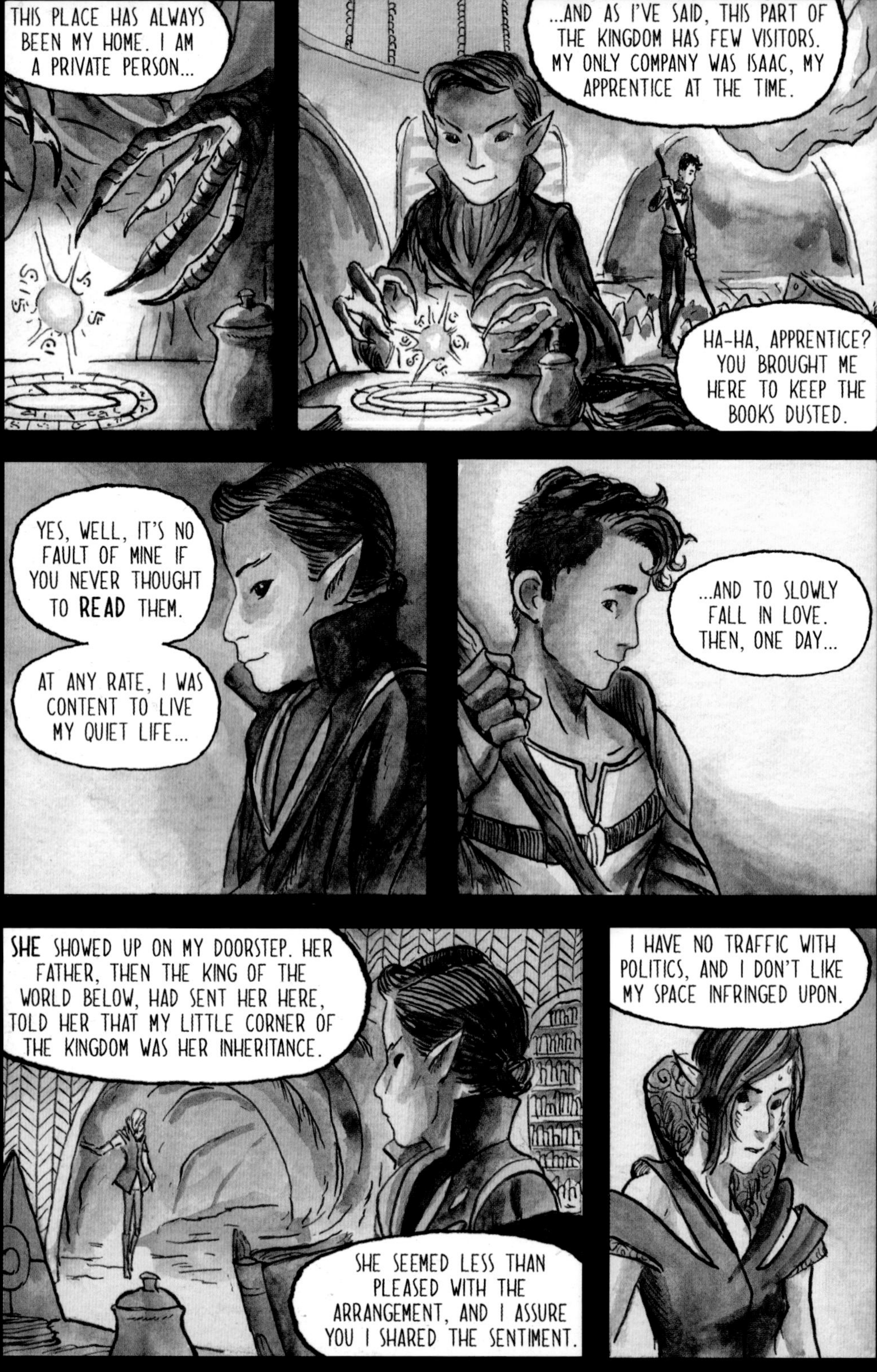
THIS PLACE HAS ALWAYS BEEN MY HOME. I AM A PRIVATE PERSON...
...AND AS I'VE SAID, THIS PART OF THE KINGDOM HAS FEW VISITORS. MY ONLY COMPANY WAS ISAAC, MY APPRENTICE AT THE TIME.
HA-HA, APPRENTICE? YOU BROUGHT ME HERE TO KEEP THE BOOKS DUSTED.
YES, WELL, IT'S NO FAULT OF MINE IF YOU NEVER THOUGHT TO **READ** THEM.
AT ANY RATE, I WAS CONTENT TO LIVE MY QUIET LIFE...
...AND TO SLOWLY FALL IN LOVE. THEN, ONE DAY...
SHE SHOWED UP ON MY DOORSTEP. HER FATHER, THEN THE KING OF THE WORLD BELOW, HAD SENT HER HERE, TOLD HER THAT MY LITTLE CORNER OF THE KINGDOM WAS HER INHERITANCE.
SHE SEEMED LESS THAN PLEASED WITH THE ARRANGEMENT, AND I ASSURE YOU I SHARED THE SENTIMENT.
I HAVE NO TRAFFIC WITH POLITICS, AND I DON'T LIKE MY SPACE INFRINGED UPON.

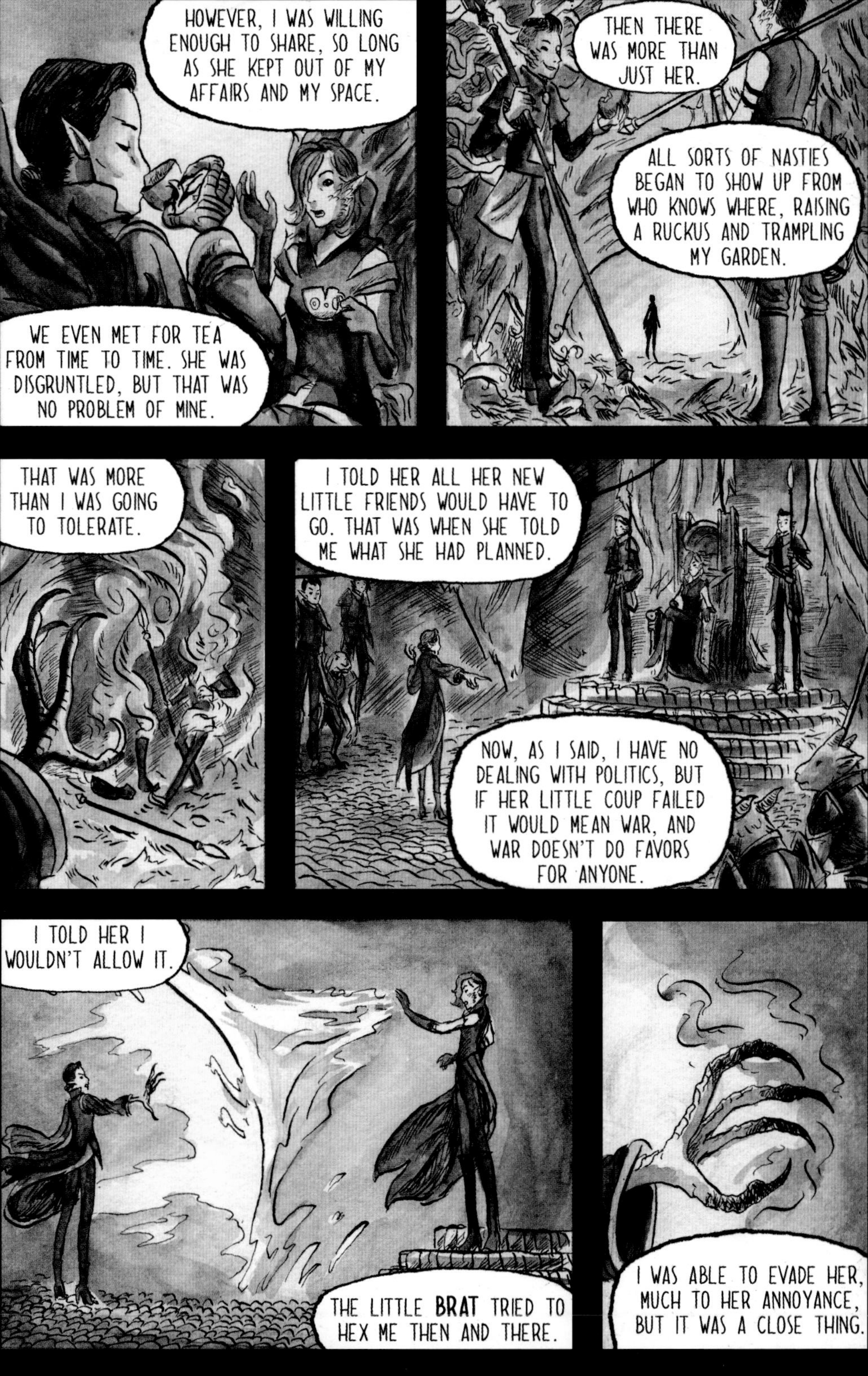
HOWEVER, I WAS WILLING ENOUGH TO SHARE, SO LONG AS SHE KEPT OUT OF MY AFFAIRS AND MY SPACE.
WE EVEN MET FOR TEA FROM TIME TO TIME. SHE WAS DISGRUNTLED, BUT THAT WAS NO PROBLEM OF MINE.
THEN THERE WAS MORE THAN JUST HER.
ALL SORTS OF NASTIES BEGAN TO SHOW UP FROM WHO KNOWS WHERE, RAISING A RUCKUS AND TRAMPLING MY GARDEN.
THAT WAS MORE THAN I WAS GOING TO TOLERATE.
I TOLD HER ALL HER NEW LITTLE FRIENDS WOULD HAVE TO GO. THAT WAS WHEN SHE TOLD ME WHAT SHE HAD PLANNED.
NOW, AS I SAID, I HAVE NO DEALING WITH POLITICS, BUT IF HER LITTLE COUP FAILED IT WOULD MEAN WAR, AND WAR DOESN'T DO FAVORS FOR ANYONE.
I TOLD HER I WOULDN'T ALLOW IT.
THE LITTLE **BRAT** TRIED TO HEX ME THEN AND THERE.
I WAS ABLE TO EVADE HER, MUCH TO HER ANNOYANCE, BUT IT WAS A CLOSE THING.

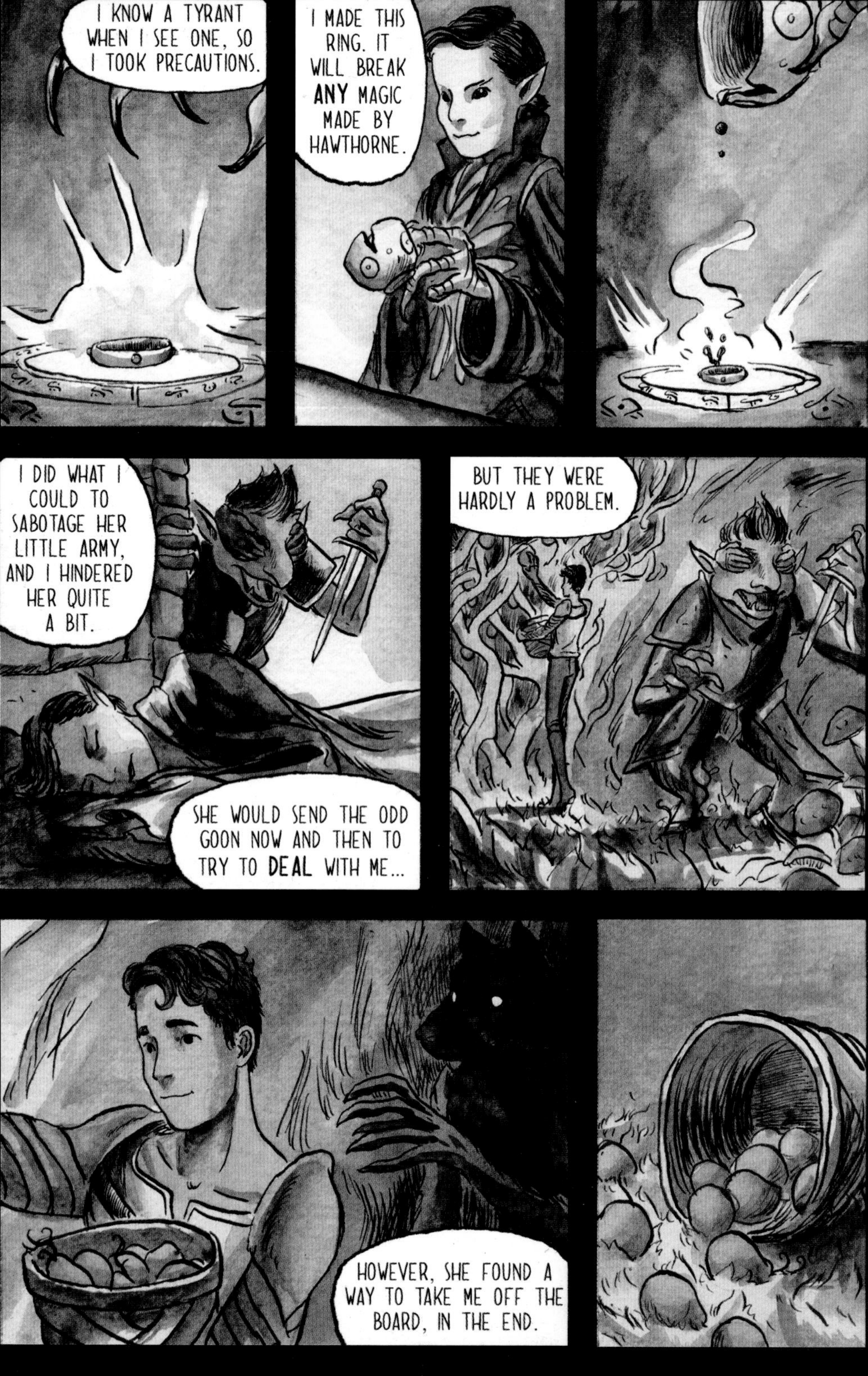
I KNOW A TYRANT WHEN I SEE ONE, SO I TOOK PRECAUTIONS.
I MADE THIS RING. IT WILL BREAK ANY MAGIC MADE BY HAWTHORNE.
I DID WHAT I COULD TO SABOTAGE HER LITTLE ARMY, AND I HINDERED HER QUITE A BIT.
SHE WOULD SEND THE ODD GOON NOW AND THEN TO TRY TO DEAL WITH ME...
BUT THEY WERE HARDLY A PROBLEM.
HOWEVER, SHE FOUND A WAY TO TAKE ME OFF THE BOARD, IN THE END.

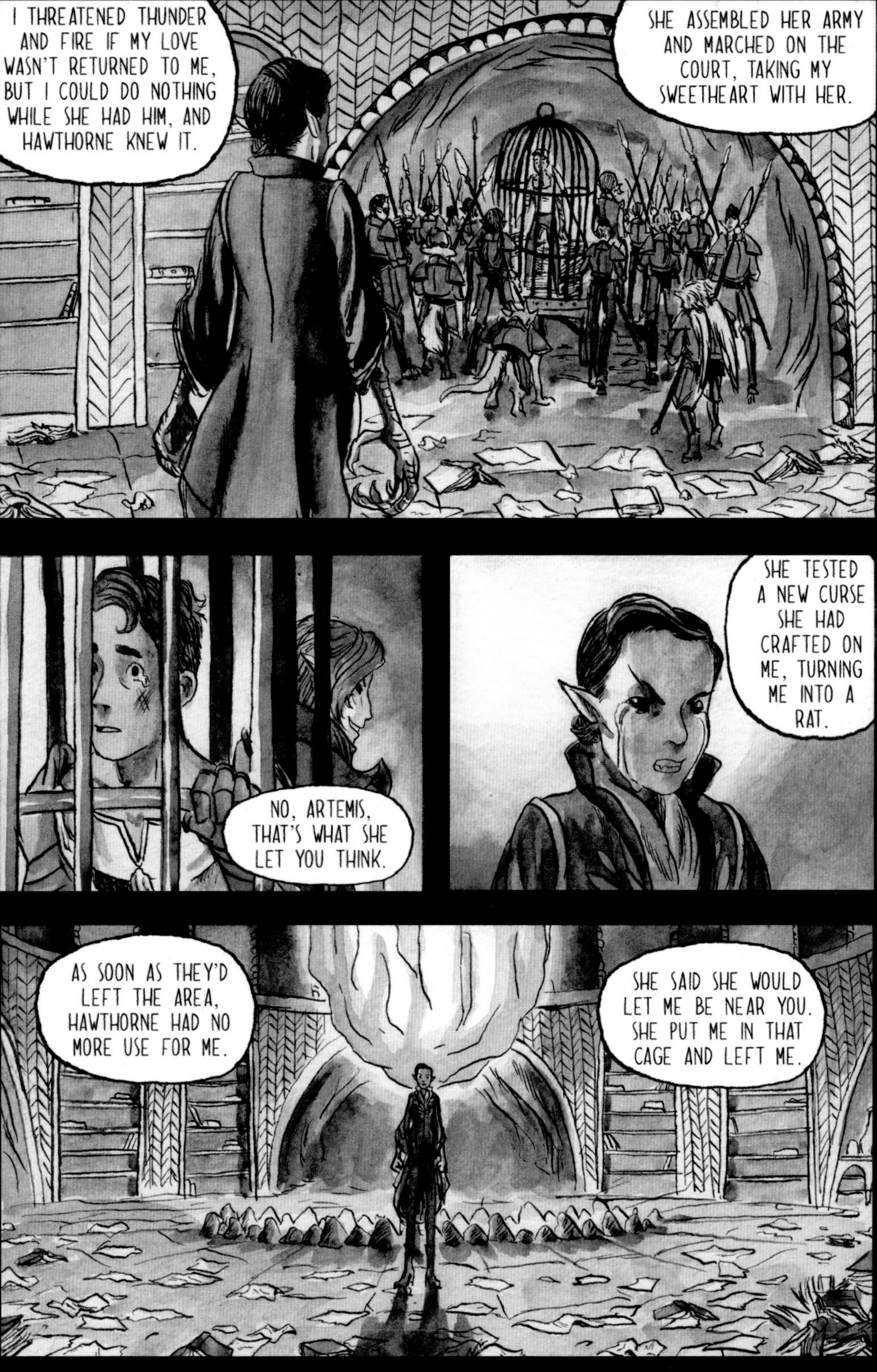
I THREATENED THUNDER AND FIRE IF MY LOVE WASN'T RETURNED TO ME, BUT I COULD DO NOTHING WHILE SHE HAD HIM, AND HAWTHORNE KNEW IT.
SHE ASSEMBLED HER ARMY AND MARCHED ON THE COURT, TAKING MY SWEETHEART WITH HER.
NO, ARTEMIS, THAT'S WHAT SHE LET YOU THINK.
SHE TESTED A NEW CURSE SHE HAD CRAFTED ON ME, TURNING ME INTO A RAT.
AS SOON AS THEY'D LEFT THE AREA, HAWTHORNE HAD NO MORE USE FOR ME.
SHE SAID SHE WOULD LET ME BE NEAR YOU. SHE PUT ME IN THAT CAGE AND LEFT ME.

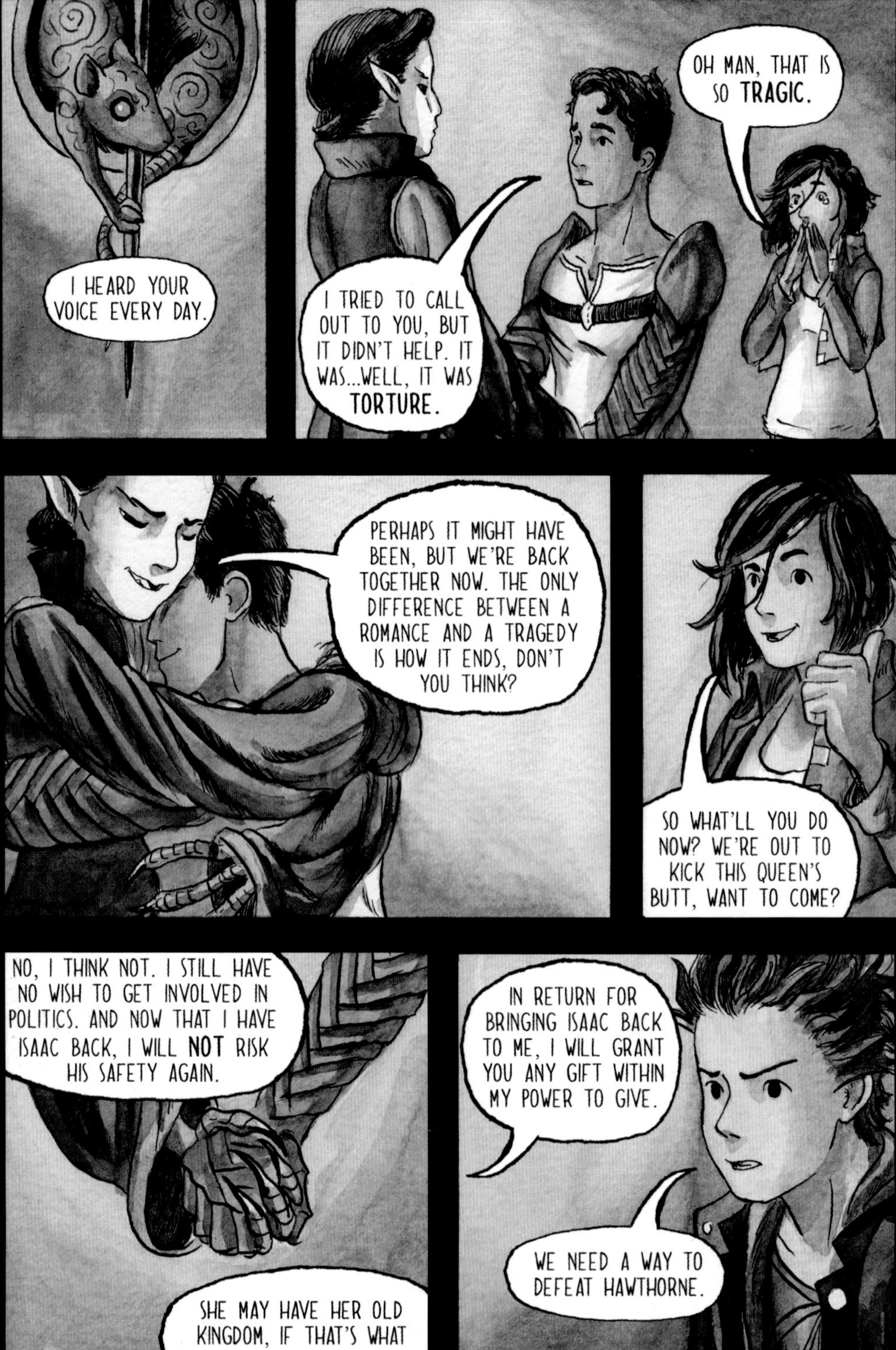
I HEARD YOUR VOICE EVERY DAY.
I TRIED TO CALL OUT TO YOU, BUT IT DIDN'T HELP. IT WAS...WELL, IT WAS **TORTURE**.
OH MAN, THAT IS SO **TRAGIC**.
PERHAPS IT MIGHT HAVE BEEN, BUT WE'RE BACK TOGETHER NOW. THE ONLY DIFFERENCE BETWEEN A ROMANCE AND A TRAGEDY IS HOW IT ENDS, DON'T YOU THINK?
SO WHAT'LL YOU DO NOW? WE'RE OUT TO KICK THIS QUEEN'S BUTT, WANT TO COME?
NO, I THINK NOT. I STILL HAVE NO WISH TO GET INVOLVED IN POLITICS. AND NOW THAT I HAVE ISAAC BACK, I WILL **NOT** RISK HIS SAFETY AGAIN.
SHE MAY HAVE HER OLD KINGDOM, IF THAT'S WHAT SHE WANTS. HOWEVER...
IN RETURN FOR BRINGING ISAAC BACK TO ME, I WILL GRANT YOU ANY GIFT WITHIN MY POWER TO GIVE.
WE NEED A WAY TO DEFEAT HAWTHORNE.

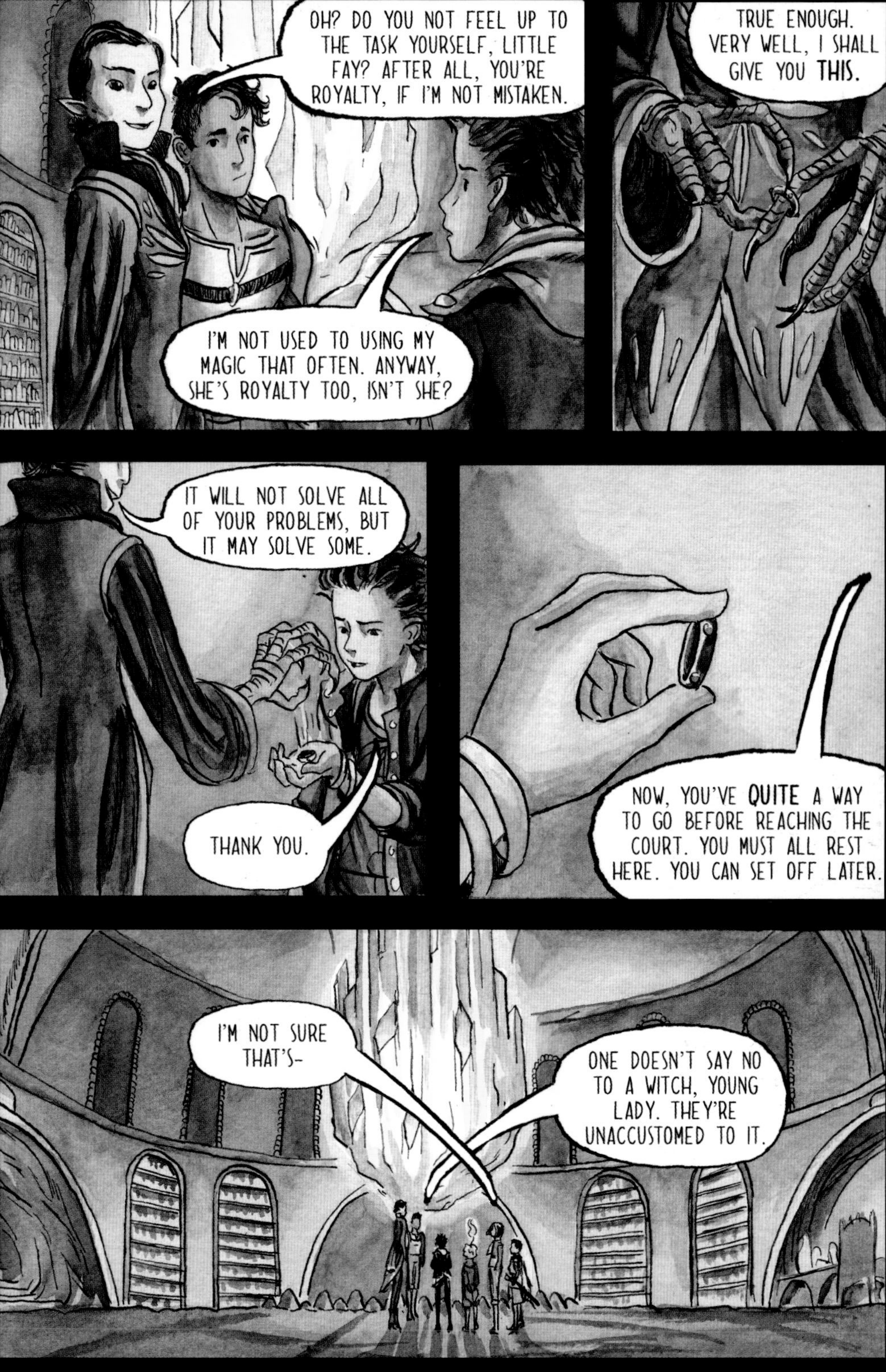
OH? DO YOU NOT FEEL UP TO THE TASK YOURSELF, LITTLE FAY? AFTER ALL, YOU'RE ROYALTY, IF I'M NOT MISTAKEN.
I'M NOT USED TO USING MY MAGIC THAT OFTEN. ANYWAY, SHE'S ROYALTY TOO, ISN'T SHE?
TRUE ENOUGH. VERY WELL, I SHALL GIVE YOU **THIS.**
IT WILL NOT SOLVE ALL OF YOUR PROBLEMS, BUT IT MAY SOLVE SOME.
THANK YOU.
NOW, YOU'VE **QUITE** A WAY TO GO BEFORE REACHING THE COURT. YOU MUST ALL REST HERE. YOU CAN SET OFF LATER.
I'M NOT SURE THAT'S-
ONE DOESN'T SAY NO TO A WITCH, YOUNG LADY. THEY'RE UNACCUSTOMED TO IT.

Chapter Ten

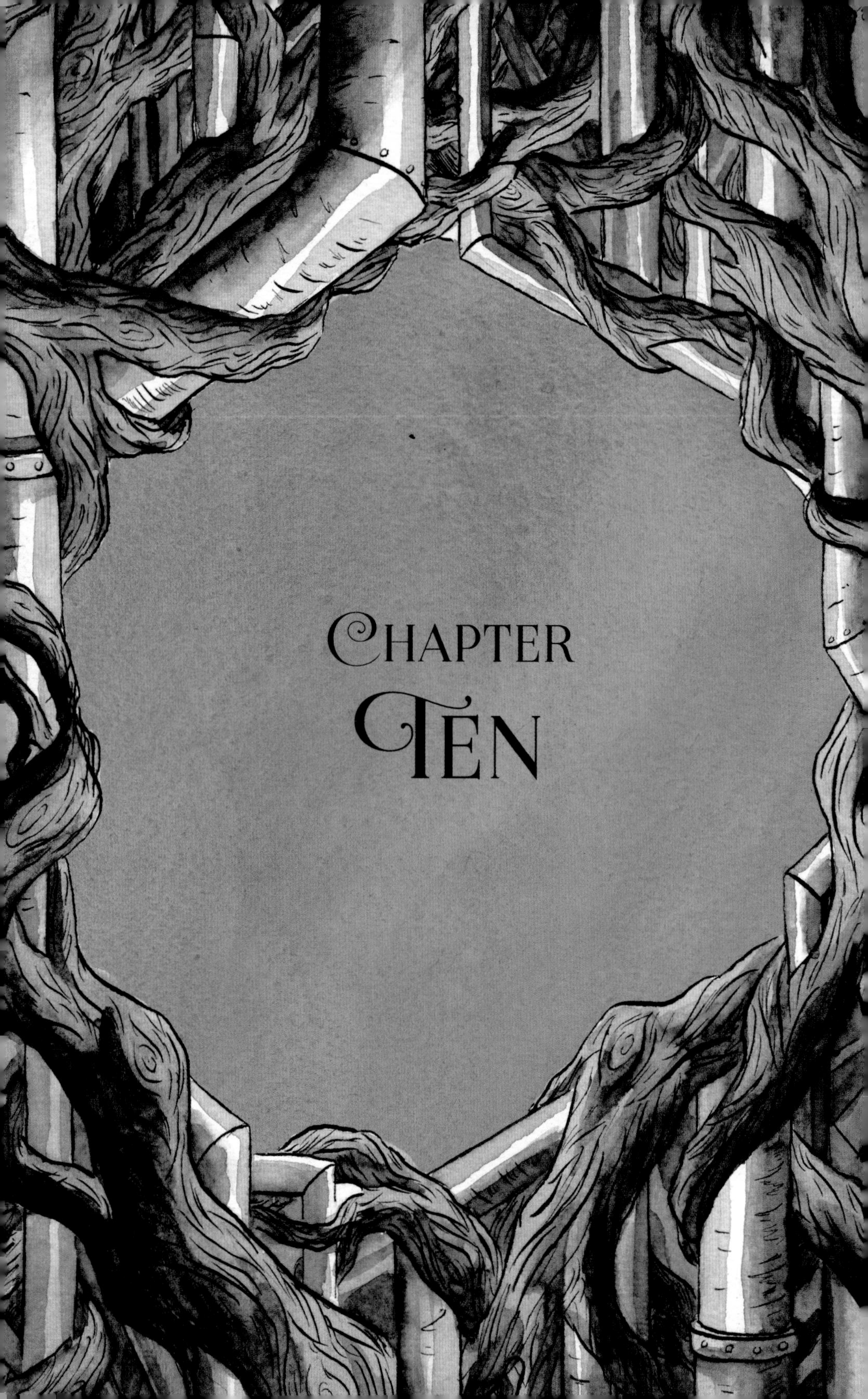

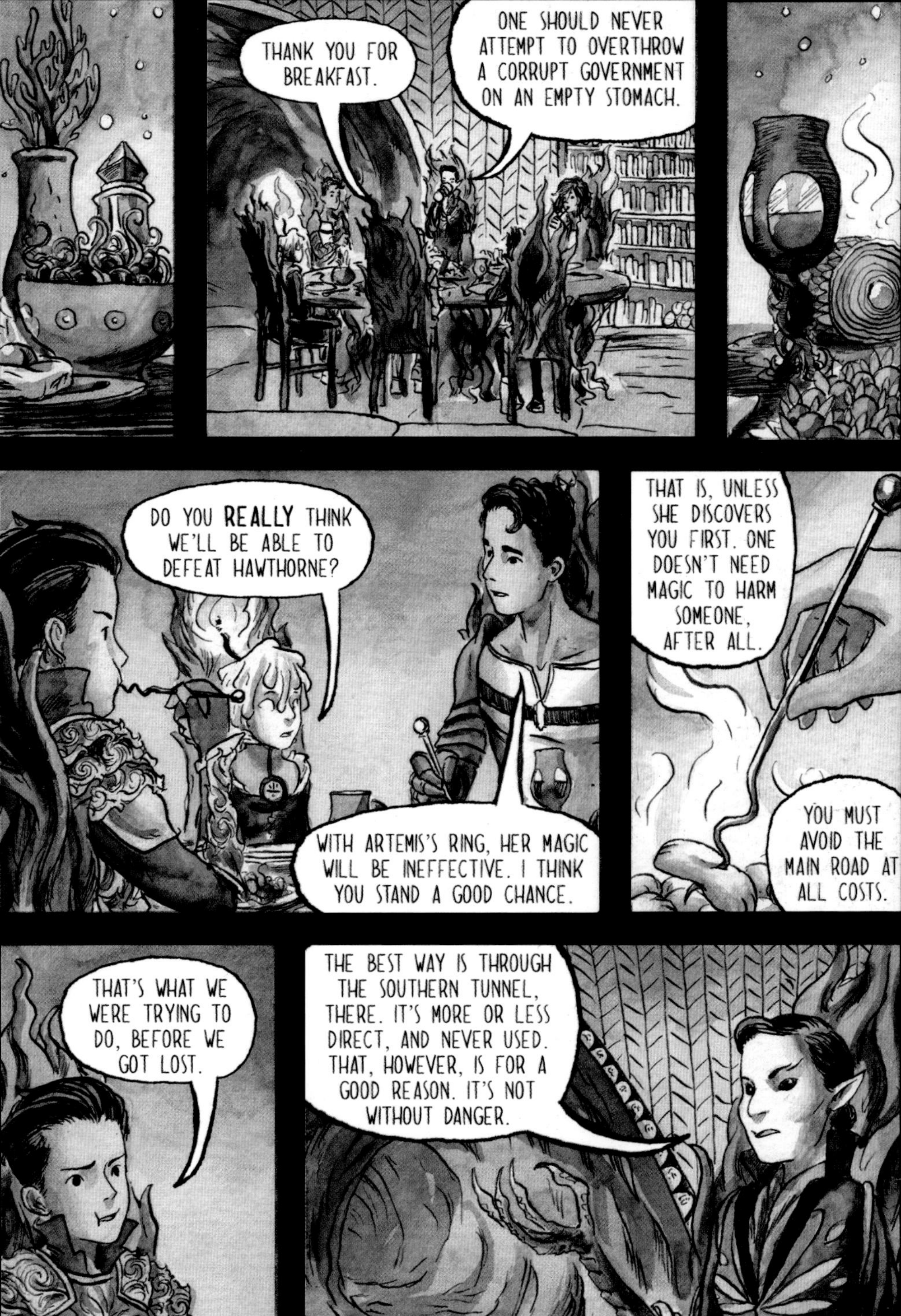
THANK YOU FOR BREAKFAST.
ONE SHOULD NEVER ATTEMPT TO OVERTHROW A CORRUPT GOVERNMENT ON AN EMPTY STOMACH.
DO YOU **REALLY** THINK WE'LL BE ABLE TO DEFEAT HAWTHORNE?
WITH ARTEMIS'S RING, HER MAGIC WILL BE INEFFECTIVE. I THINK YOU STAND A GOOD CHANCE.
THAT IS, UNLESS SHE DISCOVERS YOU FIRST. ONE DOESN'T NEED MAGIC TO HARM SOMEONE, AFTER ALL.
YOU MUST AVOID THE MAIN ROAD AT ALL COSTS.
THAT'S WHAT WE WERE TRYING TO DO, BEFORE WE GOT LOST.
THE BEST WAY IS THROUGH THE SOUTHERN TUNNEL, THERE. IT'S MORE OR LESS DIRECT, AND NEVER USED. THAT, HOWEVER, IS FOR A GOOD REASON. IT'S NOT WITHOUT DANGER.

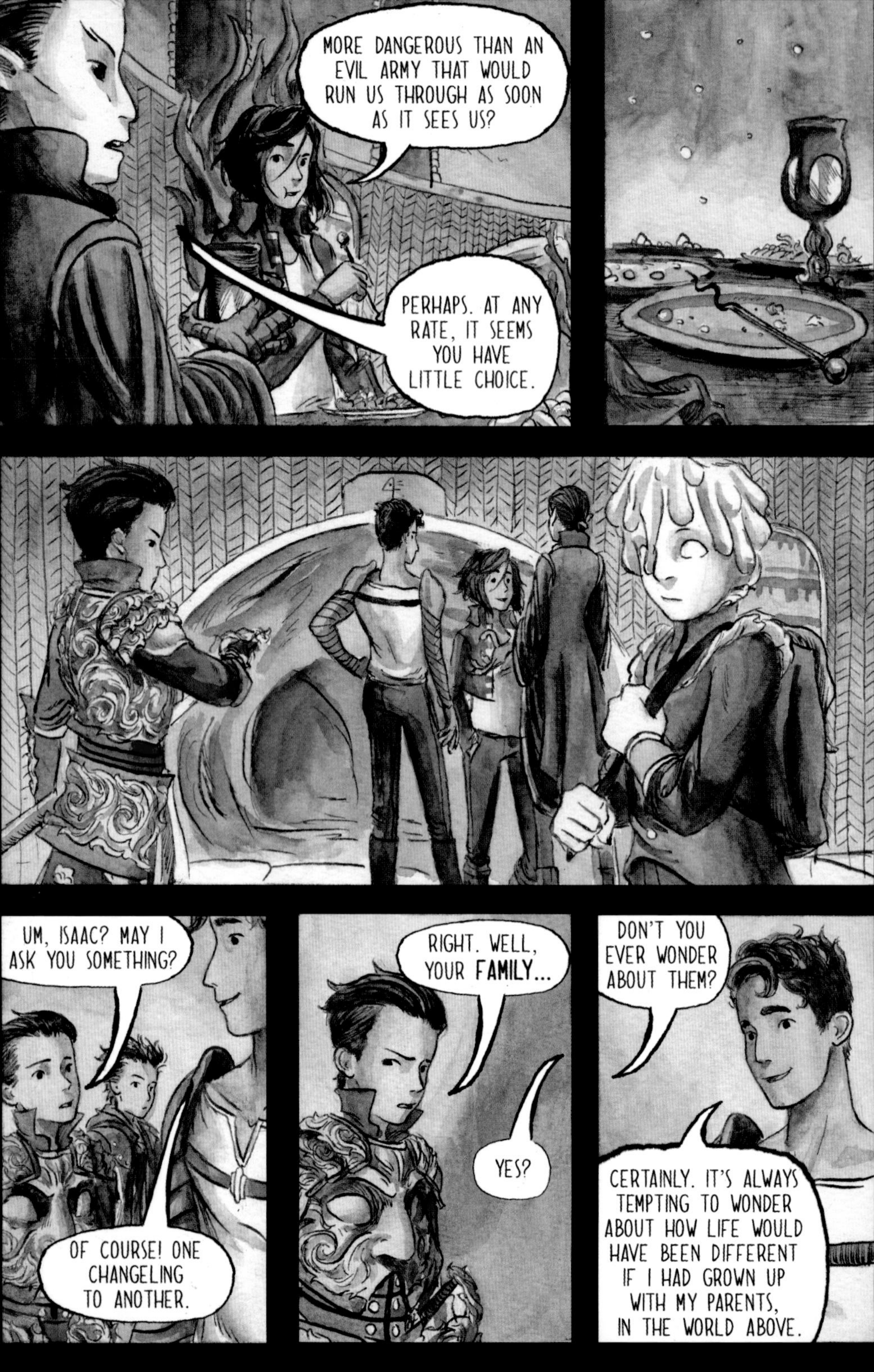
MORE DANGEROUS THAN AN EVIL ARMY THAT WOULD RUN US THROUGH AS SOON AS IT SEES US?
PERHAPS. AT ANY RATE, IT SEEMS YOU HAVE LITTLE CHOICE.
UM, ISAAC? MAY I ASK YOU SOMETHING?
OF COURSE! ONE CHANGELING TO ANOTHER.
RIGHT. WELL, YOUR **FAMILY**...
YES?
DON'T YOU EVER WONDER ABOUT THEM?
CERTAINLY. IT'S ALWAYS TEMPTING TO WONDER ABOUT HOW LIFE WOULD HAVE BEEN DIFFERENT IF I HAD GROWN UP WITH MY PARENTS, IN THE WORLD ABOVE.

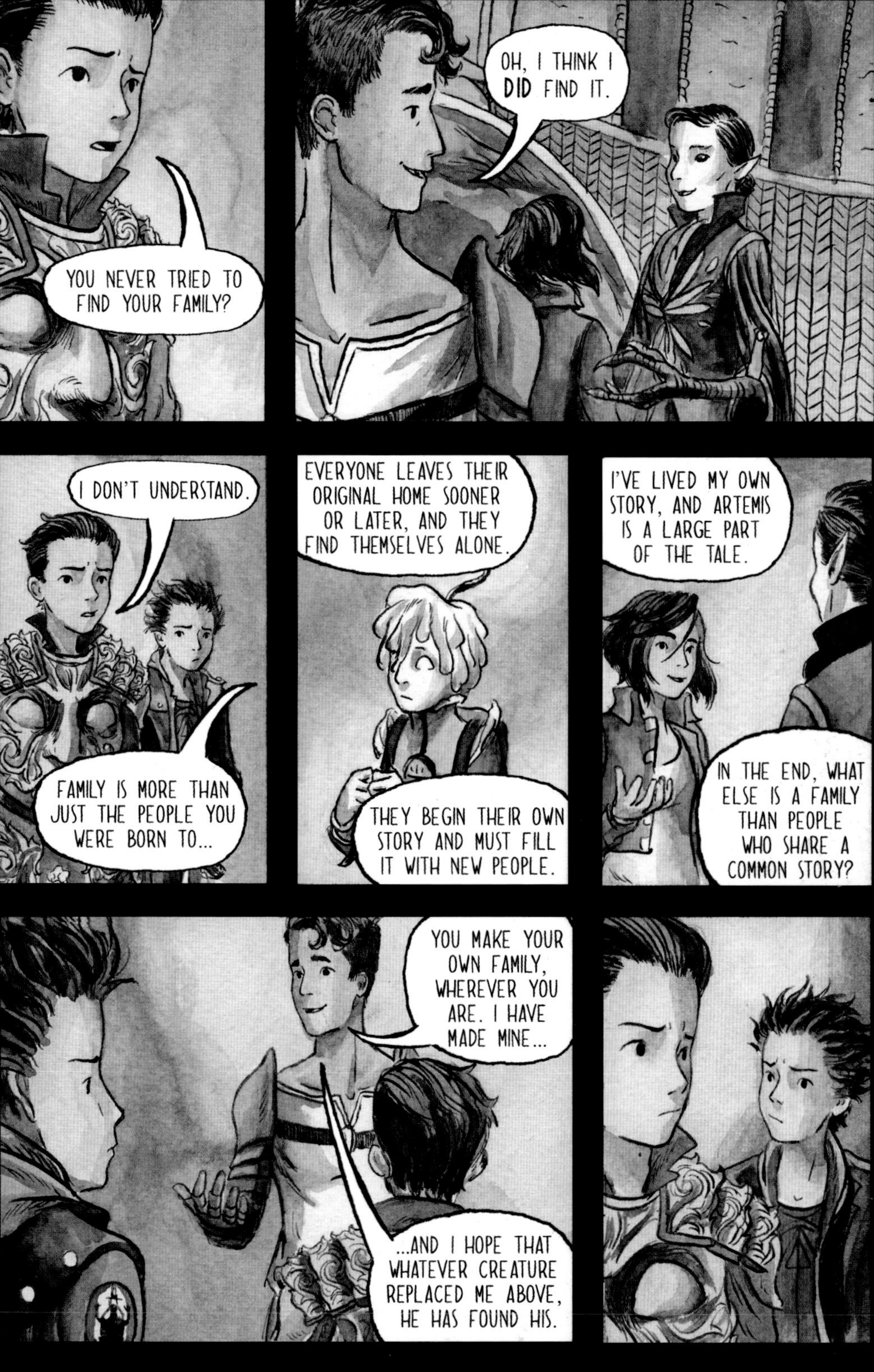
YOU NEVER TRIED TO FIND YOUR FAMILY?
OH, I THINK I **DID** FIND IT.
I DON'T UNDERSTAND.
FAMILY IS MORE THAN JUST THE PEOPLE YOU WERE BORN TO...
EVERYONE LEAVES THEIR ORIGINAL HOME SOONER OR LATER, AND THEY FIND THEMSELVES ALONE.
THEY BEGIN THEIR OWN STORY AND MUST FILL IT WITH NEW PEOPLE.
I'VE LIVED MY OWN STORY, AND ARTEMIS IS A LARGE PART OF THE TALE.
IN THE END, WHAT ELSE IS A FAMILY THAN PEOPLE WHO SHARE A COMMON STORY?
YOU MAKE YOUR OWN FAMILY, WHEREVER YOU ARE. I HAVE MADE MINE...
...AND I HOPE THAT WHATEVER CREATURE REPLACED ME ABOVE, HE HAS FOUND HIS.

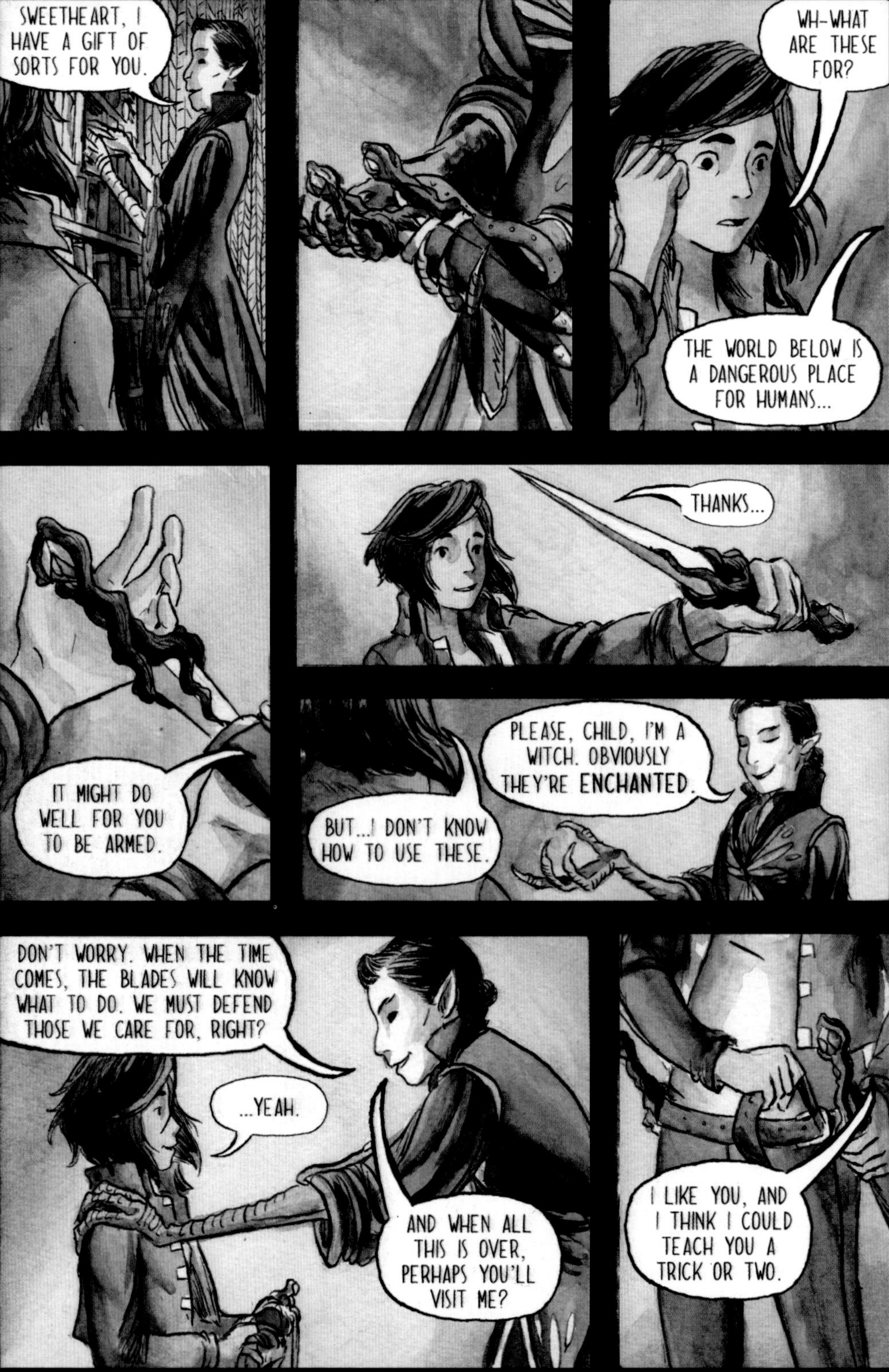
SWEETHEART, I HAVE A GIFT OF SORTS FOR YOU.
WH-WHAT ARE THESE FOR?
THE WORLD BELOW IS A DANGEROUS PLACE FOR HUMANS...
IT MIGHT DO WELL FOR YOU TO BE ARMED.
THANKS...
BUT...I DON'T KNOW HOW TO USE THESE.
PLEASE, CHILD, I'M A WITCH. OBVIOUSLY THEY'RE ENCHANTED.
DON'T WORRY. WHEN THE TIME COMES, THE BLADES WILL KNOW WHAT TO DO. WE MUST DEFEND THOSE WE CARE FOR, RIGHT?
...YEAH.
AND WHEN ALL THIS IS OVER, PERHAPS YOU'LL VISIT ME?
I LIKE YOU, AND I THINK I COULD TEACH YOU A TRICK OR TWO.

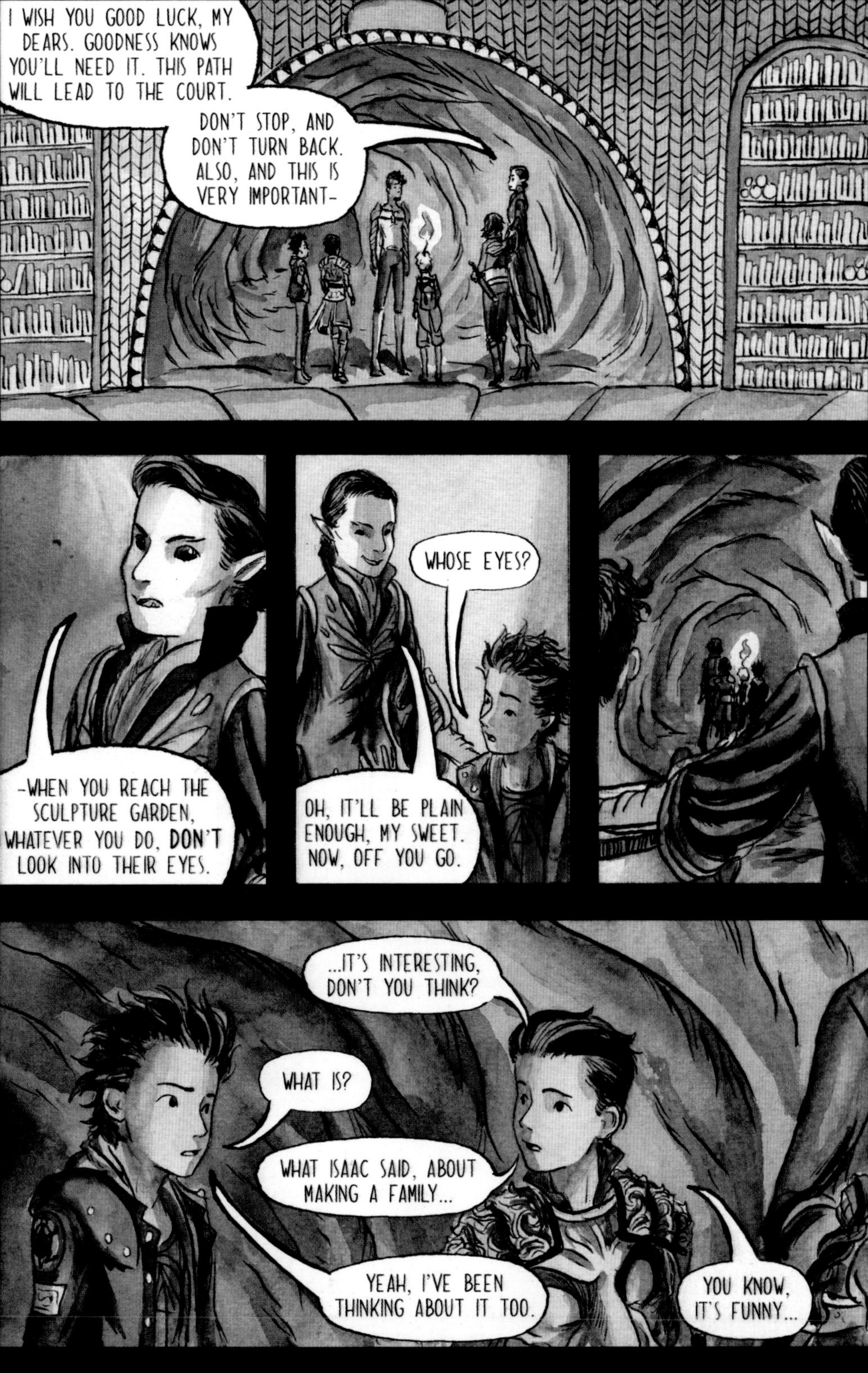
I WISH YOU GOOD LUCK, MY DEARS. GOODNESS KNOWS YOU'LL NEED IT. THIS PATH WILL LEAD TO THE COURT.
DON'T STOP, AND DON'T TURN BACK. ALSO, AND THIS IS VERY IMPORTANT-
-WHEN YOU REACH THE SCULPTURE GARDEN, WHATEVER YOU DO, **DON'T** LOOK INTO THEIR EYES.
WHOSE EYES?
OH, IT'LL BE PLAIN ENOUGH, MY SWEET. NOW, OFF YOU GO.
...IT'S INTERESTING, DON'T YOU THINK?
WHAT IS?
WHAT ISAAC SAID, ABOUT MAKING A FAMILY...
YEAH, I'VE BEEN THINKING ABOUT IT TOO.
YOU KNOW, IT'S FUNNY...

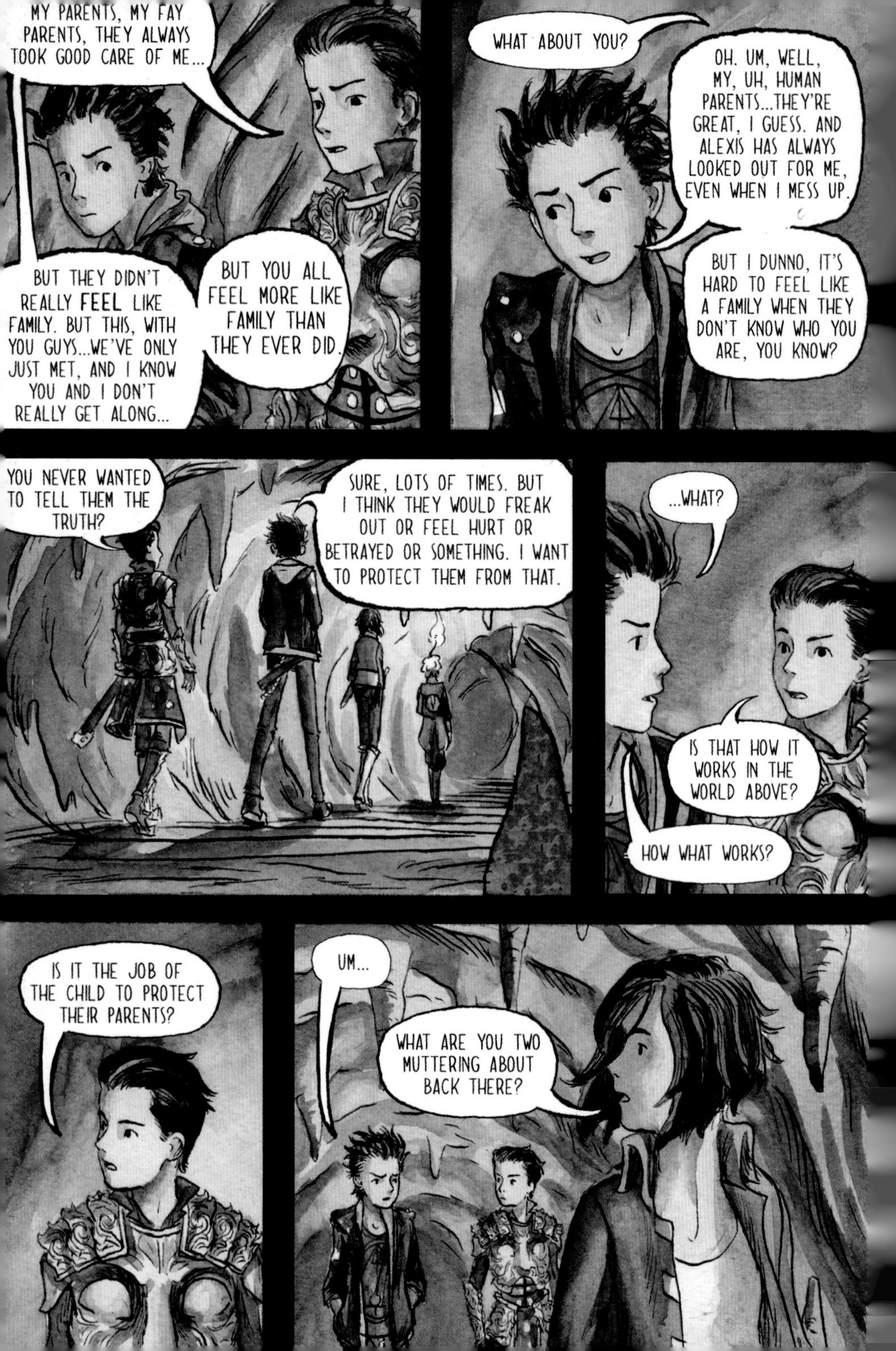
MY PARENTS, MY FAY PARENTS, THEY ALWAYS TOOK GOOD CARE OF ME...
BUT THEY DIDN'T REALLY **FEEL** LIKE FAMILY. BUT THIS, WITH YOU GUYS...WE'VE ONLY JUST MET, AND I KNOW YOU AND I DON'T REALLY GET ALONG...
BUT YOU ALL FEEL MORE LIKE FAMILY THAN THEY EVER DID.
WHAT ABOUT YOU?
OH. UM, WELL, MY, UH, HUMAN PARENTS...THEY'RE GREAT, I GUESS. AND ALEXIS HAS ALWAYS LOOKED OUT FOR ME, EVEN WHEN I MESS UP.
BUT I DUNNO, IT'S HARD TO FEEL LIKE A FAMILY WHEN THEY DON'T KNOW WHO YOU ARE, YOU KNOW?
YOU NEVER WANTED TO TELL THEM THE TRUTH?
SURE, LOTS OF TIMES. BUT I THINK THEY WOULD FREAK OUT OR FEEL HURT OR BETRAYED OR SOMETHING. I WANT TO PROTECT THEM FROM THAT.
...WHAT?
IS THAT HOW IT WORKS IN THE WORLD ABOVE?
HOW WHAT WORKS?
IS IT THE JOB OF THE CHILD TO PROTECT THEIR PARENTS?
UM...
WHAT ARE YOU TWO MUTTERING ABOUT BACK THERE?

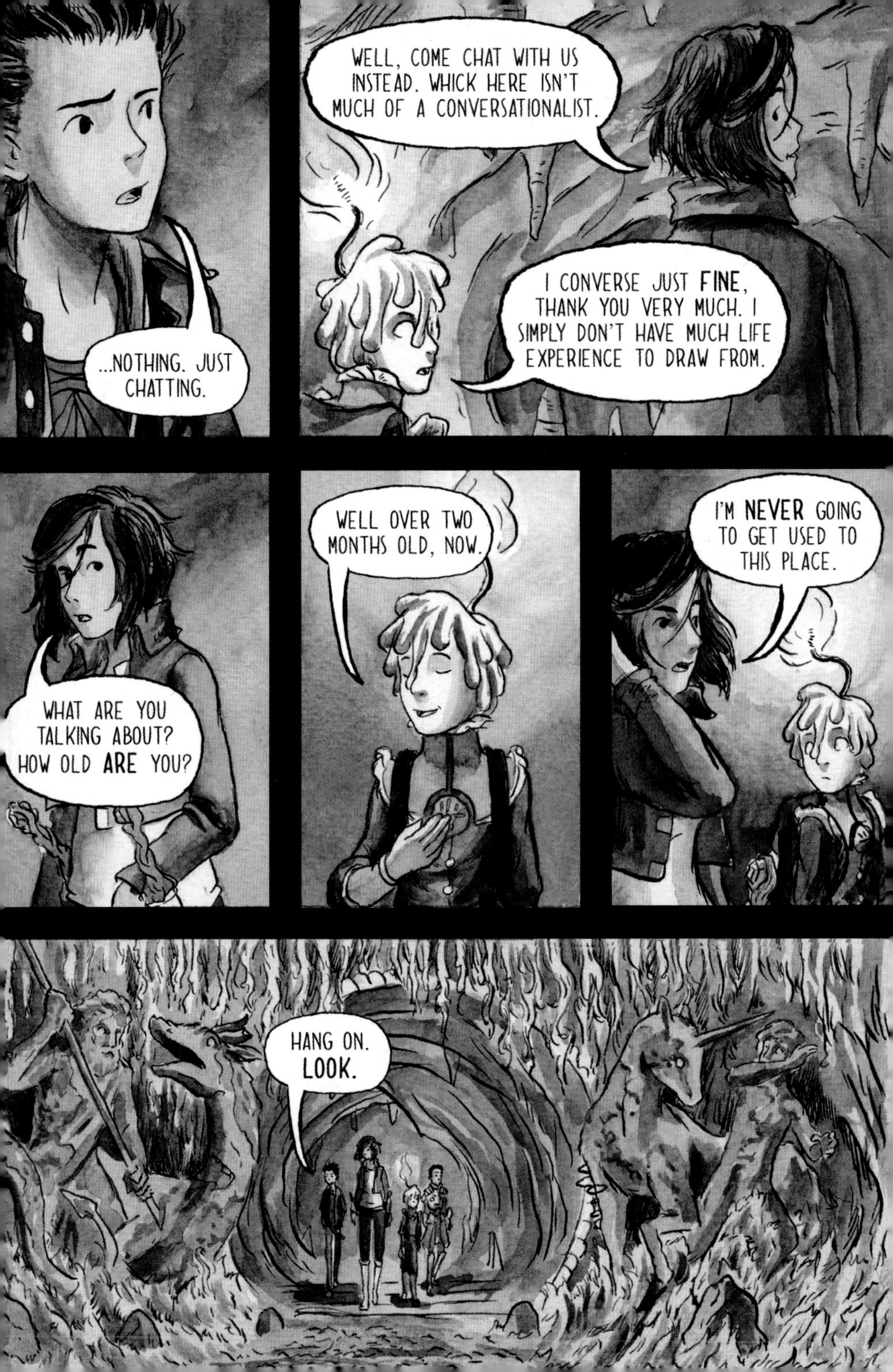
...NOTHING. JUST CHATTING.
WELL, COME CHAT WITH US INSTEAD. WHICK HERE ISN'T MUCH OF A CONVERSATIONALIST.
I CONVERSE JUST **FINE**, THANK YOU VERY MUCH. I SIMPLY DON'T HAVE MUCH LIFE EXPERIENCE TO DRAW FROM.
WHAT ARE YOU TALKING ABOUT? HOW OLD **ARE** YOU?
WELL OVER TWO MONTHS OLD, NOW.
I'M **NEVER** GOING TO GET USED TO THIS PLACE.
HANG ON. **LOOK.**

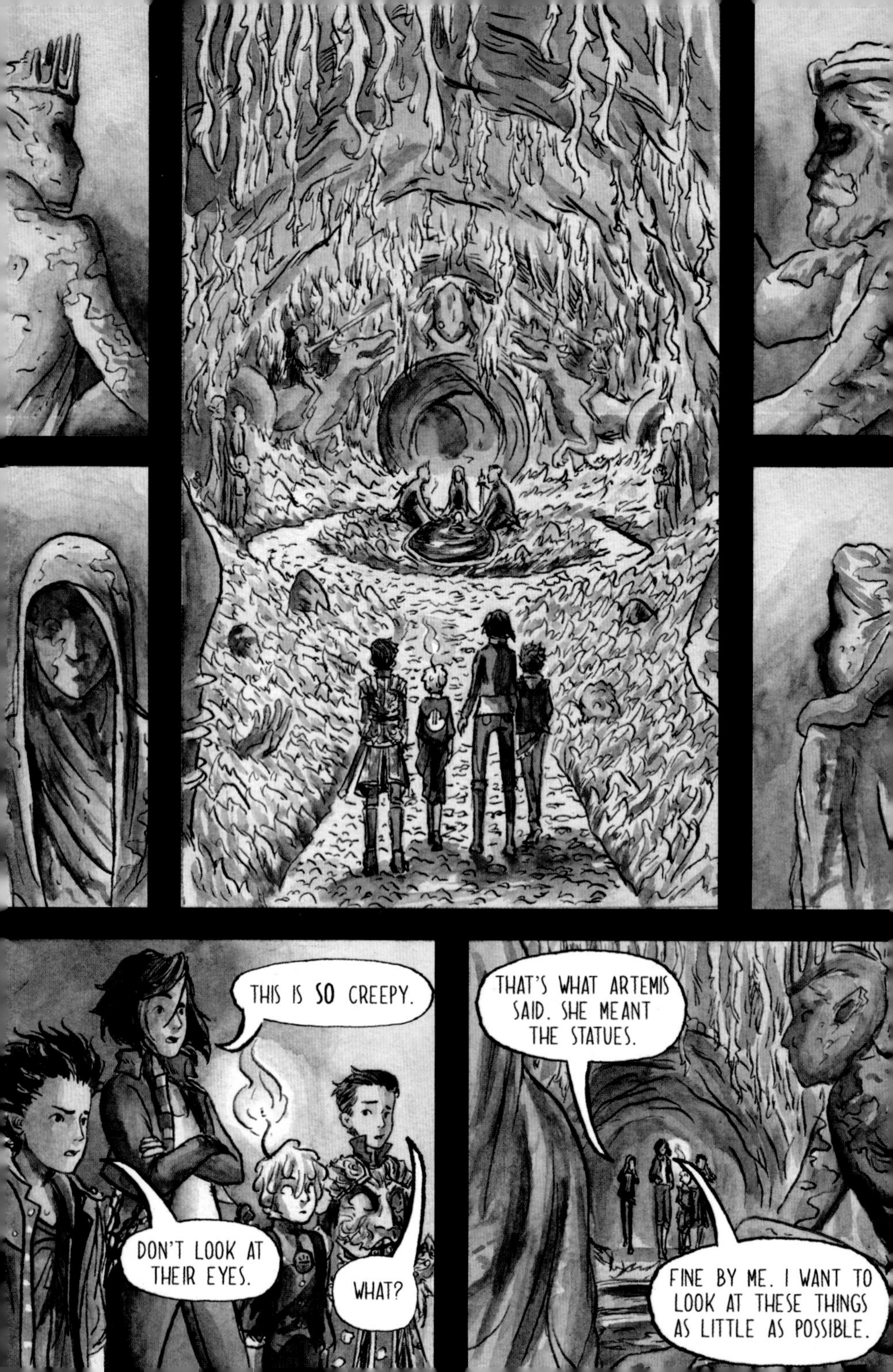
THIS IS SO CREEPY.
DON'T LOOK AT THEIR EYES.
WHAT?
THAT'S WHAT ARTEMIS SAID. SHE MEANT THE STATUES.
FINE BY ME. I WANT TO LOOK AT THESE THINGS AS LITTLE AS POSSIBLE.

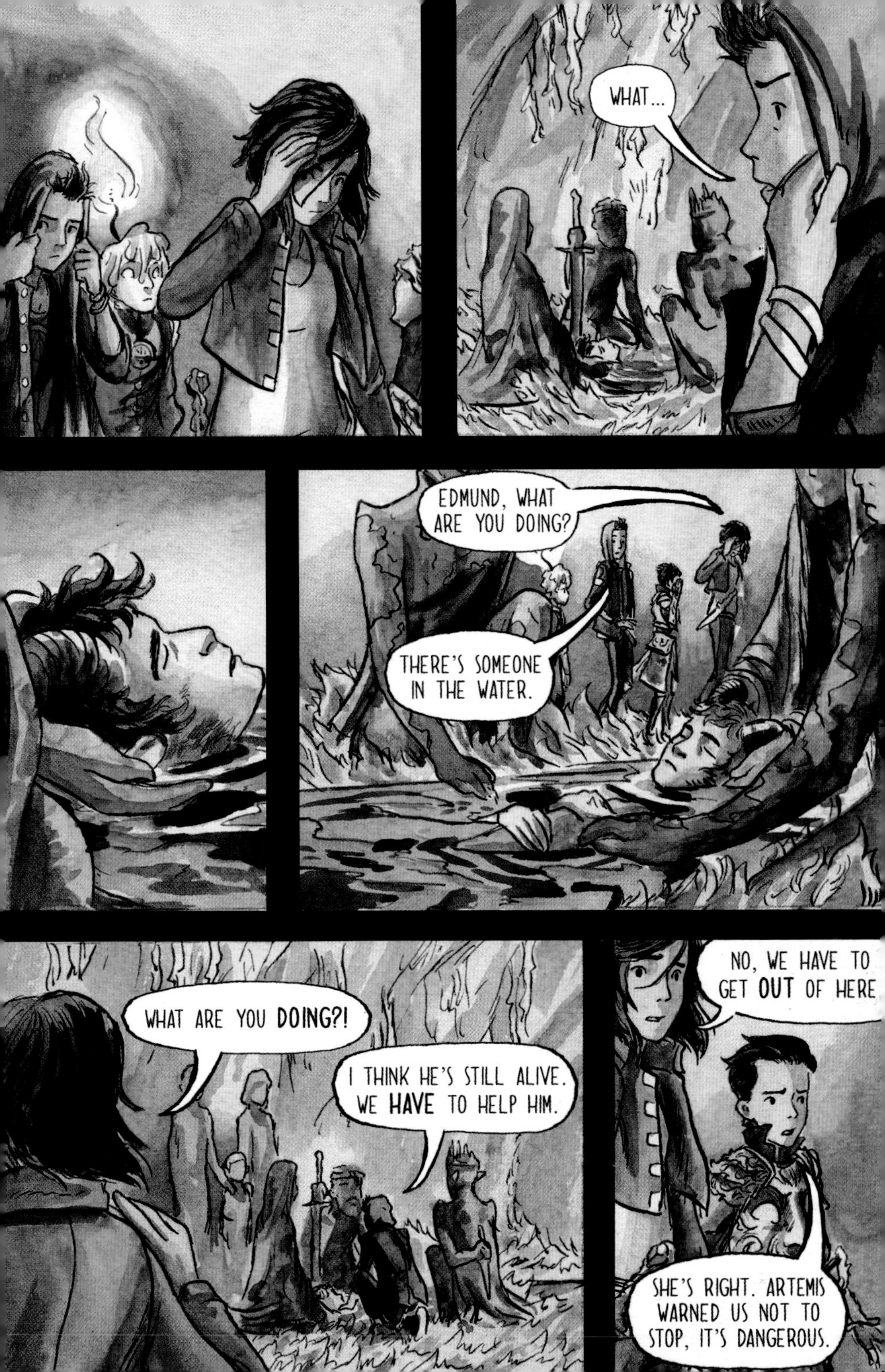
WHAT...
EDMUND, WHAT ARE YOU DOING?
THERE'S SOMEONE IN THE WATER.
WHAT ARE YOU DOING?!
I THINK HE'S STILL ALIVE. WE HAVE TO HELP HIM.
NO, WE HAVE TO GET OUT OF HERE
SHE'S RIGHT. ARTEMIS WARNED US NOT TO STOP, IT'S DANGEROUS.

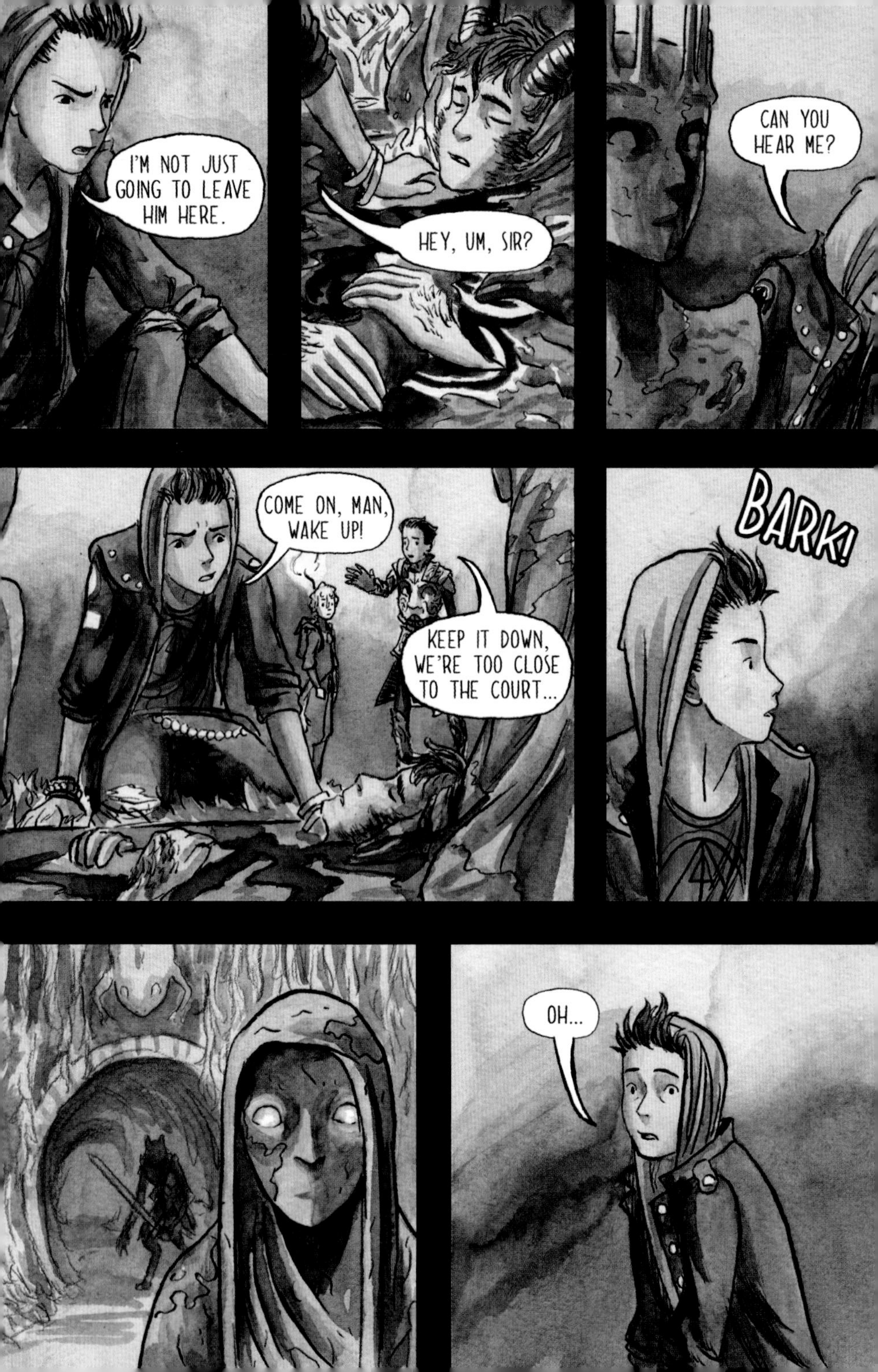
I'M NOT JUST GOING TO LEAVE HIM HERE.
HEY, UM, SIR?
CAN YOU HEAR ME?
COME ON, MAN, WAKE UP!
KEEP IT DOWN, WE'RE TOO CLOSE TO THE COURT...
BARK!
OH...

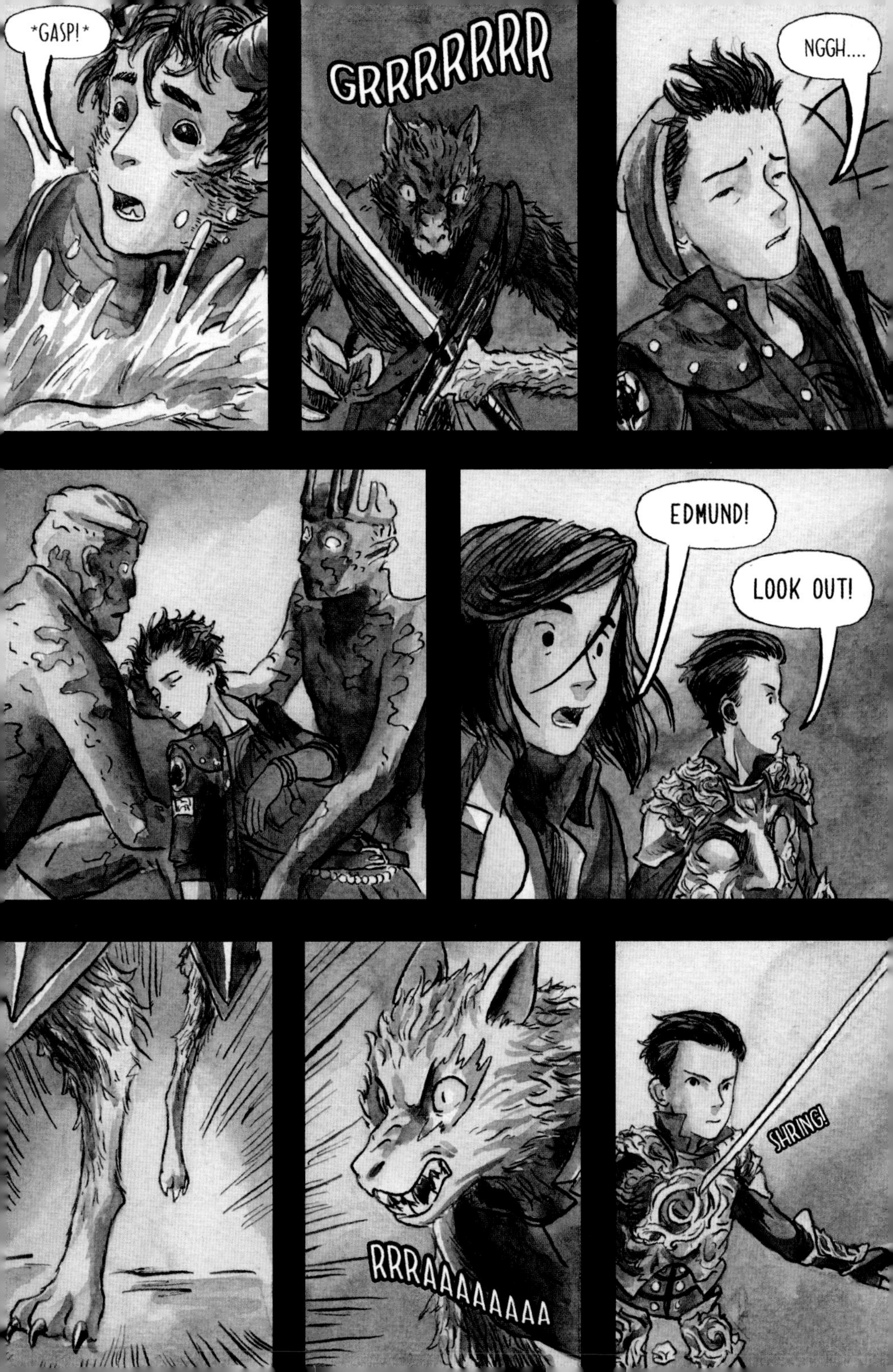
GASP!
GRRRRRRR
NGGH....
EDMUND!
LOOK OUT!
RRRAAAAAAAA
SHRING!

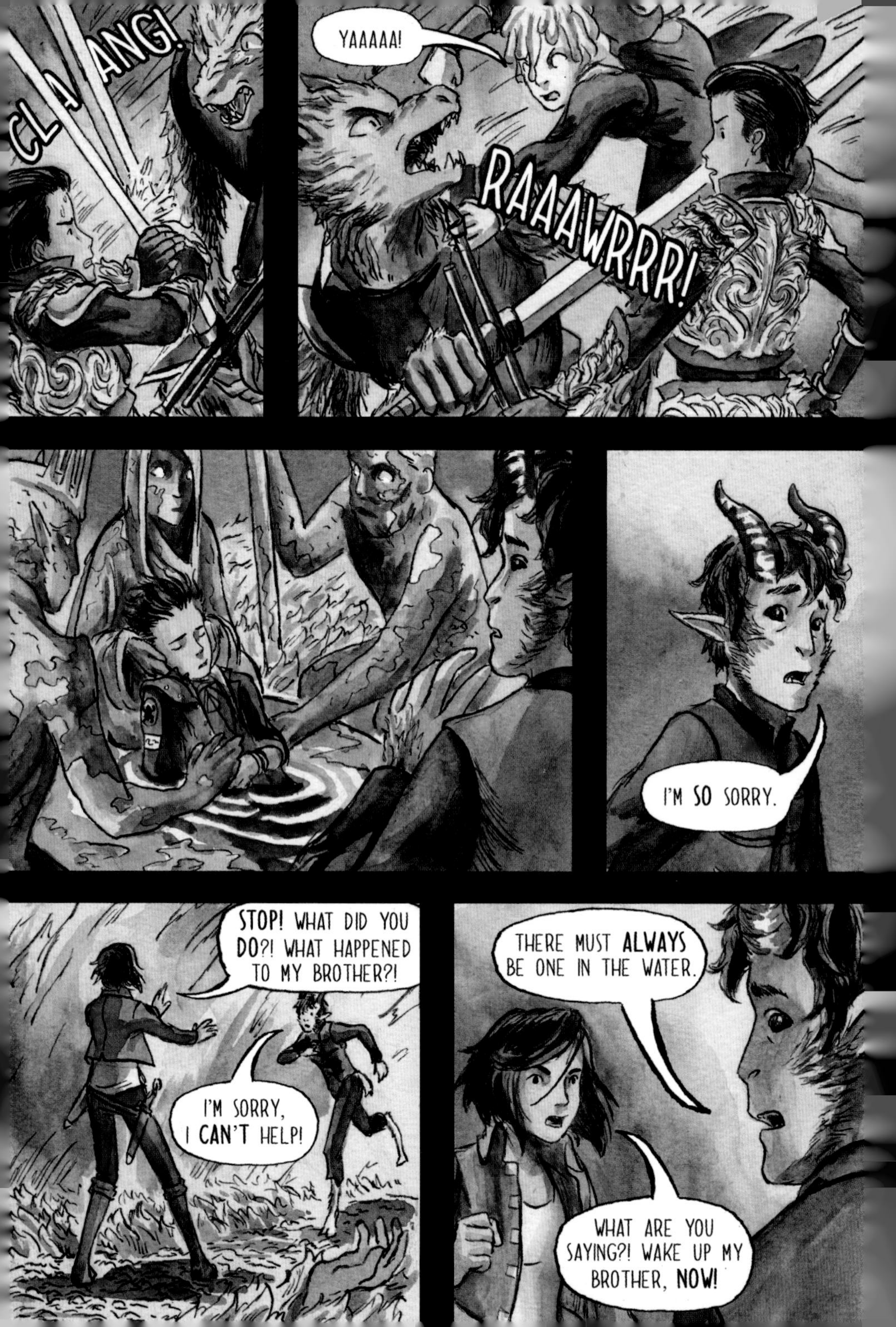
CLANG!
YAAAAA!
RAAAWRRRR!
I'M SO SORRY.
STOP! WHAT DID YOU DO?! WHAT HAPPENED TO MY BROTHER?!
I'M SORRY, I CAN'T HELP!
THERE MUST ALWAYS BE ONE IN THE WATER.
WHAT ARE YOU SAYING?! WAKE UP MY BROTHER, NOW!

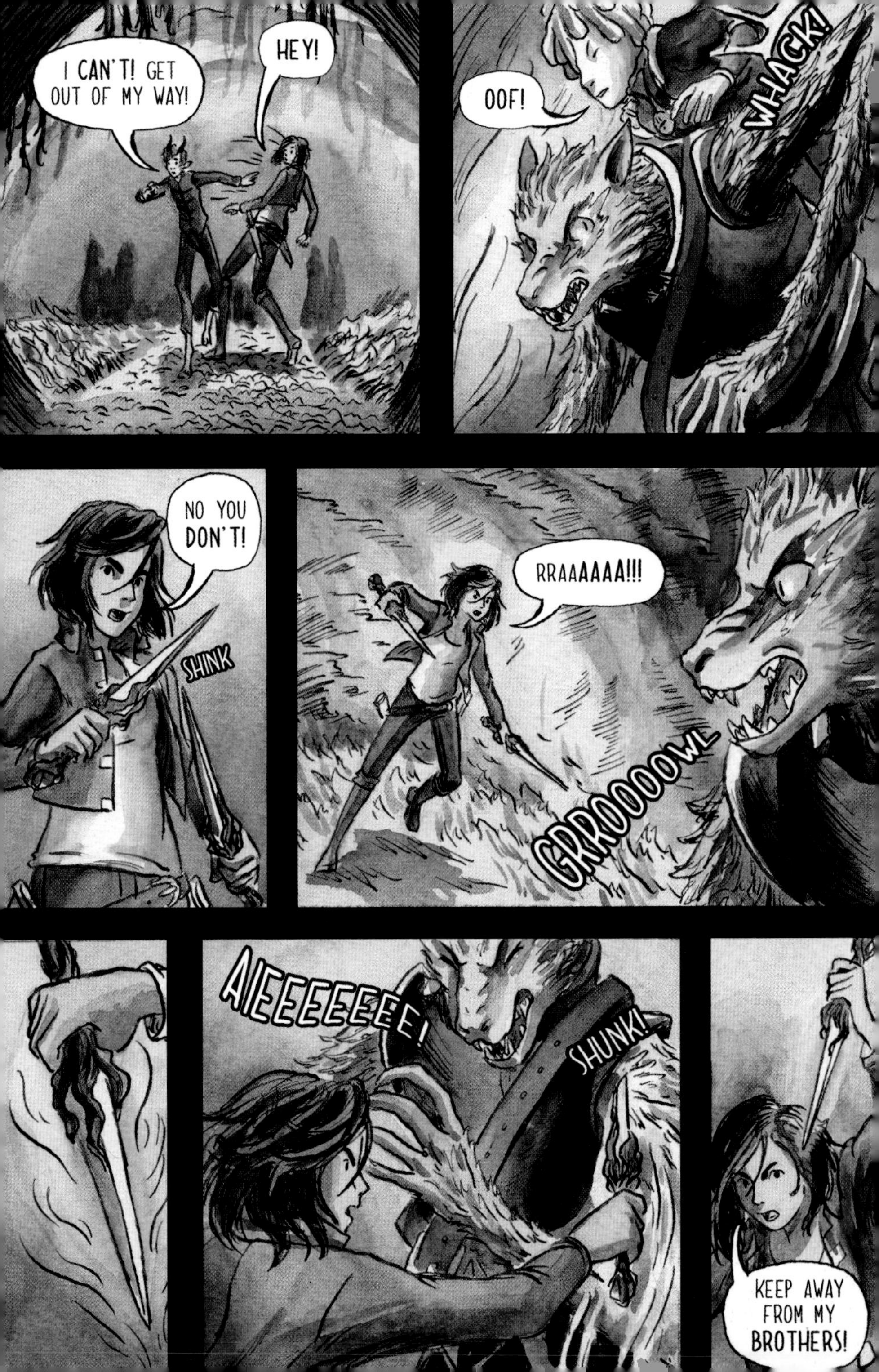
I CAN'T! GET OUT OF MY WAY!
HEY!
OOF!
WHACK!
NO YOU DON'T!
SHINK
RRAAAAAA!!!
GRROOOOOWL
AIEEEEEEEE!
SHUNK!
KEEP AWAY FROM MY BROTHERS!

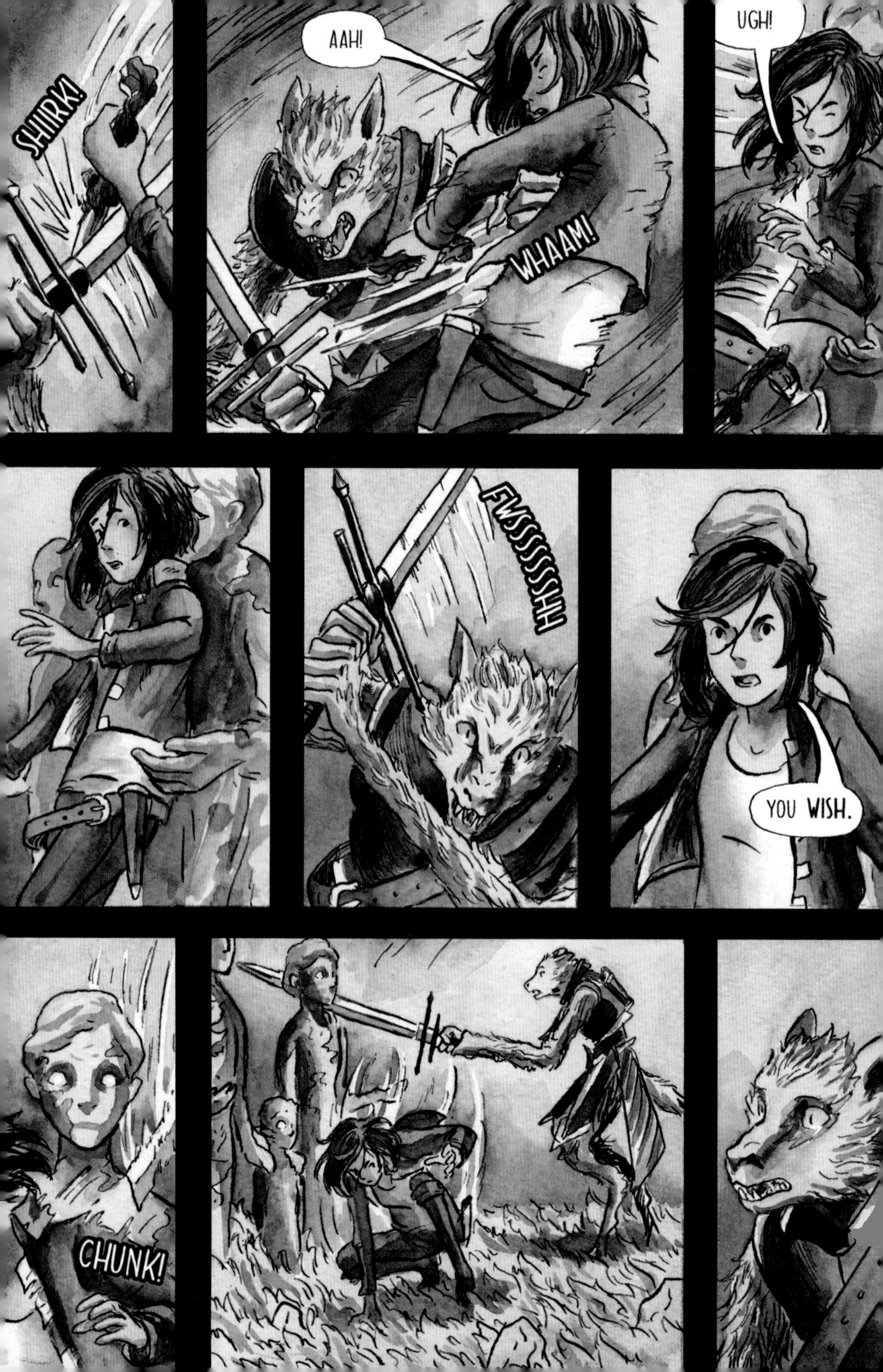
SHIRK!
AAH!
WHAAM!
UGH!
FWSSSSSSH!
YOU WISH.
CHUNK!

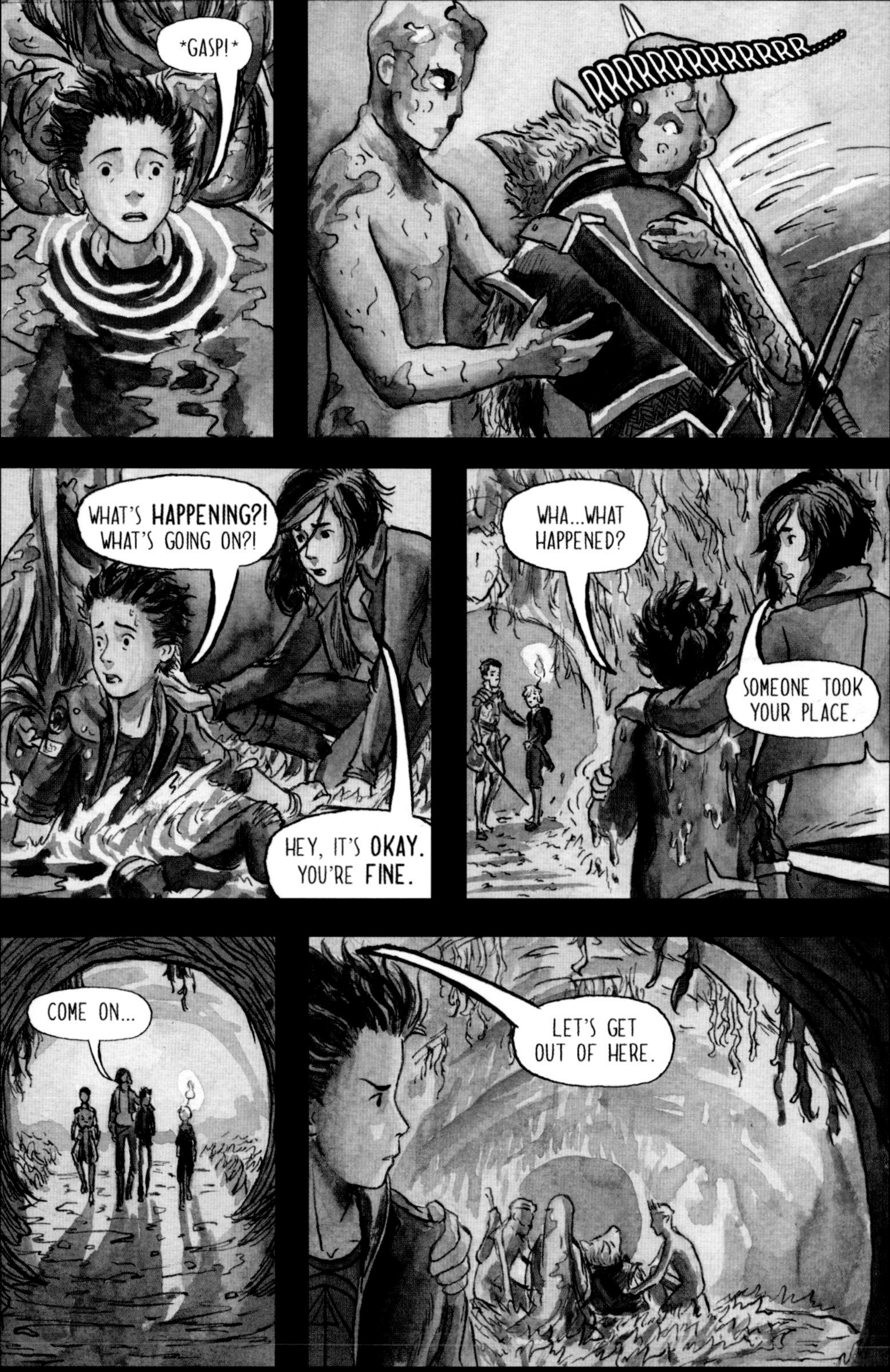
GASP!
RRRRRRRRRRRRR...
WHAT'S **HAPPENING?!** WHAT'S GOING ON?!
HEY, IT'S **OKAY.** YOU'RE **FINE.**
WHA...WHAT HAPPENED?
SOMEONE TOOK YOUR PLACE.
COME ON...
LET'S GET OUT OF HERE.

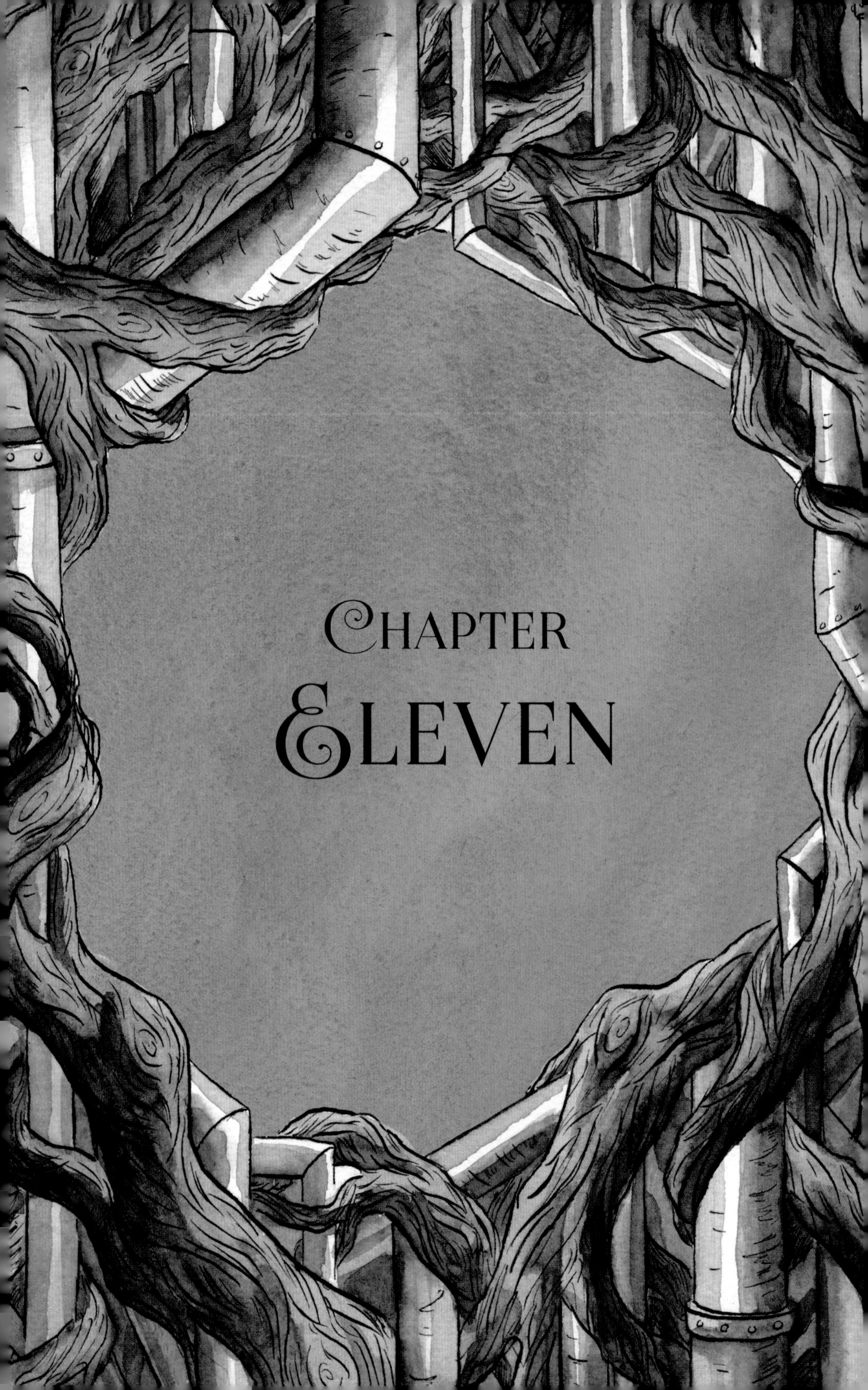

Chapter Eleven

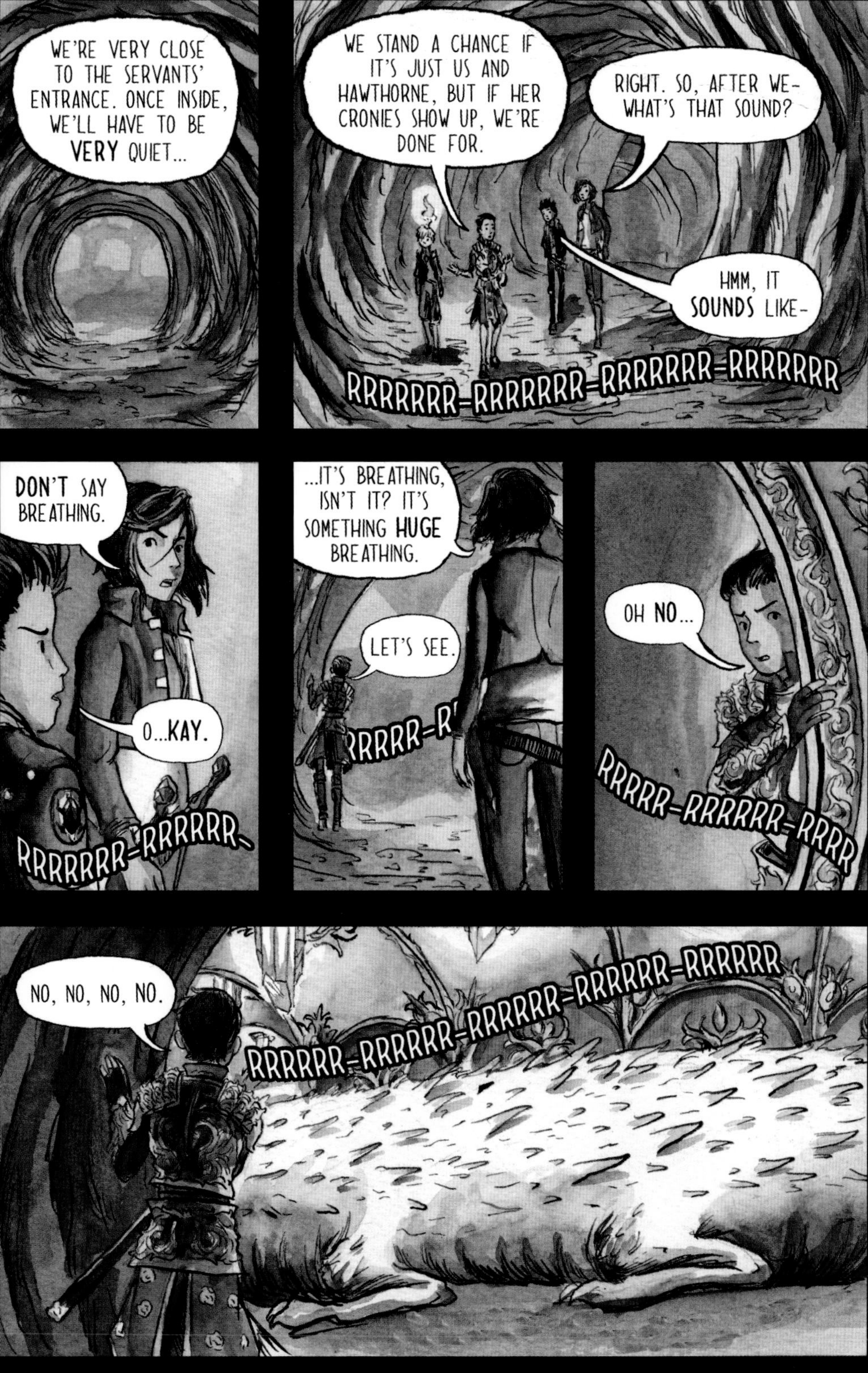
WE'RE VERY CLOSE TO THE SERVANTS' ENTRANCE. ONCE INSIDE, WE'LL HAVE TO BE VERY QUIET...
WE STAND A CHANCE IF IT'S JUST US AND HAWTHORNE, BUT IF HER CRONIES SHOW UP, WE'RE DONE FOR.
RIGHT. SO, AFTER WE- WHAT'S THAT SOUND?
HMM, IT SOUNDS LIKE-
RRRRRRR-RRRRRRR-RRRRRRR-RRRRRRR
DON'T SAY BREATHING.
O...KAY.
RRRRRRR-RRRRRR-
...IT'S BREATHING, ISN'T IT? IT'S SOMETHING HUGE BREATHING.
LET'S SEE.
RRRRRR-R
OH NO...
RRRRR-RRRRRR-RRRR
NO, NO, NO, NO.
RRRRRR-RRRRRR-RRRRRR-RRRRRR-RRRRRR

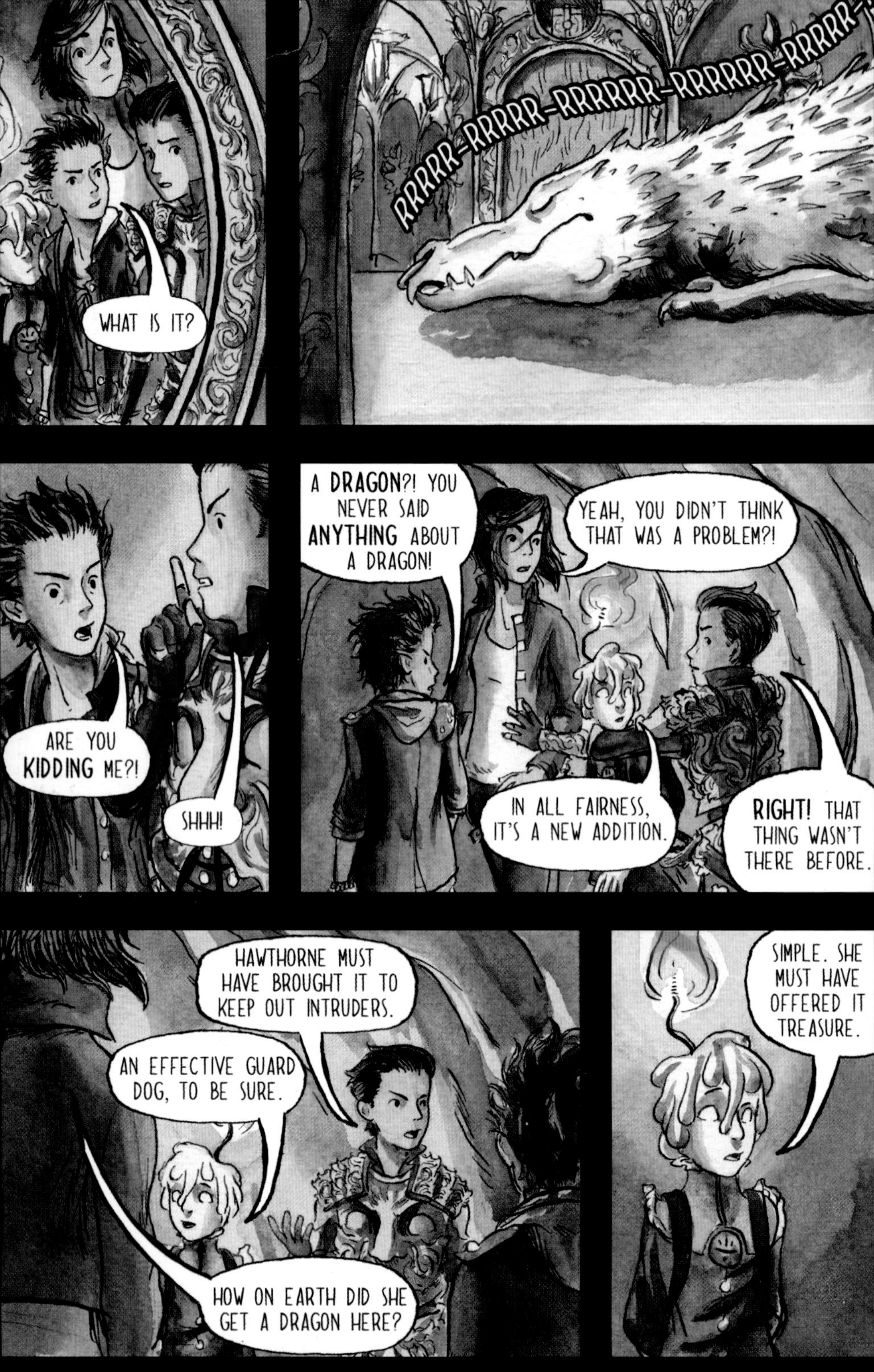
WHAT IS IT?
RRRRR-RRRRR-RRRRRR-RRRRRR-RRRRR-
ARE YOU KIDDING ME?!
SHHH!
A DRAGON?! YOU NEVER SAID ANYTHING ABOUT A DRAGON!
YEAH, YOU DIDN'T THINK THAT WAS A PROBLEM?!
IN ALL FAIRNESS, IT'S A NEW ADDITION.
RIGHT! THAT THING WASN'T THERE BEFORE.
HAWTHORNE MUST HAVE BROUGHT IT TO KEEP OUT INTRUDERS.
AN EFFECTIVE GUARD DOG, TO BE SURE.
HOW ON EARTH DID SHE GET A DRAGON HERE?
SIMPLE. SHE MUST HAVE OFFERED IT TREASURE.

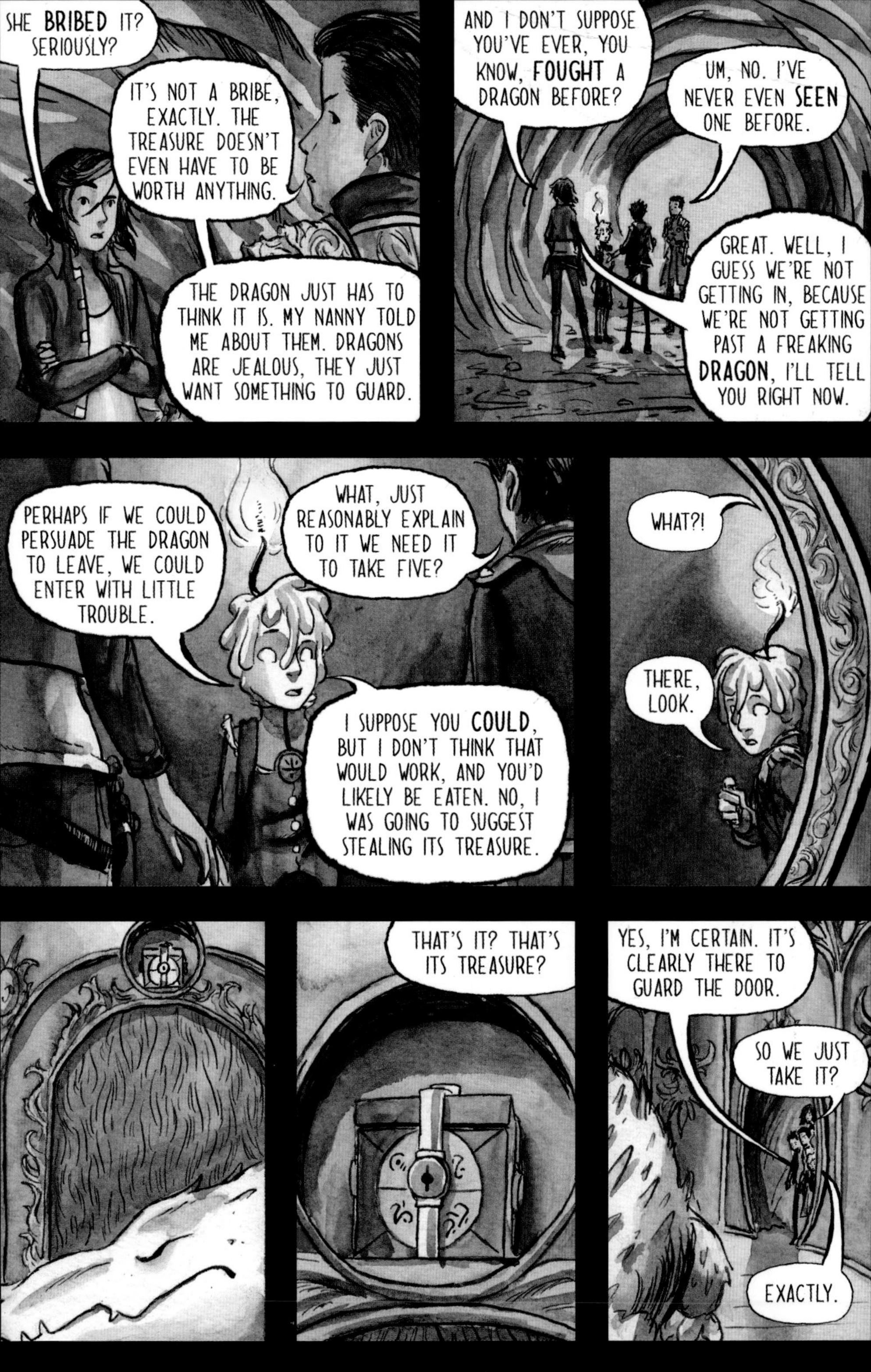
SHE BRIBED IT? SERIOUSLY?
IT'S NOT A BRIBE, EXACTLY. THE TREASURE DOESN'T EVEN HAVE TO BE WORTH ANYTHING.
THE DRAGON JUST HAS TO THINK IT IS. MY NANNY TOLD ME ABOUT THEM. DRAGONS ARE JEALOUS, THEY JUST WANT SOMETHING TO GUARD.
AND I DON'T SUPPOSE YOU'VE EVER, YOU KNOW, FOUGHT A DRAGON BEFORE?
UM, NO. I'VE NEVER EVEN SEEN ONE BEFORE.
GREAT. WELL, I GUESS WE'RE NOT GETTING IN, BECAUSE WE'RE NOT GETTING PAST A FREAKING DRAGON, I'LL TELL YOU RIGHT NOW.
PERHAPS IF WE COULD PERSUADE THE DRAGON TO LEAVE, WE COULD ENTER WITH LITTLE TROUBLE.
WHAT, JUST REASONABLY EXPLAIN TO IT WE NEED IT TO TAKE FIVE?
I SUPPOSE YOU COULD, BUT I DON'T THINK THAT WOULD WORK, AND YOU'D LIKELY BE EATEN. NO, I WAS GOING TO SUGGEST STEALING ITS TREASURE.
WHAT?!
THERE, LOOK.
THAT'S IT? THAT'S ITS TREASURE?
YES, I'M CERTAIN. IT'S CLEARLY THERE TO GUARD THE DOOR.
SO WE JUST TAKE IT?
EXACTLY.

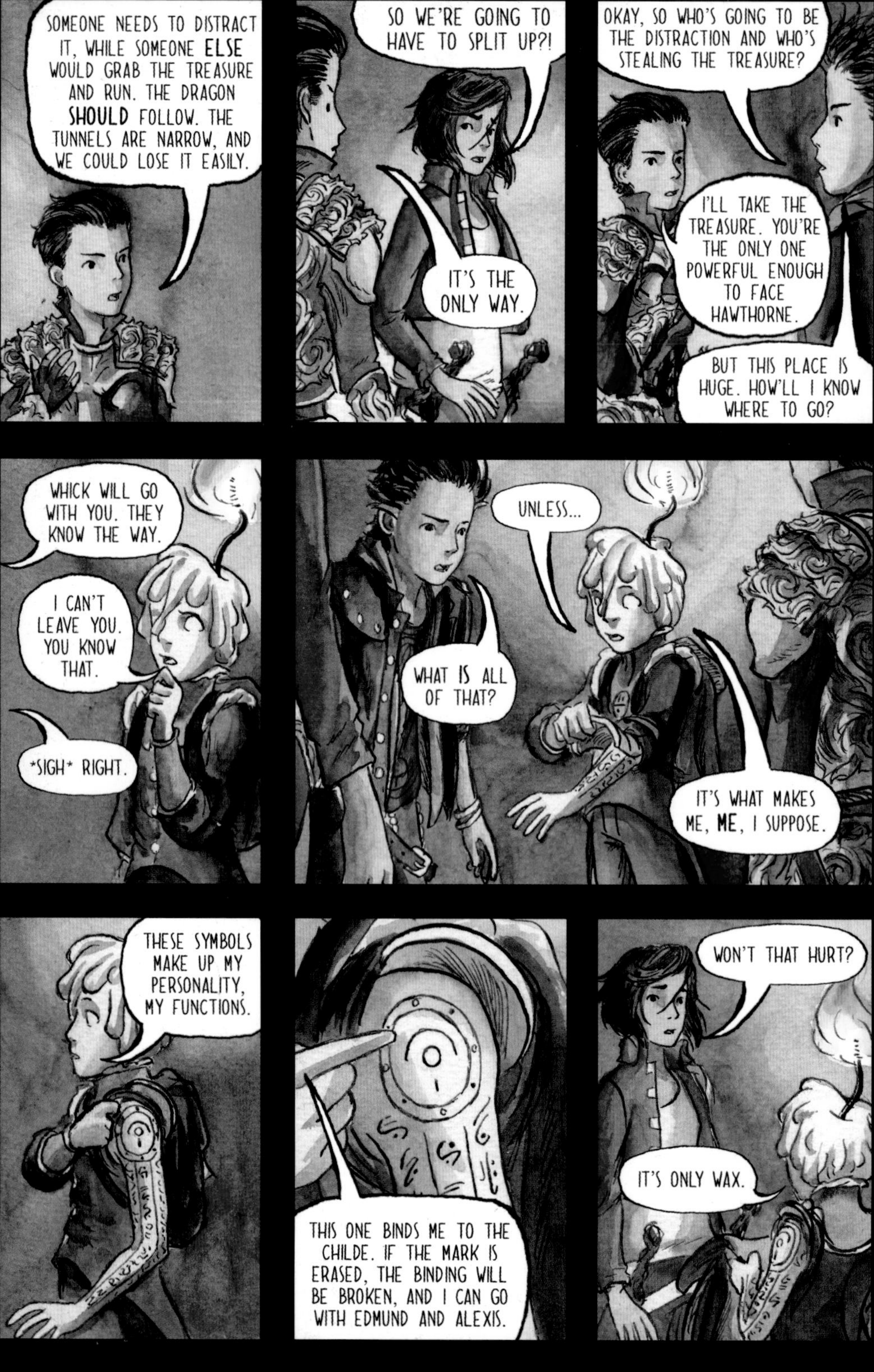

SOMEONE NEEDS TO DISTRACT IT, WHILE SOMEONE ELSE WOULD GRAB THE TREASURE AND RUN. THE DRAGON SHOULD FOLLOW. THE TUNNELS ARE NARROW, AND WE COULD LOSE IT EASILY.
SO WE'RE GOING TO HAVE TO SPLIT UP?!
IT'S THE ONLY WAY.
OKAY, SO WHO'S GOING TO BE THE DISTRACTION AND WHO'S STEALING THE TREASURE?
I'LL TAKE THE TREASURE. YOU'RE THE ONLY ONE POWERFUL ENOUGH TO FACE HAWTHORNE.
BUT THIS PLACE IS HUGE. HOW'LL I KNOW WHERE TO GO?
WHICK WILL GO WITH YOU. THEY KNOW THE WAY.
I CAN'T LEAVE YOU. YOU KNOW THAT.
SIGH RIGHT.
UNLESS...
WHAT IS ALL OF THAT?
IT'S WHAT MAKES ME, ME, I SUPPOSE.
THESE SYMBOLS MAKE UP MY PERSONALITY, MY FUNCTIONS.
THIS ONE BINDS ME TO THE CHILDE. IF THE MARK IS ERASED, THE BINDING WILL BE BROKEN, AND I CAN GO WITH EDMUND AND ALEXIS.
WON'T THAT HURT?
IT'S ONLY WAX.

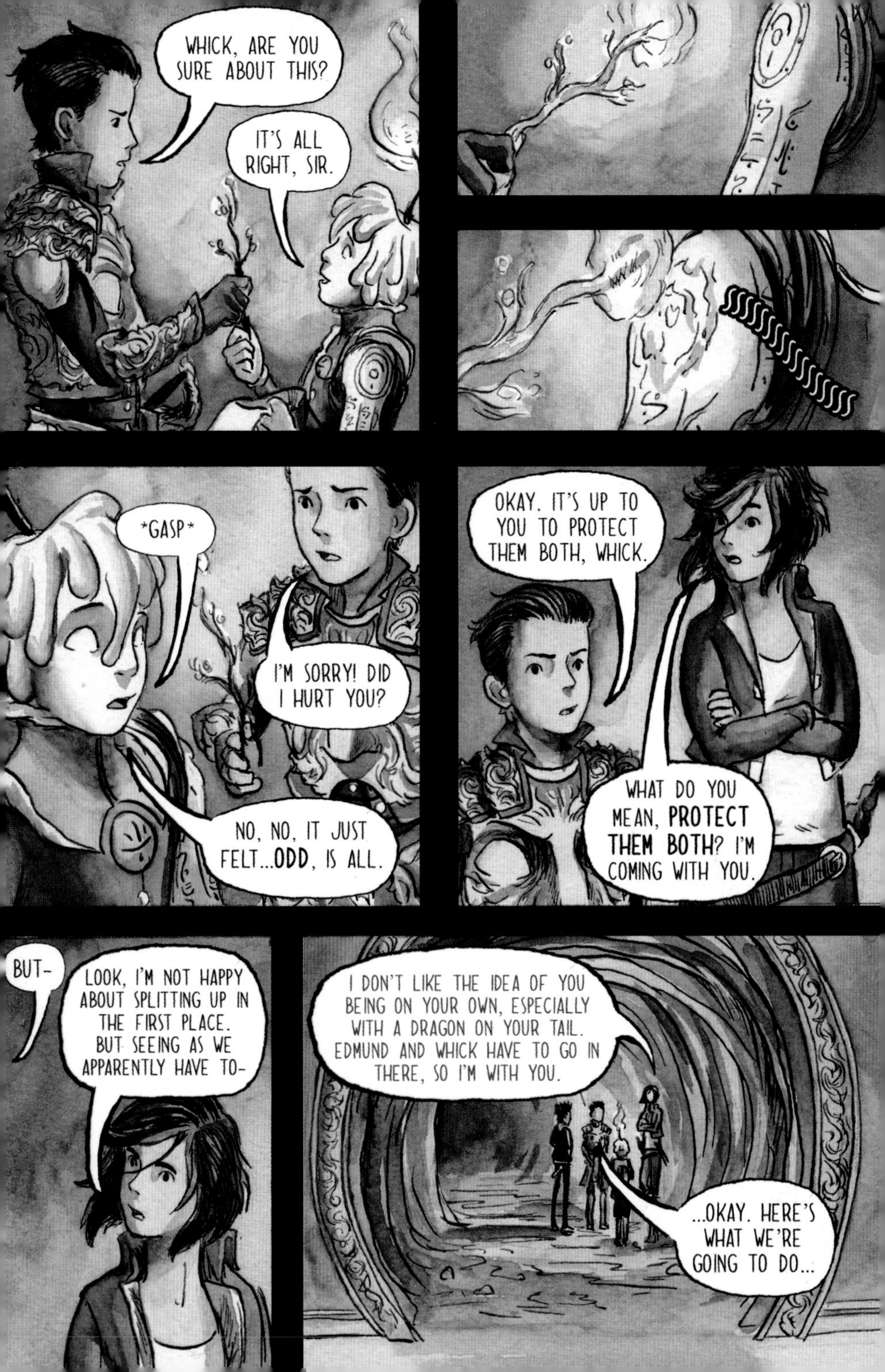
WHICK, ARE YOU SURE ABOUT THIS?
IT'S ALL RIGHT, SIR.
SSSSSSSSSSS
GASP
I'M SORRY! DID I HURT YOU?
NO, NO, IT JUST FELT...ODD, IS ALL.
OKAY. IT'S UP TO YOU TO PROTECT THEM BOTH, WHICK.
WHAT DO YOU MEAN, PROTECT THEM BOTH? I'M COMING WITH YOU.
BUT-
LOOK, I'M NOT HAPPY ABOUT SPLITTING UP IN THE FIRST PLACE. BUT SEEING AS WE APPARENTLY HAVE TO-
I DON'T LIKE THE IDEA OF YOU BEING ON YOUR OWN, ESPECIALLY WITH A DRAGON ON YOUR TAIL. EDMUND AND WHICK HAVE TO GO IN THERE, SO I'M WITH YOU.
...OKAY. HERE'S WHAT WE'RE GOING TO DO...

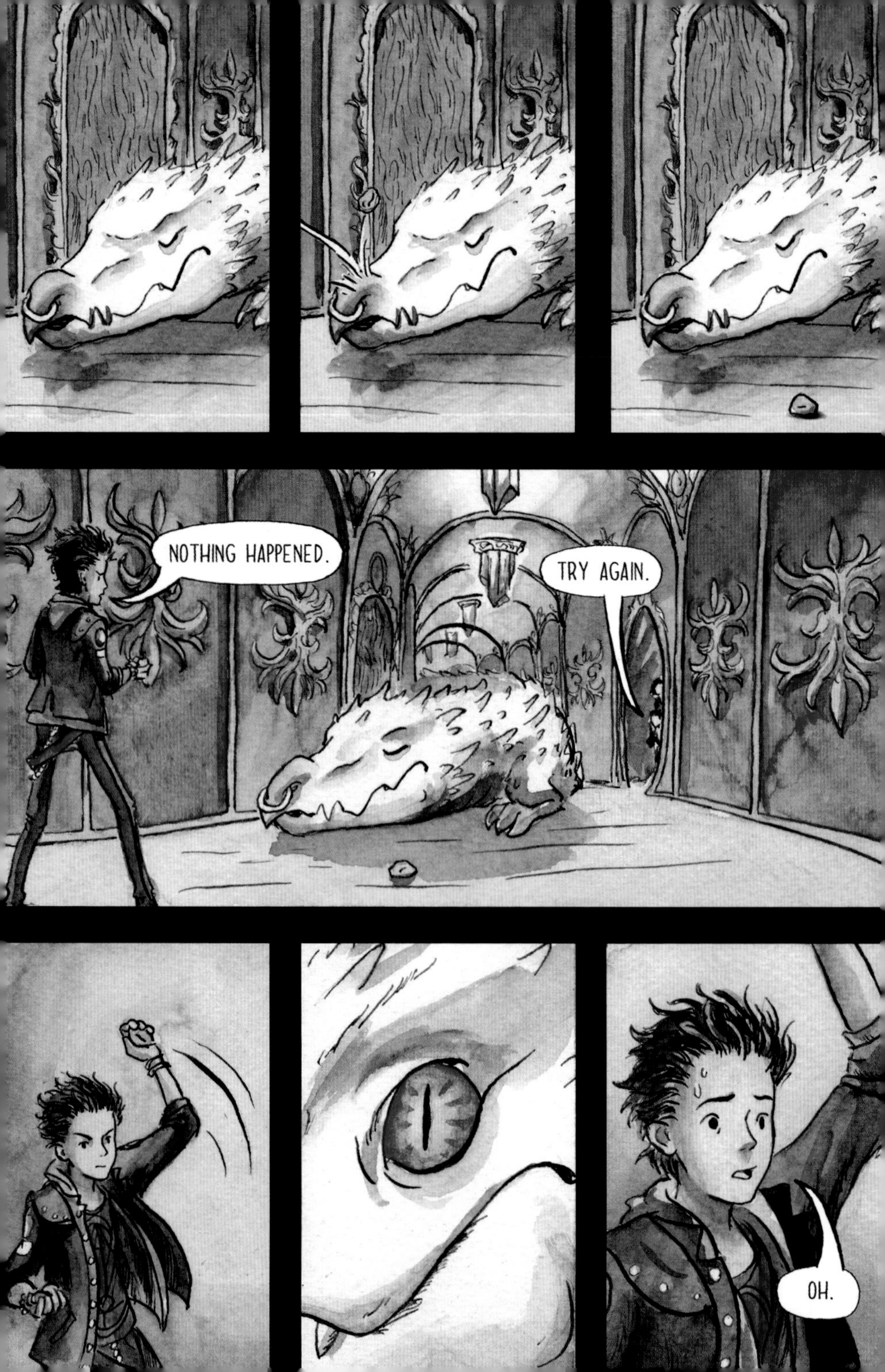
NOTHING HAPPENED.
TRY AGAIN.
OH.

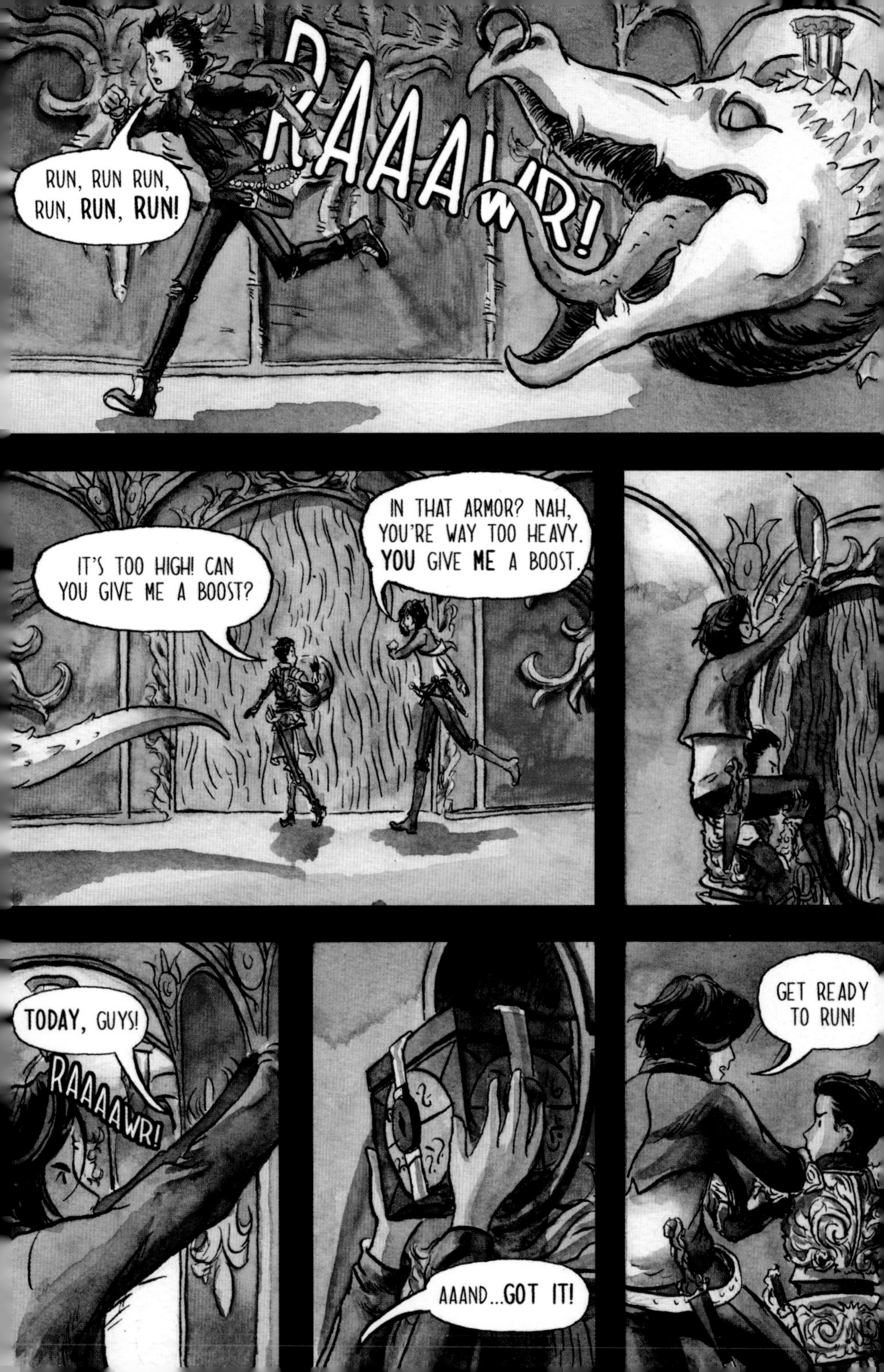
RUN, RUN RUN,
RUN, **RUN**, **RUN!**
RAAAAWR!
IT'S TOO HIGH! CAN YOU GIVE ME A BOOST?
IN THAT ARMOR? NAH, YOU'RE WAY TOO HEAVY. **YOU** GIVE **ME** A BOOST.
TODAY, GUYS!
RAAAAWR!
AAAND...**GOT IT!**
GET READY TO RUN!

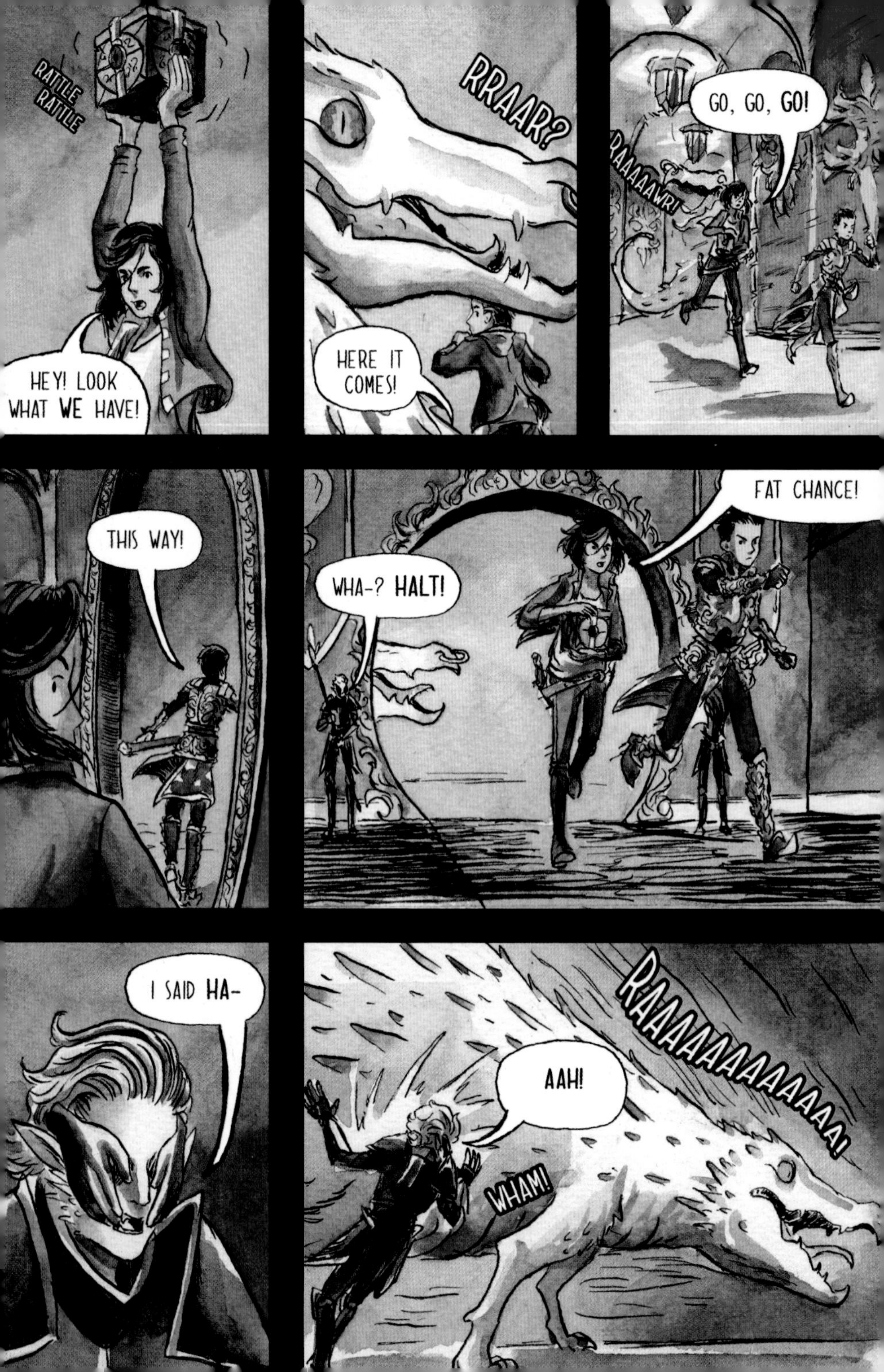
RATTLE RATTLE
HEY! LOOK WHAT WE HAVE!
RRAAR?
HERE IT COMES!
GO, GO, GO!
RAAAAAAWR!
THIS WAY!
WHA-? HALT!
FAT CHANCE!
I SAID HA-
RAAAAAAAAAAAAA!
AAH!
WHAM!

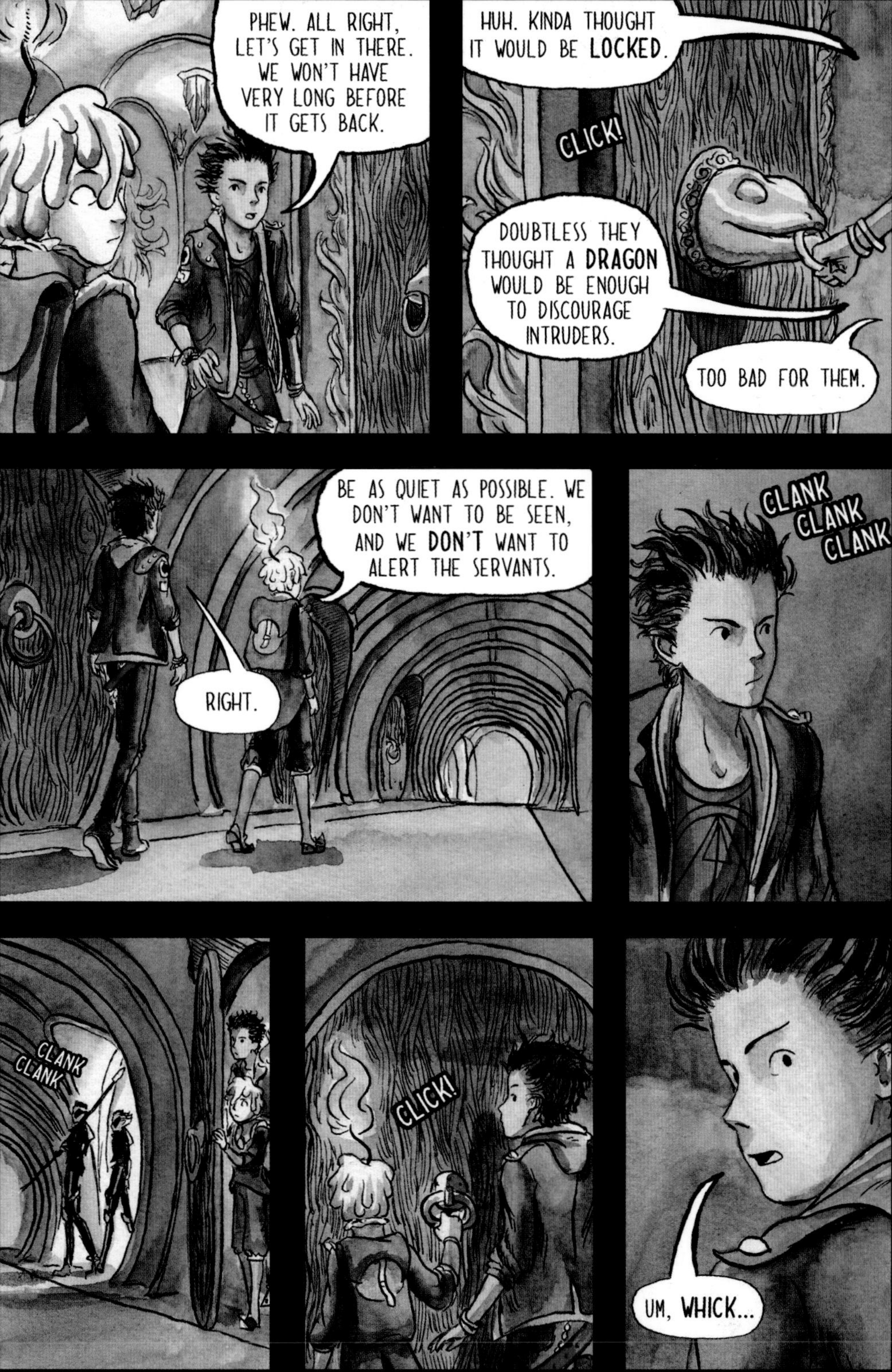
PHEW. ALL RIGHT, LET'S GET IN THERE. WE WON'T HAVE VERY LONG BEFORE IT GETS BACK.
HUH. KINDA THOUGHT IT WOULD BE **LOCKED**.
CLICK!
DOUBTLESS THEY THOUGHT A **DRAGON** WOULD BE ENOUGH TO DISCOURAGE INTRUDERS.
TOO BAD FOR THEM.
BE AS QUIET AS POSSIBLE. WE DON'T WANT TO BE SEEN, AND WE **DON'T** WANT TO ALERT THE SERVANTS.
RIGHT.
CLANK CLANK CLANK
CLANK CLANK
CLICK!
UM, **WHICK**...

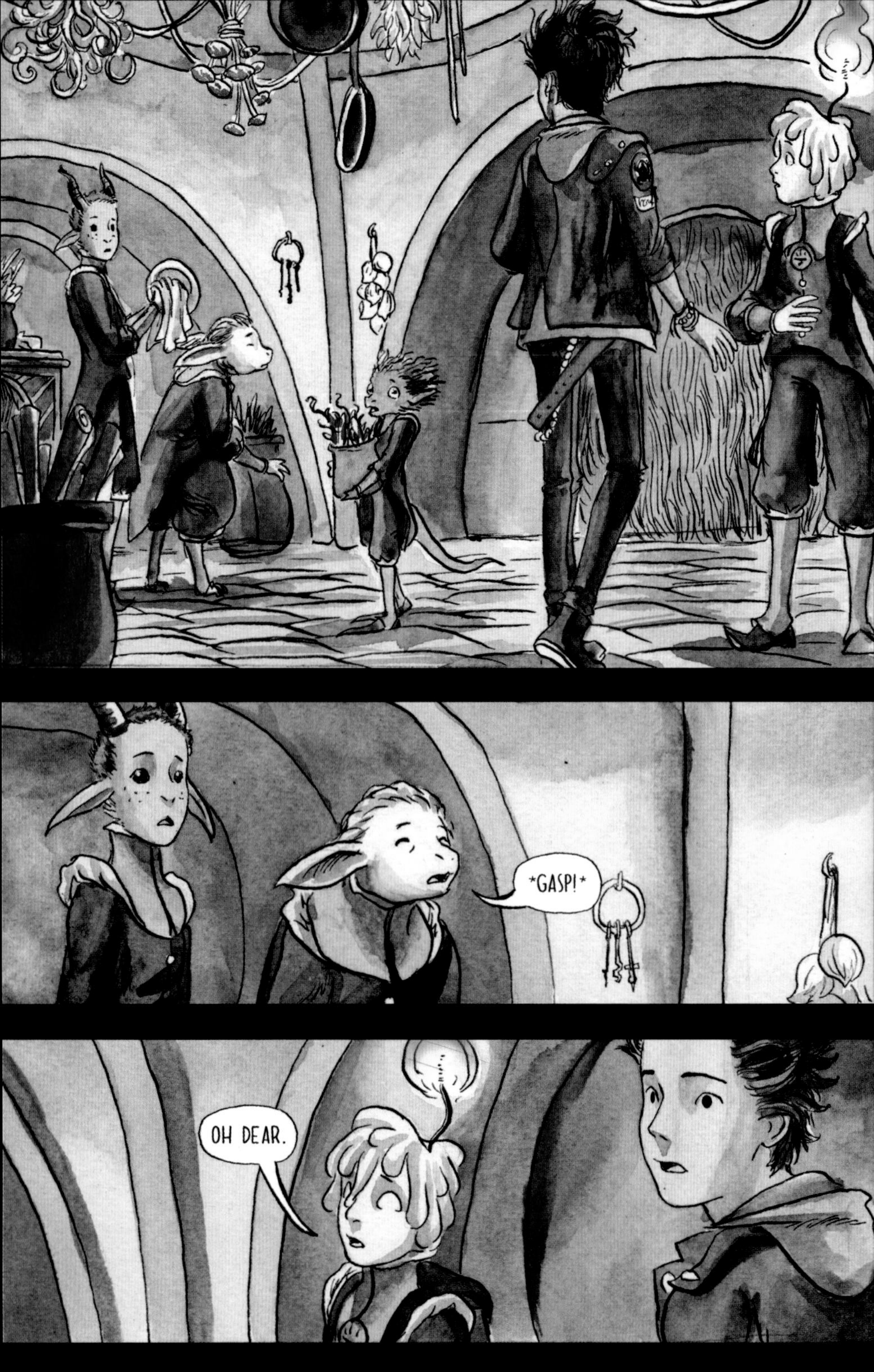
GASP!
OH DEAR.

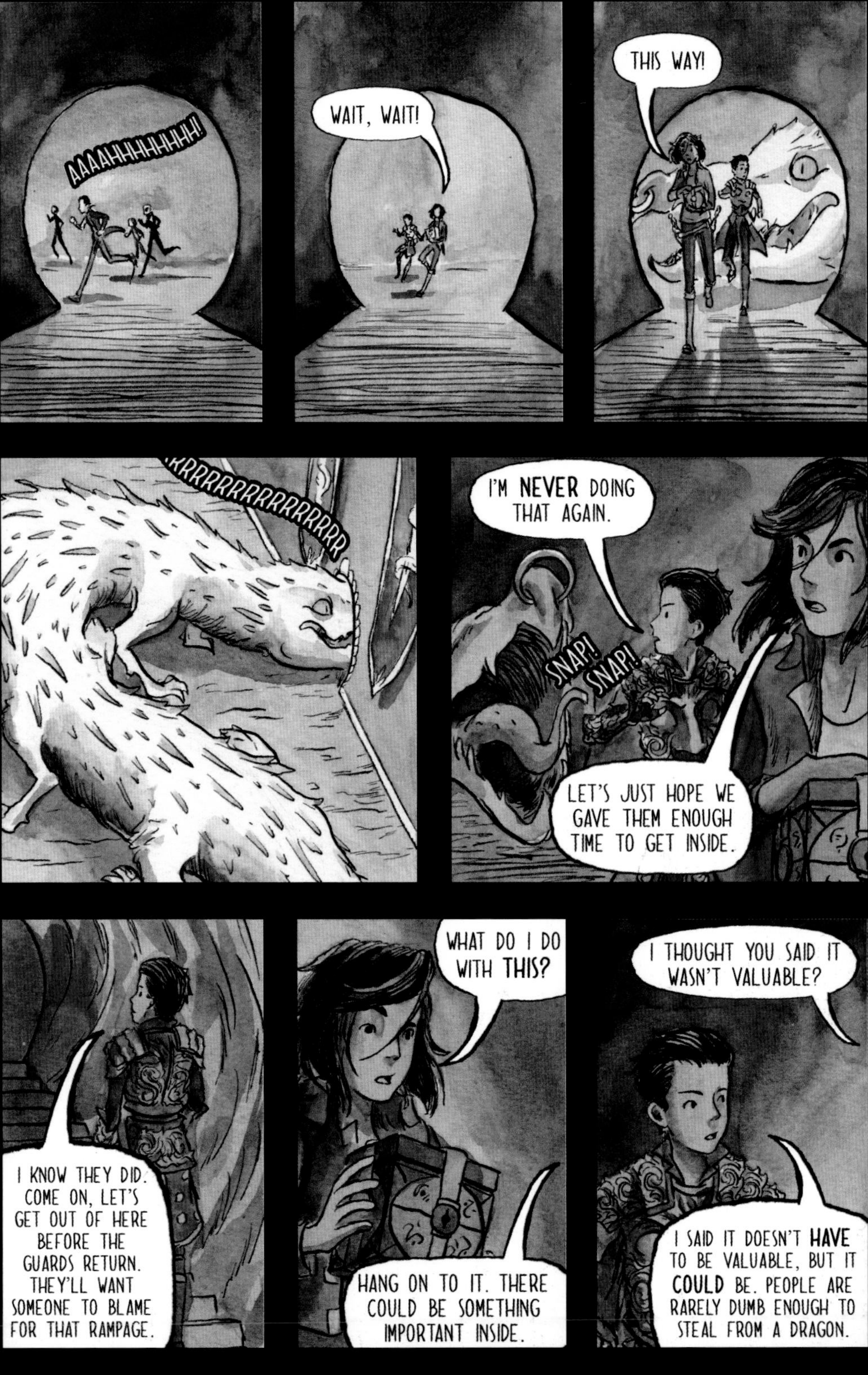
AAAAHHHHHHHH!
WAIT, WAIT!
THIS WAY!
RRRRRRRRRRRRRRRRRR
I'M **NEVER** DOING THAT AGAIN.
SNAP! SNAP!
LET'S JUST HOPE WE GAVE THEM ENOUGH TIME TO GET INSIDE.
I KNOW THEY DID. COME ON, LET'S GET OUT OF HERE BEFORE THE GUARDS RETURN. THEY'LL WANT SOMEONE TO BLAME FOR THAT RAMPAGE.
WHAT DO I DO WITH **THIS**?
HANG ON TO IT. THERE COULD BE SOMETHING IMPORTANT INSIDE.
I THOUGHT YOU SAID IT WASN'T VALUABLE?
I SAID IT DOESN'T **HAVE** TO BE VALUABLE, BUT IT **COULD** BE. PEOPLE ARE RARELY DUMB ENOUGH TO STEAL FROM A DRAGON.

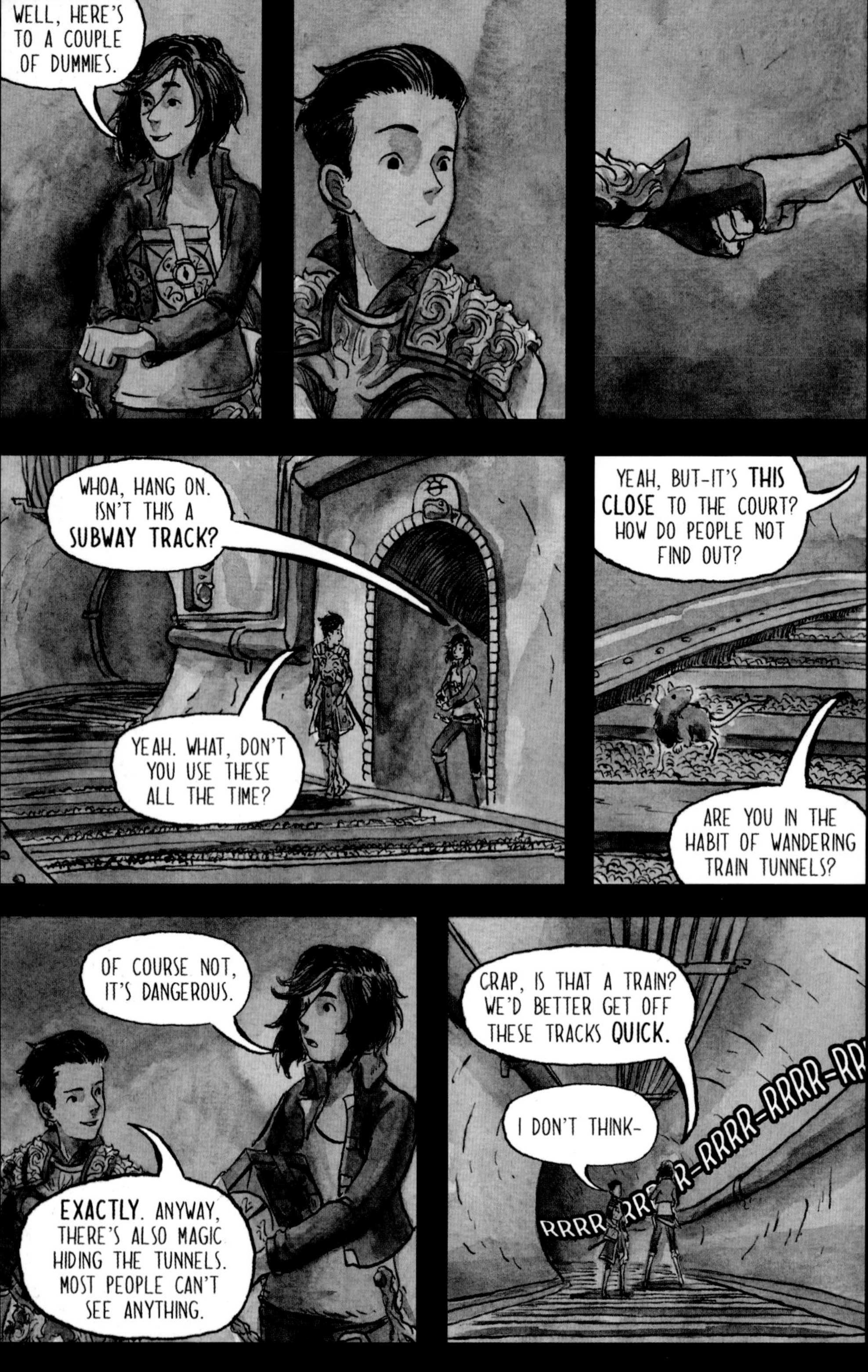
WELL, HERE'S TO A COUPLE OF DUMMIES.
WHOA, HANG ON. ISN'T THIS A **SUBWAY TRACK?**
YEAH. WHAT, DON'T YOU USE THESE ALL THE TIME?
YEAH, BUT–IT'S **THIS CLOSE** TO THE COURT? HOW DO PEOPLE NOT FIND OUT?
ARE YOU IN THE HABIT OF WANDERING TRAIN TUNNELS?
OF COURSE NOT, IT'S DANGEROUS.
EXACTLY. ANYWAY, THERE'S ALSO MAGIC HIDING THE TUNNELS. MOST PEOPLE CAN'T SEE ANYTHING.
CRAP, IS THAT A TRAIN? WE'D BETTER GET OFF THESE TRACKS **QUICK.**
I DON'T THINK-
RRRR RRRR-RRRR-RRRR-RR

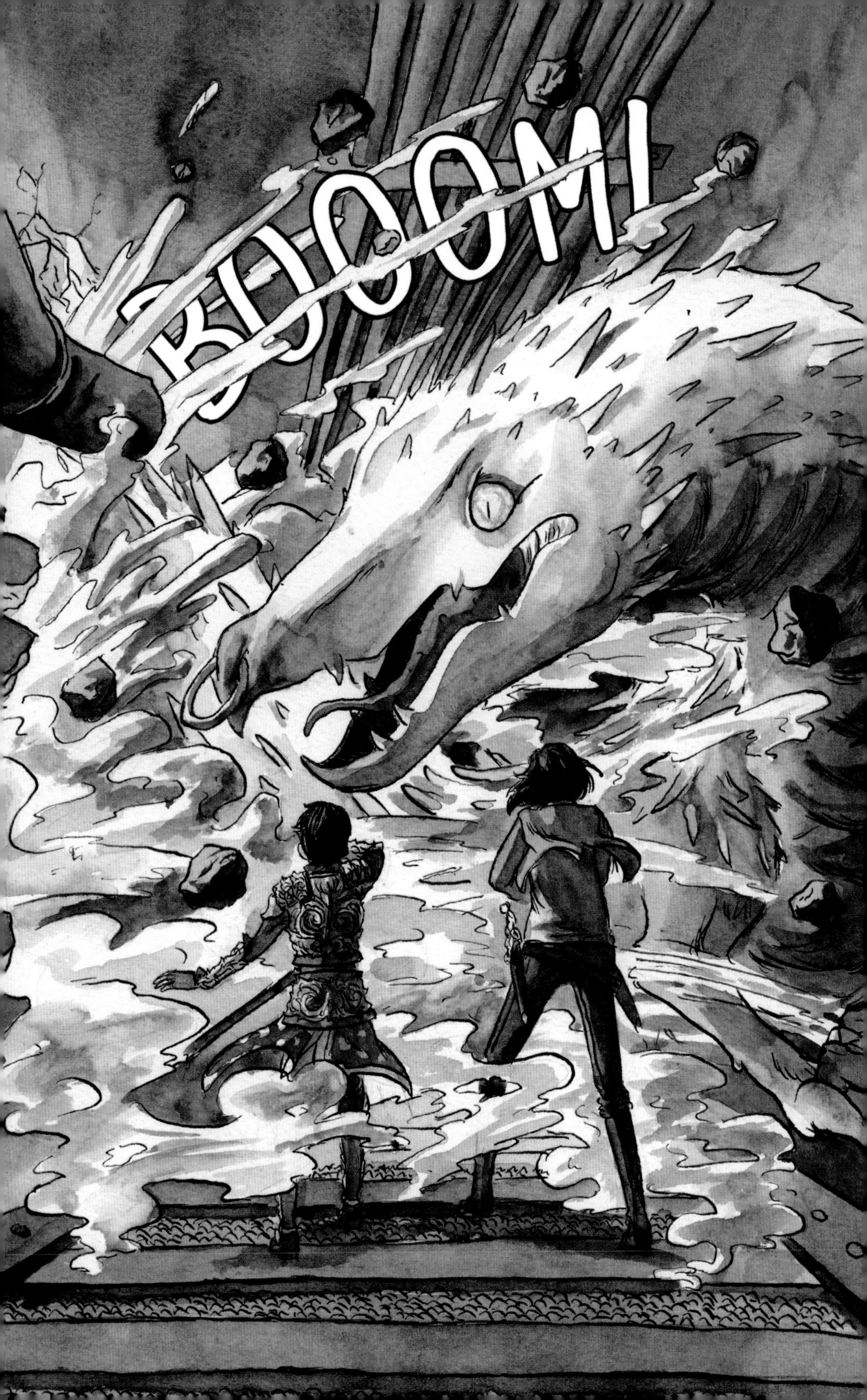
BOOOM!

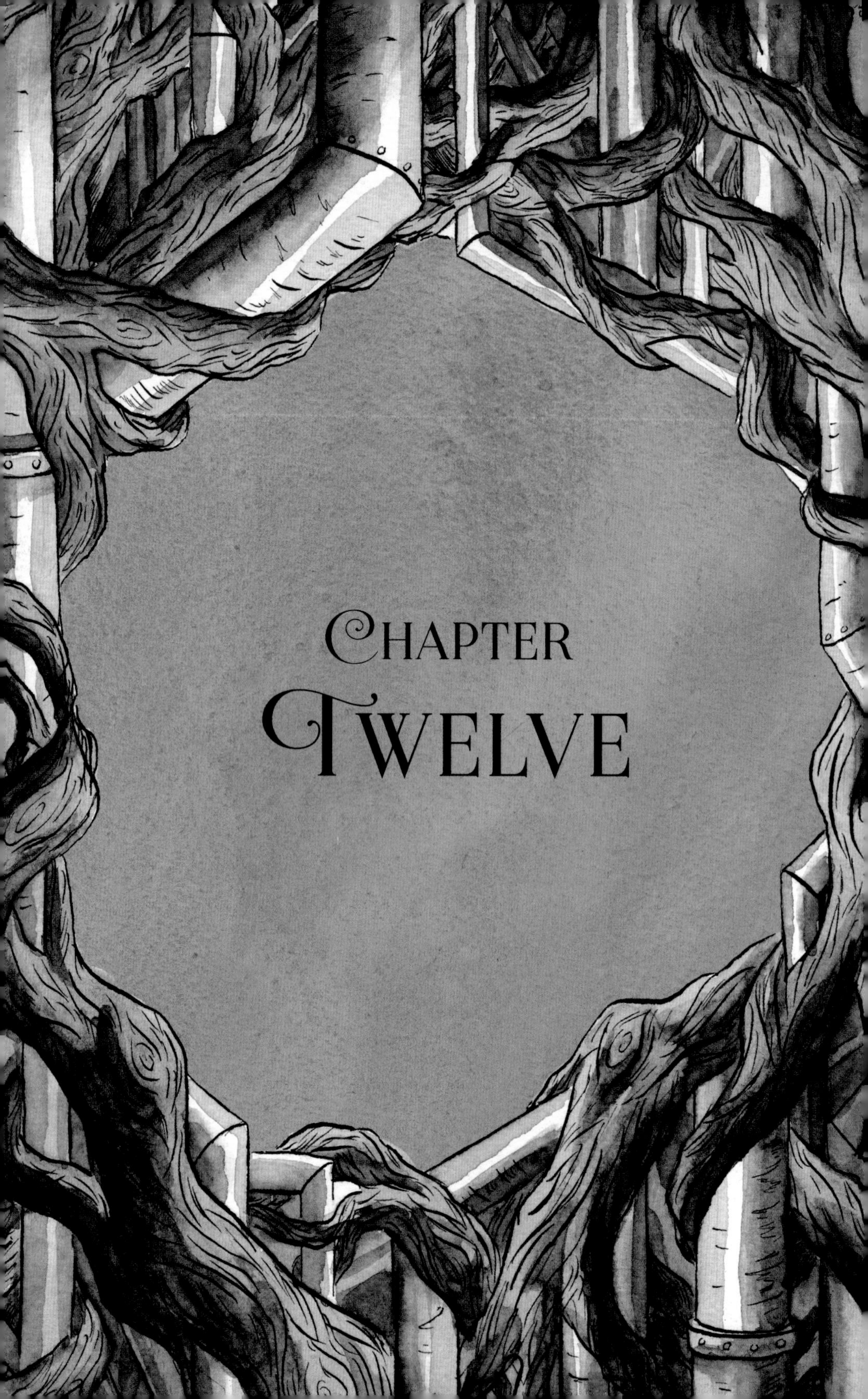

CHAPTER TWELVE

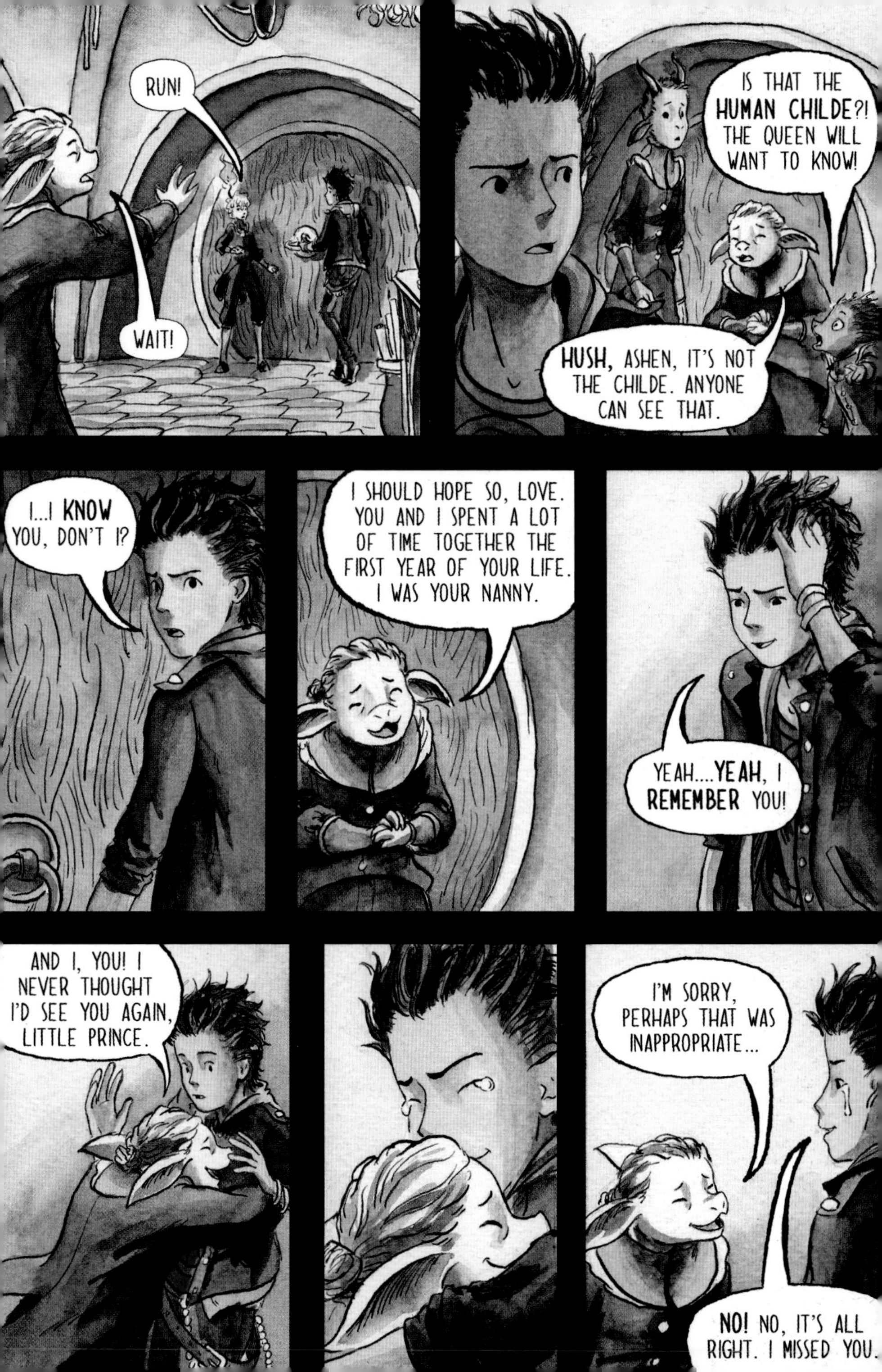
RUN!
WAIT!
IS THAT THE HUMAN CHILDE?! THE QUEEN WILL WANT TO KNOW!
HUSH, ASHEN, IT'S NOT THE CHILDE. ANYONE CAN SEE THAT.
I...I KNOW YOU, DON'T I?
I SHOULD HOPE SO, LOVE. YOU AND I SPENT A LOT OF TIME TOGETHER THE FIRST YEAR OF YOUR LIFE. I WAS YOUR NANNY.
YEAH....YEAH, I REMEMBER YOU!
AND I, YOU! I NEVER THOUGHT I'D SEE YOU AGAIN, LITTLE PRINCE.
I'M SORRY, PERHAPS THAT WAS INAPPROPRIATE...
NO! NO, IT'S ALL RIGHT. I MISSED YOU.

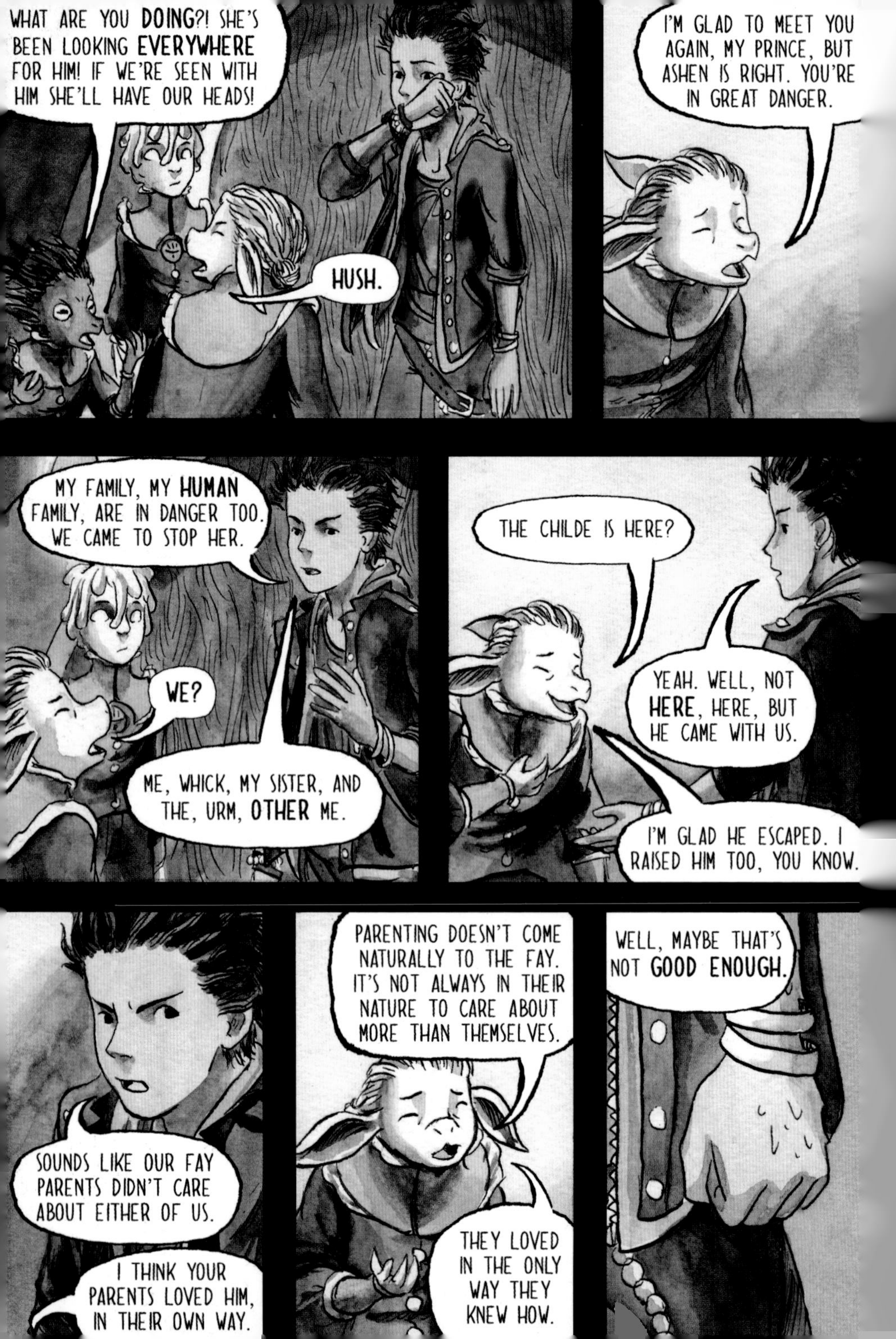
WHAT ARE YOU DOING?! SHE'S BEEN LOOKING EVERYWHERE FOR HIM! IF WE'RE SEEN WITH HIM SHE'LL HAVE OUR HEADS!
HUSH.
I'M GLAD TO MEET YOU AGAIN, MY PRINCE, BUT ASHEN IS RIGHT. YOU'RE IN GREAT DANGER.
MY FAMILY, MY HUMAN FAMILY, ARE IN DANGER TOO. WE CAME TO STOP HER.
WE?
ME, WHICK, MY SISTER, AND THE, URM, OTHER ME.
THE CHILDE IS HERE?
YEAH. WELL, NOT HERE, HERE, BUT HE CAME WITH US.
I'M GLAD HE ESCAPED. I RAISED HIM TOO, YOU KNOW.
SOUNDS LIKE OUR FAY PARENTS DIDN'T CARE ABOUT EITHER OF US.
I THINK YOUR PARENTS LOVED HIM, IN THEIR OWN WAY.
PARENTING DOESN'T COME NATURALLY TO THE FAY. IT'S NOT ALWAYS IN THEIR NATURE TO CARE ABOUT MORE THAN THEMSELVES.
THEY LOVED IN THE ONLY WAY THEY KNEW HOW.
WELL, MAYBE THAT'S NOT GOOD ENOUGH.

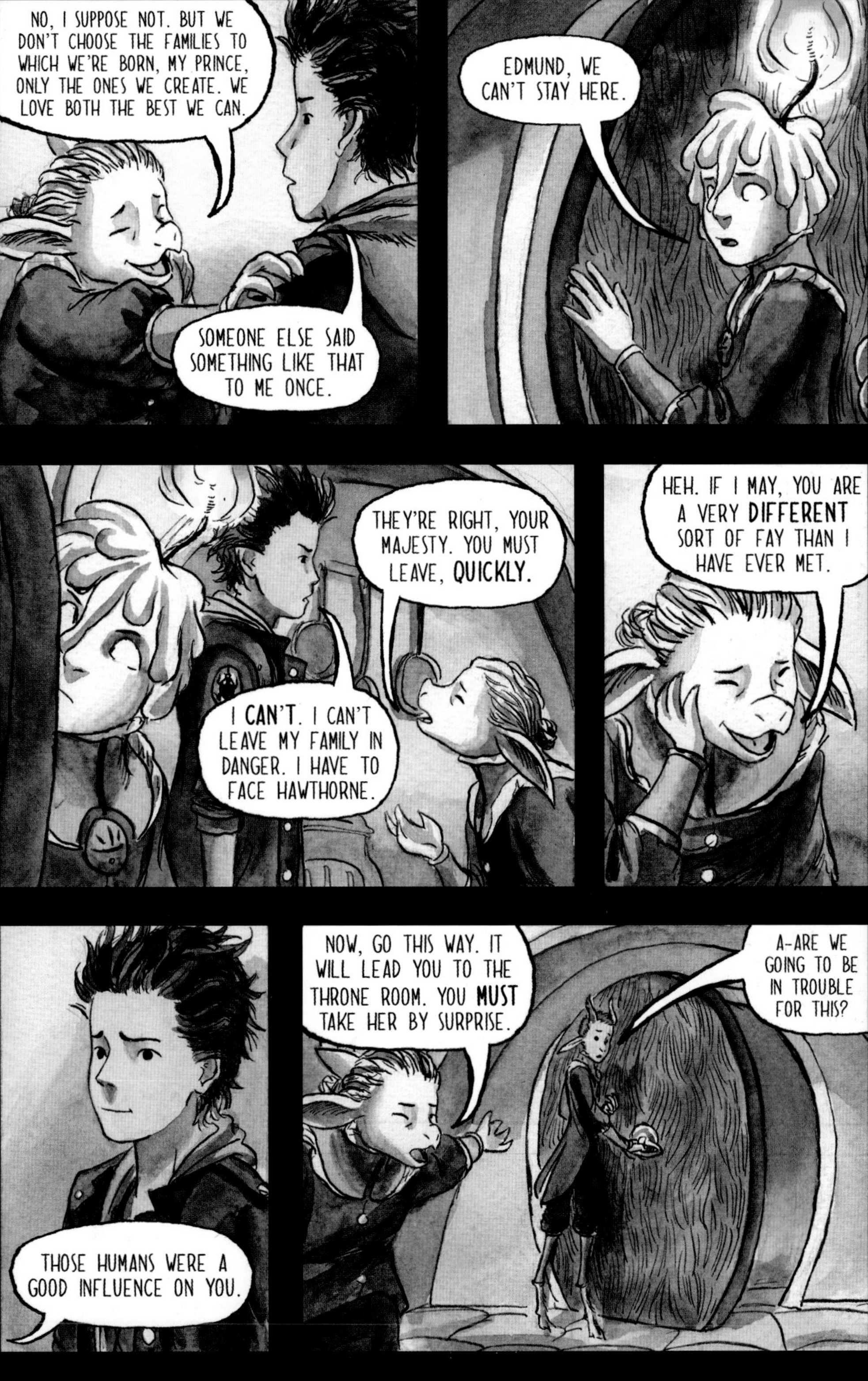
NO, I SUPPOSE NOT. BUT WE DON'T CHOOSE THE FAMILIES TO WHICH WE'RE BORN, MY PRINCE, ONLY THE ONES WE CREATE. WE LOVE BOTH THE BEST WE CAN.
SOMEONE ELSE SAID SOMETHING LIKE THAT TO ME ONCE.
EDMUND, WE CAN'T STAY HERE.
THEY'RE RIGHT, YOUR MAJESTY. YOU MUST LEAVE, **QUICKLY.**
I **CAN'T**. I CAN'T LEAVE MY FAMILY IN DANGER. I HAVE TO FACE HAWTHORNE.
HEH. IF I MAY, YOU ARE A VERY **DIFFERENT** SORT OF FAY THAN I HAVE EVER MET.
THOSE HUMANS WERE A GOOD INFLUENCE ON YOU.
NOW, GO THIS WAY. IT WILL LEAD YOU TO THE THRONE ROOM. YOU **MUST** TAKE HER BY SURPRISE.
A-ARE WE GOING TO BE IN TROUBLE FOR THIS?

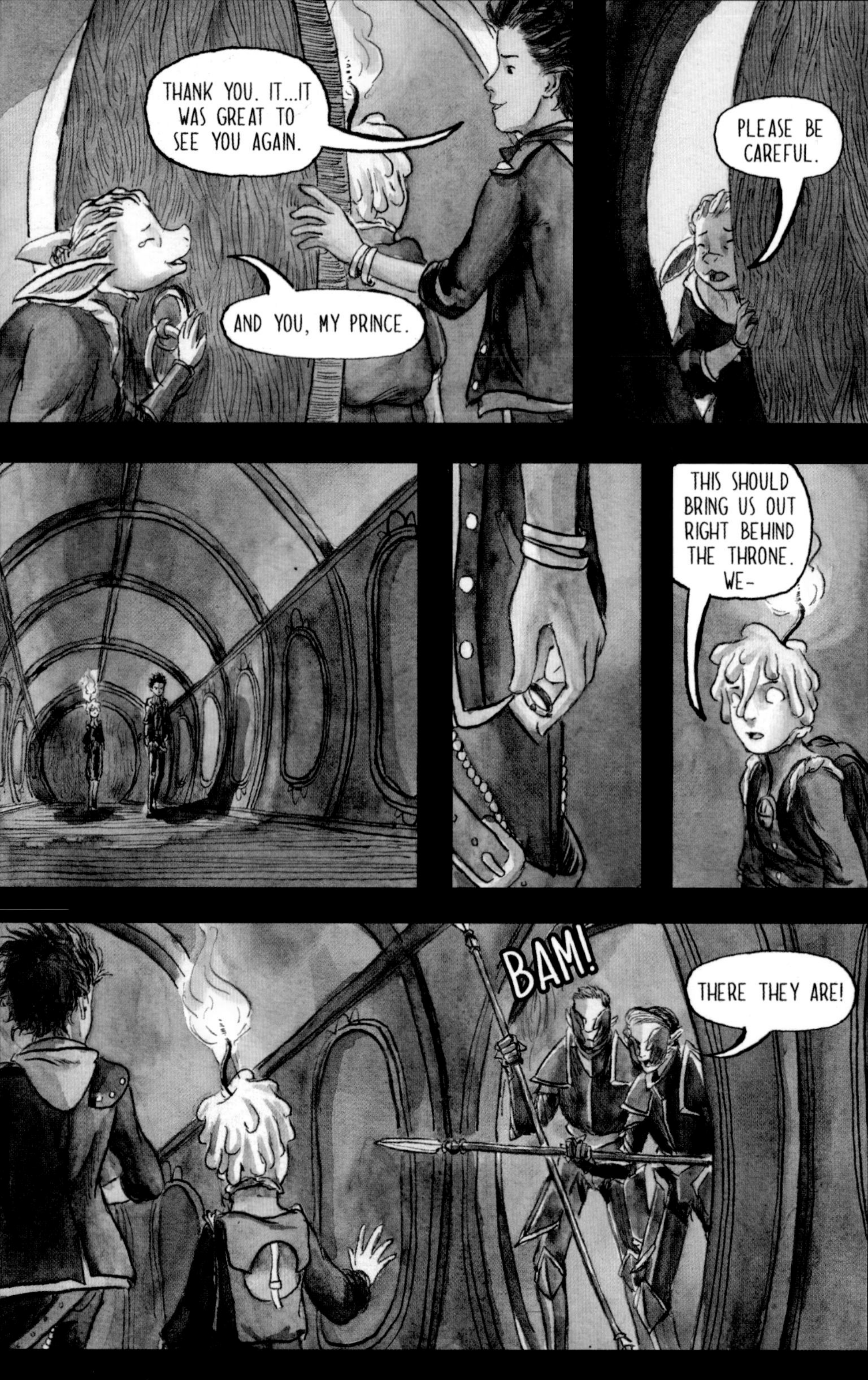
THANK YOU. IT...IT WAS GREAT TO SEE YOU AGAIN.
AND YOU, MY PRINCE.
PLEASE BE CAREFUL.
THIS SHOULD BRING US OUT RIGHT BEHIND THE THRONE. WE-
BAM!
THERE THEY ARE!

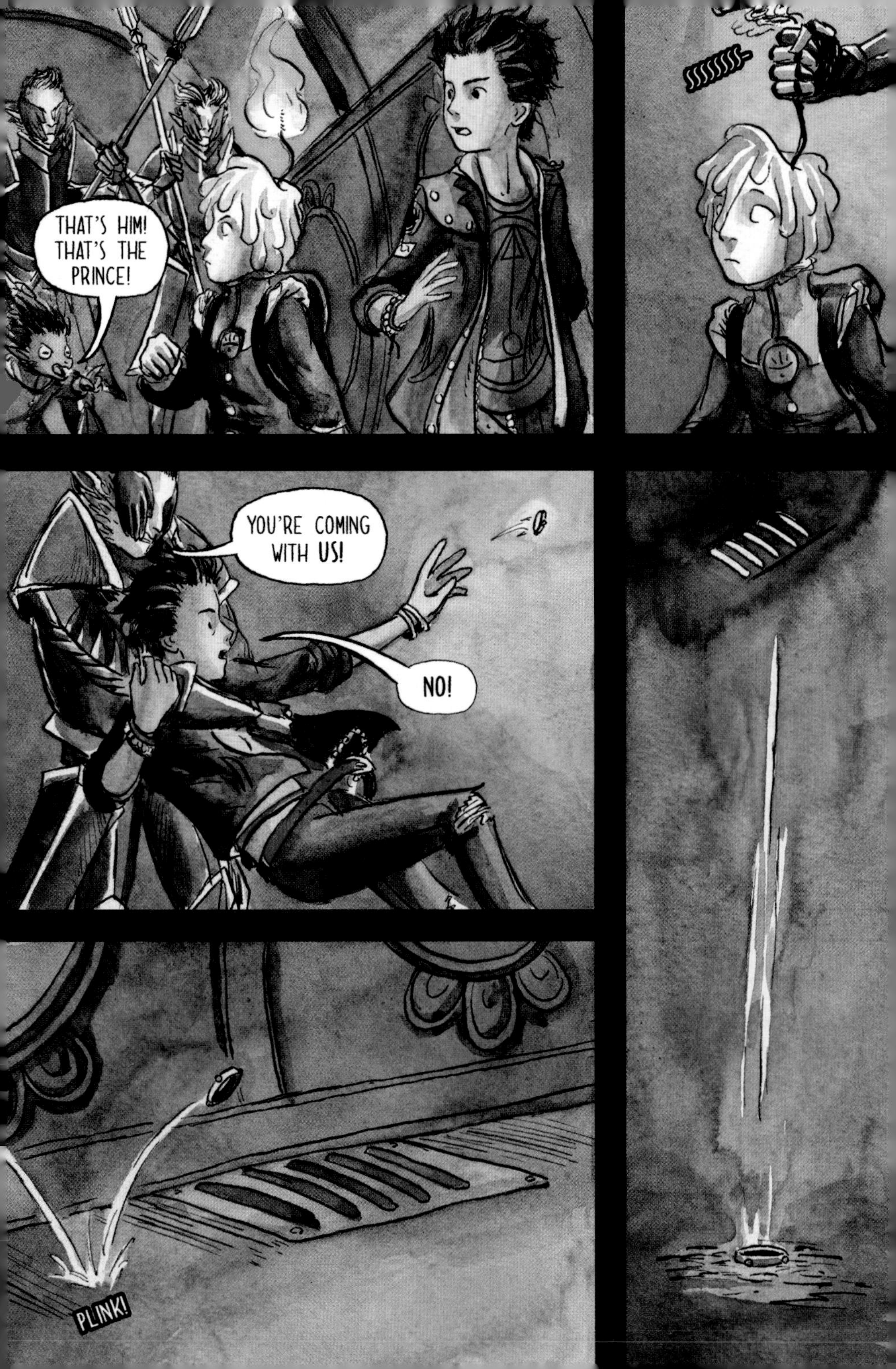
THAT'S HIM! THAT'S THE PRINCE!
SSSSSSS
YOU'RE COMING WITH US!
NO!
PLINK!

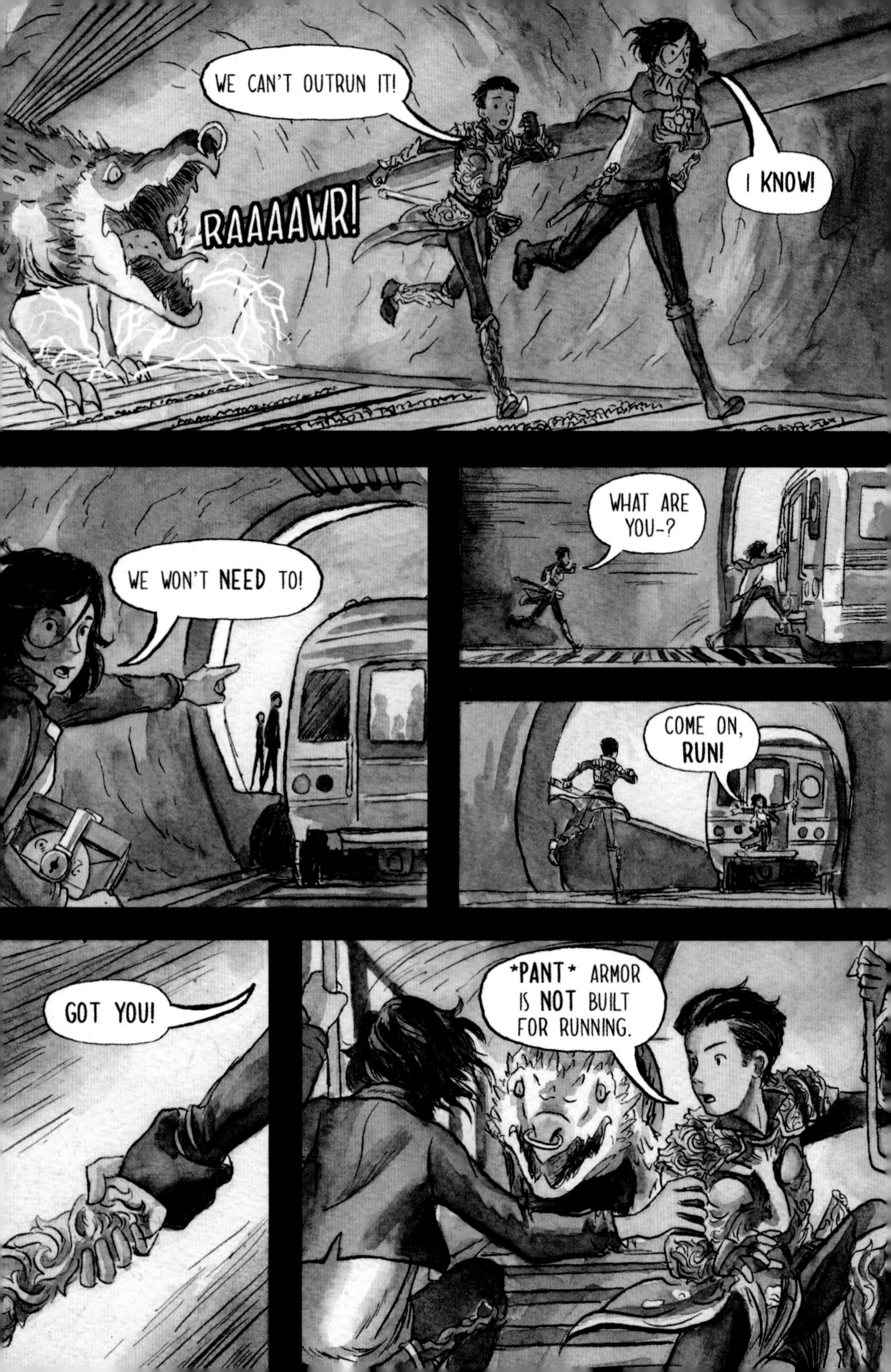
WE CAN'T OUTRUN IT!
RAAAAWR!
I KNOW!
WE WON'T NEED TO!
WHAT ARE YOU-?
COME ON, RUN!
GOT YOU!
PANT ARMOR IS NOT BUILT FOR RUNNING.

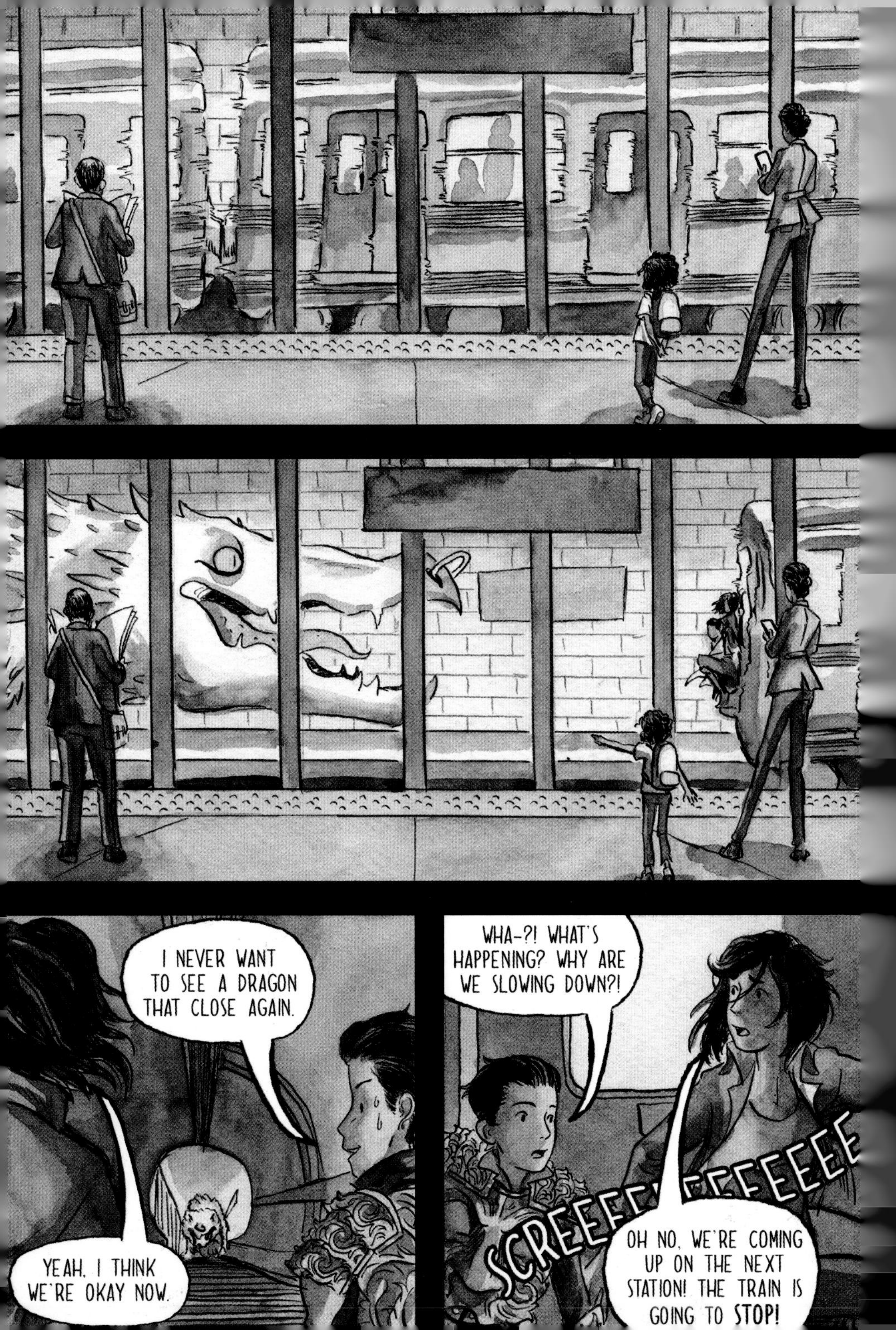
I NEVER WANT TO SEE A DRAGON THAT CLOSE AGAIN.
YEAH, I THINK WE'RE OKAY NOW.
WHA-?! WHAT'S HAPPENING? WHY ARE WE SLOWING DOWN?!
SCREEEEEEEEEEEE
OH NO, WE'RE COMING UP ON THE NEXT STATION! THE TRAIN IS GOING TO STOP!

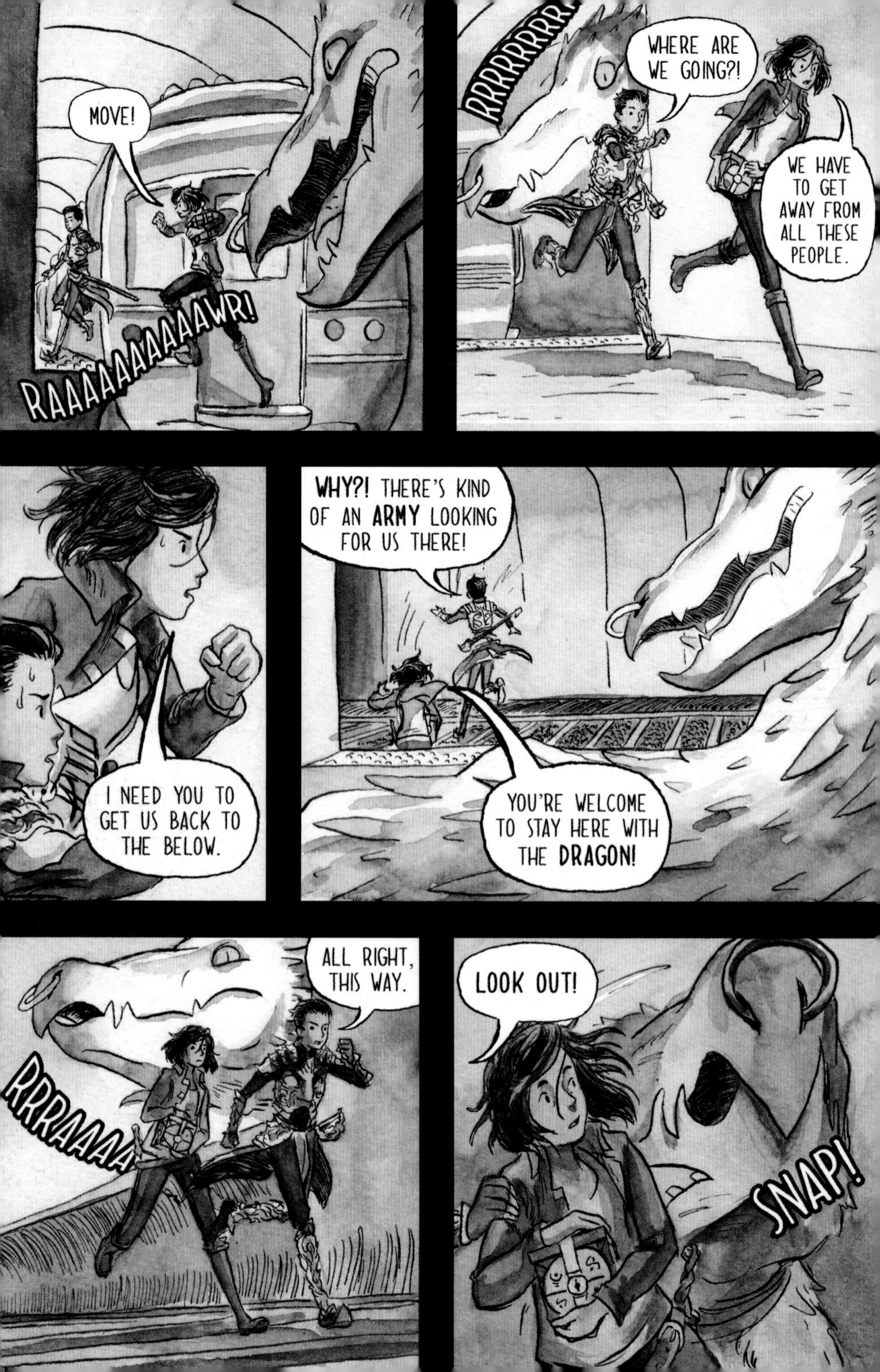
MOVE!
RAAAAAAAAAAAAWR!
RRRRRRRR
WHERE ARE WE GOING?!
WE HAVE TO GET AWAY FROM ALL THESE PEOPLE.
I NEED YOU TO GET US BACK TO THE BELOW.
WHY?! THERE'S KIND OF AN ARMY LOOKING FOR US THERE!
YOU'RE WELCOME TO STAY HERE WITH THE DRAGON!
RRRAAAA
ALL RIGHT, THIS WAY.
LOOK OUT!
SNAP!

RAAAAAAAAAAAAAAAAWR!
HONK! HONK!
-RRRRRR?
HONK!
WHAM!
SCREEEEEE!
COME ON. IF IT WASN'T MAD BEFORE, IT SURE IS NOW.
HISSSSSSSSSSSSSSSS!
SSSSSSSSSSSRRRRRR
RRRRRAAAAAAAAAAAAA

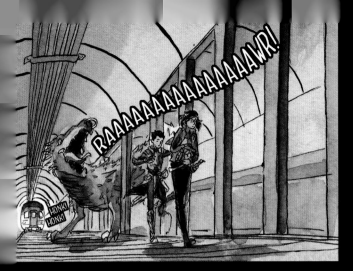

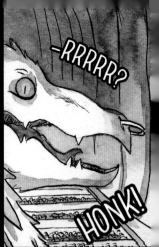

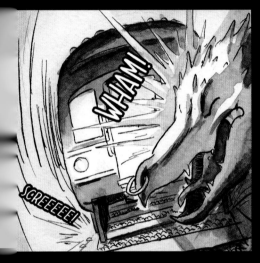

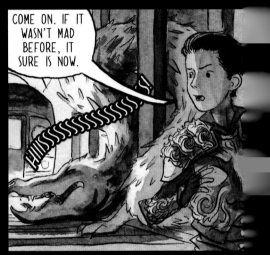

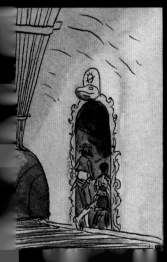

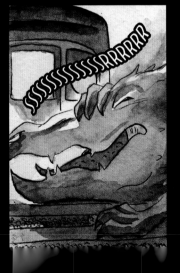

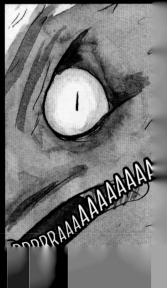

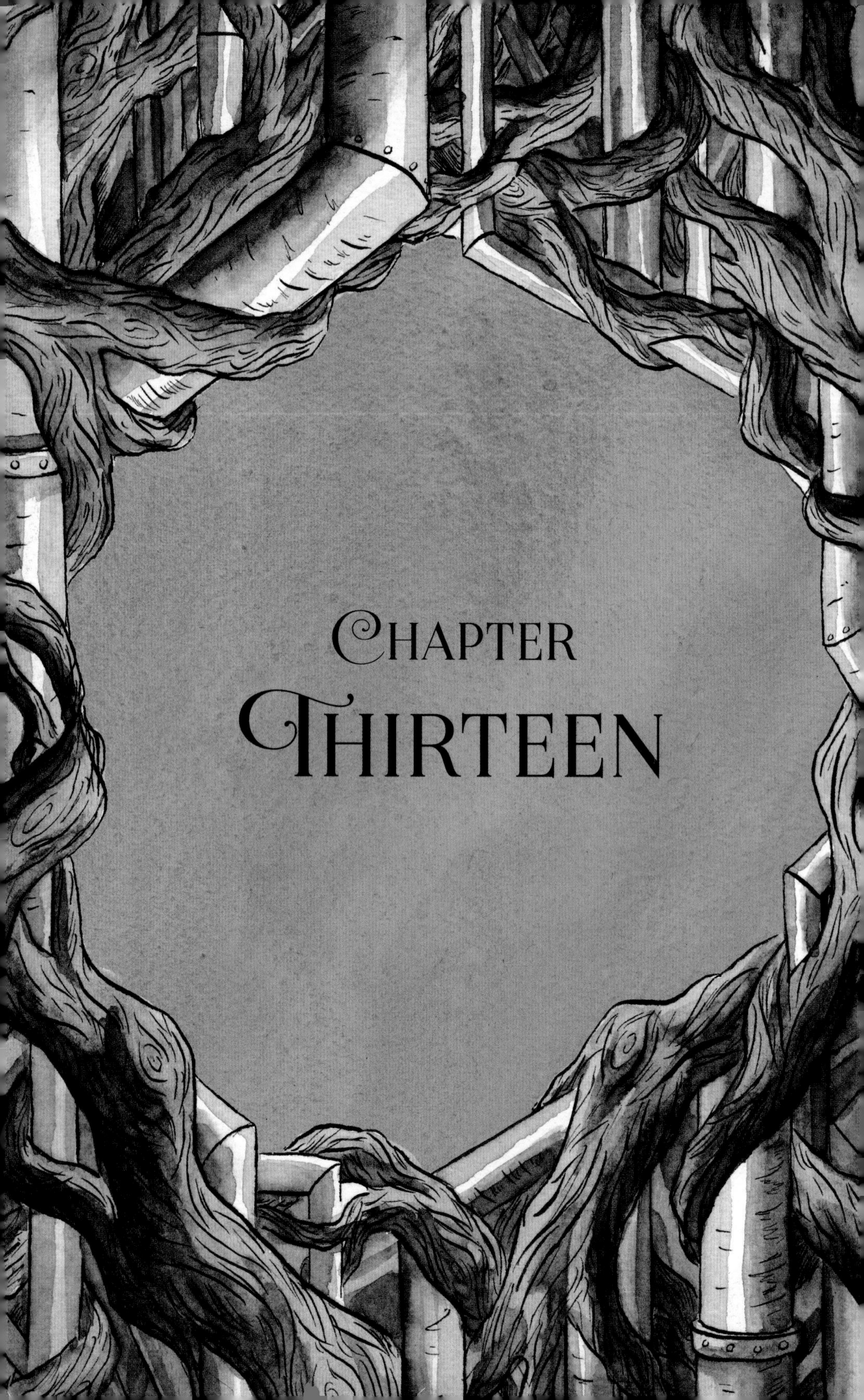

Chapter Thirteen

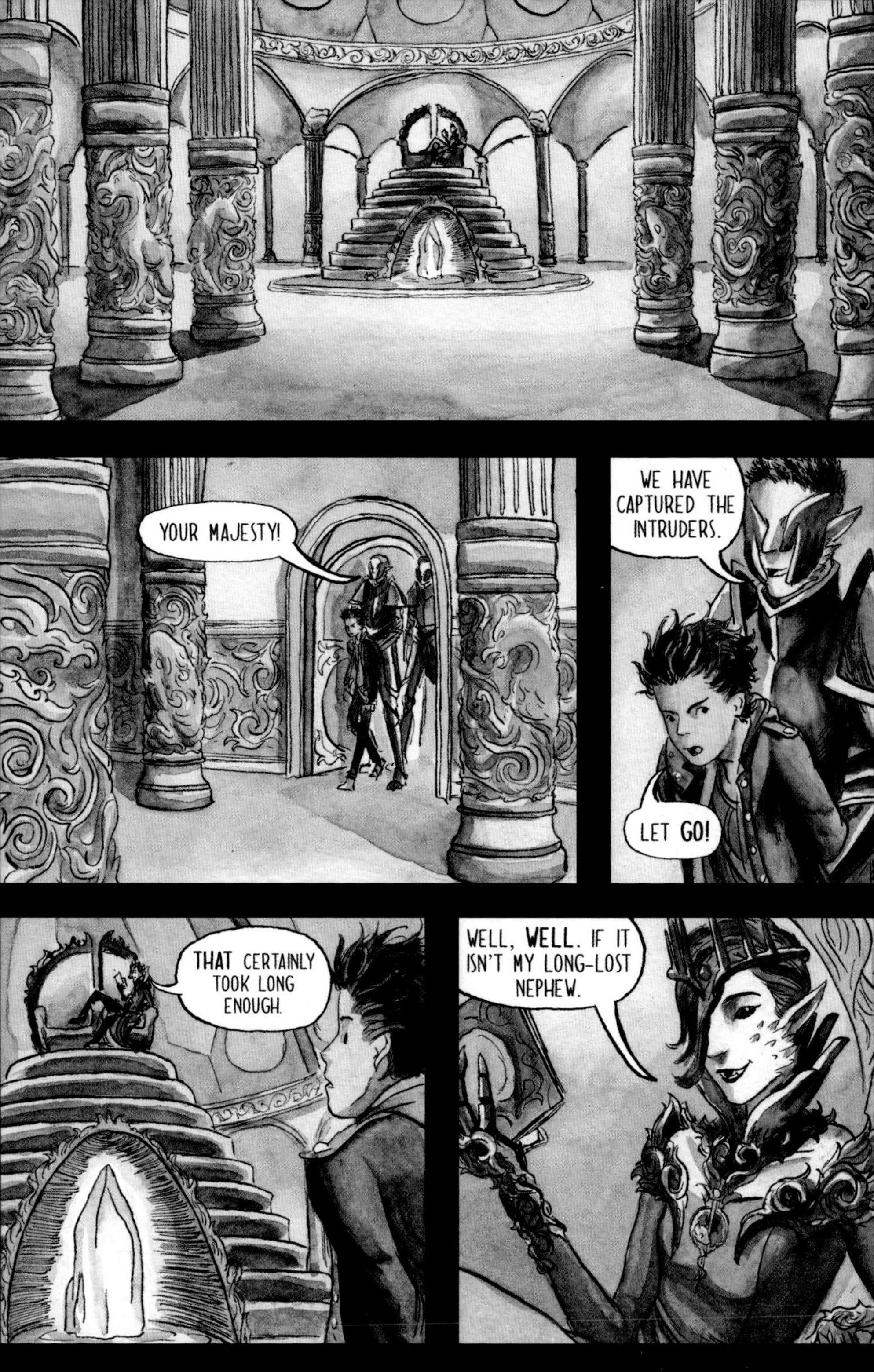
YOUR MAJESTY!
WE HAVE CAPTURED THE INTRUDERS.
LET GO!
THAT CERTAINLY TOOK LONG ENOUGH.
WELL, WELL. IF IT ISN'T MY LONG-LOST NEPHEW.

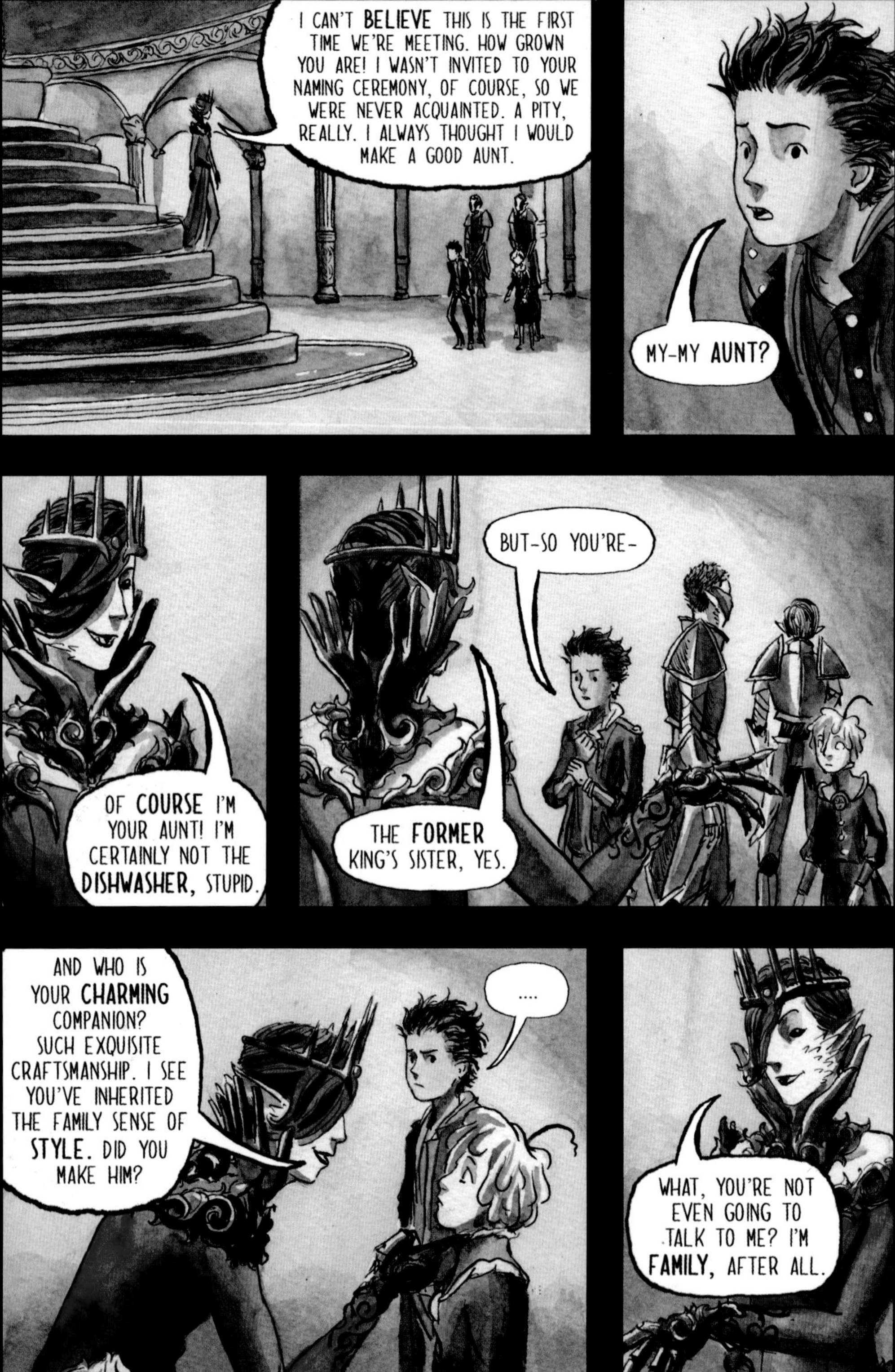
I CAN'T BELIEVE THIS IS THE FIRST TIME WE'RE MEETING. HOW GROWN YOU ARE! I WASN'T INVITED TO YOUR NAMING CEREMONY, OF COURSE, SO WE WERE NEVER ACQUAINTED. A PITY, REALLY. I ALWAYS THOUGHT I WOULD MAKE A GOOD AUNT.
MY-MY AUNT?
OF COURSE I'M YOUR AUNT! I'M CERTAINLY NOT THE DISHWASHER, STUPID.
BUT-SO YOU'RE-
THE FORMER KING'S SISTER, YES.
AND WHO IS YOUR CHARMING COMPANION? SUCH EXQUISITE CRAFTSMANSHIP. I SEE YOU'VE INHERITED THE FAMILY SENSE OF STYLE. DID YOU MAKE HIM?
....
WHAT, YOU'RE NOT EVEN GOING TO TALK TO ME? I'M FAMILY, AFTER ALL.

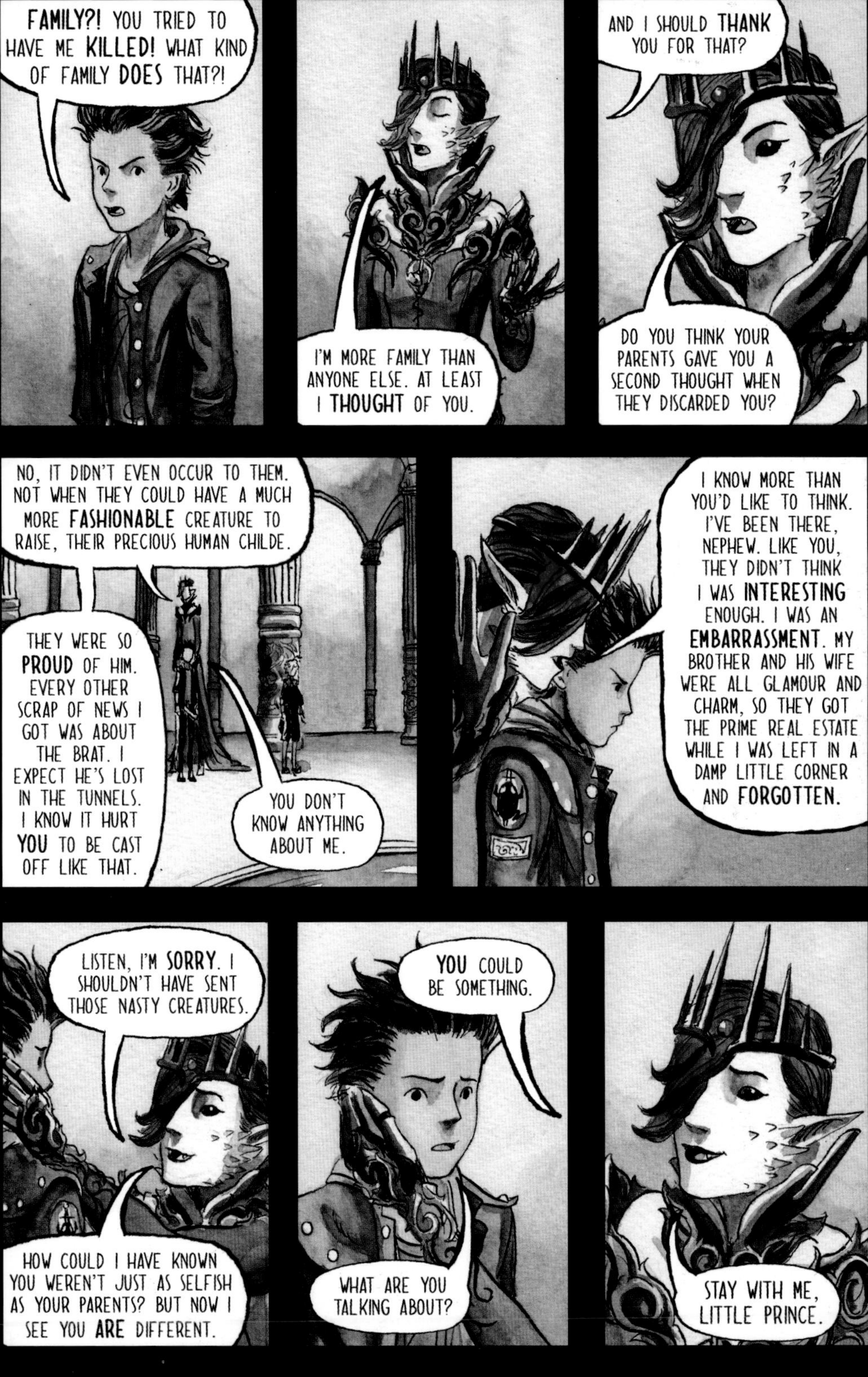
FAMILY?! YOU TRIED TO HAVE ME KILLED! WHAT KIND OF FAMILY DOES THAT?!
I'M MORE FAMILY THAN ANYONE ELSE. AT LEAST I THOUGHT OF YOU.
AND I SHOULD THANK YOU FOR THAT?
DO YOU THINK YOUR PARENTS GAVE YOU A SECOND THOUGHT WHEN THEY DISCARDED YOU?
NO, IT DIDN'T EVEN OCCUR TO THEM. NOT WHEN THEY COULD HAVE A MUCH MORE FASHIONABLE CREATURE TO RAISE, THEIR PRECIOUS HUMAN CHILDE.
THEY WERE SO PROUD OF HIM. EVERY OTHER SCRAP OF NEWS I GOT WAS ABOUT THE BRAT. I EXPECT HE'S LOST IN THE TUNNELS. I KNOW IT HURT YOU TO BE CAST OFF LIKE THAT.
YOU DON'T KNOW ANYTHING ABOUT ME.
I KNOW MORE THAN YOU'D LIKE TO THINK. I'VE BEEN THERE, NEPHEW. LIKE YOU, THEY DIDN'T THINK I WAS INTERESTING ENOUGH. I WAS AN EMBARRASSMENT. MY BROTHER AND HIS WIFE WERE ALL GLAMOUR AND CHARM, SO THEY GOT THE PRIME REAL ESTATE WHILE I WAS LEFT IN A DAMP LITTLE CORNER AND FORGOTTEN.
LISTEN, I'M SORRY. I SHOULDN'T HAVE SENT THOSE NASTY CREATURES.
HOW COULD I HAVE KNOWN YOU WEREN'T JUST AS SELFISH AS YOUR PARENTS? BUT NOW I SEE YOU ARE DIFFERENT.
YOU COULD BE SOMETHING.
WHAT ARE YOU TALKING ABOUT?
STAY WITH ME, LITTLE PRINCE.

WHAT?

THEY DIDN'T WANT YOU, BUT **I** DO. I PUNISHED THEM, FOR **BOTH** OF US, AND NOW WE CAN HAVE OUR FAMILY, OUR **HOME**. ISN'T THAT WHAT YOU WANT?

YES, BUT...BUT—

BUT **WHAT**? NO ONE IS GOING TO GIVE US A PLACE IN THIS WORLD. WE HAVE TO **TAKE** IT.

COME ON, LET'S BE THE FAMILY WE NEVER HAD, THE ONE WE **DESERVE**.

NO.

PARDON?

NO. I'M SORRY. I KNOW YOU WANT A HOME...

AND YOU'RE RIGHT, I WANT THAT TOO. BUT NOT LIKE THIS.

I...I SEE. IT BREAKS MY HEART TO HEAR YOU SAY THAT, IT REALLY DOES. I GUESS YOU'RE JUST LIKE THE REST OF THEM AFTER ALL.

AND I **WON'T** LET YOU TAKE MY HOME FROM ME.

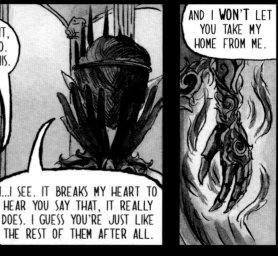

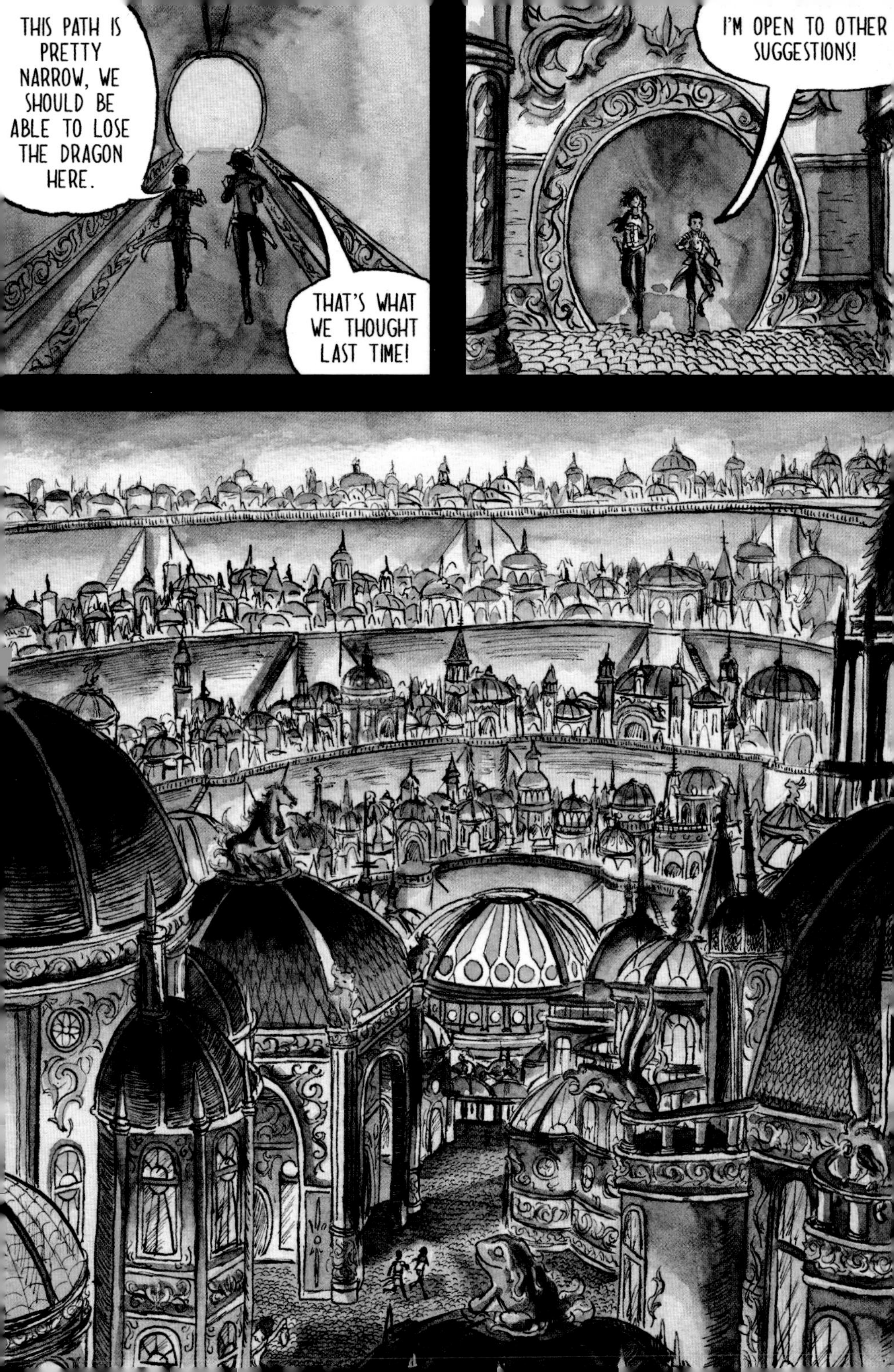
THIS PATH IS PRETTY NARROW, WE SHOULD BE ABLE TO LOSE THE DRAGON HERE.
THAT'S WHAT WE THOUGHT LAST TIME!
I'M OPEN TO OTHER SUGGESTIONS!

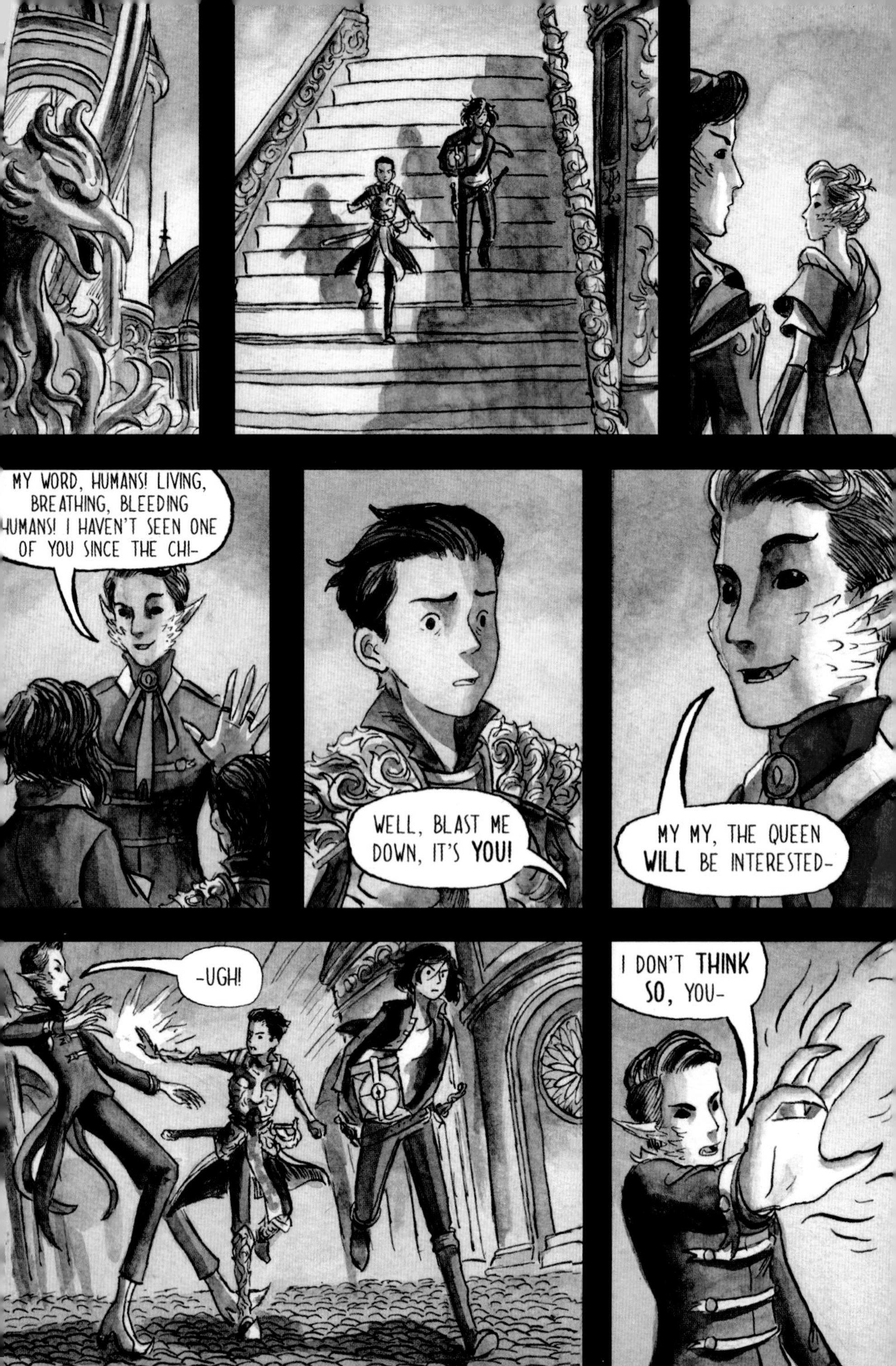
MY WORD, HUMANS! LIVING, BREATHING, BLEEDING HUMANS! I HAVEN'T SEEN ONE OF YOU SINCE THE CHI-
WELL, BLAST ME DOWN, IT'S **YOU!**
MY MY, THE QUEEN **WILL** BE INTERESTED-
-UGH!
I DON'T **THINK SO,** YOU-

BOOOM!

AAAAAAAH!

HIIISSSSSSSSSSSSSSSSS

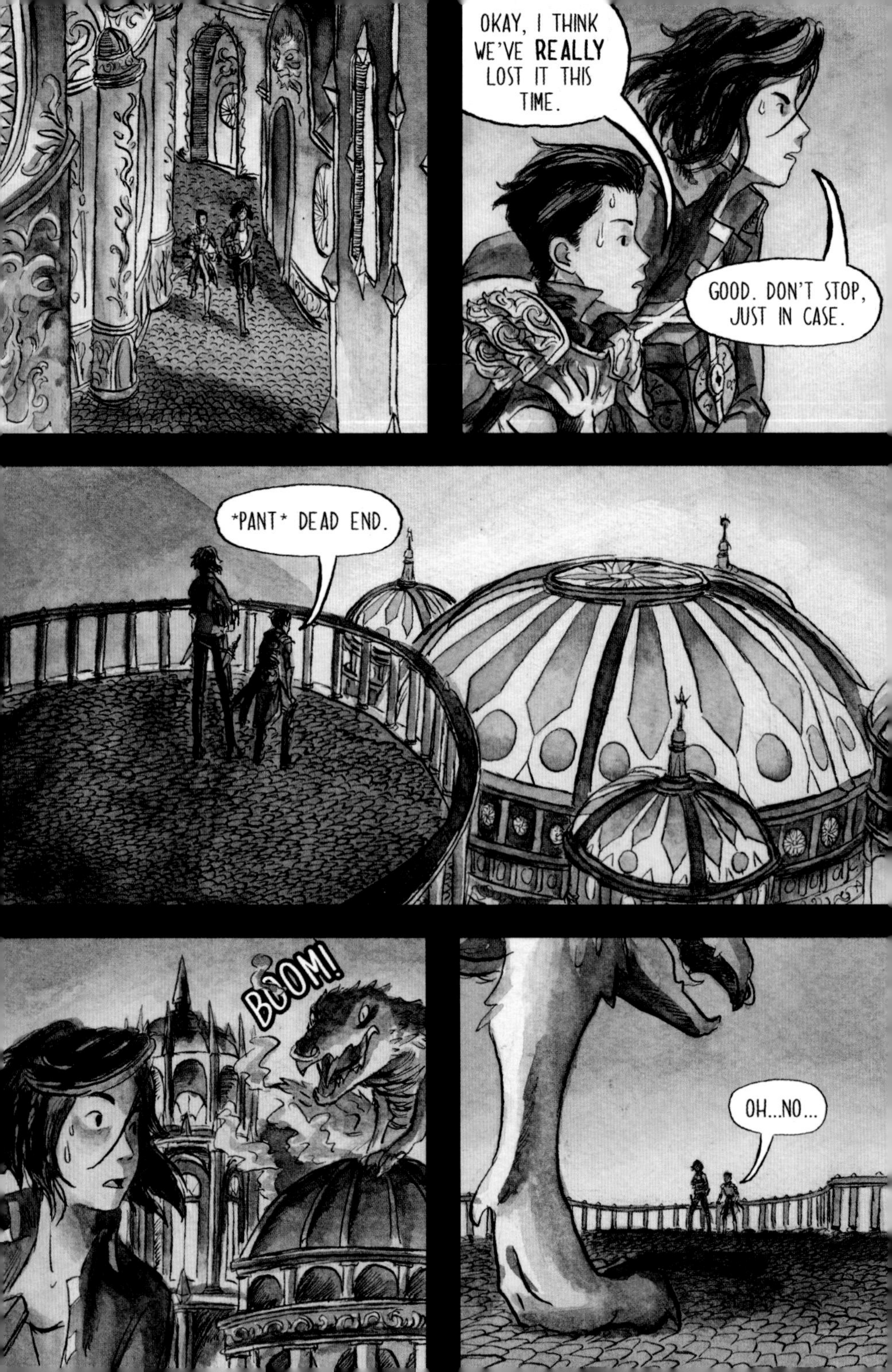
OKAY, I THINK WE'VE **REALLY** LOST IT THIS TIME.
GOOD. DON'T STOP, JUST IN CASE.
PANT DEAD END.
BOOM!
OH...NO...

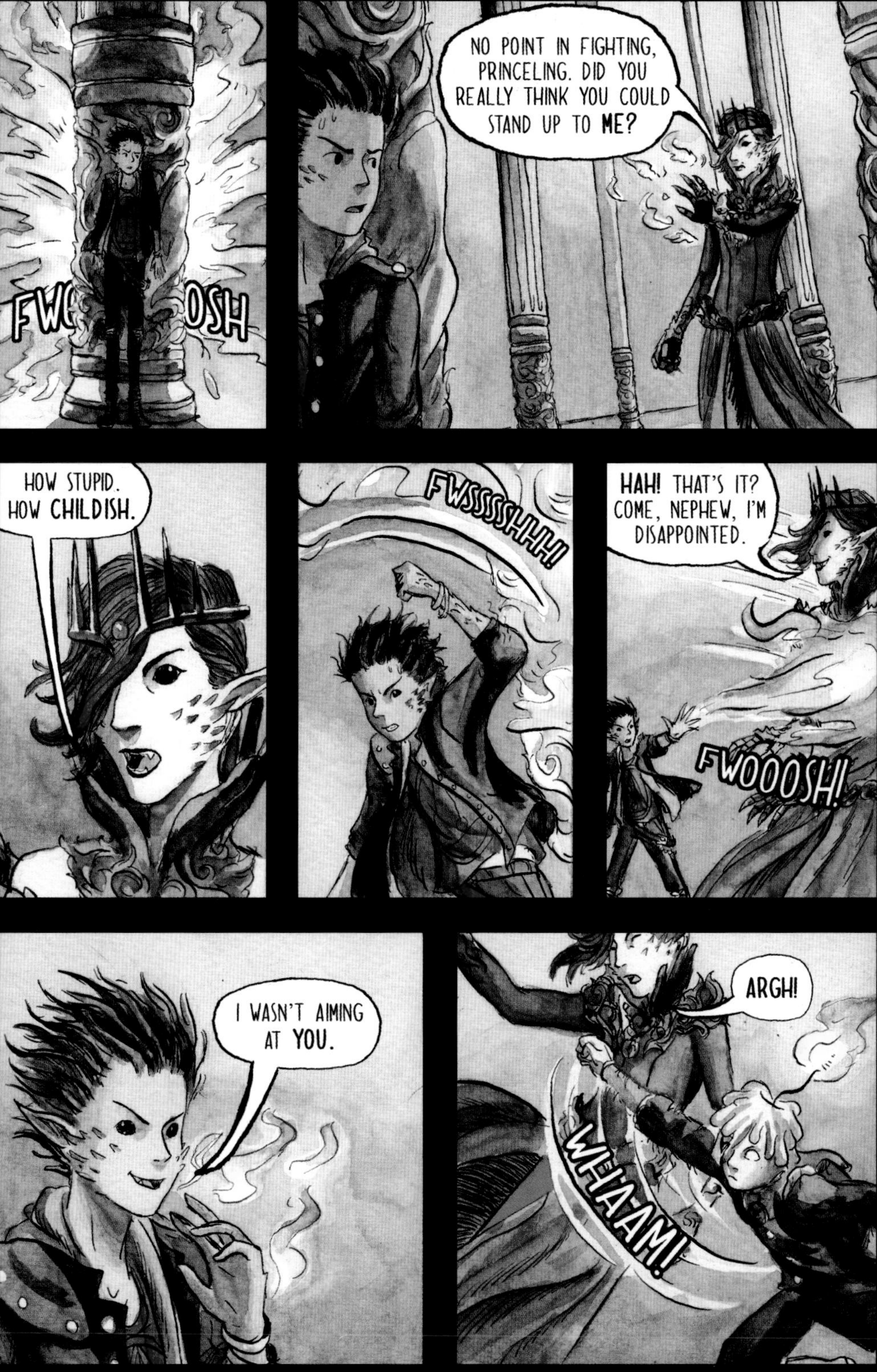
FWOOSH
NO POINT IN FIGHTING, PRINCELING. DID YOU REALLY THINK YOU COULD STAND UP TO ME?
HOW STUPID. HOW CHILDISH.
FWSSSSSHHH!
HAH! THAT'S IT? COME, NEPHEW, I'M DISAPPOINTED.
FWOOOSH!
I WASN'T AIMING AT YOU.
ARGH!
WHAAM!

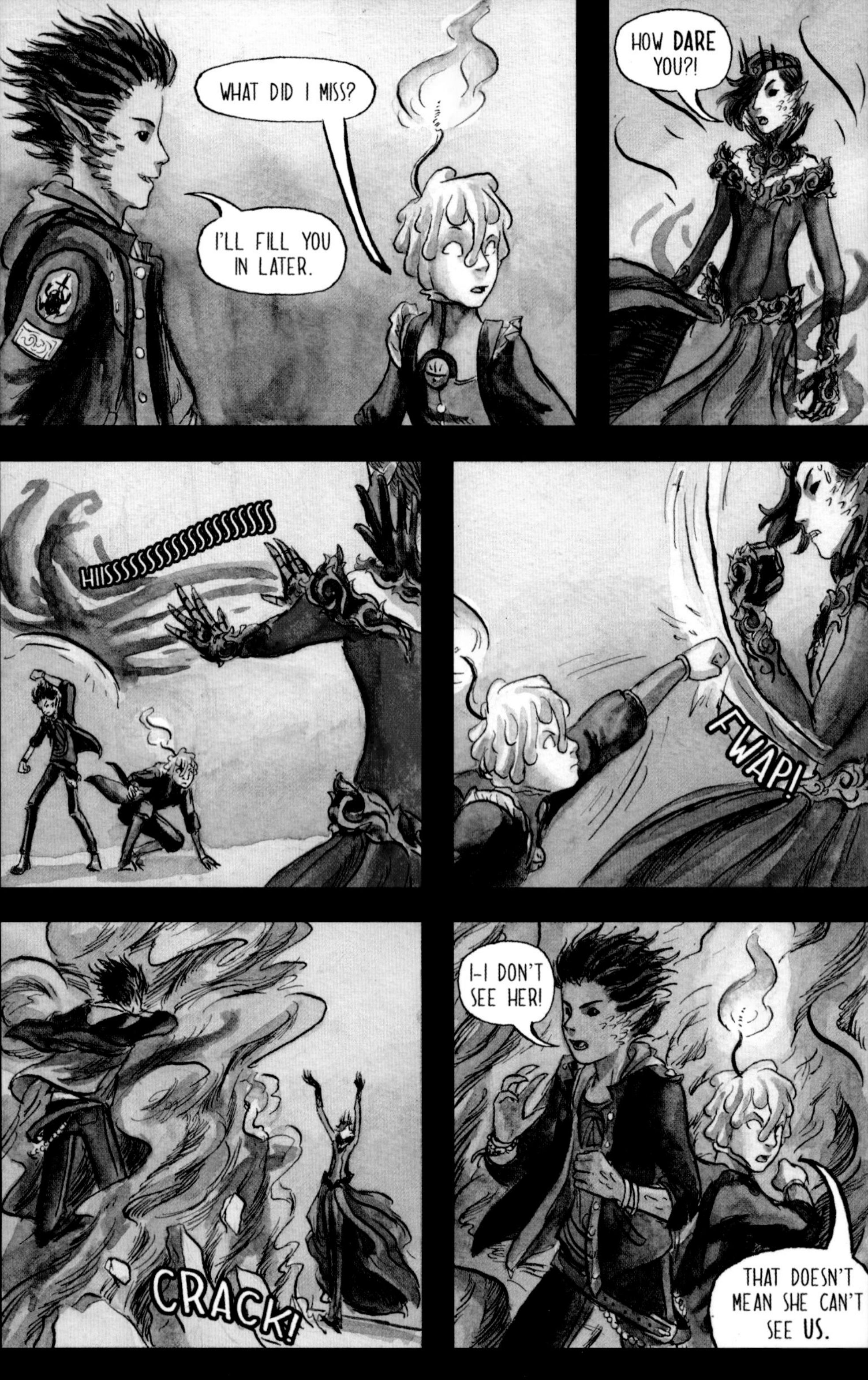
WHAT DID I MISS?
I'LL FILL YOU IN LATER.
HOW DARE YOU?!
HIISSSSSSSSSSSSSSSSSSSS
FWAP!
CRACK!
I-I DON'T SEE HER!
THAT DOESN'T MEAN SHE CAN'T SEE US.

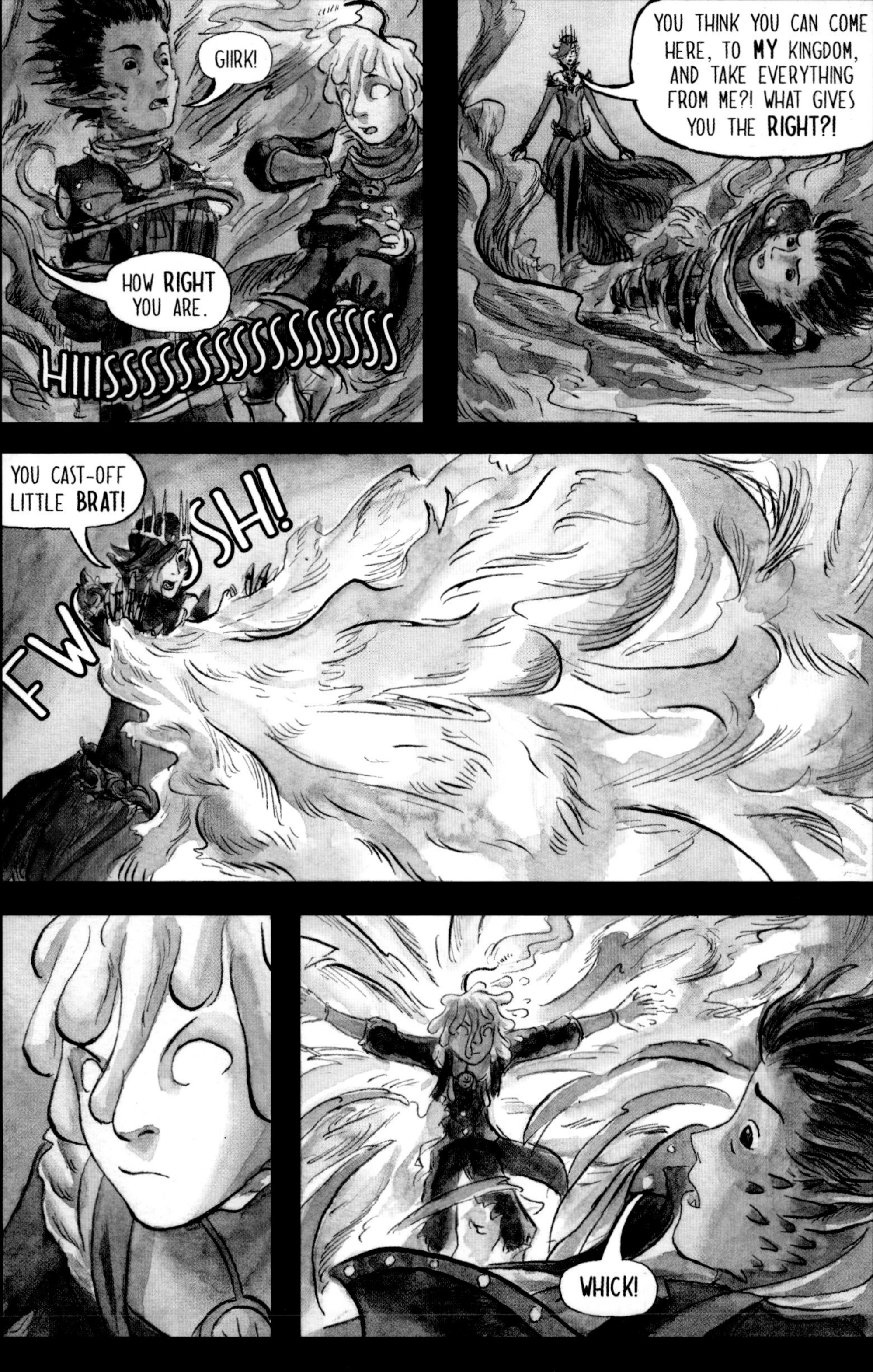
GIIRK!
HOW RIGHT YOU ARE.
HIIISSSSSSSSSSSSSSSS
YOU THINK YOU CAN COME HERE, TO MY KINGDOM, AND TAKE EVERYTHING FROM ME?! WHAT GIVES YOU THE RIGHT?!
YOU CAST-OFF LITTLE BRAT!
FW SH!
WHICK!

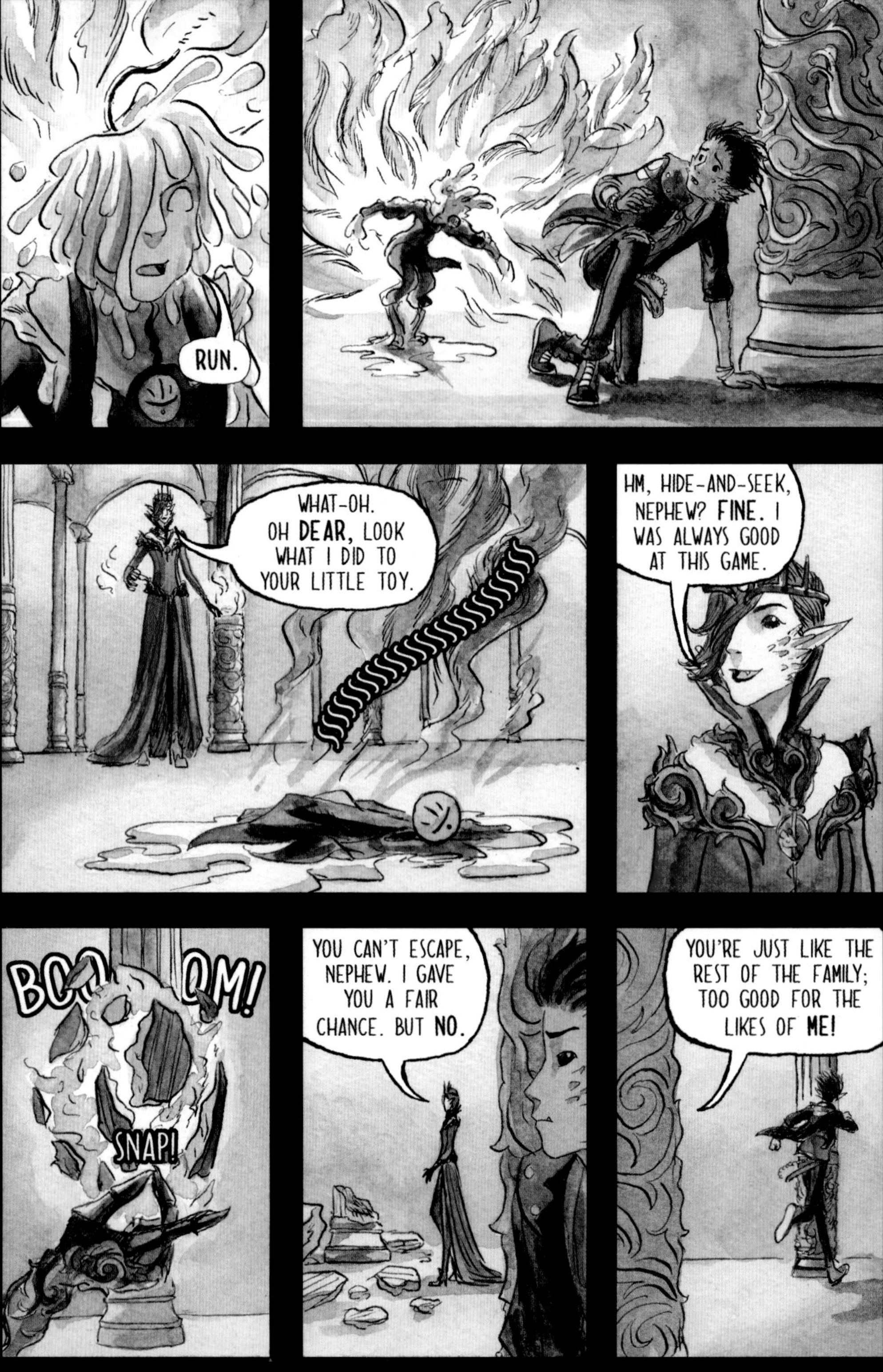
RUN.
WHAT-OH.
OH DEAR, LOOK WHAT I DID TO YOUR LITTLE TOY.
HM, HIDE-AND-SEEK, NEPHEW? FINE. I WAS ALWAYS GOOD AT THIS GAME.
BOOM!
SNAP!
YOU CAN'T ESCAPE, NEPHEW. I GAVE YOU A FAIR CHANCE. BUT NO.
YOU'RE JUST LIKE THE REST OF THE FAMILY; TOO GOOD FOR THE LIKES OF ME!

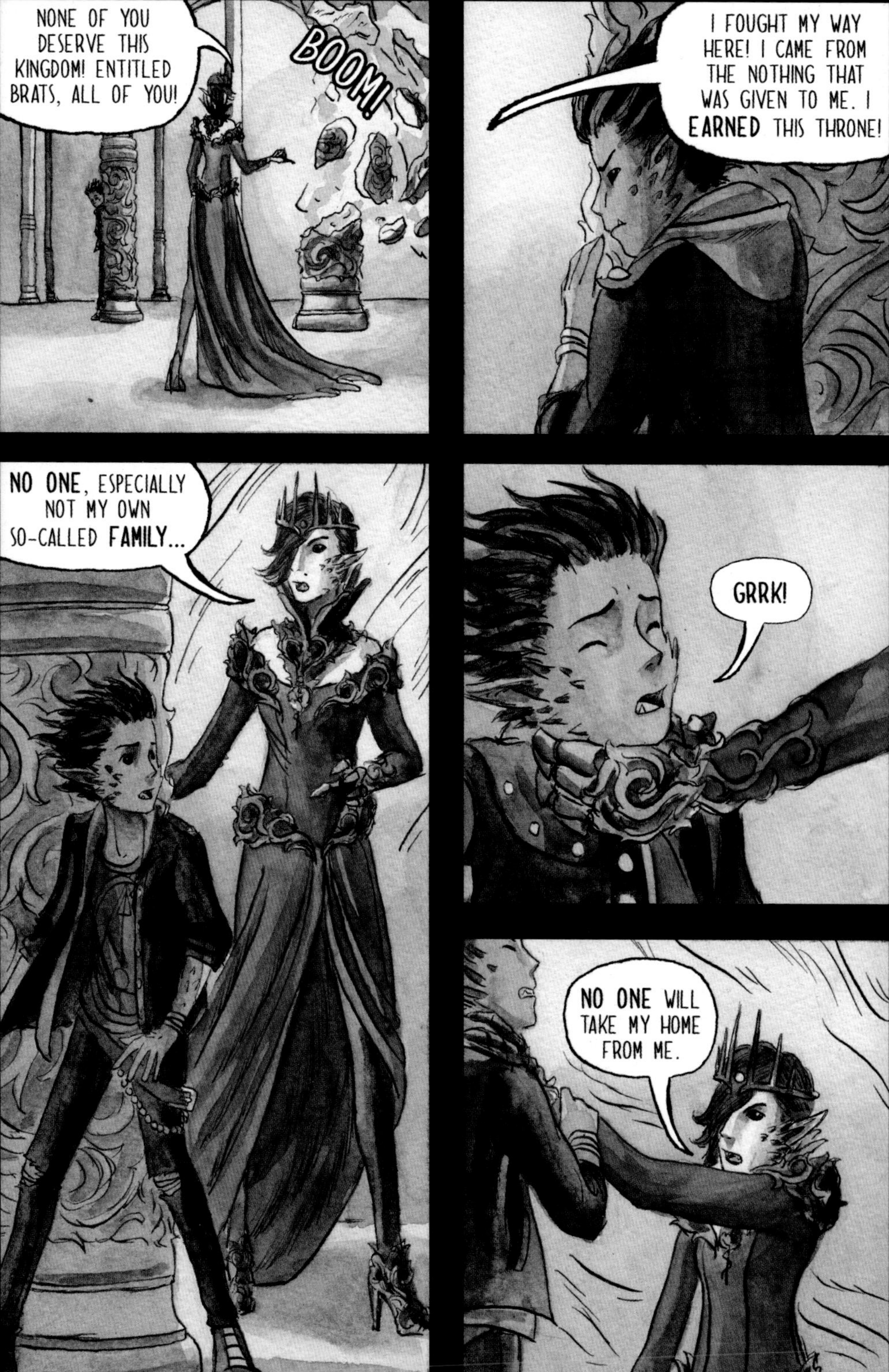
NONE OF YOU DESERVE THIS KINGDOM! ENTITLED BRATS, ALL OF YOU!
BOOM!
I FOUGHT MY WAY HERE! I CAME FROM THE NOTHING THAT WAS GIVEN TO ME. I **EARNED** THIS THRONE!
NO ONE, ESPECIALLY NOT MY OWN SO-CALLED **FAMILY**...
GRRK!
NO ONE WILL TAKE MY HOME FROM ME.

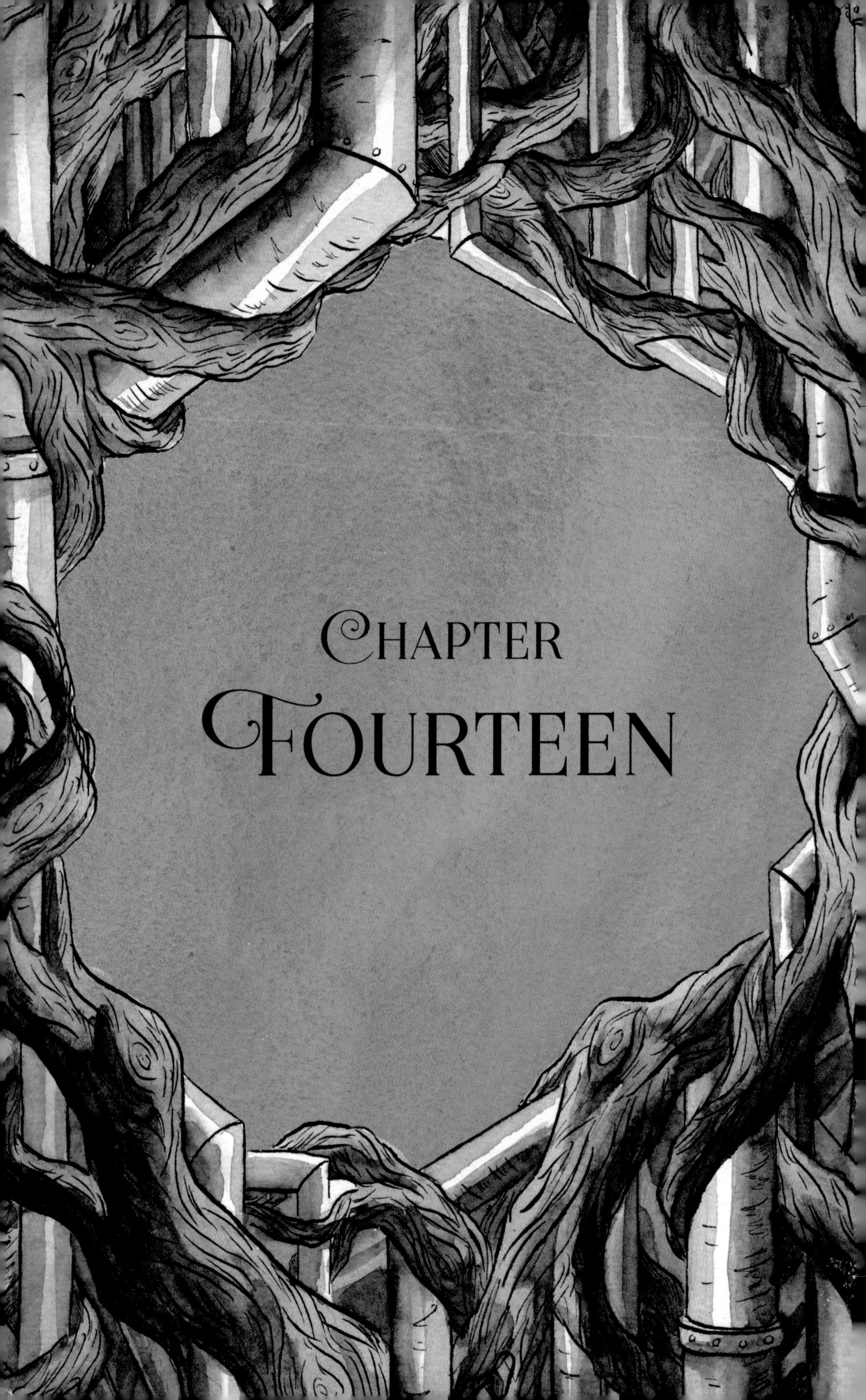

Chapter Fourteen

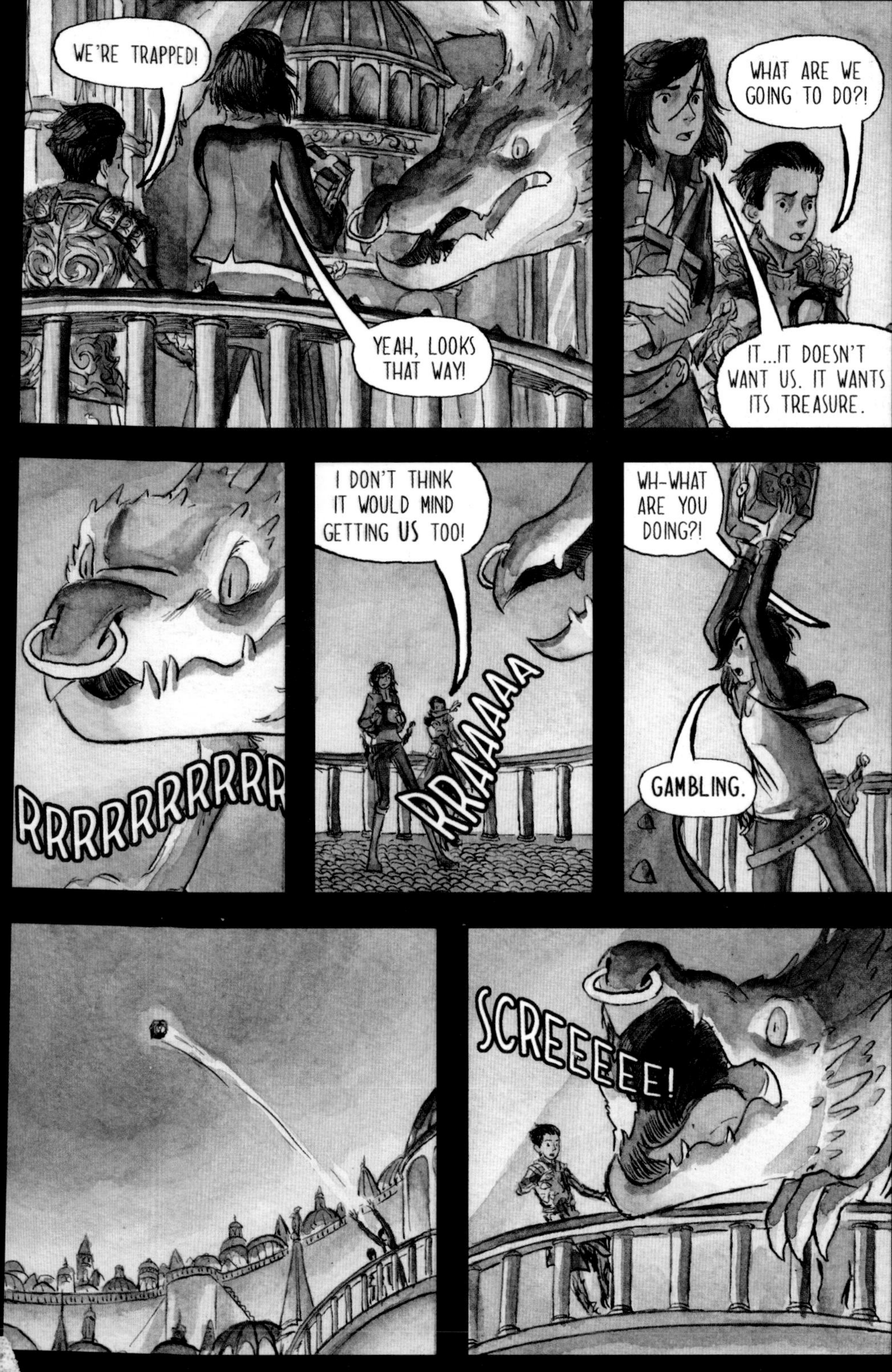
WE'RE TRAPPED!
YEAH, LOOKS THAT WAY!
WHAT ARE WE GOING TO DO?!
IT...IT DOESN'T WANT US. IT WANTS ITS TREASURE.
RRRRRRRRRR
I DON'T THINK IT WOULD MIND GETTING US TOO!
RRAAAAA
WH-WHAT ARE YOU DOING?!
GAMBLING.
SCREEEEEE!

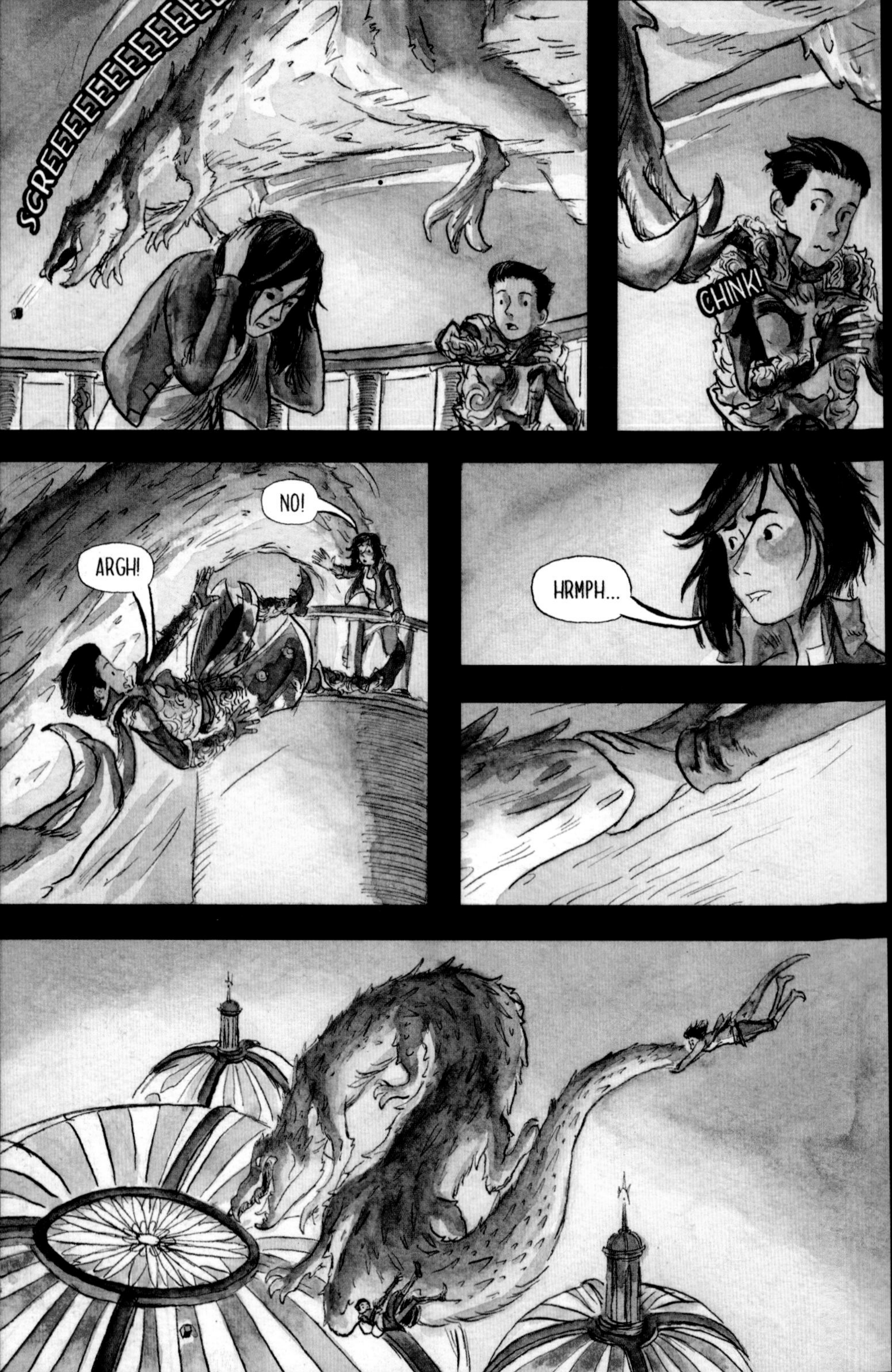

SCREEEEEEEEEE
CHINK!
NO!
ARGH!
HRMPH...

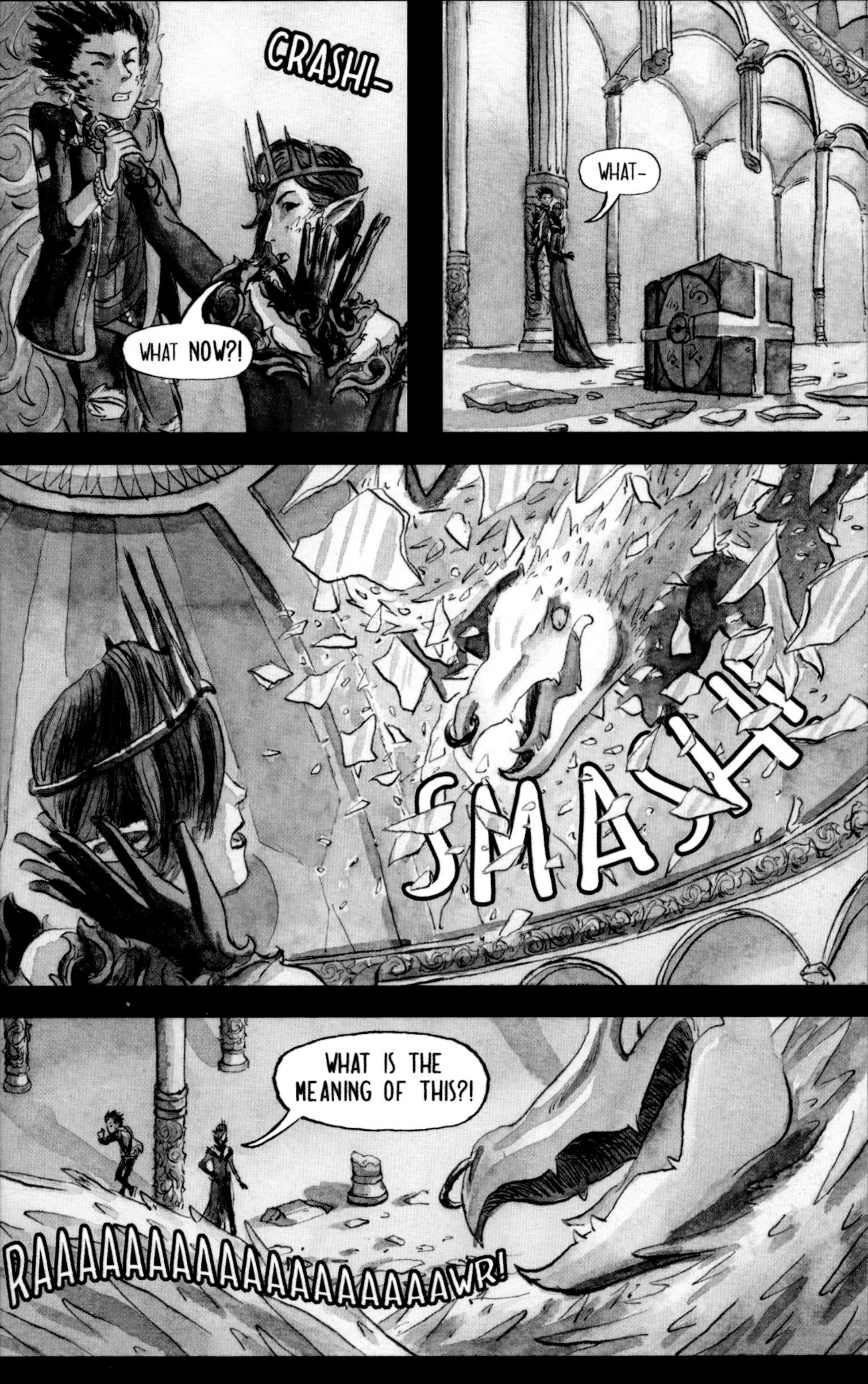
CRASH!-
WHAT NOW?!
WHAT-
SMASH!
WHAT IS THE MEANING OF THIS?!
RAAAAAAAAAAAAAAAAAAAAAWR!

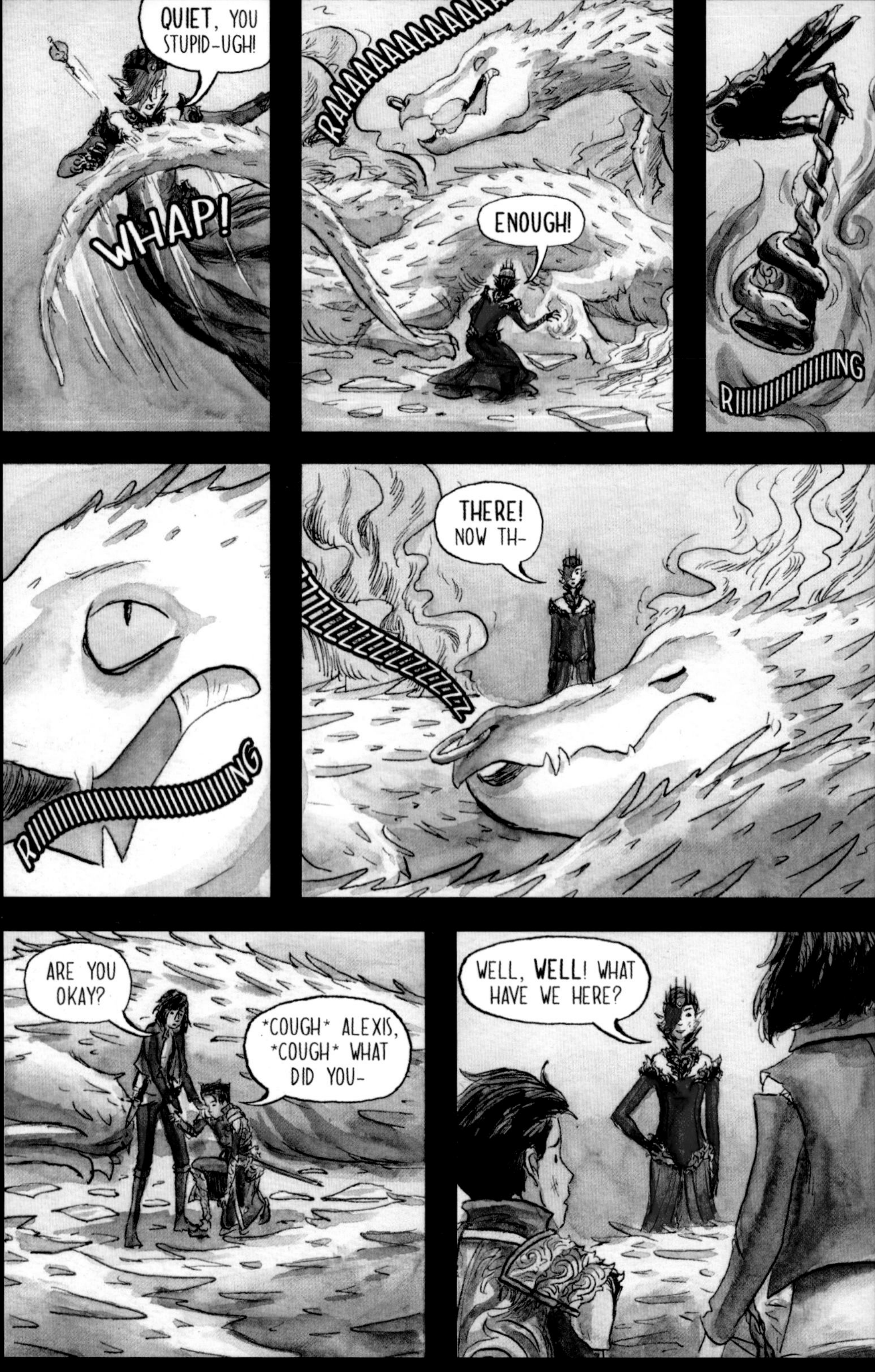
QUIET, YOU STUPID-UGH!
WHAP!
RAAAAAAAAAAAAAA
ENOUGH!
RIIIIIIIIIIIIING
RIIIIIIIIIIIIIIING
THERE! NOW TH-
ZZZZZZZZZZZ
ARE YOU OKAY?
COUGH ALEXIS, *COUGH* WHAT DID YOU-
WELL, **WELL**! WHAT HAVE WE HERE?

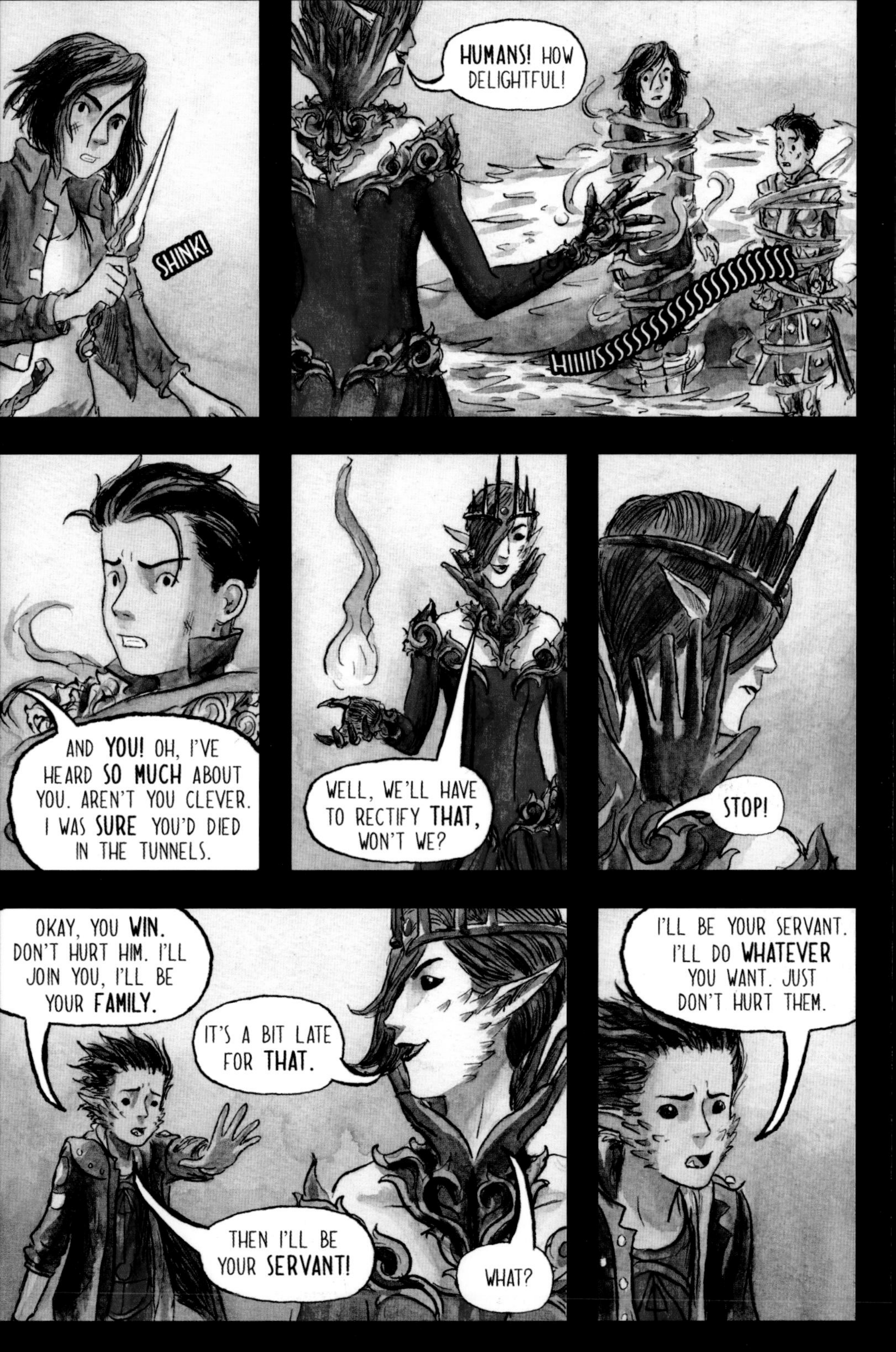
SHINK!
HUMANS! HOW DELIGHTFUL!
HIIIISSSSSSSSSSSSSSSSSSSS
AND YOU! OH, I'VE HEARD SO MUCH ABOUT YOU. AREN'T YOU CLEVER. I WAS SURE YOU'D DIED IN THE TUNNELS.
WELL, WE'LL HAVE TO RECTIFY THAT, WON'T WE?
STOP!
OKAY, YOU WIN. DON'T HURT HIM. I'LL JOIN YOU, I'LL BE YOUR FAMILY.
IT'S A BIT LATE FOR THAT.
THEN I'LL BE YOUR SERVANT!
WHAT?
I'LL BE YOUR SERVANT. I'LL DO WHATEVER YOU WANT. JUST DON'T HURT THEM.

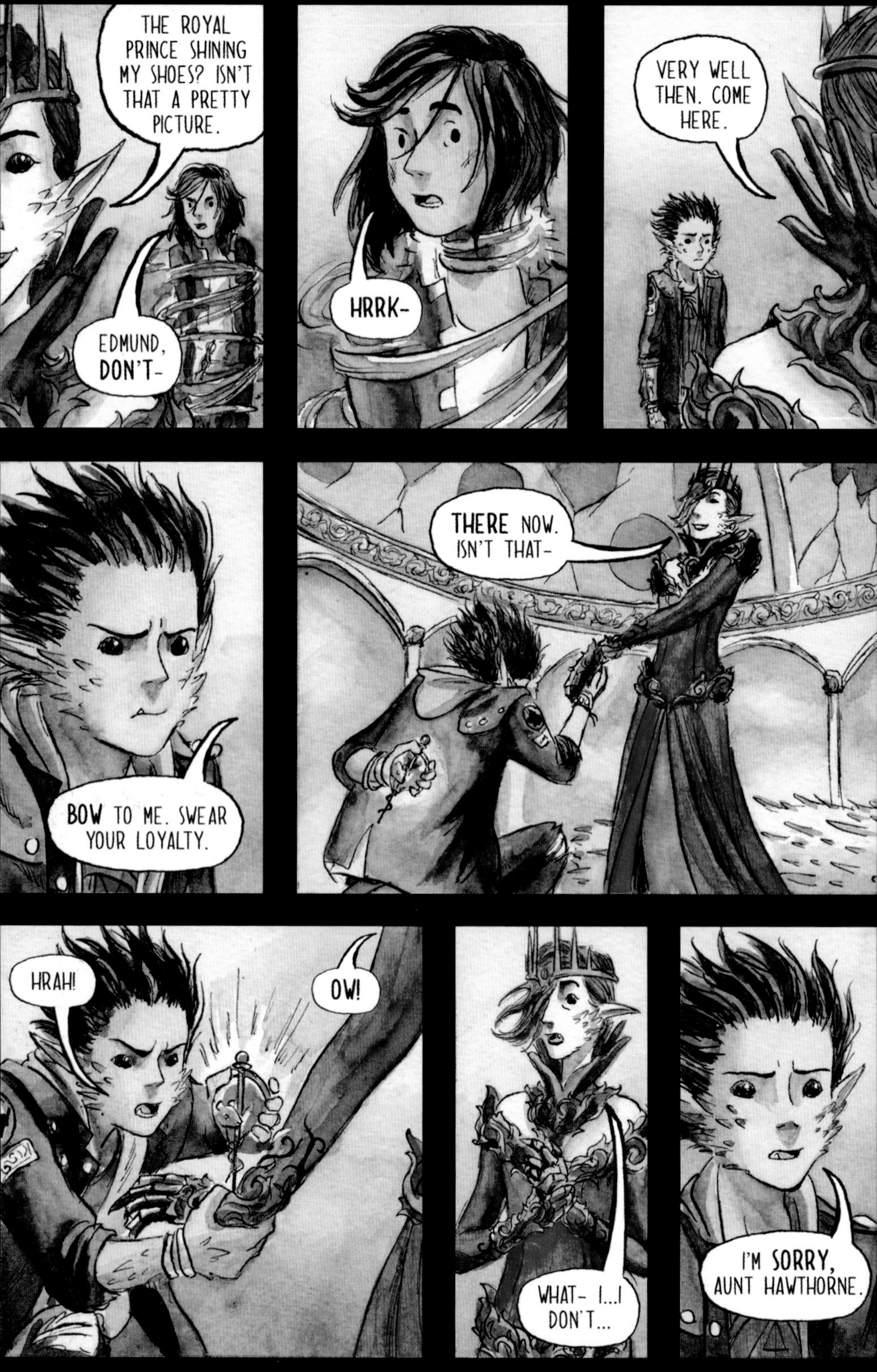
THE ROYAL PRINCE SHINING MY SHOES? ISN'T THAT A PRETTY PICTURE.
EDMUND, DON'T-
HRRK-
VERY WELL THEN. COME HERE.
BOW TO ME. SWEAR YOUR LOYALTY.
THERE NOW. ISN'T THAT-
HRAH!
OW!
WHAT- I...I DON'T...
I'M SORRY, AUNT HAWTHORNE.

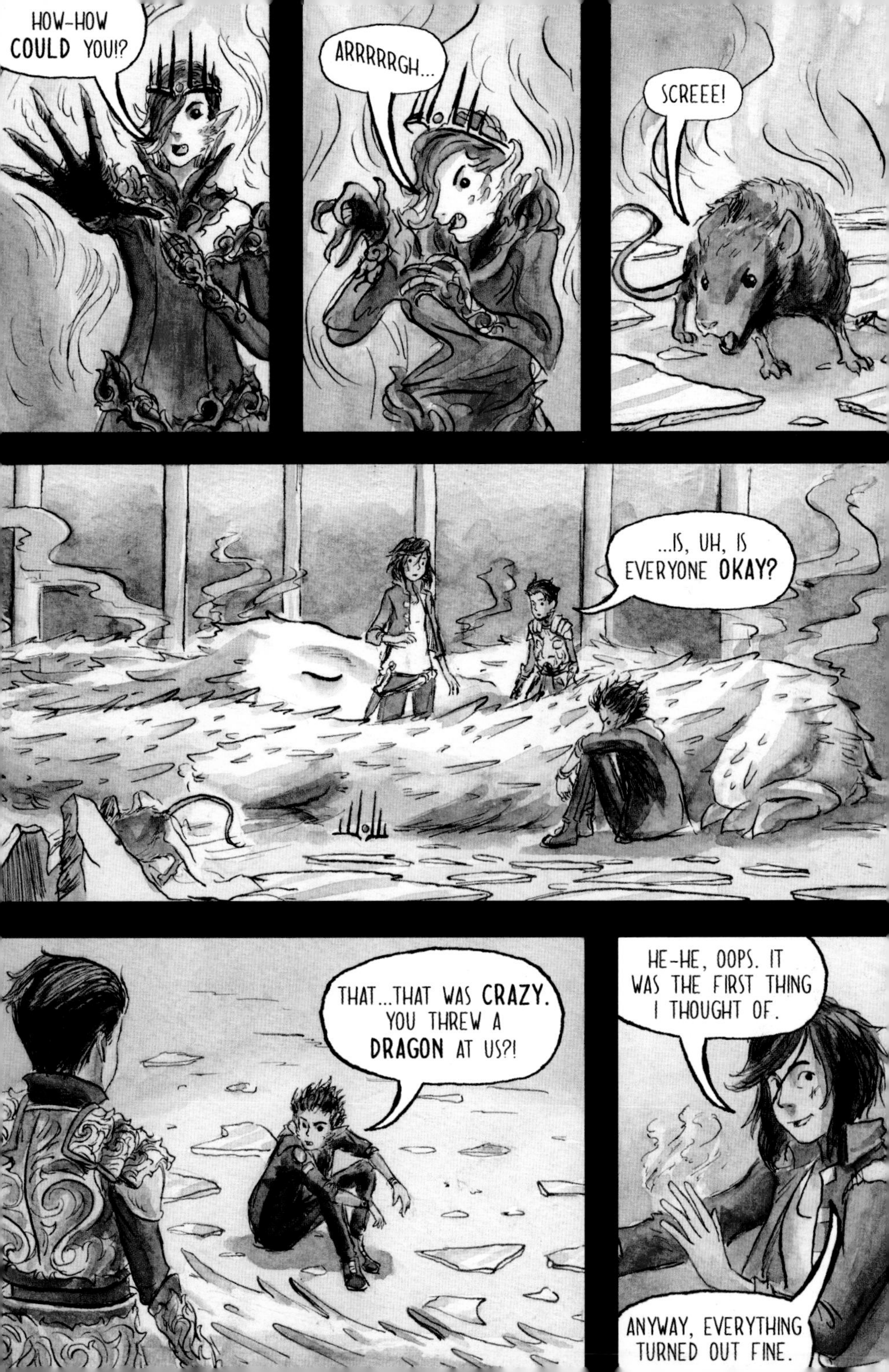
HOW-HOW COULD YOU!?
ARRRRRGH...
SCREEE!
...IS, UH, IS EVERYONE OKAY?
THAT...THAT WAS CRAZY. YOU THREW A DRAGON AT US?!
HE-HE, OOPS. IT WAS THE FIRST THING I THOUGHT OF.
ANYWAY, EVERYTHING TURNED OUT FINE.

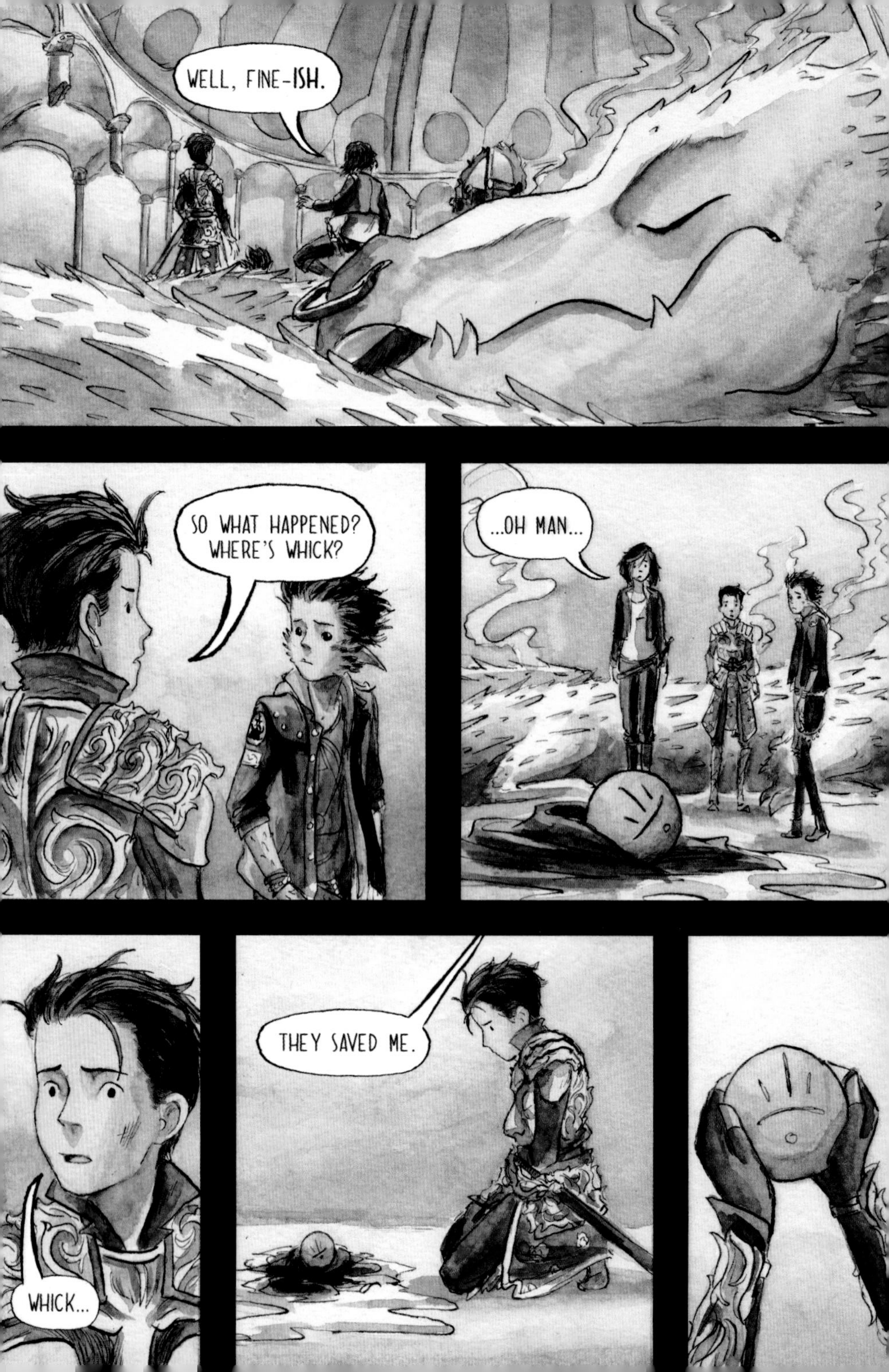
WELL, FINE-ISH.
SO WHAT HAPPENED? WHERE'S WHICK?
...OH MAN...
WHICK...
THEY SAVED ME.

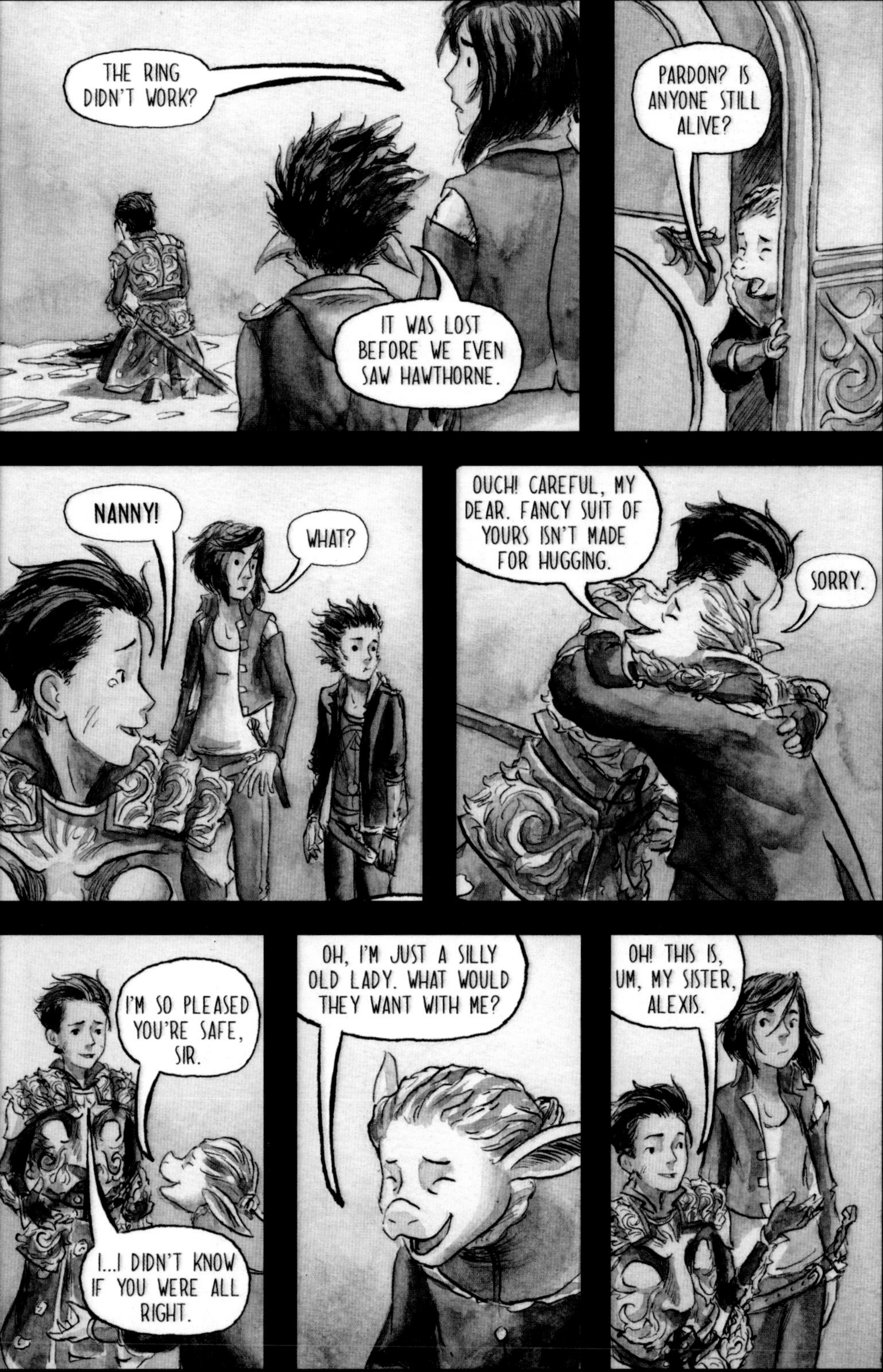
THE RING DIDN'T WORK?
IT WAS LOST BEFORE WE EVEN SAW HAWTHORNE.
PARDON? IS ANYONE STILL ALIVE?
NANNY!
WHAT?
OUCH! CAREFUL, MY DEAR. FANCY SUIT OF YOURS ISN'T MADE FOR HUGGING.
SORRY.
I'M SO PLEASED YOU'RE SAFE, SIR.
I...I DIDN'T KNOW IF YOU WERE ALL RIGHT.
OH, I'M JUST A SILLY OLD LADY. WHAT WOULD THEY WANT WITH ME?
OH! THIS IS, UM, MY SISTER, ALEXIS.

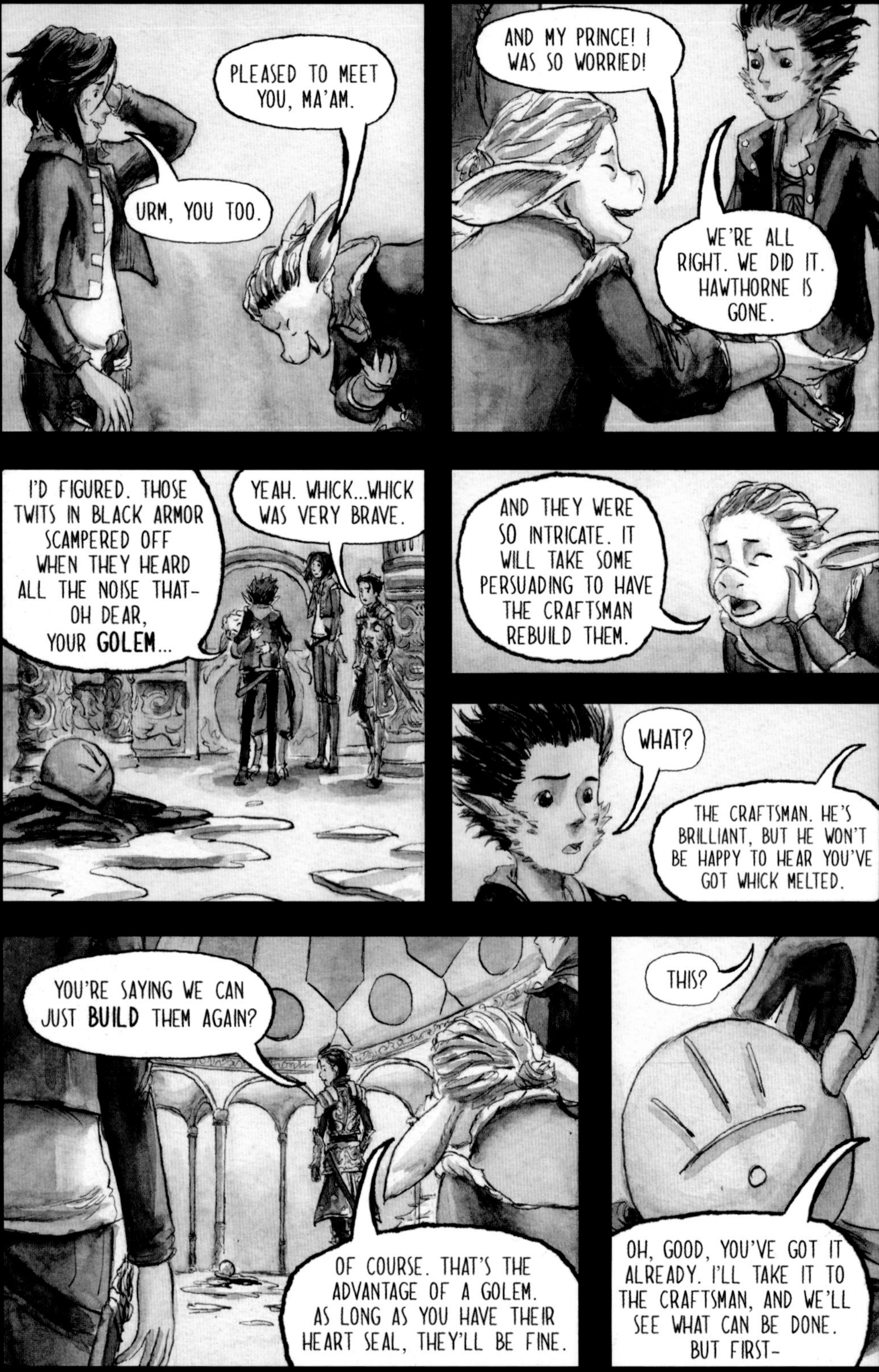
PLEASED TO MEET YOU, MA'AM.
URM, YOU TOO.
AND MY PRINCE! I WAS SO WORRIED!
WE'RE ALL RIGHT. WE DID IT. HAWTHORNE IS GONE.
I'D FIGURED. THOSE TWITS IN BLACK ARMOR SCAMPERED OFF WHEN THEY HEARD ALL THE NOISE THAT- OH DEAR, YOUR **GOLEM**...
YEAH. WHICK...WHICK WAS VERY BRAVE.
AND THEY WERE SO INTRICATE. IT WILL TAKE SOME PERSUADING TO HAVE THE CRAFTSMAN REBUILD THEM.
WHAT?
THE CRAFTSMAN. HE'S BRILLIANT, BUT HE WON'T BE HAPPY TO HEAR YOU'VE GOT WHICK MELTED.
YOU'RE SAYING WE CAN JUST **BUILD** THEM AGAIN?
OF COURSE. THAT'S THE ADVANTAGE OF A GOLEM. AS LONG AS YOU HAVE THEIR HEART SEAL, THEY'LL BE FINE.
THIS?
OH, GOOD, YOU'VE GOT IT ALREADY. I'LL TAKE IT TO THE CRAFTSMAN, AND WE'LL SEE WHAT CAN BE DONE. BUT FIRST-

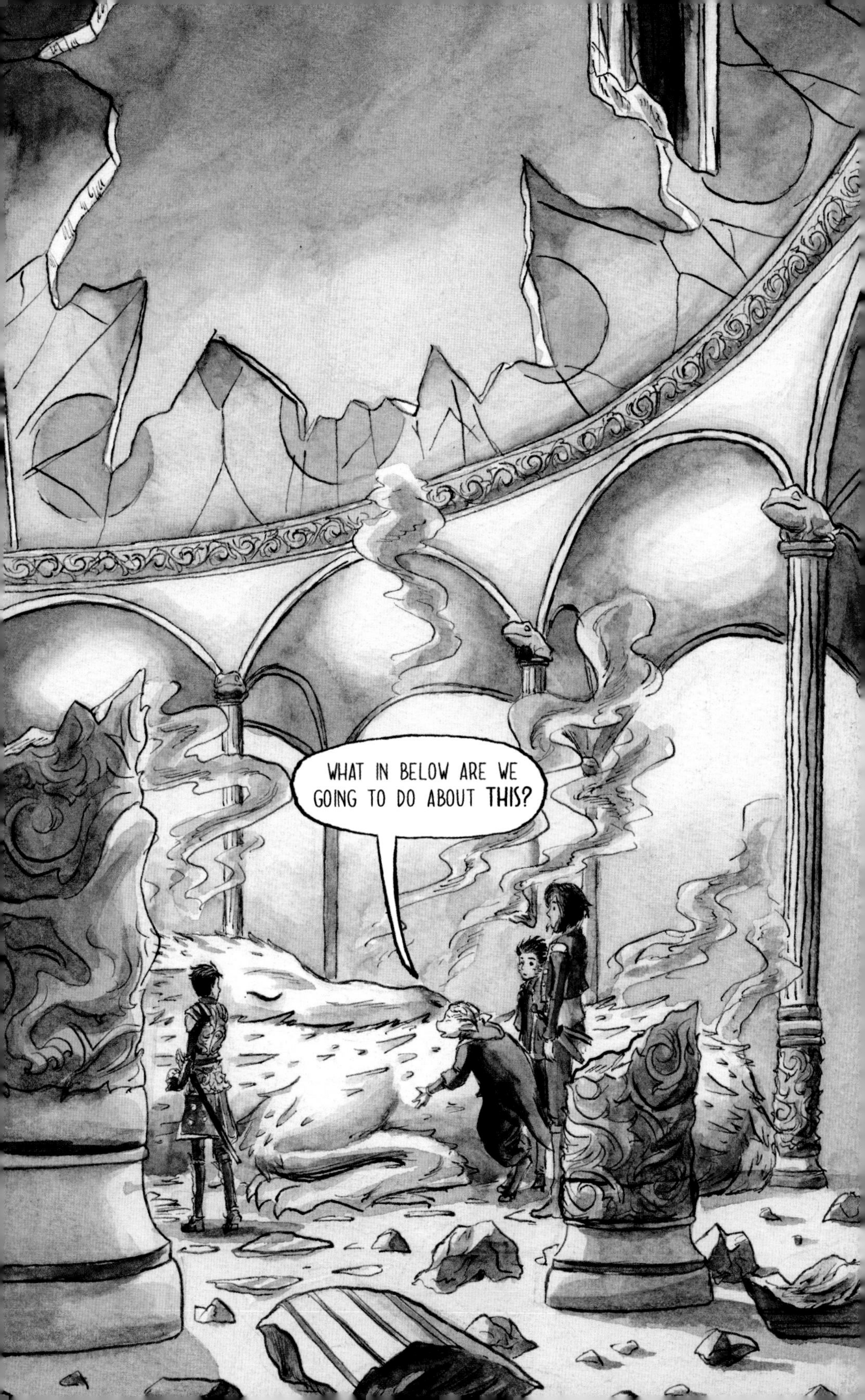
WHAT IN BELOW ARE WE GOING TO DO ABOUT THIS?

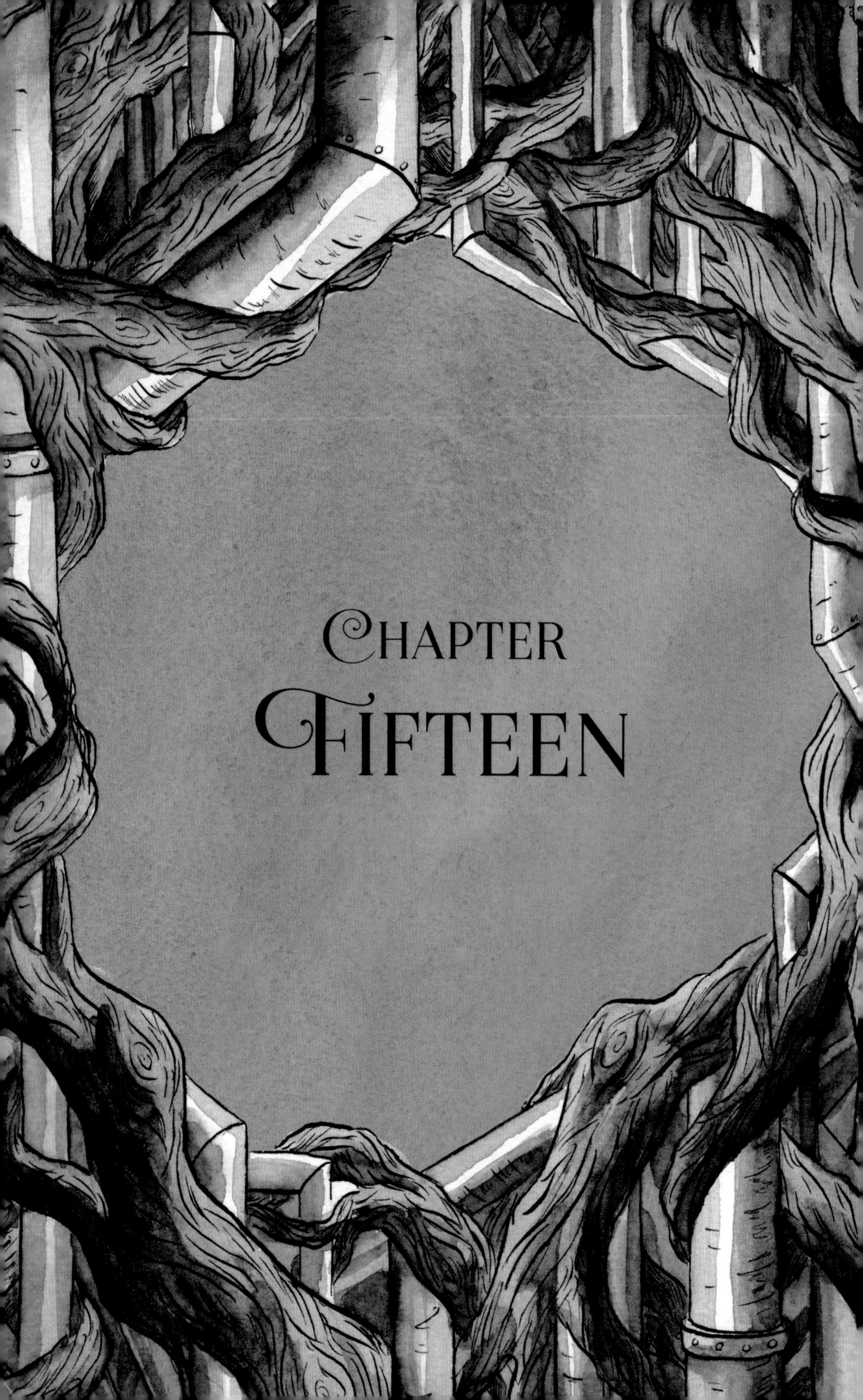

Chapter Fifteen

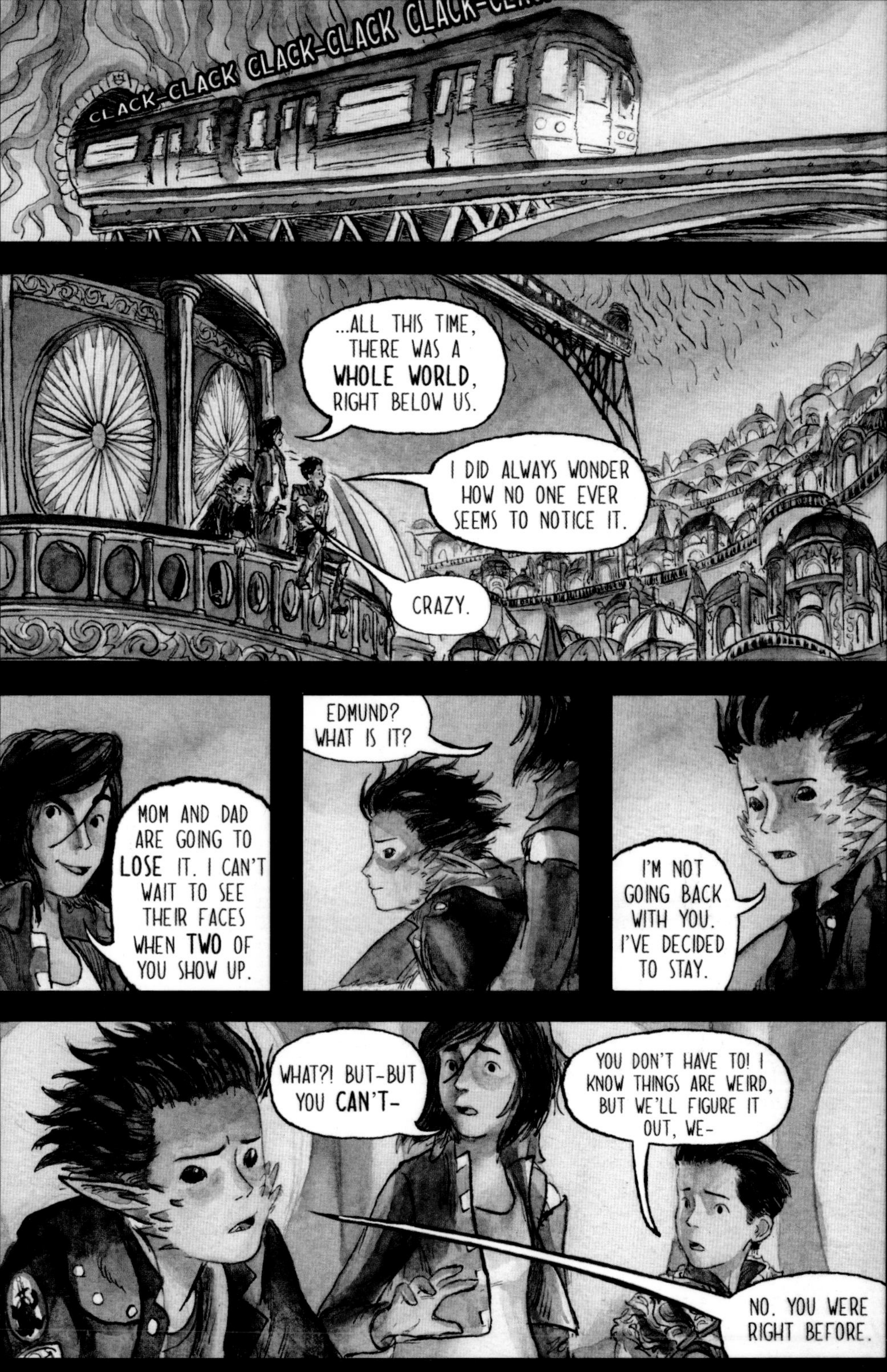
CLACK-CLACK CLACK-CLACK
...ALL THIS TIME, THERE WAS A **WHOLE WORLD**, RIGHT BELOW US.
I DID ALWAYS WONDER HOW NO ONE EVER SEEMS TO NOTICE IT.
CRAZY.
MOM AND DAD ARE GOING TO **LOSE** IT. I CAN'T WAIT TO SEE THEIR FACES WHEN **TWO** OF YOU SHOW UP.
EDMUND? WHAT IS IT?
I'M NOT GOING BACK WITH YOU. I'VE DECIDED TO STAY.
WHAT?! BUT-BUT YOU **CAN'T**-
YOU DON'T HAVE TO! I KNOW THINGS ARE WEIRD, BUT WE'LL FIGURE IT OUT, WE-
NO. YOU WERE RIGHT BEFORE.

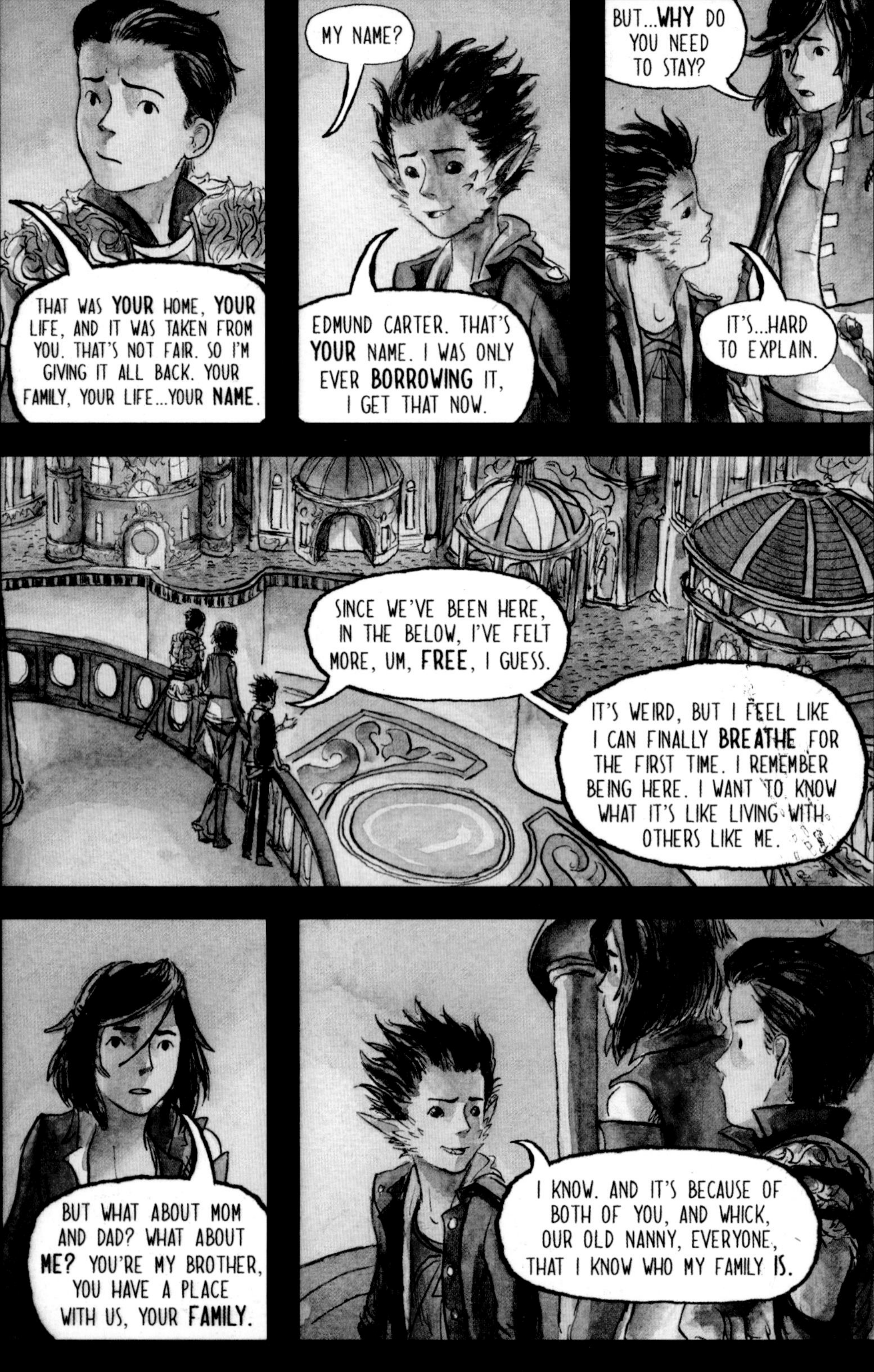
THAT WAS YOUR HOME, YOUR LIFE, AND IT WAS TAKEN FROM YOU. THAT'S NOT FAIR. SO I'M GIVING IT ALL BACK. YOUR FAMILY, YOUR LIFE...YOUR NAME.
MY NAME?
EDMUND CARTER. THAT'S YOUR NAME. I WAS ONLY EVER BORROWING IT, I GET THAT NOW.
BUT...WHY DO YOU NEED TO STAY?
IT'S...HARD TO EXPLAIN.
SINCE WE'VE BEEN HERE, IN THE BELOW, I'VE FELT MORE, UM, FREE, I GUESS.
IT'S WEIRD, BUT I FEEL LIKE I CAN FINALLY BREATHE FOR THE FIRST TIME. I REMEMBER BEING HERE. I WANT TO KNOW WHAT IT'S LIKE LIVING WITH OTHERS LIKE ME.
BUT WHAT ABOUT MOM AND DAD? WHAT ABOUT ME? YOU'RE MY BROTHER. YOU HAVE A PLACE WITH US, YOUR FAMILY.
I KNOW. AND IT'S BECAUSE OF BOTH OF YOU, AND WHICK, OUR OLD NANNY, EVERYONE, THAT I KNOW WHO MY FAMILY IS.

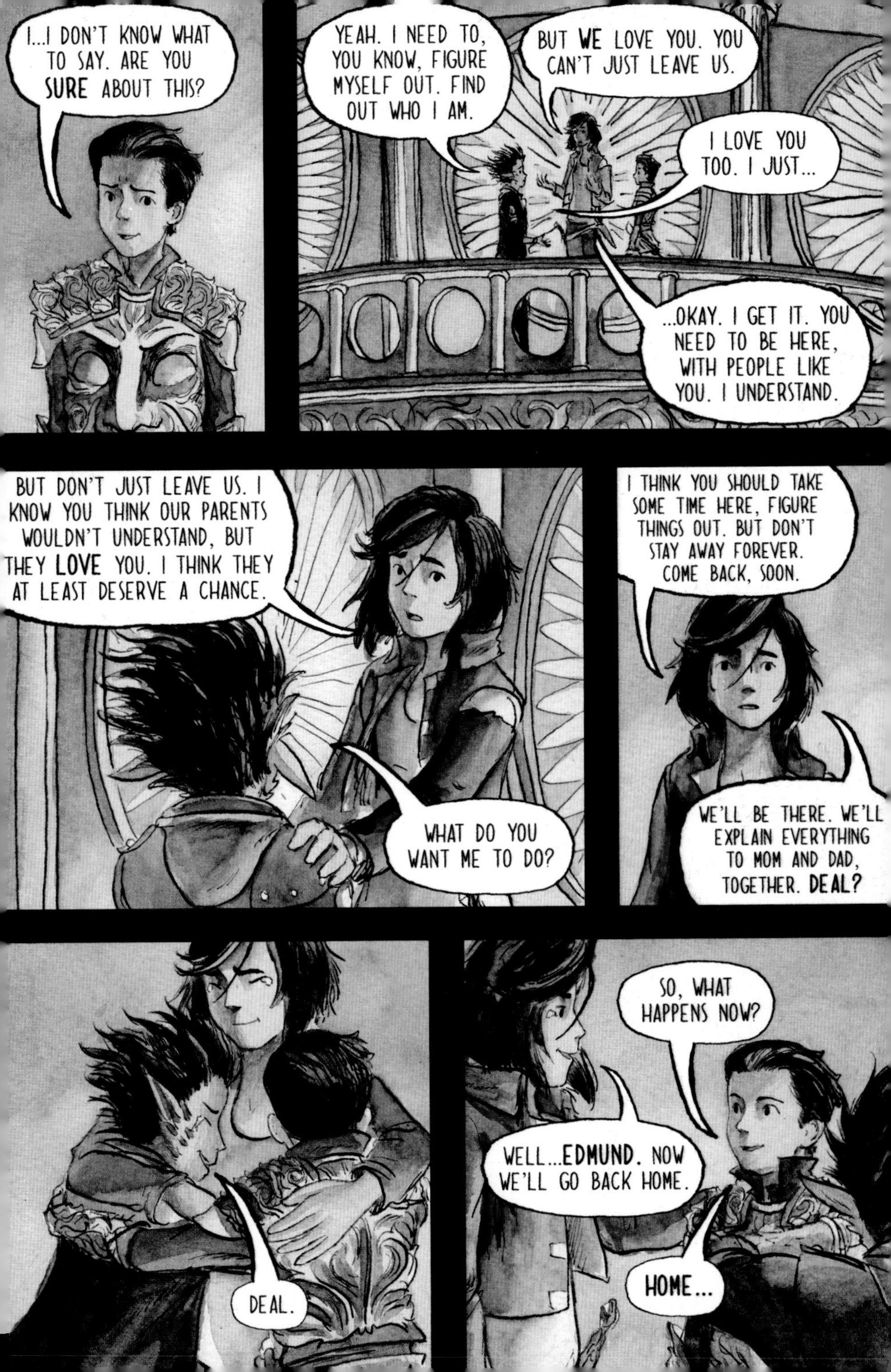
I...I DON'T KNOW WHAT TO SAY. ARE YOU **SURE** ABOUT THIS?
YEAH. I NEED TO, YOU KNOW, FIGURE MYSELF OUT. FIND OUT WHO I AM.
BUT **WE** LOVE YOU. YOU CAN'T JUST LEAVE US.
I LOVE YOU TOO. I JUST...
...OKAY. I GET IT. YOU NEED TO BE HERE, WITH PEOPLE LIKE YOU. I UNDERSTAND.
BUT DON'T JUST LEAVE US. I KNOW YOU THINK OUR PARENTS WOULDN'T UNDERSTAND, BUT THEY **LOVE** YOU. I THINK THEY AT LEAST DESERVE A CHANCE.
WHAT DO YOU WANT ME TO DO?
I THINK YOU SHOULD TAKE SOME TIME HERE, FIGURE THINGS OUT. BUT DON'T STAY AWAY FOREVER. COME BACK, SOON.
WE'LL BE THERE. WE'LL EXPLAIN EVERYTHING TO MOM AND DAD, TOGETHER. **DEAL?**
DEAL.
SO, WHAT HAPPENS NOW?
WELL...**EDMUND.** NOW WE'LL GO BACK HOME.
HOME...

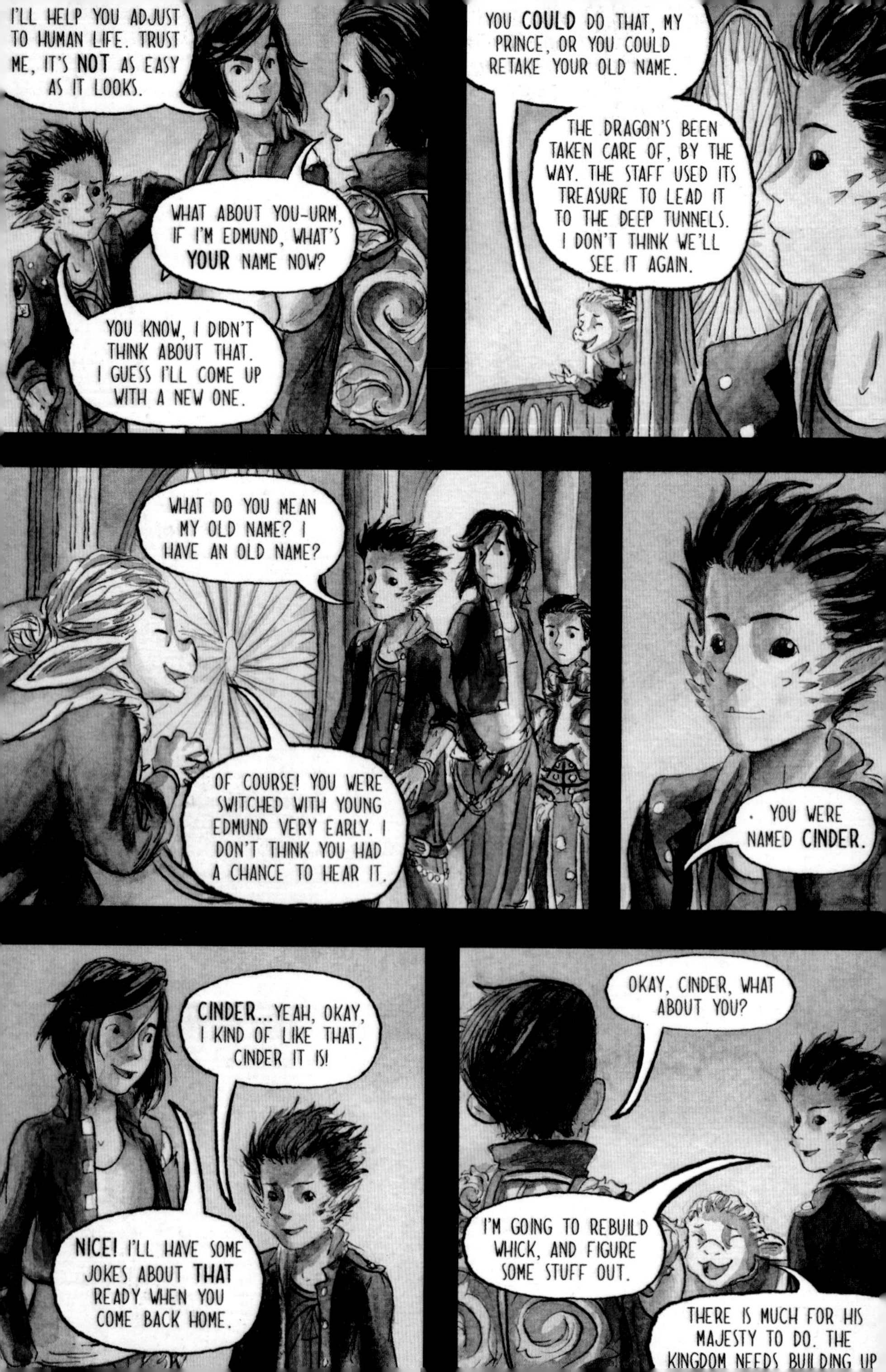
I'LL HELP YOU ADJUST TO HUMAN LIFE. TRUST ME, IT'S **NOT** AS EASY AS IT LOOKS.
WHAT ABOUT YOU–URM, IF I'M EDMUND, WHAT'S **YOUR** NAME NOW?
YOU KNOW, I DIDN'T THINK ABOUT THAT. I GUESS I'LL COME UP WITH A NEW ONE.
YOU **COULD** DO THAT, MY PRINCE, OR YOU COULD RETAKE YOUR OLD NAME.
THE DRAGON'S BEEN TAKEN CARE OF, BY THE WAY. THE STAFF USED ITS TREASURE TO LEAD IT TO THE DEEP TUNNELS. I DON'T THINK WE'LL SEE IT AGAIN.
WHAT DO YOU MEAN MY OLD NAME? I HAVE AN OLD NAME?
OF COURSE! YOU WERE SWITCHED WITH YOUNG EDMUND VERY EARLY. I DON'T THINK YOU HAD A CHANCE TO HEAR IT.
. YOU WERE NAMED **CINDER**.
CINDER...YEAH, OKAY, I KIND OF LIKE THAT. CINDER IT IS!
NICE! I'LL HAVE SOME JOKES ABOUT **THAT** READY WHEN YOU COME BACK HOME.
OKAY, CINDER, WHAT ABOUT YOU?
I'M GOING TO REBUILD WHICK, AND FIGURE SOME STUFF OUT.
THERE IS MUCH FOR HIS MAJESTY TO DO. THE KINGDOM NEEDS BUILDING UP

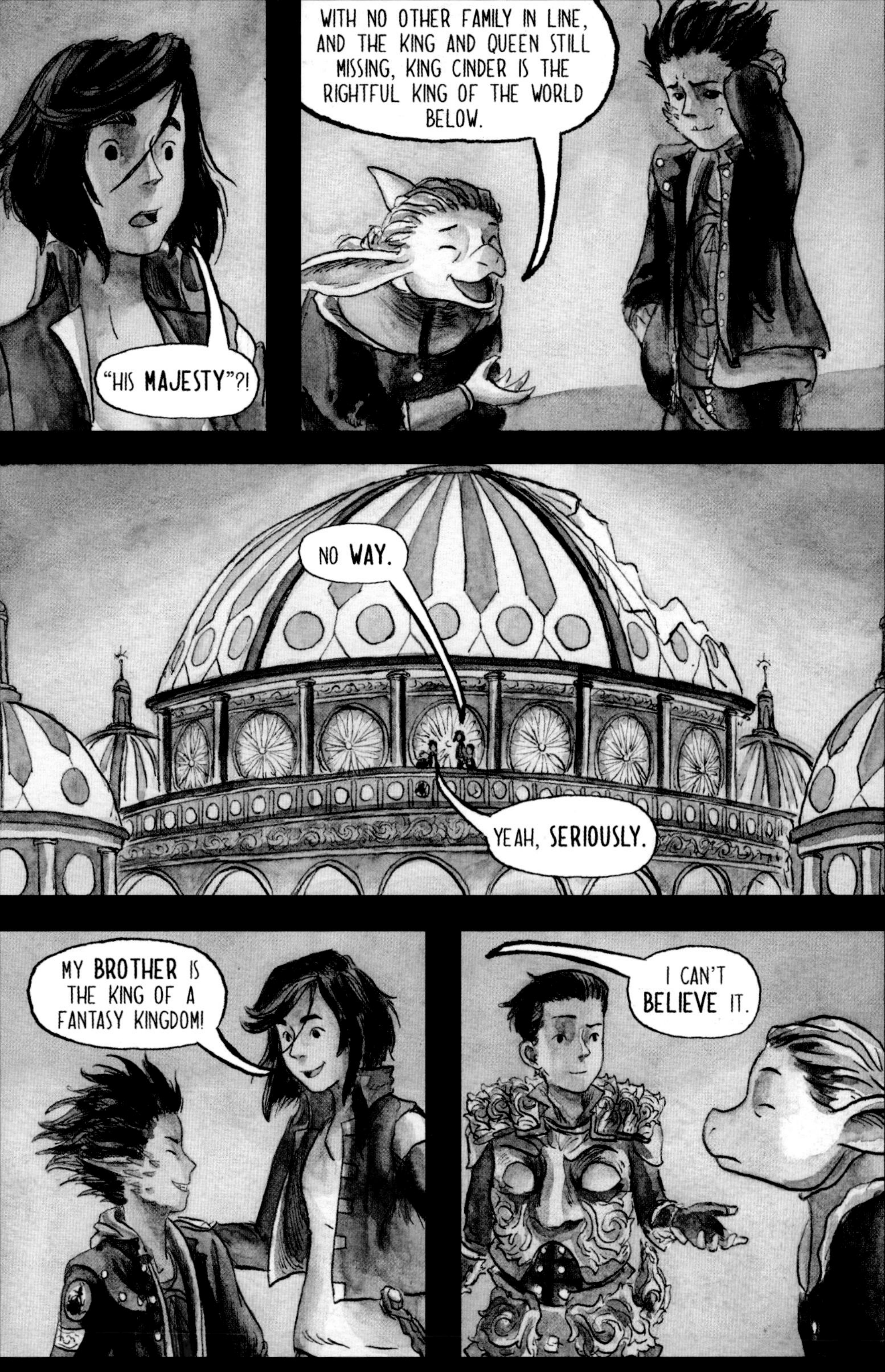
"HIS **MAJESTY**"?!
WITH NO OTHER FAMILY IN LINE, AND THE KING AND QUEEN STILL MISSING, KING CINDER IS THE RIGHTFUL KING OF THE WORLD BELOW.
NO **WAY**.
YEAH, **SERIOUSLY**.
MY **BROTHER** IS THE KING OF A FANTASY KINGDOM!
I CAN'T **BELIEVE** IT.

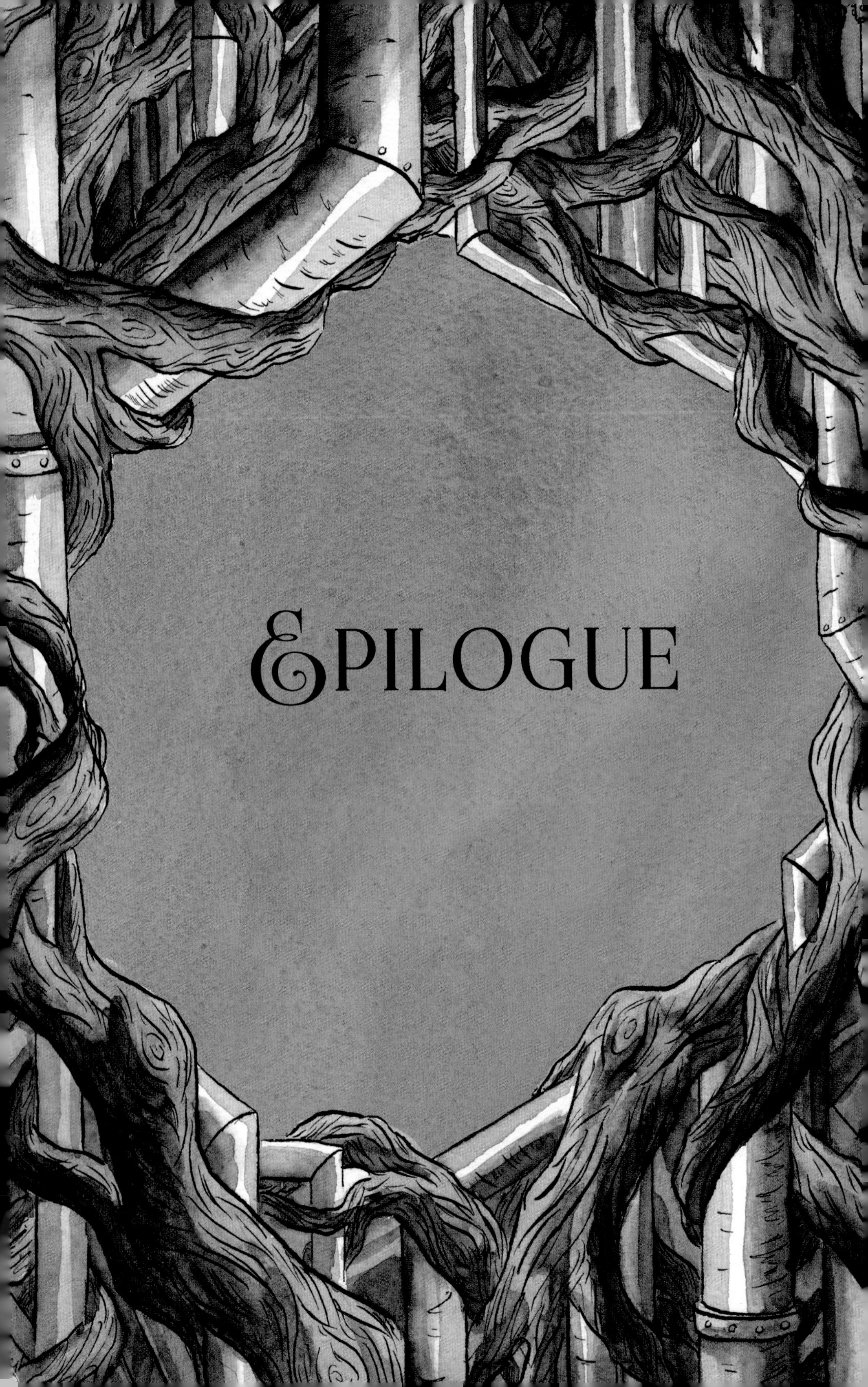

EPILOGUE

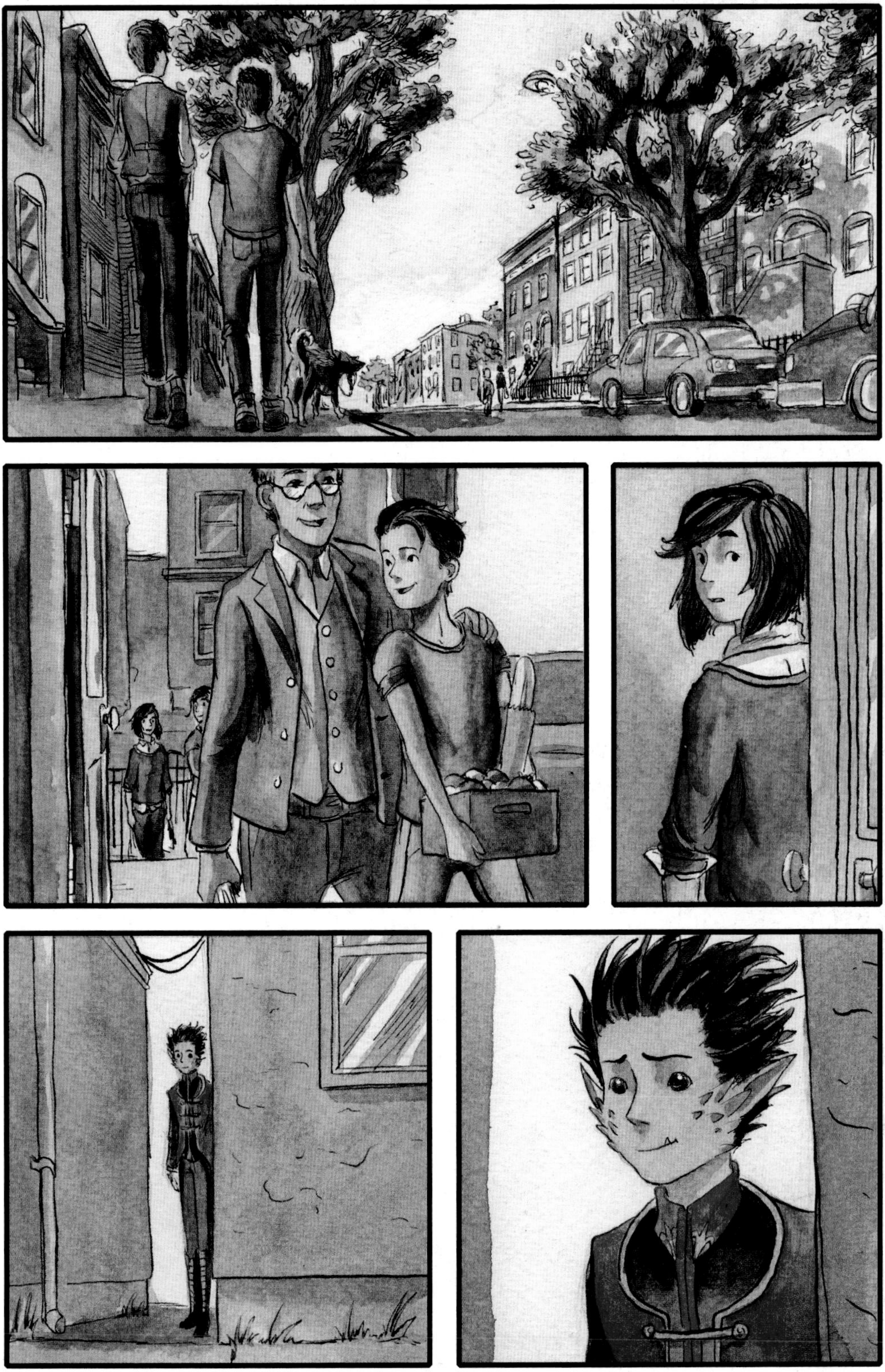

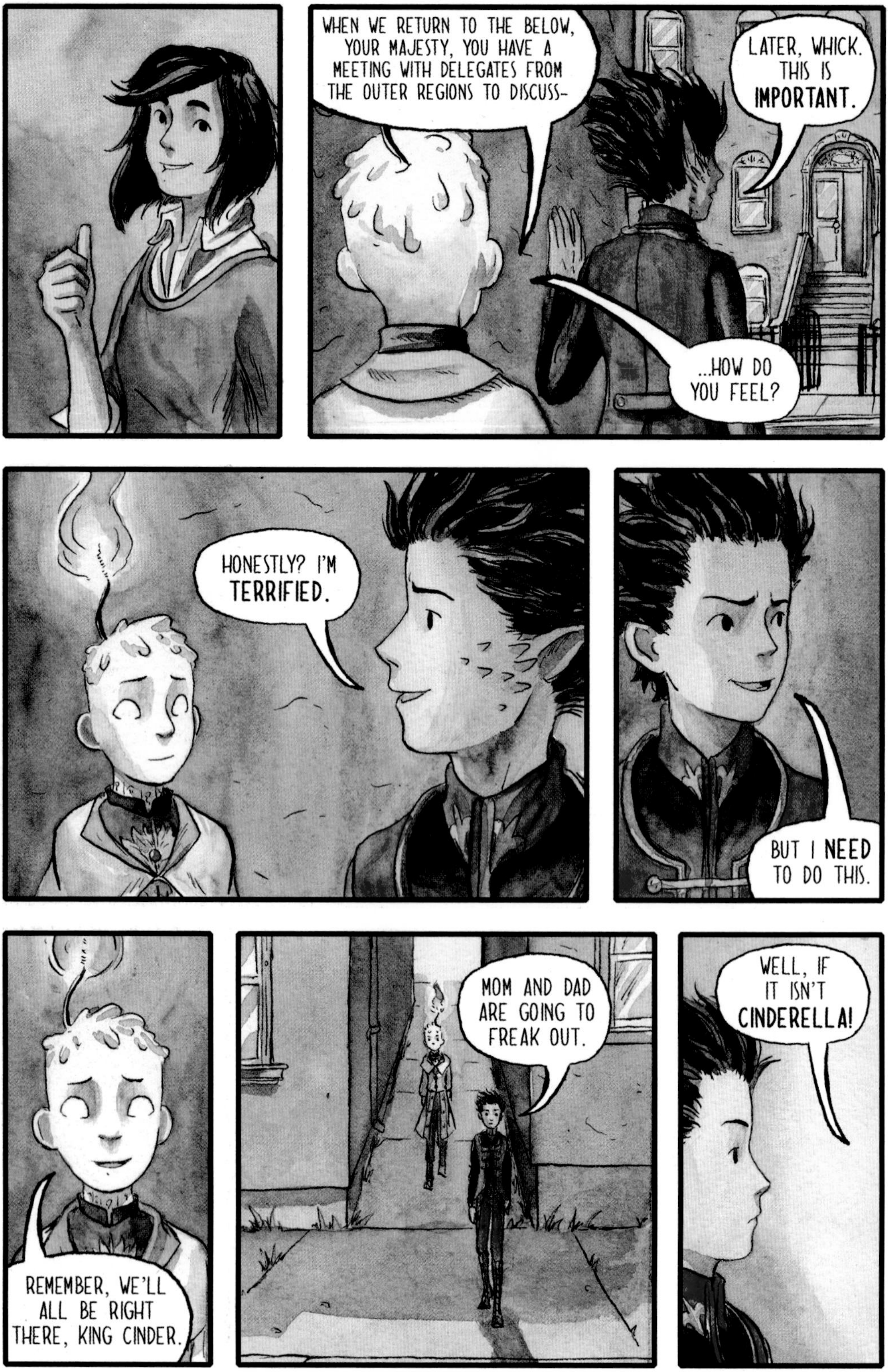
WHEN WE RETURN TO THE BELOW, YOUR MAJESTY, YOU HAVE A MEETING WITH DELEGATES FROM THE OUTER REGIONS TO DISCUSS-
LATER, WHICK. THIS IS **IMPORTANT**.
...HOW DO YOU FEEL?
HONESTLY? I'M **TERRIFIED**.
BUT I **NEED** TO DO THIS.
REMEMBER, WE'LL ALL BE RIGHT THERE, KING CINDER.
MOM AND DAD ARE GOING TO FREAK OUT.
WELL, IF IT ISN'T **CINDERELLA!**

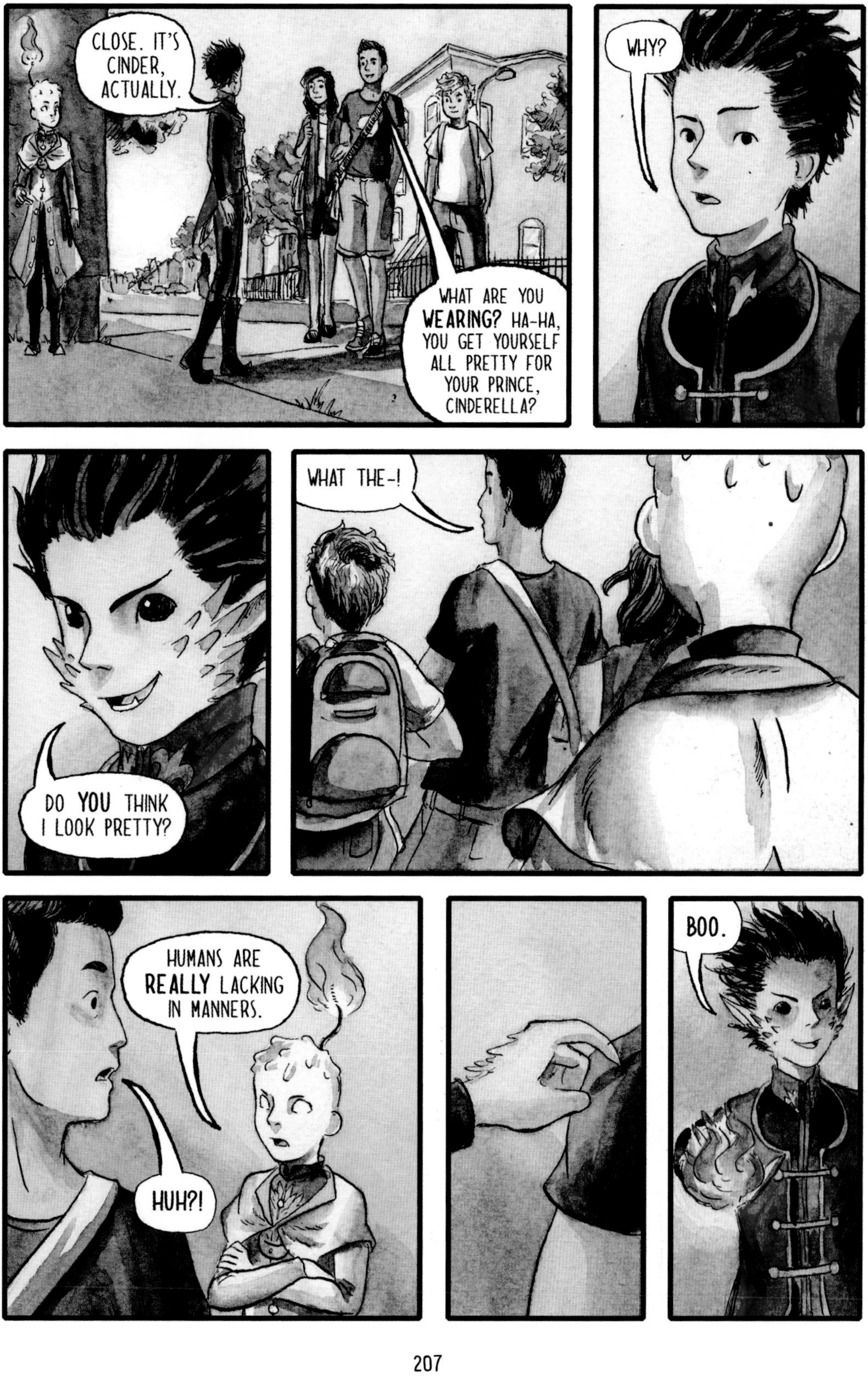
CLOSE. IT'S CINDER, ACTUALLY.
WHAT ARE YOU WEARING? HA-HA, YOU GET YOURSELF ALL PRETTY FOR YOUR PRINCE, CINDERELLA?
WHY?
DO YOU THINK I LOOK PRETTY?
WHAT THE-!
HUMANS ARE REALLY LACKING IN MANNERS.
HUH?!
BOO.

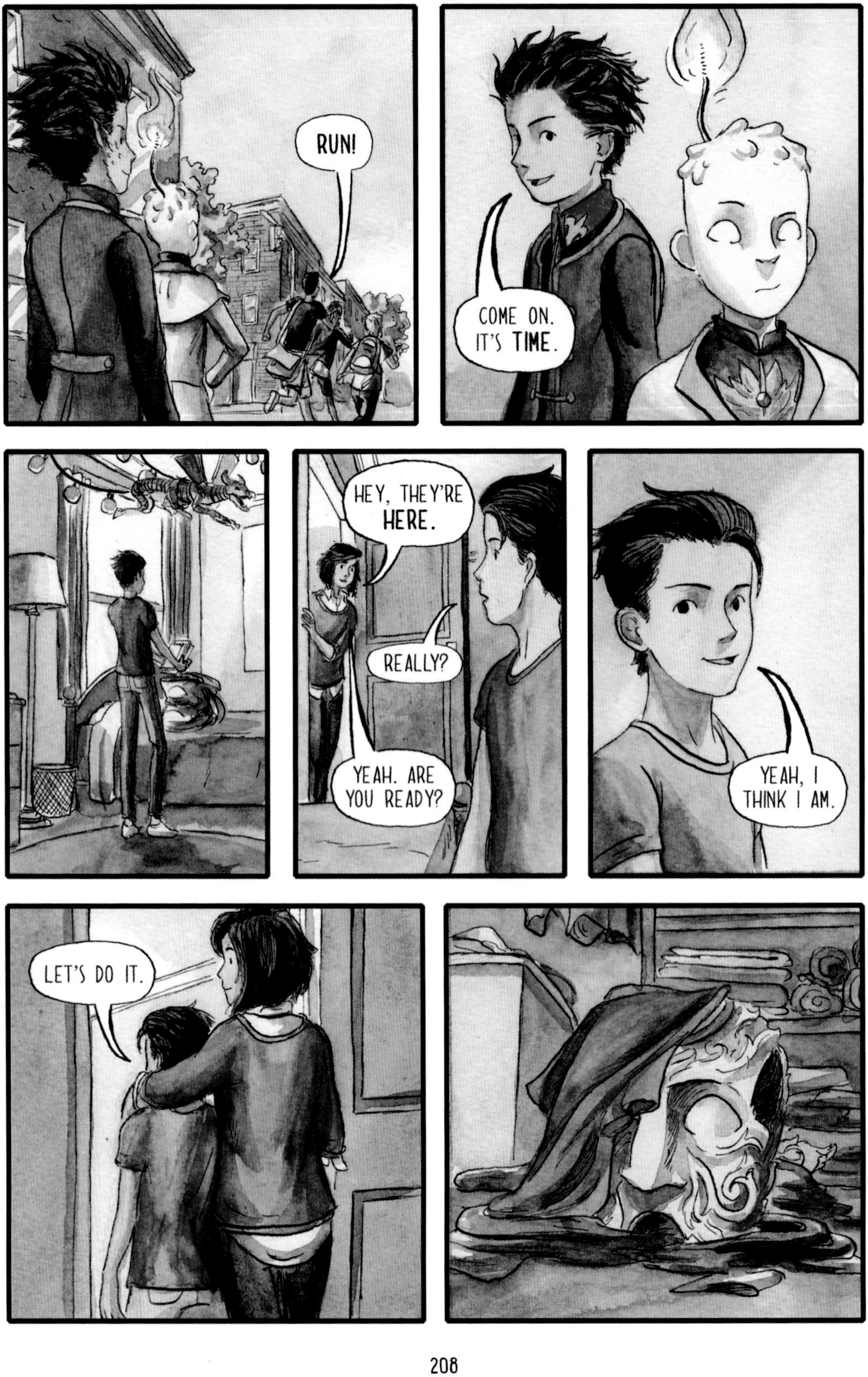
RUN!
COME ON. IT'S **TIME**.
HEY, THEY'RE **HERE**.
REALLY?
YEAH. ARE YOU READY?
YEAH, I THINK I AM.
LET'S DO IT.

THE END

Acknowledgments

First, to my parents, **BRAD** and **JULIA**, who went out of their way to make sure our home was always filled with good stories and that there was always plenty of blank paper and usable pencils lying about, in case any child should have the impulse to doodle.

To those who encouraged my ideas (no matter how strange) and helped me to make them better, including **PAUL ALLRED**, **SCOTT ALLRED**, **ADAM LARSEN**, **DUSTIN HANSEN**, **BRAD TAGGART**, and **CHARLIE OLSEN**.

To **JULIE DANIELSON**, who liked my work and introduced me to the wider publishing world at a time when no one else knew who I was.

To my wonderful agent, **STEPHEN BARBARA**, who remains my constant guide through the often confusing labyrinth of publishing.

To **BRITTANY RAGLIN**, who patiently listened to long rambling explanations of the early development of this story, and responded with insight, cleverness, and wit.

To **ANDREW ELIOPULOS**, **ERIN FITZSIMMONS**, and the entire team at Harper, for their wisdom, expertise, and unfailing dedication to making good books.

And finally to my incredible husband, **MATTHEW**, for his unwavering support, brilliant understanding of narrative, and for bringing me food when I forgot to eat, deep in what he lovingly calls my "cave-goblin" mode. This book literally could not have been made without him.

Development of Estranged

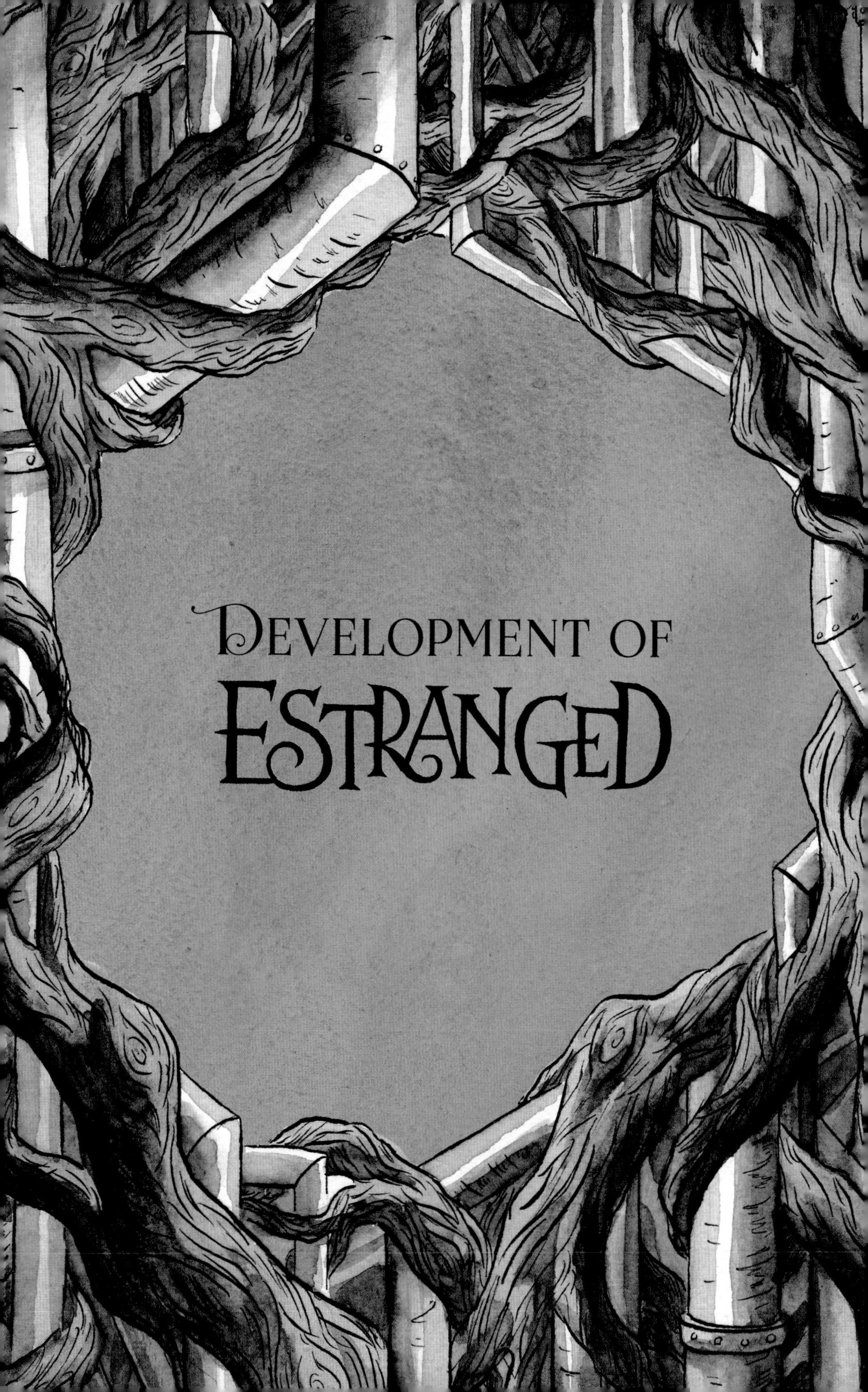

THE CHILDE

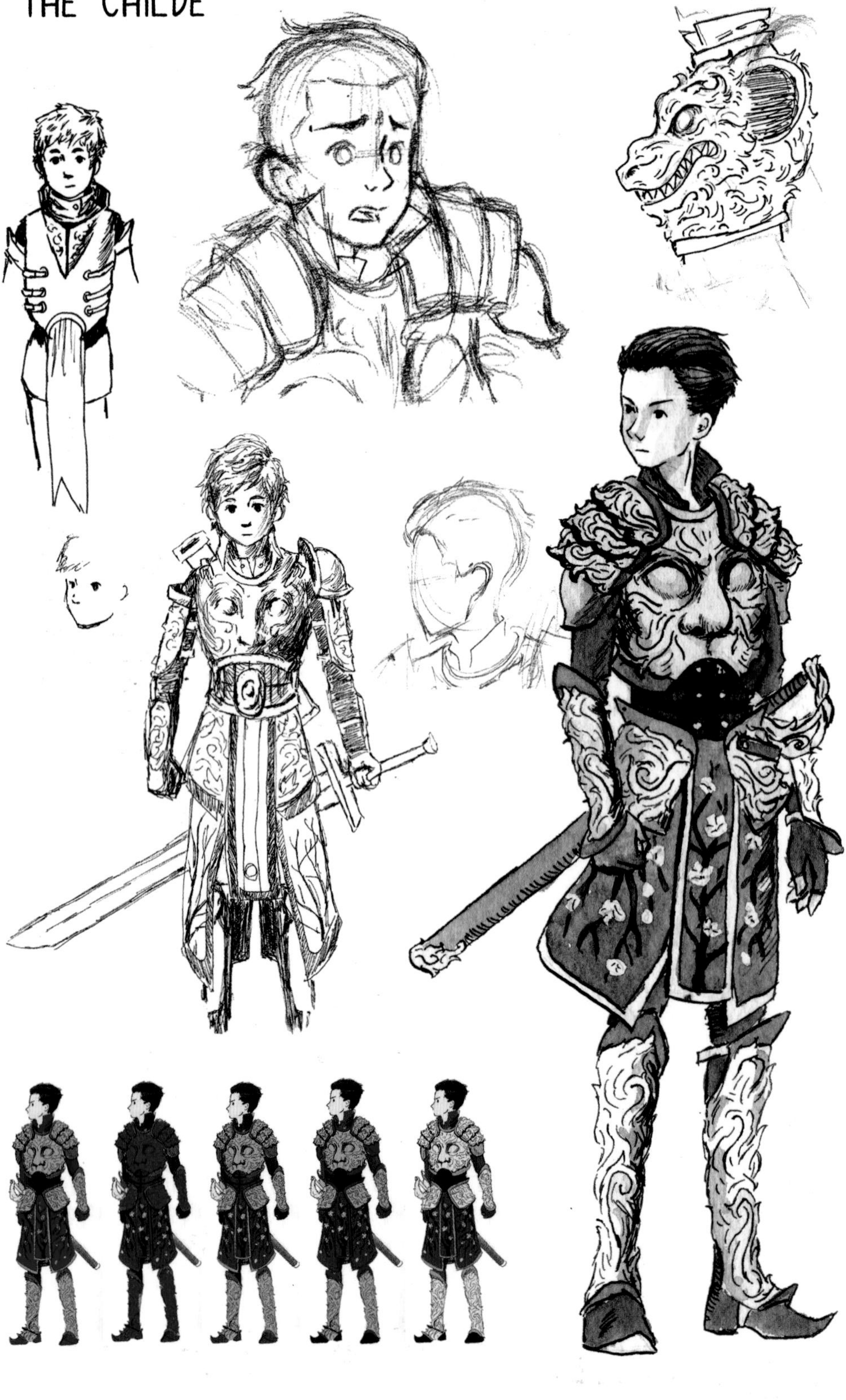

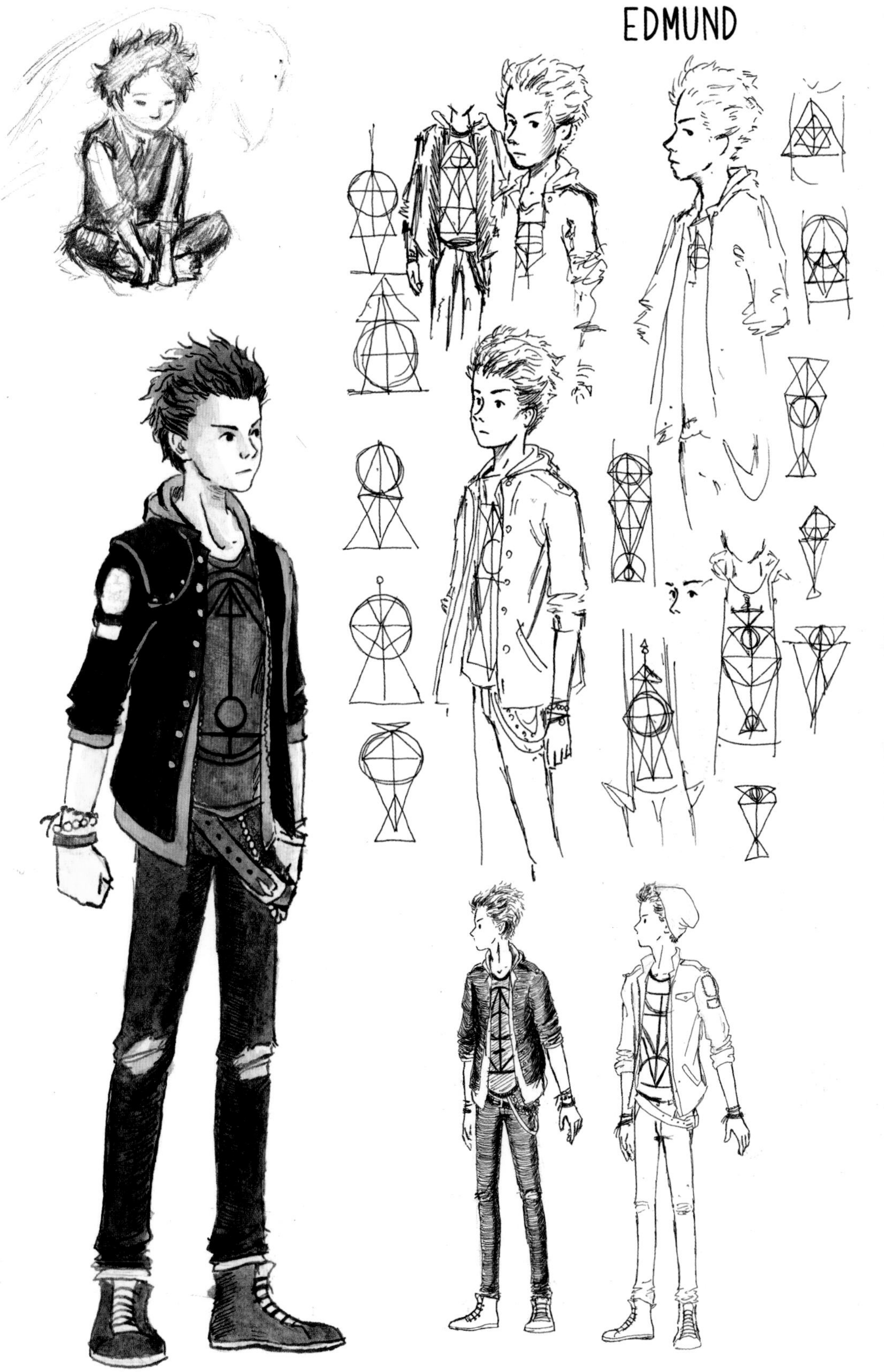
EDMUND

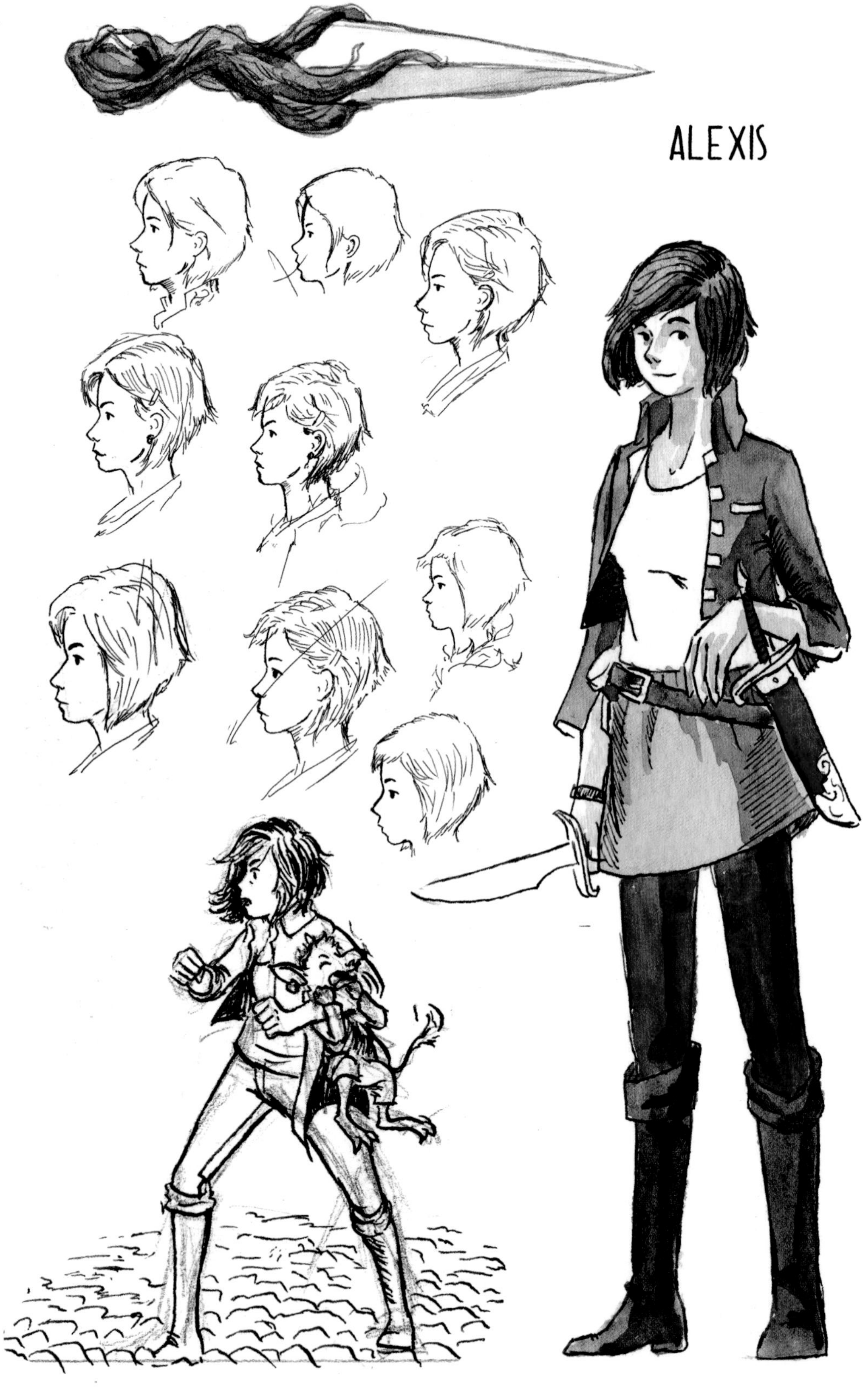
ALEXIS

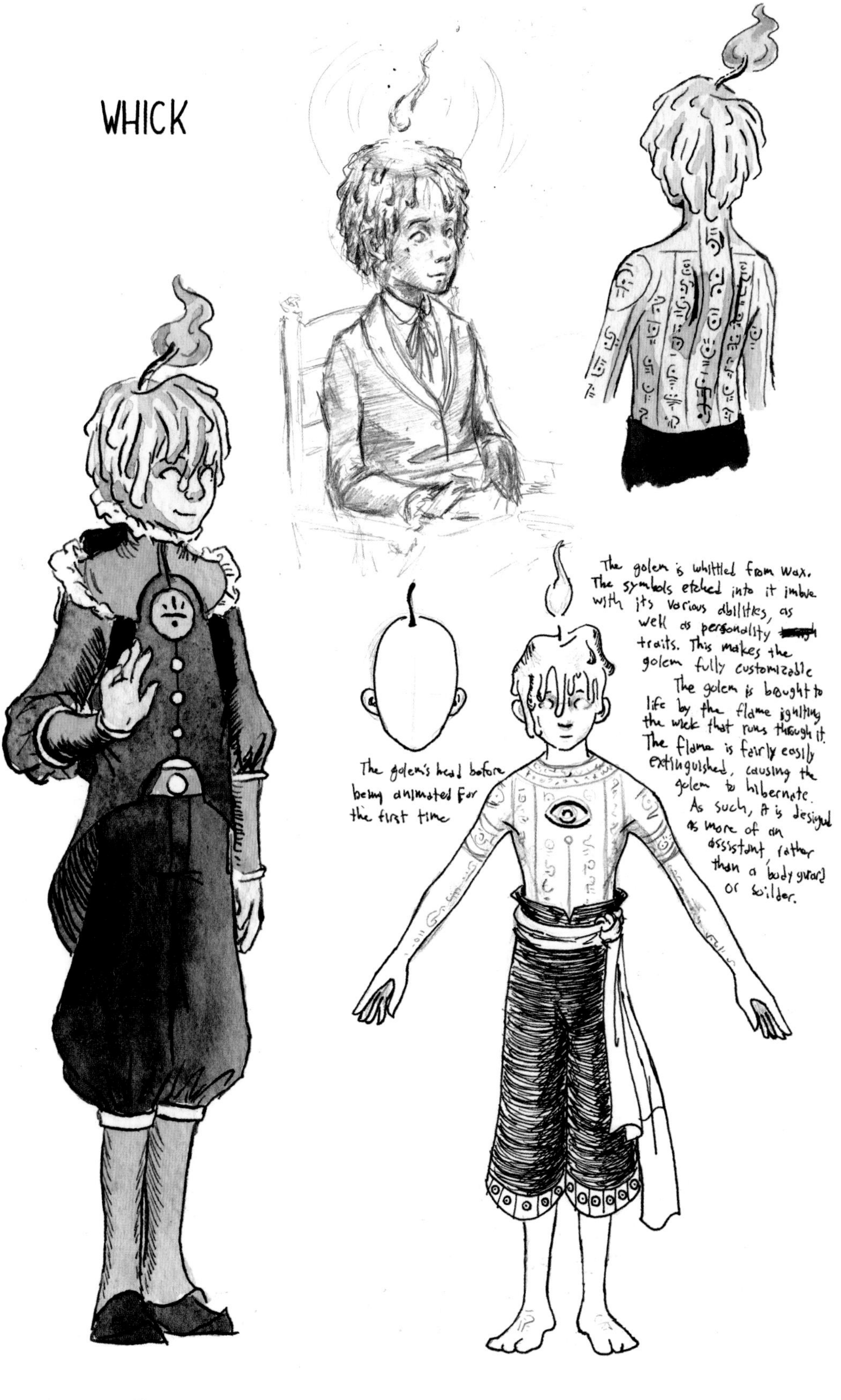
WHICK
The golem's head before being animated for the first time
The golem is whittled from wax. The symbols etched into it imbue with its various abilities, as well as personality [redacted] traits. This makes the golem fully customizable
The golem is brought to life by the flame igniting the wick that runs through it. The flame is fairly easily extinguished, causing the golem to hibernate.
As such, it is designed as more of an assistant, rather than a body guard or soilder.

THE WORLD BELOW

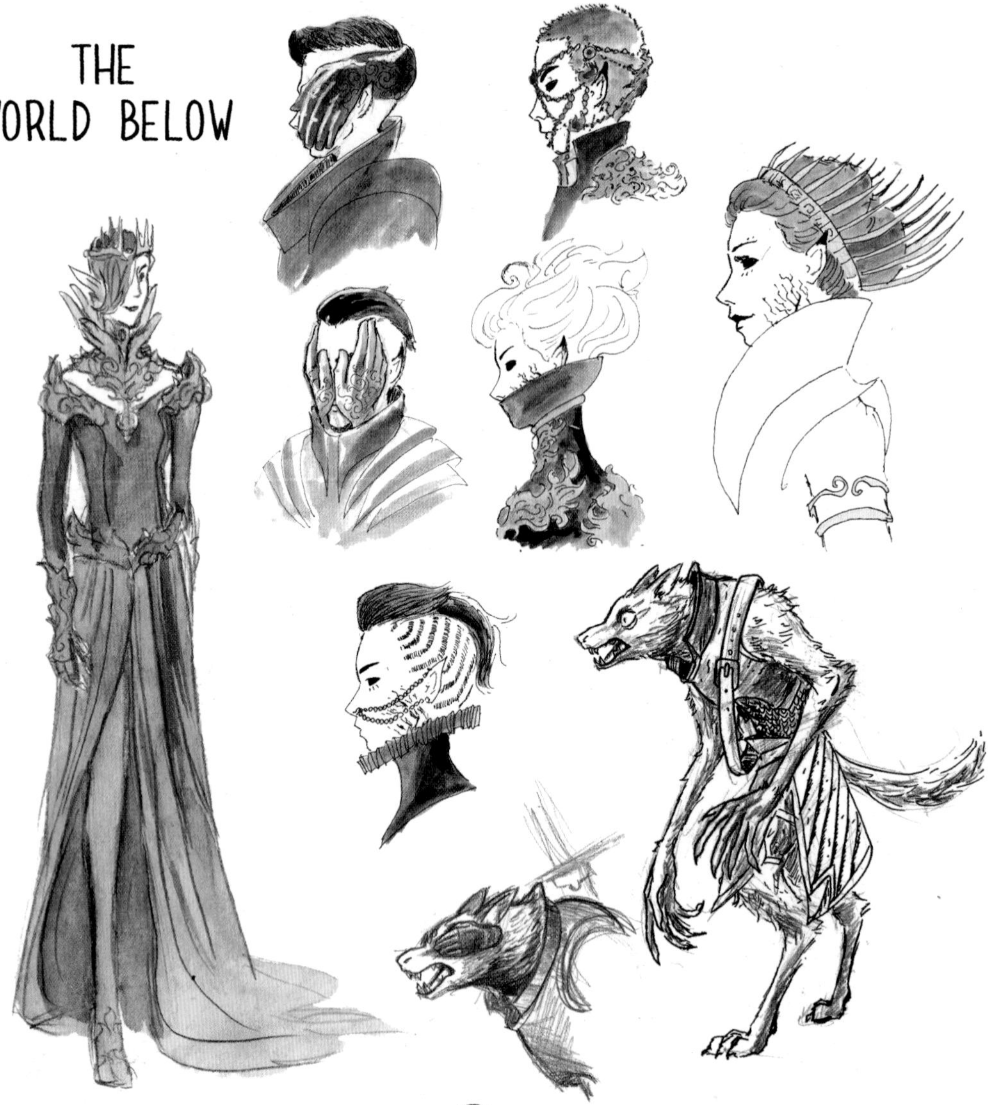

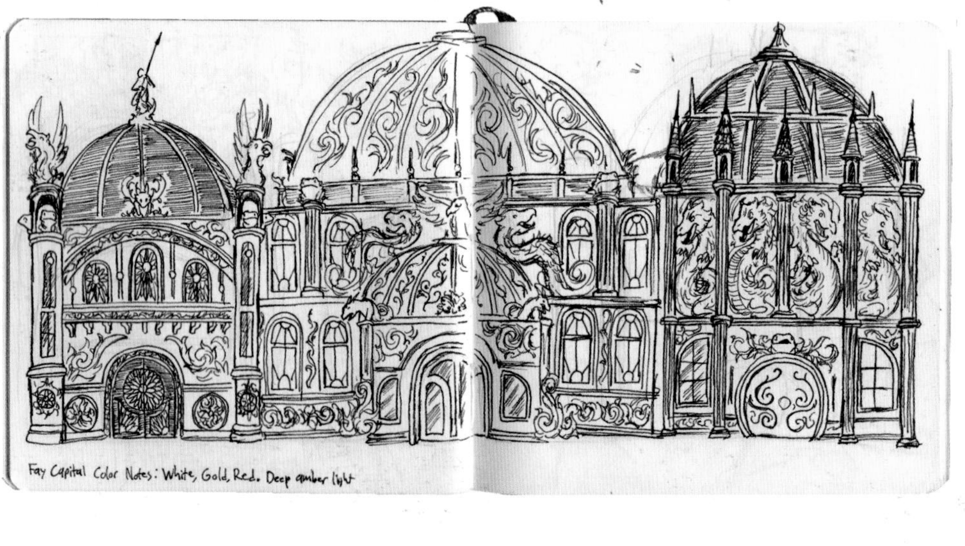
Fay Capital Color Notes: White, Gold, Red. Deep amber light

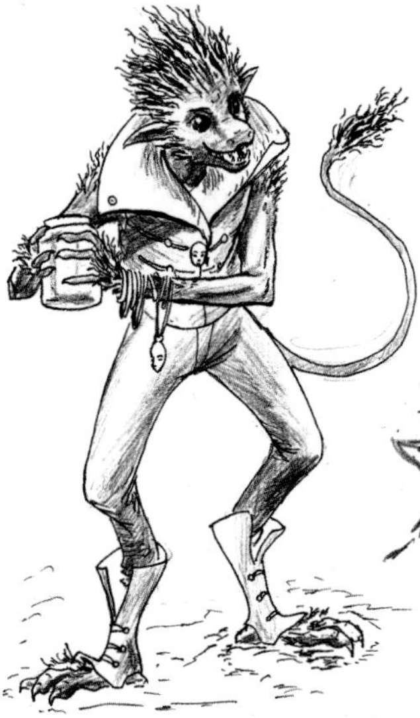
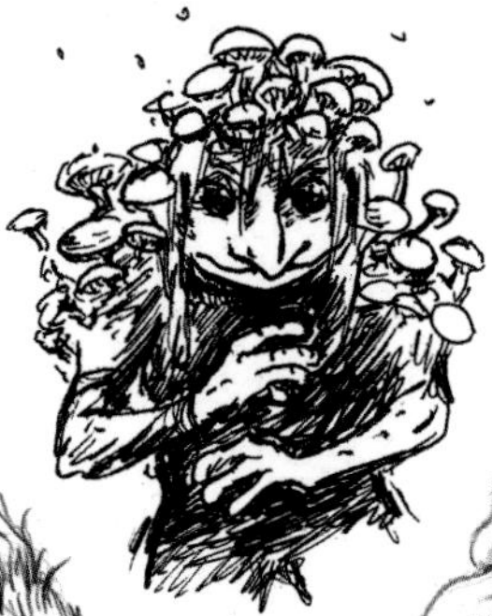
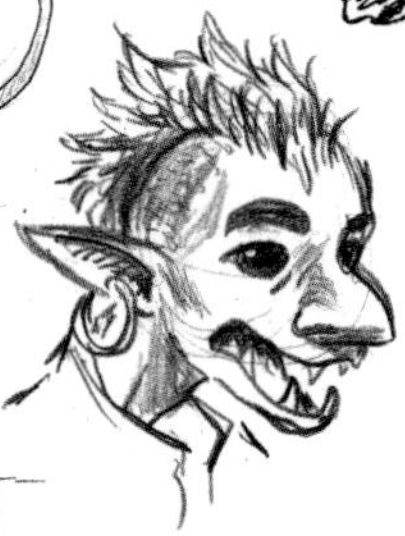
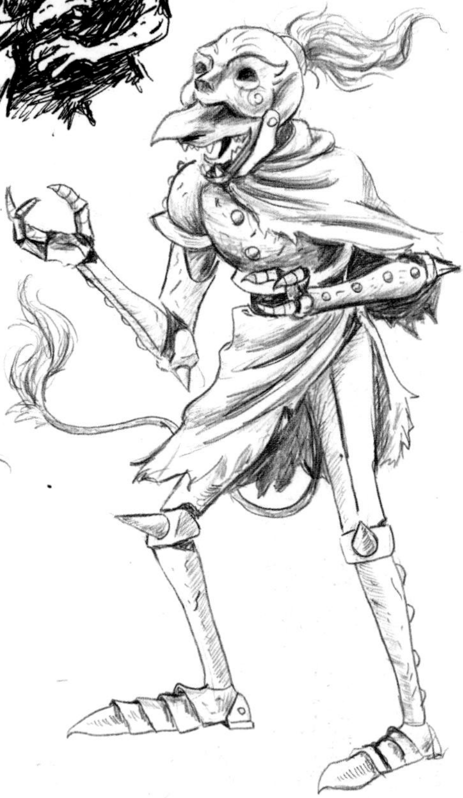
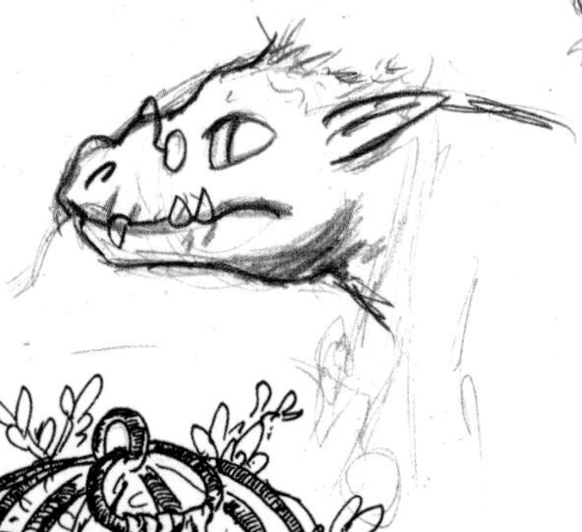
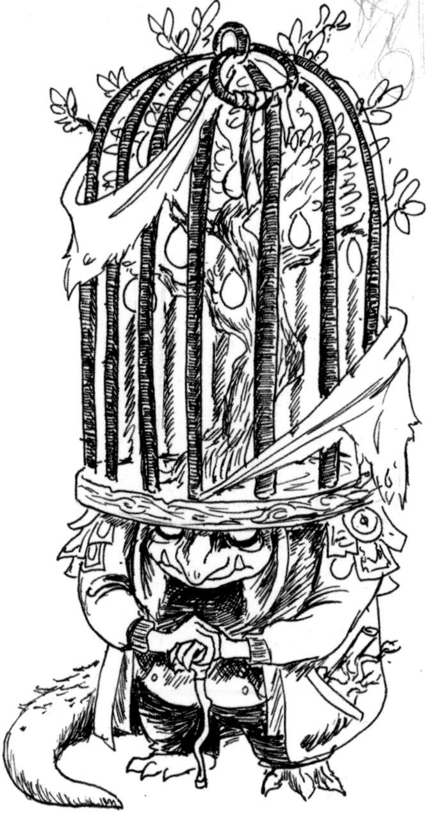
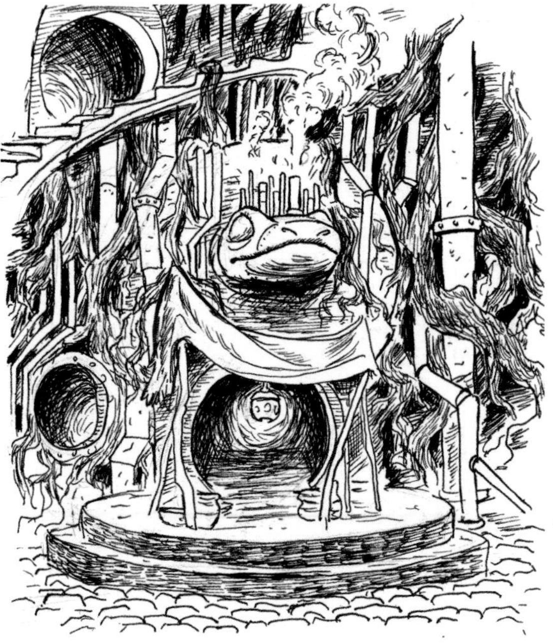

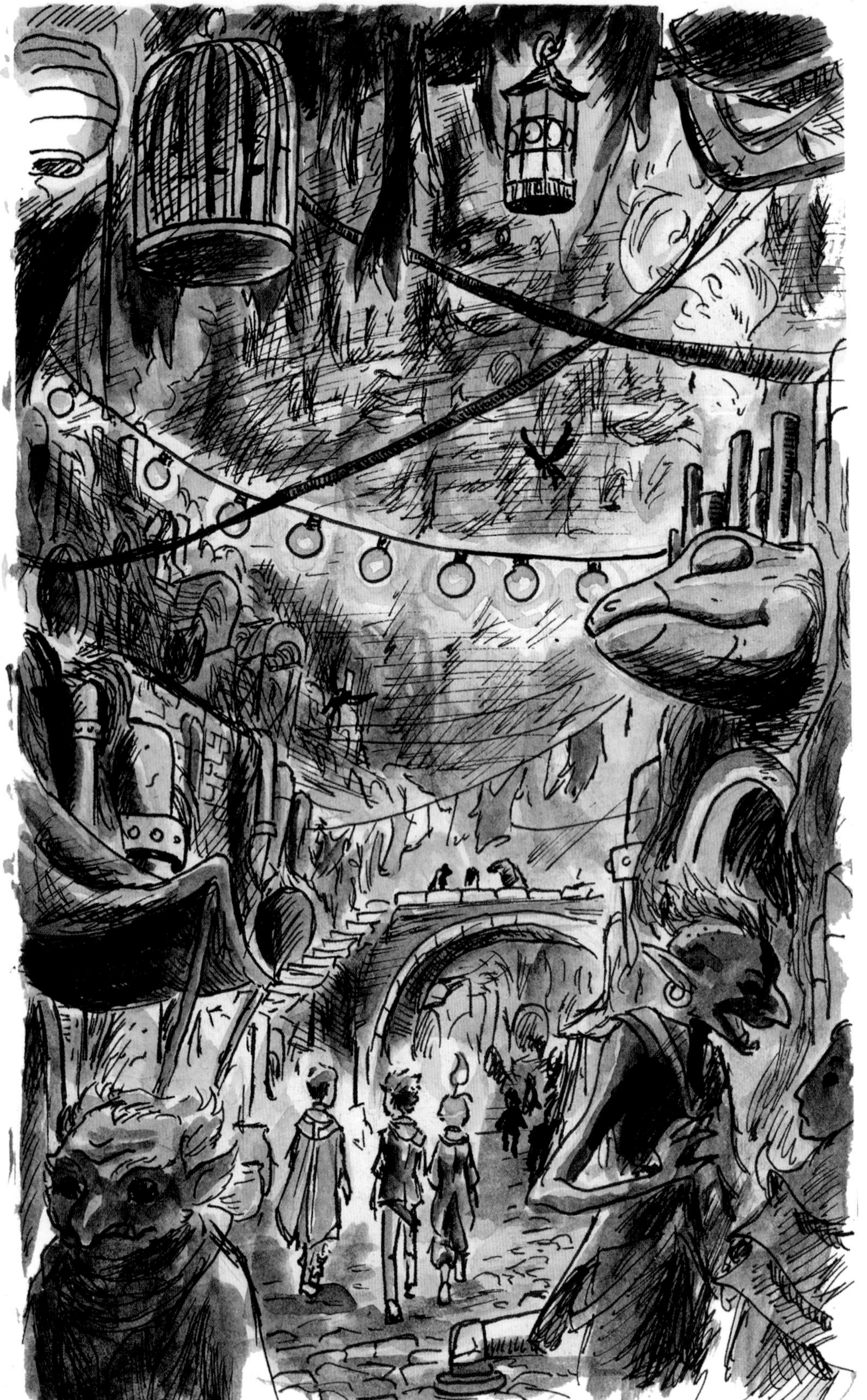